THE CANADIAN SHORT STORY

THE CANADIAN SHORT STORY

Stu Metcalf

John Metcalf

At the Toronto launch —
Oct. 2018

BIBLIOASIS
WINDSOR, ONTARIO

FIRST EDITION

Library and Archives Canada Cataloguing in Publication

Metcalf, John, 1938-, author
     The Canadian short story / John Metcalf.

Issued in print and electronic formats.
ISBN 978-1-77196-084-7 (paperback).--ISBN 978-1-77196-085-4 (ebook)

     1. Short stories, Canadian (English)--History and criticism.
I. Title.

PS8191.S5M48 2016   C813'.0109   C2016-901173-9
                                               C2016-901174-7

Readied for the Press by Daniel Wells
Copy-edited by Emily Donaldson
Typeset and designed by Chris Andrechek
The cover is after the collage by Tony Calzetta *I've got nothing against art and all that kind of stuff.*

Canada Council   Conseil des Arts   ONTARIO ARTS COUNCIL
for the Arts   du Canada   CONSEIL DES ARTS DE L'ONTARIO
                                      an Ontario government agency
                                      un organisme du gouvernement de l'Ontario

Canada   Ontario
          Ontario Media Development
          Corporation

Published with the generous assistance of the Canada Council for the Arts, which last year invested $153 million to bring the arts to Canadians throughout the country, and the financial support of the Government of Canada. Biblioasis also acknowledges the support of the Ontario Arts Council (OAC), an agency of the Government of Ontario, which last year funded 1,709 individual artists and 1,078 organizations in 204 communities across Ontario, for a total of $52.1 million, and the contribution of the Government of Ontario through the Ontario Book Publishing Tax Credit and the Ontario Media Development Corporation.

PRINTED AND BOUND IN CANADA

"'Well, I trust everyone,' says Miss Callendar, 'but no one especially over everyone else. I suppose I don't believe in group virtue. It seems to me such an individual achievement. Which, I imagine, is why you teach sociology and I teach literature.' 'Ah, yes,' says Howard, 'but how do you teach it?' 'Do you mean am I a structuralist or a Leavisite or a psycho-linguistician or a formalist or a Christian existentialist or a phenomenologist?' 'Yes,' says Howard. 'Ah,' says Miss Callendar, 'well, I'm none of them.' 'What do you do, then?' asks Howard. 'I read books and talk to people about them.' 'Without a method?' asks Howard. 'That's right,' says Miss Callendar. 'It doesn't sound very convincing,' says Howard. 'No,' says Miss Callendar, 'I have a taste for remaining a little elusive.' 'You can't,' says Howard. 'With every word you utter, you state your world view.' 'I know,' says Miss Callendar, 'I'm trying to find a way round that.' 'There isn't one,' says Howard, 'you have to know what you are.' 'I'm a nineteenth century liberal,' says Miss Callendar. 'You can't be,' says Howard, 'this is the twentieth century, near the end of it. There are no resources.' 'I know,' says Miss Callendar, 'that's why I am one.'"

Malcolm Bradbury, *The History Man*

With love for Tony Calzetta.
...the sound of charcoal...

Contents

Try Harder to Like Alice Munro's Stories

I

Quill and Quire: Canada's Magazine of Book News and Reviews reviewed three story collections not too long ago under the general heading: "Short Tales for Grown-ups." The first paragraph of the review read: "With the recent success of books such as David Bezmozgis' *Natasha and Other Stories*, as well as the relative prominence of short fiction on the shortlists for this year's big literary prizes, the perception of short stories as the publishing industry equivalent to the NDP [New Democratic Party]—admirable and virtuous, if a little foolhardy and, well, *not quite grown-up*—may be changing."

(How amused I was when in Russell Smith's novel *How Insensitive* he referred to a fictitious Canadian professional magazine of the book trade called *Reams and Reams*.)

Malcolm Bradbury edited and introduced *The Penguin Book of Modern British Short Stories*. Bradbury was the author of, among many other books, *Eating People Is Wrong*, *Stepping Westward*, *The History Man*, and *Rates of Exchange*. He was, for twenty-five years, the Professor of American Studies at the University of East Anglia and also ran the university's famous creative writing school, whose alumni include Ian McEwan and Kazuo Ishiguro.

Bradbury wrote:

The short story has become one of the major forms of modern literary expression—in some ways the most modern of them all. For what we usually mean by the genre is that concentrated form of writing that, breaking away from the classic short tale, became, as it were, the lyric form of modern fictional prose. The great precursors were Chekhov, Henry James, Katherine Mansfield, James Joyce, and Sherwood Anderson. It took on a strong modernist evolution in the work of Hemingway, Faulkner, Babel, and Kafka which, in the period after 1940, was followed by a new wave of experiment led by Beckett and Borges, and provided the short story with a repertory of late twentieth-century forms. The modern short story has therefore been distinguished by its break away from anecdote, tale-telling and simple narrative, and for its linguistic and stylistic concentration, its imagistic methods, its symbolic potential. In it, some of our greatest modern writers, from Hemingway to Mann to Beckett, have found their finest exactitude and most finished stylistic practice. In fact, for many prose-writers it has come closest to representing the most 'poetic' aspect of their craft.

In Canada, I'm afraid that for the *nomenklatura* of big house publishers, bleating media savants, agents and low-wattage academics, hacks, hucksters, and flacks, a *nomenklatura* that reliably confuses commercial success with value, the short story remains a genre "not quite grown-up."

Alexander MacLeod recently characterized the literary effluent flowing from the large commercial publishing houses in Toronto as "industrial fiction." Those on the panel with him were delighted with this contemptuous coinage. Scant months later, the *Globe and Mail*, in shameless abdication, instituted a review column headed: Commercial Fiction.

Professor Sam Solecki of the University of Toronto's St. Michael's College, whose taste I've often jousted with (he vastly overrates Josef Skvorecky's unsubtle and rather bloated novels; Al Purdy, another Solecki enthusiasm, was a two-by-four journeyman I once described as the Stompin' Tom Connors of Canadian verse), had this to say about short stories:

The short story resembles the miniaturist in painting or the composer specializing in preludes or the featherweight boxer: the interesting action is elsewhere."

What a *deficient* judgment to pass on James Joyce, Sherwood Anderson, Ernest Hemingway, Katherine Mansfield, Eudora Welty, Flannery O'Connor, Samuel Beckett, Richard Yates, Raymond Carver, Mavis Gallant, Alice Munro... a cavalcade of the twentieth century's more powerful writers.

And these heavyweights you tout, Sam, so often turn out to be George Chuvalo.

The academic dismissal of short fiction in Canada was institutionalized with the creation of the New Canadian Library (NCL). This series of reprints of Canadian "classics" and books of significance, moraine lumps of dropped debris, were declared classic or significant not because they were good lumps, or even adequate lumps, but because, sticking up from the general desolation of the past, they were the *only* lumps.

The series was designed to make Canadian material available to Canadian students at an affordable paperback price. The NCL, simply because of its availability at a low cost, became a *de facto* canon; what was available readily and cheaply became, by default, "Canadian Literature."

What normal person, in 1967, would otherwise have endured *Wacousta* by John Richardson, originally published in 1832?

The NCL was the result of a collaboration between a milquetoast academic (Professor Malcolm Ross of Queen's University), who was more committed to Canada than to Literature, and a swashbuckling publisher (Jack McClelland of McClelland and Stewart), who was not entirely averse to profit.

Robertson Davies wrote, in 1964, in his essay "The Northern Muse": "If Canadian books are mingled with books from England and the United States and all the other lands that publish in English, they are likely to be lost, for their tone is not aggressive or eccentric. But gather them together as a Canadian Library, and consider them as the production of a land and a people, and they assume a more impressive stature."

Robertson Davies was flatly wrong.

There weren't many collections of short stories in existence in Canada, which explains why in the first period of the NCL (1958–1978) Canadian Literature was represented principally by novels. (There were some volumes of Stephen Leacock in the NCL but his work wasn't "story" in any modern sense.) But in the later NCL series, short story collections continued to be disparaged and excluded, probably because sales projections were discouraging. The result was that the Canadian "canon" missed what was turning out to be a Golden Age of the short story in Canada.

(Well, if not Golden, Silver certainly.)

In 1978, the Calgary Conference on the Canadian Novel, an M&S marketing ploy, drew up a list, in order of popularity amongst academics, of One Hundred Canadian Novels; the novels were almost uniformly chaff and could only have been read by people utterly armoured in nationalistic masochism. By that date Mavis Gallant had published *Green Water, Green Sky, A Fairly Good Time, My Heart Is Broken, The Other Paris*, and *The Pegnitz Junction* and Alice Munro had published *Dance of the Happy Shades, Lives of Girls and Women, Something I've Been Meaning to Tell You*, and *Who Do You Think You Are?*

(The Mavis Gallant titles were published in the US but not in Canada. It took years before foaming nationalists forgave her for living in Paris. At a reading in some such metropolis as Moncton, New Brunswick, a hostile questioner asked why she had committed such (implied) treachery; she replied, "Have you ever *been* to Paris?")

One only has to read the first page of *Green Water, Green Sky* (1959) to realize that, at that time in Canada, Mavis Gallant was playing in a league entirely her own.

This "Leap of the Lemmings" conference had been preceded nearly a decade earlier by Margaret Atwood's tendentious tract *Survival*, a sullen suet duff of nationalism, economics, psychobabble, and aggressive philistinism. This most popular of all commentaries on Canadian literature proclaimed that it "is not evaluative." It is not, Atwood says, "'good writing' or good style or literary excellence I 'm talking about here."

How sadly true.

She excluded from consideration "people who entered and/or entered-and-left the country at a developmentally late stage of their lives"; she denied, that is, to nearly all non-Canadian-born Canadians what their passports grant.

We must always be evaluative when considering literature, and to be evaluative we must be comparative. Cadres of ludicrous academics have asserted in recent years that evaluation is in itself delusional, that it is elitist to claim that one thing is better than another. Are they daft enough to believe that a cheap Chinese knock-off is much the same as an antique Bokhara? Rug dealers *dream* of such idiot Western customers.

We cannot make a meaningful evaluation of, say, Ernest Buckler's *The Mountain and the Valley* (1952, published in the NCL in 1961), unless we have in mind what preceded the book and when and what was published in 1952 in the States and England. We cannot be merely evaluative *within Canada*; our frame of reference must be the English-speaking world. To do otherwise is to remain in playschool.

To evaluate, say, Sinclair Ross' *The Lamp at Noon and Other Stories* (NCL 1968, though the stories were written over a long period) we must know that James Joyce had completed *Dubliners* in 1907, the book actually appearing in 1914; it is also necessary, needless to say, to know *Dubliners*. We must know that Katherine Mansfield had published *Bliss* in 1920. Ezra Pound had proclaimed imagism in 1912. "The Waste Land" appeared in 1922. H.D.'s *Sea Garden* appeared in 1916. Sherwood Anderson published *Winesburg, Ohio* in 1919 and *The Triumph of the Egg* in 1921. Hemingway published *In Our Time* in 1925 and *Men Without Women* in 1927.

These writers and titles are not, *pace* Professor Solecki, dancing featherweight footwork.

They are achieved glory.

The centrality of short-story writing in modern literature was movingly asserted by Jonathan Franzen in his *New York Times* review of Alice Munro's *Runaway*. Franzen endeared himself to me when he expressed his *shame* at having his novel *The Corrections* touted by Oprah Winfrey. His *real* shame was that under the barrage of subsequent criticism accusing him of elitism and snobbery he caved in to the vast mass of the tasteless.

Franzen wrote:

> I want to circle around Munro's latest marvel of a book, *Runaway*, by taking some guesses at why her excellence so dismayingly exceeds her fame...
>
> Discussing them [short stories] is so challenging, indeed, that one can almost forgive the *New York Times Book Review*'s former editor, Charles McGrath, for his recent comparison of young short story writers to "people who learn golf by never venturing onto a golf course but instead practicing at a driving range." The real game being, by this analogy, the novel.
>
> ...And yet, despite the short story's Cinderella status, or maybe because of it, a high percentage of the most exciting fiction written in the last 25 years—the stuff I immediately mention if somebody asks me what's terrific—has been short fiction. There's the Great One herself, naturally. There's also Lydia Davis, David Means, George Saunders, Lorrie Moore, Amy Hempel and the late Raymond Carver—all of them pure or nearly pure short-story writers—and then a larger group of writers who have achievements in multiple genres (John Updike, Joy Williams, Joyce Carol Oates, Denis Johnson, Ann Beattie, William T. Vollman, Tobias Wolff, Annie Proulx, Tom Drury, the late Andre Dubus) but who seem to me to be most at home, most undilutedly themselves, in their shorter work. There are also, to be sure, some very fine pure novelists. But when I close my eyes and think about literature in recent decades, I see a twilight landscape in which many of the most inviting lights, the sites that beckon me to return for a visit, are shed by particular short stories I've read.
>
> ...What makes Munro's growth as an artist so crisply and breathtakingly visible—throughout the *Selected Stories* and even more so in her three latest books—is precisely the familiarity of her materials. Look what she can do with nothing but her own small story; the more she returns to it, the more she finds.

This is not a golfer on a practice tee. This is a gymnast in a plain black leotard, alone on a bare floor, outperforming all the novelists with their flashy costumes and whips and elephants and tigers.

"The complexity of things—the things within things—just seems to be endless," Munro told her interviewer. "I mean nothing is easy, nothing is simple."

She was stating the fundamental axiom of literature, the core of its appeal. And, for whatever reason—the fragmentation of my reading time, the distractions and atomization of contemporary life or, perhaps, a genuine paucity of compelling novels—I find that when I 'm in need of a hit of real writing, a good stiff drink of paradox and complexity, I'm likeliest to encounter it in short fiction.

Despite the hoopla surrounding the award to Alice Munro of the Nobel Prize for Literature, the big houses in Toronto and the literary agents who feed them their daily chaff continue to regard the short story as *not quite grown-up*. The general reading public, too, continues to ignore the form, as do those with specialist interests, book dealers, and collectors. I know this because I have always preferred grubby fact to airy pronouncement and weekly I trawl through the Ottawa Public Library's Discards and Donations shop in search of treasures. Now, months after the announcement of the Nobel Prize, I am still noting pristine hardcover copies of first-edition Alice Munro collections priced at one dollar.

The general attitude to Alice Munro and to the story form might be suggested by a tedious "New Year Resolution" column that appeared in the *Ottawa Citizen* on December 28, 2013. The column was by Bruce Ward, one of the paper's lumpen stalwarts, and was headed:

TRY HARDER TO LIKE ALICE MUNRO'S STORIES
Munro won the Nobel Prize in 2013 and I'm delighted for her. But her short stories are always about ordinary people who live in rural Ontario. Sometimes they go to Toronto or some place

near Vancouver. Then they move back to rural Ontario. There's often a "years later" moment at the end of her stories, when one of the main characters spots the other crossing the street but doesn't speak. Resolution: find a way to care about these dismal small-town losers.

What interests me is what this small-town columnist is *really* objecting to, because I suspect it's an objection shared by millions of readers and explains why the short story is so widely avoided or disdained.

I like to relax with a book...
... lose myself in another world ... takes me out of myself ..
... see what happens next.
A real page-turner!

What underlies such familiar comments and Bruce Ward's grumpings is an unarticulated objection to the lack, in short stories, of traditional PLOT.

I do not begrudge readers the use of literature as narcotic, literature as Lorazepam, literature as Scotch or Class B ameliorative, but I find it rather dispiriting to see thrillers and detective stories gathered in the Ottawa Public Library into an enclave of their own, aisle upon aisle, separate from the frequently culled aisles designated "Fiction." Thrillers and detective stories and police procedurals are now designated "Crime Novels"; this terminological inflation of what once were called "Penny Dreadfuls" is rather like the emblazoning of Ottawa garbage trucks with the words "Waste Disposal Systems.'"

That's not to say that I don't read such books myself. From a few of these writers I've learned valuable tricks of the trade—writers like Elmore Leonard, Loren D. Estleman, Bill James, Denise Mina, Patricia Highsmith, Ruth Rendell as herself and as "Barbara Vine," George V. Higgins—but I quickly realized that I was drawn to "Crime Novelists" who weren't quite, novelists who were more interested in character than plot.

Genre writing's principal flaw is the tyranny of plot. When I'm tired and read "Crime Novels" there's enough to keep me turning pages—a hunt, a chase, funny dialogue, new slang, entertaining spots of mayhem, arcane information about forensics, ballistics, triads, forgery, dinky toys, the Unione Corse—but late at night, when there's no more of that kind of thing to be gleaned, and plot hammers on and on, I often can't be bothered to finish because ultimately I don't *care* who did it or why or how or if the Baddie gets caught. Because the characters are cardboard-thin, I don't *care* whether the private eye Keeps Off the Sauce, whether he wins The Girl with Auburn Hair... The onward rush of narrative initially engaged, but the plotted destination and conclusion become tiresome. And because such books pose questions and end with some kind of answer they cannot be reread.

(The only "Crime Novelist" I revisit is Raymond Chandler, and that not for characters or plot but for the comic rococo of his similes.)

The lack of traditional plot is at the heart of many readers' difficulties and explains, in part, why so many feel disaffected with modern short stories. Malcolm Bradbury, in his *Introduction*, quoted earlier, wrote that modern stories had broken away from "the classic short tale," from "anecdote, tale-telling and simple narrative" and aspired more to poetry with its "linguistic and stylistic concentrations, its imagistic methods."

Over the last eighty years there has been a shift, I think, in the connotations of the word "tale" as it applies to literature. The word was once synonymous with "story," though even years ago it carried suggestions of entertainment, improbability, fancifulness, romance. The word "tale" now implies, I think, a story whose main emphasis is on the contrivances of plot, on "what will happen next." Similarly with the word "yarn," though "yarn" is even more downmarket. W.W. Jacobs comes to mind. Both words now imply Entertainment, Adventure, Exotic Climes. "Tales" seem typical of the nineteenth century. Kipling and Robert Louis Stevenson... (I'm *still* trying to drive into my head the recently heard fact that Stevenson pronounced his middle name not as "Louis" but as *Lewis*). And along with *Kidnapped* and *Treasure Island*, Rider Haggard's tale of *King Solomon's Mines* with Gagool and the Zulu impis, A.E.W. Mason's

The Four Feathers, R.D. Blackmore's *Lorna Doone*... all, it should be noted, wonderful books for children. Stevenson refused to take his writing seriously: "Fiction," he stated, "is to grown men what play is to the child." His historical fiction he described as "tushery."

We might talk of "a pirate tale," but if we were talking about Katherine Mansfield's "The Daughters of the Late Colonel" we'd be unlikely to refer to it as "a tale about two sisters" or "Miss Brill" as "a tale about a spinster sitting in a park." "Tale" suggests the kind of story that preceded modernism and it is modernism and its developments which have dominated writing in the twentieth century.

We must remind ourselves that the word "modernism" refers to revolutionary movements in the arts that began *more than one hundred years ago*. Battle lines were quickly drawn; Sir John Squire, bluff, hearty, literary editor of *The New Statesman* and chief literary critic for the *Observer*, a reactionary old beast who dominated Katherine Mansfield's literary London in the 1920s, wrote, "...we are not moved by her stories because nothing happens to her characters."

Exactly the same observation some ninety-five years later as the *Ottawa Citizen*'s Bruce Ward's contempt for Alice Munro's "dismal small-town losers" who "spot the other crossing the street but don't speak."

Still.

Still going on.

We seem unable to escape the warfare surrounding plot.

In 1929 Evelyn Waugh wrote an appreciation of novelist Ronald Firbank, a writer still little known but rather venerated by those who've had the pleasure. His books from 1905 onwards were all but one published at his own expense and in tiny editions; many writers consider him one of the more important in the twentieth century.

Waugh wrote:

> He is the first quite modern writer to solve for himself ... the aesthetic problem of representation in fiction; to achieve, that is to say, a new, balanced interrelation of subject and form. Nineteenth-century novelists achieved a balance only by complete submission to the idea of the succession of

events in an arbitrarily limited period of time. Just as in painting until the last generation the aesthetically significant activity of the artist had always to be occasioned by anecdote and representation, so the novelist was fettered by the chain of cause and effect. Almost all the important novels of this century have been experiments in making an art form out of this raw material of narration.

Waugh is saying that traditional narrative conventions imposed on life's rush and chaos a form that betrayed that life by distortions, just as in painting the painter was forced to submit to anecdote and representation to satisfy the demands of an intensely conservative ecclesiastic world followed, in succeeding centuries, by the demands of a patrician world intent on celebrating its own magnificence and martial exploits.

All those dreary acres of Depositions, Pietàs, Flights into Egypt, Saint Jeromes mouldering… the only glint, the varnish. Even Bernard Berenson, the greatest connoisseur of Trecento and Quattrocento Italian painting, confided to his diary in old age, "…I care less and less for the "Old Masters." I really prefer the French of the so-called impressionistic period, or even from David to the death of Degas. Minor Trecento painters, merely artisans, bore me, unless indeed I take them as handicraft. I still keep asking how much of Italian paintings would affect me if I were not interested in attributing and dating them. Little, I fear."

Ronald Firbank's masterpiece is *Concerning the Eccentricities of Cardinal Pirelli* (1926). The book is very funny yet intensely sad and lonely in the Cardinal's chilly Gothic death. The vignettes of sin, homosexual desire, guilt, corruption, sensual delight are not composed as "a succession of events" or a "chain of cause and effect" but as—the best word I think, is "mosaic,"—as a mosaic of intense images.

The book opens, memorably, in the pomp and magnificence of the cathedral. "And thus being cleansed and purified I do call thee 'Crack'!" intones the Cardinal as he baptises the Duquesa's German Shepherd puppy.

II

How *exactly* does a "tale" differ from a "story"?

What does Malcolm Bradbury *mean*, exactly, when he says that the modern short story has broken away from "anecdote, tale-telling and simple narrative" and is distinguished by "linguistic and stylistic concentration" and "imagistic methods"? What does he mean, exactly, when he says that for many prose writers the story has "come closest to representing the 'poetic' aspect of their craft?"

I could say simply that if all literary writing is on a continuum, then novels would be at one end and poetry at the other, that "tales" would have to be located at the lower end, along with novels (for yes, there is a hierarchy) while "stories" are often closer to the poetry end of the continuum. This is in a large sense true, I think, but not readily understandable or helpful to readers coming to these ideas unprepared.

What does Bradbury *mean* by "poetic," by "imagistic"?

I am forced to answer these questions in oblique ways—but illustrative ways, I hope—because dogmatic statements would do nothing towards encouraging readers' sensibilities to bloom.

When I was seventeen and still in grammar school, I read a book about writing that quite literally changed my life. The book was *Enemies of Promise* by Cyril Connolly and was published in 1938. Connolly was a writer, critic, translator, and editor of the literary magazine *Horizon*, the most important literary magazine in England during the thirties and forties. *Horizon*'s financial backer, Peter Watson, described Connolly as "a disappointed uncreative critic, approaching forty, who is frightfully ugly." He was known in his circle as "Boots Connolly" because Virginia Woolf once referred to him, cattily, as "Smarty-boots." She wrote to Vanessa Bell, "We spent a night with the Bowens, where, to our horror, we found the Connollys, a less appetising pair I have never seen out of the Zoo, and the apes are considerably preferable to Cyril."

Evelyn Waugh's feelings about Connolly were ambivalent, but his feelings towards *Horizon*'s co-editor, the poet Stephen Spender, were virulent. Waugh referred to Spender in a letter to Connolly as

"your semi-literate socialist colleague." Reviewing Spender's autobiography, *World Within World*, Waugh wrote "...to see him fumbling
with our rich and delicate language is to experience all the horror of
seeing a Sèvres vase in the hands of a chimpanzee."

But for all the literary infighting around the fat and forlorn
Connolly, his reputation survives and grows and *Enemies of Promise*
continues to spread its dawn over generation after generation. The
book has never been out of print. Here, from its opening chapter, is
the passage that changed my life:

> What kills a literary reputation is inflation. The advertising,
> publicity and enthusiasm which a book generates—in a word its
> success—imply a reaction against it. The element of inflation in
> a writer's success, the extent to which it has been forced, is some-
> thing that has to be written off. One can fool the public about a
> book but the public will store up resentment in proportion to
> its folly. The public can be fooled deliberately by advertising and
> publicity or it can be fooled by accident, by the writer fooling
> himself. If we look at the book pages of the Sunday papers we
> can see the fooling of the public going on, inflation at work. A
> word like genius is used so many times that eventually the sen-
> tence "Jenkins has genius. *Cauliflower Ear* is immense!" becomes
> true because he has as much genius and is as immense as are
> the other writers who have been praised there. It is the words
> that suffer for in the inflation they have lost their meaning. The
> public at first suffers too but in the end it ceases to care and so
> new words have to be dragged out of retirement and forced to
> suggest merit. Often the public is taken in by a book because,
> although bad, it is topical, its up-to-datedness passes as original-
> ity, its ideas seem important because they are "in the air." *The
> Bridge of San Luis Rey, Dusty Answer, Decline and Fall, Brave New
> World, The Postman Always Rings Twice, The Fountain, Good-bye,
> Mr. Chips* are examples of books which had a success quite out
> of proportion to their undoubted merit and which now reacts
> unfavourably on their authors, because the overexcitable public
> who read those books have been fooled. None of the authors

expected their books to become best-sellers but, without knowing it, they had hit upon the contemporary chemical combination of illusion with disillusion which makes books sell.

But it is also possible to write a good book and for it to be imitated and for those imitations to have more success than the original so that when the vogue which they have created and surfeited is past, they drag the good book down with them. This is what has happened to Hemingway who made certain pointillist discoveries in style which have almost led to his undoing. So much depends on style, this factor of which we are growing more and more suspicious, that although the tendency of criticism is to explain a writer either in terms of his sexual experience or his economic background, I still believe his technique remains the soundest base for a diagnosis, that it should be possible to learn as much about an author's income and sex-life from one paragraph of his writing as from his cheque stubs and love-letters and that one should also be able to learn how well he writes, and who are his influences. Critics who ignore style are liable to lump good and bad writers together in support of pre-conceived theories.

An expert should be able to tell a carpet by one skein of it; a vintage by rinsing a glassful round his mouth. Applied to prose there is one advantage attached to this method—a passage taken from its context is isolated from the rest of a book, and cannot depend on the goodwill which the author has cleverly established with his reader. This is important, for in all the books which become best-sellers and then flop, this salesmanship exists. The author has fooled the reader by winning him over at the beginning, and so establishing a favourable atmosphere for putting across his inferior article—for making him accept false sentiment, bad writing, or unreal situations. To write a best-seller is to set oneself a problem in seduction. A book of this kind is a confidence trick. The reader is given a cigar and a glass of brandy and asked to put his feet up and listen. The author then tells him the tale. The most favourable atmosphere is a stall at a theatre, and consequently of all things which enjoy contemporary success that which obtains it with least merit is the average play.

A great writer creates a world of his own and his readers are proud to live in it. A lesser writer may entice them in for a moment, but soon he will watch them filing out.

One sentence from these paragraphs was the Damascus Road experience for me; the scales fell from my eyes.

Apprehending the whole by a close examination of a paragraph isolated.

An expert should be able to tell a carpet by one skein of it; a vintage by rinsing a glassful round his mouth.

This sentence changed the way I thought and felt about prose. As the sentence grew in my mind, the implications and ramifications continued to amaze me. The sentence forced me first of all to stop thinking about plot or context; that was a given and usually simple. The sentence forced me to think about *how* a writer writes; it forced me to think about verbs and nouns, adjectives and adverbs, the nature and level of diction, the placement of words within sentences, the rhythms of sentences, the functions of punctuation. In brief, it forced me to consider writing as technical performance, as rhetoric organized to achieve planned emotional effects.

(What a story is "about" doesn't really much matter. Most "abouts" are simple. What matters are "hows," *how* the story is performed. Maurice Denis, the theoretician of Les Nabis (from Hebrew, "prophet"), a group comprising Bonnard, Vuillard, and Maillol among others (1889–1899) uttered one of the great battle-cries of modern art when he said: "Remember that a picture, before being a horse, a nude, or some kind of anecdote, is essentially a flat surface covered with colours assembled in a certain order.")

Connolly's sentence also implies, of course, that the entire story, the entire book, must be written with an intensity that will live up to and survive the sort of scrutiny given to the one paragraph. Connolly is implying a prose written with the deliberation usually given to poetry.

Difficult?

Well-nigh impossible.

But as Connolly wrote in a later book, *The Unquiet Grave*, "The more books we read, the sooner we perceive that the true function of a writer is to produce a masterpiece and that no other task is of any consequence."

Connolly's sentence further implies that form and content are indivisible, that the way something is being said *is* what is being said. A profound idea which is worth prolonged thought and grappling.

The sentence also suggests that a piece of writing should be a refined pleasure—as is wine, as are the old Persian carpets made before the introduction of aniline dyes. This in turn implies that good prose is not something we read through for comprehension, for information, as a medium for getting us from A to B. Connolly suggests we taste the prose, fondle it, explore and experience it. What a radical way of looking at prose this is! For when we have explored it, we have not finished with it; we cannot then dismiss it as "understood." We do not, at the close of a Bach fugue or a Mozart concerto, say "Heard it." We do not, after looking at, say, Picasso's *Night Fishing in Antibes*, dust off our hands and say "Seen it." Similarly, we can come back again and again to brilliant prose and with a deepening of pleasure and understanding. "Understanding" in the utilitarian high-school or university sense is a barrier to understanding; if we have read with wholehearted engagement, we have not "understood" the prose—an intellectual activity—rather, we have experienced the prose by entering into a relationship with it. Prose which is brilliantly performed offers inexhaustible pleasures.

Connolly does not merely talk the talk. I was rereading *The Unquiet Grave* the other night and was arrested by the following evocation of remembered joys:

> Early morning on the Mediterranean: bright air resinous with Aleppo pine, water spraying over the gleaming tarmac of the Route Nationale and darkly reflecting the spring-summer green of the planes; swifts wheeling around the oleander, waiters unpiling the wicker chairs and scrubbing the café tables; armfuls of carnations on the flower-stall, pyramids of lemon and

aubergine, *rascasses* on the fishmonger's slab goggling among the wine-dark urchins; smell of brioches from the bakers, sound of reed curtains jingling in the barber's shop, clang of the tin kiosk opening for *Le Petit Var*. Our rope-soles warm up on the cobbles by the harbor where the *Jean d'Agrève* prepares for a trip to the Islands and the Annamese boy scrubs her brass. Now cooks from many yachts step ashore with their market-baskets, one-eyed cats scrounge among the fish-heads, while the hot sun refracts the dancing sea-glitter on the café awning.

("planes" are the plane trees planted in long lines down each side of the southern Routes Nationales. In another place, Connolly writes of driving on Nationale Sept "sizzling down the long black liquid reaches—the plane trees going sha-sha-sha through the open windows…"

Le Petit Var is a newspaper printed in Toulon.)

Hear it? See it? Smell? Feel?

If not, take up lawn bowling.

Back, however, to plot and structure. In 1982, in an essay collection entitled *Kicking Against the Pricks*, I wrote some notes on Leon Rooke's work:

> Where twenty years ago Canadian stories—and critical reaction to them—stressed content, what a story was *about*, the main emphasis now is on the story as verbal and rhetorical *performance*. Our best writers are concerned with the story as *thing to be experienced* rather than as *thing to be understood*.
>
> *Thing to be understood* implies that the reader is outside the story and looking at it intellectually as an observer. *Thing to be experienced* implies that the reader is inside the story and reacting to it emotionally. Leon Rooke has been one of those who effected in Canada the verbal and rhetorical revolution.

The key idea in all this is that modernist writers have changed the place from where the reader sees the action. I recently came across an interesting illustration of this idea in a review in the

London Review of Books (April 11, 2013) of the first two volumes of the *Edinburgh Edition of the Collected Works of Katherine Mansfield*. This extensive and important review was by Kirsty Gunn, novelist and short-story writer, whose most recent collection is *Infidelities*.

> She never wrote the novels she'd discussed with Woolf or sketched out in her notebooks. She never added, as she'd intended, a sequel to "Prelude" or gathered together her many reviews and notes and ideas about art and literature. Yet there'd been time to rearrange storytelling's priorities, making the shift from the convention of detailed, concrete description to something far more like impressionism, the aim being, as she once put it, "to push through the heavy door into little cafés and to watch the pattern people make among tables and bottles and glasses... To air oneself among these things." Her style creates the impression that there's no distance at all between the story that is told and our experience of it. Take an opening line like "In the afternoon the chairs came," from "Sun and Moon," about a dinner party and the children who observe it. So much is presumed here—to do with our relationship to the story, our position within it—that we could well know other things, too, things that happened, before "the chairs came." "And then the flowers came," Mansfield continues. "When you stared down from the balcony at the people carrying them the flower pots looked like funny awfully nice hats nodding up the path." Is it the form of address much used in New Zealand writing, both formal and informal, that does the trick here? The "you" that implies both the intimate second person and something more cool, the Edwardian-sounding "one"? It is a very particular kind of storytelling voice, open enough to merge with the reader's own, so that the fictional scenario is not owned by character or narrator but made available for all of us to enact. Not even "Mrs. Dalloway said she would buy the flowers herself," for another soirée seven years later, can compete in the transubstantiation of reader into participant

that has been effected here, in Mansfield's few opening lines. With "Sun and Moon," we haven't just been invited to the party, we're hosting it ourselves."

I *was* going to write earlier about the place from where the reader sees the action, that the reader has been transported from the red plush theatre seat onto the stage itself—but that doesn't make sense. In traditional fiction, the audience *was* separated from the lighted box wherein the figures played, but we need to escape the theatre analogy and substitute instead film.

Film immediately pulls the viewer into the screen with its fade-outs, close-ups, establishing shots, dolly shots, cuts.... The very early impact of film on literature was profound; film rewrote literature's rules. I can only thinly imagine a traditional novelist realising for the first time that getting a character out of a room and on his way need not involve the kissing of the lady's hand, the opening and closing of a door, the white-aproned maid handing him his fedora or boater in the hall, the outer door opening ....

Realizing that could all be done—and done away with—by a cut.

Traditional writers babied readers by showing pictures and then explaining them, gently shepherding readers along in the desired direction, making sure they didn't stray off the safety of the sidewalk.

A while ago, shelf-browsing in a library, I came across John Buchan's *The House of the Four Winds*. Buchan, apart from having been Governor General of Canada, was one of the most popular middlebrow novelists in the English-speaking world. His best-remembered book, one of a group he called "shockers," is *The Thirty-Nine Steps*.

(Though it is the Hitchcock film we remember.)

The narration is urbane, knowing, insinuating, and patronizing.

I was struck by the flabby, imprecise language, by the sheer padding and hackery, by the use of words and phrases as mere verbal counters which, shuffled together, clack out conventional sentences. Here is the first paragraph of the first page. I have italicized the clichés, the verbal board-pieces or chips, and the deliberate archaic usages which stand for "rusticity."

> The inn at Kremisch, the Stag with the Two Heads, has an upper room *so bowed with age* that it *leans drunkenly* over the village street. It is a bare place, which must be chilly in winter, for the old *casement* has many chinks in it, and the china stove does not look efficient, and the *rough beechen table*, marked by many beer mugs, and the seats of beechwood and hide *are scarcely luxurious*. But on this summer night to one who had been tramping all day on roads deep in white dust under a *merciless sun*, it seemed *a haven of ease*. Jaikie had eaten an *admirable supper* on a corner of the table, a supper of cold ham, an omelet, hot toasted rye-cakes and *a seductive cheese*. He had drunk wine tapped from a barrel and *cold as water from a mountain spring*, and had concluded with coffee and cream in a blue cup as large as a basin. Now he could light his pipe and watch the green dusk deepen behind the onion spire of the village church.

This was never writing; it is the equivalent, with words, of joining together bits of Lego.

Innovative shapes must be forged in language that is precise and quick to the touch. Touching that language must be like touching skin or an animal's pelt. Nothing else will do; nothing else will last.

What a different affair it is if you're in the hands of a Norman Levine, say, or a Leon Rooke. Norman Levine's images pile up and are rarely explained or commented on; *it is up to you to compose the story*.

(See the entry on Levine in the Century List.)

Here from "A Small Piece of Blue" is a young man stuck overnight in Sault Ste Marie waiting for the train to take him further north for a summer job in the Algoma Ore mine.

> ... Away from the main street I walked in a residential area. The houses were set back from the sidewalk by lawns; grass, trees, but no flowers. One wooden house with a large veranda had a cardboard sign, *Room To Let*, nailed to a veranda post. Above the bell-button was a metal plate, *L.M. Kalma. Music Teacher.*

Qualified. I rang the bell. I could hear the bell ringing inside. But the tall grey door remained closed. I rang and knocked and waited. A window on the top opened but no one looked out. Then I heard steps.

The woman who opened the door was small. She had a dressing-gown on over a nightdress. Her hair was grey, fuzzy, and held in place by a net. Though it was early afternoon the fact that she had obviously just come out of bed did not seem as startling as her face. The eyes were there. So was the mouth. But where her nose should have been there was a flat surface of scarred flesh with two small holes.

"You caught me undressed."

I told her I wanted a room for one night. She led me upstairs to a bedroom. A square room with a window and a large four-poster bed. "It's a feather bed," she said. "They are much better than spring or rubber. The feathers they sleep with you like another person."

My first impulse was to make some excuse, leave, and find another place.

"The clever doctors, to them I ought to be dead."

She said this without sadness or humour...

What exactly is going on here? Difficult to say at this point in the story, but currents are moving below the placid surface of door-knocking and room-surveying. Who is this noseless woman? Is it her disfigurement alone that disturbs the narrator? What do we know about her? Only that she is not an English-speaker by birth or upbringing. That she is most probably a speaker of Yiddish, originally.

To learn more about her place and function in the story we can only watch and listen.

The spark behind most Levine stories is usually visual, a seen detail that conjures up, draws in, other details which accumulate and, in their accumulation, plot an emotional direction.

With Leon Rooke, the story nearly always comes to life in a voice overheard, a voice speaking. As in the opening lines of "The Deacon's Tale":

Here's a story.

Although it has been going on for years, the crucial facts are fresh in my mind so I will have no trouble confining myself strictly to what's essential. Nothing made up, have no worry about that. I live in this world too: when my wife, lovely woman, tells me that people are tired of hearing *stories*, they want facts, gossip, trivia, how-to about real life, I'm first to take the hint. So this is plain fact: yesterday my foot was hurting. The pain was unbearable. I was in mortal anguish and…

"And"… on and on it goes. Leon Rooke's voices speak urgently, eager always to spill the beans.

What on earth are they talking about? All the reader has to do is listen.

Leon once found a story between the pages of a library book, a torn piece of paper on which was written, in a childish hand, "she have to do her hygiene." Whose little voice was this? What were the circumstances? What a torrent of invention *that* called forth.

He phoned me one day to say, "Ah have recently acquired some information of which Ah feel you need to be apprised. It has come to mah attention"—portentous silence followed by the Full Plantation—"it has come to mah attention that while an English-speaking man of the Christian West about to climax might say 'Ahm coming,' a *Japanese* fellah—you're following me here?—a Japanese fellah would say, 'Ahm going,' 'Ahm going.'"

Leon chuckled.

"Don't that," he said, "beat the band?"

Days later in the mail arrived a story set in some Faulknerian, cornpone, white-lightning-swilling Southern US hellhole that opened with a young brother and sister climbing up on a rain barrel below a window to watch area men watching on a TV a pornographic, subtitled Japanese movie. "Itu," says the actor, "itu"; *I'm going, I'm going* reads the subtitle.

This, the story's opening scene, leads into the father stripping off his belt preparing to leather his son and daughter for leaving the house, while in the rear of the shotgun structure, in a room the children call "the Fatal Care Unit" or "the Coma Room," Mama, dying of asbestos fibre, somehow signals for water.

Don't ask; it's the way his mind works.

The story was called "Daddy Stump."

After his deformity, of course.

One last example of how "modernist" writing banishes the urbane, charming Master of Ceremonies who explains, provides a commentary, suggests where laughter or tears are required. How do writers themselves think about what they are creating?

In 1984 I delivered a speech in Grainau, Bavaria, to the German Association of Canadian Studies. I was trying to suggest that there were subtleties in contemporary Canadian stories for which academic criticism had no adequate critical terms, that Canadian writers now found academic enthusiasm for the writing of Ernest Buckler and Morley Callaghan, say, bizarre, if not insulting. I described what young writers were doing as inventing, or refining, "new verse forms" and urged on academics the need to find ways to talk about these "verse forms." The speech was greeted with a degree of chill.

I tried to direct attention towards the *sort* of thing that was currently happening by casting modesty aside and discussing some lines from my then-recently completed novella *Polly Ongle*.

The scene describes a middle-aged man in a hotel bar with a beautiful young girl. They have sought shelter from a torrential summer downpour. The man is the owner of an art gallery. The girl is his employee. Paul is restless with his life, dissatisfied, and his obscure longing for that elusive "more" has centered itself on Norma. At the same time, he realizes that his undeclared desire for her is slightly ludicrous because she is so young and so difficult to talk to.

The opening section of the story reads like this:

> *"Tabarouette!"* said the waitress, depositing on their table a bowl of potato chips. "Me, I'm scared of lightning!"
>
> Turning the glass vase-thing upside down, she lighted the candle inside.
>
> "Cider?" she repeated.

"No?" said Paul.

"Oh, well," said Norma, "I'll have what-do-you-call-it that goes cloudy."

"Pernod," said Paul. "And a Scotch, please."

"Ice?"

"They feel squishy," said Norma, stretching out her leg.

"Umm?"

"My sandals."

He looked down at her foot.

It was the Happy Hour in the bar on the main floor of the Chateau Laurier. People drifting in were pantomiming distress and amazement as they eased out of sodden raincoats or used the edge of their hands to wipe rain from eyebrows and foreheads. Men were seating themselves gingerly and loosening from their knees the cling of damp cloth; women were being casually dangerous with umbrellas. Necks were being mopped with handkerchiefs; spectacles were being polished with bar napkins.

How to describe what this passage does?

The first thing to say is that it is concerned with more than the ordering of drinks.

This is the first time we have met the girl, Norma, outside Paul Denton's thoughts and picturings of her, and so this brief passage is concerned with characterization. The characterization is traditional enough though economical in its compression. What do we learn about her?

We learn that she asks—presumably through Paul—for cider, a drink not normally available in most bars and definitely not available in the bars of large hotels. We learn that she doesn't know the name Pernod. The hyphenating of "what-do-you-call-it" and the awkwardness of "that goes cloudy" suggest a slight childishness. Her use of the word "squishy" and her stretching out of her leg to show him the squishiness reinforce this suggestion.

Now let's look at the same lines from a different point of view. Their arrangement is meant to convey something of the rush to shelter they've made from the downpour; they're still a little breathless, perhaps. The *movement* of the lines is slightly confused and intentionally so. In the line, "'Cider?' she repeated," the speaker *must* be the waitress responding to the question that does not appear in the text. But I intended a fraction of confusion. The "she repeated" is intended to suggest the waitress' surprise at the request. The speaker of the line "'Ice?'" is intentionally not identified or answered.

These tiny ambiguities also serve the function of drawing the reader more actively into the dialogue.

After the line "He looked down at her foot," the writing changes focus. If the first twelve lines were in close-up, the camera, as it were, now draws back into a longer shot that more thoroughly establishes locale. But notice the camera movement from people, men, women, down to necks and spectacles. It is a sequence that starts wide and then moves into a series of cuts which are much closer up. This is because the next line of the story moves back into the close-up of dialogue between Norma and Paul.

Notice in passing (he said modestly) the felicity of "loosening from their knees the cling of damp cloth"; it is the *sound* to which I wish to draw your attention.

Everything about the writing that I've so far mentioned is traditional enough. Only its extreme compression is a departure.

But now I want to draw your attention to what is my central point.

The first twelve lines are certainly concerned with the ordering of drinks, and with characterization, and with setting, but at the same time the *essence* of the lines is the *awkwardness* that exists between Norma and Paul. Although most of the lines are *speech*, they are, essentially, a mapping of *silences*. There is an *emotional* movement in these lines. They wind down to silence. They are stopped by the line "He looked down at her foot." This is a "heavy" line, a "plonking" line, a line, if you'll notice, of successive heavy stresses; it captures, I feel, something central in the scene and in the relationship.

These lines are what I meant by 'new verse forms.'"

III

To return now more specifically to the idea of plot.

At the beginning of the twentieth century, writers were beginning to feel plot as a constraint, traditional baggage which burdened and prevented them from grappling with the new ferment in the world. It was a world in a ferment of change—world war, traditional pieties under siege, secularization, universal education, art nouveau, marcelled hair, jazz, transport and travel, suffragettes, Freud, Jung, Adler...

Change was charging all the arts, Diaghilev and the Ballets Russes, Nijinsky, Gertrude Stein, Picasso, Braque, Stravinsky, Brancusi, Chekhov, James Joyce, Sergei Eisenstein, D.W. Griffith's *The Birth of a Nation*, Erich von Stroheim, Ezra Pound, Buster Keaton, Katherine Mansfield, Sherwood Anderson, Ernest Hemingway...

Given the way the world was expanding, writers were not interested in writing tales about Zulu impis or about such heroes as Alan Quartermain or Richard Hannay. They were more interested in character, in emotional states, more interested in the inner lives of people than in their exploits.

This shift of interest from the external world to the inner meant, obviously, that the writer's focus had to change, the light he or she shone had to be spot rather than flood and that, in turn, meant that language had to change, becoming sharper, clearer, more concentrated, intense—a use of language far different from Lego and the bagginess that afflicted so much writing in the Victorian and Edwardian periods.

With the advent of the new writing, the gap between "Literature" and "Entertainment" widened. In the nineteenth century, writers like Dickens, Thackeray, Disraeli, Hardy, and even Conrad spoke to most readers; in the last years of the century and into the 1920s, such writers as Firbank, Eliot, Osbert Sitwell, and Joyce, definitely did not. There gradually arose, as the century progressed and the gap widened, the concept of "Middlebrow" writing. A typical "Middlebrow" writer, author of *The Good Companions* (1929) and *Angel Pavement* (1930), much beloved by the populace generally but disdained by "literary" writers particularly, was J.B. Priestley, a figure who always provoked Evelyn Waugh's considerable ire.

"Literary" writing became increasingly difficult to read, allusive, fragmented, subtle to the point of obscurity. Readers still wrestle with "The Waste Land" (1922), a work which, until Ezra Pound got his hands on it, was—unbelievably—entitled "He Do the Police in Different Voices."

Some critics have said that this acceptance of complexity and obscurity was the deliberate strategy of an elite defending itself against what it felt to be an attack by "the masses." British writers in particular deplored the levelling effects of social change represented by bad architecture and the spread of suburbs; they loathed what they described as "the century of the common man."

The British elite found delectable the effete charms of Saki— *I think oysters are more beautiful than any religion.*

Revelled in the glitter of his wit: *Children with Hyacinth's temperament don't know better as they grow older,—they merely know more.*

They rallied to John Betjeman's hymn of hatred for the "Common Man," in his 1937 poem "Slough":

> *Come friendly bombs and fall on Slough!*
> *It isn't fit for humans now,*
> *There isn't grass to graze a cow,*
> *Swarm over, Death!*

British writers tended to embrace the aristocratic and the rural.

American writers went to Paris.

Canadian writers ....

Canada, languishing in its time warp through all the furore and ferment, slumbered on. The Ryerson Press, owned by the Methodist Church, published a few titles annually under the authority of The Book Steward. The barrenness and artistic bankruptcy of Canadian writing in the early years of the twentieth century are suggested by the illiterate jacket copy on Paul A.W. Wallace's *The Twist and Other Stories* published by the Ryerson Press in 1923.

> A purely Canadian book of short stories is considerable of a novelty. Those included in this volume are characteristic, striking tales of romance, adventure and whimsical nonsense written in a most vigorous style and set in such familiar locations as Banff...

I must record, however, that the first really significant book in Canadian prose was *Flying a Red Kite* by Hugh Hood, which was published in 1962 by... the Ryerson Press.

Canada's first prose writer with modernist ambitions was Raymond Knister (1899–1932). He imbibed these ideas in Iowa City, where he was associate editor of the avant-garde literary magazine *The Midland*. In 1925 he published a poem and two stories in the important American literary magazine *This Quarter*.

What follows is an extract from his story "The Strawstack" published in *The Canadian Forum* in 1923. In 1972, Michael Gnarowski, one of our more eminent Canadianists, singled out "The Strawstack" in his *Selected Stories of Raymond Knister* as—Gawd 'elp us—"fascinating and rewarding."

In this story a fugitive murderer pursued by a "posse" is making his way back by night to the now-abandoned homestead of his childhood. He is consumed by guilt and anguished by the sordid horror his life has become. The story ends with his braiding binder twine with which to hang himself:

> Dark splotches in one little field were peacefully still, and the cool munching of cows had something obscene about it, like the ravening of wolves at the finding of a dead hunter: the field, dead, was not the less silently complaining, he saw.
>
> He came nearer, and they woofed and scampered leadenly away, turning about to face him at a distance. He went on without seeing them.

The wind lifted again, and he stopped with a jerk which drew his head back, stiffened as before a brink. His face was compressed in a colour of terror which made his unshaven features frightful. Then he stepped on again after an instant, with limp strides as before...

Cows "ravening" like wolves?

"... scampered leadenly"? Cows that "woof"?

"stepped on . . . with limp strides?"

And as to what "the field, dead, was not the less silently complaining, he saw" might mean, your guess is as good as mine.

Three years before Knister wrote "The Strawstack," Katherine Mansfield had written one of the loveliest stories of early modernism, "Miss Brill."

Here are its crystalline opening lines:

> Although it was so brilliantly fine—the blue sky powdered with gold and great spots of light like white wine splashed over the Jardins Publiques—Miss Brill was glad that she had decided on her fur. The air was motionless, but when you opened your mouth there was just a faint chill, like a chill from a glass of iced water before you sip, and now and again a leaf came drifting—from nowhere, from the sky.

Knister was attempting to use description of landscape and object to suggest an emotional state, using *things* to suggest, to stand for *feelings*, a typical modernist practice. He was trying to lead Canada away from "tale" and towards "story"; unfortunately, his writerly endowments were negligible.

Knister was striving towards image.

Most contemporary writers would immediately recognize and most probably embrace the following paragraph from *The White Album* by Joan Didion.

> During the years when I found it necessary to rewire the circuitry of my mind I discovered that I was no longer interested

in whether the woman on the ledge outside the window on the sixth floor jumped or did not jump, or in why. I was interested only in the picture of her in my mind: hair incandescent in the floodlights, her bare toes curled inward on the stone ledge.

This quotation encapsulates the living centre of this chapter's concerns.

Jump?

Not jump?

Why?

Irrelevant, irrelevant

mere PLOT.

All is contained in the image, all is stated, suggested, implied in the image of the woman caught in the insane light, *bare toes curled inward.*

Grampaw Ez

I

Ford Maddox Ford described Ezra Pound as he looked when he descended on London literary society in 1909:

> Ezra had a forked red beard, luxuriant chestnut hair... He wore a purple hat, a green shirt, a black velvet jacket, vermilion socks, openwork, brilliant tanned sandals, trousers of green billiard cloth, in addition to an immense flowing tie that had been hand-painted by a Japanese Futurist poet.

He is described at a dinner as eating the table's centerpiece, a vase of tulips. Peter Ackroyd says of Pound that he was

> seen everywhere and with everyone, and was as a consequence, someone to be feared, respected, or consciously snubbed. Gertrude Stein, whom Pound met in 1933, did a little of all three. Pound visited her, lectured her on her own collection of paintings, and, in his eagerness to explain, toppled out of her favourite armchair. Miss Stein has left a description of the occasion in *The Autobiography of Alice B. Toklas*: 'He came home to dinner with us and he stayed and he talked about Japanese prints among other things. Gertrude Stein liked him but did not find him amusing. She said he was a village explainer—excellent if you were a village, but, if you were not, not.'
> (*Ezra Pound and His World*. Peter Ackroyd.)

Ford Maddox Ford (1873–1939) was one of the key writers, editors, and impresarios of modernism. He was the author of *The Good Soldier* and *Parade's End*, co-author of three novels with Joseph Conrad, editor from Paris of *The Transatlantic Review*.

In Humphrey Carpenter's biography of Pound, *A Serious Character*, he describes Ford's editorial practice:

> Pound delighted in Ford's off-the-cuff literary judgements, which were nearly always right, and his ability as an editor to detect the quality of a manuscript almost by its smell.
>
> ("I don't read manuscripts," Ford would say, "I know what's in 'em.")

In an interview later in life, Pound said, "one was hunting for a simple and natural language and Ford was ten years older, and accelerated the process towards it... Ford knew the best of the people who were there before him, you see, and he had nobody to play with until Wyndham [Lewis] and I and my generation came along."

Ford Maddox Ford's editing techniques still enchant me. When he read Pound's *Canzoni* of 1911, a volume still gummed up with languorous and fruity diction, Ford's critical response was "to roll on the floor in paroxysms of embarrassment and glee."

Pound apparently later said: "That roll saved me ten years."

Wyndham Lewis, another modernist contemporary, seething with habitual malice, described Ford Maddox Ford thus:

> A flabby lemon and pink giant, who hung his mouth open as though he were an animal at the Zoo inviting buns—especially when ladies were present. Over the gaping mouth damply depended the ragged ends of a pale lemon moustache. This ex-collaborator with Joseph Conrad was himself, it always occurred to me, a typical figure out of a Conrad book—a caterer, or cornfactor, coming on board—blowing like a porpoise with the exertion—at some Eastern port.

Astonishingly, this corpulent horror was a legendary womanizer, "protector," among many others, of the helplessly alcoholic Jean Rhys. Thomas Underwood, Ford's biographer, describes Caroline Tate (wife of Allen Tate) in New York typing, at Ford's dictation, the text of *The Last Post*, the final volume of *Parade's End*, a tetralogy considered by many to be among the greatest achievements of modernism.

> …she was undoubtedly distressed by Ford's personal habits. Clad in his underwear and perspiring heavily, the obese Englishman sat dictating his novel to her without a trace of self-consciousness.

Ford Maddox Ford and Ezra Pound, an unappetizing pair, through their direct and indirect influences, transformed writing in English.

This massive and tectonic achievement began formally with Pound's proclamation of the advent of Imagism. Hilda Doolittle, a young American poet in Pound's orbit and the young English poet, Richard Aldington, had adopted Pound's habit of working in the British Museum Reading Room. Meeting one afternoon in the Museum's tea room, Pound declared H.D., as she was known, an "Imagist." Writing to Harriet Monroe, editor of *Poetry: A Magazine of Verse*, the most influential of all American literary magazines, sending her H.D.'s first poems, Pound said that they were "the sort of American stuff I can show here and in Paris without its being ridiculed. Objectivity— no slither; direct—no excessive use of adjectives, no metaphors that won't permit examination. It's straight talk, straight as the Greek!"

Helen

All Greece hates
The still eyes in the white face,
the lustre as of olives
where she stands,
and the white hands.

All Greece reviles
the wan face when she smiles,
hating it deeper still
when it grows wan and white,
remembering past enchantments
and past ills.

> Greece sees, unmoved,
> God's daughter, born of love,
> the beauty of cool feet
> and slenderest knees,
> could love indeed the maid,
> only if she were laid,
> white ash amid funereal cypresses.

H.D.

(from *Heliodora* 1924)

Pound went on, in the letter to Harriet Monroe, to describe Imagist's intentions:

> Objectivity and again objectivity, and no expression, no hind-side-beforeness, no Tennysonianness of speech—nothing, nothing that you couldn't in some circumstance, in the stress of some emotion, actually say. Every literaryism, every book word, fritters away a scrap of the reader's patience, a scrap of his sense of your sincerity. It is only in the flurry, the shallow frothy excitement of writing, or the inebriety of a metre, that one falls into the easy, easy—oh, how easy!—speech of books and poems that one has read.

At the back of his 1912 volume of poems *Ripostes* Pound referred to H.D. and Aldington as "Les Imagists" who had the "the future... in their keeping."

What *precisely* was the Imagist ferment and who were its practitioners?

The theoretician of the movement was T.E. Hulme. He was killed, in 1917, in the Great War near Nieuport. His influence spread, however, by the dissemination of two posthumously published volumes edited by Herbert Read, *Speculations* (1924) and *Notes on Language and Style* (1929). T.S. Eliot grew close to Hulme's positions.

In a review in the *TLS* (*Times Literary Supplement*) by Len Gutkin
of a book by Henry Mead on Hulme, he writes:

> To his aficionados he is, despite his brief output and short life, some-
> thing like the secret heart of pre-war British modernism. Among the
> most important of his contributions was to provide "philosophical"
> ballast to the aesthetic doctrines of Imagism as developed by Ezra
> Pound. A born polemicist and an acidulous phrase-maker, Hulme
> articulated what was arguably the British avant-garde's guiding doc-
> trine: the supremacy of "classicism" ("beauty may be in small, dry
> things") over "Romanticism" (denigrated as disgustingly "damp").
> "Romanticism", he wrote, "is spilt religion."

The querulous quotation marks around the word "philosophical"
are supplied.

Among the imagist poets were Amy Lowell, Richard Aldington,
William Carlos Williams, James Joyce, John Cournos, Ford Maddox
Ford, and we must include, I think, D.H. Lawrence's early work.

Giorno dei Morti

Along the avenue of cypresses,
All in their scarlet cloaks and surplices
Of linen, go the chanting choristers,
The priests in gold and black, the villagers...

And all along the path to the cemetery
The round dark heads of men crowd silently,
And black-scarved faces of womenfolk, wistfully
Watch at the banner of death and the mystery.

And at the foot of a grave a father stands
With sunken head, and forgotten, folded hands;
And at the foot of a grave a mother kneels
With pale shut face, nor either hears nor feels

The coming of the chanting choristers
Between the avenue of cypresses,
The silence of the many villagers,
The candle-flames beside the surplices.

D.H. Lawrence
(from *Look! We Have Come Through* 1917
The poem itself was first published in 1913)

And the movement's aims?

The Oxford Companion to English Literature describes the movement's aims as being "to avoid abstraction, and to treat the image with a hard, clear precision rather than with overt symbolic intent."

The Reader's Encyclopedia describes Imagism as "the creation of precise, concentrated, sharply delineated images to evoke a unified impression, in which the emotion or association represented and the object itself are balanced equally in importance."

Ezra Pound said, more succinctly, "... the natural object is always the adequate symbol."

(All three descriptions describe what T.S. Eliot rather obscurely referred to as "the objective correlative"; that is, the thing in the context corresponding to the emotion the writer wishes to evoke.)

In an article with F.S. Flint in *Poetry* in 1913, Pound laid down the principles of Imagism:

1) Direct treatment of the "thing," whether subjective or objective.
2) To use absolutely no word that does not contribute to the presentation.
3) As regards rhythm: to compose in the sequence of the musical phrase, not in the sequence of a metronome.

Most now agree that the *locus classici* of the Imagist movement were *Sea Garden* by H.D., *Cadences* by F.S. Flint, and *Lustra* by Ezra Pound, all culminating, perhaps, in "The Waste Land" by T.S. Eliot. Pound later described all this ferment as the "revolution of the Word."

The modernists in prose and poetry pared and cut.

John Updike, in *Due Considerations: Essays and Criticism*, wrote of Hemingway in Paris "honing language to a fresh starkness." And of Isaac Babel, a writer much admired by Hemingway: "He [Babel] used to say, 'your language becomes clear and strong, not when you can no longer add a sentence, but when you can no longer take away from it.'"

What this honing of language was revealing, of course, was images. The keener the honing, the more brilliantly revealed was "the natural object" and we should recall Pound's dictum " ... the natural object is always the adequate symbol." It was as if the writers were sculptors who were chipping images out from the overlaying marble of familiarity, conventional diction, routine deadness of observation, academicism, windbaggery.

II

The years from 1908 to the First World War, the exact period of Pound's European initiation, were a time when each of the arts evolved the use of a new idiom. For Pound these were the ebullient years, but also a time of militance, of attack on entrenched values in literature or culture that made him stand closer and closer to the edge of things...

Pound had organized the Imagists as the first phalanx in his private campaign to make a modern literature, and in the next few years he recruited Yeats, Eliot, and Joyce to his modernist standards.

(From *Ezra Pound: Poet: A Portrait of the Man and his Work*
by A. David Moody)

He remained, however, embattled.

Although the modernist world Sydney and Violet [Schiff] inhabited was internally disorganized, modernism had no organized competition. If you were a writer, painter, or composer during those years there was no escaping its influence. None of this, however, presupposed tranquil acceptance of a single view of modernism. To the contrary, divisions about the meaning of modernism, both as an aesthetic idea and as a way of life, although sometimes intellectually trivial, were often socially divisive. As a result, factions were formed, fences were built, and vituperation emerged as the extreme sport of the day. The two principal factions were deliciously contrasted by the acid-tongued poet Edith Sitwell.

"On the one side," she wrote, "was the bottle-wielding school of thought to which I could not, owing to my sex, upbringing, tastes, and lack of muscle, belong." With this taut description, as with a wave of the hand, she dismissed Ezra Pound, Eliot, Lewis and their cohorts, most of whom lived in the London district known as Bayswater. She saved her undiluted invective, however, for the relatively effete intellectual alternative whose members resided in the neighborhood known as Bloomsbury. The "society of Bloomsbury," according to Sitwell, was "the home of an echoing silence." She said it was described by Gertrude Stein as "'the Young Men's Christian Association—with Christ left out, of course.' Some of the more silent intellectuals, crouching under the umbrella-like deceptive weight of their foreheads, lived their toadstool lives sheltered by these. The appearance of others raised the conjecture that they were trying to be fetuses."

(From *Sydney and Violet* by Stephen Klaidman)

Alfred Orage, the editor of *New Age,* a radical literary journal, wrote a farewell to Ezra Pound when he decamped for Rapallo in Italy.

Mr. Pound has been an exhilarating influence for culture in England; he has left his mark upon more than one of the arts, upon literature, music, poetry and sculpture; and quite a number of men and women owe their initiation to his self-sacrificing stimulus; among them being relatively popular successes as well as failures. With all this, however, Mr. Pound, like so many others who have striven for the advancement of intelligence and culture in England, has made more enemies than friends. Much of the Press has been deliberately closed by cabal to him; his books have for some time been ignored or written down; and he himself has been compelled to live on much less than would support a navvy. His fate, as I have said, is not unusual... by and large England hates men of culture until they are dead.

(From *Ezra Pound: Poet: A Portrait of the Man and his Work* by A. David Moody)

Pound's influence was far from over; the move from London to Rapallo was not defeat but strategic withdrawal. In London, Pound had known two other American expatriates, E.J. O'Brien and John Cournos, the latter a protégé and contributor to Imagist publications. E.J. O'Brien was the editor of the annual *Best American Short Stories*, an anthology he had founded in 1915 and which continues to this day. In 1922, O'Brien was paying homage in Rapallo to the Maestro (T.S. Eliot had called Pound *il miglior fabro*) at exactly the same time as the young Ernest Hemingway.

O'Brien asked Hemingway if he had any examples of his work and Hemingway pulled out of his knapsack the typescript of "My Old Man." O'Brien, breaking from his custom of republication from the magazines only, accepted the manuscript and dedicated to Hemingway *The Best Short Stories of 1923*. This was Hemingway's first publication in book form. Unfortunately, the dedication was spelled: *To: Ernest Hemenway*—as was his name throughout; Hemingway bemoaned the fact the no one believed he was the now-celebrated "Hemenway."

O'Brien's acute antennae picked up nearly every important American writer from the very beginnings of their careers in the little magazines: Sherwood Anderson, Ernest Hemingway, Fitzgerald, Lardner, Faulkner... and behind most of them, in some aspect or other, stood Ezra Pound. Through these anthologies, O'Brien sculpted our understanding of the modern short story, a role that few have grasped or acknowledged. When O'Brien started a British counterpart to the American anthology in 1922—publishing with uncanny discernment D.H. Lawrence, Katherine Mansfield,

Dorothy Richardson, Elizabeth Bowen, Sylvia Townsend Warner, V.S. Pritchett—who should he choose as his co-editor but ex-Imagist John Cournos.

Pound's influence resounding on...

Pound's vast correspondence is a chore to read because he used odd contractions, deliberate misspellings, and favoured an invented cornpone, chawbaccy language he seemed to think funny.

What follows is a brief letter, written in 1929, to Wyndham Lewis on the subject of sailing to the States on the Italian liner *Rex*.

(Wyndham Lewis was a powerful portrait painter but his novels are verbose and unleavened. He was secretive and paranoid. He saw himself as an outsider and "by his dress created an aura of villainy, wearing steeple-jack hats and a huge black cape." When he and Pound first met, Lewis' impression was that Pound was a "cowboy songster" and that he might be a "disguised Jew." Lewis' friend, the painter C.R.W. Nevinson, said of Lewis that: "Being misunderstood was one of his pleasures.")

"I have bin TOLD that it is 'necessary' to go FIRST CLAWSS to Amurika, if anything is to be accomplished. Do you advise it. I shall go on Rex or something large / prefer 2nd on colossus to capn's kaBIN on a small tub. Purrvided they don't stik one 80 quid for a foist."

The letter was signed EZ with the E in the shape of a swastika.

The P.S. read: sig.chur for use in Murka? or not."

III

The necessity remains for some comment on Ezra Pound the man.

Pound was rarely temperate. Even as early as 1914 he was addressing his audience as, "You funghus, you continuous gangrene." I incline to the view that Pound actually *was* insane. A genius but... His anti-semitism was virulent. Some have linked it to his father's having worked for the American mint, others have linked it to his espousing the ideas of Social Credit as expressed by Major C.H. Douglas, but medieval views on "usury" can scarcely account for Pound's constant spew of hatred.

Norman Levine's postgraduate studies were in Pound's work, a
fact of particular significance given Levine's subsequent lifelong preoccupation with stylistic innovation. I remember Norman's saying
to me, "When I actually read the transcripts of the broadcasts he
made for Italy during the war I no longer wanted anything to do
with him." I too have read the transcripts and they are vile.

Pound was captured in Italy by the Americans and charged
with treason for his active support of Mussolini and the Axis powers. He faced execution. Powerful literary figures in the States, to
save his life, had him declared insane and he was committed for
years to St. Elizabeths Hospital in Washington. On his eventual
release he returned to Italy and retreated into profound—perhaps
self-punishing?—silence.

He *did* say towards the end, "… the worst mistake I made was
that stupid suburban prejudice of anti-semitism. All along that
spoiled everything."

But having read what I've read, I rather doubt his contrition. I
incline towards considering him insane rather than evil because "evil"
seems to me an inescapably religious judgement. But whatever
judgement one arrives at, it is not really possible to deny his literary
greatness. I waver about *The Cantos* as poetry, though I freely admit
to not understanding reams of them, freely admit my inadequacy of
response. But I give perfect assent to Pound's originality, vision, influence, and to his total victory in the "Revolution of the Word."

IV

What have all these antique figures and this ancient warfare to do
with short stories now and particularly with Canadian short stories?
The simple answer is that nearly all significant writers in English
derive in some aspect or another from Pound and the ideas of
Imagism. We are all Pound's descendants, inheritors of the revolution of the word.

In the early years of the twentieth century, the ideas that were to
be codified by Pound were much in the air and were certainly well

known and understood by Katherine Mansfield. Pound, impressed by Hemingway's "imagism in prose," taught him how to be yet more sparse and unadorned. Hemingway later remembered that Pound had taught him more about "how to write and how not to write than anyone else." From these two writers alone—Hemingway and Mansfield—flowed immense and on-going influence.

Gertrude Stein's stylistic influence on Sherwood Anderson and Ernest Hemingway must also be acknowledged. What follows, in much-abbreviated form, is taken from *Geniuses Together* by Humphrey Carpenter, who himself acknowledges poet Ian Crichton Smith's insights into prose-style.

> Leo [Stein] sometimes wrote burlesques of his sister's word-portraits, but this was scarcely necessary, for the originals often seem to set out to parody themselves. For example this is what Gertrude has to say about Picasso:
>
> "This one always had something being coming out of this one. This one was working. This one always had been working. This one was always having something that was coming out of this one…" (etc.)
>
> Nevertheless the word-portraits are far more genuinely experimental than *The Making of Americans*—a real attempt at Cubism in prose. When some of them were published in Gertrude's *Tender Buttons* (1914), they excited a number of young writers who were hoping to struggle free from the constraints of nineteenth-century diction. Among these was the American novelist Sherwood Anderson, who says of his discovery of her prose: "It excited me as one might grow excited in going out into a new and wonderful country where everything is strange."
>
> [Anderson] had already written some fiction, which he now reworked under the influence of Gertrude Stein's word-portraits. For days he carried around a notebook in which he experimented with new combinations of words. "The result," he says, was "a new familiarity with the words of my own vocabulary… I really fell in love with words, wanted to give each word I used every chance to show itself off at its best."

Hemingway had begun a story called "Up in Michigan" a few months earlier. It was about a young waitress' feelings for a blacksmith, and its style was derived from Sherwood Anderson, hence from Gertrude Stein:

"Liz liked Jim very much. She liked it and the way he walked over from the shop and often went out the kitchen door to watch for him to start down the road. She liked it about his moustache. She liked it about how white his teeth were when he smiled. She liked it very much that he didn't look like a blacksmith. She liked it how much D.J. Smith and Mrs. Smith liked Jim. One day she found that she liked it the way the hair was black on his arms and how white they were above the tanned line when he washed up in the washbasin outside the house. Liking that made her feel funny."

Gertrude Stein had used the "insistence" technique non-naturalistically, choosing for repetition words that seemed irrelevant or unimportant, but Hemingway was identifying the element of "insistence" in real speech, the fact that people repeat the same word rather than search for a synonym. This substantiates his claim that he was trying to achieve "one true sentence"—but only this, for in every other respect "Up in Michigan" is thoroughly artificial and non-naturalistic. An incantatory manner has replaced the wham-bam narrative style of the Stuyvesant Byng and Il Lupo stories, and a carefully contrived syntax is being developed, on the principle of "unpacking" the sentence's meaning piece by piece rather than compressing its ideas or fitting them together. Meanwhile the subject matter remains the same as in the juvenilia—the worship of he-man masculinity.

"The boards were hard. Jim had her dress up and was trying to do something to her. She was frightened but she wanted it. She had to have it but it frightened her." etc.

The short story is an international form; Canadians came late to it. E.J. O'Brien started the annual *Best American Short Stories* in 1915; the Oberon Press equivalent, which became *Best Canadian Stories*, started in 1971, nearly sixty years later.

43

Canada was so inhospitable and unliveable in literary and cultural terms that its best writers, Alice Munro and Mavis Gallant, lived their literary careers through *The New Yorker*; Norman Levine and Mordecai Richler decamped for England; Clark Blaise's reception was lukewarm possibly because of his dual American/Canadian citizenship, and the visible "foreignness" of his wife, Bharati Mukherjee.

Canadians, meanwhile, celebrated Al Purdy, and revelled in the ponderous wit of Robertson Davies, old before his time in silver beard and portentous knickerbockers. Mindless nationalism beatified a succession of schmaltz-merchants adjudged—in ascending order of awfulness—"loved," "much-loved," "beloved," and "national treasure."

Nationalist academics scurried about inventing spurious ancestors for the non-existent "Canadian tradition," coming up with our gateway "ancestor," the text from which, as story writers, we all allegedly descend. The new ancestor will come as a huge surprise to general readers, none of whom will ever have heard of him. The founding Canadian text in the writing of stories is, according to these academic dimwits, *In the Village of Viger*, a soppy little confection written by Duncan Campbell Scott in 1896 and published, ironically enough, in Boston.

England, with its "imperial" standards, was excoriated as the snooty mother vainly attempting to repress her ebullient young.

The US was anathema.

The academic grip on, and formulation of, CanLit was a stranglehold precisely because there wasn't a large or informed readership to laugh at it.

Students were taught to value Frederick Philip Grove.

Professor David Staines, editor of the refurbished New Canadian Library, in 1990 declared Morley Callaghan a better writer than Ernest Hemingway.

This intellectually disgusting morass puts me in mind of a Yiddish saying often employed by Vancouver rare-book dealer William Hoffer:

The worst truth is better than the best lie.

The Precious Particle

I

Malcolm Bradbury described the modern short story as "the lyric poem of modern fictional prose." Before digging a little deeper into what is meant in this context by "poem," "poetry," and "image," let us quickly recap.

The modern short story broke away from the traditional "tale" because its writers had become more interested in inner worlds than in exploits. To capture inner worlds, new forms of plot had to be invented: for "tale" to become "story" it was necessary to find a new language with which to capture and evoke the new experiences. Abandoning the traditional plot in order to get at the new material meant abandoning the affable, shepherding Master of Ceremonies, the commentator, the interpreter. For "tale" to become "story," the reader had to be moved into a closer viewing position and had to be forced into a new relationship with events, had to be forced not to be passive recipient but to become active participant, which, in turn, meant being forced into a new relationship with the honed and spotlighted language which presented pictures, images that the reader had to experience and arrange into cumulative and larger significances.

Before exploring the idea of prose as poetry, let's look a little more closely at writers who worked hard at flattening readers' faces against the glass, at turning the reading of prose into an almost physical experience. Necessary because "image" and "poetry" depend on honed language to be seen and heard.

A writer I regard almost reverentially is Henry Green. [*vere* Henry Yorke (1905–1973), friend and contemporary, at Oxford, of Evelyn Waugh.] Green presents descriptions like a pile of fragments purposely scrambled, with normal links eliminated or turned against the reader so as to emphasize that observation is not a passive undertaking but a rigorous examination of disparate elements. He chooses to forgo what Lionel Trilling calls, following Henry James, "the grace of ease" in favour of "the grace of uncertainty or difficulty," the kind of style that chooses to violate its own beauty to retain some of the difficulty of actual perception.

The elimination of certain words prevents familiarity, while redundancy and inversion prevent the ease that Green felt was inimical to good prose. The result is passages like this well-known one:

> Evening. Was spring, Heavy blue clouds stayed over above. In small back garden of villa small tree was with yellow buds. On table in back room daffodils, faded, were between ferns in a vase.

Green always fought against "an elegance that is too easy." He was a defender and champion of Charles Montagu Doughty's *Travels in Arabia Deserta* (1888), a book much derided and decried. Green felt that Doughty bravely resisted the urge to make experience simple and intelligible, instead of crabbed and difficult as he himself found it.

(Doughty once said his aim in travelling to Arabia was "to rescue English Prose from the slough into which it has fallen." In Henry Green's "Apologia" (*Folios of New Writing*, 4. Autumn 1941), Green refers to "the constraint of his adventures" as the key to Doughty's style, indicating that the benefit of travel to an entirely strange place is not that it frees the imagination but that it forces the imagination up against restrictions that habit has made disappear.)

> Doughty randomly drops his article, but he is also fond of the redundant conjunction: "The nomad's fantasy is high, and that is ever clothed in religion." He compresses conventional phrases into constructions like "at four afternoon" but enjoys like Green,

the biblical "who": "and reached it to him, who sat all feeble murmuring thankfulness." Doughty favours inversions that increase the difficulty of communication. "All along by the haj road from hence were, as they tell, of old time villages... no need was then to carry provisions for the way'. He sometimes simply scrambles what he wants to say: "Their aching is less which are borne lying along in covered litters, although the long stooping camel's gait is never not very uneasy."

(Notes from Henry Green and the
Writing of His Generation. Michael North)

The style, as Green observes in "Apologia," is meant *to prevent experience from being swallowed too quickly*.

In Doughty's intentionally awkward prose I can feel in my bones the never not very uneasy lurching ache of that camel's gait; and in Green's description of the villa is it fanciful to imagine behind the picture a cameraman?

(The very intimate connection between early modernist writing and cinema could fill another book. All I have space for here is to say that I believe that much modernist writing actually *derives from cinema;* that D.W. Griffith is as significant a genius as James Joyce. Before 1909 Katherine Mansfield was earning money as a walk-on, an extra, in early films; James Joyce, in 1909, opened a cinema in Dublin.)

John Carey, sometime Merton Professor of Poetry, in his charming autobiography *The Unexpected Professor: An Oxford Life in Books* wrote:

> Stendhal also uses external appearance, as Tolstoy was to do with the Tsar and his gold lorgnette, to fix a character in a single shot. Julien Sorel [in *The Red and Black*] is torn between a longing for military glory and hopes of attaining eminence in the church. On the occasion of a royal visit to Verrières he serves as a member of the guard of honour and also, arrayed in ecclesiastical gear, assists the priest at mass in the ancient abbey church. As he kneels, his spurs poke out beneath the folds of his cassock, capturing his dilemma in a single comic image.

I suppose I could be accused of reducing these great novels to picture shows, and that's probably true. They did seem primarily visual to me. When, later, I saw the 1956 film of *War and Peace* Natasha is always Audrey Hepburn. Besides, I'd argue that from the perspective of cultural history the nineteenth century was essentially a struggle towards visual representation. Dioramas, daguerreotypes, lithographic newspaper illustrations—step by step they all brought camera and film closer. So it's not surprising the centuries great novels should strive in the same direction.

Carey seems on the verge of suggesting that the advent of Imagism was inevitable, predictable.)

Norman Levine, like Doughty and Green, spent his writing life exploring the effects of deliberate sentence fragmentation and denial of cadence to jolt the reader against the "real," to force the reader into stark experience of the "thing."

Cynthia Flood, in her essential and defining essay on Levine ("All the Heart Is in the Things") *Canadian Notes & Queries* No. 85 (2012), wrote: "I reread six of his books one after the other without stylistic boredom. A surprise, then, when I went back to other writers whom I admire. Something awful had happened to their prose. Stodgy and larded with words, it waddled thick-thighed down the page".

Here are the last four paragraphs of Norman Levine's story "Champagne Barn." In the context of the whole story, of course, these paragraphs are far more powerful, but even isolated here they quiver with energy and significance, and elegiac intensity.

Outside it was like walking into a hothouse. It had just gone seven. I walked by Anglesea Square. The row of poplars was still. But now and then their leaves caught a passing breeze. York and Clarence had all the houses bulldozed to the ground. And all that remained standing were the trees. And a signpost saying *Clarence Street*. Another said *York*.

On St. Patrick—Percy the Barber was closed. The door boarded up. But from a window I could see the layers of the years still on the walls. Haircuts 10 cents… minnows for sale…

Ken Maynard at the Français... pictures of King Clancy... Albert
Battleship Leduc... Howie Morenz...
By the river it was quiet. The water hardly moving. The sun
was coming through a haze. Trees. White bridges. A silver church
steeple on the opposite shore. It was like an Impressionist painting.
Then in Murray Street. The wooden houses, with the
wooden verandahs, only on one side. As I came near Reinhard's
Foods I began to hear the hacking. Then I saw the men. Their
window was open. They were the same five men I saw before.
By the thick wooden tables... with the knives... the choppers...
attacking the meat from the bone. Hack, hack, hack. While the
birds sang. The black squirrels moved quickly and stopped on
the grass. And now and again a breeze set the small leaves of the
poplars moving. Hack, hack, hack... Hack, hack, hack...
I would carry that sound with me long after I left.

This passage, within the context of the story, is an image, a poetic
embodiment of the story's concerns.
Slowly, obliquely, we approach what is poetic in prose.
An Aside.
Which is not an aside at all.
Before moving on from Henry Green, Charles Doughty, and
Norman Levine, all now dead, I want to stress how alive they are
and with us constantly. John Updike wrote of Henry Green, "At its
highest pitch Green's writing brings the rectangle of printed page
alive like little else in English fiction of this century—a superbly rendered surface above a trembling depth, alive not only with the reflections of reality, but with the consolations of art."
And Updike again: "Henry Green is a novelist of such rarity, such
marvellous originality, intuition, sensuality, and finish, that every
fragment of his work is precious..."
Alice Munro and I talked more than once about Eudora Welty's
fiction, Alice saying how much she'd been involved by, influenced by
A Curtain of Green and *The Golden Apples*. As, too, had I.
Eudora Welty said of Green, "Green remains the most interesting and vital imagination in English fiction in our time."

Evelyn Waugh, friend and contemporary of Green at Oxford, wrote in a review of *Living*:

> It is a work of genius... Technically, *Living* is without exception the most interesting book I have read. Those who are troubled with school-ma'am minds will be continually shocked by the diction and construction. In a great number of instances, Mr. Green omits the definite article where we expect to find it; he does worse violence to our feelings by such sentences as 'this was only but nervousness because her he was taking in was so pretty,' and 'he still had some of his Friday's money which he had not been able to drink away all of it.' These are the very opposite of slovenly writing. The effects which Mr. Green wishes to make and the information he wishes to give are so accurately and subtly conceived that it becomes necessary to take language one step further than its grammatical limits allow.

This was Evelyn Waugh writing *eighty-five years ago*.

Waugh and Green acknowledged the influences of Ronald Firbank; Waugh, in a letter to Green, specifically mentioned the similarity between Green's and Firbank's method of plot construction.

Alice Munro, John Updike, Eudora Welty, Henry Green, Evelyn Waugh, Ronald Firbank—we are back almost in the blink of an eye to the first decade of the twentieth century, all these writers caught up in the mesh of literary influence, literary inheritance.

Before leaving discussion of the revolutionary nature of modernist prose I want to illustrate the subject starkly by offering two descriptions of seascapes by writers contemporary with each other. Both passages will repay repeated readings. The first passage is clogged with cleverness, with swollen literariness, its similes barely comprehensible, and is dreadful. It is by Virginia Woolf and is from *The Waves*. The second is almost magically fresh, seemingly simple, acutely seen and felt. It is by Katherine Mansfield and is from *At the Bay*.

> The sun had not yet risen. The sea was indistinguishable from the sky, except that the sea was slightly creased as if a cloth had

wrinkles in it. Gradually as the sky whitened a dark line lay on the horizon dividing the sea from the sky and the grey cloth became barred with thick strokes moving, one after another, beneath the surface, following each other, pursuing each other, perpetually.

As they neared the shore each bar rose, heaped itself, broke and swept a thin veil of white water across the sand. The wave paused, and then drew out again, sighing like a sleeper whose breath comes and goes unconsciously. Gradually, the dark bar on the horizon becomes clear as if the sediment in an old wine-bottle has sunk and left the glass green. Behind it, too, the sky cleared as if the white sediment there had sunk, or as if the arm of a woman couched below the horizon had raised a lamp and flat bars of white, green and yellow spread across the sky like the blades of a fan. Then she raised her lamp higher and the air seemed to become fibrous and to tear away from the green surface flickering and flaming in red and yellow fibres like the smoky fire that roars from a bonfire. Gradually the fibres of the burning bonfire were fused into one haze, one incandescence which lifted the weight of the woollen grey sky on top of it and turned it to a million atoms of soft blue. The surface of the sea slowly became transparent and lay rippling and sparkling until the dark stripes were almost rubbed out. Slowly the arm that held the lamp raised it higher and then higher until a broad flame became visible; an arc of fire burnt on the rim of the horizon, and all round it the sea blazed gold.

The light struck upon the trees in the garden, making one leaf transparent and then another. One bird chirped high up; there was a pause; another chirped lower down. The sun sharpened the walls of the house, and rested like the top of a fan upon a white blind and made a blue finger-print of shadow under the leaf by the bedroom window. The blind stirred slightly, but all within was dim and unsubstantial. The birds sang their blank melody outside.

(*The Waves*. Virginia Woolf.)

Very early morning. The sun was not yet risen, and the whole of Crescent Bay was hidden under a white sea-mist. The big bush-covered hills at the back were smothered. You could not see where they ended and the paddocks and bungalows began. The sandy road was gone and the paddocks and bungalows the other side of it; there were no white dunes covered with reddish grass beyond them; there was nothing to mark which was beach and where was the sea. A heavy dew had fallen. The grass was blue. Big drops hung on the bushes and just did not fall; the silvery, fluffy toi-toi was limp on its long stalks and all the marigolds and the pinks in the bungalow gardens were bowed to the earth with wetness. Drenched were the cold fuchsias, round pearls of dew lay on the flat nasturtium leaves. It looked as though the sea had beaten up softly in the darkness, as though one immense wave had come rippling, rippling—how far? Perhaps if you had waked up in the middle of the night you might have seen a big fish flicking in at the window and gone again...

Ah-Aah! sounded the sleepy sea. And from the bush there came the sound of little streams flowing quickly, lightly, slipping between the smooth stones, gushing into ferny basins and out again; and there was the splashing of big drops on large leaves, and something else—what was it?—a faint stirring and shaking, the snapping of a twig and then such silence that it seemed that some one was listening.

Round the corner of Crescent Bay, between the piled-up masses of broken rock, a flock of sheep came pattering. They were huddled together, a small, tossing, woolly mass, and their thin stick-like legs trotted along quickly as if the cold and the quiet had frightened them. Behind them an old sheep-dog, his soaking paws covered with sand, ran along with his nose to the ground, but carelessly, as if thinking of something else. And then in the rocky gateway the shepherd himself appeared...

(From: *At the Bay*, Katherine Mansfield)

II

Malcolm Cowley, American writer and literary impresario, friend of Hemingway and Faulkner, wrote an introduction to *Writers at Work:*

The Paris Review Interviews (1958) which brings us usefully closer to what is meant by the "poetic" in prose.

> There would seem to be four stages in the composition of a story. First comes the germ of the story, then a period of more or less conscious meditation, then the first draft, and finally the revision, which may be simply "pencil work" as John O'Hara calls it—that is, minor changes in wording—or may lead to writing several drafts and what amounts to a new work.
>
> The germ of a story is something seen or heard, or heard about, or suddenly remembered; it may be a remark casually dropped at the dinner table (as in the case of Henry James' story *The Spoils of Poynton*), or again it may be the look on a stranger's face. Almost always it is a new and simple element introduced into an existing situation or mood; something that expresses the mood in one sharp detail; something that serves as a focal point for a hitherto disorganized mass of remembered material in the author's mind. James describes it as "the precious particle... the stray suggestion, the wandering word, the vague echo, at a touch of which the novelist's imagination winces as at the prick of some sharp point," and he adds that, "its virtue is all in its needle-like quality, the power to penetrate as finely as possible."
>
> ... For short-story writers the four stages of composition are usually distinct, and there may even be a fifth, or rather a first, stage. Before seizing upon the germ of a story, the writer may find himself in a state of "generally intensified emotional sensitivity... when events that usually pass unnoticed suddenly move you deeply, when a sunset lifts you to exaltation, when a squeaking door throws you into a fit of exasperation, when a clear look of trust in a child's eyes moves you to tears." I am quoting from Dorothy Canfield Fisher, who "cannot conceive" she says, "of any creative fiction written from any other beginning." There is not much doubt, in any case, that the germ is precious largely because it serves to crystallize a prior state of feeling.

What Cowley is describing here is crucial in understanding what is meant by the "poetic" in prose. It is vitally important to stress that the writer about to enter upon a short story is nearly always in a state of "generally intensified emotional sensitivity," that the germ of the story "is precious largely because it serves to crystallize a prior state of feeling."

It is significant that Cowley uses the word "germ" rather than the word "idea." "Germ" carries a group of meanings associated with new life, germination, growth process; "idea" suggests thought rather than feeling, the gaze from outside, divorce from *things*, abstraction.

When someone says to me, "I have a really good idea for a story" I politely turn my mind off because I know I'm going to have to endure a plot. If, on the other hand, someone says to me, "I've found myself lately thinking again and again about an old Player's *Navy Cut* cigarette tin—they used to hold fifty cigarettes, dark blue with a sailor's head on it with a beard, the picture's inside a gold-coloured circle—was it a lifesaver?—my father kept brass screws in it on his workbench"—yes, if they told me that, then they'd capture my immediate attention.

In the days when I taught writing and literature I used to say to my students: *If you have an idea, have a little lie down until you feel better.*

Or, if irritated, *Any fool can have an idea.*

Glare,

AND MOST DO.

What Dorothy Canfield Fisher describes as "a prior state of feeling" is referred to very early on in the short history of the short story. Ezra Pound's dictum about Imagism, that "... the natural object is always the adequate symbol" worked perfectly well for very brief lyrics but longer and more complex works needed more obvious control and direction.

Katherine Mansfield herself pointed out this flaw in Pound's theorizing and stated the solution. In a book review for *The Athenaeum* she wrote:

> Without emotion writing is dead... To contemplate the object, to let it make its own impressions... is not enough. There must

be an initial emotion felt by the writer, and all that he sees is saturated in that emotional quality. It alone can give incidence and
sequence, character and background, a close and intimate unity.

"The prior state of feeling" is referred to again and again. Alice
Munro said: "What happens as event [i.e. plot] doesn't really much
matter. When the event becomes the thing that matters, the story
isn't working too well. There has to be a feeling in the story."

She has called "the prior state" that "indescribable 'feeling' that is
like the soul of the story"; Norman Levine refers to it as "a magnet
that pulls these pieces from my past"; Chekhov called it "the necessary tune" in the head that prompts the act of writing; I have always
thought of it in my own fiction as "the current."

In 1982—at this time of writing, thirty-two years ago—I edited
Making it New, an anthology of Canadian stories with accompanying commentaries. Alice Munro wrote for me the following comments: they have puzzled and distressed some readers ever since.

What is Real?

What I would like to do here is what I can't do in two or three
sentences at the end of a reading. I won't try to explain what
fiction is, and what short stories are (assuming, which we can't,
that there is any fixed thing that it is and they are), but what short
stories are to me, and how I write them, and how I use things
that are "real." I will start by explaining how I read stories written by other people. For one thing, I can start reading them anywhere; from beginning to end, from end to beginning, from any
point in between in either direction. So obviously I don't take up
a story and follow it as if it were a road, taking me somewhere,
with views and neat diversions along the way. I go into it, and
move back and forth and settle here and there, and stay in it for
a while. It's more like a house. Everybody knows what a house
does, how it encloses space and makes connections between one
enclosed space and another and presents what is outside in a new
way. This is the nearest I can come to explaining what a story
does for me, and what I want my stories to do for other people.

So when I write a story I want to make a certain kind of structure, and I know the feeling I want to get from being inside that structure. This is the hard part of the explanation, where I have to use a word like "feeling," which is not very precise, because if I attempt to be more intellectually respectable I will have to be dishonest. "Feeling" will have to do.

There is no blueprint for the structure. It's not a question of "I'll make this kind of house because if I do it right it will have this effect." I've got to make, I've got to build up, a house, a story to fit around the indescribable "feeling" that is like the soul of the story, and which I must insist upon in a dogged, embarrassed way, as being no more definable than that. And I don't know where it comes from. It seems to be already there, and some unlikely clue, such as a shop window or a bit of conversation, makes me aware of it. Then I start accumulating the material and putting it together. Some of the material I may have lying around already, in memories and observations, and some I invent, and some I have to go diligently looking for (factual details), while some is dumped in my lap (anecdotes, bits of speech). I see how this material might go together to make the shape I need, and I try it. I keep trying and seeing where I went wrong and trying again.

Also in *Making It New*, Norman Levine wrote the following notes:

I wrote "A Small Piece of Blue" towards the end of 1955 in St. Ives, Cornwall. I was waiting to go to Canada in order to do a trip across the country (the trip was to form the background of the book *Canada Made Me*) and I had made a list of the places I would visit. One of the places was Helen Mine, an iron mine in northern Ontario, where I had worked during the summer of 1948 after graduating from McGill. In the autumn I would return to McGill for my M.A. then go off to England. Meanwhile I had to earn some money. A summer job, in the past, usually meant working in Ottawa, for the government, in an office. But there had been a war. I had been in the RCAF. And I didn't want to go back to what I was used to. So going to work in the mine was also an act of bravado.

I didn't have a clear notion of the story when I started. Only a definite intention—of wanting to show something of what living and working in this iron mine was like. Yet, some of the ingredients in this story came not from the mine but from people and incidents I had met elsewhere.

The woman with no nose—she came from Barnstaple, in North Devon. She was a music teacher and let out a room. I took it for a few months in 1954.

The shooting with a gun, indoors, at a lit candle was told to me about what went on aboard the French Crabbers, anchored in the bay off St. Ives, at night.

The poem that begins:

All your experiences:
Those bits.
Those pieces you carried away with you.
How long will they last?

I wrote that separately, as a poem, in 1952. I had not long been married and we were staying, very briefly, with my wife's parents in London. I remember I was in a pub reading a newspaper. An American professor had come over to England to exhume a tomb to try and prove that Bacon had written Shakespeare's plays. There was another customer in the pub as well. We got talking. He said he worked at an undertakers. And he told me some technical things about his job; what was the best wood to have and how even that didn't last very long...

I did not think of these separate pieces as part of a jigsaw that I had to get to fit in order to make the story. As I remember it, all I wanted was to write a story about the experience of living and working in the mine. And it was the pressure of writing the story that made me remember these disconnected memories. The pressure of writing the story was like a magnet that pulled these pieces from my past.

In 1972—at this time of writing, 42 years ago—Alice Munro wrote for me the following brief commentary for my anthology *The*

Narrative Voice. The commentary was untitled, and I called it "The Colonel's Hash Resettled" to echo the title of an essay by Mary McCarthy which explores the meaning of "symbol"; that essay can be found in *The Humanist in the Bathtub*.

Alice was writing about the significantly titled story "Images" from her then-recently published first book *Dance of the Happy Shades*.

The Colonel's Hash Resettled

A Toronto critic, discussing the story "Images," said that the house in the ground—the roofed-over cellar that the hermit character lives in—symbolized death, of course, and burial, and that it was a heavy gloomy sort of story because there was nothing to symbolize resurrection. Typical of Canadian fiction, he went on to say, but I didn't follow him very far because I was feeling gloomy myself, about what he had said, and angry, and amazingly uneasy. Surely a roofed-over cellar doesn't mean any such thing, I thought, unless I want it to? Surely it's not that simple? I wrote the story, didn't I? If I hadn't sat down and written the story he wouldn't be able to talk about it, and come to all these interesting and perhaps profitable conclusions about Canadian Literature—well, he probably would have come to those conclusions all the same, but he would have had to dig up somebody else's story (I notice the choice of verb and never mind) to do it—so I get to say, don't I, whether a house in the ground is death and burial or whether it is, of all unlikely things, *a house in the ground*?

Well, the answer is no, I do not get to say, and I should have known that already. What you write is an offering; anybody can come and take what they like from it. Nevertheless I went stubbornly back to the real facts, as I saw them, the real house in the real world, and tried to discover what it was doing in the story and how the story was put together in the first place.

I grew up on the untidy, impoverished, wayward edge of a small town, where houses were casually patched and held together, and there was a man living in a house exactly like that—the roofed-over cellar of a house that had been burned down. Another man and his wife, I remember, lived in the kitchen of a burned-out house, whose blackened front walls still stood, around a roomful of nettles. (What is that going to symbolize, if I use it in a story some day?) Such a choice of living-quarters was thought only mildly eccentric. It was a cheap and practical way of getting shelter, for people with no means to build, or buy, or rebuild. And when I think of the slanting, patched roof and the stove pipe, the house as a marvellous, solid, made, final thing, I feel as if I have somehow betrayed it, putting it in a story to be extracted this way, as a bloodless symbol. There is a sort of treachery to innocent objects—to houses, chairs, dressers, dishes, and to roads, fields, landscapes—which a writer removes from their natural, dignified obscurity and sets down in print. There they lie, exposed, often shabbily treated, inadequately, badly, clumsily transformed. Once I've done that to things, I lose them from my private memory. There are primitive people who will not allow themselves to be photographed for fear the camera will steal their souls. That has always seemed to me to be not an unreasonable belief. And even as I most feverishly, desperately practice it, I am a little afraid that the work with words may turn out to be a questionable trick, an evasion (and never more so than when it is most dazzling, apt and striking), an unavoidable lie. So I could not go now and look at that house with a perfectly clear conscience, symbol or not.

I do think symbols exist, or rather, things that are symbolic, but I think that their symbolism is infinitely complex and never completely discovered. Are there really writers who sit down and say yes, well, here I need a symbol, let's see what I have in the files? I don't know; you never know how other writers work. In the case of that house, I gave it to the character without thinking about it, just as I gave him the whiskey-drinking cat that actually belonged to the father of a friend of mine. I don't remember deciding to do this. I do remember how the story started. It started with the picture in my mind of a man met in the woods, coming obliquely down the river-bank, carrying the hatchet, and the child watching him, and the father unaware, bending over his traps. For a long time I was carrying this picture in my mind, as I am carrying various pictures now which may or may not turn into stories. Of course the characters did not spring from nowhere. His ancestors were a few old men, half hermits, half madmen, often paranoid, occasionally dangerous, living around the country where I grew up, not living in the woods but in old farm-houses, old family homes. I had always heard stories about them; they were established early as semi-legendary figures in my mind.

From this picture the story moved outward, in a dim uncertain way. When this was happening I was not so much making it as remembering it. I remembered the nurse-cousin, though she was not really there to remember; there was no original for her. I remembered the trip along the river, to look at traps, with my father, although I had never gone. I remember my mother's bed set up in the dining-room, although it was never there. It has actually become difficult to sort out the real memories.—like the house—used in this story from those that are not "real" at all. I think others are real because I did not consciously plan, make, or arrange them. I found them. And it is all deeply, perfectly true to me, as a dream might be true, and all I can say, finally, about the making of a story like this is that it must be made in the same way our dreams are made, truth in them being cast, with what seems to us often a rather high-handed frivolity in any kind of plausible, implausible, giddy, strange, humdrum terms at all. This is the given story (I hate to use that adjective because it calls to mind a writer in some sort of a trance, and seems to wrap the whole subject in a lot of trashy notions, but it will have to do) and from that I work, getting no more help, doing the hard repetitive work of putting in words that are hardly any good at all, then a little better, then quite a bit better, at times satisfactory.

It was cheering to see Alice Munro insisting that the old man with the hatchet in "Images" is not Death but an old man with a hatchet and that he inhabits not the Underworld but a cellar with a roof over it. The whiskey-drinking cat is not a feline Cerberus; it is a drunk cat.

"Incandescent memories," precious particles, inform the work of many writers. Many children, particularly children who become painters or writers, apprehend their early world as holy, overpowering in its physicality, immediacy, and wonder, and the images that sear them burn for the rest of their lives. When they write or paint, they are enshrining—and that is the exact word—enshrining the Real.

Again, a pertinent quotation from Kirsty Gunn's review of the *Edinburgh Edition of the Collected Works of Kathleen Mansfield*.

> "The death of Mansfield's brother early in the war," the editors of these works write in their introduction, "is often read as the turning point where a good writer moves towards becoming something more"; though as they point out, "that devastating loss was part of the change but not all… incandescent memories of Wellington [Cook Strait, her hometown on the North Island] were being quarried before Leslie's death added its imperative." Still, in general, it's in the stories collected here from after 1917 that we see how the change in content—that ransacked childhood—leads also to a change in form as she frees herself of convention, of all these lessons of storytelling she has set about learning, as her work comes to reflect more and more the mind's seizing, sometimes apparently randomly, sometimes urgently, on the details of the remembered life. Anything may happen in this kind of story, or very little. It's the telling itself—not plot, not development, not narrative arc—that provides the imperative. "I shall tell you everything, even how the laundry basket squeaked," she wrote in her journal. "I must play my part."

"Playing her part" means, I presume, playing her part by writing of their past childhood, in honouring the memory of her brother and bearing witness to particularity.

That the sacred encompassed "how the laundry basket squeaked"—how wonderful that is, the remembering! It reminded me instantly of Del Jordan's resolution in Alice Munro's *Lives of Girls and Women* to preserve forever each shining particle of Jubilee.

(*Now,* I can't get that laundry basket out of my mind. I know, *know,* it was made of wicker.)

It did not occur to me then that day I would be so greedy for Jubilee. Voracious and misguided as Uncle Craig out at Jenkin's Bend, writing his History, I would want to write things down.

I would try to make lists. A list of all the stores and businesses going up and down main street and who owned them, a list of family names, names on the tombstones in the Cemetery and any inscriptions underneath. A list of the titles of movies that played at the Lyceum Theatre from 1938 to 1950, roughly speaking. Names on the Cenotaph (more for the First World War than for the second.) Names of the streets and the pattern they lay in...

And no list could hold what I wanted, for what I wanted was every last thing, every layer of speech and thought, stroke of light on bark or walls, every smell, pothole, pain, crack, delusion, held still and held together—radiant, everlasting.

These engrossing details, these "precious particles," are not crude equivalences. Detail X does *not* equal intellectual meaning Y. Rather, they are details that set up suggestions, leave the air quivering with reverberations until the next note is struck whose reverberations will merge with those that are still sounding so that the air of the story is alive with gathering music.

Be not afeard, the air is full of noises,
Sounds and sweet airs that give delight and hurt not.

The reading of a story well-performed (and well-read) is somehow like experiencing the Bach unaccompanied cello suites or shimmering sitar *ragas* played by Ravi Shankar.

Seamus Heaney in his 1968 T.S. Eliot Memorial Lecture, published as *The Government of the Tongue,* said of "The Waste Land" that it is a poem of images, textures, and suggestiveness.

It represents a defeat of the will, an emergence of the ungainsayable and symbolically radiant out of the subconscious deeps. Rational structure had been overtaken or gone through like a sound barrier. The poem does not disdain intellect, yet poetry, having to do with feelings and emotions, must not submit to the intellect's eagerness to foreclose. It must wait for a music to occur, an image to discover itself...

... *the intellect's eagerness to foreclose*...

Now *there's* a pregnant thought, a red danger flag cracking in the wind.

...*an image to discover itself*...

Heaney is using the word "discover" in its slightly archaic sense of "reveal itself"; open its petals, come into full bloom. A story's images then, are not always rational or explicable. Imagism was an austere impulse, yet essentially a continuation of Romanticism. I am not about to tout the *more than dubious* merits of Surrealism, but most writers experience and celebrate the *inevitability* of images. In my own writing I think of images as magical and feel perfectly unashamed doing so. The "unconscious mind" and such anemic constructions convey nothing of the power, the mystery, the joy of such births from the dark.

I have been haunted for many months now by the description in Penelope Fitzgerald's *The Bookshop* of a man in a field filing the teeth of a horse. The description ("the natural object") becomes an image for the book's concerns; it makes me shudder.

Conscious surrealism, the Full-Dali, as it were, always was a freak show.

London had its first major introduction to surrealist painting in 1936 at the New Burlington Galleries. It was announced that Salvador Dali would speak on one of the following topics: Paranoia, The Pre-Raphaelites, Harpo Marx, or Phantoms.

The London *Star* reported the lecture:

Mr Dali and an audience of 300 turned up at the lecture, and Mr Dali dressed for his part. He wore a diving suit, decorated like a Christmas tree. The diver's helmet had a motor car radiator on top. Plasticine hands were stuck on the bodice. Round his waist was a belt with a dagger. He carried a billiard cue and was escorted by two dogs. To make the performance more mystifying he spoke in French, through loudspeakers. Half-way through his patter he began to get warm and asked somebody to take his helmet off. It had stuck and a spanner was no use, but the billiard cue came in handy as a can opener. Now and again the lanternist put the slides in sideways or upside down but nobody knew or minded. Surrealism is like that... Mr Dali was asked why he wore the diving suit. "To show that I was plunging down deeply into the human mind," he replied.

This is not what I meant when I wrote of the power, the mystery, the joy of the birth of images from the dark.

Alice Munro's "Images" is not "a heavy gloomy sort of story" as the Toronto critic described it. Too many readers have assumed too firmly that "Images" is concerned with the child's learning about Death; they seem to have given little weight to the story's sexual concerns. Readers seem to have overlooked the fact the Mary McQuade, Death's harbinger, has come to the house to deliver the girl's mother of another baby, that the girl is making a connection between death and birth and sex and being female. The robust Mary McQuade, the focus of earthy laughter, who is always being teased about possible husbands, makes the child uneasy, wary. She watches the shadows cast by her father and the flirtatious Mary McQuade and tries "to understand the danger, to read the signs of invasion."

Both "Walker Brothers Cowboys" and "Images" are initiation stories, stories about the gaining of knowledge. The girl in "Images" is slightly younger than the girl in "Walker Brothers Cowboy," but in both cases the stories are richer for us if we accept that the girls in each are sensitive to the sexual currents around them, are hungry for sexual knowledge, are eager to learn how this sexuality will affect *their* lives.

In "Images" we should note the father, whom the daughter adores, takes the child into a new world of experience, gentles the hatchet-man, disarms him, soothes danger away, leaving only wonderment, delight in strangeness.

While I'm enthusiastically a "house in the ground" man, I can feel something else in the story; I can sense, under the surface, shapes not quite visible. The Quest Perilous. The Castle, Cave, Entrance. The Hidden World. The Ogre. The Keeper of the Secret. The Triumphant Return with the Treasure… a story profoundly "real" yet at the same time are those *pentimenti* we can discern? An earlier version complicating the work? Are we possibly looking at an underlying half-lost structure of fairy tale?

This "lyric" type of story, more or less naturalistic, is now fairly standard, but a good short story is whatever an author can get away with. There is only one rule: the story must somehow persuade us of its truth and engage us emotionally. Stories range from the lyricism of Eudora Welty to the often painful flatness, the anti-rhetoric, of the masterly Raymond Carver, from the wild rhetoricals of Leon Rooke which dance, and keep us dancing, like ping-pong balls on a jet of water, to the heightened vernacular of Hugh Hood. One of the strengths of short stories is that they are always changing shape and direction; without continual formal innovation, a breaking through crusted convention to emotion and significance, stories become arteriosclerotic and spread, portly, in the club's leather chairs, gesturing with fat cigars.

As I read manuscripts in my editing for Biblioasis and Oberon's *Best Canadian Stories*, the opening lines of Howard Nemerov's poem "Blue Swallows" are often in my mind:

> *O swallows, swallows, poems are not*
> *The point. Finding again the world,*
> *That is the point…*

The one constant is that the world is found again through images, through "poetry." But not, as should already be becoming clearer, by outdated artificialities; we are not concerned with "poetry" in the sense of Robert Burns'

O my Luve's like a red, red, rose.

(So few writers use similes at all these days. Similes usually clog up the works and do nothing a well-chosen verb can't do better, and besides, tempt writers into "Look, Ma! No hands!" showing off.

O, swallows, swallows, *cleverness* is not the point.

Let someone else say this, the gifted and always startling Shaena Lambert.

> Years ago, when I hadn't yet written a full, satisfying story and was struggling and confused, I read Flannery O'Connor's famous essay on symbols and surface, in her book *Mystery and Manners*. This essay had a huge impact on me. Her theory is that symbols (and I think we could add in theme here as well) can only be created when the writer pays close attention to the surface details of life; how things smell, taste, look, feel. This is fascinating and true. If you want to talk about death, life, youth, eternity, redemption, you can only do it through dirty socks, rancid butter, mustard stains, a flock of geese.

(Ever since first reading it I have loved this comment of Flannery O'Connor's from an address she gave in Atlanta to the Georgia Council of Teachers of English. "The Georgia writer's true country is not Georgia but Georgia is an entrance to it for him.")

The elegiac passage quoted earlier from Norman Levine's story "Champagne Barn," the "precious particles" drawn from his memory or invention by magnet, charged and given significance in the current of his prevailing melancholia, is almost pure poetry, that overwhelming feeling of diminishment and loss detailed in picture after picture, the palimpsest of posters in the boarded-up shop of Percy the Barber, the bulldozed houses, the contrast of this destruction with the rural scene glimpsed across the river in Quebec, the village, the silver church spire, like a pretty Impressionist painting, an aesthetic rebuke to the *Hack, hack, hack* of the butchers in Reinhard's Foods.

The unrelieved current in Norman's fiction, its settled unvarying, fixèd melancholy, puts me in mind, perhaps irreverently, of an anecdote in Anthony Cronin's *Samuel Beckett: The Last Modernist*.

> When in the mid-sixties he was staying with John Calder [his publisher] in London they went with some of his BCC friends to Lord's cricket grounds to see England play Australia. In fine

weather one could sit in the members' enclosure drinking beer and watching cricket, both of which Beckett appeared to enjoy. As they sat there someone remarked on the lovely summer weather, and everyone else, including Beckett, concurred. It was a truly beautiful summer day. "The sort of day that makes one glad to be alive," remarked someone else.

"Oh," replied Beckett, "I don't think I would go quite so far as to say that."

III

I have been taking a slow, oblique approach to what "poetic" means in relation to prose because I don't wish to be prescriptive, to hand down definitions from on high. The subject is complex and complicated and needs to be listened to, grown into. I want the reader to listen to a conversation that's going on, piece together what the others are talking about, follow up hints, asides, make mental notes to explore that remark, *sidle* into an understanding.

Everyone would, I imagine, be able to sense the following paragraph as "poetic." In the context of the novel from which it comes, it is, being an image in the novel's larger design, even more intense in its impact.

The roses, when they came to the rose garden, were full out, climbing along brick walls, some, overpowered by their heavy flowers, in obeisance before brick paths, petals loose here and there on the earth but, on each bush and tree of roses, rose after rose after rose of every shade stared like oxen, and came forward to meet them with a sweet, heavy, luxuriant breath...

stared like oxen...
... and came forward to meet them

This truly extraordinary writing is from the novel *Caught* (1943) by Henry Green.

Also immediately recognizable as "poetic," this passage from *Loving* (1945), Green's novel set in wartime Ireland in a grand Country House, two young housemaids waltzing among the dust-sheet-shrouded furniture in the deserted ballroom:

> They were wheeling wheeling in each other's arms heedless at the far end where they had drawn up one of the white blinds. Above from a rather low ceiling five great chandeliers swept one after the other almost to the waxed parquet floor reflecting in their hundred thousand drops the single sparkle of distant day, again and again red velvet panelled walls, and the two girls, minute in purple, dancing multiplied to eternity in these trembling pears of glass.

Those double 'ee's' on "wheeling" and "heedless," the breathtaking "again and again red velvet panelled walls," the hard g's asserting the waltz time, the red velvet panelled walls coming past again and again as the girls wheeled—so simple yet so brilliant!

But even more extraordinary, and perhaps even *more* poetic, are the three opening lines of his novel *Party Going* (1939). These lines, in a strange way, capture the emotional impact of the whole novel, plug you, as it were, directly into the current.

> Fog was so dense, bird that had been disturbed went flat into a balustrade and slowly fell, dead, at her feet.
>
> There it lay and Miss Fellowes looked up to where that pall of fog was twenty feet above and out of which it had fallen, turning over once. She bent down and took a wing then entered a tunnel in front of her, and this had DEPARTURES lit up over it, carrying her dead pigeon.

The first two Henry Green quotations are extraordinary writing: lush, ripe, stuff to gorge on until the juice runs down your chin. But this does not make them "poetic." What makes them poetic is their having been charged by the novels' emotional currents; they are poetic because they serve a poetic function within the novels' larger structure and purposes.

I say of the opening three lines of *Party Going* that they are *more* poetic than the two previous Green quotations and I say that because they are the entire novel, in capsule. Those three lines are the opening chords of a piece of music; the sounding of the emotional themes that will be played out; they are *freighted*.

"Fog was so dense, bird that had been disturbed..."

Experiencing the omission of the definite and indefinite articles is in itself already like sticking your licked forefinger into an electric socket.

Then Miss Fellowes carries the dead pigeon into the tunnel marked DEPARTURES; we are heading into the novel's less-than-jolly journey.

"Poetry" then, in the sense in which we are talking, is nothing like what we think of as "a poem"; it has nothing much to do with *O, my Luve's like a red, red rose*. Lyric loveliness does not equal the "poetic" in prose.

Gore Vidal criticized John Updike, saying that he "describes to no purpose," and even admirers will know what Gore Vidal meant. In the early sixties, when I was teaching myself to read, I remember an Updike story which had a scene in a school classroom. Updike described the electric bell on the wall near the ceiling as looking like a swallow's nest under the eaves. I was so arrested by this, I remember, that I stopped reading the more fully to visualize it. Wow! I said to my younger self. It was probably several years before I realized that it was an image destructively obtrusive.

Look, Ma! No hands!

Martin Amis wrote in *The Moronic Inferno and Other Visits to America*:

> Something needs to be added, in a tone of baffled admiration, about Mr Updike's prose. In common with all his post-*Couples* fiction, the new novel is "beautifully written." That phrase has of course been devalued—it now means little more than freedom from gross infelicity; but Updike's style is melodious, risky, detailed, funny and fresh. (An example, more or less random: "He flopped into a canvas chair and kept crossing and recrossing

his legs, which were so short he seemed to Bech to be twiddling his thumbs.") This is so *good*, you keep thinking; why isn't it the best? Such prose is never easily achieved, and yet Updike produces an awful lot of the stuff ... In the end, it reminds you of the best cinematography. Using talent and technique, lens and filter, the artist enjoys a weird infallibility, producing effects that are always rich, ravishing and suspiciously frictionless.

There are, of course, many kinds of stories, many kinds of poetry in prose, which have evolved from the sort of story created by James Joyce, Katherine Mansfield, and Ernest Hemingway. There are stories which glitter with swordplay wit, stories of voices explaining, beseeching, confessing, ranting—think of Dylan Thomas' bombast, of Leon Rooke's shake, rattle, and roar. There are stories of voices revealing what they don't realize they are revealing. There are stories that say by not saying—Hemingway's "Hills Like White Elephants"—and there are stories employing the rhetoric of not being rhetorical, the flat, dredged-up heartbreak of Ray Carver.

> I've seen some things. I was going over to my mother's to stay a few nights. But just as I got to the top of the stairs, I looked and she was on the sofa kissing a man. It was summer. The door was open. The TV was going. That's one of the things I've seen. My mother is sixty-five. She belongs to a singles club. Even so, it was hard. I stood with my hand on the railing and watched as the man kissed her. She was kissing him back, and the TV was going.
>
> Things are better now. But back in those days, when my mother was putting out, I was out of work. My kids were crazy, and my wife was crazy. She was putting out too. The guy who was getting it was an unemployed aerospace engineer she'd met at AA. He was also crazy."

Poetry almost unbearable.

Though funny, too.

(An aside. There are very few funny short stories. I suspect this is because the mood of most stories is elegiac, flat, lyric, tragic, memorializing. I often recommend V.S. Naipaul's "The Nightwatchman's Ocurrence Book," from *A Flag on the Island*, as a comic gem. It is a "voice" story, as are many of Leon Rooke's performances, and seems to long for the stage or the stand-up microphone.

In Canada, humour, like so much else, has fallen to the Bureaucracy and is now regulated by the Leacock Award for Humour, given annually to the most commercially funny book; this often leads, fatally, to becoming "beloved."

Edwardian humour is suggested exactly in the laboriously "funny" opening sentence of Saki's "The Match-Maker" (From: *The Chronicles of Clovis* 1911)—"The grill-room clock struck eleven with the respectful unobtrusiveness of one whose mission in life is to be ignored"—and lingers archly with us yet in the spirit of the nominations for the aforementioned Medal. And let us never forgive ourselves for taking seriously Robertson Davies' Edwardian knickerbockers.)

Leacock himself plonked.

And there is the poetry of repetition, of silences. Think of Harold Pinter's *The Caretaker, The Homecoming, Old Times,* or *No Man's Land.* Think of the merciless tension in the theatre as Estragon and Vladimir wait for Godot and relapse into silence after each bout of bickering or speculation.

There is the poetry, too, of *timing;* think of silent movies, not the sentimental-sweet Chaplin but Buster Keaton, Harold Lloyd, Jacques Tati. I once owned a letter of John Betjeman's wherein he said to a friend about P.G. Wodehouse, "I have an idea P.G.W. is a saint..."

And, if a saint, certainly the Patron Saint of Timing.

This from *The Code of the Woosters*:

I reached out a hand from under the blankets and rang the bell for Jeeves.

"Good Evening Jeeves."

"Good morning, sir."

This surprised me.

"Is it morning?"

"Yes, sir."

"Are you sure? It seems very dark outside."

"There is a fog, sir. If you will recollect, we are now in Autumn—season of mists and mellow fruitfulness."

"Season of what?"

"Mists, sir, and mellow fruitfulness."

"Oh? Yes, Yes, I see. Well, be that as it may, get me one of those bracers of yours, will you?"

"I have one in readiness, sir, in the ice-box."

But in this chapter I am concentrating on the basics, on stories now seen as "traditional," (they are, after all, about one-hundred years old) stories which replaced the old kind of plot with a new kind of plot that worked through the impact of accumulating images.

In such stories, *the accretion of images*, images charged in the dominant emotional current, *becomes the plot*.

Old hat now, of course.

In 1970, Kent Thompson (writer, professor of English, editor of *The Fiddlehead*) staged a conference at the University of New Brunswick in Fredericton on the state of Canadian fiction, to which he invited a mix of writers and academics. This three-day event intensified debate among the writers and confirmed for some of us that an academic grasp of what we were doing lagged years behind us and that we'd be well advised to take care of our own analysis and criticism.

What we were talking about so passionately was, in essence, how to go beyond—even escape from—the "epiphany" story (basically the subject of this chapter) into new forms that could express new worlds, new sensibilities. Kent Thompson was speaking for many of us when he described our literary inheritance as having become ossified, Academy Stuff. Our education had been the great modernist story writers of the early twentieth century: *The Garden Party, Dubliners, In Our Time, Winesburg, Ohio, A Curtain of Green...* Our problem was that the forms these masters had created had hardened into classicism. We could no longer write in *their* forms. They cast a very long shadow from under which we *had* to escape; there was no point in our writing yet another Hemingway or Eudora Welty story.

My own answer to this challenge was a slow, unplanned, drift towards caricature. I certainly couldn't have articulated this at the time and only realized it much later with a certain level of shock. My early and abiding interest in Joyce Cary's first trilogy (*Herself Surprised*, 1941; *To Be a Pilgrim*, 1942; *The Horse's Mouth*, 1944) and my obsessive rereadings of Nathanael West's *The Dream Life of Balso Snell, Miss Lonelyhearts, A Cool Million*, and *The Day of the Locust* and my somewhat later absolute addiction to Keith Waterhouse's *Jubb*, should have perhaps tipped me off, but it didn't. In the way Topsy just growed, I just drifted into it.

I've never really been persuaded by E.M. Forster's *Aspects of the Novel*, by his idea of "flat" and "round" characters. I pretended agreement because I was young and thought that my elders and betters must have understanding more respectable than mine. But, furtively, I thought that all characters were flat. I knew I wasn't supposed to feel this (I was, after all, only an ignorant schoolboy) but I felt that Mr. Micawber and Mr. Pickwick and the Beadle in *Oliver Twist* (all "flat") were far more vivid than Jane Austen's (round) Emma, Falstaff (flat) more real than any of the (round) characters in *A Passage to India*.

Still do.

And I thought, rather defiantly, that Ben Jonson was getting the short end of the stick.

In visual art I became interested, while at university, in Hogarth, late-state pulls of *The Rake's Progress* decorating my room and stacked under my bed along with Thomas Rowlandson and James Gillray cartoons. Yet, at the same time I was obsessed with the abstract painting of William Scott. I was also becoming attracted to Max Beerbohm's caricatures. As was Evelyn Waugh, I later discovered. Some rather brilliant critic—an offhand remark somewhere—said that Waugh's characters derived not from literary models but from Beerbohm's caricatures citing Waugh's stylized book illustrations and bookplates.

In a 1901 article, Beerbohm said:

> When I draw a man, I am concerned simply and solely with the
> physical aspect of him... But I see him in a peculiar way: I see all

his salient points exaggerated (points of face, figure, port, gesture and vesture), and all his insignificant point proportionally diminished... It is when (and only when) my own caricatures hit exactly the exteriors of their subjects that they open the interiors, too.

In retrospect, I had been more deeply impressed than I realized at the time by the work of George Grosz and Otto Dix, by Honoré Daumier, Toulouse-Lautrec, Japanese "Floating World" prints, coloured lithographs from the end of the nineteenth century by Bonnard, the portraiture of Max Beckmann...

I enjoy caricature, the fast impression, the Group of Seven cigarbox lids rather than the worked-up studio canvases, which always seem to have expired in their transition, the few vivid strokes...

Despite earlier disparaging remarks about "Crime Novels," there are some masterly writers and Denise Mina chief among them. I was reading recently *The Field of Blood* and came upon this pleasingly snarky little sketch; it describes a wake at the house of Annie, an Irish Catholic in Glasgow.

> Annie had been a strict adherent to pre-Vatican II old-style Voodoo Catholicism, and it showed everywhere in the house. Holy pictures were hanging on every wall above the grab rails, novenas neatly tucked into the corners of toothy school photos of her grandchildren. A romantic plaster statue of St. Sebastian, shot through with arrows and wilting in ecstasy, sat under a grimy plastic dome on the window sill, and a chipped Child of Prague was on the mantel, tipped at an angle by the silver tenpence coin placed underneath it, a fetish that would invite prosperity into the house. Apart from superstition, sanctimony and general distrust of Protestants, Annie's only real weakness was the Saturday-afternoon wrestling on the television. She had a signed photo of Big Daddy on the wall below the Sacred Heart.

Crisply performed.

I was surprised to see that in the anthology *Making It New* (1982) I had written about "Gentle as Flowers Make the Stones"; I had forgotten. The story was in my collection *The Teeth of My Father* (1975), which means that I probably wrote the story in 1973 or '74, far earlier than I would have thought those interests were coalescing. Caricature and a growing interest in theatricality would chart my progress in the years that lay ahead.

Here's what I wrote in 1982 about "Gentle as Flowers Make the Stones."

The young poet has been lured to a ghastly evening of suburban culture by the offer of money and food.

"Gentle as Flowers Make the Stones" has its share of caricatures; Mr. Pevensey is an obvious example, but there are more complicated performances. Pevensey, by the way, is a portrait of a real person, now dead. It's a caricature of John Richmond, who used to be the book pages editor on the Montreal *Star*. The caricature was widely recognized and Richmond, reportedly enraged, "blacklisted" me from reviewing. And I thought I was being *charitable*.

(A hugely comic portrait of John Richmond can also be found in John Mills' essay collection *Thank Your Mother for the Rabbits*, a book I never tire of touting as Canada's finest collection of literary essays and memoirs.)

Consider the following passage from "Gentle as Flowers":

> Alone in the cream and gold sitting room, he examined the mantelpiece with its tiny fluted columns, shelves, alcoves, its three inset oval mirrors. He examined the silver-framed bride and groom. He examined the Royal Doulton lady in the windblown crinolines, the knick-knacks, the small copper frying-pan-looking thing that said *A Gift from Jerusalem*, the Royal reclining Doulton lady. Glancing round at the open door, he turned back and peered into the central mirror to see if any hairs were sticking out of his nose.
>
> He sank for a few minutes into the gold plush settee.
>
> The doorbell kept ringing; the litany continued.
>
> *Bernice! It's beautiful!*
>
> *We only finished the move three weeks ago.*

The pair of brass lamps which flanked the settee were in the form of huge pineapples. He touched the prickly brass leaves. The lampshades were covered in plastic. On the long table at the far end of the room, a white tablecloth covered food; he stared at the stacked plates and cups and saucers, at the tablecloth's mysterious bumps and hollows. He took a cigarette from the silver box. Which of the little things on the occasional tables, he wondered were ashtrays? Each time the door opened, the chandelier above him tinkled.

Oh, Bernice! And quarry-tile in the kitchen too!

Would you like the tour?

And as the tramplings went upstairs, faintly:

Master-bedroom...

Cedar-lined...

A plump woman wandered in. He nodded and smiled at her. She hesitated in the doorway staring at him. The green Chinese lady gazed from the gilt frame. The plump woman went around the other end of the settee and stood fingering the drapes. He tried to remember the painter's name; Tetchi, Tretchisomething, ended with "koff" or "kov"?—a name that sounded vaguely like a disease.

"Are you the poet?" said the plump woman.

"Yes, that's right."

He smiled.

"We had a nudist last week," she said.

The description of the objects and furnishings exists for its own sake, of course, but it also functions as a description of Bernice. The random collection of *things* suggests Bernice, the milieu, the vapidity of the evening to come. ("Natural" objects as image.) And as the things are seen more or less through the poet's eyes, the description *also* functions as a portrait of the poet himself. "Setting" and "character," then, are not divisible; three different sets of information are being delivered simultaneously.

The overheard fragments of conversation are set in italic (unconventionally) for a variety of reasons: because the speech is not directed to him, because the speakers are not visible, because italic seems to suggest, in this context, faintness and distance, and because italics here somehow suggest *prattle*.

I would claim, you see, that the use of italic is, in itself, an aspect of characterization.

The word "litany" ironically suggests something of the women's values while also suggesting a ritual, almost mechanical, quality in the conversation.

The invented word "tramplings" does triple duty. I wanted the idea of trampling feet and the idea of *weight* that implies—the idea that these young women are not exactly sylph-like—and I also wanted a faint suggestion of "little tramps."

The ornate mantelpiece with its "silver-framed bride and groom" and its conventionally "beautiful" knick-knacks—which as a whole suggests Bernice and her life and the lives of her friends and which, through the language used to describe it, reveals something of the poet's sensibility—is set up for the contrast with the poet's peering into one of its mirrors to see if "hairs were sticking out of his nose."

What is the effect, in context, of "Royal reclining Doulton lady"?

The sentence rhythms in the paragraph before the final dialogue are deliberately flat and, as Stephen Potter would say, "plonking." The plump woman fingers the material of the drapes; she stares at him; he stares at her; the green Chinese lady (presumably by Pavel Tchelitchew, but who knows?) stares out of her gilt frame at both of them in the silence.

These bits and pieces, then, are just a very few of my pleasures. Writing is very hard work but at the same time it is delightful play. When I think about writing, I often think it's like the play of small children on the beach absorbed in building sandcastles and towns with roads and tunnels all decorated with flags made from popsicle sticks and bits of cigarette packets.

And then the wonderful application of water.

Writing stories has something about it of that tranced pleasure, and I'm convinced that if readers are to share fully in the delight of writing they must be prepared to play *with* writers; they must launch a car through the tunnel to judge the banking and texture of the sand. Does it need more water? They must pat and stroke and probe. They must roll up trousers, tuck skirts into knickers, get down on hands and knees, and muck about.

Hello Central, Give Me Doctor Blaise

Clark Blaise is one of Canada's most important writers; he is, of course, little known. The Prize Machine grinds past him in the opposite direction; in bookstores, libraries, universities, he is unstocked, unshelved, untaught; the CBC's *Canada Reads* doesn't. Along with Mavis Gallant, Norman Levine, and Alice Munro, he is one of the chief glories of Canadian literature.

His story "Broward Dowdy" appeared in his second collection, *Tribal Justice*, in 1974 but had been written a decade earlier and first appeared in the Summer 1964 issue of *Shenandoah*. It was his third published story but first to appear in a magazine of national scope and reach. His first two stories had appeared in college magazines. The final, brilliant image of "Broward Dowdy" announced the arrival on the literary scene of a massive talent. The picture insinuated itself and has been in my mind for forty years. "Broward Dowdy" can now be found in *Southern Stories (The Selected Stories, Vol. I)*.

Over the years, Clark has written essays to accompany stories of his I was anthologizing. These essays, "To Begin, To Begin," "The Cast and the Mold," and "On Ending Stories" have come to be seen by young writers as essential. The three are gathered in *Selected Essays*. Clark Blaise. (Ed. John Metcalf and Tim Struthers) Windsor, ON: Biblioasis, 2008.)

Prompted by my remarks on the encapsulating nature of the first three lines of Henry Green's *Party Going*, an approach I'd learned from Clark, I realized that the reader needed and deserved extensive exposure to the Blaisian sensibility at full snap and crackle.

What follows is an extensive quotation from "To Begin, To Begin":

> The most interesting thing about a story is not its climax or dénouement—both dated terms—nor even its style and characterization. It is its beginning, its first paragraph, often its first sentence. More decisions are made on the basis of the first sentences of a story than on any other part, and it would seem to me after having read thousands of stories, and beginning hundreds of my own (completing, I should add, far fewer), that something more than luck accounts for the occasional success of the operation. What I propose is theoretical, yet rooted in the practice of writing and of reading-as-a-writer; good stories *can* start unpromisingly, and well-begun stories can obviously degenerate, but the observation generally holds: the story seeks its beginning, the story many times *is* its beginning, amplified.
>
> The first sentence of a story is an act of faith—or astonishing bravado. A story screams for attention, as it must, for it breaks a silence. It removes the reader from the everyday (no such imperative attaches to the novel, for which the reader makes his own preparations). It is an act of perfect rhythmic balance, the single crisp gesture, the drop of the baton that gathers a hundred disparate forces into a single note. The first paragraph is a microcosm of the whole, but in a way that only the whole can reveal. If the story begins one sentence too soon, or a sentence too late, the balance is lost, the energy diffused.
>
> It is in the very first line that the story reveals its kinship to poetry. Not that the line is necessarily "beautiful," merely that it can exist utterly alone, and that its force draws a series of sentences behind it. The line doesn't have to "grab" or "hook" but it should be striking. Good examples I'll offer further on, but consider first some bad ones:
>
> Catelli plunged the dagger deeper in her breast, the dark blood oozed out like cherry syrup.
>
> The President's procession would pass under the window at 12:03, and Slattery would be ready.

Such sentences can be wearying; they strike a note too heavily, too prematurely. They "start" where they should be ending. The advantages wrested will quickly dissipate. On the other hand, the "casual" opening can be just as damaging:

> When I saw Bob in the cafeteria he asked me to a party at his house that evening and since I wasn't doing much anyway I said sure, I wouldn't mind. Bob's kind of an ass, but his old man's loaded and there's always a lot of grass around...

Or, *in media res:*

> "Linda, toast is ready! Linda, are you awake?"

Now what's wrong with those sentences? The tone is right. The action is promising. They're real, they communicate. Yet no experienced reader would go past them. The last two start too early (what the critics might call an imitative fallacy) and the real story is still imprisoned somewhere in the body.

Lesson One: As in poetry, a good first sentence of prose implies its opposite. If I describe a sunny morning in May (the buds, the wet-winged flies, the warm sun and cool breeze), I am also implying the perishing quality of a morning in May, and a good, sensuous description of May sets up the possibility of a May disaster. It is the singular quality of that experience that counts. May follows from the sludge of April and leads to the drone of summer, and in a careful story the action will be mindful of May: it must be. May is unstable, treacherous, beguiling, seductive, and whatever experience follows from a first sentence will be, in essence, a story about the May-ness of human affairs.

What is it, for example in this sentence from Hugh Hood's story "Fallings from Us, Vanishings" that hints so strongly at disappointment:

> Brandishing a cornucopia of daffodils, flowers for Gloria, in his right hand, Arthur Merlin crossed the dusky oak-panelled

foyer of his apartment building and came into the welcoming sunlit avenue.

The name Merlin? The flourish of the opening clause, associations of the name, Gloria? Here is a lover doomed to loneliness, yet a lover who seeks it, despite appearances. Nowhere, however, is it stated. Yet no one, I trust, would miss it.

Such openings are everywhere, at least in authors I admire:

The girl stood with her back to the bar, slightly in everyone's way. (Frank Tuohy)

The thick ticking of the tin clock stopped. Mendel, dozing in the dark, awoke in fright. (Bernard Malamud)

I owe the discovery of Uqbar to the conjunction of a mirror and an encyclopedia. (Jorge Luis Borges)

For a little while when Walter Henderson was nine years old he thought falling dead was the very zenith of romance, and so did a number of his friends. (Richard Yates)

One group is against the war. But the war goes on. (Donald Barthelme)

The principal dish at dinner had been croquettes made of turnip greens. (Thomas Mann)

The first time I saw Brenda she asked me to hold her glasses. (Philip Roth)

The sky had been overcast since early morning; it was a still day, not hot, but tedious, as it usually is when the weather is gray and dull, when clouds have been hanging over the fields for a long time, and you wait for the rain that does not come. (Anton Chekhov)

I wanted terribly to own a dovecot when I was a child. (Isaac Babel)

... Lesson Two: Art wishes to begin, even more than end. Fashionable criticism—much of it very intelligent—has emphasized the so-called "apocalyptic impulse," the desire of fiction to bring the house down. I can understand the interest in endings—it is easier to explain why things end than how they begin, for one thing. For another, the ending is a contrivance—artistic and believable, yet in many ways predictable, the beginning, however, is always a mystery. Criticism likes contrivances, and has little to say of mysteries. My own experience, as a writer and especially as a "working" reader, is closer to genesis than apocalypse, and I cherish openings more than endings. My memory of any given story is likely to be its first few lines.

Lesson Three: Art wishes to begin *again*. The impulse is not only to finish, it is to capture. In the stories I admire, there is a sense of a continuum disrupted, then re-established, and both the disruption and re-ordering are part of the *beginning* of a story. The first paragraph tells us, in effect, that "this is how things have always been," or, at least, how they have been until the arrival of the story. It may summarize, as Faulkner does in "That Evening Sun":

> Monday is no different from any other workday in Jefferson now. The streets are paved now, and the telephone and electric companies are cutting down more and more of the shade trees...

Or it may develop a life in a single sentence, as Bernard Malamud's often do:

> Manischevitz, a tailor, in his fifty-fifth year suffered many reverses and indignities.

Whereupon Malamud embellishes the history, a few sentences more of indignities, aches, curses, until the fateful word that occurs in almost all stories, the simple terrifying adverb:
Then.

Then, which means to the reader: "I am ready." The moment of change is at hand, the story shifts gears, and, for the first time, *plot* intrudes on poetry. In Malamud's story, a Negro angel suddenly ("then") appears in the tailor's living room reading a newspaper.

Suddenly there appeared...

Then one morning...

Then one evening she wasn't home to greet him...

Or, in the chilling construction of Flannery O'Connor, there appeared at her door three young men:

They walked single file, the middle one bent to the side carrying a black pig-shaped valise.

A pig-shaped valise! This is the apocalypse, if the reader needs one; whatever the plot may reveal a few pages later is really redundant. The mysterious part of the story—that which *is* poetic yet sets it (why not?) above poetry—is over. The rest of the story will attempt to draw out the inferences of that earlier upheaval. What is meant by "climax" in the conventional short story is merely the moment that the *character* realizes the true, the devastating, meaning of "then."

... the purest part of a story, I think, is from its beginning to its "then." "Then" is the moment of the slightest tremor, the moment when the author is satisfied that all the forces are deployed, the unruffled surface perfectly cast, and the insertion, gross or delicate, can now take place. It is the cracking of the perfect, smug egg of possibility.

And here is the final tantalizing paragraph of "On Ending Stories."

Stories begin mysteriously but end deliberately. A writer can't really *will* a story to open, but, in the act of writing, the appropriate ending (event, tone, revelation, effect) will probably suggest itself. Most endings arise in the act of writing... and they all share a single purpose: to give a final emphasis to a particular aspect of the story. Literally, it's the writer's last word on the subject: he'd better choose those words carefully. The opening anticipates the conflict. The ending immortalizes the resolution.

Miss Brill

Although it was so brilliantly fine—the blue sky powdered with gold and great spots of light like white wine splashed over the Jardins Publiques—Miss Brill was glad that she had decided on her fur. The air was motionless, but when you opened your mouth there was just a faint chill, like a chill from a glass of iced water before you sip, and now and again a leaf came drifting—from nowhere, from the sky. Miss Brill put up her hand and touched her fur. Dear little thing! It was nice to feel it again. She had taken it out of its box that afternoon, shaken out the moth powder, given it a good brush, and rubbed the life back into the dim little eyes. "What has been happening to me?" said the sad little eyes. Oh, how sweet it was to see them snap at her again from the red eiderdown! . . . But the nose, which was of some black composition, wasn't at all firm. It must have had a knock, somehow. Never mind—a little dab of black sealing-wax when the time came—when it was absolutely necessary... Little rogue! Yes, she really felt like that about it. Little rogue biting its tail just by her left ear. She could have taken it off and laid it on her lap and stroked it. She felt a tingling in her hands and arms, but that came from walking, she supposed. And when she breathed, something light and sad—no, not sad, exactly—something gentle seemed to move in her bosom.

There were a number of people out this afternoon, far more than last Sunday. And the band sounded louder and gayer. That was because the Season had begun. For although the band played all the year round on Sundays, out of season it was never the same. It was like someone playing with only the family to listen; it didn't care how it played if there weren't any strangers present. Wasn't the conductor wearing a new coat, too? She was sure it was new. He scraped with his foot and flapped his arms like a rooster about to crow, and the bandsmen sitting in the green rotunda blew out their cheeks and glared at the music. Now there came a little "flutey" bit—very pretty!—a little chain of bright drops. She was sure it would be repeated. It was; she lifted her head and smiled.

Only two people shared her "special" seat: a fine old man in a velvet coat, his hands clasped over a huge carved walking-stick, and a big old woman, sitting upright, with a roll of knitting on her embroidered apron. They did not speak. This was disappointing, for Miss Brill always looked forward to the conversation. She had become really quite expert, she thought, at listening as though she didn't listen, at sitting in other people's lives just for a minute while they talked round her.

She glanced, sideways, at the old couple. Perhaps they would go soon. Last Sunday, too, hadn't been as interesting as usual. An Englishman and his wife, he wearing a dreadful Panama hat and she button boots. And she'd gone on the whole time about how she ought to wear spectacles; she knew she needed them; but that it was no good getting any; they'd be sure to break and they'd never keep on. And he'd been so patient. He'd suggested everything—gold rims, the kind that curve round your ears, little pads inside the bridge. No, nothing would please her. "They'll always be sliding down my nose!" Miss Brill had wanted to shake her.

The old people sat on a bench, still as statues. Never mind, there was always the crowd to watch. To and fro, in front of the flower beds and the band rotunda, the couples and groups paraded, stopped to talk, to greet, to buy a handful of flowers from the old beggar who had his tray fixed to the railings. Little children ran among them, swooping and laughing; little boys with big white silk bows under their chins, little girls, little French dolls, dressed up in velvet and lace. And sometimes a tiny staggerer came suddenly rocking into the open from under the trees, stopped, stared, as suddenly sat down "flop," until its small, high-stepping mother, like a young hen, rushed scolding to its rescue. Other people sat on the benches and green chairs, but they were nearly always the same, Sunday after Sunday, and—Miss Brill had often noticed—there was something funny about nearly all of them. They were odd, silent, nearly all old, and from the way they stared they looked as though they'd just come from dark little rooms or even—even cupboards!

Behind the rotunda the slender trees with yellow leaves down drooping, and through them just a line of sea, and beyond the blue sky with gold-veined clouds.

Tum-tum-tum tiddle-um! tiddle-um! tum tiddley-um tum ta! blew the band.

Two young girls in red came by and two young soldiers in blue met them, and they laughed and paired and went off arm-in-arm. Two peasant women with funny straw hats passed, gravely, leading beautiful smoke-coloured donkeys. A cold, pale nun hurried by. A beautiful woman came along and dropped her bunch of violets, and a little boy ran after to hand them to her, and she took them and threw them away as if they'd been poisoned. Dear me! Miss Brill didn't know whether to admire that or not! And now an ermine toque and a gentleman in gray met just in front of her. He was tall, stiff, dignified, and she was wearing the ermine toque she'd bought when her hair was yellow. Now everything, her hair, her face, even her eyes, was the same colour as the shabby ermine, and her hand, in its cleaned glove, lifted to dab her lips, was a tiny yellowish paw. Oh, she was so pleased to see him—delighted! She rather thought they were going to meet that afternoon. She described where she'd been—everywhere, here, there, along by the sea. The day was so charming—didn't he agree? And wouldn't he, perhaps? . . . But he shook his head, lighted a cigarette, slowly breathed a great deep puff into her face, and even while she was still talking and laughing, flicked the match away and walked on. The ermine toque was alone; she smiled more brightly than ever. But even the band seemed to know what she was feeling and played more softly, played tenderly, and the drum beat, "The Brute! The Brute!" over and over. What would she do? What was going to happen now? But as Miss Brill wondered, the ermine toque turned, raised her hand as though she'd seen someone else, much nicer, just over there, and pattered away. And the band changed again and played more quickly, more gayly than ever, and the old couple on Miss Brill's seat got up and marched away, and such a funny old man with long whiskers hobbled along in time to the music and was nearly knocked over by four girls walking abreast.

Oh, how fascinating it was! How she enjoyed it! How she loved sitting here, watching it all! It was like a play. It was exactly like a play. Who could believe the sky at the back wasn't painted? But it wasn't till a little brown dog trotted on solemn and then slowly trotted off, like a little "theatre" dog, a little dog that had been drugged, that Miss Brill discovered what it was that made it so exciting. They were all on stage. They weren't only the audience, not only looking on; they were acting. Even she had a part and came every Sunday. No doubt somebody would have noticed if she hadn't been there; she was part of the performance after all. How strange she'd never thought of it like that before! And yet it explained why she made such point of starting from home at just the same time each week—so as not to be late for the performance—and it also explained why she had a queer, shy feeling at telling her English pupils how she spent her Sunday afternoons. No wonder! Miss Brill nearly laughed out loud. She was on the stage. She thought of the old invalid gentleman to whom she read the newspaper four afternoons a week while he slept in the garden. She had got quite used to the frail head on the cotton pillow, the hollowed eyes, the open mouth and the high pinched nose. If he'd been dead she mightn't have noticed for weeks; she wouldn't have minded. But suddenly he knew he was having the paper read to him by an actress! "An actress!" The old head lifted; two points of light quivered in the old eyes. "An actress—are ye?" And Miss Brill smoothed the newspaper as though it were the manuscript of her part and said gently; "Yes, I have been an actress for a long time."

The band had been having a rest. Now they started again. And what they played was warm, sunny, yet there was just a faint chill—a something, what was it?—not sadness—no, not sadness—a something that made you want to sing. The tune lifted, lifted, the light shone; and it seemed to Miss Brill that in another moment all of them, all the whole company, would begin singing. The young ones, the laughing ones who were moving together, they would begin and the men's voices, very resolute and brave, would join them. And then she too, she too, and the others on the benches—they would come in with a kind of accompaniment—something low, that scarcely rose or fell, something so beautiful—moving... And Miss Brill's eyes filled with tears and she looked smiling at all the other members of the company. Yes, we understand, we understand, she thought—though what they understood she didn't know.

Just at that moment a boy and girl came and sat down where the old couple had been. They were beautifully dressed; they were in love. The hero and heroine, of course, just arrived from his father's yacht. And still soundlessly singing, still with that trembling smile, Miss Brill prepared to listen.

"No, not now," said the girl. "Not here, I can't."

"But why? Because of that stupid old thing at the end there?" asked the boy. "Why does she come here at all—who wants her? Why doesn't she keep her silly old mug at home?"

"It's her fu-ur which is so funny," giggled the girl. "It's exactly like a fried whiting."

"Ah, be off with you!" said the boy in an angry whisper. Then: "Tell me, ma petite chère—"

"No, not here," said the girl. "Not yet."

*

On her way home she usually bought a slice of honeycake at the baker's. It was her Sunday treat. Sometimes there was an almond in her slice, sometimes not. It made a great difference. If there was an almond it was like carrying home a tiny present—a surprise—something that might very well not have been there. She hurried on the almond Sundays and struck the match for the kettle in quite a dashing way.

But today she passed the baker's by, climbed the stairs, went into the little dark room—her room like a cupboard—and sat down on the red eiderdown. She sat there for a long time. The box that the fur came out of was on the bed. She unclasped the necklet quickly; quickly, without looking, laid it inside. But when she put the lid on she thought she heard something crying.

Listening to Miss Brill

I

Sixteen, browsing the shelves in the deserted school library. That week I was reading, I remember, the newly published *Victorian People* by Asa Briggs. Another essay loomed on the agricultural and industrial revolutions, Jethro Tull, James Hargreaves, etc., Farmer George, enclosures, field drainage, etc. mangelwurzels.

I much preferred Dates and Great Men.

Browsing L—to—M

D.H. Lawrence, Linklater, Jack London, Compton Mackenzie, Katherine Mansfield, A.E.W. Mason, Somerset Maugham…

Mansfield. *The Garden Party*

Associated somehow with H.D. Died young—in France?—TB or somesuch, that was all I knew of her. She wasn't a *poet;* it was poets, I felt, who deserved reverence. Especially H.D., for whom I felt a noble teenage *tendresse* tinged with lust.

I sat at one of the oak refectory tables, blue and rose light through the stained glass onto the silence, reading the first paragraph of "Miss Brill" until the hair on my nape and forearms stood.

What was so magical and entrancing about this opening of "Miss Brill" was that it was written in the third person yet I could hear Miss Brill's voice as clearly as if she were present and talking to me. And just as magical, although she is nowhere described, that voice enabled me to *see* Miss Brill—though more of that idea in the next chapter.

Nowadays, of course, the trick is no longer so magical. I know how to perform that particular sleight of hand. And many another. But "Miss Brill" was written in 1920—now nearly a hundred years ago. We would be wise to recall T.S. Eliot's "Tradition and the Individual Talent," wherein he says, "Someone said: 'The dead writers are remote from us because we *know* so much more than they did.' Precisely, and they are that which we know."

Just *en passant*, I make no apologies for being so personal, so emotional, in my response to "Miss Brill"; it is as much a part of my life as crunching breakfast cornflakes. If you prefer to read "Miss Brill" as a study of the economic and social plight of single women in the early twentieth century, in my opinion you'd be better employed playing Go Fish. Literature is *about* emotion; it must be as Kafka wrote "... the axe for the frozen sea within us."

What, then, is "Miss Brill"—and here is the inevitable reduction and the intellect's eagerness to foreclose—"about"? A reduction inevitable as soon as the reader asks "What?" rather than "How?"

How does a story mean?

Always the preferred question.

Put crudely, it is a story, constructed in a chain of images, which presents an afternoon in Miss Brill's life, an afternoon during which she is brought to realize, to acknowledge, that she will never have a romantic or sexual relationship, will never have children; that she herself was one of the old, the odd, the ones she observed in the park, who sat on the benches looking "as though they'd just come from dark little rooms or even—cupboards."

The first two lines of the story encapsulate the story in its entirety. We should recall Clark Blaise's words in "To Begin, To Begin": "The most interesting thing about a story is not its climax or dénouement—both dated terms—not even its style and characterization. It is its beginning, its first paragraph, often its first sentence... the story seeks its beginning, the story many times *is* its beginning, amplified."

How exactly Blaise's words apply here... "the blue sky powdered with gold and great spots of light like white wine splashed over the Jardins Publiques..." The colours of the sky are the delicate washes of a watercolour but there is so much more going on in this sentence than prettiness. The pale lemony spots of light like chilled white wine are suggestive not only of bouquet and taste but of festivity, perhaps of a picnic, a luncheon *à deux*. The sky "powdered" with gold, a word natural only to a woman and conjuring make-up, a woman beautifying herself, yet, in this context, an extremely odd word to use when one thinks about it. Though less odd when in conjunction with *spots of light,* for here Mansfield is suggesting the idea of a stage and an actress preparing for a performance. Katherine Mansfield is more than capable of such intentional packed suggestions; indeed, the idea of the park and its habitués as stage and cast becomes central as the story proceeds.

This Sunday is the first Sunday of the Season. The band sounds "louder and gayer," playing not just for the regulars, for "family," but now for tourists and the annual invasion of the Riviera by the English wealthy.

("Miss Brill" was written in 1920, in Menton.)

If this Sunday is the beginning of the Season, the time of year must be spring yet Miss Brill is "glad she had decided on her fur" because the air has a faint underlying chill "like a chill from a glass of iced water before you sip." This homely simile is a tiny nudge before the stronger shove of the drifting leaf alerting us to a hostility in the beauty of the day. The chill of the glass of iced water is, even if desired, invasive, a tiny shock. And "now and again a leaf came drifting—from nowhere, from the sky." This drifting leaf from "nowhere," from no apparent nearby tree, suggests that its swirling, fluting fall is a little mysterious. We are intended to read it as poetic image. The leaf is, of course, a leaf; but remembering Ezra Pound's "the natural object is always the adequate symbol" we should feel the leaf as symbolic of fall and winter and further, and obviously, of what these seasons imply poetically in terms of human life. *But* this leaf and others "now and again" are appearing "—from nowhere, from the sky." Rhythmically and rhetorically in the sentence, and within the entire paragraph, the drifting leaf has considerable *presence.* Test this by reading aloud the first ten lines or so of the story several times.

Obviously, Mansfield wishes us to *see* the leaf and she is prompting us to wonder *where* these odd leaves are coming from and *why this is happening in the spring*. To which there are no ready answers. She is prompting us to see and feel the dead leaves as a power, a force, visitants, *spectres at the feast*.

We follow Miss Brill and her fur through the rest of the story to that awful point where she realizes that the afternoon's happiness she feels through her connection with the "cast" of the "play" in the park is a delusion, to her realization and acknowledgement of "fall" and "winter" in her life.

The sad burden of the story is carried by Miss Brill's cherishing of her fur. To welcome the Spring, Miss Brill has taken the fur from its box and "rubbed the life back into the dim little eyes." (Not, you will notice, "polished" or "rubbed dust from.")

For the benefit of younger readers, the fur would probably have been fox, mink, or ermine, the head realistically reconstructed and hooking by a clasp under its jaw onto the tail. Mansfield describes the fur as a "necklet" which the *Oxford Canadian Dictionary* defines as a necklace (or, sadly now, as a gasoline-filled tire fitted around a victim's neck). The words "stole" or "tippet" better suggest its appearance.

The fur's nose, made of some black "composition" (probably some form of hardened plaster of Paris), has been damaged while the fur was in its box, but some black sealing-wax would repair it "when the time came—when it was absolutely necessary..."

I *think* that Katherine Mansfield meant us to understand by this talk of repair "when it was absolutely necessary" that Miss Brill would go on treating "Little Rogue!" like something living until she was *forced* to treat it as a "thing" by mending it with sealing-wax; that she would give up the *pretence* of its being alive when the time came for a blob of wax. Mildly ambiguous.

She could have "laid it on her lap and stroked it. She felt a tingling in her hands and arms, but that came from walking, she supposed. And when she breathed, something light and sad— no, not sad, exactly—something gentle seemed to move in her bosom."

The derided fur opens the story and closes it. When Miss Brill gets home to her room, "her room like a cupboard," she puts the fur away in its box and "thought she heard something crying."

All the foregoing suggests that Miss Brill somehow has sexual and maternal feelings towards the tippet, that it might represent for her a surrogate child, this inanimate creature into whose eyes she had "rubbed the life."

That Katherine Mansfield fully intended all this wealth of meaning is confirmed by the sentence, "She felt a tingling in her hands and arms, but that came from walking, she supposed."

It's that final comma that halts us, that small pause the comma forces us to make before "she supposed," which informs us that *we*, the readers, should suppose no such thing.

Here, then, in the story's first paragraph is the entire story in compressed, poetic form, a perfect illustration of Blaisian perceptions. Here is the story's theme perfectly embodied in the swirling leaf and the fur with the damaged, composition nose. The structure seems to directly suggest comparisons with music, a sonata perhaps.

(Alice Munro uses an almost identical structure in "Walker Brothers Cowboy" in *Dance of the Happy Shades*. Shaena Lambert, writing on her website about William Trevor, made an image in reference to an Alice Munro *multum in parvo* opening, so delicious I can't help quoting her.

> Alice Munro's stories...may need to be read twice or even three times before they reveal themselves completely. With the story "Vandals," for instance, in her book *Open Secrets*, you can't *actually* understand this story... unless you read it more than once. There is a longish dream told in letter form at the beginning which is laden, like a water balloon, with the story's meaning. But it's impossible to "get" unless you finish the story, and then begin again at the start.

Laden like a *water balloon!*)

This prelude played, the story flows out into its amplification.

The camera now draws back, as it were, to allow us to see what Miss Brill is seeing. She is an observer, part of the audience at a play.

Theatre was one of Katherine Mansfield's passions: it plays a part, too, in "The Garden Party," and in "The Lady's Maid," which is essentially a dramatic monologue, a one-woman show.

Mansfield suggests so much about Miss Brill's life without being intrusively expositional. That Miss Brill has a "special seat," that she can recognize that the conductor's tunic is new, that she is familiar with the band's repertoire, all tell us that Miss Brill frequents the park Sunday after Sunday.

And then her observations begin. All the descriptions—which become images because, in Mansfield's words, "saturated in that emotional quality"—have sexual reference or implication. The sexual current of the imagery is relentless: the characterization of the park's regulars as "family," the band's "rooster" conductor, the English couple sharing her bench, "a fine old man" with his wife, "a big old woman." A couple she recalls from the Sunday before, the wife critical and querulous with her "patient" husband.

"Miss Brill wanted to shake her."

She is impatient with those women who seem so unappreciative of their husbands.

In front of the flower-beds, the "couples and groups paraded"; "little children ran among them"; sometimes "a tiny staggerer came suddenly rocking" until its mother "like a young hen" rushed to its rescue.

("Behind the rotunda the slender trees with yellow leaves down drooping"—a curious line I've always fancied was intended as a foreshadowing device and then abandoned. Trees with yellowish leaves in the spring and "down drooping" suggests weeping willows but quite possibly she thought "weeping" too obvious or even the "weeping" silently implied in "willows," and pulled back, leaving a description uncharacteristically vague.)

"Two young girls in red came by and two young soldiers in blue met them, and they laughed and paired and went off arm-in-arm." A "cold, pale nun" hurried by. A beautiful woman alone drops her bunch of violets and throws it away in irritation after it's been returned by a small boy instead of a potential suitor; the "gentleman in grey" brutally rejects the advances of "the ermine toque" and

Miss Brill, also be-furred, imagines the band's bass drum is sounding "The Brute! The Brute!"

Watching all this performance going on, and prompted by "a little brown dog" which "trotted on solemn and then slowly trotted off, like a little theatre dog" Miss Brill suddenly realizes that "they were all on the stage." She was in a play, was a part of it; she was not audience but cast. She was an actress!

She thinks of the old invalid gentleman to whom she read the newspaper four afternoons a week while he slept in the garden. "But suddenly he knew he was having the paper read to him by an actress!" The old head lifts a little from the pillow and a gleam returns to his eyes.

"An actress—are ye?"

This relatively long image says more about Miss Brill than a casual reader might understand. The reputation of actresses has been, historically, low. By the late Victorian-Edwardian period it was scandalous. For women charged with solicitation, the old police-court formulaic deposition was "Giving her profession as actress." Actress meant then something like the word "model" meant in England in the fifties and sixties; "models" like Christine Keeler and Mandy Rice Davies were notorious in the Profumo scandals not for modelling their clothes but for removing them. Miss Brill, then, is playing with the fantasy that she is, if not a courtesan, then on the fringes of being "no better than she should be." This mild fantasy is reined back as Miss Brill imagines smoothing the newspaper "as though it was the manuscript of her part"; after all, Miss Brill is still *Miss* Brill.

It explains the quivering light she imagines in the old invalid's eyes, a last hurrah.

Following this fancy, the band strikes up again and Miss Brill is filled with a melting feeling of community and inclusion; she is a member of the company.

"…And Miss Brill's eyes filled with tears and she looked smiling at all the other members of the company."

Then, at this moment of openness and exaltation, the boy and girl seat themselves at the other end of her bench. This is the last sexually tinged encounter of the story. The boy is persistent, the girl reluctant because of Miss Brill's presence. They audibly insult Miss Brill and deride the appearance of the presumably rather mangey-looking fur.

"It's exactly like a fried whiting" is a peculiar simile. I've tried to visualize in what way "fried whiting" might resemble a fur "necklet" but nothing occurs. A whiting is usually about nine inches or so long, and narrow, its eyes are large and its jaws somewhat beaky. I cannot imagine frying the entire creature as one does with whitebait. Perhaps we are not meant to see any similarity but to hear the words simply as teenage derision. Perhaps in the *lack* of resemblance between fish and fur her words convey the girl's feeling about the fur as outlandish, preposterous; she simply lacks the language to express what is, for her, the fur's ridiculousness and so throws in the silliest comparison that comes to mind. Her words explode within the scene, not only insulting Miss Brill but attacking the fur, into whose little eyes she has "rubbed the life."

Devastated, she leaves the park.

The penultimate paragraph is a heart-tugger with its single brilliant detail that tells the reader so much about the horizons and constraints of Miss Brill's life—whether or not a Sunday was "an almond Sunday."

The final paragraph of the story topples over into sentimentality and too overtly pulls tight the story's drawstrings of meaning. But we must remember that the story was written nearly a hundred years ago and we must realize that it was then an incomparably greater achievement than it seems now. Though, speaking personally, it still floods me with admiring envy.

II

This might be a good point to look back at the dominant expectations of plot and character against which Katherine Mansfield was writing.

Sir John Squire, you will recall, wrote:

"... we are not moved by her stories because nothing happens to her characters."

Sir John, literary editor of the *New Statesman* and chief literary critic for the *Observer*, was the power broker in literary London. He was firmly hidebound in his opinions. Most of his own verse was unmemorably conventional and he led a group of poets and critics who shared an antipathy to modernism. His detractors, notably the Sitwells, referred to this camp as "the Squirearchy."

When Squire complains that "nothing happens," the old huffer and puffer was bemoaning the lack of plot and drama. What was he pining for? The flimsily clad maiden tied to the railroad tracks with the 11:15 bearing down?

Exactly the same objection as the *Ottawa Citizen's* Bruce Ward's dismissal, some ninety-five years later, of Alice Munro's "dismal small-town losers" who "spot the other crossing the street but don't speak."

Even a writer as monumental as Thomas Hardy enquired when Katherine Mansfield was going to write more stories about those girls in "Daughters of the Late Colonel," revealing thereby that he had not understood the unique world so glintingly achieved in that story, which had been presented for his delight.

To say of the Colonel's daughters and of Miss Brill that "nothing happens" to them when the daughters are set free from a lifetime of repression into a sunlit world of expanding possibility and Miss Brill is forced into the realization and acceptance that she is doomed to a world closing in, to a life "in a room like a cupboard," it's difficult to think of what wilder drama critics desired.

Elizabeth Bowen crisply turned this "nothing happens" pontificating on its head. In *The Mulberry Tree: Writings of Elizabeth Bowen* (Ed. Hermione Lee) Bowen wrote:

> How good is Katherine Mansfield's character-drawing? I have heard this named as her weak point. I feel one cannot insist enough upon what she instinctively grasped—that the short story, by reason of its aesthetics, is not and is not intended to be the medium either for exploration or long-term development of character. Character cannot be more than shown—it is there for use, the use is dramatic.

Clark Blaise wrote of story writers in "The Craft of the Short Story":

> We are not in the business of establishing any of the *whys*. The pre-
> conditions are fine where they are; they were built by another civ-
> ilization, carved out by different glaciers and hurricanes. Novelists
> like those things, journalists can deal with them, memoirists need
> to get to the bottom of them. The story traces what lingers after
> the whirlwind, after the fracture. Or before it. We're not in the
> business of establishing the reasons, social, historic, economic,
> psychological, why things happen. They've already happened...
>
> By turning away from the need to explain too much, to cre-
> ate, to construct, and establish, the story opens a space that is
> not available to the novel.

Story writers, in this particular mold of the story form, are writing
towards Clark Blaise's THEN.

THEN and its aftermath are dramatic.

III

Readers and writers return again and again to "Miss Brill" and other
Katherine Mansfield stories for the pure pleasure of listening to
her music. I made reference in the first chapter to the sentence of
Connolly's in *Enemies of Promises* that turned my life upside down.

*An expert should be able to tell a carpet by one skein of it; a vintage by
rinsing a glassful round his mouth.*

This led me on to realize that brilliant prose could be returned to
time and again with deepening pleasure. As I also said in the first chapter: "For when we have explored it, we have not finished with it; we
cannot then dismiss it as 'understood.'

Maurice Denis, a theoretician of les Nabis, said: *Remember that a
picture before being a horse, a nude, or some kind of anecdote, is essentially
a flat surface covered with colours assembled in a certain order.*

We return to Katherine Mansfield and other great writers—the
ones we honour in the personal pantheons we have built over the

years—to revel in their "colours assembled in a certain order." We long ago absorbed the nude, the anecdote, the horse; the assembled colours in a certain order are, however, inexhaustible.

The following passage from "Miss Brill" has always charmed and captured me.

> And now an ermine toque and a gentleman in grey met just in front of her. He was tall, stiff, dignified, and she was wearing the ermine toque she'd bought when her hair was yellow. Now everything, her hair, her face, even her eyes, was the same colour as the shabby ermine, and her hand, in its cleaned glove, lifted to dab her lips, was a tiny yellowish paw. Oh, she was so pleased to see him—delighted! She rather thought they were going to meet that afternoon. She described where she'd been—everywhere, here, there, along by the sea. The day was so charming—didn't he agree? And wouldn't he, perhaps?... But he shook his head, lighted a cigarette, slowly breathed a great deep puff into her face, and, even while she was still talking and laughing, flicked the match away and walked on. The ermine toque was alone; she smiled more brightly than ever. But even the band seemed to know what she was feeling and played more softly, played tenderly, and the drum beat, 'The Brute! The Brute!' over and over. What would she do? What was going to happen now? But as Miss Brill wondered, the ermine toque turned, raised her hand as though she'd seen someone else, much nicer, just over there, and pattered away. And the band changed again and played more quickly, more gaily than ever, and the old couple on Miss Brill's seat got up and marched away, and such a funny old man with long whiskers hobbled along in time to the music and was nearly knocked over by four girls walking abreast.

I'm sure I've seen the colours but I sometimes wonder if I *have* seen the horse. I mean by that, do "the gentleman in grey" and the "ermine toque" know each other prior to this encounter or is Miss Brill witnessing an act of solicitation? And does Miss Brill understand what she is watching?

101

She is too far away to hear the conversation. The "ermine's" words are what Miss Brill imagines the woman is saying. Miss Brill imagines the "ermine" saying that "she rather thought they were going to meet that afternoon." This would seem to imply that Miss Brill imagines they have known each other prior to this Sunday meeting. But the contemptuous behaviour of the "gentleman in grey" would seem to suggest either that they were strangers or had previously quarrelled violently. Then the "ermine toque" raises her hand "as though she'd seen someone else, much nicer just over there" which suggests that she is in search of clients.

The scene is surely somewhat ambiguous. Miss Brill would be extremely reluctant to allow the word "prostitute" to surface; her gentility can only approach the possibility circuitously and she immediately fudges definition by imagining that the band is playing more tenderly to comfort the "ermine" in her rejection.

The ambiguity resides in this: would the "ermine" *need* such comfort from the band, and would the band offer it, if what has taken place is understood by all as a failed commercial transaction? Or does Miss Brill's sympathy and her imagining that the band is playing more "tenderly" suggest that she thinks "the gentleman in grey" is spurning the flirtatious invitation of an acquaintance?

Or None of the Above?

The "ermine's" imagined speech not only plays its part in the scene Miss Brill is watching but is a subtle way of describing how Miss Brill thinks and speaks, the words giving us a version of the thing described and the personality of the observer.

Mansfield eases us out of this scene with the old man hobbling along in time to the music and nearly getting knocked down by the girls "abreast."

(These thoughts of prostitution lead me to meander into Virginia Woolf's *Diaries*. She wrote, of Katherine Mansfield, that she "dressed like a tart and behaved like a bitch" and topped this off with "she stinks like a—well, civet cat that had taken to street walking.")

If the "ermine toque" is indeed a prostitute and if indeed Miss Brill understands what she has witnessed, then the segue into the scene of Miss Brill reading to the old invalid in the garden where she imagines herself an "actress" is, logically and emotionally, very smoothly managed.

The extract is verbal; though it is rendered in the third person we are listening to Miss Brill's voice. The extract is also very freshly visual. The fast strokes sketch in the now-rather-haggard "ermine toque" with her fading allure, the penny-pinching shifts she is put to with her aging gloves, and the "gentleman in grey" shaking his head in refusal, "tall, stiff, dignified." Both of these caricatures bring to my mind Toulouse-Lautrec lithographs: *Poster for the Moulin Rouge* featuring La Goulue and Valentin-le-Désossé, or the poster for *Le Divan Japonais* or *The Englishman at the Moulin Rouge*.

The passage also brings inescapably to mind film, and I'd be rather surprised if this wasn't exactly what was in Katherine Mansfield's mind too; she herself had worked as a film "extra," and in the years leading up to 1920, film was much on the minds of artists in all forms.

All these currents flow together in this brief paragraph and the only way to savour them all and apprehend all the pleasures on offer is to listen—repeatedly. This wonderful shorthand into Miss Brill's mind—

everywhere, here, there, along by the sea.

IV

There are many different kinds of music in prose and the key to their pleasures is, obviously, learning to listen. At one end of a continuum is Leon Rooke, a veritable brass band; also up at the noisy end are Mark Anthony Jarman, Terry Griggs, some of Keath Fraser's stories. The music of K.D. Miller, Elise Levine, Annabel Lyon, Linda Svendsen, and Caroline Adderson is quieter but immediately distinctive. All good prose has its own singular music; we simply have to teach ourselves to hear it.

In my 2003 memoir, *An Aesthetic Underground*, I wrote of Leon Rooke "… the central reason for his early neglect is that most readers were not hearing what Leon was up to. Their attention was directed elsewhere, to theme, perhaps, or form. They were in a similar situation to an earnest gallery-goer standing in front of a Rothko and asking 'What does it mean?' The answer is, 'Look.'

To the reader who asks 'What does it mean?' of Rooke's 'Sixteen-Year-Old Susan March Confesses to the Innocent Murder of All the Devious Strangers Who Would Drag Her Down', the answer is, 'Listen.'"

(I am not proposing some sort of hippy-dippy Zen koan; I'm offering some simple advice. I used to snarl into the ears of my very brightest students: *Stop Thinking!*)

Listen.

Rooke has published four or five plays, and many of the stories are essentially *scripts*—monologues or voices arguing. The insistent direction in his work is theatrical. Leon is never happier than on a stage, the rhetoric flying high and wide and often over the top. Leon is a performer. Leon is a self-confessed ham. His stories are *performances*.

He is very prolific, having published by now some three hundred short stories in literary magazines. Most are uncollected because, on further reflection, he felt they simply did not work. Leon doesn't brood for months over the shape and detail of what he hopes will be a masterwork; he picks up his horn, softens the reed, and tries out a few runs, a few phrases, to see if something is going to happen.

I sometimes think that Rooke's academic acceptance has been slow because academics have been slow to think of Leon as, say, a tenor sax player and the story as a jazz improvisation. If the reader *does* respond in those terms it becomes immediately obvious what Leon is up to.

Leon is leading the parade. He doesn't want a tweed-with-leather-elbow-patches response. He wants celebrants performing along with him. He wants a Second Line. At other times he wants to preach, a big Texas tenor sound, wave after wave of impossibly mounting fervour.

(The results are sometimes simply noodling, at others, electrifying as he erupts into dirty Eddie "Lockjaw" Davis or Illinois Jacquet solos.)

Leon preaching always reminds me of recordings I've heard of the Reverend Kelsey leading his Washington congregation in "Lion of the Tribe of Judah"; the preacher's voice probes at the words, repeats, hums, slides into falsetto, repeats and finds a form and then all rhythmic hell breaks loose, hands clapping, jugs grunting and booming, a trombone's urging. All rather glorious.

At entirely the other end of the continuum, I've been haunted for years by the delicate music of James Salter. His two collections of stories, *Last Night*, *Dusk and Other Stories*, and the *Collected Stories* (2013), are not much mentioned and are masterly. But the book that has been so much in my mind is Salter's memoir of West Point and his years as a fighter pilot in the American air force. It is called *Burning the Days*.

Here's a scene from his cadet days at West Point.

> I remember sweating, the heat and thirst, the banned bliss of long gulping from the spigot. At parades, three or four a week, above the drone of hazing floated the music of the band. It seemed part of another, far-off world. There was a feeling of being on a hopeless journey, an exile that would last for years. In the distance, women in light frocks strolled with officers, and the fine house of the Superintendent gleamed toylike and white. In the terrific sun someone in the next rank or beside you begins to sway, take an involuntary step, and like a beaten fighter falls forward. Rifles litter the ground. Afterwards a tactical officer walks among them as among bodies on a battlefield, noting down the serial numbers.

The whole scene is almost dreamlike. So many pleasures. "Long gulping," "light frocks," the restoration of meaning to the word "terrific." The officer, stepping among the littered rifles, noting down serial numbers for the subsequent punishment of their owners. The "strolling officers" and the Superintendent's "fine" house gleaming "toylike and white."

It is exactly like an American primitive painting, a piece of vivid folk art.

The end of the memoir sings with enormous power, with weight, with love. I've handled Salter's lines for years and know, largely, how his rhetoric works, but there's something in these final lines of *Burning the Days*, a magic, a music I can't explicate, much in the same way I can't express why *exactly* the line

> *Time hath my golden locks to silver turned*

has such elegiac power. The *trying* is like the frustration at not being able to find in an eighteenth-century desk the pressure point that will release the hidden drawer. Perhaps I should less uneasily accept magic as an explanation.

At the end of the memoir, friends have been for dinner at Salter's country house.

Here are the book's final seven sentences, sentences that continue to move me intensely:

> The fire had burned to embers, the company was gone. We walked in the icy darkness with the old, limping dog. Nothing on the empty road, no cars, no sound, no lights. The year turning, cold stars above. My arm around her. Feeling of courage. Great desire to live on.

★

For years I taught at the Humber College School for y with an old friend, Bruce Jay Friedman. I persuaded Bruce to write a memoir, which we published at Biblioasis; it is entitled *Lucky Bruce*. He refers in the book to a regular social lunch gathering of area writers, one of whom was Joseph Heller. Something of Heller's personality is caught in this anecdote recorded in Catalogue 75 of Peter Ellis— Bookseller: "Apparently, he was once asked why he had never written anything else as good as *Catch-22;* 'Who could?' was the reply."

Popular opinion, however, got Heller completely wrong. The humour of *Catch-22* is ponderous, lumbering. The book was too easy; it seemed to speak for an anti-Vietnam War generation but, after the uproar and the froth subsided, *Catch-22* subsided with them. Heller's *real* claim to fame is *Something Happened.*

In *Lucky Bruce,* Friedman wrote:

> We scheduled a regular lunch at Bobby Van's, then switched to Barrister's in Southampton where the waitresses were prettier. The core group was made up of Puzo, Heller, Speed Vogel, Mel Brooks, when he was in the area, and the screen writer David Zelag Goodman.
>
> From time to time we thought of inviting others to join us. I proposed the novelist James Salter.
>
> Puzo objected. "He is too good a writer."

V

If I were in a classroom again and talking about "Miss Brill," the first thing I would do would be to engage students with the text. This sounds stupidly obvious, but these days seems to happen rarely. I would want to slow everything down so that the prose could dampen, soak slowly into the fabric of their minds and emotions, render it eventually sopping wet. I would ask the students to copy out, say, the first paragraph. *Not* typing or keying-in but by hand, on paper. I would particularly wish them to eschew the mechanical, the speed of technology, and revert to the slow, considered, monastic labour of the scriptorium.

Then I would have them copy it out again, stopping at every sentence to reread the sentence preceding.

This pedagogical heresy alone would have me burned at the educational stake; good money had not changed hands to be squandered on childish copying; my "clients" would lodge complaints; the Head of the Department would send for me to have a friendly but corrective chat as between colleagues. Then, of course, when I persisted in my practice, I would receive the pink slip.

But what does such copying *do?*

It teaches in a way that nothing else can.

Anyone who has proofread a newsletter, a bulletin, an obituary, a letter to the editor, a university essay, knows that, despite concentration, errors appear—incorrect spellings, odd punctuation, ambiguities, grammatical mistakes, cacophonies. Slow copying by hand locks the mind onto the words on the page rather than onto the slop of omissions, invented words, homonyms, garble, that the skimming eye produces. Laboriousness becomes a virtue.

I will go into the matter of slow copying more fully (or "fulsomely" as our dimmer Cabinet Ministers have recently taken to saying on TV pundit-panels) by referring to a lovely book about Andrea Palladio by Witold Rybczynski called *The Perfect House*. Rybczynski describes Palladio (1508–1580) as the equivalent in architecture to Shakespeare in literature. I know a professional architect, graduate of the McGill architecture school, who had never heard of Palladio; this revelation left me thoughtful.

Rybyczynski wrote of Palladio's first visit to Rome:

> He made precise drawings of the capitals, friezes, and entablatures, meticulously dimensioning each torus and fillet. He copied details. He sketched mouldings, either drawing them by eye or modelling their outlines with a thin strip of lead that he used as a drawing template. The purpose of this activity was twofold. *Drawing, which involves long periods of intense scrutiny, internalizes the subject (in a way photography does not begin to approximate); Palladio was schooling his eye and trying to better understand what he was seeing. He was also compiling a visual lexicon to which he could refer when he was working.* (Emphasis added.)

Stories are intended as unique and intense experiences; they cannot be gobbled up like packets of verbal Smarties.

The last sentences of Mavis Gallant's preface to her *Selected Stories* read:

> There is something I keep wanting to say about reading short stories. I am doing it now, because I may never have another occasion. Stories are not chapters of novels. They should not be read one after another, as if they were meant to follow along. Read one. Shut the book. Read something else. Come back later.

Stories can wait.

The reader may recall Henry Green's defence of the awkwardness of Doughty's style as being a device *to prevent experience from being swallowed too quickly...*

Here is Susan Cheever on e.e. Cummings and the necessity of difficulty:

> In a world seduced by easy understanding, the modernists believed that difficulty enhanced the pleasures of reading. In a Cummings poem the reader must often pick his way toward comprehension, which comes, when it does, in a burst of delight and recognition. Like many of his fellow modernists (the audience walked out of Stravinsky's *Rite of Spring*, and viewers were scandalized by Marcel Duchamp's *Nude Descending a Staircase*), Cummings was sometimes reviled by the fakirs and fanatics of the critical establishment. Princeton poet Richard P. Blackmur said Cummings poems were "baby talk," and poetry arbiter Helen Vendler called them repellent and foolish: "What is wrong with a man who writes this?" she asked.

> Nothing was wrong with Cummings—or Duchamp or Stravinsky or Joyce, for that matter. All were trying to slow down the seemingly inexorable rush of the world, to force people to notice their own lives. In the twenty-first century, that rush has now reached Force Five; we are all inundated with information and given no time to wonder what it means or where it came from. Access without understanding and facts without context have become our daily diet.

> (From the preface to *E.E. Cummings: A Life* by Susan Cheever.)

The next thing I would do if talking about "Miss Brill"—worse even than copying—would be to ask student after student to read the first paragraph aloud, to *perform* the prose. For if a reader cannot convey the life of the prose—its rhythm, emphases, volume, pauses, silences—cannot get at its life, its *breathing*, but reads as if reading the packaged assemblage instructions for a floor lamp manufactured in China, then for that reader the prose is inert, incomprehensible, null.

And what an anguish such teaching is!

Though I strive to forget, I remember with horrid vividness a "service English" class I taught at Loyola College in Montreal. I was foolish enough to require them to read aloud the first few lines of one of John Donne's Holy Sonnets.

> Batter my heart, three-personed God; for you
> As yet but knock, breathe, shine, and seek to mend;
> That I may rise, and stand, o'erthrow me, and bend
> Your force, to break, blow, burn, and make me new.
> I, like an usurped town, to another due,
> Labour to admit you, but oh! to no end;
> Reason, your viceroy in me, me should defend,
> But is captiv'd and proves weak or untrue.
> Yet dearly I love you, and would be lovèd fain,
> But am betroth'd unto your enemy.
> Divorce me, untie or break that knot again,
> Take me to you, imprison me, for I,
> Except you enthrall me, never shall be free,
> Nor ever chaste, except you ravish me.

I explained what "due," "fain," and "enthrall" meant and explained that the consensus on "knock, breathe, shine, and seek to mend" (given the following pattern of forge imagery "break, blow, burn, and make me new") was that the verbs described the actions of, say, a tinker, an itinerant mender of kettles and pans. The tinker is tapping, then huffing on the pot, then wiping it, perhaps, with his sleeve, the better to see how the work is going. The poet rejects such delicacy and tentative tapping and begs that the damaged vessel not be "knocked" but, rather, "battered."

I pointed out how the poem is constructed on apparent contradictions:

That I may rise, and stand, o'erthrow me...

...

Nor ever chaste, except you ravish me.

When we'd finished this arcane trudging, I asked them, trying to lead them towards the *emotional* point, to read aloud the first two lines.

Batter my heart..
Batter my heart...

Dutifully they read.

Batter my heart...

"No, no," I half-begged them, waving the next reader to silence. "Logic and passion *dictate...*"

They stare silent and leery.

"... *dictate...*"

I survey them.

"BATTER," I say, "my heart..."

And they did.

But I was young then.

If I were trying to lead students into "Miss Brill," I would stand listening to their reading, wondering if one of them has begun to hear the music.

... and now and again a leaf came drifting—from nowhere, from the sky.

What timing? The length of pauses? What weight of emphases? How best to catch Miss Brill's social background? Upbringing and education? Age and manners?

I always read this partial line with a small emphasis on *leaf* and a tiny pause before *came drifting* to suggest she's watching it; the pause and the "f" sounds suggest the leaf's slow, swirling fall.

Pause on the dash.

From nowhere; between these two words, a tiny pause, the *nowhere* to carry a tone of tiny puzzlement; the pronunciation should be slightly breathy, an imperceptible shrug.

from the sky; here *from* is slightly stronger in emphasis than *the sky.* There is a fractional pause after *from* which highlights *the sky* as a sort of answer to the implicit question in *nowhere.*

So for me the line works like this:

"... and now and again a *leaf* (tiny pause) *came drifting*—(longer pause at the dash) *from nowhere* (slight emphasis on *from* followed by a fractional pause) *from the sky* (fractional emphasis on *from* and fractional pause after it.)

Then these footprints in the rhetorical sand must be brushed out to leave Miss Brill spotlighted on her bench and us emotionally moved and held in the flow of her speaking.

Though she is not speaking at all.

Well, I imagine one saying, *I didn't know this was supposed to be about acting!*

I mean, says another, *a theatre or something.*

How do you know all this—what you're saying—demands another—*how do you know what she meant?*

What she intended...

Katherine Mansfield was a practising musician and, before becoming a writer, had planned on becoming a professional cellist. She wrote in her diary, "I have a pretty bad habit of spreading myself at times, of overwriting and understating—it's just carelessness." Kirsty Gunn, the admirably accomplished reviewer mentioned earlier, writes: "It's through her 'carelessness,' all the rewrites and the false starts, that Mansfield found her way. To keep practising was the lesson, and 'practising,' as though playing the cello, was the word she herself used to describe the process of writing."

In 1921 Katherine Mansfield wrote to Richard Murry:

> It's a queer thing how *craft* comes into writing. I mean down to details. Par example. In "Miss Brill" I chose not only the length of every sentence, but even the sound of every sentence. I chose the rise and fall of every paragraph to fit her, and to fit her on that day at that very moment. After I'd written it I read it aloud—numbers of times—just as one would *play over* a musical composition—trying to get it nearer and nearer to the expression of Miss Brill—until it fitted her.

Don't think I'm vain about the little sketch. It's only the method I wanted to explain. I often wonder whether other writers do the same—if a thing has really come off it seems to me there mustn't be one single word out of place, or one word that could be taken out. That's how I AIM at writing. It will take some time to get anywhere near there.

It will take some time...

Two years later, at the age of thirty-four, Katherine Mansfield was dead.

★

All of the foregoing has been the general approach to literature I have wanted to stress throughout this book. "Social ends," to use Clive James' phrase, may emerge, the reader's engagement with the world may be deepened, enriched, but such possible experiences are always strictly a by-product. The by-product of pleasure and joy, the by-product of being aesthetically devastated, the pleasure and joy I first felt, nearly sixty years ago, when, in the silence of a grammar school library in Kent, I answered to the voice of Miss Brill.

Dandelions

George Kenway straightened his shoulders and sat upright to ease the pang of heartburn. He breathed deeply until the pain began to fade, its sharpness settling into a dull ache in his teeth on the left side. He took the bottle of aspirins from the centre drawer of the desk and shook a couple out onto his palm. When the pains had first started he had thought he was suffering heart attacks.

It was probably lack of exercise. That, and sitting hunched over the desk. When the spring came again he would really try to get himself into shape. He pulled his stomach in and looked down, but the grey cardigan Mary had knitted him still bulged. Tennis might do the trick. He stared down at the mother-of-pearl buttons. Or walking. Walking was quite pleasant. He pushed his spectacles higher on the bridge of his nose.

On both sides of the central aisle, the shelves stretched down the length of the narrow shop. There were no customers. In the silence, he could hear the sounds of the old beams and floor boards. On the desk lay *Imprint* and *Book News*; he had not yet read them. The paperback order forms, too, were waiting to be completed. The pencil in his hand doodled over the yellow pad drawing tiny, interlocking circles in endless repetitions.

The bell above the door jangled. A woman with a child came in. He looked at her over his glasses and inclined his head in welcome. He never approached customers now. He did not want to say *Can I help you?* and hear the ritual *I'm just looking, thank you.*

"A book for a boy, madam? This boy? Over in the far corner."

Over in the far corner with all the trains and planes, the fire engines and the spaceships, the brown bunnies and the cuddly bears; with all the fat, pink pigs in trousers, the winsome pups and patient horses. He glanced at his pocket watch. The glass was scratched and yellowed. It had belonged to his father. Mary had made a shammy-leather pocket for it in the waistband of his trousers.

Business was slow, even for a Monday. Twenty-odd paperbacks, a book about the care of budgies, two copies of *Middlemarch* because they were doing it on TV and an enquiry:

I can order it for you.

And the traditional lie:

I especially wanted it for today.

He wrapped the book in brown paper, sticking down the flaps with tape. So much more sensible than string. *Farm Friends*. And change from the tin cash box in his drawer. He walked toward the door with the woman but stopped to straighten the Penguins and Pelicans. He would have to re-order, too, on the new gardening books. A very popular line.

He moved back past Gardening and Cookery, Religion (Common Prayers in white leatherette and Presentation Bibles), Modern Literature (low again on the Cronins and Shutes), Hobbies, Travel, and Adventure, towards his desk.

He had put his sandwiches in the desk drawer. He wondered what they were today. Cheese and tomato, perhaps? He hoped they weren't fish-paste or luncheon-meat. Those always left him so thirsty. She'd promised shepherd's pie tonight. He'd always liked that. It was an attractive name, too. Shepherd's pie. As he put his hand down to open the drawer, he noticed the sticking plaster across the back of his thumb. He thought, as he always did, what an unpleasant colour it was; that unnatural flesh colour, almost salmon, that children produced in their paintings. A nasty scrape on one of the wing nuts of Roy's bicycle. And the wheel still wasn't straight. That would be another job for tonight. He'd probably have to take off the brake blocks. And the front hedge couldn't go much longer. It was silly, though, how upset she got about things like that. He would have to buy a bottle of machine oil for the clippers on the way home.

The sandwiches were wrapped in grease-proof paper and secured with an elastic band. He looked at his watch again and decided to wait until one o'clock. Another ten minutes. Perhaps he could lose weight if, every day, he left one sandwich. But then, he knew that he would eat it with his afternoon cup of tea.

Sometimes, in the long afternoons, after the day had been divided by the sandwiches, he saw the shelves as he had always imagined them, the rows of calf-bound volumes, gilt titles, gilt decoration on the spines, the light hinting on the mahogany richness of the old leather. Standing along the bottom shelves, the massive folios—Heraldry, County Visitations, Voyages, Theological Disputations, and Chronicles. The air would be heavy with the must of old paper. Lying open on his desk, or perhaps propped against his works of reference, would be a sixteenth-century German blackletter with quaint woodcuts of vigorous tortures and martyrdoms, and in the glass-fronted cases behind him a few incunabula and the Aldines and Elzevirs and the volumes with the fore-edge paintings. In the heavy portfolio beside the desk there would be the Speed and Bartholomew maps, single leaves from Caxton, a few autographs, and pages of medieval manuscript brilliant with gold, blue, and scarlet illumination. And to his few customers—for most of his trade would be through his scholarly catalogues—he would say:

"Well, the title's foxed and there's some worming in the last signature, but it's a rare volume. Not recorded in Wing, I believe."

Or he'd say:

"It's a pleasing book. A very representative binding."

He still bought catalogues of the sales and read the report from Sotheby's every week in the *Literary Supplement*. It was Friday's chief pleasure.

He unwrapped the sandwiches, leaving them out of sight in the open drawer in case a customer came in. They were egg and lettuce. The coffee in his thermos flask was the kind without caffeine. She was always worrying about his health. On winter mornings, when he stooped to kiss her goodbye, she always tucked his muffler more firmly inside the old mac.

The afternoon sun was quite strong for September and the narrow room was becoming uncomfortably warm. He got up from his desk and walked down to the window where he lowered the Venetian blind. He checked to see that the sign on the door said Open and then went back to his desk.

He took out his fountain pen, a gift from Mary eleven years ago, and unscrewed the cap. He took the bottle of Permanent Black from its place in the left-hand drawer and filled the pen, wiping it clean on a piece of rag he kept with the ink bottle. He placed the pen beside his memo pad on the blotter and then started to work his way through *Book News* but it was difficult to concentrate; his eyes jumped lines of print and he had to keep on going back to grasp what he was reading. He did not like to admit it, but he often felt quite sleepy after lunch. It would have been most refreshing to stretch out, just for a few minutes.

With the blind down, the room was rather dim, except for a single patch of sunlight where a slat in the blind was buckled. He took off his glasses and rubbed his eyes. The bridge of his nose, too, was sore from the pressure.

He raised his head and stared down the warm gloom towards the window. His eyes were caught and dazzled in the burst of light. As he stared, the light seemed to grow brighter like a climbing candle flame, and larger, until he saw nothing else. Then, slowly, in the white centre of the light, a picture grew.

He saw a small boy standing in a familiar room looking towards the window. The boy was himself. He was standing alone in the big stone-flagged kitchen. He could feel the coolness of the stone through his stocking-feet. Behind him, on the mantelpiece, the black clock was ticking.

On the red-tiled windowsill stood a jam jar full of dandelions. The window burned. Between the lace curtains, sunlight, sunshine glittering off the silver tap, gleaming in the white sink, glowing on the crowded yellow heads.

He had picked them in the orchard.

The details of the picture faded, faded until he saw only the burning flowers in the jam jar, and then, blinking, he found that he was staring at the sunpatch, the Venetian blind with its buckled slat, the shelves of books, and his desk in front of him with his glasses lying on the green blotter. For a few moments, he stared at the glasses as though he did not know what they were for. Then he reached out and picked them up, settling them cautiously on his nose. He sat motionless in his chair and the afternoon ebbed quietly away.

The bell above the door jangled. A young man, an untidy young man in jeans and a sweater, a student, walked up the shop towards him and stood in front of the desk.

"*Economic Theory* by Woodall? I don't believe I have . . . no, I'm sure . . . I beg your pardon? Order it for you? Oh, yes. *Order* it. Certainly, sir. Certainly."

When the young man had gone, he took out his watch and, looking at it, shook his head. He felt rather fuzzy; a cold coming on perhaps, or possibly the aspirins. He put the thermos flask into his briefcase and snapped shut the clasp. His raincoat was in the cupboard behind the desk and he took it out and shrugged his shoulders into it. He pulled the belt tighter and stood looking round the shop.

He was surprised to see his fountain pen still lying on the blotter. He put it in the right-hand drawer in its proper place in the *Castañeda* cigar box.

He put the lock down on the door and turned the Open sign around. He pulled the door shut after him and shook the handle to make sure, as he always did. And as he always did, he looked up at the sign above the door: Geo. Kenway: Bookseller.

Because he was earlier than usual, there was not such a long queue at the bus stop and when the bus came he managed the luxury of a seat to himself. The familiar landmarks passed in their usual order and he got automatically to his feet just before his stop.

The fresh air seemed to clear his head as he walked down Cherril Avenue and turned into The Grove. Down at the far end, by the bowling green, a group of boys were straddling their bikes and talking. He recognized Roy, and Peter from next door.

He had forgotten to empty the tin cash box.

The painters were at work at number fifty-three. He hoped the green they were using was an undercoat. Mr. Glover waved to him.

"How are you keeping, Mr. Glover?"

"Sprightly for an old one. Keeping busy, you know. And yourself?"

"Oh, very well, thank you," he called.

"Yes, it's been a beautiful afternoon."

He turned in at number forty-seven. The front door was ajar. As he hung up his raincoat and pushed his briefcase under the hall table, he called, "Hello? Mary?"

She came out from the kitchen and as he bent to kiss her she said, "Is anything wrong, George?"

"Wrong?"

"You're so early."

"Oh, no. I had a bit of a headache and things were quiet. I just thought I'd come home."

"Would you like a cup of tea?"

"Yes," he said. "Yes, that'd be nice."

"It was so lovely this afternoon," she said, "just like summer, so I made a salad for you. With salmon. And Roy's off somewhere playing speedbike."

"Speedway," he said.

He had forgotten the oil for the clippers.

"Whatever he calls it," she said.

"I think I'll do the hedge before supper," he said, as he followed her into the kitchen.

It was still warm, although, as the sun set, a breeze was springing up. He moved gradually into the rhythm of the work. It became enjoyable and he frequently stepped back to see if the line was straight. The higher sprigs would have to be tackled from the other side. But he had managed a smooth curve towards the crown of the hedge. Very smooth, in fact. He stepped back to look again and then moved in to trim a straggling spray.

His hands were hot and sweaty and a heavy pulse beat in his neck. Leaning on the front gate, he rested for a few minutes before starting on the other side.

The light was thickening and the houses opposite were becoming shapes against the flushed sky. Shepherd's delight. Shepherd's pie. Another fine day tomorrow. He could hear the distant whirr and

clack of a lawnmower, and across the road the Romilly girl was practising scales on the piano, the notes falling softly into the evening.

There was a light, sharp scent in the air, a faintly acid smell. The
smell of sap and bruised privet leaves. It seemed to move a memory
in him . . . a recollection . . . but he could not remember what it was.

Dandelions Is All My Love

"Dandelions" was written fairly early in my writing career and collected in my first book *The Lady Who Sold Furniture* (1970). Although my interests now, as I've mentioned earlier, are in caricature and theatrical flourish, "Dandelions" is a useful story to look at in the context of this book because although stories have evolved in many different directions and in a variety of styles, they all still are the inheritors of the "revolution of the Word," of honed diction, imagery, dominant currents of feeling within stories.

The story, written in the sixties, was my belated entry into "modernism." Behind the times as it was, however, it now offers a way of reiterating this book's central concerns. "Dandelions" and stories like it are a necessary template for understanding subsequent developments in the form. In this story we can watch this book's abstract ideas, earlier discussed, given concrete embodiment; given as *A Midsummer Night's Dream*, has it:

> ... *to airy nothing*
> *A local habitation and a name.*

The story started for me with a real memory of a jam-jar of dandelions. Stories still start for me in exactly the same way, remembered pictures which begin to return, then haunt, obviously important, significant, portentous, but incomprehensible. Portentous of what? Early on, I used to nag at the pictures but soon learned to relax and, in Seamus Heaney's words, let them *discover* themselves.

The dandelions were an acute visual memory, a vision, a revelation. I was ten or eleven at the time and this memory was of the kitchen at Low Bracken Hall, my uncle's farm in Cumberland. The sunlight, the white enamel sink chipped and pitted through here and there to reveal the biscuit-yellow beneath, the curve of the gleaming tap. The glowing flower heads on the tiled sill, though almost holy in themselves, have no larger meaning until they are given meaning by being placed in a context, by being charged with a pre-existing feeling. The "pre-existing feeling" in "Dandelions" is easy to describe. I feared the smother of dailiness; I feared (at the age of thirty!) the death of passion; despite whatever consequent privations, I wanted a passionate life.

Looking back now over earlier work, I realize that this "pre-existing feeling" has been a constant. In a story called "Single Gents Only," I wrote about an eighteen-year-old boy leaving home:

> But he found it easier to approach what he would become by defining what he was leaving behind. What he most definitely *wasn't*—hideous images came to mind; sachets of dried lavender, Post Office Savings Books, hyacinth bulbs in bowls, the *Radio Times* in a padded leather cover embossed with the words *Radio Times,* Sunday best silver tongs for removing sugar cubes from sugar bowls, plump armchairs.

The dreariness of this life, as he sees it, its stifling effects, are conveyed in the "plonking" repetition of the *Radio Times*, the pretentiousness of a leather cover for this weekly magazine-cum-programme guide to the BBC's cultural offerings, the everything-in-its-placeness, the offensive daintiness of sugar tongs for removing sugar cubes from sugar bowls, the smug comfort of "plump."

Given such a current, George Kenway, bookseller, seemed an almost inevitable invention.

George Johnston's poem "Bedtime" might have been written for him.

Edna the dog is dead and so is Min;
Mr. Smith's diet worked and now he's thin;
Walter has left the park for his loving wife:
Better warm than happy defines his life.

The next part of the story to arrive was insistent memories of an actual second-hand bookstore I frequented in Bristol when I was a student. It was at the top of the picturesque Christmas Steps, a steep, descending row of ancient, ramshackle shops, seedy, beautiful. I can even remember particular books I bought there: the wonderful Joyce Cary first trilogy in the Carfax uniform edition: *Herself Surprised, To Be a Pilgrim,* and *The Horse's Mouth.* I brought these to Canada and gave them to Amanda Jernigan, when she was still a girl in school, fairly confident that *The Horse's Mouth* would lure her into a life of art and penury, a confidence later justified. I also remember buying there an omnibus edition published by Grey Walls Press of the first British publication of the four works of Nathanael West.

But in these memories, it was the store itself, the long, narrow central aisle and its gloom, which seemed important. Gradually the store became in my mind a different *kind* of store, not the solid, tasteful second-hand bookstore it actually was, but a new bookstore, a store that sold Georgette Heyer, Neville Shute, A.J. Cronin, Richmal Compton's "William" books, Daphne Du Maurier, and books bound in white leatherette, propped up at a slight angle in their white fancy cardboard gift boxes, leatherette Bibles, hymnals, and the *Book of Common Prayer,* white Autograph Albums with padded, puffy covers. Slowly, the store's owner began to appear as I began to hear his voice.

This peculiar sentence needs elaboration. In humdrum novels that described characters—five-foot-eight, wispy moustache, grey eyes etc.—*my* eyes glazed quickly and I saw nothing. The same seemed to hold true for landscape and housing; I always skipped until the dialogue started. I slowly realized that voice seemed to deliver *something essential of physical appearance.*

Writing a story called "Single Gents Only," which appeared in *Adult Entertainment* in 1986, I was attempting to describe the unappealing denizens of a boarding house. One in particular, an old man addressed always as "Father," gave me endless trouble. I expended on him hours of clever phrase-making but, try as I might, he lay dead on the page until, finally, I stood back and listened as I let him talk. *Then* I discovered he had an Irish accent and a garrulous mind awash in non sequiturs and he stirred to immediate life.

Here is Father manufacturing a spill from newspaper with which to light the gas under the hot-water heater, the geyser, in the bathroom, a terrifying undertaking. The scene is observed by David, a newly arrived lodger, his room door slightly ajar.

"*Evening Post*. Now that should serve her nicely, the *Evening Post*. Six pages of the *Post*. Read the newspapers, do you? Not much of a fellow for the reading. Scars, though! Now that's a different story entirely. Did I show you me scars?"

Through the banisters, an old man's head with hanging wings of white hair. Behind him, a stout boy in a brown dressing gown.

The boy stood holding a sponge bag by its strings; his calves were white and plump.

"Now there's a dreadful thing!" said the old man, who was scrabbling about on hands and knees with the sheets of newspaper manufacturing a giant spill. "A dreadful thing! Two hundred homeless. Will you look at that! There, look, there's a footballer. Follow the football, do you? Fill in the Pools? Never a drop of luck I've had. Spot the Ball? But a raffle, now! A raffle. I fancy the odds in a raffle. A raffle's a more reasonable creature than Spot the Ball."

He disappeared into the bathroom.

The front door slammed, shaking the house.

Boots.

"PERCY?"

"WHAT?"

"PERCE!"

"Quick, now!" shouted the old man. "Quick! Holy Mother, she's in full flow!"

Matches shaking from the box, he secured one against his chest and then rasped it into flame. He set fire to the drooping spill.

"BACK, BOY! BACK!"

Body shielded by the door, face averted, he lunged blindly. The expanding sheet of light reminded David of war films. The old man's quavering cry and the explosion were nearly simultaneous.

Brown shoulders blocking the view.

Suddenly from below, at great volume, Paul Anka.

I'M JUST A LONELY BOY....

The old man was in the smoke stamping on the spill.

Ash, grey and tremulous, floated on the air.

In "Dandelions," however, there is very little speech; that in the shop is ritualistic, that between George Kenway and his wife is brief and, intentionally, on my part, inconsequential. Why did I avoid direct speech? I hadn't realized it at the time but now, forty years later, it seems obvious to me that I was trying to write "Miss Brill."

Katherine Mansfield had an essential reason for not giving Miss Brill speech; Miss Brill was habitually alone; *she had no one to speak to*; she could live life only vicariously. George Kenway, too, lives life inside his head but... well, I was experimenting and trying to pay my debt to genius.

I was trying to suggest, by the rhythms and repetitions of the prose, George Kenway's voice and, through his voice, his appearance and being.

He wrapped the book in brown paper, sticking down the flaps with tape. So much more sensible than string. *Farm Friends.* And change from the tin cash box in his drawer. He walked towards the door with the woman but stopped to straighten the Penguins and Pelicans. He would have to re-order, too, on the new gardening books. A very popular line.

He moved back past Gardening and Cookery, Religion (*Common Prayers* in white leatherette and Presentation Bibles), Modern Literature (low again on the Cronins and Shutes), Hobbies, Travel and Adventure, towards his desk.

"So much more sensible than string."

"And change from the tin cash box in his drawer."

"A very popular line."

Perfectly believable as part of the lifelong conversation in his head, easily believable, too, as *spoken* words. George Kenway *would* have a little "tin cash box"—how easily though those words translate into "And your change, Madam." Each word builds towards a picture of George Kenway: the preciseness of his wrapping, his little tin cash box, his straightening the Penguins and the Pelicans; fussy, caught up in routines and obligations that are a little resented, yet embraced as comforting. George Kenway wears cardigans, has what polite British people might call "a bit of a tummy," is a creature of habit, a place for everything and everything in its place, the Permanent Black ink, the fountain pen, the fountain pen's special rag, the *Castañeda* cigar box, the chamois leather pocket for his pocket watch. He is uxorious and is, in turn, somewhat infantilized by Mary's decaffeinated coffee, by her sandwiches, by his letting her tuck his muffler firmly about his throat on winter mornings.

... *moved back past... Adventure towards his desk.*

"A book for a boy, Madam? This boy?"

I imagine him regarding the child over his spectacles with less than enthusiasm.

"Over in the corner."

Before she'd come in he'd been facing the to-be-completed order forms, his pencil doodling "interlocking circles in endless repetitions." Over in the far corner with "the fat, pink pigs in trousers"... "the winsome pups and patient horses," the "p" sounds suggesting disparagement, suggesting tedium. He had consulted his watch to see how much longer he would have to wait until sandwich-time.

This boredom, this mild dissatisfaction, seem to be setting us up for what will happen *after* the dandelions. For George Kenway is sometimes still visited by wistful visions of might-have-beens; set against "white leatherette" (i.e. plastic) is the romance of the antiquarian trade.

> Sometimes, in the long afternoons, after the day had been
> divided by the sandwiches, he saw the shelves as he had always
> imagined them, the rows of calf-bound volumes, gilt titles, gilt
> decorations on the spines, the light hinting on the mahogany
> richness of the old leather. Standing along the bottom shelves
> the massive folios—Heraldry, County Visitations, Voyages,
> Theological Disputations, and Chronicles. The air would be
> heavy with the must of old paper. Lying open on his desk, or
> perhaps propped against his works of reference, would be a
> sixteenth-century German blackletter with quaint woodcuts
> of vigorous tortures and martyrdoms, and in the glass-fronted
> cases behind him a few incunabula and the Aldines and Elzevirs
> and the volumes with the fore-edge paintings... And to his few
> customers—for most of his trade would be through scholarly
> catalogues—he would say:
> "Well, the title's foxed and there's some worming in the
> last signature, but it's a rare volume. Not recorded in Wing, I
> believe."

(Wing is a reference to *Short-Title Catalogue of Books printed in
England, Scotland, Ireland, Wales and British America, and of English
Books printed in other Countries 1641–1700*. Compiled by Donald Wing
of the Yale University Library. Printed for the Index Society by
Columbia University Press, New York.)

This Wing world is not the world of egg-and-lettuce sandwiches.

The logic of "Dandelions," the "feel" of the story, would suggest
that its structure *ought* to fall into roughly the following pattern:

1) Small indications, hints, that the protagonist's life could
offer more fulfillment.

(His boredom, depressive inability to fill in ordering-forms, the
ritual quality of shop conversations (conveyed by use of italic) *I'm
just looking, thank you / I especially wanted it for today*. His anticipation of comfort food. His imagining of an antiquarian store with

its weight of old leather and pale vellum bindings, the maps of Bartholomew and John Speed.)

2) The vision of the dandelions, which ought, in turn, to prompt some kind of self-awareness, some movement, however slight, towards change.

3) Some example, on the close of the story, of such change, beginning or imminent.

That would be the now-classic pattern for a "modernist" story, for what is called an "epiphany" story.

"Dandelions" is a variant on this structure.

During the 1970 conference in Fredericton—"conference" sounds so *tedious* for what was simply an opportunity to meet other writers and drink too much—Kent Thompson suggested that the "epiphany" story, which had been an escape from plotted tales with a tacked-on moral, had itself now become the problem, stories which neatly delivered little packages of emotional "growth" and "fulfillment." It was from *these*, the Academy Stuff, that the young writer now had to escape. And by "Academy Stuff," Kent Thompson meant such giants as Eudora Welty and John Cheever.

(The varieties of that escape can be read in the Century List.)

The word "epiphany" means "a sudden and important manifestation or realization" and, from Greek, indicates the apprehension or advent of a god. In the Western Church it refers to the manifestation of Jesus to the Magi; in the Orthodox Church to Jesus' baptism.)

I rather like the fancy of the dandelions as the manifestation or apprehension of a god.

But what, seriously, are we to understand the dandelions to mean? Principally, of course, *themselves*. The beauty of the packed, glowing crowns. The smell of them. The unique odour of the milky sap inside the hollow stems.

One could put the flowers at a remove, abstract them by thinking of "beauty," or "intensity," or "promise." They're certainly associated with sap and all that is implied in that word of youth, growth, power, sexuality. These words, though, are reductive, the intellect's "eagerness," as Seamus Heaney put it, "to foreclose."

Better to let the dandelions *discover* themselves in all their smell and floweriness.

Remember the words of Grampaw E "... the natural object is always the adequate symbol."

What, then, happens post-dandelions?

Kenway is unsettled as the vision of dandelions recedes and the burning light becomes again merely sunshine through a buckled slat in the blind. He re-enters the world slowly, recognizing his glasses on the blotter, settles them on his nose cautiously, fumbles the student's request for Woodall's *Economic Theory;* he feels, to use a word my wife often uses comically, discombobulated.

He is a little "fuzzy." The aspirins he's taken earlier perhaps? A cold coming on? He decides to go home early. Surprised at his forgetfulness, he puts the fountain pen on his desk back into its place in the Castañeda cigar box. He locks up, tests the lock, looks up "as he always did" at the sign above the door: Geo. Kenway: Bookseller.

He is soon settling back into his accustomed world. On the bus on the way home "... the familiar landmarks passed in their usual order" and he gets to his feet before his stop "automatically."

Then occurs the story's only extended conversation. He exchanges ritual and neighbourly pleasantries with Mr. Glover, talks briefly with Mary about dinner, shares with her a nice cup of tea, then decides he must tackle the front-garden hedge, a duty done that will please Mary, a duty done that has been on his mind all day.

The story ends with his clipping the privet, achieving a smooth curve, trimming away straggling sprays.

This is all to say that the now-classic pattern, the epiphany model, has been broken, for George Kenway is unchanged by the vision of the dandelions. He has quickly re-entered the world as it was before. His looking up at his shop sign, Geo. Kenway: Bookseller, defines himself, confirms again who and what he is in the world. As he travels home "automatically" we begin to realize his unsettling vision has not unsettled him for long, that he remains ungalvanized, that incunabula and the world of Wing will remain notions; Geo. Kenway's world will remain white leatherette.

My story, then, is an attempt to break out of the mold, to escape what Kent Thompson had called "Academy Stuff"; I had written an epiphany story that had no epiphany, an anti-epiphany story. It began in its first sentence much in accordance with Clark Blaise's prescription in "To Begin, To Begin", i.e., with Geo. Kenway suffering a "pang of heartburn," but the pang turns out to be less a burning of the heart and more a digestive indisposition.

(Odd actually, because Clark wrote that essay for my anthology *The Narrative Voice*, which appeared in 1972, and "Dandelions" was written in 1968 and appeared in 1970 in *The Lady Who Sold Furniture* and so preceded the essay by four years. Perhaps we'd been talking about such concerns but I can't now remember conversations from forty-five years ago.)

It is the end of the story, where *ta-dah!* is supposed to happen, which gave me then the most trouble and now the greatest pleasure.

I wrote "Dandelions" in Montreal during the summer holidays from school. I was staying with a friend, Gordon Callaghan, a fellow teacher at Chomedey High School; we were working together every day compiling a poetry anthology called *Rhyme and Reason*, which appeared in 1968 with Ryerson Press.

"Dandelions" was going well; Geo. Kenway filled my world. The emotional current of the story was fierce; I was in that state known, I'm sure, to all writers, of writing with great power and command. I was, in the vernacular, "hot," "on a roll." Everything I saw and heard and read was drawn in towards the story; words in books, advertisements, photographs, memories, the classical flute music Gordon often played in the evenings, the name of a brand of cigars seen in a shop window. I was invincible. I was like a professional snooker player who doesn't even bother to watch the ball falling into the pocket; while the ball's still rolling he's walking round the table chalking the cue-tip, watching in his mind the geometry and fall of the next colour.

Until the two final paragraphs.

This ending was difficult to sculpt. I needed something intensely lyrical, poetic. Something that summed up what Geo. Kenway *was*. At the same time that I wanted these lines to be *devastating*, I wanted them not noisy but *quietly* devastating. And the ending wouldn't come. These two brief paragraphs became longer, then shorter, self-conscious, clever, preachy, *wrong*.

Wrestling with the angel.

I was happy with:

> The light was thickening and the houses opposite were becoming shapes against the flushed sky. Shepherd's delight. Shepherd's pie. Another fine day tomorrow.

"The light was thickening"; and so it was but I also had in mind Macbeth's "Light thickens and the crow / Makes wing to the rooky wood," wanted to suggest a drawing in of day, the approach of some kind of darkness.

"… the flushed sky" leads Kenway into the automatic, almanac folk-wisdom of

> *Red sky at night, shepherd's delight.*
> *Red sky in the morning, shepherd take warning.*

I was pleased with the complacency of this.

But the timing was disastrously wrong. My sentences were like actors in the finale staring at the lead who has dried. I needed to extend this scene for a few more beats before the final three sentences could flow.

Poetic, Defining. But *what?*

And then, sitting at the table by the open window in that middle-class, suburban house, the current jolted me into *listening* to what I had been hearing.

> He could heat the distant whirr and clack of a lawnmower, and across the road the Romilly girl was practicing scales on the piano, the notes falling softly into the evening.

Both details suggest middle-class orderliness and social cohesion, neat grass, banned weeds. And "the Romilly girl" practicing scales, unwillingly undergoing the discipline which, if she perseveres, will enable her to eventually play the least-demanding little exercises of a world of formality and elegance that she, like thousands of other pubescents, will never understand or attain. (With, of course, the suggestion that Kenway will never attain the world of Wing.)

Now the final three sentences. The faintly acid smell of the sap.

"It seemed to move a memory in him... a recollection... but he could not remember what it was."

What it was, of course, was the dandelions.

What delighted me then and still does is the way the sentence seems to halt and grope for the memory; it follows the pattern of someone talking. It is a third-person version of someone saying, "It reminds me of something... something quite recent... but, no, it's gone."

But the line's greatest pleasure for me is that, in writing these notes, I realized that the groping break exactly mirrors and pays homage to the dash and comma and repetition in the opening lines of "Miss Brill."

> The air was motionless but when you opened your mouth there was just a faint chill, like a chill from a glass of iced water before you sip, and now and again a leaf came drifting—from nowhere, from the sky.

> *—from nowhere, from the sky*

> *seemed to move a memory in him... a recollection... but he could not remember what it was.*

Pride and Prejudice

I have so far in this book expressed great enthusiasm for modernism. My interest has been mainly in the *how* rather than the *what*, in technique rather than content. I have for years promoted the idea that the two are actually inseparable, that the how *is* the what. I continue to celebrate the cleansing of the Augean Stables of pre-modernist prose, to celebrate Pound's Revolution of the Word. I treasure the technical equipment modernism handed down to us. But I would feel intellectually dishonest if I did not draw the attention of readers to an opposing view of modernism, one that concentrates almost exclusively on the *what*, on modernism's content, on its social and reactionary class concerns.

The account I would urge on readers is the brilliant polemic by John Carey, Merton Professor of English at Oxford. The book is entitled *The Intellectuals and the Masses: Pride and Prejudice among the Literary Intelligentsia 1880-1939.* (Published in 1992.) It is a devastating assault touched everywhere with wry humour.

Carey's preface opens:

> This book is about the response of the English literary intelligentsia to the new phenomenon of mass culture. It argues that modernist literature and art can be seen as a hostile reaction to the unprecedently large reading public created by nineteenth-century educational reforms. The purpose of modernist writing, it suggests, was to exclude these newly educated (or

'semi-educated') readers, and so to preserve the intellectual's seclusion from the "mass."

The "mass" is, of course, a fiction. Its function, as a linguistic device, is to eliminate the human status of the majority of people—or, at any rate, to deprive them of those distinctive features that make users of the term, in their own esteem, superior.

Carey claims the classic account by an intellectual of the advent of mass culture to be *The Revolt of the Masses* by the Spanish philosopher José Ortega y Gasset published in 1930. The root of its worries is population explosion. From the time European history began, in the sixth century, up to 1800, Europe's population never exceeded 180 million. But from 1800 to 1914 it rose from 180 to 460 million.

The consequences were:

> First, overcrowding. Everywhere is full of people—trains, hotels, cafés, parks, theatres, doctors' consulting rooms, beaches. Secondly, this is not just overcrowding; it is intrusion. The crowd has taken possession of places which were created by civilization for the best people. A third consequence is the dictatorship of the mass... This triumph of the "hyperdemocracy" has created the modern state, which Ortega sees as the gravest danger threatening civilization. The masses believe in the state as a machine for obtaining the material pleasures they desire, but it will crush the individual.

Ortega's ideas derive in part from the demonically loony German philosopher Nietzsche (1844–1900) whose message in *The Will to Power* is that "a declaration of war on the masses by higher men is needed... Everywhere the mediocre are combining in order to make themselves master." The conclusion of this "tyranny of the least and the dumbest" will be socialism—"a hopeless and sour affair" which "negates life." This train of thought was espoused by D.H. Lawrence, H.G. Wells, Aldous Huxley, T.S. Eliot, W.B. Yeats, and by F.R. Leavis who in his *Mass Civilization and Minority Culture* (1930) deplored mass circulation newspapers and advertising in general and asserted that "culture is at a crisis" unprecedented.

These proto-fascist thoughts and feelings were shared by a host of minor writers who ranged from the gentle Henry Williamson *(Tarka the Otter* and *A Chronicle of Ancient Sunlight)* to the flamboyant Roy Campbell *(The Flaming Terrapin* and *The Georgiad)* who actually went to Spain and fought for Franco.

In the first issue of the magazine *The Criterion,* edited by T.S. Eliot from 1922 to 1939, and funded by Lady Rothermere, Eliot introduced the magazine with these words:

> The object is not to create more experts, more professors, more artists, but a type of man or woman for whom their efforts will be valuable and by whom they may be judged... A cultured aristocracy cannot indeed create genius, but it can keep the national intelligence vigorous and it can check what is crude, tedious, and impudent.

The word "impudent" speaks, as they say, volumes.

These "aristocratic" trends, mirrored in the rise of the "science" of eugenics which promoted the idea of euthanizing inferior or diseased human stock, created an enabling climate of thought and feeling, Carey suggests, which came to fruition in the gas chambers of Auschwitz.

That Carey is not being fanciful is suggested by a letter written in 1908 by D.H. Lawrence explaining how he would dispose of the unproductive in society:

> If I had my way, I would build a lethal chamber as big as Crystal Palace, with a military band playing softly, and a Cinematograph working brightly; then I'd go out in the back streets and bring them in, all the sick, the halt, and the maimed; I would lead them gently, and they would smile me a weary thanks; and the band would softly bubble out the "Hallelujah Chorus."

The words "in the back streets" also speak volumes.

The hatred of "the mass" found expression in the vitriol poured upon the new newspapers which were geared to appeal to those made literate by the Education Act of 1871. "The principle of his [Lord Northcliffe's *Daily Mail*] new journalism was 'giving the public what it wants.' To intellectuals," writes Carey, "this naturally sounded ominous. Intellectuals believe in giving the public what intellectuals want; that, generally speaking, is what they mean by education."

The other great focus of hatred of the "mass" was hatred of the raw suburbs created to house the growing population. Suburbs destroyed the centuries-old shapes and patterns of the countryside—patterns essentially aristocratic and feudal. The suburbs were populated by "the clerks," that section of the middle and lower-middle class employed in commerce, banks, insurance, and real estate. Northcliffe's *Daily Mail* was aimed specifically at clerks whose education did not extend much beyond basic skills. "The paper," said one intellectual critic, "reeks of the concerns of villadom with its cycling column, its fashion section, and its home hints."

In hatred and contempt for suburban life, Waugh erected his fantasy country house, Brideshead.

Analysing the social messages behind *Brideshead Revisited*, Connor Cruise O'Brien remarks that in Catholic countries Catholicism is not invariably associated with big houses or the fate of the aristocracy. Waugh, however, was romantically enthralled by the idea of the "Catholic squires of England," who were doomed to die "so that things might be safe for the travelling salesman, with his polygonal pince-nez, his fat wet hand-shake, his grinning dentures."

Even the consumption of tinned food by the underclasses provoked the intellectuals.

> In the intellectuals' conceptual vocabulary tinned food becomes a mass symbol because it offends against what the intellectual designates as nature: it is mechanical and soulless. As a homogenized, mass product it is also an offence against the sacredness of individuality, and can therefore be allowed into art only if satirized and disowned.

Leonard Bast in E.M. Forster's *Howards End* "eats tinned food, a practice that is meant to tell us something significant about Leonard, and not to his advantage…"

John Betjeman deplores the appetite of the masses for "tinned fruit, tinned meat, tinned milk, tinned beans."

All these hatreds, of tinned food, of newspapers, of advertising, of the ugly sprawl of suburbs, of the class of intrusive clerks, are drawn together in the opening pages of Graham Greene's *Brighton Rock*.

Carey writes:

> Loathing of what the masses have done to England reverberates throughout the novel. Around Brighton the suburbs spread—bungalows, half-made roads, hoardings, advertisements for Mazawattee Tea. It is a scarred, shabby terrain, littered with empty corned-beef tins. On the day Greene's novel opens, 50,000 trippers are cramming into the town. Bank-holiday trains leave Victoria every five minutes, carrying "clerks, shop girls, hairdressers"... an aeroplane, advertising patent medicine, does sky-writing overhead.

Carey, however, considers *Brighton Rock* to be Graham Greene's "masterpiece" and leaves it up to his readers to deal with the complexities of that judgement.

In a summary passage, Carey writes:

> The intellectuals could not, of course, actually prevent the masses from attaining literacy. But they could prevent them reading literature by making it too difficult for them to understand—and this is what they did. The early twentieth century saw a determined effort on the part of the European intelligentsia, to exclude the masses from culture. In England this movement has become known as modernism... Realism of the sort that it was assumed the masses appreciated was abandoned. So was logical coherence. Irrationality and obscurity were cultivated.

Carey then cites Ortega.

> Orega y Gasset in *The Dehumanization of Art,* reckons that it is the essential function of modem art to divide the public into two

classes—those who can understand it and those who cannot. Modern art is not so much unpopular, he argues, as anti-popular... The time must come, Ortega predicts, when society will reorganize itself into "two orders or ranks: the illustrious and the vulgar."

This skeleton account has been unable to do more than merely hint at the queasy riches of Carey's book. The first section lays out its themes; in the second section, "Case Studies," the gloves *really* come off as Carey digs into George Gissing, H.G. Wells, Arnold Bennet, Wyndham Lewis, and Virginia Woolf. *The Intellectuals and the Masses* is a disquieting book and forces us to revisit and re-evaluate received judgements. Speaking personally, I felt on page after page that I could make powerful rebuttals in defence of the *necessity* of logical incoherence and of the abandonment of realism, powerful arguments in defence of the technical subtleties the art itself demands. John Carey's book continually provokes me into mental retort and riposte. What more could be asked of a critic?

Backlash

The imagist ideas of Ezra Pound and the other inventors and practitioners of the "modern" subsequently became the legacy of all writers. The work of Firbank, Anderson, Hemingway, Stein et al. diminished plot, brought image to the foreground in construction, repositioned the reader, and altered dialogue forever.

(The efforts of writers to capture the vernacular or construct a version of it that will persuade readers of its verisimilitude are constant: names thrown out almost at random, Dickens, Mark Twain, Anderson, Ring Lardner, Hemingway, Faulkner, Malamud, Barry Hannah, Cormac McCarthy, Chester Himes, Leon Rooke, George V. Higgins, Elmore Leonard, and a young writer I'm currently working with, Kevin Hardcastle...)

But the initial successes of imagism had been in poetry, and when imagist ideas were applied to the greater lengths of prose the results invited greater debate and posed new problems. The great novels of the modernist movement—let us say Firbank's *The Flower Beneath the Foot, Sorrow in Sunlight*, and *Concerning the Eccentricities of Cardinal Pirelli*; Joyce's *Ulysses*; Ford Madox Ford's *The Good Soldier* and *Parade's End*; Faulkner; the later Conrad; Wyndham Lewis' *Tarr, The Childermass, The Apes of God*; Dorothy Richardson's *Pilgrimage* (and most particularly *Pointed Roofs*); Ivy Compton-Burnett's speech-scapes, the first, *Pastors and Masters*, appearing in 1925; John Cooper Powys' *Rodmoor* and *Ducdame*; Henry Green's *Living, Blindness*, and *Loving*; all these books were successful in the sense of marvellously accomplishing what the authors had set out to do, but they were all *sui generis*; for the writers who succeeded them, the modernist masters were dead ends.

Henry Green put the idea more gracefully in a 1958 *Paris Review* interview with his unlikely interlocutor, Terry Southern. Asked about the stylistic future of the novel, Green said:

> I think Joyce and Kafka have said the last word on each of the two forms they developed. There's no one to follow them. They're like cats which have licked the plate clean. You've got to dream up another dish if you're to be a writer.

The pendulum began to swing back.

It is impossible to deny the elitism of the modernist movement, its complexity and, at times, obscurity; impossible to ignore its dandyism and the class attitudes of most of its practitioners; impossible to pretend to ignore Firbank's scarlet nail polish.

Evelyn Waugh, himself a "modernist," (*Vile Bodies*) and devotee of Firbank, came the crusty patriarch, at the age of forty-one, in his review of Cyril Connolly's *Enemies of Promise*, referring to "Mr. Connolly's preference for the epicene," a criticism rather rich given the passionate homosexual attachments of Waugh's own young-manhood.

"... in all he admires and all that strikes him as significant, whether for praise or blame'" wrote Waugh, "there is a single common quality—the lack of masculinity. Petronius, Gide, Firbank, Wilde... names succeed one another of living and dead writers, all, or most of them, simpering and sidling across the stage ...'"

Waugh's bluff-squire act.

Many writers had, of course, ignored modernism, but they were, in the main, more dull than defiant. By 1950, however, there was a deliberate assault on modernist practice in England. The "revolution of the word" achieved, the pendulum was swinging back to more traditional practices. Modernism had been essentially romantic; the challenge to it was committedly anti-romantic. This backlash was prompted, some feel, by the changes in social and political attitudes engendered by the Second World War. Whatever the accuracy of that perception, the backlash was certainly tinged, and in some cases driven, by class warfare. The book we might take as emblematic was the 1950 *Scenes from Provincial Life* by William Cooper (*vere* Harry Summerfield Hoff).

Looking back now on "modernism," one of my fondest images is of Harold Acton, clad, as I imagine him, in Oxford "bags," taunting from the balcony of his rooms in Christchurch the muddied rugby oafs and returning sweaty oarsmen in the Meadows below by declaiming, *through a megaphone*, Eliot's "The Waste Land" and his own dreadful poems.

> *Within, the heat is curdling into flesh,*
> *Vague, supple limbs to weave a night of lust*
> *And throats lain back to kiss at my desire*
> *White, soft and curving, I may nibble then*
> *Such mad caresses as will flay my lips.*

Scenes from Provincial Life had considerable influence on what became known later as the Movement, poets and novelists who included Kingsley Amis, John Wain, Robert Conquest, and Philip Larkin. West Indian playwright and novelist Caryl Phillips wrote, in a recent review, that "Amis made clear his hostility toward those who continued to believe that experimentation with form was indicative of a higher literary purpose." He quotes Amis as writing, "Shift from one scene to the next in mid-sentence, cut down on verbs or definite articles, and you are putting yourself right in the forefront, at any rate in the eyes of those who were reared on Joyce and Virginia Woolf and take a jaundiced view of more recent developments."

"More recent developments" were Larkin's *Jill* (1946), *A Girl in Winter* (1947), *The Less Deceived* (1955), and *The Whitsun Weddings* (1964), Amis' *Lucky Jim* (1954) and *That Uncertain Feeling* (1955), John Wain's *Hurry on Down* (1953), and John Braine's *Room at the Top* (1957).

A few more title citations will give the flavour of what was happening: Alan Sillitoe's *Saturday Night and Sunday Morning* (1958) and *The Loneliness of the Long Distance Runner* (1959); David Storey's *This Sporting Life* (1960); Stan Barstow's *A Kind of Loving* (1960); and in 1963, triumphantly, a book far funnier than *Lucky Jim*, Keith Waterhouse's haunting masterwork, *Jubb*.

(I'm sure much of the snooty dismissal of Waterhouse is because he wrote a column for—horrors! —*The Daily Mirror*, but try arguing convincingly against the sheer vitality of *Jubb*, *The Bucket Shop*, *Office Life*, or *Maggie Muggins*. I've treasured for years the name of a boutique in *The Bucket Shop*, a boutique run by a gay couple, a boutique delicately called *Trousers Primarily*. I enthusiastically agree with Auberon Waugh, who wrote: "For several years I have been engaged in a lonely campaign to persuade anyone who would listen that Keith Waterhouse is one of the few great writers of our time.")

In the theatre, the Movement was reflected in the "kitchen sink drama" (as opposed to Rattigan, Coward, etc.) of John Osborne's *Look Back in Anger* (1956) and *The Entertainer* (1957); in Shelagh Delaney's *A Taste of Honey* (1958) and the Arnold Wesker Trilogy (1958–60) and his subsequent tin-eared embarrassments in similar vein.

In poetry the Movement was showcased in the *New Lines* anthologies of 1956 and 1963, edited by Robert Conquest; poets included Amis, Larkin, Donald Davie, D.J. Enright, Thom Gunn, and Conquest himself. The poems were anti-romantic, rational, witty, and often sardonic. In his introduction, Conquest attacked obscurity and overwrought metaphor and championed the claims of "rational structure and comprehensible language," aims which explain the Movement's marked hostility to the poetry of Dylan Thomas.

The writers associated with the Movement were not members of the Bullingdon, the Oxford dining club for rich sportsmen (in Waugh's *Decline and Fall* called the Bollinger) at whose festivities could be heard "the sound of the English county families baying for broken glass." Many of the "backlash" writers were not "County," coming mostly from middle-class suburbs or from the factory floor in the grimmer, grimier Midlands and industrial North.

The essence of the poetry and prose of the Movement writers, the *feel* of what they were up to, is strongly suggested in the following poem by Kingsley Amis from *A Look Around the Estate*.

Nothing to Fear

All fixed: early arrival at the flat
Lent by a friend, whose note says *Lucky sod*;
Drinks on the tray; the cover story pat
And quite uncheckable; the husband off
Somewhere with the kids till six o'clock
(Which ought to be quite long enough);
And all worth while: face really beautiful,
Good legs and hips, and as for breasts—my God.
What about guilt, compunction and such stuff?
I've had my fill of all that cock;
It'll wear off, as usual.

Yes, all fixed. Then why this slight trembling,
Dry mouth, quick pulse-rate, sweaty hands,
As though she were the first? No, not impatience,
Nor fear of failure, thank you, Jack.
Beauty, they tell me, is a dangerous thing,
Whose touch will burn, but I'm asbestos, see?
All worth while—it's a dead coincidence
That sitting here, a bag of glands
Tuned up to concert pitch, I seem to sense
A different style of caller at my back.
As cold as ice, but just as set on me.

The most interesting account I know of how the Movement felt to its participants is in John Wain's *Sprightly Running*, an autobiography written in 1960.

The word "experiment," when I was an undergraduate was still a holy one; if you could say of a poem, novel, or play that it was "experimental" that automatically placed it in a worthy category. Only in a few, not very influential, quarters was the suspicion beginning to arise that a work could be experimental and good or it could be experimental and bad. The arts were still partitioned into "modern" and "traditional" and it was assumed that all ardent, youthful spirits would naturally write in a "modern" manner, leaving the established forms to the timid, the exhausted and the elderly.

This idea, which may have had some validity thirty years earlier, was manifestly absurd by 1950, when I first began to publish criticism. I, and most of my contemporaries, simply took it for granted that any writer just beginning his life's work was free to choose whether to use the already matured "experimental" forms, or go back to the traditional. The choice, if need be, could be made afresh for each separate work. One didn't have to join a club; to use a form learnt from Eliot or Proust, from Pound or Breton, didn't mean that you were *never* going to find usefulness in, say, the sonnet, the ballad, the picaresque novel or the "well made play." They were all just forms, existing in a democracy of forms.

Our elders could never understand this attitude; to many of them, it seemed that the new writers must be "middlebrow," intellectually timid and perhaps lower-middle-class; why otherwise did they not declare themselves pledged to "experimentation" and progress generally? I have bumped into this attitude many times, and some of my most peaceable utterances, things I was saying as a matter of course and without dreaming of controversy, have aroused an (to me) astonishingly vicious comeback. I have been sneered at dozens of times, for instance, for saying that literature in our time had entered on "a period of consolidation." This still seems to me to be so self-evident that I cannot be bothered to argue the point ...

To drive home this point, Wain quotes the German poet Hans Egon Holthusen, lecturing at the Library of Congress in Washington on January 25, 1960:

... when we—with some justification—speak of "modern poetry" or "modern art," we are guided by a concept of "epoch" big enough to comprehend at least the last 50 years. The idiom of modern literature has emerged from a revolution that occurred roughly between 1910 and 1925. It was then that the great decisive breakthroughs were made, in Germany as well as in England, France, America, Italy and Russia. It was then that the new territories of expression, within which we still have our literary homes, were conquered; and so far-reaching a revolution in significant themes and forms can neither be completed nor out-lived in a few decades. It naturally must be followed by a lengthy period of assimilation in which language becomes acclimatized to new experiences, by a phase of cultivation and cautious expansion of the newly won fields. If today we find nothing absolutely new in any national literature of the West, this is because we have been living in a post-revolutionary situation for at least 30 years ...

A slightly more acerbic account of the century's literary shenanigans is offered by the literary critic Al Alvarez in his *Beyond All This Fiddle: Essays 1955–1967*.

During the first thirty-odd years of this century the arts were sustained by a vague but optimistic feeling that a specifically Modernist style was emerging. What precisely it was to be was never agreed, though the theoretical shapes and possibilities were clear enough. It would certainly be anti-traditional, breaking with the old conventions, old rules, old gods; yet at the same time it would be concerned, in a worried way, with the breakdown of traditions, and so prone to nostalgia for a lost classical culture—as in early Pound and Eliot. It would also be highly, self-consciously intellectual—as in Cubism or the Jesuit Cubist language of James Joyce, or in the whole movement to reinstate the title "Metaphysical Poet" as a fighting term. It would make use of the newly popularized insights of psychoanalysis (Kafka, the Surrealists), and yet somehow be attuned to the Marxist vision of reality (Mayakovsky, Attila József). And so on. If the details were imprecise, the hopes were considerable. Whatever else, the Modernist style would be freer and more strenuous than anything before: difficult, disciplined, complex, aware, elliptical and unprecedented, as was appropriate for the bewildering and bewildered society that had emerged.

Even the least optimistic agreed that certain advances were being made from which there was no going back. Where, say, Eliot or Pound led, others would follow. Given *New Bearings in English Poetry*, the line of march was assured even if the destination wasn't. Yet it didn't finally turn out that way. In England a relatively inert traditionalism gradually reasserted itself until, by the end of the 1950s, poetry was more or less back at the place where the Moderns had left it in 1914. Even in the U.S.A., where most of the Modernist writers originated, the movement also backtracked into another kind of nostalgia: instead of returning to traditional forms, the poets resurrected traditional experiments. Hence the odd phenomenon of the latest *avant-garde* being largely a rewrite of that of fifty years ago. Hence, too, the even odder phenomenon of no one being bothered that Pound looms behind Charles Olson's shoulder and William Carlos Williams towers over Robert Creeley's. The stuff is felt to *be* modern simple because it *looks* modern. The *avant-garde* is acceptable because it is essentially reactionary, harmless.

...the revolutionary spirit that motivates every genuinely new movement in the arts—the desire to have done with the old clichés, and make it new—in this instance is a revolution of the academy, not of the market place. In the fifties the accepted Academic-Modern style—the style that would help a struggling poet to a comfortable university job—was the Pound-Eliot-Wallace Stevens line. That has now been replaced by the Pound-Williams-Cummings line. That is, the cosmopolitan bias in American poetry had been abandoned in favour of something altogether more chauvinistic.

Whatever emphases one wishes to make, there can be no doubts that Pound's "Revolution of the Word" triumphed. Any persuasion necessary is provided by reading prose and poetry from both sides of the 1912–1925 divide.

The "backlash" against "experimental" writing in England gathered strength, then, between 1945–50. The short story was not much
involved then, or later. As the years after Joyce and Mansfield passed,
there were a few distinguished British and Irish short-story writers—Elizabeth Bowen, V.S. Pritchett, Jean Rhys, Mary Lavin, Angus
Wilson, John McGahern, Bernard MacLaverty, David Constantine—
but, though given lip-service, it was not a form favoured generally and nor was it given any weight in criticism or curricula. The
dynamo of the genre was the United States.

A useful way to look at the genre in the States—for what I am
writing is necessarily broad brush-strokes—is to look at the career of
Edward J. O'Brien. In 1915, O'Brien published an anthology entitled
*The Best Short Stories of 1915 and the Yearbook of the American Short
Story*. The "Roll of Honour" was listings of other distinguished
short stories singled out but not actually published in the volume.
This anthology has appeared every year, uninterruptedly, since 1915
and continues still. O'Brien edited the anthology from 1915 until his
death in 1941. He was succeeded by his friend Martha Foley, who
edited from 1941 until her death, in 1977. Following that, a new
editorial system was introduced, each volume being selected and
introduced by a prominent writer working from a professional editor's initial cull.

Our understanding and appreciation of the story form was
moulded and guided by O'Brien; it was he who focussed attention
and then directed our gaze as each new talent appeared. Very little
escaped his radar. What he did for many years and what Martha
Foley did as his disciple shaped our understanding of the genre;
there seems to be no academic recognition of this and there exists,
to the best of my knowledge, only one study of O'Brien's life and
massive achievement, and that difficult to acquire.

Why am I not surprised?

(The sole work on O'Brien, *Edward J. O'Brien and His Role in the
Rise of the American Short Story in the 1920s and 1930s* is published by
the Edwin Mellen Press and is print-on-demand and is expensive.)

O'Brien was born in 1890 and grew up in Boston in a household of women. He developed an interest in nude male beauty and a

mystical Catholicism about which he felt evangelical. His emotions drove him towards "poetic" expression. In 1917 he published, in Boston, a *throbbing* volume of verse entitled *White Fountains*; three completely representative stanzas from the poem "Flower" will suggest everything that could be written at great length.

> *The Poet, naked on a Sunny Hill, speaketh to the little Flower*
> Little Flower, open thine heart and tell me, why
> > thou dost smile and blow in thine innocence:
> thou art gentle as laughter, and pure as the
> > wonder of children.

> Why art thou so wise and fair in the Grasses?
> Thou art little as Love, and fragrant as meditation.

> Sunlight laugheth on the Flesh, and on mine:
> Little brother Flower, whisper to me thy secret.

> *'Strewth!*

Not a great deal seems to be known about O'Brien's early years in the States. We know he was busy writing and publishing poems in such magazines as *Scribner's Magazine*, *The Poetry Review of America*, *The Little Review*, *The Midland*, *The Smart Set*, and *Contemporary Verse*. We know that he travelled about in the States giving poetry readings, selling chapbooks of his own, and that of others manufactured for that purpose, delivering talks and lectures. We know he was frequently pitching projects to publishers. He was a young poet on the hustle.

(It has always amazed me that a man capable of such soppy emissions as "Flower" saw the true poetry in prose with such deadeye authority and speed. It amazes me, in the same way, that exquisitely poetic prose writers produce such embarrassing verse: James Joyce himself, Katherine Mansfield, Ernest Hemingway, even Beckett does not exactly grip, while Harold Pinter, a prose master, produced unforgivable verse, copiously.)

O'Brien moved to London and later Oxford, where he remained for most of his life. His first wife was the beautiful young writer Romer Wilson; she was the winner of the Hawthornden Prize and her contemporaries compared her with Katherine Mansfield. I read, or tried to read, a 1921 novel of hers called *The Death of Society*, but it was too grimly bad to pursue. She became increasingly mentally unstable and died young. O'Brien's second wife was a German girl of sixteen who, with the connivance of her parents, was conveyed to England. She spoke no English. O'Brien's personal life remains somewhat veiled.

By 1924, the *Best* series was establishing itself with such offshoots as a chapbook (fifty-eight pages) *Study Questions on "The Best Short Stories of 1924." Compiled for Home, Class, or Club Use.* The publicity machinery was grinding into gear. By 1940, shortly before his death, the Houghton Mifflin dust jacket read: "He is considered by many to be the world's foremost authority on the short story and to have the finest eye among editors for picking new writers."

In my library I have a complete run of the anthologies from 1915 to the present and the experience of reading the early years is fascinatingly tedious. Here is O'Brien throwing down the gauntlet in the introduction to the 1915 volume.

> In reaffirming the significant position of the American short story as compared with the English short story, I am more impressed than ever with the leadership maintained by American artists in this literary form. Mr. James Stephens has been criticising us for our curiously negative achievement in novel writing. He has compared the American novelist with the English novelist and found him wanting. He is compelled to deny literary distinction to the American novel, and he makes a sweeping indictment of American fiction in consequence. But does he know the American short story?
>
> If you turn to the English magazines, you will find a certain form of *conte* of narrow range developed to a point of high literary merit in such papers as the *Nation* or the *New Statesman*. But if you look for short stories in the literary periodicals, you will not find them, and if you turn to the popular English magazines,

you will be amazed at the cheap and meretricious quality of the English short story.

It would be idle to dispute about the origin of the short story, for several literatures may claim its birth, but the American short story has been developed as an art form to the point where it may fairly claim a sustained superiority, as different in kind as in quality from the tale or *conte* of other literatures.

In his introduction in 1916 O'Brien wrote:

Last year I was moved to compare the American short story with that of other countries, and was driven to the conclusion that we were developing a new literary form, organically different from everything that preceded it, and still in the interesting process of developing its own technique."

In 1917 he wrote:

The critic, when he approaches American literature, cannot regard it as he can regard any foreign literature. Setting aside the question of whether our cosmopolitan population, with its widely different kinds of racial heritage, is at an advantage or a disadvantage because of its conflicting traditions, we must accept the variety in substance and attempt to find in it a new kind of national unity, hitherto unknown in the history of the world.

But despite these brave assertions, he was, from 1915 until 1921, if not flatly lying, then whistling Dixie. The stories, whatever his claims, are not distinguished. What he described was not what he saw but, rather, what he desired to see.

Years later he was to admit this.

In his introduction in 1932 he wrote:

... the years from 1915 to 1922 were a lean time ... From 1922 to 1930 was the shaping period ... I found Sherwood Anderson. A little later I found Ernest Hemingway.

What liveliness there was in those lean times comes from stories flavoured by the presence, in the background, of Yiddish. Stories by Benjamin Rosenblatt, Fannie Hurst, and Anzia Yezierska *almost* linger from the early volumes, but they don't linger, as Kingsley Amis would have said, *enough.*

The general flavour of the prose in the annuals from the first years is sufficiently suggested in such sentences as these:

> The old mail-sled running between Haney and Le Beau, in the days when Dakota was still a Territory, was nearing the end of its hundred-mile route … (1920)
>
> A man was standing in the shadow, almost at his elbow.
>
> He was old, the oldest man Blagden had ever seen, and he wore the long brown gown of a monk. His face was like a withered leaf, lined and yellow, and his hair was silver white.
>
> Only the small, saurian eyes held Blagden with their strange brilliance. The rest of his face was like a death mask. (1915)

> There is sometimes melancholy in revisiting after years of absence a place where one was joyous in the days of youth. That is why sadness stole over me on the evening of my return to Florence.
>
> To be sure, the physical beauties of the Italian city were intact … (1920)

Stories creaking in their plots, weakened by explanation and exposition, studded with similes, language variously pompous, humdrum, stale. Yet, despite being so limited in choice, O'Brien *was* able to recognize Sherwood Anderson. In the "Roll of Honour," in 1916, he cited Anderson's stories "Hands" and "Queer" *three years* before their appearance in *Winesburg, Ohio.*

He wrote of Anderson "…a new and original artist of power who belongs to an important literary group in Chicago which bids fair to dominate the course of American literature during the next ten years …"

(This "literary group" was essentially Amy Lowell and co. under the tutelage of, who else, but Ezra Pound, and O'Brien's recognition of "modernism" came via Gertrude Stein (via Anderson) and then directly from Hemingway and Pound.)

> By 1922, we see a splendid cavalcade beginning to assemble, horses tossing their heads, bits jingling, brocade and silk in the sun, an almost ceremonial coming-together, a cavalcade that O'Brien *had imagined into being.*
>
> 1922: Conrad Aikin, Sherwood Anderson, F. Scott Fitzgerald, Ring Lardner
>
> 1923: Ernest Hemingway
>
> 1925: Anderson, Lardner, Fitzgerald, Hemingway
>
> 1926: Hemingway, Lardner, Kay Boyle, F. Scott Fitzgerald, Edith Wharton
>
> 1929: *A comparison of the stories which I published in 1915 with those which I am publishing in 1929 reveals an interesting contrast. Fifteen years ago, it was almost impossible to find more than one or two stories in a year's file of all American periodicals which revealed literary gifts of more than a technical order …*
>
> *Today such men as Sherwood Anderson, Ernest Hemingway, Ring Lardner, and Morley Callaghan, to mention no other names, have educated a considerable public sufficiently for it to distinguish between ready-made stories and works of art.*
>
> 1930: *The period of ferment is over. The period of integration has begun.*
>
> *The credit for all that is good in this change is due to the small magazines. The younger writers who represent the future, finding that the older magazines were not open to them except upon terms they decline to accept, founded magazines of their own. It is in those magazines that the best stories are being published.*
>
> *The Midland, The Prairie Schooner, The Frontier, This Quarter, The Gyroscope…*
>
> 1931: Caroline Gordon, Katherine Anne Porter.
>
> *The old conception of an artificial plot imposed too much strain on the form, and turned the short story into something very much like a potted novel. In the new short story, plot is a servant and not a master, as a machine should be.*

1932: Faulkner

1938: Eudora Welty, John Cheever

1940: Kay Boyle, Ernest Hemingway, William Faulkner, F. Scott Fitzgerald, Katherine Anne Porter, William Saroyan, Irwin Shaw, Eudora Welty

As the years went by the annuals almost unerringly represented the cream of American story writers.

O'Brien died in 1941 and Martha Foley took over the editorship. After her death in 1977, a new system was instituted, each annual volume being edited by different noted writers. A representative array of authors who have edited the annual since Martha Foley's death: Stanley Elkin, John Gardner, John Updike, Raymond Carver, Anne Beattie, Margaret Atwood, Richard Ford, Robert Stone, Tobias Wolff, E.L. Doctorow, Lorrie Moore, Salman Rushdie, Jennifer Egan …

American writing did not undergo the same anti-experimental backlash that happened in England in the fifties and sixties. In his introduction to the 1930 *Best American*, O'Brien wrote: "The period of ferment is over. The period of integration has begun." If he meant that the precepts of the "Revolution of the Word" were finding a wider audience he was probably right, but "ferment" in the short story was most definitely not over. American authors embraced and explored the image far more than had been the case in the UK and they pushed the image into new and fascinating directions.

Glancing along my shelves, names at random: Amy Hempel, Anne Beattie, Mary Robison, Deborah Eisenberg, Richard Yates, Raymond Carver, James Salter, Thom Jones, Tobias Wolff, Joy Williams, Jane Anne Phillips, Barry Hannah, Lorrie Moore, Junot Diaz, David Means…

Far from reverting to "traditional forms," American writing became a positive cornucopia of continuing ferment.

*

When I inherited, from David Helwig, in 1975, the editorship of the Oberon Press annual series of short-story anthologies he'd initiated in 1971 with Tom Marshall, entitling their first volume *Fourteen Stories High* and subsequent volumes *New Canadian Stories*, I changed the policy and title in 1977 to *Best Canadian Stories* and downplayed "newness" in favour of republication of the best work from the literary magazines. I announced this forthcoming change in the foreword of the 1976 volume by saying it was "in frank emulation of Martha Foley's *Best American Stories*"; I never forget emotional debt.

This announcement of my allegiance to the American anthology and to the dazzling accomplishment of American short-story writers more or less coincided with the beginnings of what cultural and literary critic Jeet Heer has called my "informal blacklisting," which seems to have become my portion in life.

From 1980 on, my writing was excluded from every trade anthology of national scope. I was excluded from *The Oxford Book of Canadian Short Stories in English* edited by Margaret Atwood and Robert Weaver; from Weaver's *Canadian Short Stories: Fourth Series* and *Fifth Series*; from Wayne Grady's *Penguin Book of Canadian Short Stories*; from Wayne Grady's *Penguin Book of Modern Canadian Stories*; from Michael Ondaatje's *From Ink Lake*; from Jane Urquhart's *Penguin Book of Canadian Stories* (2007).

The names of these editors came to my mind with sadness and contempt when I read, in Adam Gopnik's *Paris to the Moon*, "The logic of nationalism always flows downhill, towards the gutter."

From 1976–82 I edited the Oberon anthologies, with Joan Harcourt, then with Clark Blaise, and finally with Leon Rooke. In 2007 I took over the editorship again after Douglas Glover retired.

Our early experience was utterly different from O'Brien's.

We did not have to imagine some shimmering future.

From the very beginning we offered brilliance.

1976: Norman Levine, Hugh Hood, Audrey Thomas, Clark Blaise, Elizabeth Spencer, Leon Rooke.
1978: Alice Munro, Hugh Hood, Elizabeth Spencer
1980: Mavis Gallant, Alice Munro, Guy Vanderhaeghe
1981: Clark Blaise, Mavis Gallant, Norman Levine, Alice Munro, and a fledgling Linda Svendsen

The only fly in the Canadian literary ointment was that there was no audience. In over forty years of editing and nurturing Canadian writers, we have failed in finding people to read them. Canada remains a country where, in public library discard and donation shops, in St. Vincent de Paul and Salvation Army stores and other charity outlets, pristine hardcover first editions by Alice Munro, upon whom was recently bestowed the world's highest literary honour, the Nobel Prize for Literature, can be purchased for one dollar.

Introducing the Century List

An earlier version of the Century List was published by Biblioasis in my 2007 memoir *Shut Up He Explained*. In that version, the List started nominally in 1900 (but effectively in 1950) and the cut-off date was 2000: therefore "Century." This present version of the Century List has been expanded by the addition of ten more writers because the 2000 cut-off date could be seen as being somewhat arbitrary and the added writers can be considered an integral part of what the first version chronicled; we might think of 1950–2015 as a Hobsbawmian "long" fifty years. And anyway, the writers were treading too closely on my heels to be ignored.

In alphabetical order, these writers are: Joan Alexander, Sharon English, Zsuzsi Gartner, Dayv James-French, Shaena Lambert, Alexander MacLeod, Kathy Page, Alice Petersen, Rebecca Rosenblum, and Kathleen Winter. The additions bring the List to fifty entries. I would like the list to be considered as the starting point for a literary discussion which has not yet taken place but that is essential for our literary sanity.

When I was looking over the List, it occurred to me that I'd feel pushed to find even ten novels worthy of inclusion in a companion list. There's something wickedly accurate about Randall Jarrell's line that a novel is "a prose work of a certain length with something wrong with it." And international comparisons are pulverising.

(Randall Jarrell's comic novel *Pictures From an Institution*, however, is firmly lodged in my affections.)

We have produced so few collections of tolerable literary essays that a List would be impossible. We have little to compare with Randall Jarrell's *A Sad Heart at the Supermarket* and *Poetry and the Age*, or W.H. Auden's *The Dyer's Hand* and *Secondary Worlds*, or Kingsley Amis' chatty *What Became of Jane Austen?* or Orwell's *Inside the Whale, The Lion and the Unicorn, Shooting an Elephant*, and *Such, Such were the Joys*, or V.S. Naipaul's *The Overcrowded Barracoon*, or Shiva Naipaul's *Beyond the Dragon's Mouth* and *An Unfinished Journey*.

Canadian readers *should* pay attention, however, to *Director's Cut* by David Solway, *A Lover's Quarrel* by Carmine Starnino, and *Attack of the Copula Spiders* by Douglas Glover. I continue to be dismayed at the refusal of Canadian readers to acknowledge—acknowledge, hell! *Delight* in!—John Mills' essay collection *Thank Your Mother for the Rabbits*. The Irving Layton—Steam Laundry—John Richmond—Aviva Layton rigamarole is alone worth the price of admission.

Making a List is, of course, an act of literary criticism. Lists always seem to provoke discussion and argument and this is obviously important for the literature. Lists can champion unexpected or forgotten works, as was the case with Anthony Powell's support of Jocelyn Brooke, author of "The Orchid Trilogy" *(The Military Orchid, A Mine of Serpents*, and *The Goose Cathedral)* or Philip Larkin's and Lord David Cecil's resurrection of the delightful novels of Barbara Pym. They can also suggest a re-ordering within the hierarchy of a writer's work; when I choose Margaret Laurence's *The Tomorrow-Tamer* (stories set in Africa) over *A Bird in the House* (stories set in Canada), my list is jousting with conventional wisdom; I am choosing craft over nation. Perhaps most importantly, Lists can pull a period into a clearer focus; instead of readers being faced with many hundreds of volumes which range from the superb to the execrable, the List enables readers to see an informed estimate of the size and shape of the period's accomplishment.

Anthologies are Lists, as it were, in the flesh, while Lists are virtual Anthologies. The first nationally important anthology of Canadian short stories was published in 1928. *Canadian Short Stories* was edited by Raymond Knister. This volume contained stories by Duncan Campbell Scott, Frederick William Wallace, Edward

William Thomson, Sir Gilbert Parker, Charles G.D. Roberts, Marjorie Pickthall, Merill Denison, Morley Callaghan, Stephen Leacock, Norman Duncan, Alan Sullivan, Walter McLaren Imrie, Will E. Ingersoll, Mazo de la Roche, Harvey O'Higgins, Thomas Murtha, and Leslie McFarlane.

A chore to trudge through, the anthology represents the exhausted end of a tradition of magazine writing by "professional" writers; the stories are more "tale" or "yarn" than story in the modernist tradition.

(As late as 1963, Hugh Garner, a writer very much in this "professional writer" milieu, won the Governor General's Award for *Hugh Garner's Best Stories*. That this honour was conferred upon such an appalling book is mildly astonishing; Garner wrote only one half-way decent story, "The Yellow Sweater," and even that one was scarcely light on its feet. Though to put this in perspective, it should always be remembered that the Governor General's Award for Fiction, in 1954, was bestowed upon *Fall of a Titan*, a saga of Stalin, by the Russian defector Igor Gouzenko, who was memorable chiefly for appearing on television with a shopping bag over his head.

When the Ryerson Press published Alice Munro's *Dance of the Happy Shades*, they thought it helpful to have this unknown flower introduced by a stalwart; the result is typical Garner, bluff, no-nonsense, and, as Nancy Mitford might have written, "cringe-inducing.")

Raymond Knister himself, he of the aforementioned "woofing cows" and "limp strides," has faded from all but antiquarian memory.

Morley Callaghan wrote to Knister:

> Dear Raymond,
>
> Today I got a copy of the Canadian Stories. I read the introduction and then I read D.C. Scott's story in the book. What is the matter with you?
>
> Though it will come as a relief to many schoolmarms throughout the country to learn that the venerable Duncan is a great writer, since they have always suspected it, you know better. Then why do you do it? ...You had a chance to point the way in that introduction, and you merely arrived at the old values

that have been accepted here the last fifty years: *id est*, Duncan C. Scott, G.D. Roberts and Gilbert Parker are great prose writers. In any other country in the world they are not taken seriously...

What explains this barren literary moonscape of our past? I have often borrowed the science fiction idea of a time warp. Canada seemed to exist many years behind the rest of the English-speaking world and seemed impervious to innovation. It was a country largely indifferent to art or literature. The National Gallery of Canada was not founded until 1913 and the National Library of Canada, now in headlong decline and dissolution, was founded as recently as 1953.

(The most recent National Librarian, hired to chop the Library's already skimpy budget, was unqualified as a librarian, holding a snake-oil degree in some sub-branch of Sociology, Human Engineering or somesuch, and, while dismantling the nation's collection, always referred to libraries as "memory institutes"; this in itself should have been grounds for his dismissal, but he was actually fired for bloated expense claims amounting to peculation.)

The Auditor General's Report, in 2014, stated that the basements of the Library and Archives house ninety-eight thousand unopened boxes of archival material. The Library has not bought significantly from Canadian rare-book dealers for years and no longer enforces its status as a national deposit library.

During the first half of the century, Canada had few magazines and a publishing industry that was comatose and which existed to import British and American books. What few Canadian books did get published appeared, usually, from Macmillan of Canada and from the Ryerson Press, which was owned by the United Church of Canada and administered by a gentleman known as The Book Steward, a man I imagine as a fusspot, vicar-ish, dentures, clad in a suit shiny at seat and elbows from twenty-three years of faithful wear, a face harried into creases of bonhomie. The Press's most famous editor was the Methodist minister Lorne Pierce, an ardent nationalist booster of stupefying books by the likes of Sir Charles G.D. Roberts and Frederick Philip Grove.

Raymond Knister's 1928 anthology represented the work of seventeen writers. Thirty years later, in 1958, Robert Weaver edited the first international anthology, *Canadian Short Stories*, in the Oxford University Press' *World's Classics* series. Only five of Knister's magazine deadbeats appear in Weaver. Not a single one survives on the Century List, not Knister, not Leacock, not Callaghan himself.

Between the anthologies of Knister and Weaver, Professor W.C. Desmond Pacey of the University of New Brunswick published *A Book of Canadian Stories* (1947). The "modern" was represented by P.K. Page, Raymond Knister, William McConnell, Sinclair Ross, John Leo Kennedy, Morley Callaghan, and Mary Quayle Innis. Again, not a single one appears on the Century List.

Why is that? The simplest answer is that these writers were not in touch with the genre. This seemingly brutal, wholesale dismissal of our literary past, doubtless strikes some, and especially necrophilic scholars of Canadian minutiae, as arrogant if not impious, but we must always face and answer the stark question posed by Mavis Gallant: *Is it dead or alive?*

It is hard to imagine anything much deader than the afore-listed job lots of "professional" fiction.

In the introduction to his 1960 anthology, *Canadian Short Stories*, Weaver wrote:

> There have been so few collections of Canadian short stories that there is no tradition which an editor is required either to follow or to explain away...

Later, in the introduction, he wrote: "Knister and Callaghan published abroad in the 1920s because there were almost no outlets in Canada for serious and experimental short fiction. This fugitive existence of the short story has continued until today in this country."

That was written in 1960.

(When I came to Canada in 1962 there were, to the best of my knowledge, four single-author collections of short stories in print.)

Today, fifty-six short years after Weaver's "fugitive existence," there have been hundreds of anthologies and individual collections published. It would be intensely gratifying were this sudden efflorescence the result of the joyous discovery by Canadians of astonishing achievement in an hitherto scarcely known form. Sadly, it was the result of government gold.

The House of Anansi was founded, in 1967, by young writers raging against the impossibility of publishing and finding an audience; publishing Canadian books was, for Anansi, a political statement, an assertion of nationalism. (Readers interested in the underlying ideas of Anansi are advised to read Dennis Lee's meditative poem "Civil Elegies.") The government funded the small-press movement generously because it saw in it an instrument to mold and nourish Canadian identity and nationalism, a persistent delusion of the Liberal Party.

Seed subsidy was scattered broadcast; the busy scene was like the literary equivalent of a Soviet Five Year Plan or a Chinese Great Leap Forward. The defining comment on the entire farcical, sad fandangle was, for me, the Saga of Book Kits Canada. In 1987 I took up pamphleteering and wrote *Freedom from Culture*, a guerrilla attack against the idea of state subsidy.

Here is an extract from that nineteen-page pamphlet.

> A literature is the possession and expression of individuals or it is nothing. Lord Goodman, Chairman of the Arts Council of Great Britain, once said, "One of the most precious freedoms of the British people is freedom from culture"; since the establishment of the Canada Council in 1957 that freedom has been eroding here more and more rapidly. Small-c culture in Canada is becoming Culture—a possession and expression of the State. The Council has no real constituency. Its members and officers are not elected from a broader base below; all are appointed. The Council has no real connection with an audience or readership. It only goes through the motions of consulting; it invents its own policies and implements them. The manifold literary activities of the Council proclaim literary culture in Canada to be a thing apart, a thing of government, just one more weird expression of that Ottawa which urged us to insulate our homes with foam, that subsequently turned out to be toxic.

Because the Council is a thing apart with its own logic and its own dynamic and because it wields a huge budget, it skews and distorts the nature of our literature and the workings of our literary world. The Council is not, however, the only source of subsidy; we must also bear in mind the massive interventions of the Department of Communications, External Affairs, and the various provincial cultural agencies.

The big commercial publishing houses are subsidized. The smaller literary presses are subsidized. The still smaller regional presses are subsidized. The magazines are subsidized. The writers are subsidized. The literary critics are subsidized. Translation is subsidized. Publicity is subsidized. Distribution is subsidized. More bizarre than perhaps anything else, the Writers' Union of Canada is subsidized.

The literary world in Canada is a huge boondoggle operating with government gold and Mad Hatter logic.

I once sat on a Council jury whose purpose was to purchase books from Canadian publishers so that the books could be made up into kits and distributed free of charge to schools, hospitals, asylums, prisons, and the like. Depending on the number of books it had published and the size of its gross, each publishing house was entitled under Council regulations to a certain sum in subsidy. The task of the jury was to select, from the publishers' catalogues, books whose price added up more or less to the sum to which the company was entitled.

So there the three of us sat reading catalogues of publishers we'd never heard of and buying by the dozen, the score, the gross, such non-fiction as *Outhouses of Western Canada* and novels called *Hurt Not the Hills*.

Now and again, one or the other of us would burst out:

"We can't buy *that!* I've read it. It was *awful!*"

And the presiding Literary Officer would reply with mounting impatience:

"We're not here to make judgements. You have to purchase $250,000 dollars worth from their catalogue."

The long day squandered on.

The purpose of the Book Purchase Programme was to give added subsidy to the publishers and to get Canadian books into the hands of Canadian readers. Year after year of purchase passed until the news leaked out that the Council had been unable to give many of the Book Kits away: even such truly captive audiences as the inmates of prisons spurned them. Kits composed of Canadian fiction were met with particular opprobrium. By 1985, in a rented warehouse on Richmond Street in Toronto, the Canada Council had accumulated 70,000 volumes of unwanted CanLit.

(My own hardcover copy of my own story collection, *The Teeth of My Father*, bears on the pastedown a complimentary sticker from the Canada Council and on the next page the ownership stamp of the recipient: *The Thamesville Happy Club*.)

This anecdote has several particularly interesting features— features characteristic of the Canadian literary world: it shows books being treated in an emotionally and spiritually deadening way as a commodity; it shows a total disregard for any standards of taste or excellence; it shows members of the literary community in baffled collusion—but in collusion—with the bureaucracy; and lastly, it shows that the exercise failed entirely in one important respect—it failed to connect with an audience.

The anecdote could be considered emblematic.

No one seems to find quite as Monty Python as I do the idea of a Literature administered by a Bureaucracy.

Writers and academics suborned, the literature Bureaucratized, the infant tottered forward; Nanny's cry was *Read Canadian!* Rabid anti-Americanism turned Canadian writing in on itself so that it became ever more parochial. The work of writers who fled— Richler, Blaise, Levine,—was ostracized. Concurrent with this turning inward, style and craft were decried as suspect, un-Canadian attributes. Thematic Criticism dominated and obviously had nothing whatever to say about style or language. Thematic Criticism was concerned with Themes. Critics thought up Themes such as Immigration then gathered up stories and extracts from novels and odd chunks of non-fiction and used them to illustrate Immigration.

Sociology was easier than literature to explicate and expound and seemed to suit nearly everyone's I.Q.

A refusal by critics to evaluate accommodated the mediocre. The nascent literature turned not only inward but also looked to the rural past. Terry Rigelhof wrote recently of "the hostility many Canadian cultural nationalists showed towards the urban and urbane in art through much of the second half of the twentieth century..." Russell Smith put it more pithily when he said that Canadian literature was about "angst on farms."

When I urged looking outwards rather than inwards, I seemed to provoke hysterical hostility.

Professor Sam Solecki of St. Michael's College of the University of Toronto wrote, in rebuttal of my arguments:

> ... by characterizing the best work of the past twenty-five years as modern or international in style Metcalf, consciously or unconsciously, leaves the Canadian writer and critic without a Canadian tradition.

Consciously, Sam, consciously.

Professor David Jackel, who wrote the chapter on the short story in volume IV of the *Literary History of Canada*, had me in his sights when he wrote:

> The recognition given [to the short story] within Canada was accompanied by serious international attention to the work of Gallant, Munro, Atwood, and others. Less encouraging was the tendency to find the short story a ground on which to battle over the merits of experimental and self-reflexive fiction at the expense of more traditional forms. As well, the promotion of a vague and rootless cosmopolitanism which would somehow accord with "international standards" invoked but never defined, seemed to deny the Canadian-ness of Canadian short fiction .... T.D. MacLulich has properly observed that Canada's continued existence, as George Grant claimed, [see Grant's *Lament for a Nation*] has traditionally been based on an assertion of particularity against

the homogenizing claims of continentalism and universalism. "Canadian fiction," MacLulich asserts, "has provided some of the most eloquent expressions of our devotion to such particularity." Writers who seek to attune themselves with currently fashionable theories of art, and neglect the realities of their time and place, add to the risk that literature will become merely source material for social scientists and cultural historians. Fortunately, the variety, the substance, and the quality of many short stories published between 1972 and 1984 give some reason to hope that dogmatic, doctrinaire, and ill-grounded "international" views will not in the end prevail.

And here is the same dumb beast seen from a slightly different angle, T.D. MacLulich from his *Between Europe and America: The Canadian Tradition in Fiction:*

> ... Canadian literature, especially Canadian fiction, has never been notable for its innovations of form. Indeed, its conservatism has contributed to its distinctiveness from American literature. Until very recently, much of the best Canadian fiction has sought to occupy a middle ground, using the conventions of the bourgeois novel to make significant statements about life in particular parts of our country, at particular times. As a result, the central tradition in our fiction is found in the work of writers such as Grove, Callaghan, MacLennan, Buckler, Ross, Mitchell, Wilson, Laurence, Richler, Davies, and Munro. These authors do not produce "popular" literature in the vulgarly commercial sense; yet neither do they rely on superficial treatments of trendy subjects nor on clever tricks played with narrative point of view. They write books that are accessible to a wide readership, and they do so without sacrificing their private vision to commercial demands. We should be encouraging such writing (and some of us are), rather than calling for experimental or language-centered fiction. After all, what will we get if Canadian fiction joins our poetry in adopting the international style?

(As our poets were trading Bliss Carman for W.H. Auden it seems to me that we would've been getting a hell of a lot.)

MacLulich is calling for more fiction "using the conventions of the bourgeois novel"; no innovation, please, we're Canadian. He calls for books "accessible to a wide readership" but which do not sacrifice themselves to "commercial demands." Notice that, implicitly, he is talking about novels only; short stories seem not to have been on his mind. What he *really* wants, fifty years after the fact, is another, but Canadian, version of J.B. Priestly's *The Good Companions.* Or perhaps something along Maeve Binchy lines? Ooh! I wonder if he's read Roger Lemelin's *The Plouffe Family;* he'd like *that* one.

Professor MacLulich espouses that strain in Canadian writing which seems to pride itself on being, well, Canadian. And what "Canadian" seems to mean in this context is utilitarian, lumpy, old-fashioned, innocent of stylistic sophistication. *Homespun,* that's the word! The writing he seems to champion prides itself on appearing in longjohns and gumboots; W.O. Mitchell and David Adams Richards could stand for its rural expression; or it presents itself in frocks: Jane Urquhart, Elizabeth Harvor, and Carol Shields its urban counterpart.

I was amused by MacLulish's "central tradition in our fiction," the crackpot assertion of a "tradition" comprising eleven writers.

Eleven! A tradition!

I was amused, too, in that of the eleven names he cites I'd junk eight without a moment's hesitation.

MacLulich's fellow rearguardist, Professor Jackel, has entirely misunderstood me when he implies that I have urged writers to "neglect the realities of their time and place" in favour of—*Circle the wagons, boys!* —internationalism. Quite the reverse is true. What I've been saying for forty years is that to write well about Livelong, Saskatchewan, one must draw on the entire range of technique and sensibility world literature affords. Just as Alice Munro did in writing about Jubilee, Ontario; just as Mary Borsky did writing about Salt Prairie, Alberta ("Where Culture and Agriculture Meet"); just as Mordecai Richler did writing about St. Urbain Street, as Sharon English did writing about the suburb of Greenview ("Land of the Walking Dead"). Canadian writing should not doggedly pride itself for toiling onward with the rusted toolkit of a Hugh MacLennan.

What is it here, Professor, that seems beyond your comprehension?

(Faulkner and Joyce are both radically experimental and language-centered yet it is hard to imagine writers more deeply rooted in their time and place: Joyce, who is almost a Baedeker to Dublin, and Faulkner, who enshrines Yoknapatawpha.)

Professors Maclulich and Jackel don't seem to have grasped that all good writing is, to some extent, "experimental or language-centered." Language perfectly forged for the task at hand is literature's central and enduring pleasure. We do not return again and again, for example, to Shakespeare's history plays for their themes; we do not return to them to muse over his views on hierarchy or the divine right of kings or primogeniture or read them as propaganda for the legitimacy of the Tudor dynasty; we return to them to savour, again and again, the almost unbearable pleasures of language performing at high voltage.

Harry's great speech before battle is joined at Agincourt makes Churchill's wartime broadcasts sound like the work of a tyro:

> And gentlemen in England, now-a-bed
> Shall think themselves accursed they were not here,
> And hold their manhoods cheap whiles any speaks
> That fought with us upon Saint Crispins's day...

(The fusion of music and meaning in the lines relentlessly engages the reader or listener. "A-bed" is not synonymous with "in bed." Where must the stresses fall in the third quoted line? On "cheap," obviously, and with a pause after it. But also, I've always thought, on "any," because it is intended to work back against "gentlemen" who are "a-bed." In other words, Shakespeare is talking about class, rank, and enoblement. Even a "gentleman" will shut his poncy mouth if one of these old sweats...)

All good writing is, to some extent, experimental. Writers have to push at the conventions, have to experiment to discover their own voices within the tradition or in opposition to it. They cannot keep working in the dominant manner of a great predecessor; they cannot write in someone else's voice. The search for new forms is not some mere "technical" preoccupation of writers; the new forms *are* the new voices, the new voices and sensibilities *are* the stories.

It follows, then, that traditions themselves do not stand still. The "traditional forms" to which Professor Jackel would have us hold allegiance are in fact *fossil moments in an endless process of change*, a process without which literature cannot remain alive. When he calls for loyalty to "traditional forms," he reveals a profound lack of thought about literary history and an amazing insensitivity to the pulse of creation going on about him. Who, exactly, is Professor Jackel to instruct Annabel Lyon, say, or Terry Griggs, that they ought to be writing like Duncan Campbell Scott or Sinclair Ross? His pronouncements are not the sensitive and percipient judgments of a finely honed literary mind; they're merely old-fartism.

As new stories started to invade the bounds of Professor Jackel's "traditional forms," academics fought a nationalistic rearguard action, touting the drear likes of Ernest Buckler in the face of Eudora Welty, John Cheever, Bernard Malamud, Richard Yates, Andre Dubus, Raymond Carver... and attempted to inculcate in students a devotion to the works of Frederick Philip Grove.

I felt blessed to be co-editing the work of beginning and young writers with Clark Blaise, and, later, Leon Rooke, because their knowledge and vision was international and expansionist—nothing costively Canadian in *their* literary embrace.

I remember, hazily, being in New York with Leon Rooke in 1985 or thereabouts, an expedition which seemed to require much driving, many martinis, and little sleep. I had guest-edited a polemical issue of *The Literary Review*, a quarterly published by Fairleigh Dickinson University, entitled *On the Edge: Canadian Short Stories*. Leon and I were on a mini-tour reading in various universities beginning in Hartford, Connecticut and ending at Fairleigh Dickinson in New Jersey. In Connecticut we were greeted by Maureen Forrester, who was singing there that night, Mahler's *Second Symphony*, the contralto solo "Urlicht" in the fourth movement, and we moved quickly from "How do you do?" to being "my boys" to whom she told an inexhaustible string of dirty jokes.

In a library at Fairleigh Dickinson, a somewhat oiled Leon performed "Some People Will Tell You the Situation at Henny Penny Nursery Is Getting Intolerable." So deeply did Leon *become* the nursery principal, Mr. Beacon, he started to climb library shelves, the audience rigid in apprehension.

At some point in the phantasmagoria of this American foray we were visiting Gordon Lish, a friend of Leon's, at his Alfred Knopf office, where he gave us copies of *What We Talk About When We Talk About Love* and Barry Hannah's *Captain Maximus*; volumes, I felt, unlikely to appeal to Professor Jackel. We drifted on to the Strand Book Store, where I bought an advance reading copy of Cormac McCarthy's *Blood Meridian* and we then drifted on for a boozy lunch at a favoured joint of Leon's where the house specialty was a plate of chitlins and collard greens served with a flute of champagne. Not exactly a lordly dish, and one Leon refused on the grounds that it reminded him of childhood privations, but certainly memorable for *texture*.

In the subsequent weeks of recovery I devoured the rest of what Cormac McCarthy had written to that date and decided that the richly Faulknerian *Suttree* was his finest work.

The good young writers did not need guidance; they had no problems with "better" and "best"; they knew what the best was. They were in accord with the spirit of the young Montreal pianist Paul Bley, who said: "You go to where the heat is and you *become* the heat." Bley had moved to New York, where he'd played with Charlie Parker, Mingus, Sonny Rollins, Art Blakey, and Ornette Coleman. Post-Coleman, his playing was a major influence on Keith Jarrett. Canada, even decades after the fact, still preferred the cocktail-loungerie of Oliver Jones.

Academic interest in Canadian literature had always been nationalist fantasy masquerading as literary judgement; academic teaching, writing, and "research" during the sixties and seventies amounted to a *trahison des clercs*. Professor David Staines, university Dean, General Editor of the New Canadian Library, Pooh-Bah, authority on King Arthur stories, actually asserted *in print* that Morley Callaghan was a better writer than Ernest Hemingway.

He was not fired.

(Impossible to resist a meander into Morley Callaghan. His most interesting book is probably *That Summer in Paris*—and interesting mainly because of its portraits of Hemingway, Fitzgerald, and other literary expatriates. Norman Mailer reviewed it and wrote, in part,

It is dim writing. One only has to compare the chapter he gives to Sinclair Lewis (one of the more elaborate cameos) against some equivalent number of pages Wolfe devoted to a similar portrait, and the result is no contest. A deadness comes back from Callaghan's echo. His short portraits are written at the level of a conversation with somebody who might tell you he met Truman Capote.

—And here Mailer pins *exactly* Callaghan's "Aw, shucks" tone and persona—

"Well," you might respond, "what is he like?"

"Well," says your friend, "he's small you know, and he's kind of bright.")

This squabbling about Morley Callaghan is not an unedifying spat between a disgruntled writer and an authority on the Knights of the Round Table; it is about a central defect of received wisdom concerning Canadian literature.

Consider two examples—entirely typical and representative—of sentences from opening paragraphs of Callaghan stories:

Mrs. Massey, a stout, kindly woman of sixty, full of energy for her age, and red-faced and healthy except for an occasional pain in her left leg which she watched very carefully, had come from Chicago to see her son who was a doctor.

And:

She stood on the corner of Bloor and Yonge, an impressive build of a woman, tall, stout, good-looking for forty-two, and watched the traffic signal.

The sentences are so stunningly bad they're comic. I have suggested in my memoir, *Shut Up He Explained*, that Callaghan never was a modernist short-story writer but rather a writer of parables, homilies, Catholic *exempla*, little sermons; he was interested not in prose but in preaching. Yet he has been hailed, decade after decade, by Professor Staines and his fellow authorities as "The Father of the Canadian Short Story" and his work, which I've described as "stumblebum," is generally accepted in literary histories, and in the *Canadian Encyclopedia*, as "classic."

The importance of the "spat" is this: if we accept that writing such as the sentences quoted is "classic" then that acceptance deforms judgement of Canadian literature entirely. If Callaghan is "classic" then how can we say anything meaningful in praise *or* criticism of Alice Munro? If she is "classic," as world opinion by way of the Nobel Prize would suggest, how can Canadians accept that estimation if at the same time they *also* hold Callaghan to be "classic"? If all concur that sentimental, simple-minded, ill-written religiosities are "classic," how can Canadians make *any* meaningful evaluation of the work of Mordecai Richler, Norman Levine, Mavis Gallant, Alice Munro, Clark Blaise, or Keath Fraser?

The reader can probably sense by now that, slowly and obliquely, I'm working my way towards answering the question that lies behind the Century List: how, and with what authority, does one make the choices that are behind its compiling? I am not being intentionally irritating when I say that the answer must be roundabout.

Randall Jarrell wrote, in 1953, in *Poetry and the Age*, that critics are "the bane of our age because our age so fantastically over-estimates their importance and so willingly forsakes the works they are writing about for them."

Criticism, obviously a secondary activity, has arrogated to itself primacy. I am not deluded that this book is anything but secondary. I often feel guilty thinking of Cyril Connolly's statement in *The Unquiet Grave*:

> The more books we read, the sooner we perceive that the true function of a writer is to produce a masterpiece and that no other task is of any consequence.

Critics have abdicated responsibility to the literature and have arrogated primacy to their paddling in the abstract shallows. They are hostile to aesthetic concerns and to elegance because they know that elegance eludes them, laughs at their ponderous ponderings. They feel, however, no guilt or shame in their arrogance. Rather than elucidating, helping readers to widen and deepen their understanding and pleasure, *serving* literature, criticism has wandered into its own funhall of mirrors and talks to itself in barbarous yawp.

In my novella *Forde Abroad*, Forde eavesdropped on an academic conference scene:

> They were arguing about a poet.
> "… but surely he's *noted* for his deconstruction of binaries."
> "… and by the introduction of chorus avoids the monological egocentricity of conventional lyric discourse."
> *Christ!*
> "Let me say," brayed one of the men, "let me say, in full awareness of heteroglossia…"
> *Christ!*

My admiration for my wife deepened when, many years ago now, she walked out on an academic paper we'd been cajoled into attending, saying, *sotto voce*, "It's like listening to a washing machine."

In 1955 Evelyn Waugh wrote: "It is a matter for thankfulness that the modern school of critics are unable or unwilling to compose a pleasurable sentence. It greatly limits the harm they do."

The *modern* school of critics!

It is, perhaps, a blessing he died before the advent of Derrida.

There exists now an almost total rift and mutual hostility between practicing artists and critics. Critics have turned the traditional function of criticism on its head by distorting literature entirely, treating it as the fodder for their scarcely comprehensible forays into sociology, politics, philosophy, race, feminism, sexual orientation, etc. much of their musing nihilistic, not a whit of it celebrating or luxuriating in:

> *Look, stranger, on this island now*
> *The leaping light for your delight discovers,*

> *Stand stable here*
> *And silent be,*
> *That through the channels of the ear*
> *May wander like a river*
> *The swaying sound of the sea.*
>
> *Here at the small field's ending pause*
> *When the chalk wall falls to the foam and its tall ledges*
> *Oppose the pluck*
> *And knock of the tide,*
> *And the shingle scrambles after the sucking surf,*
> *And the gull lodges*
> *A moment on its sheer side.*

"Deconstruction," at base an assertion that, despite decades of refined thought and practice, writers actually have no idea what they're doing or saying, is regarded by many writers as gross impertinence; "political correctness" is simply regarded by most as a tedious joke.

David Lodge, witty novelist and sometime professor of English at the University of Birmingham, wrote:

> Since serious literary criticism was virtually monopolized by the universities, it has become of all-absorbing interest to its practitioners, and a matter of indifference or incomprehension to society at large.

He also suggested that the aim of Derridean deconstruction is "the mystification and intimidation of the reader."

John Carey, sometime Merton Professor of Poetry at Oxford, appalled by structuralism, suggested that it "pretty clearly called for a spell of sedation and devoted nursing."

(These bracing quotations are drawn from D.J. Taylor's *The Prose Factory: Literary Life in England since 1918.*)

In *Bellow: A Biography*, James Atlas quoted Saul Bellow's challenge to "politically correct" academics who insist that all cultures are equal. It was delivered with the self-delighting laugh, head thrown back, that accompanied his funniest one-liners: "Who is the Tolstoy of the Zulus? The Proust of the Papuans? I'd be glad to read him."

Hugh Hood, I remember, used to say, similarly, "And who is the Haydn of the Huron?"

Critics delight in their obscure jargon, the flapdoodle of deconstruction, hermeneutics, *parole, langue,* binary oppositions, analytico-referential discourse, signified and signifier.

Like dotty alchemists, brains addled by the noxious fumes, they transmute gold to dross.

In a recent review, James Wood wrote: "There is no greater mark of the gap that separates writers and English departments than the question of value. The very thing that most matters to writers, the first question they ask of a work—is it any good?—is often largely irrelevant to university teachers. Writers are intensely interested in what might be called aesthetic success: they have to be, because in order to create something successful one must learn about other people's successful creations."

What artists know is a very different kind of thing from what theorists about the arts know. Les Mundwiler, poet, critic, and proprietor of Highbrow Books in Winnipeg, expressed this succinctly and suggestively in an essay called "Theory and Literary Knowledge":

> ... in observing my sister and other painters at work in appraising a painting, I've noticed that their greatest interest is often in very tiny areas and very subtle elements of technical detail. And this is the way any accomplished writer reads any other accomplished writer with the ever-present assistance, at interesting moments, of a kind of technical microscope. Even to recognize those moments, the writer has to have achieved a certain level of technical mastery, whatever level permits the writer to perceive the problem in question and to understand how another writer bungled it or solved it. What Booth [Wayne Booth], Genette [Gérard Genette] and others have to offer then is, by and large, a *macro* view of literary structures, which has only a rough-and-ready, mostly simplistic, significance for technically skilled

writers. Writers must still learn the tricky stuff from other writers, and good writers know that even something so apparently
straightforward as a page of unadorned dialogue between two
characters is filled, in practice, with a great many subtle narrative moves, well beyond the map-work of narratology.

These comments of Mundwiler's about the greatest interests of artists being in "very tiny areas and very subtle elements of technical
detail" is exactly so. The experience of Ben Nicholson in Paris in
1921 came to mind. He wrote in his autobiography:

> I remember suddenly coming on a cubist Picasso at the end of a
> small room at Paul Rosenberg's Gallery. It must have been a 1915
> painting—it was what seemed to me then, completely abstract.
> And in the centre there was an absolutely miraculous green—
> very deep, very potent and absolutely real. In fact, none of the
> actual events in one's life have been more real than that...

Anyone can see the whole thing, the nude, the horse, the anecdote; the
interest for the fellow-maker is what has gone into achieving that whole.
How is it made? Part of that interest is, of course, in stealing a trick-of-
the-trade for future personal use, but the larger part is the pleasure given
and taken in mastery. And that larger pleasure can be learned by people
not themselves practitioners. Indeed, it is vital to art and literature that
readers and viewers move into that relation with books or canvas.

Looking back at my own earlier work, I find that in 1972, in an
anthology called *The Narrative Voice*, I had written helpful suggestions for the writing life entitled "Soaping a Meditative Foot: Notes
for a Young Writer."

I'd quoted these words of novelist Herbert Gold:

> Particular life is still the best map to truth. When we search our
> hearts and strip our pretences, we all know this. Particular life—
> we know only what we *know.*

Another of my *dicta* read:

Avoid literary criticism which moves away from the word on the printed page and ascends to theories of God, Archetypes, Myth, Psyche, The Garden of Eden, the New Jerusalem, and Orgone Boxes. Stick to the study of the placement of commas.

In the spirit of Mundwiler's "very tiny areas," and my own "placement of commas," I offer a small sample, taken from "crime novels," of the sort of things that cause writers to pause when reading, and make mental note.

Recently, I was reading Denise Mina's *Still Midnight* and was stopped considering the next five fragments:

"Police!" shouted Omar from the footwell, pointing past Mo to the door. "'S police car!"

*

"Shots fired?"
"One, sixteen-year-old girl's hand blown off."
"'Kin hell."
He hummed in agreement.

*

"Mon," said Pat, anxious to get back.

*

"'F you don't mind."

*

"'S get the fuck out of here before we catch something."

*

These contracted forms, their accuracy, were a pleasurable jolt, left me thoughtful.

Also read recently, *Panicking Ralph* by Bill James (*vere* James Tucker), a masterly writer of baroquely comic dialogue. In addition to his crime novels, he has written a book on Anthony Powell's *Dance to the Music of Time*, and I think of the Harpur and Iles books as a "Dance to the Music of Crime." *Kirkus Review* said of Bill James that "he is probably the most undervalued Brit writing crime fiction today." A conclusion I'd arrived at many years ago.

In these lines, the wife of a drug-dealer has been murdered by two hired London gunmen. The local thug, Foster, says:

> "Women, they hear things, spy things," Foster replied. "I've seen pictures of her. She looked good. Tits. Women like that get told secrets, get invited into big people's confidence."

And from *Cold Light* by John Harvey; Dana's thoughts about Police Inspector Charlie Resnick after a one-night stand.

> Dana lit another cigarette, poured herself another drink. She had already had several, finding her courage to phone him when he hadn't phoned her. And at work. Probably she shouldn't have done that, probably that had been a mistake. Except he had said yes, hadn't he? Agreed to come around for a drink. She smiled, raising her glass: he was worth a little seeking out, a little chasing after. She liked him, the memory of him; big; there was something, she thought, about a man who was big. And she laughed.

Any serious writer could be proud of any of these quoted passages; packed with pleasures; they abundantly pass the test of being alive rather than dead.

In a tumult of punctuation, how I loved that
; big;!

I launch now into an attempt to describe my own stance in all this bizarre critical warfare and to describe why and how I selected the writers in the Century List and how I select the stories that appear in the annual *Best Canadian Stories*. The attempt will be oblique, I fear, and characteristically meandering.

The essence of all judgement is comparison followed by evaluation.

(Postmodern hackles will already be rising.)

The art critic Robert Hughes wrote in *Culture of Complaint: The Fraying of America:*

> It is in the nature of human beings to discriminate. We make choices and judgements every day. These choices are part of real experience. They are influenced by others, of course, but they are not fundamentally the result of a passive reaction to authority. And we know that one of the realest experiences in cultural life is that of inequality between books and musical performances and paintings and other works of art. Some things do strike us as better than others—more articulate, more radiant with consciousness. We may have difficulty saying why, but the experience remains. The pleasure principle is enormously important in art, and those who would like to see it downgraded in favour of ideological utterance remind me of the English Puritans who opposed bear-baiting, not because it gave pain to the bear, but because it gave pleasure to the spectators.

In *Shut Up He Explained* I wrote about tradition.

> The past is not an oppressive, rigid constant but grows larger all the time as experiment and reaction and schism and innovation and unique visions pass into history and become part of what we use to measure and to judge.
>
> The past has to be our constant present; it is our yardstick.

From a critical book I wrote in 1988, *What Is a Canadian Literature?*

> A literature is a relationship between books and readers. A tradition implies an audience. A tradition honours and bequeaths;

it is a gift handed down from generation to generation. A literature is a living thing; it is the involvement of writers and readers, of publishers, printers, scholars, critics, reviewers, teachers, librarians, booksellers, collectors, antiquarians, bibliographers, and historians, in the cherishing of language.

T.S. Eliot writes in "Tradition and the Individual Talent," in *Selected Essays*, that the tradition of the European poet

> ... involves in the first place, the historical sense, which we may call nearly indispensable to anyone who would continue to be a poet beyond his twenty-fifth year; and the historical sense involves a perception, not only of the pastness of the past, but of its presence; the historical sense compels a man to write with not merely his own generation in his bones, but with a feeling that the whole literature of Europe from Homer, and within it the whole literature of his own country, has a simultaneous existence and composes a simultaneous order.

Sven Birkerts wrote lovingly of Cyril Connolly:

> For Connolly, every realized work had an equal claim on our attention, not in spite of its pastness, but because of it. "Culture" and "history" were words referring to an ever-changing entity—human life—in which we are implicated. And of which every part mattered. The critic's job, along with greeting and assessing the new, was to keep alive in the present an image of the whole. In this capacity, Connolly patrolled the past incessantly—as a seeker, not an archivist. He tested the works and reputations of other periods for their value to our ongoing endeavour. And when he brought a neglected treasure in to the light, he celebrated not only its beauty, but its capacity to recall to us the mysterious larger life of culture.
>
> The reappearance of Connolly's books may be a sign of reaction against the prevailing thrust of critical theory. If so, it will generate the slightest of ripples, nothing more. The

various doctrinaire isms have taken their place at the table and are happily masticating the legacy of centuries. They will not disappear. New styles of "reading" will succeed one another, but the underlying tendency—towards reduction and abstraction—is no more likely to die out than is the collateral trend toward the technological transformation of the social and natural order. Where will Connolly fit in? Nowhere near the centre, that much is certain. His books— those wonderful auscultations of the tradition—are fated to return to the underground. There they will command interest among a small public of unregenerate back-pedal-ers. How could it be otherwise? The arrow of modern life and the arrow of private sensibility have passed going in opposite directions.

From: *An Artificial Wilderness*. Sven Birkerts

I have little to say to ideologues, to those who deny the validity of "better" and "best," who profess that all cultures are of equal value, whose lip curls at the thought of comparison, evaluation, history, and hierarchy. I prefer the emotional and intellectual company of people who actually *know* things, people like booksellers, paint-ers, antique dealers, carpenters, gardeners, enthusiasts who collect horse-brasses, Colt revolvers, teaspoons, or *tulwahs,* people who know *things.*

If trapped with one who disparages the idea of "better" and "best" and if a polite smile will not suffice, I say that I suppose that *connoisseurship* probably comes closest...

If pressed, tediously, about the utter subjectivity of connoisseur-ship—*yes, yes, for Christ's sake!*—I might say that if I wished to buy a drawing from the Italian *quatrocentro* I'd seek out the advice of Bernard Berenson or Kenneth Clark before that of Joe Blow or (a pretty little Osric-from-*Hamlet* tumbling gesture of the hand) you.

"There is a huge envious world," wrote Evelyn Waugh, "to whom elegance is positively offensive."

Connoisseurs bring to their enthusiasms long years of passion-ate study, knowledge, and taste deriving from the experience of handling (or reading) hundreds, if not thousands, of the items in question, the knowledge gained from the daily conversation of their community, the guidance and benediction of elders… All this combines with the kind of knowledge potters have of clay, cabinet-makers of wood, smiths of steel and heat.

One of my culture-heroes is the polished connoisseur Kenneth Clark. He is the author of *Leonardo da Vinci, The Leonardo da Vinci Drawings at Windsor Castle, Florentine Painting, Piero della Francesca, The Romantic Rebellion, The Nude: A Study of Ideal Art* (probably his greatest book), *The Gothic Revival, Landscape Into Art, Rembrandt and the Italian Renaissance, Ruskin Today, Looking at Pictures, Moments of Vision,* and *Civilization.*

Kenneth Clark, later Sir Kenneth Clark, later Lord Clark, a protégé of Bernard Berenson at Villa I Tatti, was director of the National Gallery at the incredible age of thirty-one, Slade Professor of Fine Art at Oxford, Keeper of Fine Arts at the Ashmolean, Surveyor of the King's Pictures, Chairman of the Arts Council, Trustee of the British Museum…

And author of two absorbing volumes of autobiography, *Another Part of the Wood* and *The Other Half.*

Rather than talk *about* him, I'd prefer to let the reader hear his voice. From *Another Part of the Wood*, his invitation to Australia to give advice on holdings and acquisitions.

Melbourne

Facing the Tiepolo was a stuffed horse named Pharlap, which was the supreme attraction of the Gallery. Pharlap had been, without doubt, the greatest racehorse of all time. It was the god of Australia… This sacred animal had been sent to race in America, and had died mysteriously… After its death there arose a violent controversy between Sydney and Melbourne as to which should have its remains. Finally its heart… was consigned to Sydney and its stuffed body was exhibited in Melbourne. Around it was a fair collection of impressionists…

Sydney

I was taken to visit an exhibition of contemporary landscape painting, and it was sad to see how the excellent Australian land-scape painters of the late nineteenth century had exhausted the genre. As I was leaving the exhibition I noticed, hung high up above the entrance stairs, a work of remarkable originality and painter-like qualities. I asked who it was by. "Oh, nobody." "But you must have his name in your catalogue." "Let's see; here it is, Nolan, Sidney Nolan. Never heard of him." I said I would like to see more of his work. "Well he's not on the telephone." "But you must have his address." More angry scuffling finally produced an address in a suburb of Sydney. I took a taxi there that afternoon, and found the painter dressed in khaki shorts, at work on a series of large paintings of imaginary birds. He seemed to me an entirely original artist, and incidentally a fascinating human being. I bought the landscape in the exhibition, not that it was necessarily the best, but in order to annoy the exhibition secretary, and was confident that I had stumbled on a genius.

Here, from *The Other Half,* Clark's visit in Japan to a temple (Nishi Hongan-ji):

The Abbot is married to a niece of the Emperor, called Lady Ohtai, and she did me the great honour of receiving me and showing one of the temple's greatest treasures, an anthology of poems in six volumes, said to have been written by some aristocratic calligrapher in about 1118. It is the most ravishing example of the fusion of drawing and writing I have ever seen, and I would gladly have spent the whole day looking at it. Of course I could not read the poems, but nor, I was delighted to find, could the Japanese. The calligraphy is so exquisite as to be incomprehensible. The Lady Ohtai spoke a little English in the quiet, modest voice of a genuine aristocrat. We seemed to be in sympathy with each other, when she said, "There is one more question I must ask you. What is the state of calligraphy in your country?" and in a flash I realized what deserts of incomprehension exist between our two cultures.

And finally, a very moving vignette of Kenneth Clark as a small boy.

> These Sunday afternoons with Mr. Macdonald's Japanese prints were among the happiest and most formative of my life. They confirmed my belief that nothing could destroy me as long as I could enjoy works of art, and for "enjoy" read "enjoy": not codify or classify, or purge my spirit or arouse my social consciousness, just enjoy. From this hedonist, or at best epicurean, position I have never departed. It is true that I tried to communicate my pleasure to other people, but that is not because I feel it my duty to do so, but simply because I cannot contain myself.

Even the most refined of connoisseurs, however, is not infallible. In *Another Part of the Wood* there is a photograph of a dapper Kenneth Clark, one elegantly clad buttock lodged on the edge of a table or desk, proudly posing beside a carving in wood of a Madonna and Child sold to him by the uncouth Lord Duveen as by Simone Martini (c. 1284–1344), but subsequently exposed as being a fake manufactured by one Alceo Dossena; (1878–1937) a forger born in Cremona. Thomas Hoving (ex-director of the Metropolitan) in his book *False Impressions*, called Dossena's work "sketchy, untutored, and mostly laughable."

The joy of connoisseurs is to grapple with actual things, to look long and scrupulously. To handle and heft. To ask: Is it right? Is the patina as it should be? Is the wear in the right places? Are there any repairs? Any retouches? Are the pigments right? Has someone used potassium permanganate to dull the gleam of new brass? Has kola nut-compound aged the appearance of this mask, possibly recently crafted?

Does the piece have "presence?"

And then the connoisseur would say: Compare, and having compared, rank and evaluate.

And it is with comparison and evaluation that Canadian literature and Canadian criticism implode. The epitome of Canadian reluctance to evaluate and judge is the Conclusion to the *Literary History of Canada*, under the general editorship of Carl F. Klinck (1965), written by Northrop Frye.

Here is what the massively influential Frye wrote, in part, in the Conclusion:

> The evaluative view is based on the conception of criticism as concerned mainly to define and canonize the genuine classics of literature. And Canada has produced no author who is a classic in the sense of possessing a vision greater in kind than that of his best readers (Canadians themselves might argue about one or two, but in the perspective of the world at large the statement is true)...
>
> ... If no Canadian author pulls us away from the Canadian context toward the centre of literary experience itself, then at every point we remain aware of his social and historical setting. The conception of what is literary has to be greatly broadened for such a literature. The literary in Canada is often only an incidental quality of writings which, like those of many of the early explorers, are as innocent of literary intention as a mating loon. Even when it is literature in its orthodox genres of poetry and fiction, it is more significantly studied as a part of Canadian life than as a part of an autonomous world literature.

This rather bland dismissal of nearly one hundred years of Canadian writing, a dismissal with which I'd totally agree, is at the same time oddly unregretful and lacking apparently in any desire to spur future writing on towards significance. Frye's unengaged and somewhat remote, priestly response to literary inadequacy put me in mind of Matthew 27:24.

When Pilate saw that he could prevail nothing, but rather a tumult was made, he took water, and washed his hands before the multitude...

My problem with Frye is that nothing of his I've read connects with literature as I think and feel about it. I'm interested enough in myth and symbol, in Jung, *The Golden Bough*, Robert Graves, Jessie L. Weston, Lévi-Strauss... it's all a sort of background mental furniture, ticked off in my mind, NOTED, but I think about none of these things when I'm reading and, later, evaluating short stories. Frye was concerned with grand patterns, with abstruse reference, with the pursuit of abstractions; I am hopelessly wedded to the "natural object," particular life, the label on the tin of cocoa.

It is probably shameful to admit that I find Frye's syntheses about as gripping as newspaper Christmas or New Year Giant Crossword Puzzles.

The University of Toronto Press is publishing *The Collected Works of Northrop Frye* in thirty-three volumes.

Lévi-Strauss was a mind from the same sort of mold as Frye and I'm interested, vaguely, in his writing on religion, kinship, and myth. I've picked, in a desultory way, at a version of his *Mythologiques*, but I'm passionate about the power and beauty of the Dan, Pende, Baule, Mama, and Bambara masks on my walls, the masks that topped the painted sackcloth costumes, the cloaks of straw and cascading raffia shimmering in the firelight, the masks hieractic, the masks *dancing* those myths.

Nothing in Frye is as vital and vivid to me as:

Aisla's bedroom used to shine with prettiness, with its pony wallpaper, and the jewellery box with the ballet dancer that spun to *"Für Elise,"* and the wooden dollhouse. While Aisla went to swim class on Saturday mornings, you used to tidy her room, and then make the beds in that little house and set the tiny table. Now Aisla's floor is covered in towels, discarded clothes, dirty cereal bowls. The pony wallpaper is still there, but a few months ago Aisla circled the ponies with Magic Marker, then put question marks coming from their heads.

Aisla lies in bed, her short platinum hair sticking every which way, her face pure as a piece of crystal, though beneath her eyes the skin is faintly blue—the only hint that she returned home at two in the morning, on a school night, then showered for ages before throwing herself into bed. Worry sings in you, sings and sings. Briefly you imagine picking her up, carrying her to safety across a burning landscape. Instead you lean down and shake her awake.

"Fuck off," says the perfect mouth.

A pause. Then you pull the pillow out from under her head. Aisla sits up. She looks like an angry pixie.

"Fuck off, Mum, I'm sleeping."

"Don't you dare say 'fuck off' to me."

"Then don't come in and shake me."

"I was waking you."

"Okay. Fuck off. I'm awake."

You stare at Aisla. Aisla stares back.

"You're such a cow," says Aisla, and this hurts so much you draw in your breath.

"You are cruel."

"You are a fucking cow."

(*Oh, My Darling* by Shaena Lambert.)

Or the visit to Nora, the father, Ben's ex-girlfriend, and the farmhouse as seen through the eyes of Ben's young daughter in "Walker Brothers Cowboy" in Alice Munro's *Dance of the Happy Shades.*

There is a gramophone and a pump organ and a picture on the wall of Mary, Jesus' mother—I know that much—in shades of bright blue and pink with a spiked band of light around her head. I know that such pictures are found only in the homes of Roman Catholics and so Nora must be one. We have never known any Roman Catholics at all well, never well enough to visit in their houses. I think of what my grandmother and my Aunt Tena, over in Dungannon, used to always say to indicate somebody was a Catholic. *So-and-so digs with the wrong foot,* they would say. *She digs with the wrong foot.* That was what they would say about Nora.

...We go across the yard ("Excuse me taking you in this way but I don't think the front door has been opened since Papa's funeral, I'm afraid the hinges might drop off"), up the porch steps, into the kitchen, which really is cool, high-ceilinged, the blinds of course down, a simple, clean, threadbare room with waxed worn linoleum, potted geraniums, drinking-pail and dipper, a round table with scrubbed oilcloth. In spite of the cleanness, the wiped and swept surfaces, there is a faint sour smell—maybe of the dishrag or the tin dipper or the oilcloth, or the old lady, because there is one, sitting in an easy chair under the clock shelf. She turns her head slightly in our direction and says, "Nora? Is that company?"

"Blind," says Nora in a quick explaining voice to my father. Then, "You won't guess who it is, Momma. Hear his voice."

My father goes to the front of her chair and bends and says hopefully, "Afternoon, Mrs. Cronin."

..."He's married, Momma," says Nora cheerfully and aggressively. "Married and got two children and here they are." She pulls us forward, makes each of us touch the old lady's dry, cool hand while she says our names in turn. Blind! This is the first blind person I have ever seen close up. Her eyes are closed, the eyelids sunk away down, showing no shape of the eyeball, just hollows. From one hollow comes a drop of silver liquid, a medicine, or a miraculous tear.

In forty-odd years I've forgotten much but never the "faint sour smell" and the miraculous silver tear.

Frye wrote further in the Conclusion to the *Literary History*, speaking of the literary scholars who contributed topic essays to the book:

> Had evaluation been their guiding principle, this book would, if written at all, have been only a huge debunking project, leaving Canadian literature a poor naked alouette plucked of every feather of decency and dignity...

This wholesale absolution, this condoning of general ineptitude and crudeness, this remission of the country's literary sins, gave the imprimatur and *nihil obstat* of the country's best university and its most revered literary scholar and led us not onward and upward, but into international irrelevance.

What we needed then, and need now, is to be *thoroughly* plucked.

Choosing the Best

In this period, when traditional verities are under fierce assault and when the very ideas of evaluation and hierarchy are, to many university teachers of English, intellectually embarrassing, how can I feel confident in my ability to select the best writers for the anthologies I edit? How can I even continue to use expressions like "the best writers"? Isn't the age of such anthologies over, played out? How can such elitist anthologies speak to the concerns of a pluralistic society, to the concerns of women, visible minorities, native peoples, the differently abled, the transgendered, the aged?

The anthologist likes to claim—indeed, does claim—that he sees more clearly than most the shape of a decade or a generation, but the anthologist is probably as much molded by the times as the next man. Who could now ignore gender and colour and, in Canada particularly, native people and regions? They *should* be ignored, of course, but we are all susceptible to the pressures and assumptions of the *zeitgeist*.

The anthologizer betrays art to select stories and writers to serve or bolster political ends or to mirror fashionable orthodoxies. I was disturbed by Robert Weaver's Oxford University Press anthology *Canadian Short Stories: Fifth Series*. The aim of the anthology was to present the best story writers of the second half of the eighties. One of the selling points of the book in the catalogue advertising was: "New Canadian and native Canadian writers included." How horribly revealing is that word "included." Examination of the contents further revealed that "New Canadians" meant "of West Indian origin." Being "new" or "native" seems a less-than-adequate qualification for being selected for an anthology of the best writing of the second half of the eighties. And it was doubly unfortunate that the three stories in question were among the weakest in the book. It is hard to avoid the conclusion that Weaver was deliberately indulging in the lunacy of literary affirmative action.

(Though on his part, I wish to believe, under protest.)

There is a simple answer to these questions: they're the wrong questions to ask. Such concerns, the concerns of pluralistic society, how one "self-identifies," how one should or shouldn't respect the wishes of an individual who wishes to be addressed as "they," whether "safe rooms" should be provided for university students liable to be "triggered" into wounded hysteria by texts which represent the Patriarchy uncensored, or describe warfare, or contain racial epithets and episodes of sexual aggression, such concerns are the business of bureaucrats, politicians, self-censoring editors in textbook publishing, the quaveringly "correct" in universities, the cohorts of those with very little else to occupy their minds. Writers do not sit down to address "society," pluralistic or otherwise; they sit down to wrestle with language. The anthologist must understand that struggle and concern himself solely with the words on the page, the placement of commas.

(Another meander, though on intimately connected with the above. I have not been able to erase from my memory seeing a girl, sixteen or so, skateboarding down the hill outside Ottawa's *Chateau Laurier*. She fell and her head hit the sidewalk terrifyingly. I ran towards her but as I reached her a young man, a student in appearance, had knelt beside her half-conscious sprawl and was saying,

"Do I have your permission to touch your body?")

All anthologists are liable to lapses of taste and exhibitions of bad judgement. The anthologist who puts together annual collections is particularly prone to errors of judgement because the constraints of an annual tend to mean that he or she cannot watch a promising newcomer over a period of time and form considered opinions about the writing and the writer's staying power. It is easy to be momentarily dazzled by flashy work which turns out to be a flash in the pan—as I was by the first few stories of Patrick Roscoe.

The first story of his I read I thought charming. It was *faux-naïf* but well-handled. The second story was also charming. By the time I'd read five, the charm and sweetness had become cloying and that which had at first seemed lyrical began to sound more like a monotonous and deliberate incantation, the expression of an extravagant, if not hysterical, sensibility.

Who am I, then, given these deficiencies, to assume the mantle of critic and connoisseur?

I was born in England in 1938 into a middle-class family. I attended state schools and studied at Bristol University on a state scholarship. I was eleven before I learned how to tell time.

The writers I grew up on—say, until the age of twelve—were mainly the middlebrow writers of the first third of the century but with some nineteenth-century titles thrown in. Where are the looming figures of that period now? Where are the easier Dickens, *Oliver Twist, A Tale of Two Cities, The Pickwick Papers, David Copperfield?* Where are Scott's *Ivanhoe, Quentin Durward, Redgauntlet, Rob Roy?* Where are Stevenson's *Kidnapped, Treasure Island,* and *Catriona?* Rider Haggard? Where are H.G. Wells, Arnold Bennett, John Masefield, John Drinkwater, Hilaire Belloc, G.K. Chesterton, Hugh Walpole, J.B. Priestley, Somerset Maugham. Aldous Huxley... and, on a more popular level, Daphne du Maurier, Nevil Shute, A.J. Cronin...?

Though "on a more popular level" is an understanding from a later time because I was quite happily reading *The Pickwick Papers* at the same time as Richmal Crompton's "William" books and Rupert Bear Annuals.

It is all now rather like a fading sepia photograph... *is that him in the back row?*

And what happened to the critical reputations of their contemporary modernists?

Those reputations are still high but they have suffered a diminishment—D.H. Lawrence, Ford Madox Ford, Virginia Woolf, Ezra Pound, T.S. Eliot... still very much *there* but more admired, I'd venture, than read.

A single anecdote can suggest the ephemeral nature of literary reputation and serve as a memento to the complacent pundit.

In 1924 Michael Arlen (*vere* Dikran Kouyoumdjian) published a novel called *The Green Hat*. Who has heard of it now? Who remembers Michael Arlen? *The Green Hat* is described, in *The Oxford Companion to Twentieth Century Literature in English* (Ed. Jenny Stringer), as "one of the best-selling books of the 1920s." In the same year, but to no fanfare whatsoever, and to almost total critical neglect, a pathetically shy, wildly eccentric, flamboyantly homosexual writer called Ronald Firbank paid to have published a most peculiar, slim volume entitled *Sorrow in Sunlight*.

Here are its opening sentences:

> Looking gloriously bored, Miss Miami Mouth gaped up into the boughs of a giant silk-cotton tree. In the lethargic noontide nothing stirred: all was so still, indeed, that the sound of someone snoring was clearly audible among the cane-fields far away.
>
> "After dose yams an' pods an' de white falernum, I dats way sleepy too," she murmured, fixing heavy, somnolent eyes upon the prospect that lay before her.
>
> Through the sun-tinged greenery shone the sea, like a floor of silver glass strewn with white sails.
>
> Somewhere out there, fishing, must be her boy, Bamboo!

When I first read those lines it was as if shock troops had opened the door into the room where I was sitting, tossed in a verbal stun grenade, and pulled the door shut again before the explosion.

For its American publication, the book's sponsor and advocate, Carl Van Vechten, entitled it *Prancing Nigger*, a title that earned Firbank and Van Vechten unwarranted animosity as both were much in sympathy with the aspirations of what is now called the Harlem Renaissance.

All Firbank's books were printed, in his lifetime, in editions of five hundred copies and at his own expense. His reputation has been kept alive by other writers and by a tiny but always-growing readership. Those five hundred copies eventually had a profound effect on

Waugh, Green, Connolly, the Sitwells... and, whether we realize it or not, us.

I have long held to the lonely view that *Vile Bodies* is Evelyn Waugh's most important book. It is certainly his most Firbankian.

(Numbers in literary matters are always interesting. *Poems* (1918) by Gerard Manley Hopkins, one of the great poets, was published by Oxford University Press in seven hundred copies; the edition took years to sell.)

Fully aware, then, of the subjectivity of judgement and of what a damn fool history can prove one to be, let me try to answer the question: How can you be so arrogant as to presume to judge contemporary work?

The beginning of my answer must be: How can I *not* judge? Academic opinion may currently dislike such words as "better" and "best," yet to reject evaluation and hierarchy is a refusal to engage with the book or painting for what it is; to reject evaluation and hierarchy is to reject art's importance.

The whole of the artistic life is concerned with evaluation. When an artist puts down a line on a sheet of paper, he is comparing that line, consciously or unconsciously, with the line he's seen in the work of others and with every other line he himself has previously drawn. Every stroke is made against the accumulated knowledge and taste of his entire life as an artist.

It is this kind of knowledge that as a writer, editor, critic, reader, I bring to anthologizing. I feel comfortable as an anthologist because, as a writer myself, I know why and how the new writers are doing what they are doing. To be somewhat paradoxical, I *recognize* new writers and new expressions of the art and I intend the word "recognize" in its sense of "identify something or someone *as being known before.*"

That doesn't and does make sense.

The Canadian literary landscape was the recent construct of a tiny number of people. That was, and is, its central problem; the literature was the possession of a faction, not of a class or a people, and it is now largely a product owned by a megacompany and sold as a commodity.

I still look back with pleasure at the beginnings in the late sixties and seventies—the manning of the barricades, the astounding simultaneous release of five *Spiderline* novels by Anansi and the emotional call to arms of Dennis Lee's *Civil Elegies*.

Bliss was it in that dawn to be alive!

But it did not take long to descend to the Centre for the Editing of Early Canadian Texts. It is hard not to smile at the industry of D.R. Cronk's *unutterably* definitive edition of John Richardson's *Wacousta* (1832).

> "Ha! Ha! By heaven, such cold, pompous insolence amuses me," vociferated Wacousta.

What brought us from the revolutionary hope of the sixties and seventies to the threadbare present?

The answer to all such questions is always the ferocious nationalism that dismissed comparisons and evaluation as kowtowing to what Robin Matthews, professor and demagogue, referred to as the "imperial centres" (i.e., England and the United States). This denial of what should have been overwhelmingly obvious to even *his* meagre mind suggests, again, Bill Hoffer's oft-quoted Yiddish saying:

The worst truth is better than the best lie.

And what the extreme nationalists urged was the lousiest of lies.

I always urged the worst truth as our necessary starting point.

(I cannot expunge from my mind a sentence in one of Robin Mathews' feeble fictions:

The beach was like a croissant.

No, Professor Matthews, it was not.)

When I first came to Canada, Hugh Garner was considered a story writer to reckon with. Morley Callaghan's reputation was high and inviolable; he was hailed as the Father of the Canadian Short Story. Reputations which then hung over the literary battlefield like searing flares quickly burned down to ash and cinder. Margaret Laurence once seemed to dominate our literary world but now seems a transitional writer, a writer more at the end of a tradition, less our contemporary than we had thought. Rudy Wiebe is more celebrated in the Western canon of "prairie literature"(!) than in the Eastern canon. And where now is Dave Godfrey?

All, you will notice, winners of the Governor General's Award for Literature.

Dave Godfrey, founder of presses, spokesperson, *animateur* of nationalist *brouhaha*, won the Governor General's Award for his 1970 novel *The New Ancestors*, a tome the *Oxford Companion to Canadian Literature* describes, admiringly, as "an Einsteinian vision of relative values."

Strewth!

The indefatigable Professor John Moss of the University of Ottawa judged the book

"as monumental an achievement as our literature has yet produced."

Strewth!

In the same year, Norman Levine published *From a Seaside Town*. *The New Ancestors* drifts down towards history's footnotes while Norman Levine, who never won anything and ended his life on a stipend from a charity for indigent writers, stands more and more clearly revealed as at the centre of our literature, one of its most radiant figures. Unheralded as he is, he is my daily companion.

The English-Scottish-Irish-Empire Loyalist canon celebrated in Margaret Atwood's *Survival* is now no canon at all but simply a curiosity in our literary history, a dead, closed little world of wretchedly bad writers to whom nationalist fervour gave a brief semblance of life.

Canadian anthologies, too, have been something of a trainwreck. From Knister's *Canadian Short Stories* (1928) to Pacey's *A Book of Canadian Stories* (1947; fourth edition 1967) to Robert Weaver's *Canadian Short Stories* (1960), nothing much remains. These were followed by the volumes selected by "celebrities"; *From Ink Lake* (1990) edited by Michael Ondaatje and *The Penguin Book of Canadian Short Stories* (2008) edited by Jane Urquhart, a volume so outrageous in its ignorance that Dan Wells of Biblioasis, Kim Jernigan of *The New Quarterly*, and I felt compelled to organize a simultaneous attack upon it in issues of *CNQ (Canadian Notes and Queries)* No. 74 and in *The New Quarterly* No. 107. These *Salon des Réfusés* issues confronted

Urquhart's admitted ignorance of the genre and her exclusion from the wretched book of a rather long list of the country's best writers. Both magazines contain engaging stories, solid commentary, and much good, nasty fun.

What went wrong and so *consistently* so?

The answer is inescapable: the lack of an informed audience. There have never been enough people to comment on the emperor's willie.

In his introduction to *Canadian Short Stories* (1960), Robert Weaver calls Canada "a provincial literary society" and goes on to say, "What we do not have is much of that sophistication and intellectual intensity that distinguishes a good deal of the contemporary fiction appearing in the older literary societies abroad."

John Meisel, Professor of political science at Queen's University and ex-Chairman of the Canadian Radio-Television and Telecommunications Commission (CRTC), ascribed all Canada's artistic ills to "the thinness of a cultural class in Canada."

Northrop Frye wrote "even [Canadian] poetry and fiction is more significantly studied as a part of Canadian life than as a part of an autonomous world literature."

Philip Marchand, the distinguished books columnist for the *National Post* and author of *Ripostes* wrote:

> There is something both heartening and disheartening about the fact that so much of the strength of Canadian literary culture lies in the short story form. It is heartening because there are now many Canadian writers who are truly proficient in the art— so much so that whatever is enduring in our literature will be more likely found in their work than in over-stuffed prose epics such as [Rohinton Mistry's] *A Fine Balance* or [Timothy Findley's] *The Piano Man's Daughter*.
>
> The situation is in some respects similar to Elizabethan and Jacobean England, where a cultural climate favoured the production of an enormous amount of good lyric verse, sonnets, and so on. Most of this good verse has since been classified by academic critics as "minor" but it was wonderful minor stuff and it has remained undimmed by time.

Something similar may be said about Canadian short fiction in the late twentieth century. The disheartening element in the situation, of course, is that few people actually read it.

Decorum urges me not to recall David Mamet's striking phrase "... savage shitheads in the wilderness."

Earlier, I said that a literature is a relationship between books and readers and I wish to return to that idea. The book does not exist—it is merely paper and ink—until a reader reads it, until a reader "creates" the book by establishing a relationship with it, by "composing" it. Reading is not a passive activity.

It follows, then, that every response to a work of literature or a painting is a subjective response. To criticize connoisseurship, therefore, as being subjective is not a criticism exactly devastating.

The critic F.R. Leavis, tieless and grinding, disdained by some for not being socially from "the top drawer," gritty, irritating, was described by Isaiah Berlin in *Affirming: Letters 1975–1997* as having "the hectoring, bullying tone of the infallible Savonarola, dispensing praise and blame as an instrument of divine justice."

Yet what Leavis wrote, calmly and gently, in *Education and the University*, goes to the heart of the discussion about evaluation and judgement:

> Analysis is not a dissection of something that is already and passively there. What we call analysis is, of course, a constructive or creative process. It is a re-creation...

And in *Letters in Criticism* he wrote:

> You cannot be intelligent about literature without judging. A judgement is a personal judgement or it is nothing—you cannot have your judging done for you... And it is a further truism ... that only by the collaborative-creative process I have alluded to can a living literary culture—and all that goes with it—be created and maintained.

And that is what all this book has been for me: nudging, shoving, pointing, showing, urging relationship.

(It's wildly unfair, but F.R. Leavis will probably be remembered by many as the butt of Sir John Sparrow's vicious but brilliant class jibe:

"If he'd wash his neck, I'd wring it."

Almost in the class of Dr. Johnson, to an offending bargee or wherryman, "Sir, your wife, under the guise of keeping a bawdy-house, is a receiver of stolen goods.")

★

What drew me to the stories in the Century List was, ultimately, language. I was looking to experience tension in the sentences, that tension as I somewhere wrote, of a taut rope invisibly aquiver. I was looking for language that was, as I wrote in *The New Story Writers*, "precise and quick to the touch. Touching that language must be like touching skin or an animal's pelt. Nothing else will do: nothing else will last."

I was not averse to initial difficulty. We will remember the hard, chewy stories of a Mavis Gallant long after we've forgotten Richard Brautigan's soft centres. W.B. Yeats offered some advice to poets which also applies, in spirit, to prose writers *and to readers.*

> When your technic is sloppy your matter grows second-hand—
> there is no difficulty to force you down under the surface—diffi-
> culty is our plough.

Yeats is saying that, out of imposed technical difficulty (metre, enjambment, rhyme, etc.), constraints overcome, arises energy, power, depth. The deeper the plough the more abundant the crop.

I craved rhetoric in the stories, rhetoric that dominated the stage and violated the audience.

> ... swinging hard across the blue plains and raggedly-ass cot-
> tonwoods, the endless flight through pale aspens and truckstop
> botulism, Kmart snakeskin cowboy boots, cheating songs, box

elders. This is just after the grain elevator blew over in Missouri: burnt for days and they couldn't get at the bodies. In the blind pigs and roadhouses lizards cringe under the crashing rain of Wurlitzers and chicken bones.

(Mark Jarman honking and Texas-tenor raucous in the story "Cowboys Inc." from *Dancing Nightly in the Tavern.*)

I hungered to be *moved*.

I hungered for even *one word* that lit up for me the dim recesses of the stage, that in Francis Bacon's words "returned me to life more violently."

I'll repeat an anecdote I've told before in *Freedom from Culture*, (1994):

I was reading a story the other day by a beginning writer, perhaps the second story she has published. Within four sentences I knew she was a writer I wanted to read and keep an eye on. What will happen to her writing in the future I have no idea; I can find good writing but I can't predict careers. I will preserve her anonymity, but here are the story's first four sentences.

They call it a state of emergency. White dervishes scour Stephenville, the blue arm of the plough impotently slashes through the snow. In St. John's where my mother is, the wires are frozen with sleet and the electricity is out. She's in the plaid chair, I know, one emergency candle and a flashing drink of rye.

The spark?

Well, yes, of course—*Flashing*.

Good writing is, quite simply, *alive*.

(That anonymous young beginner? Lisa Moore.)

I wrote in the introduction to *Best Canadian Stories 2013:*

I'm sometimes asked how I pick these stories, how I recognize them—"Aren't your choices and judgements purely subjective?"

Yes, absolutely and joyously.

Recently I'm returned from a holiday in Rome. There are twenty-two or twenty-three Caravaggio paintings in Rome in national collections housed in the Borghese, Barberini, Corsini, and Pamphilj palazzos, and in the churches which commissioned them for their chapels. I visited them all.

The church interiors are usually tenebrous. Through the gloom one can make out Depositions, Pietas, Dormitions, Martyrdoms, Flights into Egypt—acres of conventional paint until suddenly, a trumpet blast in the mouldering silence, *there* is a Caravaggio. One doesn't have to search for them. They proclaim themselves.

Just as these stories do.

They pick *me.*

Fresh from the Mountain on Tablets of Stone

In a rather doleful book, *Beauty and Sadness,* published in 2010, André Alexis took me to task for my critical shortcomings in general, and my "shaky arguments" in particular.

> Foremost among the shaky arguments is the idea that "good writing" is easily distinguished from bad. Anyone who has actually tried to set down rules to help discriminate between good and bad writing knows just how difficult this is. Metcalf doesn't set down rules, though. He takes sentences or paragraphs that he considers examples of "brilliant" writing and then does the written equivalent of pointing and saying "There, you see?" Having spent so much time arguing against the "academic," there really isn't much more that Metcalf *can* do. He has painted himself into a corner where any introduction of system or method would itself be considered "academic." Not suprisingly, Metcalf and his followers do a lot of pointing.

Followers, yet!

There's much I could say to André but it would be like talking to someone from Brussels; I will content myself by saying that I was *astounded* to read such boilerplate coming from a *writer.* Metcalf doesn't "set down rules" because there aren't any. Metcalf hasn't "painted himself into a corner" because no such corner exists. Metcalf wouldn't attempt to introduce "system or method" because there is not and cannot be such a method, such a system.

What system, what set of rules, can encompass both Alexander Pope and William Faulkner?

Rules and methods lead inevitably to Canons and Academies, steady work for the taxidermist.

Great art—and vibrant criticism—are alive and often contrary. Think of the work of Gerard Manley Hopkins, Ezra Pound, T.S. Eliot, James Joyce, William Faulkner, Samuel Beckett, Harold Pinter, and, to be provocative, Russell Hoban. All of it once reviled or ignored by literature's placemen and the Ivory Tower's gatekeepers.

Worth remembering that "The Waste Land" was reviewed in a contemporary journal as the ravings of "a drunken helot."

(The allusion is to the practice of the Spartans of making a slave (helot) drunk as an object-lesson to their youth of the evils of intemperance.)

It is usually more enlightening to listen to great practitioners:

> Academic training in beauty is a sham ... The beauties of the Parthenon, Venuses, nymphs, Narcissuses, are so many lies. Art is not the application of a canon of beauty but what the instinct and the brain can conceive beyond any canon. (Pablo Picasso)

Metcalf does a lot of "pointing" and saying "There, you see?" agreed; it helps, of course, to know what books to point *to*, and in them, what to point *at*. What more reliable sort of criticism *is* there than saying: "Weigh this in your palm; heft that; give this a gentle squeeze; smell that; taste this; is this apple larger, juicier, nicer-tasting than that? What should we do about a tomato with spots of black rot?"

Does André wish to make fruits and vegetables conform to the Rules of the EU, whose monstrous regiment of bureaucrats has recently ruled against knobbly potatoes?

Would André have me lay a ruler along a cucumber?

Would he have me, with calipers, measure for conformity the circumference of a kumquat?

What puppy-piddle!

"When a man talks of a system," said Lord Byron, "his case is hopeless."

Anthony Burgess, in the introduction to his *99 Novels: The Best in English since 1939* [1984], wrote:

> ...I do know that we carry a scale of values whereby we know that *Anna Karenina* is a great novel and *The Carpet Baggers* an inferior one, and that our standards have something to do with the management of language and concern with the human personality. Sometimes the management of language will be so remarkable that we will be prepared to forgive the lack of human interest; sometimes character interest will condone verbal and structural incompetence. Judging a novel is a rule-of-thumb matter; we cannot appeal to any aesthetic tribunal which will lay down universal laws.

A short story is whatever a writer can get away with.

If it works, it works.

It is either dead or alive.

THERE ARE NO RULES.

Each time a new talent and a new sensibility arrives to challenge "traditional forms" with "clever tricks" (professors Jackel and MacLulich) we are not watching, in Housman's words

> *... the day when heaven was falling,*
> *The hour when earth's foundations fled*

After the little disturbances of man, the tradition will enfold the vital new and that which is greater than us will flow onwards as it has for hundreds of years, and that apple will always taste nicer than this apple.

The Century List

I want to make clear that I am not claiming the Century List as a new or contrarian canon, or indeed as canon of any stripe. I think of the List as the beginning of a necessary conversation, a conversation that welcomes argument, enthusiasm, conviction, and dissent.

A canon cannot be promulgated by an elite as ours has been; a genuine canon represents the accumulated responses of informed readers over a long period of time. Virgil wrote: *omnia vinci amor*; Love *may* conquer all but it is *stone certainty* that Time *diminishes* all.

Professor Nick Mount of the University of Toronto, in his authoritative and engrossing new book *Arrival: The Story of CanLit*, annotates the "received" version of the score card. Of Dave Godfrey's novel, *The New Ancestors* (1970) he writes:

> ... the least enjoyable novel I have ever read. There's no plot to follow, no style to admire, no characters to feel for... Margaret Laurence thought it a work of genius.

The book was awarded the Governor General's Award and was much-trumpeted.

Of Rudy Wiebe's *The Temptations of Big Bear* (1973) he writes:

> Judging by the typos alone, Wiebe's editors had the same problem with his fourth novel that legions of undergraduates have had: staying awake while reading it... Wiebe's plodding

style—obese, ungainly sentences that trudge across the pages like the story's vanishing buffalo.

The book was awarded the Governor General's Award and was much-trumpeted.

In similarly breezy tone, so welcome a tone, Mount kisses off Hugh Hood, George Bowering, Audrey Thomas, etc.

Ninepin reputations falling.

I have already said that were I to rewrite the Century List, I would drop Margaret Laurence. If the List were to remain at fifty, I would be forced to immediately bump five more to make room for better writers of astonishing promise, four of whom I'm currently working with: Kevin Hardcastle, David Huebert, Martha Wilson, Kerry-Lee Powell, and Paige Cooper.

Cynthia Ozick in her *Critics, Monsters, Fanatics, and Other Literary Essays*, writes about the responses to literature of America's pre-eminent literary critic, Harold Bloom.

Bloom writes:

> There is no mystery about canons. A canon is a list. That's all. We need it because we *have* to read Shakespeare; we *have* to study Dante; we *have* to read Chaucer, Cervantes, the Bible, at least the King James Bible; we *have* to read certain authors; we have to read Proust, Tolstoy, Dickens, George Eliot and Jane Austen. It is absolutely inescapable that we have to read Joyce and Samuel Beckett. These are absolutely crucial writers. They provide an intellectual, I dare say a spiritual, value which has nothing to do with organized religion, or the history of institutional belief. They not only tell us things we have forgotten but they tell us things we couldn't possibly know without them. And they reform our minds. They make our minds stronger; they make us more vital. They make us alive!

And again:

> Everybody should make their own list, really, *particularly for the last fifty years or so.* [my italics]

What, for Bloom, goes into such making, such ecstatic making? What, by implication, are *we* called upon to do?

Again:

> Walt Whitman overwhelms me, possesses me, as only a few oth-ers—Dante, Shakespeare, Milton—consistently flood my entire being... Without vision, criticism perishes.

Again:

> True criticism recognizes itself as a form of memoir.

(What does he mean by "a form of memoir"? He means that criticism is a remembering, a re-creation of how one experienced a text, of how it made one *feel*, so Bloom sees criticism as a form of autobiography which is offered as a map or guide book for others to follow.)

Again:

> I believe there is no critical method except yourself.

With this, he drives down to the very core of his vast knowledge and experience of literature. He is here *bearing witness*; he is attesting to the need for each individual reader to recognize the work, *to fuse with it* at white hot heat, to consume it and to be consumed. At exalted pitch, he is talking about—surprise, surprise—an intense form of connoisseurship.

Bloom himself writes of his own "perilous [mental] balance." Ozick writes of him: "... the self that surrenders to the oracular, the self that willingly submits to submersion in ecstasy. Whatever it is that poets of the Orphic (or call it mystical) variety experience, Bloom too experiences, or longs to. In this he is like no other critic: why then, since he knows in his marrow what poets know, and long ago uncovered this knowledge as poets do, in childhood, is he not a poet? He tells us why he is not:

> I have been rereading *Moby-Dick* since I fell in love with the book in 1940, a boy of ten enthralled with Hart Crane, Whitman,

William Blake, Shakespeare. *Moby-Dick* made a fifth with *The Bridge, Songs of Myself,* Blake's *The Four Zoas,* and *King Lear,* a visionary company that transformed a changeling child into a exegetical enthusiast adept at appreciation rather than a poet. A superstitious soul, then and now, I feared being devoured by ravenous daemons if I crossed the line into creation.

After this discomforting brush against rapture, I must descend to sordid housecleaning. I see the Century List less as list than as an invitation to a process. I see this process of unseating, of "bumping," of "musical chairs," as a continual process taking place over a long period of time.

Past judgements stand as a silent reproach. Margaret Atwood's *Survival* gave entirely undeserved prominence to scriveners; this would be of no great importance had the wretched book duly faded, but it has recently been republished to inflict continuing damage.

In 1963, the Governor General's Award for Fiction was given to *Hugh Garner's Best Stories*; today, if he is remembered at all, he is rightly regarded as an acute embarrassment; in 1968 he was so respected that he was asked to write a foreword to Alice Munro's first book, *Dance of the Happy Shades.* It was, needless to say, uncouth and uncomprehending.

Garner situated himself among the elect and concluded:

> *These are women's stories that will appeal to women and men alike, unless somebody's been kidding me all this time.*

After some considerable stretch of time and much jostling and unseating, there will remain an irreducible core. Meanwhile, it is our responsibility to our literary culture to make the best-informed judgments of which we're at present capable, judgments made, one would hope, with as great a degree of asperity as we can muster.

In the introduction to *The Sacred Wood,* T.S. Eliot wrote: "It is the perpetual heresy of English culture to believe that only the first order mind, the Genius, the Great Man matters; that he is solitary and produced best by the least favourable environment."

Lesser writers, claims Eliot, in what might be a defense of the Century List, are important because

> ... a great literature is more than the sum of a number of great writers. Secondary writers provide collectively, and individually in varying degrees, an important part of the environment of the great writer... The continuity of a literature is essential to its greatness; it is very largely the function of secondary writers to preserve this continuity, and to provide a body of writings which is not necessarily read by posterity but which plays a great part in forming a link between those writers who continue to be read.

Tinkering with and adjusting the Century List, extending its dates, reconsidering omitted writers, considering dropping others—all this is a part of what literary criticism should be doing. Evelyn Waugh objected to

> ... the abandonment of the hierarchic principle. It has hitherto been assumed that works of art exist in an order of precedence with the great masters, Virgil, Dante and their fellows, at the top and the popular novel of the season at the bottom. The critic's task has been primarily to preserve and adjust this classification ... This, I believe, is still the critic's essential task...

The Century List runs, inclusive, from 1900–2015, and the order is simply alphabetical. When writers have published a Selected Stories I have always accepted their estimation of their own work rather than choosing a story they have not. In two cases—Clark Blaise and Leon Rooke—I have cited more than one title because the titles are, in effect, Selecteds.

Eleven of the fifty writers are given lengthier consideration than others because of the weight and presence their accumulated work has built over the years; such attention is simply their due. These eleven are, in alphabetical order, Caroline Adderson, Clark Blaise, Cynthia Flood, Keath Fraser, Mavis Gallant, Hugh Hood, K.D. Miller, Alice Munro, Kathy Page, Leon Rooke, and Diane Schoemperlen.

The necessarily brief quotations throughout are intended as a *menu degustation.*

Volume Titles

Caroline Adderson	*Bad Imaginings*
Joan Alexander	*Lines of Truth and Conversation*
Margaret Atwood	*Good Bones*
Mike Barnes	*Aquarium*
Clark Blaise	*Collected Stories* (4 Volumes)
Mary Borsky	*Influence of the Moon*
Ann Copeland	*The Golden Thread*
Libby Creelman	*Walking in Paradise*
Sharon English	*Uncomfortably Numb*
Shirley Faessler	*A Basket of Apples*
Cynthia Flood	*My Father Took a Cake to France*
Keath Fraser	*Thirteen Ways of Listening to a Stranger*
Mavis Gallant	*Selected Stories*
Zsuzsi Gartner	*All the Anxious Girls on Earth*
Paul Glennon	*How Did You Sleep?*
Douglas Glover	*Bad News of the Heart*
Terry Griggs	*Quickening*
Steven Heighton	*Flight Paths of the Emperor*
Jack Hodgins	*The Barclay Family Theatre*
Hugh Hood	*Light Shining Out of Darkness*
Isabel Huggan	*The Elizabeth Stories*
Dayv James-French	*The Afternoon of Day Five*
Mark Anthony Jarman	*Dancing Nightly in the Tavern*
Susan Kerslake	*The Book of Fears*
Shaena Lambert	*Oh, My Darling*
Margaret Laurence	*The Tomorrow-Tamer*
Elise Levine	*Driving Men Mad*

Norman Levine	*I Don't Want to Know Anyone Too Well: Collected Stories*
Annabel Lyon	*Oxygen*
Alistair MacLeod	*Island*
Alexander MacLeod	*Light Lifting*
K.D. Miller	*A Litany in Time of Plague*
Lisa Moore	*Degrees of Nakedness*
Alice Munro	*Selected Stories*
Kathy Page	*Paradise & Elsewhere*
Alice Petersen	*All the Voices Cry*
Gayla Reid	*To Be There with You*
Patricia Robertson	*City of Orphans*
Leon Rooke	*Painting the Dog* and *Hitting the Charts*
Rebecca Rosenblum	*Once*
Robyn Sarah	*Promise of Shelter*
Diane Schoemperlen	*Red Plaid Shirt: Stories New and Selected*
Carol Shields	*Collected Stories*
Ray Smith	*Cape Breton Is the Thought-Control Centre of Canada*
Russell Smith	*Young Men*
Linda Svendsen	*Marine Life*
Audrey Thomas	*The Path of Totality: New and Selected Stories*
Guy Vanderhaeghe	*Man Descending*
Kathleen Winter	*boYs*
Michael Winter	*One Last Good Look*

Individual Stories

Caroline Adderson	"Shiners"
Joan Alexander	"Five Months"

Margaret Atwood	"Poppies: Three Variations"
Mike Barnes	"Bitter Lake"
Clark Blaise	"A North American Education"
Mary Borsky	"Maps of the Known World"
Ann Copeland	"At Peace"
Libby Creelman	"Three Weeks"
Sharon English	"Clear Blue"
Shirley Faessler	"Henye"
Cynthia Flood	"The Animals in Their Elements"
Keath Fraser	"Healing"
Mavis Gallant	"Luc and His Father"
Zsuzsi Gartner	"How to Survive in the Bush"
Paul Glennon	"The Museum of the Decay of Our Love"
Douglas Glover	"Bad News of the Heart"
Terry Griggs	"Suddenly"
Steven Heighton	"Five Paintings of the New Japan"
Jack Hodgins	"The Lepers' Squint"
Hugh Hood	"Getting to Williamstown"
Isabel Huggan	"Jack of Hearts"
Dayv James-French	"Cervine"
Mark Anthony Jarman	"Cowboys Inc."
Susan Kerslake	"Push-Me Pull-You"
Shaena Lambert	"Crow Ride"
Margaret Laurence	"The Perfume Sea"
Elise Levine	"Boy"
Norman Levine	"Champagne Barn"
Annabel Lyon	"Joe in the Afterlife"
Alexander MacLeod	"The Loop"
Alistair MacLeod	"In the Fall"
K.D. Miller	"A Litany in Time of Plague"
Lisa Moore	"Ingrid Catching Snowflakes on Her Tongue"

Alice Munro	"Meneseteung"
Kathy Page	"Low Tide"
Alice Petersen	"Scottish Annie"
Gayla Reid	"To Be There with You"
Patricia Robertson	"City of Orphans"
Leon Rooke	"The Deacon's Tale"
Rebecca Rosenblum	"ContEd"
Robyn Sarah	"Looking for My Keys"
Diane Schoemperlen	"A Simple Story"
Carol Shields	"Good Manners"
Ray Smith	"Peril"
Russell Smith	"Crazy"
Linda Svendsen	"The Edger Man"
Audrey Thomas	"The More Little Mummy in the World"
Guy Vanderhaeghe	"King Walsh"
Kathleen Winter	"You Can Take One Thing"
Michael Winter	"Archibald the Arctic"

Caroline Adderson

Short Story Collections: *Bad Imaginings* (1993) and *Pleased to Meet You* (2006).

Novels: *A History of Forgetting* (1999), *Sitting Practice* (2003), *The Sky is Falling* (2010), *Ellen in Pieces* (2014), and *A History of Forgetting* [revised] (2015).

Book critic Philip Marchand once hailed Caroline Adderson as one of the four most notable emerging writers in Canada.

The stories in *Bad Imaginings* have an astonishing range both in subject matter and emotion. Adderson moves, always with great authority, from stories about troubled children— "Bread and Stone," "And the Children Shall Rise," and "Shiners"—to the complex comedy of "The Planet Earth," to fanciful pastiche of nineteenth century memoir-writing in "Gold Mountain: A Tale of Fortune-Seeking in British North America." She is somewhat drawn, perhaps, to the macabre, but any Gothic tendency is countered in the crispness of her language and the directness of her gaze. Nothing she writes is touched by sentimentality.

Her stories tend to make the reader uncomfortable; there is nothing emotionally easy in any of them and the poetry of her language increases our unease as it makes us work closer and closer in to the depth of the experience she is creating and making us share.

At the Wild Writers We Have Known conference in Stratford in 2000, recorded in *The New Quarterly Volume XXI, Nos. 2 and 3*, Terry Griggs began her comments on Caroline Adderson's writing by talking about the story "Shiners":

> *Laurence is wading stiff-legged into the lake, plastic bucket in one hand, the other reassuring the top of his head. Their grandmother has got him to put on a little sailor cap. Blue trunks, Thad's of two years before, sag at the crotch. On his chest are raw pink marks, a tender mottling where scabs were peeled off too soon.*

The writing is deft and swift and telling: Laurence's tentative "stiff-legged" wade into the lake, his own hand "reassuring the top of his head," the "little sailor cap" (a wrenching detail), the "sag at the crotch" (another one), the "raw pink marks," the "scabs... peeled off too soon." The effect this has is an immediate plunge into uneasiness, if not dread—you know this story is going to hurt, that something unpleasant is going to happen to this vulnerable child, that scabs are going to be ripped off too soon and that very likely they will be yours. Instinctively, protectively, one wants to turn away and not read further, but that is really not possible because of the appeal of the writing itself, the sheer loveliness of it. It is as alluring as the minnows, the "shiners," that attract Laurence's attention: "Sun-warmed shallows show minnows. Like the blades of small new knives, they are painfully silver, alluring. A cluster hovers over grey-green pebbles." By loveliness of the writing it's clear that I'm not referring to a lushly romantic style, but to a style of exactitude and particularity, in which words have been chosen very carefully and are placed just-so on the page with an economy—and an economy of metaphor—that nonetheless resonates, that has poetic impact.

This is the essence of Caroline Adderson's writing, but there is another aspect of her work that Terry Griggs only touches on but which I consider central—Caroline Adderson is very, very funny. Her humour flashes and glints throughout the book in a controlled way, but when deliberately let rip, as in the story "The Planet Earth," a comedienne stands revealed. The story records the friendship of two school friends, Denise and Barbara.

Denise was sick of her parents. Sick, sick, sick. It wasn't that they hounded or cramped her. Rather, they left her too much alone, starring in their own little melodrama with Denise as their audience. She booed and cat-called. "Get a divorce!" were her parting words. As for Barbara, her three older sisters were all pregnant at the same time. When the extended family united for Sunday dinner the vomiting terrified her. She wanted to live a little before that happened to her.

They rented a furnished bachelor suite in Kitsilano, its proximity to the beach compensating for the mildew. "Furnished" meant a kitchen table, two unmatching chairs and a Murphy bed that pulled out of the wall like a drawer. Opening the bed that first night, they shrieked in disgust; the mattress was a record in splotches of all the previous tenants. Or, as Denise imagined, it was an astigmatic cartographer's projection of the earth—the stains the continents misshapen and askew. South America was obviously blood. Barbara thought menstrual blood; Denise said, "Somebody picked a cherry." Neither wanted to lie down on it so they bought a cot and made this rule: the last one home sleeps with Murphy.

Denise didn't show her skinny legs. She wore long tie-dyed skirts and got a job in a café on Fourth Avenue, the Planet Earth, that specialized in vegan cuisine.

"I don't get it," said Barbara. "It's called Planet Earth but you sell food from Venus." Tofu made her fart so they instituted another rule: Denise couldn't bring any home. Instead she brought her contempt for the clientele of the Planet Earth. "I am a flower" she sang, swaying on the Murphy bed, arms swirling around her. "Feel my good vibrations." She claimed to despise everyone in Kitsilano except Barbara, Max—bus boy from the Planet Earth—and her boss, Peter, who owned the café but was at the same time a supposedly penniless Hare Krishna distributing the *Bhagavad Gita* downtown in front of the Bay.

Denise also brought home men she met in the café.

"This is Frank. Frank, tell Barb your favourite colour."

"Psychedelic."

Such fast, deft characterization. Such verbal pleasures ...

A profile of Caroline Adderson appears in *CNQ* No. 71, 2007.

A Fixed, Discerning Light, A Knowing Joy

Before discussing Caroline Adderson's short stories, I must record that I was involved editorially with *Bad Imaginings* and with her first novel, *A History of Forgetting*, and am involved with Caroline herself in long friendship. The same is true of many of the writers on the Century List. I hope that such association has not affected my literary judgement unduly. I'm not pleading guilty or apologizing for such familiarity; I've always thought one's relation to literature should be as daily as cornflakes.

Whenever I set out to write a story or an essay I can never settle to it until I've arrived at a title, and that might take days dithering; I suppose what I'm doing is probing gingerly towards the very heart of what I want to say. For this essay's title, I found myself drawn to, and mentally wandering about in, religious poems of the seventeenth century: Richard Crashaw, John Donne, George Herbert, Henry Vaughan, Thomas Traherne. I wasn't quite sure why, until, browsing, I came across a poem of Henry Vaughan's "Quickness," which contains the following stanza:

> *Life is a fixed Discerning light,*
> *A knowing joy;*
> *No chance, or fit; but ever bright,*
> *And calm and full, yet doth not cloy.*

I thought that this did capture much of what I wanted to say about Caroline's work. "Fixed" because she has a steady gaze; "discerning," showing good judgement and taste, because she does; "light" because she casts it; "a knowing joy" because, despite her shrewdness, her grip on the world's realities, there is always joy in her detail of the observed world, a joy in her fresh-minted language.

The last two lines of "Quickness" play with the word in its old meaning of "living" or "alive," a meaning now only surviving in such expressions as "cut to the quick" and "the quick and the dead."

> But in life is what none can express,
> *A quickness which my God hath kissed.*

But why was I thinking of Caroline Adderson in, vaguely, religious terms? To the best of my knowledge, she hasn't had much connection with religion, organized or otherwise, since Sunday School. But her work seems to me to carry a moral weight.

What does "moral" mean? Well, not adherence to any set of precepts. Rather, a fundamental seriousness. Though, at the same time, she is among the funniest of Canadian writers. I think I might mean by "moral" closely paid attention that expresses itself in fastidious and brilliantly constructed sentences. "Moral," then, because deeply caring, because deeply observed.

Detail observed like the tumult of welcome greeting the first troop ship to return to Vancouver at the end of World War I in the story "The Hypochondria Club":

> Boys on bicycles zip up and down Dallas Road, playing cards salvo in their spokes.

The noun "salvo" used ambiguously as verb and noun; the context of its use, the return of the veterans; auxiliary to "salvo," *zip*; the boys innocent of salvoes the trench troops have endured. The *noise*. All caught in a word.

In the same story, the wealthy hotel resident Mr. Stone, at whom all the female staff set their caps, is observed:

> Surprisingly, none of the younger maids seemed to appeal to him, despite their coyness, the way, for example, they tickled the furniture with their feather dusters.

"Tickled"! And the way the sentence unnecessarily lingers before it gets there, just as the maids are lingering. "Tickled" is so "frothily" naughty, so cartoonishly funny.

In *A History of Forgetting*, Denis, the aging hairdresser is observed:

> Despite decades of dishes laced with butter and, yes, lard, Denis had never gone to fat. Almost imperceptible, his transition from blond to grey.

The alliteration of the first three words *embodies* the repetitions, the hundreds of dishes. The second sentence make us wait for its meaning until it fades to its final "grey."

Lesser writers would have written: "this transition from blond to grey had been almost imperceptible."

These two versions of a sentence vividly demonstrate *how* being *is*.

Again in *A History of Forgetting*, the young thug Vorst is observed, a white supremacist accused of the "gay-bashing" murder of Alison's hairdresser friend, Christian. Alison and Malcolm stare at Vorst as he appears in the dock.

> Above his shirt collar, the Adam's apple could have been a fist. A blocky head and a face sullen and appallingly young and irredeemable. Then Vorst turned his blond close-cropped head to look back at his judge. The girl clutched Malcolm's arm; Malcolm, too, was shaken. In his long career he had seen his

share of scalp afflictions—scales and shingles, baldness in patches, unhealed sores—but here, on this teenager's square skull, was a disease of an entirely different magnitude marked out in right angles with a razor.

A magnificent build to the unwritten word: swastika. A word all the more powerful because we have been forced to supply it.

In the following scene from *A History of Forgetting*, Alison and her mother are delivering bread rolls to the Mission for the Christmas Dinner:

Her mother took the bags into the kitchen, reappearing a few minutes later empty-handed. "Mission accomplished." They went back out into the rain.

"Pretty depressing," said Alison.

"I know. I always have a little cry on Christmas night. Your father thinks I'm crazy."

"Why do you do it then?" She and Jeffy had been raised agnostic. "Do you believe in God after all?"

"No. I just add that extra letter," said her mother. "I believe in Good."

They got into the car and her mother found her keys, but before she turned on the ignition, Alison reached out and stopped her hand. "What about Jeffy?"

"What about him?"

"Would you mind if he was?"

"Gay?" Instantly, she cheered up. "They're very good to their mothers, I hear."

I set out to quote this scene because I wanted, soppily I admit, to associate Caroline with goodness of the mother's kind, thereby committing the cardinal sin of reading fiction as autobiography. The second I'd finished copying out the passage, however, I realised that I'd been waylaid, yet again, by Caroline's prose.

Alison reached out and stopped her hand.

I marvelled at these words in their context. Alison's touch does not grasp or pull or hold; it arrests with butterfly delicacy. The touch creates sudden intimacy of feeling between mother and daughter, intimacy that enables Alison to broach the emotional question of her young brother's sexual orientation.

Who but Caroline Adderson could have invented "stopped"?

"Moral" or "weight," then, seems to mean to me the texture of the writing, observation and invention translated into language that has been loved into honed service. My struggles to express this and to assert language's value, are, perhaps, a struggle against ideas, simplifications, generalities, grand encompassing theories, against the Northrop Fryes, against the intellect's eagerness to foreclose. The struggle crops up again in my notes on Ann Copeland and Alice Petersen. With Ann Copeland I talk about clarity. With Alice Petersen I talk about "a special intensity of light, a luminosity" and go on to say, "If talking *connoisseur*, paintings, say, or pots, the word 'presence' would be in the air."

"Presence" is not an airy-fairy notion; it is a quality of original-ity, perfection, power that proclaims itself. Stand in an art gallery or museum and some item might impress itself upon you, ravish you away from your quotidian surroundings so that only you and it exist. That commanding impression is instantaneous; explaining it to yourself or others, the how and why of it, might take years.

How does one explain a *coup de foudre*?

(Though it is also true that the lightning bolt is more likely to strike if the viewer has undergone education in, and exposure to, the class of objects to which the magic item belongs.)

To return, however, to the matter of language.

Novelist and literary critic David Lodge wrote *Language of Fiction* in 1966. Routledge re-issued the book in 2002 as a "Routledge Classic." Lodge as a novelist is so unweighty as to be in the Soufflé division; *Language of Fiction*, however, plods mightily to arrive at what, decades ago, I simply assumed as my starting point.

Lodge's conclusion:

What I hope to have shown is that, if we are right to regard the art of poetry as an art of language, then so is the art of the novel; and that the critic of the novel has no special dispensation from that close and sensitive engagement with language we naturally expect from the critic of poetry.

Again

> ... Amis's use of language may be inextricably part of his importance as Henry James's was of his, or Joyce's was of his. That James and Joyce are vastly *more* important writers need not disturb us. They use language more ambitiously and with more consistent success; Amis less ambitiously and with less consistent success; [John] Braine less and less still. The important thing is that they can all be measured on the same scale—the creative use of language. For ultimately language is the only tangible evidence we have for those vast, vague, unreliable, qualities which we bandy about in literary criticism: "truth to life," "moral seriousness," "psychological insight," "social awareness."

Time, then, to return to *Bad Imaginings*.

The collection appeared twenty-five years ago. It was obviously brilliant and was well-received. Its impact at the time, its sophistication, its glitter against the background of dull contemporaries, can now scarcely be imagined. The stories ranged widely. There were stories rather gothic, "The Hypochondria Club," "Oil and Dread," "Grunt If You Love Me," this last with an almost Flannery O'Connor flavour. "And the Children Shall Rise" edges towards Shirley Jackson territory. As does "Bread and Stone." Both stories are deeply unsentimental. Then there's "Shiners," a story in the Eudora Welty mold or Alice Munro-via-Welty. "Gold Mountain" is a pastiche of Victorian memoirs, of travel writing, with such gothic flourishes as cross-dressing, buggery, and the wholesale murder of Celestials gold-panning in the claim next to the narrator.

I've never talked to Caroline in depth about who she was reading, but I know she lived in New Orleans for a time and so assume she was familiar with Southern writing. What aspiring writer wouldn't have been?

My favourite story in the book is "The Hanging Gardens of Babylon," about Lillian and her brother Rory, frogs mating, and Lillian's sudden apprehension of the world's threating sexuality.

But behind all this hovers a but...

The collection is undoubtedly brilliant and remains one of the high points of Canadian short fiction, but in retrospect it is a beginner's book; it pales beside what was to come. In retrospect, it is a dress rehearsal, a calling card, a job interview; the audition, as it were, of a prospective casino dealer who nonchalantly fans a deck across the baize. What I mean here is that the stories, all brilliant as they are, wear their Sunday Best and are on their best behaviour. One can sense standing behind them their immediate and distinguished progenitors. Only the story "The Planet Earth" relaxes towards the everyday, the colloquial, and the even more powerful stories that were to appear in *Pleased to Meet You*.

This second volume of stories appeared thirteen years later. In 2011, Adderson was granted a belated entry in *The Concise Oxford Companion to Canadian Literature* (Second Edition). The pedestrian and peculiar entry was almost entirely devoted to tedious plot summaries, but the contributor did make a stab at evaluation in comments on *Pleased to Meet You*: a second collection of stories "which for this reader was disappointing, in spite of the praise it received. The stories lack the depth, originality, and readability of those in her first collection; the characters and plots are thin and uninteresting, though they summon up every day behaviour and verbal exchanges convincingly, sometimes amusingly."

I do not put trust much in the literary sensibility of one who describes "conversation" as "verbal exchanges."

What Caroline was doing in *Pleased to Meet You* was struggling free from the ancestors, fighting through to new forms that would allow us to see and feel anew.

"We could not write *our* stories in *their* voices," sums up the point of the struggle. Or, I should add, "*their* forms."

Immediately following *Bad Imaginings* came the novel *A History of Forgetting* (1999). This book has a troubled history that Caroline describes in an article she wrote for *CNQ* No. 93 (2015). In brief, Porcupine's Quill delayed the publication date without informing her and in considerable umbrage she took the book away and published it with my friend, Patrick Crean at Key Porter, replacing me as editor.

Years later, when the book was out of print, we asked Caroline if Biblioasis could re-publish it in our ReSet series. She agreed but took the opportunity to rewrite the book entirely.

The first version was splendid, but the 2015 rewrite of *A History of Forgetting*, is, without reservation, superb. I would place it in the half-dozen best novels Canada has yet produced.

Both versions of the book have strong links to the story form. The novel progresses in a series of vividly realized scenes that could be read as something like miniature short stories. The omniscient narrator's role is discreet and downplayed, made unobtrusive by bringing what is seen and described close to the characters' sensibilities. The reader is brought close to what is pictured, and forced to "compose" and "deduce" the meanings of scenes, and, as a result, is the more deeply emotionally engaged. This approach culminates in *Ellen in Pieces* (2014), a novel composed entirely in discrete short stories, in pieces.

Some critics have described her novels disparagingly as "episodic." What attic muse are they harking back to? Robertson Davies? It amuses me that the word "episodic" was used to describe my first novel, *Going Down Slow*, forty years ago. *Plus ça change…*

Thinking how very hard it must be emotionally and technically to rewrite a novel, I find myself drifting into a digression.

One of my favourite British authors is Beryl Bainbridge. She completely rewrote two of her novels; *Another Part of the Wood* (1968) was rewritten in 1979 and *A Weekend with Claude* (1967) was rewritten in 1981. Her novels, too, move in scenes and in quite marvellously managed dialogue (or "verbal exchanges") of false starts, interruptions, non-sequiturs, silences, misunderstandings. She started life as an actress; Caroline is married to a filmmaker; I wonder if that has anything to do with their attraction to the episodic form?

Oddly, the very *texture* of Bainbridge's writing also reminds me of Caroline's; so does her dippy humour. I've no idea if Caroline has read her.

Here Brenda and Freda first meet each other in *The Bottle Factory Outing*:

> When they had first met in the butcher's shop on the Finchley Road, it had been Brenda's lack of control, her passion, that had been the attraction. Standing directly in front of Freda she had asked for a pork chop, and the butcher, reaching for his cleaver on the wooden slab, had shouted with familiarity 'Giving the old man a treat are you?' at which Brenda had begun to weep, moaning that her husband had left her, that there was no old man in her world. She had trembled in a blue faded coat with a damaged fur collar and let the tears trickle down her face. Freda led her away, leaving the offending cut of meat on the counter, and after a week they found a room together in Hope Street, and Freda learnt it wasn't the husband that had abandoned Brenda, it was she who had left him because she couldn't stand him coming home drunk every night from the Little Legion and peeing on the front step. Also, she had a Mother-in-Law who was obviously deranged, who sneaked out at dawn to lift the eggs from under the hens and drew little faces on the shells with a biro.

What *is* it I find so entrancing about Bainbridge? Well, the humour, obviously, but from the quotation above it is the sentence:

> She had trembled in a blue faded coat with a damaged fur collar and let the tears trickle down her face.

Another example from *Sweet William*, Ann seeing William and being smitten:

> It was then Ann saw William. He was standing with his hands on his hips, looking up at her. He wore a pair of black swimming trunks and his hair was flat to his head. For one moment Ann stopped breathing and the next she wanted to hide. She thought

everyone else was free and undressed, while she was cumbersome and conspicuous in her grey coat and her court shoes. She was even holding a bag; it was dangling over the rail, bulky with her documents and Emily's head-band. She almost let go of it. She had never really liked nudity—all that expanse of flesh touched by the grave—unless you'd been away on holiday and become less obscene. But he looked beautiful, outlined in light that seemed to waver and coalesce, though she knew it was only the reflection of the glass roof on the water. There was so much noise and movement: the screaming, the splashing, the mouths opening in one great shout, the putty-coloured bodies plunging from the diving board. A wave of sound and light rose up and engulfed her. She felt she was drowning.

Beryl Bainbridge was a scrupulous writer; the seeming ease of her writing was in fact hard-won. I was moved by the words of her daughter, Jojo Davies, in the *Observer* obituary:

> Since her death I have been rereading all her books, slowly, because I don't want them to end. They make me feel connected with her. I reread sentences because they are so exquisite, so well crafted. They are beautiful to read aloud. What she called the dum-te-um—the rhythm of the language—took hours to create. It was normal practice to write five pages to get a paragraph.

★

How utterly such writing differs from the following first page of a contemporaneous novel:

> "David Crimond is here in a *kilt!*"
> "Good God, is Crimond here? Where is he?"
> "Over in that tent or marquee or whatever you call it. He's with Lily Boyne."
> The first speaker was Gulliver Ashe, the second was Conrad Lomas. Gulliver was a versatile, currently unemployed, young

Englishman in his early thirties, pointedly vague about his age. Conrad was a more gorgeously young young American student. He was taller than Gulliver who was rated as tall. Gulliver had never hitherto met Conrad, but he had heard of him and had addressed the remark which caused such excitement to, jointly, Conrad and his partner Tamar Hernshaw. The scene was the so-much-looked-forward-to Commem Ball at Oxford, and the time about eleven p.m. It was midsummer and the night was not yet, and was indeed never entirely to be, dark. Above the various lighted marquees, from which various musics streamed, hung a sky of dusky blue already exhibiting a few splintery yellow stars. The moon, huge, crumbly like a cheese, was still low down among trees beyond the local streamlets of the river Cherwell which bounded the more immediate territory of the college. Tamar and Conrad had just arrived, had not yet danced. Gulliver had confidently addressed them since he knew, though not well, Tamar, and had heard who her escort was to be. The sight of Tamar filled Gulliver, in fact, with irritation, since *his* partner for the momentous night was to have been (only she had cried off at the last moment) Tamar's mother Violet. Gulliver did not particularly like Violet, but had agreed to be paired with her to oblige Gerard Hernshaw, whom he usually obliged, even obeyed. Gerard was Tamar's uncle, or "uncle," since he was not Violet's brother but her cousin. Gerard was considerably older than Gulliver. Gerard's sister Patricia, who was to have had Jenkin Riderhood as her partner, had also not turned up, but had (unlike Violet, who seemed to have no reason) a good reason, since Gerard's father, long ill, had suddenly become iller. Gulliver, though of course thrilled to be asked, was irritated by being paired by Gerard with Violet, which seemed to relegate Gulliver to the older generation. Gulliver would not have minded partnering Tamar, though he was not especially "keen" on her.

There, you see?

From the recipient of the James Tait Black Memorial, the Whitbread, and the Booker prizes, the opening page of *The Book and the Brotherhood* by Iris Murdoch.

An Object Lesson in writing that is DOA.

"The Hanging Gardens of Babylon" from *Bad Imaginings* dates from around 1990, appearing in book form in 1993. It is both short and powerful. The plot aspect of it is simple. Two small children are told to go out and collect the mail from the rural communal mailbox away and down the road. Their house has grown dirty, food is running out, their mother is confined to bed, close to giving birth. Their father is distracted, distraught.

The younger child, Rudy, has been "chatting happily" to his mother.

> With his two fingers he began to march up her arm, "Dee dee dee, dee dee de... At the base of her stomach, rising under the quilt like a jelly mould, he stopped and in his play-voice squealed, "My, what a big hill!"

The two children set out.

> ...the bright biting smell of new leaves. Rudy went with his face up and nostrils wide, she behind, hands deep in pockets. They heard the call of one bird to another, dee dee dee, dee dee dee, the answer in variation meaning yes, no, perhaps—meaning, *yes, soon.*

Rudy spies something in the centre of the road ahead, a squashed cat. They stand staring. "Rudy made the sign of the cross. On the wide, crusted-over eye was a pivoting fly."

The sight prompts Lilian to tell Rudy that Daddy had told her that, the next day, the doctors were going to cut Mummy open and pull out the baby.

> "What do you think happens to people when they get cut open like that?"
> Rudy still looked at the cat.
> "Answer me."
> "Poor cat," said Rudy, patting its head gently.

The children walk on down the road.

Rudy asks Lilian to tell him again about the Hanging Gardens, something she's been reading about. She liked to instruct and so tells him again about the terraces, how they held examples of every kind of animal and all the plants in the world...

"Which plants?"
"All plants. That's all I'll say."
"Easter lilies," he said.

This, in much abbreviated form, is the "set up" for the story's central event and image, the frogs.

The story is full of characteristic Adderson detail, that exactitude, that richness we have come to treasure.

"Lilian looked in the bread box. She said, talking into the box, her voice sounding hollow, "There's just crusts..."

...*sounding hollow*...

And the fly on the cat's eyeball *pivoting*.

She slips only once, the bird calls meaning "yes, no, perhaps— meaning, *yes, soon.*" Brilliant foreshadowing of the meaning that Lilian later gives to the idea of Babylon, but it is Adderson rather than Lilian. She wanted it, of course, for its reference back to Rudy's "marching" fingers, dee dee dee over their mother's "jelly mould."

The linkage of imagery is fairly obvious; the pregnant mother about to undergo a Caesarean, Spring fecundity, the dead cat, Rudy's possible linkage of the cat to what happens to cut-open people (though that is rather vague, as is Rudy.) Slightly odd and insistent is the imagery of Easter, the lack of Easter Eggs, the Easter lilies, Rudy crossing himself, the "cathedral" sound of frogs "like mass in amphibian tongue"; all references, at a remove, to the Crucifixion and Resurrection.

Then arrives the central scene that all the foregoing has prepared us for: at the mailbox, they encounter a child-stranger visiting neighbours. He wears a toque that says: Put On A Happy Face. He leads them to his frogs.

"Ours was empty too," said the boy with the toque. "It's a holiday, remember?" He was staying at his grandparents' for Easter, he told them. His face was dirty, some orange sauce circling his mouth. He tilted back his head and narrowed his eyes. "I got a secret."

"What kind of secret?" asked Rudy.

"Come on," he said.

They followed him back in the direction they had just come from, the boy looking for something in the ditch. "This is it," he said finally.

Together they jumped the ditch and pushed through the aspen scrub into the trees. Then they found themselves standing in a small clearing beside a shallow pond formed by spring run-off. All around and rising up through the trees like cathedral music was the deep, frantic, pulsing sound of frogs. It was hurried and overlapping, repetitive, an urgent chorus like mass in amphibian tongue. A plastic bucket sat next to the pond. The boy went over to it and beckoned.

They came and looked inside. The bucket was half-full of water and teeming with frogs, coupled frogs, one in front that made the motions of swimming, one in back with its ridiculous arms clutching the other's middle. This seemed like such an absurd thing for a frog to be doing, squeezing the breath out of another, not letting go even when the boy put his hand in and stirred.

"Isn't that funny?" said Rudy.

Lilian glanced at the boy and at Rudy who swayed as if the sound had hands to move him, then back at the frogs. "What are they doing?" she asked.

"Fucking," said the boy.

He waded into the pond and, splashing around, caught up a handful of doubled frogs. Returning to the bucket, he dropped them in.

"What are they doing?" asked Lilian.

"I told you. They're fucking. You know what fucking is, don't you?"

"Of course," said Lilian.

"Isn't it funny?" said Rudy.

She looked again in the bucket at the piggy-back frogs swimming in circles, cycling around and around, no beginning or end. The frog song seemed louder now, insistent, listen-listen-listen.

She was dizzy, then afraid, of the song and the strange boy, this hidden centrifugal clearing revolving with frogs. Clearing, earth, everything, turning, circling.

The boy took Rudy's hand and guided it into the bucket. Rudy drew back quickly and laughed. Listen-listen-listen. The song lulled and agitated. She put her hands on her ears. The way the boy held a pair of frogs, learning their weight, they were something to throw. Listen-listen-listen.

"Funny!" cried Rudy.

"What are you going to do?" she asked.

He shrugged, then wound back his arm. Even airborne the frogs did not uncouple. They sailed straight for a tree, struck it—a terrible jellied splash on the bark.

The story from this point *could* have become too obvious, didactic almost, but it becomes instead disturbingly disordered, visionary almost.

Rudy suddenly claims to know what the frogs were doing. They were going to the Hanging Gardens. We are to understand, I think, that for Rudy, the Hanging Gardens, though nebulous, are a sort of paradisaical zoo. He says that the frogs are going there because he remembers Lilian telling him that all the kinds of animal in the world are gathered there; he also says it because he *doesn't* understand what the "funny" frogs were doing but wishes to assert himself.

The stranger boy has told Lilian the frogs are fucking. That she's unsure what this means is strongly implied in that she asks again.

The stranger-boy asks, "You know what fucking is, don't you?"

"Of course," said Lilian.

She doesn't know, exactly, but suspects.

This dawning apprehension explains her fury with Rudy.

The whole scene pivots on the stranger-boy killing the frogs—pivots on the words "a terrible jellied splash," words that immediately take us back to the mother's "jelly mould."

And suddenly she was furious. "Don't you know there's no hanging gardens of Babylon? Have you ever heard of that place before? There's no such place as Babylon! It's *made up!*"

She was shaking and he was backing away from her with a fierce angry face.

"There is so!" he cried. "Too bad, Lilly. Too bad you don't know where Babylon is."

"There is no Babylon!"

Rudy ran away up the road.

Through the aspen stand the breeze was filtering. Again she heard that call, dee dee dee, dee dee dee—the bird-call, Rudy-call, then the sound of snow melting in the ditch. Gradually the sound grew louder, becoming the roar of a river, of a waterfall, water gushing up out of the open earth, pushing things forward. She saw the tumble of waking insects on the crest, and animals, cats, dogs, snakes, all animals, *which ones? tell me,* all animals and people, sweeping forward, on and on and on to the beginning again. Listen-listen-listen. Listen-listen-listen.

When Rudy finally disappeared, a dark bird flew by. She watched as it dipped and swooped and circled, circled again. Then it vanished too, in the direction of Babylon. Everything in the direction of Babylon.

The story ends, then, with Lilian's disillusionment and disgust, her first bite of The Apple. The beauty and poetry of the fabled "Babylon" cannot exist in the same world as the "pulsing sound of frogs." With her new, unarticulated knowledge, Lilian undergoes something like an apocalyptic vision, seeing "Babylon" not as a beautiful place *there* but as Horror *here,* omnipresent and always ongoing, violent, murderous, the songs no longer dee dee dee but listen-listen-listen to the *real* songs, the songs that croak and pulse.

The emotional linkage by female children of sex with violence and death is scarcely new. See, for example, the entry on Alice Munro's story "Images" discussed in the essay "Signs of Invasion." Or read K.D. Miller's story "To Hell and Back" in *Give Me Your Answer.* There aren't too many new themes, only new performances.

(One niggling aside: two sentences in the story discomfort me.

All around and rising up through the trees like cathedral music was the deep, frantic, pulsing sound of frogs. It was hurried and overlapping, repetitive, an urgent chorus like mass in an amphibian tongue.

When I read this twenty-five years ago, my general reaction was probably *wow*! The older me thinks: too clever and obtrusive in its cleverness. And woolly to boot. Is she implying that the noise of the frogs is the annunciation of a new, or rather, older sacrament? Or what?)

My brief synopsis of the end of Caroline's story is an example of "the intellect's eagerness to foreclose"; my plodding words capture nothing of the *how* of it. What is important about the penultimate and final paragraphs is the way they *perform themselves*.

The penultimate paragraph is a gathering wave, a welter of words, a tumbling torrent, a rhetoric that, by piling on detail checks and delays climax, tension building, until the wave casts us up on the sandbar of the Here with the admonition to Listen-listen-listen.

The final paragraph, bleakly resigned, shows us a sky, a lone dark bird circling, until it, too, vanishes towards Babylon.

Were I teaching, I'd be saying, "Read it aloud. Listen to it. Read it again."

If the stories in *Bad Imaginings* are on their best behaviour, a little stiff in their Sunday Best, the stories in *Pleased to Meet You* are unbuttoned. The imagery and lyricism are less evidently wrought and the stories give us no sense of "having a literary experience." They cheerfully assail us. It is this relaxation of style that Adderson had been working through to; she had liberated herself into it by writing the two intervening novels since *Bad Imaginings*. It would have been impossible, of course, to have written an entire new novel faithful to strict Poundian percepts. The new stories had also liberated themselves from modernist expectation that a character achieve "self-knowledge" or "richer emotional understanding," or, vaguely, "growth."

The story closest to such concerns is the story "Falling," and a honey of a story it is, a delicate poem of a story about a seemingly happy executive whose corporate armour is pierced by a line in a poem he cannot exactly recall. Of the stories more typical of this second volume, I am particularly fond of "Mr. Justice," "Knives," the extraordinary razzle-dazzle of "Ring Ring," and "The Maternity Suite."

I wish to talk about "The Maternity Suite" simply because it is Caroline Adderson at her funniest. The characters in the story are: Betty, long-suffering mother to Pauline and Anna. Anna is the younger and Good daughter, Pauline the older and Bad daughter. At the beginning of the story, Anna, married to Carey, is mildly pregnant. Pauline, married to no one, is massively pregnant, the possible father any one of a variety of Mexicans, ex-pat Germans, or Americans. These pregnancies are not coterminous.

Betty's husband, father of Pauline and Anna, dies of cancer near the story's beginning. Towards the end of his life he is reunited with the United Church and is visited and administered to by the "little Reverend" who looked "every inch his denomination in corduroys and earnestness."

Listening outside the door, Betty learns that "The Light of Christ was a radiant presence in the room."

Betty's marriage to Robert has been lacking radiance.

> Even when Robert had crept across the ravine of decency that separated their twin beds, she never let go of the reins of her senses. She focussed instead on the ingredients and steps for making bouillabaisse.

Pauline, the "wayward" first child, was born wayward.

> Pauline was born tangled in umbilical cord and with her first shrill and indignant vocalization seemed to announce that she would never be tied up or down again. Then, as if anyone could have mistaken her meaning, she continued screaming for three months. It was a demand for love fiercer than Betty had ever imagined. Her nipples cracked from giving and Pauline drew her blood.

Anna was the quiet one, so placid she was cast as the Infant Jesus in the United Church nativity play where previously they had used a big bald doll. Pauline, three years old that Christmas, flossy in her lamb's suit, clustered with the rest of the preschool flock around Anna in the manger. Betty and Robert could hear her crying "Meow," while everyone else bleated. At home after the service, Pauline insisted Anna be put to bed in a box in the garage.

In later years, Anna graduated to playing Mary. Pauline had no further interest in Sunday school theatrics; the days and nights of her real life provided drama enough. Her preteen vocational aspiration was to be a bank robber. She shoplifted for practice and got caught. Robert, in charge of discipline, of disciplining Pauline, grounded her for a year. This didn't stop the boys from coming. So skinny, shaggy and sullen, all wearing the same grey hooded sweatshirts as they filed down to the rumpus room, they reminded Betty of a chain gang. She strongly suspected Pauline had relinquished her virginity at thirteen, probably in their own basement, though she could never bring herself to ask. Whom could she blame for her daughter's loss? She and Robert were decent people. They had faults, certainly; they played too much bridge, for example, but they had never modelled lust.

Anna, in contrast, lives a life of unaffected innocence.

The professor was explaining something marvellous a little monk had done with sweet peas. Anna closed her eyes and pictured the flowers that scaled the fence in their yard every summer, a tangle of moth-winged blooms, some pink, others red or mauve or white. As a girl she believed Jesus made dawn rounds through the garden with a brush and palette, mixing paints with dew. Now, at twenty, that was the explanation she still preferred. Science was not saving her father. All it had done was disillusion her.

She remembered Pauline showing her an advertisement in *Teen*. "What's Tampax?" She was only ten at the time, too young, Betty thought, to know how tedious her fate would be. "I wish," Betty had answered, "you wouldn't read those magazines."

So perhaps her own prudishness had contributed to Pauline's preternatural curiosity. She vowed to do better by Anna. "Inside a woman's body is a nest," she told her, and from Anna's perplexed look Betty knew she was thinking of twigs and grass and tangled bits of string.

"It's made of blood."

Anna's bottom lip began to quiver. "I know! Pauline told me, but I hoped it wasn't true!"

Anna being prettier than Pauline, taller and fair, Betty had expected from her an even longer line of convict suitors. They never came. On Friday nights Anna went to the library with her girlfriends. She joined a swim club and spent every weekend at the pool or painting watercolour pictures of butterflies and flowers in her room. Into adolescence she sailed on gentle breezes.

Pauline's escape from the domination of "the patriarchy" (ie. her father) to the dubious enchantments of ex-pat Mexico is richly detailed.

She got a standby flight to Acapulco and from there took the bus. Took buses. Often she was the only *gringa* on them. The men crowded around her, clicking and whistling like starlings. The only English phrase she heard was, "Hey, Blondie." At first she didn't realize they meant her.

Almost immediately she found herself seduced. It was the fruit. The mango's hairy core as she sucked it reminded her of a Mound of Venus. So like the women's fallen breasts were the papaya, their seeds slippery, cum-coated. She bounced on the seat while the huge breasts of the peasant woman next to her, unrestrained by a brassiere, moved in the same orgiastic rhythm. The dark oily faces of the men with their ripe lips began to excite rather than repel her. When she went up to the driver it was partly to feel their cockroach eyes scurrying across her body as she pitched and swayed in the aisle. She gestured for him to stop the bus: too much fruit, too much fruit! He understood and, though they were driving through forest, did not apply the brake until they had passed the sheltering trees and come to a mile of field. She clambered down and, with nowhere to go for privacy, squatted in the ditch. A hot flux gushed exquisitely from her. Glancing back at the bus windows lined with faces, she giggled.

⋆

"You shouldn't eat those,"' someone across the aisle said. "You shouldn't eat anything that's not cooked or peeled."

She'd thought he was Mexican, but now that he had given himself away, she noticed his pallor. His accent was American. "The weirdest goddamn thing just happened to me," he told her, "so please don't eat those strawberries."

He had been working in the mountains on a development project, was heading back there now, though the way he was feeling he wasn't sure he would make it. Eight months in poverty and isolation had not agreed with his bowels. He'd lost weight steadily until the morning he knew he had to leave. Something wasn't right. "I had that, you know, gut feeling, ha ha." They got him on the Oaxaca bus, but he had to keep asking the driver to stop.

"I know, I know," said Pauline. "And everybody watched."

"I wondered what the hell could be coming out. I mean, I wasn't eating anything. There I was, hunkering. I looked and— whoa there! Whoa just a minute! A piece of my goddamn intestine!"

"What?" cried Pauline, recoiling. "Coming out?"

"I was shitting out my guts."

"No way."

"Yeah. So I stuffed it back in and got back on the bus gripping my ass. Days it seemed to take to get to Oaxaca. Months. The whole time I sat there clenching."

"Oh, God,"' said Pauline. "Oh, my God."

"Finally, I got to the clinic. My guts are coming out! My guts are coming out! Crazy *gringo*. The doctor saw me right away. No rubber glove, nothing. Just stuffed his finger up my Khyber Pass.

Señor, he said with perfect manners, I suggest you go right now to the toilet."

His white face sheening with sweat, he paused and stretched his lips in a slow, sick grimace.

"Are you okay now?" Pauline asked.

"It was as long as my arm. Jesus Christ. Have you ever *seen* a tapeworm?"

Life in the hippie enclave in which she fetches up is as languorous as that led by the mariners in Tennyson's "Song of the Lotus-Eaters."

> How sweet it were, hearing the downward stream,
> With half-shut eyes ever to seem
> Falling asleep in a half-dream!
> To dream and dream, like yonder amber light,
> Which will not leave the myrrh-bush on the height;
> To hear each other's whispered speech;
> Eating the Lotos day by day,
> To watch the crisping ripples on the beach,
> And tender curving lines of creamy spray;

Here is Adderson, Tennyson in modern dress.

The waves rolled onto the beach, then retreated—a rhythm as regular as a metronome set on largo. It was the very pace of life, the timing of those days. She rose early, took a walk, then climbed the hill to the café for breakfast. Afterward, she would lie on the sand reading a book she'd picked up some-where. Maybe the story didn't interest her, or the sun was glaring off the page, but she found herself always reading the same six pages over and over again. She'd doze off, only to wake in time for a siesta and stagger back to her hammock under the leafy roof. For dinner there was beer, fried fish, fruit. It got dark early. Someone had a guitar and would play Dylan or the Eagles. The pot was excellent. The waves rolled up. The waves rolled back.

She had no idea how long she'd been there when she began to feel unwell. There was no way of telling time, no calendar or clock. Too much of an effort, carving notches in a tree. No one had a mirror so she couldn't tell if her hair had finally bleached enough to earn her the appellation Blondie, or if the skin on her bare ass had darkened to a native shade. Her body offered no clues at all; since she'd gone off the pill, her periods had ceased. Civilization's other chronometer, laundry day, did not apply.

Meanwhile, on the home front, Anna's pregnancy proceeds, but all is not what it so visually appears to be, as Carey, Anna's husband, is not the father. The question of the actual father is not pursued nor is Anna's uncharacteristic deviation from the sweet pea behaviour we might have expected from her.

As it later becomes clear, the marriage has never been consummated. Carey has turned out to be not much of a prize in the matrimonial stakes, being a fitfully employed substitute teacher and part-time teacher of ESL to recent refugees.

Most of them had arrived here penniless from the desperate places they had fled. They were a Bosnian couple, several Kurds from Iraq, a six-foot Sudanese, three Afghan women in head scarves, a Burmese, and a stunned little Sri Lankan girl with a bindi and only one pronoun.

Poor Carey's underlying problems are suggested in the recounting of his mother's hygienic obsessions.

Carey's worst memory was of his mother with a Q-Tip. In dreams his profound dread of it would magnify to her coming at him with a majorette's baton, cotton tipped. For years and years he had stood it. He'd thought it was a ritual that went on in the home of every boy, that after your Sunday night bath your mother would come in and sit on the edge of the tub and, cringing with disgust, clean under your foreskin while you stood shivering on the bath mat. Then he started junior high school, all the naked boys crammed into one big shower stall. He was the only one born in Scotland. Unless you were born in Scotland, he discovered, you didn't even have a foreskin.

He began to lock the door. "Carey?" she would call. "What are you doing in there, Carey?" She probably thought he was abusing himself. She'd always told him, "Carey, never abuse yourself," and he was thrown into confusion. What would she call forcing a cotton swab into the hood of his penis? Hygiene, of course. She'd been a nurse until Carey's father had brought her to Canada. Eventually she let him be, but ever after on a Sunday night she would leave the Q-Tip in a saucer on the vanity.

When the time came for him to go to university, he chose a school as far away as possible from his mother, went from one coast to the other. Every Sunday night she phoned and asked if he was meeting girls, which he was. He wasn't particularly handsome, but what attracted women more than looks, he quickly learned, was a sense of humour, preferably self-deprecating, and a certain wistfulness. He would date them until that first sweet kiss, then abandon them and not return their perplexed calls. His mother never asked if he was keeping himself clean, but that was implied by the very time and day she phoned.

Back now in Mexico, Pauline, not realizing she is pregnant, has been feeling unwell. Thinking back to the American student she encountered on the bus, she becomes convinced that she is harbouring a tapeworm.

She could feel it coiling and uncoiling, nudging the walls of her gut, slithering through the folded corridors of intestine, trying doors. She pounded fists against her spongy, distended abdomen. "Get lost!"

Putting on her clothes the next morning confirmed that she was bloated. Her shorts would not close. Thankfully, she had a drawstring skirt and a baggy shirt. Clutching her phrase book, she left Paradise, not even wearing any panties.

There was no translation for "tapeworm," she discovered after arriving at the Puerto Angel clinic. "*Serpiente,*" she told the nurse, "*serpiente,*" and pointed to her ass.

"Loca," she heard the nurse tell the doctor in the next room. *"Otra gringa loca."*

"¿Esta vestida?" asked the doctor. They both laughed, then the nurse came back with a half-dozen white suppository bullets that were, naturally, ineffective.

The passage compels my deepest admiration. It is as exquisitely performed as comic passages by Beryl Bainbridge, Kingsley Amis, the Naipaul of the early novels (*The Mystic Masseur* and *The Suffrage of Elvira*) or even by Waugh himself. It's well worth considering her use off the word "ass," that sudden change of register. With all the writers I've been looking at we *must* slow down, giving the work deep and unusual attention; with such passages as the above we should reread and reread simply for the airy pleasure; rereading is, too, our bow to mastery.

The following paragraphs are more of the same:

She came home before she got too big to fly. The next week she had the ultrasound. "Look," said the technician, pressing the lubricated wand hard under Pauline's ribs. On the screen, the ghost of five little bean-shaped toes curled and uncurled.

"Great," Pauline drawled. "It has a foot." Nothing could convince her that these separate parts would come out properly strung together. No way. Pauline had done too many drugs. She planned donations to the eye bank and the foot repository after it was over.

"You don't want the baby?" asked the technician.

"I'm more of a cat person," Pauline admitted.

*

...the moment she was placed on Pauline's chest gave Pauline her first inkling as to how things were going to be. They were going to be about the baby. Already the baby was shrieking *Me! me! me!*

They sent her home the next day. How to care for an infant, Pauline had no idea. Every time they'd wheeled Rebecca into the room in her clear plastic box, Pauline had opened one eye and waved the nurse off as if refusing the fare on a dim sum trolley. She hadn't wanted to see anyone who could have used her so violently.

Once home, she hobbled around the house with a sopping, brick-thick menstrual pad between her legs, but no one paid attention. "I have a hemorrhoid," she announced to Anna and Carey and Betty convening around the bassinet. Betty was concerned because Rebecca had changed colour and now looked washed in an iodine solution. All over her misshapen head, black hair was patched like a radiation victim's. Pauline lifted the hand mirror and examined the Catherine wheel of broken blood vessels in her left eye, from pushing. No one had given her an ounce of sympathy for that either.

She'd had enough. She was going back to Mexico with her inheritance. Bowlegged, she pegged up the stairs, dressed, packed and left unnoticed. She thought she would call a cab from the grocery store on the corner, but when she had got halfway across the yard *Me! me! me!* came floating through the open window. *Me! me! me!* Panic overwhelmed her. She beat a stinging retreat and burst back in the house.

"Is she crying?" she called.

"Shh!" hissed Anna. "You're going to wake her up!" .

"...Waved the nurse off as if refusing the fare on a dim sum trolley. She hadn't wanted to see anyone who could have used her so violently." Deliciously funny, yet Adderson negotiates the next couple of paragraphs, through further comedy, into different territory, into something reluctantly tender and touching.

She's had enough. She was going back to Mexico with her inheritance. Bowlegged, she pegged up the stairs, dressed, packed and left unnoticed. She thought she would call a cab from the grocery store on the corner, but when she got halfway across the yard *Me! Me! Me!* came floating through the open window. *Me!*

Me! Me! Panic overwhelmed her. She beat a stinging retreat and
burst back into the house.

"Is she crying?" she called.

"Shh!" hissed Anna. "You're going to wake her up!"

Again, the writing is gorgeous. "Pegged up the stairs."

Pegged.

From stumped peg-legged because of the "brick-thick" menstrual pad.

I think we first read *Me! me! me!* as the baby's actual crying trans-
posed into what the crying asserts rather than the actual sound of it.
It is only when we read "Shh! You're going to wake her up!" that we
realise that the *Me! me! me!* was never a *heard* sound, but a voice felt
in Pauline's heretofore untender heart.

What an utterly brilliant skirting of the gooey.

The story proceeds; it resolutely does not resolve itself or reach
any "significant" conclusion. I have no particular interest in following the rest of the "plot" except to say that it is episodic and that that
method of construction is one of the story's great strengths; events,
emotions, are presented in small spot-like sequences that move
fluidly between past and present; the movement is film-like. Each
sequence is discrete, but the sequences gather a cumulative weight.

I find it difficult to grasp why "episodic" is a term of negative
criticism because I can't imagine what it is that critics consider superior. What do they want? Are they desiring an omniscient narrator
who comments on the action, a Master of Ceremonies, a Host, a
Presenter? Do they treasure a linear plot? Are they captive to Ideas?
Do they yearn for Henry James?

Who knows? There flashes in my mind remembered military
tombstones in Benghazi, markers of the unidentified dead incised:
Known Unto God.

Caroline Adderson's most recent book is *Ellen in Pieces: A Novel* (2014).
The book is made up of short stories, each of which features either
Ellen or one of a cast of characters in her orbit. I recall Caroline
saying to me that her intention was to write a novel composed of

discrete stories. I would have described such a venture as a book of linked stories. *Ellen* is presented, however, as a novel, part of that determination no doubt being that novels are more saleable to a recalcitrant public than story collections.

The "in Pieces" part of the title alludes to the "Pieces" being stories and to the idea that Ellen is seen differently by different people, the different pieces combining to form a portrait of her life. Although the blurby stuff on the inside front flap refers to the novel as "genre-bending" that is the last we hear of the "pieces" as stories except for the acknowledgement, on the verso of the title page, in miniscule print, that "parts of this book were previously published in slightly different forms," ie., as stories: "I Feel Lousy" in *Eighteen Bridges*; "Poppycock" in *The New Quarterly*; "Ellen-Celine, Celine-Ellen," in *CNQ*; "Your Dog Makes Me Smile" in Douglas Glover's online magazine *Numéro Cinq*. I anthologized the last three in *Best Canadian Stories*, 2012, 2013, and 2014.

The verso's acknowledgement that four of the pieces ("parts of this book") were previously published "in slightly different forms" seems to me a wily avoidance that "parts" really means "stories," and "in slightly different forms" also means—"stories." None of this really matters a damn except that the strength of the book is in those "parts" that are obviously stories and that the two final "parts"—"Absent" and "Ellen in Pieces"—are not stories like the others but a decline into a more novelistic sort of narrative, a gesture towards tying up the loose ends—Larry's new play to be performed after long arid years, the unlikely reappearance of Matt, his picking up Ellen's daughter, Mimi, in a purely fortuitous encounter, Matt going with her to see her father's opening night of the play that has been inspired by the interaction of Ellen and his Yiddishly-inflected mother, Esther—it's all rather like the last episode, the finale of a TV series.

I would imagine, being too polite to ask, that Caroline felt pressure to make the book more conventional, more commercially acceptable.

There are twelve "pieces" in the book and the ten of them that *are* stories are magnificent, driving, dancing, laced with comic observation so snortingly funny as to ensure that Caroline Adderson will never be the recipient of the Stephen Leacock Medal for humour.

"Episode" in this book reigns; the narrative thread in the stories weaves in and out of past and present, connecting episodes, vignettes that accrete towards portraits.

Ellen in Pieces is the culmination of Caroline's short-story writing thus far. The book is too complex to précis its plot entanglements, so I'll simply suggest its many pleasures by pointing and saying "There, you see?"

Ellen's two young daughters, Yolanda and Mimi.

> Every infestation a toxic ordeal, a nitpicking torture. Both had silky Rapunzel tresses that took hours to properly delouse. Mimi screeched and writhed, but Yolanda would sit quietly, her back to Ellen, paging through a picture book.
>
> During one of these sessions Ellen noticed that Yolanda had been crying the whole time. Her chest was bibbed with tears. "Oh, honey," Ellen said. "Am I hurting you?"
>
> "I feel so sorry for them."
>
> "For who?"
>
> "The baby lices."

Funny, but nifty thumbnail caricatures of both children and indicative of the emotional futures.

The Gulf Island where Ellen and Larry and the children surfed in the sixties:

> Cordova Island was also where Ellen discovered pottery. She'd been pregnant with Mimi when they first arrived and needed an outlet herself. The island so teemed with creative types that you didn't really fit in unless you batiked, or made driftwood furniture, or wove lampshades out of kelp. Ellen took lessons with an island potter, Mary Bourne, who encouraged her. Apparently Ellen had an instinctive feel for the possibilities of clay, not to mention strong hands. It made her ludicrously happy to take what was essentially a lump of dirt and transform it into something useful.

Kelp!

Look at Ellen, a single mother. Larry kept up payments on the house for those years, but that was it. He contributed shelter; Ellen food, clothing, allowance, dance lessons, drug rehab.

The placing and timing of "drug rehab," coming after "dance lessons," is a classic comic move. The recipient of rehabilitation is, of course, Mimi.

Larry stepped out of his jeans and there it was, his cock, so longed-for and pink, seemingly innocent, like something you'd cradle in your palm and feed from a dropper.

A somehow unsurprising Adderson detail; in much of her work the gothic or surreal lurk. Reading this snippet, it's easy to see from whom Yolanda inherited her empathy for baby lices.

Another of these surreal images rises to the surface in a scene where the adult Mimi is employed as daily labour to clear out from his house the strange possessions and obsessions of Mr. D'Huet, a terminal hoarder. The multiplicity and grotesqueness of his accumulations is caught in the magazine article he refuses to jettison, an article about how playing the didgeridoo reduced the symptoms of sleep apnea.

The bedrooms were on the upper floor, three of them as unlived in as museum displays. The exception was the small plaid room that must have been Mr. D'Huet's, the twin bed tousled, stuff piled everywhere. A nozzled machine sat on the bedside table. Yesterday Mr. D'Huet had refused to part with an article on how playing the didgeridoo reduced the symptoms of sleep apnea. Mimi pictured him in the bed gasping for breath in the middle of the night, the mask and nozzle attached to his face, a shrivelled old elephant god.

These wild images nail scenes and episodes. I love this tiny, almost throw-away picture following. It's as delicate in its way as an

Elizabethan miniature; Caroline Adderson as Nicholas Hilliard. Ellen has bought party presents for her grandchildren; from the "fabric artist" in the studio next to hers in Kitsilano, she bought an Arctic Hare and a Vole.

> She laughed and went to the kitchen for more wine, found Eli crouching behind the island counter with the hare that had cost her three hundred and fifty dollars, its face stained with chili now. He'd discovered chopsticks in a drawer and was carefully inserting them between the stitches into the animal's body.

I loved this capturing of the *solemnity* of small children engaged in whatever has engaged them.

"...[C]arefully inserting" chopsticks "between the stitches into the animal's body."

This image has kept popping into my mind ever since I first read it; I think it's "chopsticks" that utterly persuades me of its truth.

And here's Ellen's ex-husband, who has married Amber, a much younger woman, dictating his mother's dialogue to his iPod as he walks, his new play gestating.

> "She didn't even like *Talking Stick*," he told his iPod. "Every time I mention it, she does that thing with her mouth."
>
> He tried to describe Esther's mouth movements that had irritated him his whole life. According to Ellen, Mimi had inherited a version of it. Ellen had a term for it. What?
>
> Later, when he replayed this monologue, there would be stammering and the sound of traffic on Fourth Avenue, where he was walking now among the flip-flopped mob streaming up from the beach to fill the restaurants and pubs. They looked so young, and were, he knew from their piercings and tattoos. Amber had a bruise-like mandala on her left shoulder, and in her right nostril, a stud. Once Larry had come across her in the bathroom with the stud out, picking snot off it. *What have I done?* He'd thought.

It was vaguely insulting, their youth and robust good health. "Speaking on behalf of pain sufferers everywhere," he said into the iPod.

When he reached the end of the too-long block, he turned and left them to their pinkening sunset, their rosy futures.

Ellen has moved into a ramshackle "studio" in Kitsilano to pursue her career as a potter. In the studio on one side is Gerhard, a video artist, on the other side, Tilda, a "fabric artist," a knitter of iconic Canadian wildlife.

"Tilda looks like a thirty-year-old Joyce Carol Oates who knots, rather than writes, compulsively."

The triplex Ellen moves into that September is old. Eighty years old, even a hundred (what is time?). Three shops stood here once, but now they're artists' studios, green-shingled with large windows, in the heart of Kitsilano. Time has played a trick on the neighbourhood too. Once Kits was the Cordova Island of Vancouver, a hippy paradise, but after four gentrifying decades only pockets of this patchoulied past remain.

The studio is about a quarter the size of Ellen's former house in North Vancouver. She's had to sort and cull her life's artifacts down to a cruel minimum. Unloading her car that first day, backing up with a box of books she couldn't bear to part with, she crashes into her new neighbour Gerhard standing too close behind her. She bounces off him, one of those large, incompressible Germans with a shaved head, unnerving blue eyes, and chains. Jangling, he stoops to gather the fallen books, then carries them into the studio half filled with her scant cardboard-boxed possessions.

Adderson's caricatures are always rapier work but the descriptions of Gerhard ending in "and chains" is *so* sudden it feels as if she's jerking ours. Because of the denial of expected rhythm, so *startlingly* exact.

And the words "patchoulied past" preserve, as if in amber, an entire era. The description of the corner store fills out the picture of the neighbourhood while also adding detail to Ellen's character. (For a similar lovely take of a neighbourhood store, see entry on Rebecca Rosenblum.)

> Across the street from the studio was a corner store. This time of year Christmas cacti, poinsettia, and little bonsai pines crowded the board-and-cinderblock shelves out front. Plants, cigarettes, and lottery tickets were the store's main business. Ellen, worried the place would go under, occasionally scooted across to buy something she didn't need. Another plant to ignore to death. A can of corn. There was little else. The Frosted Flakes looked archeological.
>
> She ran across in sweats and an old loose T-shirt scabbed with drying flecks of clay. A dog was shivering in a newspaper-lined box beside the till. She couldn't tell its breed. The black kind with a goatee and plaintive eyes.
>
> "Where did it come from?" she asked.
>
> The owner of the store said, "My brother. Driving from Chilliwack? He saw it on the road. You want it?"
>
> "I just came in for some corn." Ellen set the can down, leaving fingerprints in the dust on top. "Maybe you should take it to the SPCA."

In this new studio and home, Ellen, in her forty-eighth year, takes up a very young lover, Matt. He is at first madly attentive, but in the background, never mentioned or acknowledged, is a girlfriend, Nicole. In the following snippet, Nicole is Christmas-visiting Matt's family home in Spruce Grove, a small town near Edmonton.

> "First Matty. Then Matt-a-tat-tat. Which became Machine-Gun Matt. Machine-Gun Mutt. Doggy. Dogbone. Boner. Erection Man, or just E.M. Then, for some reason, Dr. Dog. Dr. Love. Loverboy."
>
> "Loverboy?" Nicole said, still staring straight ahead. "Really?"
>
> He had made her come for this drive. "Clay Franks lived here." Slowing, he stared at the house. Snow-blown driveway, its

banks waist-high. Two-car garage. Vinyl siding. Amber glass on either side of the front door. Same as every other house.

"A.k.a. Frankster. Frankenfurter. Weiner. Weenie. Teenie-Weenie. Then just Teenie, though the guy was, and probably still is, huge."

Nicole finally broke her silence. "It's so sad about your mom. She's much worse than last summer. She seems completely blind now."

"We got mad at him and put a bag of dog shit in his mailbox."

"Charming."

"Next door there? That was Tommy Gerken's place…"

They drove in complete silence for several blocks, along the winter-locked streets of his banal childhood, the stomping ground of his appalling ordinariness, the inspiration for every-thing he would eventually not become.

The beginning of the affair between Matt and Ellen is a beautiful set-piece, early passion caught in vivid detail, then the introduction of autumnal tints and tones that presage bleakness to come.

So in her forty-eighth year Ellen took up with a man-boy in his twenties who wore shorts in any weather. She couldn't believe her luck.

At first Matt had hours (all day in fact; he was unemployed) to lie around with Ellen, who, living off her savings, was queen of her own life. Queen Ellen spread out in the loft on the hot twisted sheets, inhaling the tang of their exertions, while Matt scampered naked down the ladder to do her bidding. He brought her a glass of water, a wad of tissues to wipe the milty puddle off her belly, a cheese plate from the fridge.

One afternoon he fell back, curls fanning across the pillow. "I need to ask you something really personal. I've never asked anyone before. I need the honest truth. Please."

"What?" Ellen said. "What?"

"Is my cock too big?"

This went on for three glorious weeks that autumn while even the weather seemed to announce the return of love. The horse-chestnut trees burst into flame, the Japanese maples dripped red, burgundy, carnelian. It didn't rain.

And then it did. Lashings of it, the wind tearing off the last celebratory leaves. The trees stood around, undressed and shivering, clotted with crows' nests.

Now Matt brought his cell phone up to the loft and left it turned on. Ellen pretended she didn't see it tossed onto the clothes he'd so urgently shed, but there it lay, connecting him to someone he'd failed to mention.

She pulled the sheet up to cover her body. Too much information.

Let the suffering begin.

Notice the muscularity of the language, the "tang of their exertions," "milty puddle"; the meaning of "tang"—a penetrating taste or smell—is a metaphorical extension of meaning from what a tang actually is, an extension of the blade of a knife; and "milty" to describe human sperm when "milt" means specifically the semen of fish—both usages are obviously deliberate and are introducing—at this point subliminally—the ideas of danger and wounding and the animality of their coupling.

The weather is used to plot the course of the affair—"that autumn while even the weather seemed to announce the return of love"—"flame," "dripping red, burgundy, camelian."

Then came the rain, "tearing off the last celebratory leaves" revealing the tracery of the now-naked branches "clotted" with crows' nests.

The passage ends with what must be Ellen's thoughts:

"Let the suffering begin."

If I could point only to a single passage in Caroline Adderson's short stories as an example of her mastery, this might well be the passage.

Joan Alexander
Short Story Collections: *Lines of Truth and Conversation* (2005).

This is a story collection I wish to sidle up to. The blurbs for the book by Tim O'Brien (author of *Going After Cacciato*) and Nino Ricci

(Lives of the Saints) are both unusually accurate. O'Brien said " ... powerful and quirky ... among the most daring, most original, and most wholly successful works of fiction I have read in a long while." Nino Ricci said "At once eccentric and precisely observed, they seem to hum with the energy of everything in life that is unreasonable and can't quite be contained."

I want to approach Joan's work by talking first about Saul Bellow, because Alexander expresses a particular sensibility in a particular accent, which to some degree she and Bellow share. The following quotations are taken from *Bellow: A Biography* by James Atlas.

> I was, in 1937, a very young, married man who had quickly lost his first job and who lived with his in-laws. His affectionate, loyal, and pretty wife insisted he must be given a chance to write something.

But what? In "Starting out in Chicago," originally delivered as a Brandeis commencement address in 1974, Saul Bellow provided a memorable portrait of his beginnings as a writer. This brief memoir, more than anything else he ever wrote, captures the early stage of that momentous confrontation in which "American society and S. Bellow came face to face." He was twenty-two years old.

> His in-law's apartment on North Virginia Avenue in the Northwest Side neighborhood of Ravenswood was drab and anonymous, one of the thousands of identical brick dwellings that sprawled mile upon mile across a dull, orderly grid of streets. While his wife, Anita, attended classes at the School of Social Service Administration at the university, Bellow sat at a bridge table in the back bedroom:
>
> > My table faced three cement steps that rose from the cellar into the brick gloom of a passageway. Only my mother-in-law was at home. A widow, then in her seventies [actually, her mid-sixties], she wore a heavy white braid down her back.

She had been a modern woman and a socialist and suffrag-ette in the old country. She was attractive in a fragile, steely way. You felt Sophie's [Sonya's] strength of will in all things. She kept a neat house. The very plants, the ashtrays, the pedestals, the doilies, the chairs, revealed her mastery. Each object had its military place. Her apartment could easily have been transferred to West Point.

Lunch occurred at half-past twelve. The cooking was good. We ate together in the kitchen. The meal was followed by an interval of stone. My mother-in-law took a nap. I went into the street. Ravenswood was utterly empty. I walked about with something like a large stone in my belly. I often turned into Lawrence Avenue and stood on the bridge looking into the drainage canal. If I had been a dog I would have howled.

★

His mandate, as he defined it, was "to write about American life, and to do with Chicago or Manhattan or Minneapolis what Arnold Bennett had done with the Five Towns or H.G. Wells with London." And to do it, he might have added, in the American language—even if he had to make it up himself. *The Victim*, Martin Greenberg declared in a prescient review in *Commentary*, was "the first attempt in American literature to consider Jewishness not in its singularity, not as constitutive of a special world of experience, but as a quality that informs all of modern life, as the quality of modernity itself." It was through Bellow's efforts that Jewish literature was to become American.

★

And now, from Bellow's collection of essays and occasional pieces *It all Adds Up:*

You must have felt on writing Augie *that you were on some quite major departure.*

I knew it was major for me. I couldn't judge what it might be for anyone else. What I found was the relief of turning away from mandarin English and putting my own accents into the language. My earlier books had been straight and respectable. As if I had to satisfy the demands of H.W. Fowler. But in *Augie March* I wanted to invent a new sort of American sentence. Something like a fusion of colloquialism and elegance. What you find in the best English writing of the twentieth century—in Joyce, or E.E. Cummings. Street language combined with high style. I don't today take rhetorical effects so seriously, but at the time I was driven by a passion to *invent*.

I felt that American writing had enslaved itself without sufficient reason to English models—everybody trying to meet the dominant English standard. This was undoubtedly a very good thing, but not for me. It meant that one's own habits of speech, daily speech, had to be abandoned. Leading the "correct" grammatical forces was *The New Yorker*. I used to say about Shawn that at *The New Yorker* he had traded the Talmud for Fowler's *Modern English Usage* ...

This use of language you were talking about in Augie ... *It always seemed an inner necessity.*

Paris in 1948 was a good year for this *grisaille*. Paris was depressed; I was depressed. I became aware that the book I had gone there to write had taken a stranglehold on me. Then I became aware one morning that I might break its grip, outwit depression, by writing about something for which I had a great deal of feeling—namely, life in Chicago as I had known it in my earliest years. And there was only one way to do that—reckless spontaneity.

Didn't the book take off once you had decided to do that?

It did. I *took* the opening I had found and immediately fell into an enthusiastic state. I began to write in all places, in all postures, at all times of the day and night. It rushed out of me. I was turned on like a hydrant in summer. The simile is not entirely satisfactory. Hydrants are not sexually excited. I was wildly excited.

★

What now follows are some notes on her writing life Alexander recently sent me.

I didn't grow up with my head in a book, a flashlight under the covers. There weren't books around. Not at home, not at school, not out in the community (a few city blocks on the south side of Chicago). Somehow at the age of nine I decided to become a writer though I had no idea what that meant for about fifteen more years. By the end of high school, however, the idea began to dawn on me that I was at the bottom of the canon. This was after I read Camus's *The Stranger* and realized that I hadn't yet read Kafka. Oh dear, that was an agony with Sartre in the wings.

In university, I liked Borges and Joyce and Hemingway. This liking came from trying to carefully analyze stories for essays assigned by old-fashioned English professors who expected their students to grapple with texts. At this time I thought John Barth and Thomas Pynchon were cool for devising brilliant clever puzzles, what I then thought of as pinnacles of modernity. I also read Dostoyevsky's novels and watched in awe as Raskolnikov, Prince Myshkin, and Aloysha Karamazov followed their collision courses with emotional and spiritual complexity and depth.

Then it was Ann Beattie and Raymond Carver for style, Penelope Gilliatt and Deborah Eisenberg for an outlook of kindness: I also read Jean Stafford's stories with much admiration; her writing is very precise. By then I had already discovered Katherine Mansfield; I always carried around something by her in my purse. Her journals, letters, and stories meant a great deal to me, especially "Je ne parle pas français" for its grand sensitivity. Later came all the superb stories of Alice Munro and Mavis Gallant, and the long novels of I.B. Singer and the short novels of Natalia Ginzburg. My favorite writer is Chekhov. The best novella I ever read was Tillie Olsen's "Tell me a Riddle." The best novel: Vasily Grossman's *Life and Fate.*

Many stories come to mind. Robert Stone's "Helping," James Baldwin's "Sonny's Blues," Tim O'Brien's "The Things They Carried," Paul Bowles' "A Distant Episode," Thom Jones'

"The Pugilist at Rest," Grace Paley's "A Conversation with My Father," Lamed Shapiro's "White Challah," Paula Fox's "News from the World," Breece D'J Pancake's "Trilobites," Charles D'Ambrosio's "Screenwriter," and Nabokov's "Spring in Fialta": these stories woke me up to big possibility and changed the way I read and think and feel. If these writers had never written another word ... *Dayenyu*: It would have been enough.

So after falling in love with these writers, I asked myself: How do they do it? And then this question became more refined: How can I do it?

In Alexander's notes on individual stories which influenced her she says, "If these writers had never written another word ... *Dayenyu*: It would have been enough."

The *weight* of what she is saying here, the religious seriousness of literature she is stressing, probably needs a little explanation. The word *Dayenu* is Hebrew and means "it would have been enough for us." The word is a refrain in a song that has been traditionally sung at Passover *Seders*; the song appears in the *Haggadah* after the telling of the story of the exodus from Egypt. The song is about being grateful to God for all the gifts he has given the Jews—taking them out of slavery, giving them the Torah, giving them Shabbat—had God given only one of these gifts, it would have been enough.

She mentions a story by Grace Paley, and that revived my memory of my first encounter with her 1959 collection *The Little Disturbances of Man*. In turn, that flooded me with memories of Shirley Faessler's *A Basket of Apples* and Philip Roth's *Patrimony*.

The first Grace Paley story I read was "Goodbye and Good Luck," I think the first story she wrote. Here are the lovely opening sentences:

> I was popular in certain circles, says Aunt Rose. I wasn't no thinner then, only more stationary in the flesh. In time to come, Lillie, don't be surprised—change is a fact of God. From this no one is excused. Only a person like your mama stands on one foot, she don't notice how big her behind is getting and sings in

the canary's ear for thirty years. Who's listening? Papa's in the shop. You and Seymour, thinking about yourself. So she waits in a spotless kitchen for a kind word and thinks …

In the introduction to the *Collected Stories*, Grace Paley wrote about this and other stories of that period:

> … in 1954 or '55 I needed to speak in some inventive way about female and male lives in those years. Some knowledge was creating a real physical pressure, probably in the middle of my chest—maybe just to the right of the heart. I was beginning to suffer story-teller's pain: Listen! I *have* to tell you something! I simply hadn't known how to do it in poetry. Other writers have understood easily, but I seem to have been singing along on the gift of one ear, the ear in charge of literature …
>
> I began the story "Goodbye and Good Luck" and to my surprise carried it through to the end. So much prose. Then "The Contest." A couple of months later I finished "A Woman Young and Old". Thinking about it some years later I understood I'd found my other ear. Writing the stories had allowed it—suddenly—to do its job, to remember the street language and the home language with its Russian and Yiddish accents, a language my early characters knew well, the only language I spoke. Two ears, one for literature, one for home, are useful for writers.

Which brings me to the wonder—not of Yiddish, though Yiddish has given us so many indispensible words and phrases—but to the wonder of English as spoken by people whose first language was Yiddish, the habits of thought, the vocabulary, the syntax; it is an entrancing poetry. Which perhaps explains why I meandered off into Saul Bellow, Philip Roth, Grace Paley, and Shirley Faessler even though the main connection between Joan and Bellow is that both came from Chicago.

Alexander's "Five Months" is a long story—perhaps better described as a novella—about the death, from cancer, of Pa. It is narrated by Pa's daughter-in-law and concerns his sons and grandson and his predatory female live-in caregivers, illegals without right of abode. It is intensely sad but grotesquely funny and is crammed with everything in life, as Nino Ricci said, "that is unreasonable and can't be quite contained."

It was early January and Pa had been waiting inside while the snow piled up around his house on Hove Street. Frail and aggrieved, he answered the door … How could we make the ride back to Toronto in a station wagon sound so difficult when Pa had crossed Siberia on foot?

In the afternoon Pa vomited … Four nights in Emergency waiting for a room and a diagnosis—fecal impaction, gallstones, appendicitis, pneumonia. What was it? I visited Pa in the middle of icy nights … listened to his stories with a new intensity. He had done what he could for his wife … His efforts had added three years to her life. Three extra years! It was nothing to sniffle at. I agreed Pa was a hero.

And Europe. How glorious was Europe in his childhood! There wasn't divorce, lunacy or retardation. It had been a nearly perfect world. I couldn't imagine.

Pa's last girlfriend, Svetlana, wasn't mentioned. He'd found her in a Russian food shop, buying sprats. She was a mathematics professor from the Ukraine.

"Do you know how old she is?" Pa's voice had boomed proudly. "Thirty-seven."

★

Pa's kidney biopsy:

The next day, in the morning, Pa fell and hit his head when the nurse took him down for tests … He remained upbeat.

"The test was fast," Pa said, "Why? Machines are making it. And machines are fast and they talk. When it pierces the kidney, a man's voice cries out, 'I got 'em. Pom!'"

"How do you feel, Pa?" I said. "That cut looks nasty. Does your head hurt?"

"The way I feel now, I can live another year. We can make dinners. I'll make a chicken soup. I'll make a brisket if I feel like this. I got 'em. Pom!"

⋆

"Sheldon made me my breakfast. I had grits—what I call a kasha. With milk and sugar. I had a tea, a glass of apple juice. I had a normal breakfast." He paused at the summit. "And then I had my own stomach. The stool was almost perfect."

⋆

Finally the funeral parlour came to pick up the body. Two young men went upstairs and zipped Pa into a body bag. I watched them carry him down the stairs. Davey stood at the window. "They're putting Pa in an Econo-van. With another corpse already in the trunk."

"Person," Barbara said. "Do you mind saying person?"

"It's a business," Michael said. "They make millions. Figure three to five funerals a day. They stand to make thirty-five thousand every twenty-four hours."

Barbara said, "We should have a contents sale. Rory wants that lamp in the basement with the bulb that says B-A-R."

⋆

Pa had said weeks earlier:

"Take amicably what you want. You're not jealous people."

When it came to the division of the spoils, Pa was proven disastrously wrong.

Joan Alexander's writing is so sad. So funny. So stubbornly alive.

In Emergency a nurse stripped off his clothes and set up the IV. Pa burped, groaned, peed himself. "See what becomes of a man," he said. Never before had I noticed the deplorable state of Pa's T-shirts and underwear, his worn leather watchband, fastened by a grubby and fraying piece of string.

Magaret Atwood

Short Story Collections: *Dancing Girls* (1977), *Murder in the Dark* (1983), *Bluebeard's Egg* (1983), *Wilderness Tips* (1991), *Good Bones* (1992), *Good Bones and Simple Murders* (1994), *The Labrador Fiasco* (1996), *The Tent* (2006), *Moral Disorder* (2006), and *Stone Mattress* (2014).

Novels: *The Edible Woman* (1969), *Surfacing* (1972), *Lady Oracle* (1976), *Life Before Man* (1979), *Bodily Harm* (1981), *The Handmaid's Tale, Cat's Eye* (1988), *The Robber Bride* (1993), *Alias Grace* (1996), *Oryx and Crake* (2003), *The Penelopiad* (2005), *The Year of the Flood* (2009), *MaddAddam* (2013), *The Heart Goes Last* (2015), and *Hag-Seed* (2016).

Poetry Collections: *Double Persephone* (1961), *The Circle Game* (1964), *Expeditions* (1965), *Speeches for Doctor Frankenstein* (1966), *The Animals in That Country* (1968), *The Journals of Susanna Moodie* (1970), *Procedures for Underground* (1970), *Power Politics* (1971), *You Are Happy* (1974), *Selected Poems* (1976), *Two-Headed Poems* (1978), *True Stories* (1981), *Love Songs of a Terminator* (1983), *Snake Poems* (1983), *Interlunar* (1984), *Selected Poems 1966–1984 Canada, Selected Poems II: 1976–1986, Morning in the Burned House* (1995), *Eating Fire: Selected Poems 1965–1995* (1998), and *The Door* (2007).

Non-Fiction: *Survival: A Thematic Guide to Canadian Literature* (1972), *Days of the Rebels 1815–1840* (1977), *Second Words: Selected Critical Prose* (1982), *Through the One-Way Mirror* (1986), *Strange Things: The Malevolent North in Canadian Literature* (1995), *Negotiating with the Dead: A Writer on Writing* (2002), *Moving Targets: Writing with Intent 1982–2004* (2004), *Writing with Intent: Essays Reviews Personal Prose 1983-2005* (2005), *Payback: Debt and the Shadow Side of Wealth* (2008), and *In Other Worlds: SF and the Human Imagination* (2011).

Margaret Atwood has been internationally lauded for these volumes but I remain unconvinced. While her wit and intelligence are obvious, the stories in general fill me with disquiet. My unease revolves around what she wrote in "An End to Audience?" which I quoted from in a talk I gave at Alcalá de Henares at the Eighth International Conference on the Short Story in English:

> I believe that fiction writing is the guardian of the moral and eth-
> ical sense of community. Especially now that organized religion
> is scattered and in disarray, and politicians have, Lord knows,
> lost their credibility, fiction is one of the few forms left through
> which we may examine our society not in its particular but in
> its typical aspects; through which we can see ourselves and the
> ways in which we behave towards each other, through which we
> can see others and judge them and ourselves.

She goes on: "Writing is a craft, true, and discussions of the position of colons and the rhyming of *plastic* and *spastic* have some
place in it ..."

Her statement in the first quoted passage, that fiction enables
us to examine our society "not in its particular but in its typical
aspects," and the implication, in the second, that the craft of writing
is separable from and subsidiary to the "message" of the writing,
fundamentally differentiates Margaret Atwood from most of the
other writers on the Century List. Characteristically, she is committed to presenting ideas and political positions. The central problem
with fiction that advances ideas is that we can take issue with the
ideas advanced *as ideas*; we can disagree intellectually with particular moral and ethical positions or with the political ideas of left,
right, and centre. But it is impossible to "disagree" with our experience of the particularities of a Mavis Gallant story.

All too often her messages seem to me to urge a feminism which
is in conflict with artistry. Bill Hoffer used to grump that Atwood's
work was most appreciated "by girls of the most unpromising
kind." Doubtless this is less perceptive criticism than irritated misog-
yny. Yet the work *does* have designs on us. She does indeed want to
send us messages. And, like telemarketing, they're messages I'm not
interested in listening to. The messages are minatory and destroy
the fabric of fiction. I would stand, rather, with William Faulkner,
who is supposed to have said to a lady who asked him what message

he had wished his book to send that had he wanted to send messages he would have used Western Union.

Clark Blaise reviewed *Wilderness Tips* (1991) in the *Chicago Tribune* and wrote:

> ... she works a secure but narrow band of settings and characters. Men still murder, women still create. The stories are not profound and certainly not charming. What they are is stylish, very, very Atwoodian.

He went on:

> In the duality of the sexes, men and women can never be intimate. They can never fully trust or be worthy of trust. Like great scarred hunting cats, they gather in temporary prides for gorging and breeding and seem curiously susceptible to urges unworthy of their cunning and experience. Atwoodian men are especially ineffectual, over-matched little boys, worthy of giggles even in the height of their passions.

Despite such savage and ghastly stories as "Hairball," in *Wilderness Tips*, Atwood can be generously funny. What follows is an excerpt from "Hurricane Hazel," from *Bluebeard's Egg* (1983). The story is an almost perfect comic performance. The feminist position inherent in the story is not advanced as an argument; the uncouth young male, Buddy, is seen through the grave eyes of the narrator as something as alien as a being from Mars, and the rituals of teen courtship are described almost as by an anthropologist observing the rites of savages.

"Hurricane Hazel" has, for me, only one flaw and it is that place in the story where Margaret Atwood intrudes into the comic texture to hammer home unnecessarily a point that was being made delicately by the whole shape of the scene. I draw attention to this because it illustrates my reservations about her editorializing, her deforming didacticism.

The narrator and Buddy, along with Trish and Charlie, are swimming in Pike Lake and, typical Atwoodian detail this, "Part of a hot-dog wiener floated near where we waded in, pallid, grey-ish-pink, lost-looking."

Under a shady tree Buddy plights his troth.

> Then he said, "I want you to have something." His voice was offhand, affable, the way it usually was; his eyes weren't. On the whole he looked frightened. He undid the silver bracelet from his wrist. It had always been there, and I knew what was written on it: *Buddy*, engraved in flowing script. It was an imitation army I.D. tag; a lot of the boys wore them.
>
> "My identity bracelet," he said.

...

> It was years later too that I realized Buddy had used the wrong word: it wasn't an identity bracelet, it was an identification bracelet. The difference escaped me at the time. But maybe it was the right word after all, and what Buddy was handing over to me was his identity, some key part of himself that I was expected to keep for him and watch over.
>
> Another interpretation has since become possible: that Buddy was putting his name on me, like a *Reserved* sign or an ownership label, or a tattoo on a cow's ear, or a brand. But at the time nobody thought that way. Everyone knew that getting a boy's I.D. bracelet was a privilege, not a degradation, and this is how Trish greeted it when she came back from her walk with Charlie.

Messages. Messages.

It may be that Margaret Atwood's best work in short fiction will turn out not to reflect the bleak world of "great scarred hunting cats gathering in temporary prides for gorging and breeding" as Clark Blaise put it. She is not so much "stylish," as Blaise said, but, rather, fashionable. Her talent is, as he said, "not profound" and her best work in short fiction just might be in the idiosyncratic bits and pieces in *Murder in the Dark: Short Fictions and Prose Poems, Good Bones,* and *The Tent,* cleverness rather than artistry.

In the December 19 and 26, 2014 double issue of the *TLS* (*Times Literary Supplement*) there was a review of Margaret Atwood's latest story collection, *Stone Mattress: Nine Tales*. The feminist "messages" that made me uneasy in 1983 seem to have bloated into a pathological condition.

> In "Stone Mattress," Verna has already murdered at least four husbands when she runs into the man who raped her more than fifty years before, when she was in her teens. Her whole life since the assault has been conceived as a revenge against men in general; now she has a chance to revenge herself against this man in particular. When she recognized him, she feels "a combination of rage and an almost reckless mirth." It's a good description of Atwood's prevailing attitude to her male characters: almost all the men in this collection are philanderers, letches, spongers and bullies, while almost all the women have been wronged. It isn't very subtle, or very flattering to anyone—but we are in the realm of abstractions and archetypes, in which characters get defined by their gender alone.

Mike Barnes

Short Story Collections: *Aquarium* (1999), *Contrary Angel* (2004), and *The Reasonable Ogre: Tales for the Sick and Well* (2012).

Novels: *The Syllabus* (2002), *Catalogue Raisonné* (2005), and *The Adjustment League* (2016).

Memoirs: *The Lily Pond* (2008).

Poetry Collections: *Calm Jazz Sea* (1996) and *A Thaw Foretold* (2006).

Mike Barnes' *Aquarium* was the winner of the first Danuta Gleed Award for the best first story collection of the year.

Calm Jazz Sea was the first Barnes book I read, and poetry is probably at the centre of everything he writes. His observation is keen, observations, which, to use Robyn Sarah's phrase, "resonate in more than one frequency," observations which the story elevates to the status of image.

The story "Dr. Lekky's Rose," in *Aquarium*, for example, concerns the efforts of an alcoholic couple to make a new start and achieve sobriety. By the end of the story we realize that life for them is going to be simply more of the same. Here is the story's opening.

> Paul was on his way into the liquor store when he heard a small, bright sound. *Chip. Chip.* He looked up. A little above him, large white letters spelling Liquor Control Board projected from the brick wall. Inside the O in Liquor, a sparrow was sitting on an untidy nest, chirping. It looked down at him, switching its head from side to side. When it opened its beak the bright sound sprang out. Other letters—the C, the B, and D—had bits of sticks and dried grass stuck in them, the beginnings or remains of other nests.

This seems, as we read, simply observed detail, but as we read on it becomes clearer that the paragraph is, in fact, an image informing the story's emotional direction. The image is not defined; there is no "equals" sign. But the bird presides over the Liquor Board amid "the beginning or remains" of nests and utters "the bright sound." Two emotional states, or currents, are being suggested here. And observations become images repeatedly as incident follows incident.

In my 1972 anthology *The Narrative Voice*, Clark Blaise wrote in "To Begin, to Begin"

> ... the story seeks its beginning, the story many times *is* its beginning, amplified... The first paragraph is a microcosm of the whole, but in a way that only the whole can reveal.

In light of this, consider the following paragraph near the opening of the story "Bitter Lake." Don Tremaine, a teacher on a remote northern Ojibway reserve, who's estranged from his wife, Becky, receives from her a box of supplies.

> He was glad that Becky had got his letter in time to send the food-stuffs he had requested: Red River cereal, oatmeal, dried fruit; but disappointed that she had sent them in such small quantities. Her little twist-tied bags bespoke a proximity to malls and supermarkets. Around them she had packed useless, sentimental things. Another

mug, his desk lamp, two brass duck heads (he leaned back and shook his head at those), two framed pictures. The glass over the Monet print had cracked. Glass! Broken parts rattled in the clock radio.

Broken, broken.

So much going on here.

At the Stratford Conference, David Bergen said, "As a writer, Mike Barnes circles a problem or a character, dropping hints and pulling back, drawing closer, lifting the lid slightly and then closing it, as if we are voyeurs with the author and are being invited to look."

Jim Bartley, once the *Globe and Mail*'s reviewer of first literary fiction, captured the *shape* of a Barnes story when he wrote of *Aquarium*: "Barnes chooses his narrative turns with delicacy, avoiding high drama and epiphanies in favour of keen, incremental observation of characters. His climaxes approach like dawning understanding."

"Dr. Lekky's Rose" ends with Paul and Jean sitting on the balcony of their new apartment watching the sunrise. They had been awakened in the night by the scrabblings of an animal above their heads—another detail turning into image. Paul later awakes again to hear sounds from the kitchen and suspects Jean might have been drinking more gin.

The story ends bleakly with these three paragraphs.

> She flicked her cigarette over the railing.
>
> 'Hey,' he said. 'We live here.'
>
> Jean said something back to him, but he didn't catch it because he was watching the butt go spinning end over end down to the grass. It had already landed but he could still see it falling, like a scene on video loop. There was a good inch left beyond the filter. He would have to go down in a minute and pick it up, before Mr. Rice found it and decided that he'd rented to a couple of bums.

And that butt, falling, falling, falling, is our "dawning of understanding" of the sparrow's "bright sound" in the first paragraph.

Chip. Chip.

Not all, however, is brooding poetry. Mike Barnes is disgracefully funny in writing sex scenes –see *The Syllabus*—and capable of lively humour modulating to sudden warm depth as in this polished paragraph from *Catalogue Raisonné*:

> Angela rolled her eyes my way at Robert's "jitterbugging," but she was having fun. Her cheeks flushed, laughing when he cranked her around in a spastic spin. But next up she got Jason, who shuffled awkwardly to "Start Me Up," the usual masculine jerks and jolts, like a man forced to be sprightly in body armour. Our registrar was an earnest, thoroughly decent guy, a fitness buff capable of telling you far more than you wanted to know about lactic acid and proteins. Executing a neat turn away from him, Angela shot me a pained look of appeal. I spoke to Ramon, and rescued her when the next song started. "Avalon" by Roxy Music, one of her current favourites. We danced in a slow tight circle, her body humid and warm. It felt like high school. Almost that magical again.

With his second collection, *Contrary Angel*, Mike Barnes dramatically extended his range and ambition.

Kim Jernigan conducts an interesting interview with Barnes in *The New Quarterly Volume XX, No. 4* (Winter/Spring 2001).

David Bergen writes on the stories in *Aquarium* in "The Blue Bic Pen" in *The New Quarterly XXI, Nos. 2 and 3*.

Clark Blaise

Short Story Collections: *A North American Education* (1973), *Tribal Justice* (1974), *Resident Alien* (1986), *Man and His World* (1992), *If I Were Me* (1997), *Southern Stories* (2000), *Pittsburgh Stories* (2001), *Montreal Stories* (2003), *World Body* (2006), and *The Meagre Tarmac* (2011).

Novels: *Lunar Attractions* (1979) and *Lusts* (1984).

Memoirs: *Days and Nights in Calcutta* (1977) and *I had a Father* (1992).

Non-Fiction: *The Sorrow and the Terror: The Haunting Legacy of the Air India Tragedy* (1987), *Time Lord: Sir Sandford Fleming and the Creation of Standard Time* (2000), *Selected Essays* (Ed. J. Metcalf and J.R. Tim Struthers), and *The Interviews*. (Ed. J.R. Tim Struthers) (2016).

Clark Blaise's *Selected Stories* appeared from The Porcupine's Quill in four volumes: *Southern Stories* (with an introduction by Fenton Johnson), 2000; *Pittsburgh Stories* (with an introduction by Robert Boyers), 2001; *Montreal Stories* (with an introduction by Peter Behrens), 2003; and *World Body* (with an introduction by Michael Augustin), 2006. Since then he has also written *The Meagre Tarmac*, stories of the Indian diaspora in California.

Along with the Selected Stories of Mavis Gallant, Norman Levine, and Alice Munro, these five books constitute one of the most important bodies of work in Canadian fiction.

In his afterword to *World Body*, Blaise wrote:

> Fate, family and marriage have conspired to make me into a hydroponic writer: rootless, unhoused, fed by swirling waters and harsh, artificial light. In Canadian terms, a classic un-Munro. A Manitoba mother and a Quebec father, an American and Canadian life split more or less equally, can do that to an inquisitive and absorptive child. I never lived longer than six months anywhere, until my four-year Pittsburgh adolescence and fourteen years of Montreal teaching. As a consequence, when I was a young writer, I thought that making sense of my American and Canadian experience would absorb my interest for the rest of my life.
>
> But a five-minute wedding ceremony in a lawyer's office in Iowa City forty-two years ago delivered that inquisitive child an even larger world than the North American continent. I married India, a beautiful and complicated world, and that Canadian/American, French/English, Northern/Southern boy slowly disappeared. (I wonder what he would have been like, had the larger world never intervened.) The stories in *World Body* reflect a few of those non-North-American experiences. I now live in California, but my California, strangely, presents itself through Indian eyes.

When I first knew Blaise, forty years ago, as a member of the Montreal Story Tellers, I was a young English immigrant from a still-insular England. We gathered from his stories that he had spent his childhood among redneck crackers having chigger-like worms removed from his feet with the aid of carbolic acid and pouring fresh quicklime down the seething, hissing squatty-hole. In Cincinnati he attended school with Israelites and the "coloured," elementary school students who were either balding or with moustaches. He spoke French; even more impressive, he understood *joual*. His mother had studied art in Germany during Hitler's rise to power; his father, a thuggish, illiterate womanizer, was, in Clark's words, "a salesman, a violent, aggressive, manipulative man specializing in the arts of spontaneous misrepresentation." Bernard Malamud was his friend. He had been at Iowa in much the same years as Raymond Carver, Andre Dubus, and Joy Williams. And to top off all this outré richness, he was married to Bharati Mukherjee, a novelist and story writer of great beauty, who dazzled us with her saris. I found him (and her), exotic.

A few years ago my son Daniel married Chantal Filion and Blaise said to me, "At last your people have joined my people." But by then I was less clear who my people were. I was no longer, as I had been, simply a part of the Metcalf diaspora from Wensleydale in North Yorkshire. I had acquired another country, another citizenship. My first wife was of Lebanese origins, her people from a village not far from Mount Hermon, so my daughter is half-British, half-Lebanese-Canadian, though American in upbringing. My wife is Jewish as, therefore, is my stepson. My wife connects me to Quebec, where she was born, and to Romania, Poland, and Israel. My younger son and daughter are from Kerala or Tamil Nadu State—no one knows. My wife and I were the guardians of boat children, a brother and sister from Cholon in Saigon. Over the forty years I've known Blaise, my life, I realized slowly, had become a Clark Blaise-life, a Clark Blaise-story.

Alexander MacLeod wrote an interesting essay on Blaise in *CNQ* No. 67 entitled "I once was lost but now am found: Re-reading Clark Blaise in 2005.":

> After so many years of emigration and immigration, and after decades of cultural and linguistic inter-marriage, and

after generations of ever-increasing personal mobility and travel, I think the world outside Blaise's fiction has caught up to lives led inside the books. When we re-read these stories in 2005, we see that Blaise's characters are not nearly as unusual as we may once have thought. Rather than imagining that they are lost and alone, it seems now that Blaise's characters are actually leading the way, carving out a path that millions have followed in recent decades. It may be true that seventy years ago most of the North American population lived and died within fifty miles of the places where they were born, but that simply is no longer the case. "The past" as L.P. Hartley famously put it "is another country" and we do not live there any more. When scholars study Blaise's work they are not reading anthropological reports on some strange group of lonely overeducated misfits who just can't fit in no matter where they go. If it were only possible to shake off the nostalgic fog that so often clouds our reading on the issue of place, we might finally see the mirror Blaise is holding up. We might finally understand that when we look at his people, we see ourselves—an entire population haunted by visions and stories of a stable home place that never actually belonged to us.

In "A North American Education" Blaise wrote a story that is one of the glories of Canadian literature, though it touches on Canada only briefly. It begins:

> Eleven years after the death of Napoleon, in the presidency of Andrew Jackson, my grandfather, Boniface Thibidault, was born.

In the opening paragraphs, Blaise refers to Flaubert's *A Sentimental Education* and Flaubert's novel is to be understood as a ghostly presence, a running commentary on and contrast to the events of Blaise's story. Though the latter is less about sexual love than it is about the love the boy longs for from his father.

A Sentimental Education takes place largely in Paris in the years leading up to the overthrow of Louis-Philippe, in 1848, and the establishment of the Second Republic. Paris serves as a vibrant backdrop to the obsessional love affair between Frederic Moreau and Mme Marie Arnoux.

> The Seine, mud-coloured, had risen almost to the keystones of the bridges. A chilly breath came off the river. Frederic sniffed it with all his strength, savouring that delicious Paris air, which seems to be fraught with the redolence of love and the exhalations of the intellect.

The book climbs towards the events of 1848 and the early rapture of those who took to the streets is suggested by Dussardier's speech to Frederic during the fighting.

> The Republic has been proclaimed! We shall be happy now. I heard some journalists talking just now; they said we were going to liberate Poland and Italy. No more kings! Do you understand? The whole world free! The whole world free!

This fervour is wonderfully undercut by the subsequent scenes of rioting, wanton destruction, and drunken looting.

Frederic's unconsummated and consuming love for Marie Arnoux, which is the book's central strand, is summed up in his final speech to her:

> Your figure, your smallest movement seemed to me of more than human significance on earth. When you passed by, my heart lifted like dust after your footsteps. The effect you had on me was like a moonlit night in summer, when the world is all perfume, soft shadows, milky paleness, and dim horizons; when I repeated your name, I tried to kiss it with my lips; for me it contained all the joys of the flesh and the soul.

This is the presence behind "A North American Education." The idealized, madly romantic passion between Frederic and Mme Arnoux stands in contrast to the narrator's North American education in matters sexual.

> I had known from books and articles my mother was leaving in the bathroom, that I was supposed to be learning about sex. I'd read the books and figured out the anatomy for myself; I wondered only how to ask a girl for it and what to do once I got there. Sex was something like dancing, I supposed, too intricate and spontaneous for a boy like me. And so we toured the Fair Grounds that morning, saying nothing, reviewing the prize sows and heifers, watching a stock-car race and a miniature rodeo. I could tell from my father's breathing, his coughing, his attempt to put his arm around my shoulder, that this was the day he was going to talk to me about sex, the facts of life, and the thought embarrassed him as much as it did me. I wanted to tell him to never mind; I didn't need it, it was something that selfish people did to one another.
>
> He led me to a remote tent far off the fairway. There was a long male line outside, men with a few boys my age, joking loudly and smelling bad. My father looked away, silent. So this is the place, I thought, where I'm going to see it, going to learn something good and dirty, something they couldn't put on these Britannica Films and show in school. The sign over the entrance said only: *Princess Hi-Yalla. Shows Continuously.*

So much for a *moonlit night in summer, when the world is all perfume.*

The shadow of *A Sentimental Education*, which stands behind "A North American Education" and intensifies its power and depth, also suggests other sadnesses, diminishments, varieties of loss.

An avuncular adult once asked one of Clark Blaise's sons what he wished to be when he grew up.

The child replied, "A European."

Clark Blaise and Broward Dowdy

As central to Blaise as his writing is his teaching; never impersonal or efficient, never a proponent of "chalk and talk," he pours into teaching his tireless passion. When he graduated from Denison University in Ohio, he travelled to Harvard, almost as on pilgrimage, to seek out Bernard Malamud. He was lucky enough to be allowed into Malamud's summer seminar class, and Malamud eventually became both mentor and friend. Blaise wrote of him:

> Malamud, as a reader, as a teacher, and as a writer, takes *delight*; there is no other way of putting it. It was possible to *delight* this man, to see his eyes, mouth, brow suddenly dance over a sentence, a word, an idea.

The poet Brian Bartlett interviewing Clark recalls Blaise's Concordia University fiction workshop in 1975-6 in Montreal:

> **Bartlett:** "...I just wanted to say your description of Malamud reminded me of your own approach to teaching in that workshop... The first class was on campus, then after that we met in your living room... and thank you for all those bottles of wine, and all those *hors d'oeuvres*."

This seemingly inconsequential recollection of Bartlett's reveals so much about Blaise; it reveals his generosity, his recognition of talent, his acceptance for his responsibility to the tradition, his welcoming-in and handing-on.

> **Bartlett:** "Here's another memory, about a workshopped story by Peter Behrens. In one scene he was describing a police or an ambulance siren, the way its sound moves up and down in volume. And he used the phrase "thready wail"—do you remember that?
>
> **Blaise:** Yes. Speaking of Peter Behrens, I remember something he did that I tried to point out to the class—he so perfectly described the heat that comes from an old car's heater. You know, on a cold, cold Canadian night, when you had the heat coming in from the manifold and you had to open up the two little doors. And I said that it's more worthwhile to be able to describe the

heat coming in off a heater than it is to describe anything else in the story. That *that* was the thing that gave me the assurance that this was a writer who paid attention, who noted things.

It is still received opinion that short stories are the apprentice work that a writer undertakes before tackling the really serious work of the novel, where the big bucks are. Imagine, then, how liberating and reinforcing it was for me as a young writer of short stories to read Blaise in the little mags and to listen to him as Hugh Hood drove the Montreal Story Tellers to our readings. Clark often proposed that the short story, far from being fiction's Cinderella, was actually *superior* to novels.

Most novels are watery, diluted, and bloated, and they do not have anything like the richness of a short story.

What, he asked, was the difference between a Mavis Gallant story and someone else's novel? It's that in comparison, "the novel becomes smaller and thinner than her story."

For me, the short story is an expansionist form, not a miniaturizing form. To me, the novel is a miniaturizing form. I think of the story as the largest, most expanded statement you can make about a particular incident. I think of the novel as the briefest thing you can say about a larger incident. I think of the novel as being far more miniaturist—it's a miniaturization of life. And short fiction is an expansion of a moment.

This was the sort of thing tossed back over the front seat's headrest. And there was more.

I think the job of fiction is to view life through a microscope so that every grain gets its due and no one can confuse salt with sugar. You hear a lot about cinema being a visual medium—this is false. It *degrades* the visual by its inability to focus. It takes the visual for granted. Only the word—for me—is truly visual.

I've always favoured the short story for its energy, a result of its confinement, and for the fact that its length reflects the author's ability to hold it entirely in his/her head like a musical note. You can't do that with a novel. Holding everything, meaning the syllables, the rhythms, the balance of scene and narration, long sentences and short...

When I "see" a story, it is always in terms of images... In *A North American Education*, most of the Montreal stories—"Eyes," "Words for the Winter," "Extractions and Contractions" and "Going to India" ... are stories of texture and voice—details selected with an eye to their aptness but also to their "vapour trails," their slow dissolve into something more diffuse and nameless.

At "vapour trails" and "something more diffuse and nameless," I can sense Ray Smith's glance upon me but refuse to turn my head; Ray is more comfortable, at least in public, discussing brands of beer. A pose, of course, because he's a dandy in disguise.

Recently I was reading an essay about childhood reading by Jeanette Winterson. I was reminded of it by Blaise's "diffuse and nameless."

At the library, dutifully stamping out wave upon wave of sea stories, and the battered blossoms of Mills and Boon, I recognized what I had known dimly: that plot was meaningless to me. This was a difficult admission for one whose body was tattooed with Bible stories, but it was necessary for me to accept that my love affair was with language not with what it said. Art communicates, that is certain. What it communicates is something ineffable. Something about ourselves, about the human condition, that is not summed up by the oil painting, or the piece of music, or the poem, but, rather, moves through it. What you say, what you paint, what you can hear is the means not the end of art; there are so many rooms behind it.

Blaise's details, apt but also dissolving into "something more diffuse and nameless" and Winterson's "ineffable...something," that "moves through it" are not unconnected.

And then there's the hard grind of it, the unromantic slog.

> I tend to work from the small to the large. I can worry a long time over a word and then the sentence and then the paragraph, but the real progress comes when I realise that all of that was useless. I didn't need the paragraph. I didn't even need the three or four paragraphs around it. I can go from point A to point G in a single leap and a suture, but I don't see it quickly. I have to go from the very, very fine up. That's how I work. I don't have the construction engineer's sense of "Knock this out, knock that out, and it will work." I'm a bricklayer in that sense—I have to go from brick to brick...
>
> If the reading of a story is a line-by-line discovery, the writing of it has to be much more. It's not just line-by-line, it's line-by-line creation and it's line-by-line re-presentation. It's not like choreography, with its illusion of spontaneity and its hours of rehearsal. Line by line the writer is discovering the nature of his material and each line is like the finest nozzle point holding back a great force. The best kind of writing—I'm thinking of Gallant or [Hortense] Calisher, or a few others—is that which comes out like a laser: very fine, very controlled, perfectly placed, able to do surgery, but behind it is the power to knock aircraft out of the skies."

I was recently re-reading Meryle Secrest's *Kenneth Clark: A Biography* and paused over a section recounting Clark's appointment as Slade Professor of Fine Arts at the University of Oxford. The first holder of the position had been John Ruskin. This connection meant a great deal to Kenneth Clark as, from the time he began to work on *The Gothic Revival*, Ruskin had been the predominant influence on his thought.

Ruskin's belief that no one could pretend to know about art unless he or she practiced it, would have struck a chord with Sir Kenneth. That belief of Ruskin's came to mind when I remembered a vivid instance of Blaise illuminating another writer's story in a way that only another writer could.

Here is Blaise reaching into the innards of a story. In an interview with Tim Struthers, Blaise says of Hemingway's story:

> "Cat in the Rain," yes. Just the inclusion of a waiter, standing silently in a doorway of a restaurant, waiting for the rain to go away, because the rain has totally wiped out his business. But he's there and, as I said, there's no reason why he should be there in the story. The story is eloquent enough with just the rain conveying that it's a desolate urban scene.
>
> But putting him in there alters the relationship of everything. It gives a third point, it allows for a triangulation of the rain and the desolation. It's there. And I've always felt the presence of that waiter. He has no role in the story. He disappears and we don't see him again. Nevertheless he has made his entrance, he has stood there looking out over the rain. Probably, I can imagine, with the insolence of the normal Italian waiter. But I guess he goes back inside…
>
> See, what happens here is when the young, dissatisfied, and unfulfilled wife is looking out over the rain herself, from the window of her room, where her husband is lying in bed writing, she sees the waiter. This is not in the story at all—but in my mind she sees the waiter and since that is a forbidden kind of vision for her she sees the cat trying to stay dry and focuses on "I want a kitty," "I want a cat." It's probably not what she wants. But she can't articulate, or doesn't know, what it is she really wants.

Is this groundless and eccentric speculation?

In a well-known passage from *A Moveable Feast*, Hemingway recalls writing those early stories:

> It was a very simple story called "Out of Season" and I had omitted the real end of it which was that the old man hanged himself. This was omitted on my new theory that you could omit anything if you knew that you omitted and the omitted part would strengthen the story and make people feel something more than they understood.

Put together Blaise's feeling about the waiter—that something is being said that is not being said, the feeling of a brilliant writer/critic—put this feeling together with Hemingway's "new theory" of omission and—CLICK!

To turn back to the story "A North American Education," for we are not yet done with it; the boy's ripening sexuality was confined to fantasy; he feasted his eyes on the young women who lived on the same block; the sight of them fed his hot imagination.

> There lived on that street, and I was beginning to notice in that summer before the sideshow at the county fair, several girl brides and one or two maturely youthful wives. The brides, under twenty and with their first or second youngsters, were a sloppy crew who patrolled the streets in cut-away shorts and bra-less elasticized halters that had to be pulled up every few steps. They set their hair so tightly in pin-curlers that the effect, at a distance, was of the mange.

The boy's sexual obsessions focused on his next-door neighbour, Annette; on occasion he babysat her three children. The duplexes were mirror images with only the staircases and bathrooms adjoining. In a lengthy feat of complex voyeuristic engineering, he made it possible to see through the used-razorblade slot in his medicine cabinet into the medicine cabinet in Annette's duplex. One evening while babysitting for Annette, he hears unexpected sounds in the bathroom in *his* house, unexpected because his parents are out, and looking through the interlocking razorblade slots sees "young fingers among our bottles, blond hair, and a tanned forehead: Annette."

He watches nothingness until the light's switched off.

Then he watches Annette walking down the path to the Thibidault Furniture station wagon, "the car immediately, silently, backed away, with just its parking lights on... I never asked my father why he had come home or why Annette had been in our bathroom. I didn't have to—I'd gotten a glimpse of Annette, which was all I could handle anyway. I didn't understand the rest."

But he had, we feel, understood enough to feel his world threatened.

To return now to Princess Hi-Yella in the county fair tent and the narrator's continuing sentimental education.

(High yellow, one of the South's endless calibrations of skin colour, meaning an African American with very light colouring.)

The horrified narrator watches Princess Hi-Yella's lubricious manipulations of a stick of licked gum and the cigarette she unnaturally "smokes."

A boy with "the cretinous look of fat boys in overalls: big, sweating, red-cheeked, with eyes like calves in a roping event" was "holding his crotch as though it burned. He was running in place, moaning, then screaming, 'Daddy!' and I forgot about the Princess. Men cleared a circle and began clapping and chanting, 'Whip it out!' and the boy was crying 'Daddy, I can't hold it back no more.' A navy-blue stain that I thought was blood was spreading between his legs. I thought he'd managed to pull his penis off."

The narrator's father grimly escorts his son out of the tent just as the son says, "Wait—it's happening to me too."

His father says: "'Jesus Christ—are you *sick*?' ... He jerked me forward by the elbow. 'Jesus God,' he muttered, pulling me along down the fairway, then letting me go and walking so fast I had to run, both hands trying to cup the mess I had made... 'I don't know about you,' my father said. '*I think there's something wrong with you*' and it was the worst thing my father could say about me."

"A North American Education" ends almost symphonically.

> There was another Sunday in Florida. A hurricane was a hundred miles off shore and due to strike Fort Lauderdale within the next six hours. We drove from our house down Las Olas to the beach (Fort Lauderdale was still an inland city then), and parked half a mile away, safe from the paint-blasting sand. We could hear the breakers under the shriek of the wind, shaking the wooden bridge we walked on. Then we watched them crash, brown with weeds and suspended sand. And we could see them miles offshore, rolling in forty feet high and flashing their foam like icebergs. A few men in swimming suits and woollen sweaters were standing in the crater pools, pulling out the deep-sea fish that had been stunned by the trip and waves. Other fish littered the beach, their bellies blasted by the change in pressure.

My mother's face was raw and her glasses webbed with salt. She went back to the car on her own. My father and I sat on the bench until we were soaked and the municipal guards rounded us up. Then they barricaded the boulevards and we went back to the car, the best day of fishing we'd ever had, and we walked hand in hand for the last time, talking excitedly, dodging coconuts, power lines, and shattered glass, feeling brave and united in the face of the storm. My father and me. What a day it was, what a once-in-a-lifetime day it was.

This ending has been hailed as an intense and moving affirmation, an heroic paean, an almost *operatic* finale to the story.

Which, in one way it is, and in another, isn't. I think it has been continually misread. Blaise's stories usually seem straightforward and usually are not.

The emotions in this long paragraph travel in opposing directions. What seems to be almost delirious affirmation, is, at the same time, elegy. We have been set up for this kind of reading of the final paragraph early in the story.

We were still living in a duplex; a few months later my parents were to start their furniture store and we would never fish again. We walked out, my father and I... a few young fathers would squint and ask, "Not again, Gene?"; and silently we drove, and later, silently, we fished.

Thibidault and son. He was a fisherman and I always fished at his side. Fished for what? I wonder now—he was too short and vain a man to really be a fisherman... Every cast became a fresh hope, a trout or *doré* or even a Muskie. But we never caught a Muskie or a trout, just the snake-like fork-boned pike...

Silent Hope and Silent Disappointment.

And after the sighting of Annette in his own bathroom and the mysterious presence of his father, the concluding line of that section: "*Thibidault et fils*, fishing again."

"Fishing" takes on a new meaning in this line, undefined, fishing for sex, for relationship, for love?

And then there's the hurricane blowing in, downed power lines, flying coconuts, belly-blasted dead fish.

Blaise had written about his own work:

> Water has always summoned up the binding images of terror and of love. It did so with giant turtles grinding their beaks under my Florida pillow, it did so with the ghastly images of alligator garfish, of Canadian stories, of the leeches covering my character's body.

In an interview, he said, "My feeling has always been that nature is ruthless and that nature is corrosive."

We must assume that the hurricane should be seen not simply as a hurricane but as the visible agent of general impending disaster and destruction, his parents' divorce, the collapse of family life, the end of his connection with his father. All this is prefigured in the scene. His mother's face "was raw and her glasses webbed with salt. She went back to the car on her own. My father and I sat on the bench until we were soaked…"

It is in this final paragraph that the possible meanings of "fishing" are confirmed.

the best day of fishing we'd ever had

But on this day they'd done no fishing at all.

What a once-in-a-lifetime day it was.

This catchphrase, cliché, meaning something like "very memorable" or "unforgettable," also in this particular context means, quite literally, "once only."

Blaise has said in an interview: "Each story is a metaphor. I can't say it's a metaphor with a paraphrasable meaning. It's just a metaphor, an elaborate comparison, a way of suggesting something larger and more permanent."

Blaise's stories range from the American South, to Pittsburgh, to Montreal and Quebec, to India, to the Indian diaspora in California, through Europe to Israel, but out of this array I wish to comment on a story from his apprenticeship because it was the story that taught me how to read him. "Broward Dowdy" was the third story Blaise wrote. He wrote it when he was nineteen; it appeared in the distinguished literary magazine *Shenandoah* in 1962.

He said of it, "I wrote the core of that story as a sophomore in college... But I put the frame around it when I was at the Iowa Writers' Workshop."

The "frame" was the narrator's father being away at The War and the family's consequently reduced circumstances.

He wrote of the story in an essay for my anthology *Stories Plus,* in 1979, "'Broward Dowdy' contrasts the squalor, intolerance, poverty, and brutishment of central Florida with a certain nobility of character, humility, and fundamental human decency. [That nobility of character, etc. in the person of the boy, Broward.] Two boys confront each other over the gulf of literacy and the all-important determinant of class. The narrator's family has temporarily fallen (due to The War and the absence of the father caught up in it), and that fall enables the narrator to glimpse at a life he would otherwise have dismissed."

(I can imagine what the story would have been like before he put "the frame" of The War around it; it would have been less story than vivid, energetic *sketch*; the frame raises the sketch to metaphor. In Blaise's mature view, all short fiction aspires to metaphor.)

The "life glimpsed" was *this*.

> ...the Dowdy's rusting truck loaded with children, rattling pans, and piles of mattresses in striped ticking churned down the sandy ruts I had come to call my trail. I helped them spread their gear on the floors of a pair of tarpaper shanties, and watched their boy my age, Broward, pour new quicklime down last summer's squatty-hole. Within hours, he had shown me new fishing holes, and how to extract bait worms from lily stalks...

> Broward's little brother came scampering through the tall swamp grass... It was Bruce, about three... And like the rest

of the family, his stomach was bloated out like a floating fish's. Bruce wore only a filthy pair of underpants, with large holes cut out around his rump and penis... Bruce, Broward explained to me, was "shy—real shy. He don't take up with strangers much."

The boys gut the slimy little bream on the table they're about to eat at and Broward says, "While's I'm lightn' the fire y'all scrape the leeches off and start choppin' up the fish." The bits of fish are dusted with "a handful of gray flour" and fried in the smoking skillet and there ensues a meal of near-Gothic horror, preceded by the father's prayer of thanksgiving:

We thank Thee that we have this delicious food on our humble table, health in our fambly, and that Thee, that guards all our blessings, hast kept our name and blood untainted.

The talk of Willamae, one of the daughters, was so "cracker" as to be incomprehensible.

Another daughter had declared herself too sick to be able to eat.

"She ain't sick anymore'n I am," pronounced the father. "She's fixin' to run off is all... They gets to be her age and all of a sudden they's regular ladies—they starts thinkin' how grand they can live in Leesburg and go to pitcher shows ev'ry night."

..."Here," says Broward, "y'all hold your fork like this and bring it up to your mouth." As soon as Broward let Bruce's hand go, the fork clattered to the floor. "Oh, it just ain't no use," Broward said... "Wayce, you do it," Broward pleaded. "He don't remember from one meal to the next..." Waycross Dowdy, who was fourteen and already taller than his father, and blubbery, scowled at Broward, then down at Bruce. Then he picked up the fish on Bruce's plate and stuffed it into his own mouth, and no one said a word."

On my first reading of it in the long ago, the final image of "Broward Dowdy," which is both image and metaphor, beamed down upon me like a single ray of Charleton Heston sunlight shining out of dark, portentous clouds.

Massed choirs might have been singing.

That image unlocked for me so much about the possible shaping of stories.

"The War," Blaise wrote about the story in commentary I read years later, "—an event that Broward knows nothing about, can know nothing about—has brought them together. Squalor and dignity can co-exist; the war is not confined to unnamed islands in the Pacific—the last image in the story conveys strongly the possibility that Broward Dowdy will also be a casualty."

The story's last image.

> Before the Dowdys could leave, they had to get their sole possession, the old Dodge truck, ready to roll. Over the humid summer months, rust had set in and a thorough oiling was needed. Naturally it was Broward who had been ordered under the truck to oil the bearings. The last I saw of Broward Dowdy were his legs, pale and brilliant against the sour muck, sliced cleanly by the shadow of the truck and the shanties beyond.

Mary Borsky
Short Story Collections: *Influence of the Moon* (1995) and *Cobalt Blue* (2007).

Influence of the Moon, this gem of a book of linked stories chronicles the growing up in the fifties of Irene Lychenko in the small northern Alberta town of Salt Prairie.

"Salt Prairie" is Mary Borsky's reinvention of the actual town of High Prairie. In her childhood, she said, a sign on the outskirts read:

Welcome to High Prairie
Population 2,500
"Where Culture and Agriculture Meet"

That small Ukranian world is captured with an astonishing vividness. The intensity of these stories will remind readers of Alice Munro's

"Walker Brothers Cowboy" or Dylan Thomas' "The Peaches"—evocations of an enchanted time and place. The lyricism of the stories is tempered, however, by a dry, wry humour and, as Irene grows older, by a sly and insidiously engaging feminism.

Writers' first books often recreate the intensity with which children experience and apprehend the world. Those remembered worlds, worlds outside time, live in luminous and holy detail. That impulse to enshrine is movingly expressed by Del Jordan in the epilogue to Alice Munro's *Lives of Girls and Women*. Del is thinking about the little town of Jubilee:

> I would try to make lists. A list of all the stores and businesses going up and down the main street and who owned them, a list of family names, names on the tombstones in the cemetery and any inscriptions underneath. A list of the titles of the movies that played at the Lyceum Theatre from 1938 to 1950, roughly speaking. Names on the cenotaph (more for the First World War than for the Second). Names of the streets and the pattern they lay in.
>
> The hope of accuracy we bring to such tasks is crazy, heartbreaking.
>
> And no list could hold what I wanted, for what I wanted was every last thing, every layer of speech and thought, stroke of light on bark or walls, every smell, pothole, pain, crack, delusion, held still and held together—radiant, everlasting.

We can, I like to think, recognize enshrined detail. It seems to signal itself. Here's a passage from near the opening of Dylan Thomas' "The Peaches."

> He [Uncle Jim] backed the mare into Union Street, lurching against her side, cursing her patience and patting her nose, and we both climbed into the cart. "There are too many drunken gypsies," he said as we rolled and rattled through the flickering lamp-lit town.
>
> He sang hymns all the way to Gorsehill in an affectionate bass voice, and conducted the wind with his whip. He did not

need to touch the reins. Once on the rough road, between hedges twisting out to twig the mare by the bridle and poke our caps, we stopped at a whispered "Whoa," for uncle to light his pipe and set the darkness on fire and show his long, red, drunken fox's face to me, with its bristling side-bushes and wet, sensitive nose. A white house with a light in one bedroom window shone in a field on a short hill beyond the road.

Uncle whispered, "Easy, easy, girl," to the mare, though she was standing calmly, and said to me over his shoulder in a suddenly loud voice; "A hangman lived there."

The writing in which the experience is delivered bears the hallmarks of Dylan Thomas' razzmatazz; it is carefully, even elaborately worked.

"cursing her patience and patting her nose"

"conducting the wind with his whip"

"hedges twisting out to twig the mare by the bridle"

The sentence that signals to me, a sentence unadorned and very visible, a detail I feel sure that the child-Dylan in his best suit in the frightening dark actually saw and enshrined:

"A white house with a light in one bedroom window shone in a field on a short hill beyond the road."

And Thomas starts here to really rev up the rhetoric, splashy effects which I adored when I was sixteen. But when I was sixteen I also had a liking for Harvey's Bristol Cream. It took years to rid myself of Thomas' baneful influence. The centre of the problem in the following two paragraphs is that there is something ingratiating in the performance, a betrayal of the experience itself by manipulative charm. By charm itself.

Thomas goes on:

I pushed the door open and walked into the passage out of the wind. I might have been walking into the hollow night and the wind, passing through a tall vertical shell on an inland sea-shore. Then a door at the end of the passage opened; I saw the plates on the shelves, the lighted lamp on the long oil-clothed table. "Prepare to Meet Thy God" knitted over the fire-place, the smiling china dogs, the brown-stained settle, the grandmother clock, and I ran into the kitchen and into Annie's arms.

There was a welcome, then. The clock struck twelve as she kissed me, and I stood among the shining and striking like a prince taking off his disguise. One minute I was small and cold, skulking dead-scared down a black passage in my stiff, best suit, with my hollow belly thumping and my heart like a time bomb, clutching my grammar school cap, unfamiliar to myself, a snub-nosed story-teller lost in his own adventures and longing to be home; the next I was a royal nephew in smart town clothes, embraced and welcomed, standing in the snug centre of my stories and listening to the clock announcing me. She hurried me to a seat in the side of the cavernous fireplace and took off my shoes. The bright lamps and the ceremonial gongs blazed and rang for me.

These days when I read with a colder eye, it is a relief to turn to a different kitchen, one enshrined more austerely, the kitchen of Irene Lychenko's mother in the story "Blessing."

It was cooler inside the house and the kitchen had its same sour, salty smell. The cupboards were still red and blue, each door bordered with pictures of flowers cut from seed catalogues, glued on, then covered with clear nail varnish. The window was crowded with African violets, geraniums, and various cuttings rooting in jars. Under the window sill and along the counter were stacks of margarine containers, jars of keys, tacks, ballpoints.

And here from one of Canada's stellar short story writers with *all* the elements in play—plot, characters, dialogue—is the high-octane opening of the first story in *Influence of the Moon*, "Ice."

When the Russians shot a dog up into space, my father celebrated for three days. Later, when he got sober, he took us fishing, me and my brother Amel.

"B.B. Hunt and the other guys, when it's Russian, they think it's something bad," my dad said. He almost had to shout to be heard above the pounding of the tire chains on the winter road. Amel and I sat next to him on the front seat of the dark blue Dodge. I was wearing boys' clothes, the same as Amel, a parka, extra pants, tuque, winter boots.

"But you and me, we like that dog in space, don't we Daddy?" I shouted back. "We think it's fine, right Daddy?" Amel and I were drinking root beers. It pleased me to sit with a bottle in my hand and talk of grown-up matters to my dad.

"The Russians," my father said, shifting down to go up a hill, "when they want to send a dog in space, do they ask The-Important-B.B.-Hunt, or do they just go ahead and do it?"

I took a moment to drain the last of my root beer. Sometimes I didn't understand anything my father said—Power of the Proletariat, Science and Progress, the Emancipation of the Working Man. Still, I believed every word he said.

"They just go ahead, Daddy," I said. "They don't ask anybody." Then I checked my father's face, although I was pretty sure I'd answered right.

As we neared the crest of the hill, I could at last see the lake through the grey tops of trees. The ice, mostly blown clear of snow, was grey and flat as a cookie pan, so bright in a strip where the sun reflected, it was impossible to look at. The sky was as blue as the spark from an electric plug.

Influence of the Moon ought to be on its way to becoming a Canadian classic but remains, I'm afraid, largely unknown.

There is a useful interview with Mary Borsky in *Writers Talking* (Eds. J. Metcalf and Claire Wilkshire) Erin: Porcupine's Quill, 2003.

Ann Copeland
Short Story Collections: *At Peace* (1978), *The Back Room* (1979), *Earthen Vessels* (1984), *The Golden Thread* (1989), *Strange Bodies on a Stranger Shore* (1994), and *Season of Apples* (1996).

Non-Fiction: *The ABC's of Writing Fiction.*

Ann Copeland is the pseudonym of Virginia Ann Furtwangler (née Walsh). Born in Connecticut, Copeland was educated in Catholic schools before entering the Ursuline Order as Sister John Bernard. She left the convent shortly after the reign of Pope John XXIII and the upheavals of Vatican II. After thirteen years of convent life, she married and moved, in 1971, to New Brunswick. In her fiction she calls the Ursulines the Agnetine Order, the Sisters of St. Agnes. Her short-story collections are *At Peace* (1978), *The Back Room* (1979), *Earthen Vessels* (1984), *The Golden Thread* (1989), *Strange Bodies on a Stranger Shore* (1994) and *Season of Apples* (1996). I had the pleasure of editing her first book for Oberon Press, in 1978, not that much editing was called for.

In the collection *The Golden Thread*, Copeland reworks the material in *At Peace* to focus on Claire Delaney. We follow Claire from school-girl to novice to Sister and, in the final story, to the now-married Claire revisiting her past. What Copeland sculpts here is something close to a novel. The story Copeland tells falls into fairly conventional forms. The first story, where Claire as schoolgirl deliberately misses taking her part in a religious pageant to go dancing with a "Yale man," fore-shadows Claire's sexual attraction to a priest, her general rebellious-ness against the chafing constraints of convent life, her growing long-ing for freedom. Some might say that we have here little more than the elements of a Harlequin romance—strong-willed heroine strug-gling against oppression towards eventual escape and fulfillment in the arms of a husband, a spiritual bodice-ripper, as it were.

Nor can it be denied that the material itself exerts a strong voy-euristic appeal that is extra-literary. What do they *do* in those con-vents? What is it *for*? What is it *like*? And Copeland amply satisfies our curiosity.

From "The Golden Thread":

> As she tucked hospital corners, she thought of one morning conference in the novitiate—nine years ago now but unfor-gettable. Right after spiritual reading that golden October morning the novices gathered for their usual conference with Mother Theodore, the novice mistress. As they filed in and took their places on the straight chairs lined up in the library, they found that in place of Reverend Mother's desk

an unmade cot had been set up. In those days one didn't comment by even a surreptitious whisper about such things. Their observance of silence was scrupulous and, equally fastidious about modesty of the eyes, they studiedly avoided the exchange of quizzical glances such a break in routine would normally evoke.

Then Mother Theodore came in—a stern woman in her early sixties, straight, silent, awesomely detached from the things of this world. Secretly afraid of her uncompromising otherworldliness, in moments of deepest spiritual aspiration they longed to achieve just such detached clarity of vision and practice.

"Sisters," she said after the opening prayer, "I want to impress on you this morning a lesson for your entire religious life." She paused and looked around at their attentive faces. "There is no task too small to do well for the sake of Our Lord." They knew what was coming. "You will read in Rodriguez many examples of the saints taking care in the minutiae of their daily lives to imitate the patience and humility of Our Lord. It is not given to many of us to carry a great cross. But it is in the humble, day-to-day tasks of our religious lives that we must strive to be conformed to Jesus." She paused again, gravely. "Starting with the senior in rank, Sister Jonas, I want each of you to come forward and make and unmake this cot for us this morning."

Nor do we find in the technique, the rendering, of these stories, anything unconventional or experimental. There is no pushing at the constraints of language and form as there is in the work of, say, Mark Jarman, Michael Winter, Leon Rooke, Annabel Lyon, or Elise Levine. What, then, singles out the work of Ann Copeland?

There is in everything she writes clarity and lucidity. I have, over thirty-five years of reading typescripts, come to realize that these qualities are rare indeed. Her very clarity is a form of passion. Add to this her command of telling detail—Sister Barney's cluttered cell in "At Peace," for example—and the stories sweep the reader unresistingly on. I have never read anything quite like them.

Here from "Cloister," as a further taste, is Claire Delaney's recollection of her acceptance of her vocation.

"Reverend Mother, I have failed in several ways this month in observing the rule and constitutions. I feel I've given in to my curiosity and disedified my sisters by carelessness in religious modesty. Especially during Office I have looked around a good bit."

"Yes, Sister. A few of your sisters have mentioned this to me." Reverend Mother leaned forward slightly, raising one hand to touch the wooden crucifix in her cincture. "It is very easy to become careless about mortification of the senses. Yet our Lord rewards those who curb their curiosity about the outer world by speaking to them within. Unless we quiet worldly curiosity and mortify the tendency to look about, we shall never hear Him when He speaks."

Sister Claire held her expression steady. The inner voice. She thought of Saint Bernard looking the other way as he passed the beauties of Lake Desanzano, Saint Somebody spitting out his tongue at the temptress. She remembered Keats' nightingale and Steven's Ursula. God was about, that she believed. Where should she look to find him? Yet, Reverend Mother was right. God spoke to the soul in silence, not noise. There had come that final crucial moment when, kneeling in the college chapel during her senior year, praying that she would know, she felt in the depths of her soul a stirring... a sense. That stirring—call it a voice—touched the subtle thread of her own most deeply felt freedom. "I want you," He said. And on her free response in that moment hung her future, her life. Perhaps her eternity. She was prepared. She had responded "*in toto corde.*" That had been the moment of her true profession.

In addition to the six story collections, she has written a book about writing, *The ABCs of Writing Fiction* (Story Press, 1996). There is, unfortunately, little or no commentary.

Libby Creelman
Short Story Collections: *Walking in Paradise* (2000).
   Novels: *The Darren Effect* (2010) and *Split* (2015).

The stories in Libby Creelman's *Walking in Paradise* are about, in Stan Dragland's words, "brittle adults and sharp, bewildered children." When I first read the title story "A Walk in Paradise," which describes a cavalcade of mothers and children and bikes and strollers on its way to the grocery store, it was like listening to a scintillating run of notes in a jazz-piano solo; it was like an eruption of Oscar Peterson.

The children have reached Main Street and are waiting at the stop sign, all shouting at once for the go-ahead to cross over.

> "I hope no one's trying to take a nap," Mary Catherine says.
>
> "A nap? Who takes naps?" Aunt Darby says musically. "On a beautiful day like today?"
>
> "CAN WE GO? CAN WE GO?"
>
> "Yes, yes."
>
> "Walk your bikes on Main Street. It's the law."
>
> They cross over in a tight cluster and coast up onto the sidewalk. Georgiana's son Peter crashes into the outside of the electric company office.
>
> "Oh. my. God," Georgiana says and Mary Catherine recognizes in her cousin's voice that whine of exasperation that only a mother can produce: that certainty that she will not survive one more fall-down, bloody knee, stubbed toe, broken bone or set of stitches.

The stories repay close reading and that suggests to me that an interesting way to present Libby Creelman's writing is to look at one story, "Three Weeks," in considerable detail. It is a story about a brother and sister, Mike and Rosanna, who go to stay for three weeks with their cousin, Peter, and his girlfriend, Debbie, on a family hobby farm in Maine. Later, they are joined by Louie, a college friend of Mike's. Rosanna is sixteen. Peter, Mike, and Louie are growing on a hillside a field of marijuana.

Creelman talked about the origins of the story at the Stratford Festival Conference in a panel discussion moderated by John Vardon.

> I don't keep a notebook, but I do know that, for me, there's an intellectual component and a non-intellectual component. The non-intellectual component is really important... Like everybody else, I always have my eyes open and my ears open, and I'm always collecting things, not so much in a notebook, but more as in remembering anecdotes and storing things away. Before I can start a story, I need to be emotionally charged in a certain way. It's really hard to put this into words, but I think it happens to everybody—it's a feeling. Say you look at a photograph, or the way the light hits something—or maybe it's a movie you've seen—and you get a feeling. For the story "Three Weeks," the feeling that charges that story, and charged the writing of it, was based on a visit I made to a countryside in inland Maine about twenty-five years ago, just for a weekend. It was the feeling of the landscape that weekend that stayed with me. Nothing in the story, in terms of action and characters, is related to that weekend. It was the feeling of the landscape—it was late summer, really lush and abundant and very, very sexual—that's how it struck me. I knew that it was rich, that there was something there that I could work with ...
>
> The anecdote that forms the backbone for the story, is not even a full anecdote. Someone described to me this scenario of these young kids—well, young adults—trying to grow dope in the country, having this business. What was described to me was the atmosphere, the paranoia, the tension, the youth, and some of the details of growing dope and stripping the buds, and all this business. Eventually—I don't remember how this happened—I sat down and those two components—one (the anecdote) was more intellectual, the other (the feeling of that landscape) more intuitive—were married, so to speak, and I began to write the story.

Mike and Rosanna squabble and fight from long custom. They are not only growing dope but smoking it in stunning quantities.

"You blacked out?" Mike was saying.

It was dark now in the house.

"Go away."

"Don't get stupid Rosanna."

"Shut up. Go away."

He punched her shoulder. The sofa springs creaked beneath her and someone in the room inhaled sharply. "Rosanna, go to bed. We're gonna go look for a bar, all right, so just go to bed and don't smoke any more or else."

"Maybe your sister wants to come," Louie suggested. Rosanna figured he was standing just inside the doorway; she couldn't see him where she lay.

"Or else what?" she asked.

"She's fucking sixteen, Louie. Look at her."

Along with the sweaty heat, tensions and paranoid fears rise in the house. Violence might erupt. Rosanna sleeps for long stretches and smokes dope in her room, avoiding the others. Louie seems interested in her. The world outside the farmhouse is green-swollen, luxurious, the liquid sky hazy, heat waves cast up from the earth, engulfing the house, the woodshed and barn, Rosanna and Mike.

"I thought I heard a helicopter today," Mike said one evening. He flicked a piece of oatmeal cookie across the room. It landed neatly in Rosanna's hair.

"Fuck you, Mike," she said.

Peter was looking wearily at Mike. "They don't go over with helicopters any more. I think I mentioned that to you about eighty-one times already."

At this, Debbie giggled, the sound of it a rutty laziness that Peter appeared unable to resist ...

They harvest the crop. An obliquely sensual scene in the barn.

At best, from a distance—outdoors or in the house—the smell was sweet, like cloves, like Christmas cookies, honeyed and luscious. She lay in her bed at night and it lingered in the air above her as a reminder of her day, standing across from Louie, his class ring flashing in the gloomy light as he stripped buds as thick as his thumb.

The ripening of the marijuana parallels other ripenings, hints at other possible readiness.

After swimming at Sharpe's Lake, an ambiguously erotic scene.

She had her shirt on and was balancing on one foot, poised to step into her underpants, when she heard footsteps and realized suddenly several things: she was half dressed and wet, her clothes were dirty, she would be starting grade eleven in only a week.

Louis was passing, on his way to the road.

She stepped quickly into her underpants and began yanking them up. Pine needles on the soles of her feet dropped into the crotch. She knew that Louie had stopped, that he could not resist noticing this. She swiped at the needles, gave up and pulled at her underpants but they rolled under and tangled on her wet thighs.

"Wait. Don't," he said, coming over. He leaned down and lifted the crotch at the sides and shook it until it was cleared of debris. Then he moved his fingers around one of her thighs, then the other, thoughtfully and with his face averted, like a person picking a raffle ticket from a hat, and untangled her underwear. Despite some distant, dreary mortification, she waited to see if he would pull them up.

As the squirrel rounded a trunk only a few feet away, its voice gone, its tail swishing, its need to see getting the better of it, she stared at Louie's head bent over her, at the tight curls of black hair flashing with oil and water. Here was a proximity to something she had not planned on. He was a man. And he was very near. I'm only sixteen, she wanted to remind him.

She thought he would say, "What are you afraid of?" because that's what boys had said before, but he said nothing.

It was only when she realized her underpants were stained an ugly yellow that she blushed. Louie straightened with an expression she could not read. As he walked off across the needle floor she considered how remarkable it was that his breath should have felt so hot.

Brooding, hot, pungent, violent, and sexually gamy, the complete story unfolding at Libby Creelman's pace is a memorable performance.

Sharon English

Short Story Collections: *Uncomfortably Numb* (2002) and *Zero Gravity* (2006).

The stories in *Uncomfortably Numb* map high-school life, *terra* largely *incognita.*

(See the comments on the unchronicled in the entry for Rebecca Rosenblum.)

These notes on English's work are lengthier than has been my practice in this book. I edited both of her collections and later conducted an interview with her, which was published in *Canadian Notes and Queries.* The quotations from the interview appear not for egotistic reasons, but because, for readers, they part the veil over the travails of writers and editors.

> I taught myself to write, then, by the old unavoidable process: writing and rewriting, progressing from dreck to semi-dreck... I used my journal to record things I read or witnessed—not for "material" but to sharpen my perceptive and descriptive skills. As well, I found that reading poetry helped me enter a receptive, intuitive state and to come at language musically. (I still often begin with poetry on my writing days, something non-narrative.) Around this time I also started focusing on short-story writers and following what was being published in Canada,

especially by journals and small presses such as the Porcupine's Quill, Goose Lane and others.

Eventually I was drawn from Vancouver to Toronto where I continued to work part-time jobs, usually a few at once, to write, and to collect rejection letters from literary journals—mostly form rejections, but increasingly, and oh so brightly, a handwritten note commenting on some promising aspects of the work. How I treasured those little notes! I also began writing the book that eventually became *Uncomfortably Numb,* though its first incarnation was as a novel. In 1997 I saw an ad for the Humber School for Writers' summer writing program and noticed that John Metcalf was one of the instructors. By this time I'd read a number of the writers published by him through the Porcupine's Quill, plus his own work, and I knew that he had excellent taste. I also knew I needed help: I'd been writing for four years, had no other career plans, had never taken a writing class or had anyone but the editors of journals read my work.

I took a chunk of my manuscript to John's class, expecting to learn a few concrete skills and perhaps get some encouragement. What occurred was stunning: John seemed to take to me artistically and personally. I felt a similar connection. He said that my manuscript was rough, but most interesting, and he offered to work with me through the various stages of its development, passing the manuscript back and forth and, eventually, if all went well, to publish the book with the Porcupine's Quill.

After Humber, John read the entire manuscript and provided a lengthy and supportive critique. Unfortunately, though his criticisms were clear enough, I didn't comprehend them, not deeply. Over a year I rewrote, submitted, and eventually received an agonized reply that heavy labour was still wanting to produce a publishable book, "somewhat akin to working with axe and adze," he said. A while later, John, who was quite ill at the time, withdrew from working with me. My work was suffering from several huge problems and he felt I really needed to struggle with them on my own.

Being dumped by your first editor is quite a blow. I was dev-astated. It was now 1999 and I was 33. Sacrifices had been made to be an artist, life was being lived sketchily, and I seemed to be failing. The novel really was awful, I could see. I put it away. Addressing my writing problems meant both learning technique and turning my head around. I returned to writing stories, then, which provide a smaller canvas on which one can more easily discern purpose and shape. The draft that John read now strikes me as a formless lump of good-quality clay.

John told me much later that reading this manuscript was "like being sat on by a Sumo wrestler."

John's criticism had noted that the entire manuscript was mostly devoid of "sociological markers," which come not from mere descriptions but from "concentrating intensely on a scene and *seeing* which are the *essential* details which give us this infor-mation and which also describe character." As a writer, I wasn't visualizing hard enough; I wasn't inhabiting those scenes—let-ting go of thinking about them and really experiencing them myself.

During this time I was fortunate to become acquainted with the writer Steven Heighton when I wrote to him about his work. Very kindly, Steve offered to read one of my *Numb* stories. I sent him the best one I had, and he was quite positive. He ended up responding to two of the stories, and his help, plus the support of my writing group and my partner, kept me going. When I finished the manuscript I decided to contact John and see if he'd consider reading. Although I risked walking into the flames again, his interest in the work had stayed with me, I still trusted his opinion and I wanted his approval—which he gave this time, most warmly. And so our story comes to a happy end after all: forbearance paid off, John and I were reconciled, and my book was published with the Quill in 2002, guaranteeing fame and for-tune forever. Whew.

Once *Numb* was off my desk I began writing new stories—and, to my immense frustration, falling into my old bad prose habits that I thought I'd conquered. One story would come off well enough, but the next would be bad, and I couldn't see *why*. Why? Why was I wasting *months* of my time? John Metcalf generously suggested I send him my worst, brave soul that he is. His reply letter began thus:

"Yes. You're right. It's *awful*."

One needs to picture this written in black felt pen, the underscoring looking like he was grinding that pen tip in fury.

Many other parts of the letter were so underlined.

Fortunately John suggested why, or at least how, I was going wrong. He asked me to examine an Evelyn Waugh story:

Not that I think Waugh a natural or even talented story writer—but I want you to read the first two pages of the story *Basil Seal Rides Again*. Quite apart from being funny, those pages show you triumphantly how dialogue can work and how fast a scene can be set and a story got underway. They are exactly what I mean about focal length and drama. So I want you to study [single underscoring] how [triple underscoring] he does this. It's so easy to apply what he does technically to your own work.

Off I scurried. Over the next while what I ended up doing was an architectural analysis of Waugh's story, paragraph by paragraph, then of numerous others. Picking up on John's cinematic language, I wrote up something like shot-by-shot analyses, which worked best because sometimes several paragraphs constitute one "shot": these become scenes. Besides identifying what constituted the "shot" (e.g. whether it was a close-up of two people talking, or a long-shot description of the room they were in, etc.), I also noted where the main plot, subplots and themes were introduced how they were developed, overlaid, and resolved. This exercise was among the most beneficial things I've ever done for my writing: finally, I could clearly see the motion of stories. Prose movement can be tricky to discern because we're so easily distracted by emotional and linguistic effects and meaning, whether we're writers or readers. After these exercises, I was better able to spot when my stories were seeping onto the page instead of dancing across it.

The following extract from Sharon's work is from *Uncomfortably Numb*, from the story "Clear Blue." Germaine and Regina in the desolate suburb of Greenview—"Land of the Walking Dead"—are searching the night skies hoping for a visitation by UFOs.

I called Regina and we started our vigil in my back yard the next night. Mom and Dad had all the windows open because of the heat, but their back bedroom has a cranky air conditioner that gives good cover for talking. We set up Ian's old pup tent, which reeked of armpits and putrid feet. Inside we hunched in our bras and cut-offs and burned cone after cone of patchouli incense. "What's that smell?" Mom called, her voice going all high and shaky at the end. Through the mesh screen she appeared on the lawn like a gigantic white grub with her nightie and pale limbs. She parted the flap and peeked into the flashlit haze like there might be wild beasts she'd have to tame.

"DOPE!" I said, and presented the incense box. We doubled over laughing when she'd left *Ganja! Doob! God help me Mary Jane!*

My parents' air conditioner rattled, the Blacks' pool filter burbled and hummed next door. Down along the block, house lights shut off. Darkness moved in. Once the stars were visible we slid the sleeping bags half out of the tent. Sweaty, gasping in relief. That whole week the sky was clear. Right overhead, it seemed, the Big Dipper spread itself out. I told Regina the names of the planets in order from the sun. Mars the Red, with its two mini-moons. Gaseous Jupiter. Ian taught me this stuff years ago. He loved to make me recite things, words I didn't even know the meaning of, like "logical fallacy." I was his little protégé, he said. Not that I knew what that meant either.

Regina giggled. "So what's it like on Uranus?"

"A fucking paradise," I said.

Neither Regina's nor my parents have figured out that summertime backyard camping isn't about being able to blab all night. It's about setting up a tent, waiting until the parental units are zonked, then high-tailing it out of the yard. Then you can meet up with guys, or if there aren't any, roam around. Out here on the edge of the city, no one except high school kids is up past midnight on a weekday. Sometimes you'll meet others walking or on bikes or cruising in cars, or gathered at certain places—the mulberry-tree grove in the public school yard, or behind the store. But mostly the neighbourhood's empty, still, the world outside an echo. The streets bend round and round, a shell spiralling in on itself. Along the crescents and cul-de-sacs, lawn lampposts cast small phosphorescent pools of light, marking the houses in the gloom. The shadows are friendly, let you climb fences and go pool-hopping, easily escape from snapped-on bedroom lights. You can even run down the middle of the street butt naked, which Regina and I did once, clutching our clothes, her boobs bouncing like molded Jell-O and our feet slapping concrete, singing *The night time / Is the right time / For LOOOOVE!*

Sharon's second collection of stories, *Zero Gravity*, offers protagonists older than Germaine and more careworn as the world closes in. Here is the opening sentence of the story "Cosmic Elfs":

> I grew up in small-town Ontario, moved away for university, moved to Toronto to start working, but after four years the work-station walls were closing in and I was spending part of every day in the washroom reading children's books.

Jim Bartley's response in the *Globe:* "I surrendered to English's skin-crawling ability to regress one instantly to mean corridors, clique-blighted lunchrooms and excruciating eruptions of lust in back seats and basement rec-rooms… Observing her rebel 'jeans and leather' crowd feels like watching serial car accidents of the teenage soul—ghastly and fascinating." Jim Bartley also commented that the book "displays the difficult linked-story form to fine advantage, refusing to impose a story arc on lives defined by their very lack of direction."

Shirley Faessler
Short Story Collections: *A Basket of Apples and Other Stories* (1979).
 Novels: *Everything in the Window* (1988).

Shirley Faessler died on March 24, 1997. Most of the stories were written in the late sixties and early seventies. I anthologized "A Basket of
Apples" in a high-school text I edited in 1970 called *Sixteen by Twelve*,
and through that circumstance came to know Shirley quite well. She
was then retired from running her home on Sherbourne Street in
Toronto as a boarding house catering to the actors and actresses of
the New York Yiddish theatre companies.

Shirley spent most of the day secluded in her bedroom. She
descended at about four o'clock in the afternoon and settled herself
in the kitchen with the first drink of the day. Her brother, Louis,
would also drift in at about the same time, just awake and gradually assembling himself into evening dress, cufflinks, tea, shirt
studs, toast, black-leather shoes burnished with an orange Ilford
Anstaticum camera cloth. He dealt cards every night at high-stakes
poker games. Drivers would arrive later to take him to the houses
where the games were played.

The stories flowed with the whiskey. "Stories," as she wrote
in *Sixteen by Twelve* "of my stepmother, my stepmother's relatives
(whom my father called the Russian Hordes), stories of my sister,
my brother, myself. I established a reputation as a raconteur and it
was flattering to be sought after, to be coaxed to tell again the story
of Mrs. Baskin's love affair with Katz the fishmonger; the story of
the two prostitutes who rented a room with the Oxenbergs next
door to us, claiming they were office workers; the story of Mrs.
Spinner who, while her husband (an amputee) was still in hospital,
had gambled away at rake-off five-card stud poker the money he had
put aside for an artificial limb."

One afternoon I was treated to a story of Louis' younger days.
Louis had spent some years in Kingston, segregated from society
because he had a weakness for banks. On this particular afternoon,
said Shirley, her mother was baking in the kitchen when Louis ran
in, through, out down the outside stairs, having handed off to her a

revolver, which she buried in the flour bin. Seconds later, madly in pursuit, two policemen burst in.

"Oy, gevald!" screamed Shirley's mother. "It's a pogrom!"

The stories in *A Basket of Apples* are all about Jewish immigrants from Russia and Romania who settled in the Kensington Market area of Toronto in the years before the Second World War. Mordecai Richler said of his novels that he wanted to be a witness to his time and place and that he wanted to "get it right." The same kind of impulse lies behind Shirley's work, which chronicles the activities of what her father, known as "The Romanian Beast" or "The Mamaliga Eater," called, in turn, "The Russian Hordes."

Reading *A Basket of Apples* it is impossible not to think of a Mordecai Richler story like "The Summer my Grandmother Was Supposed to Die," collected in *The Street*, a book which would have been on the List were it not that some of the pieces are more essays blurring into sketches. Shirley's stories are certainly not essays but might, perhaps, share something with the sketch.

The Richler comedy of St. Urbain Street is often supplied by smart-ass adolescent boy narrators with slicked-back hair.

> "Knock, knock."
> "Who's there?"
> "Freda."
> "Freda who?"
> "Fre-da you. Five dollars for any one else."

> *Question:* What happened to Helena Rubinstein?
> *Answer:* Max Factor

Shirley Faessler's comedy is more layered, often tinged with sadness, emotionally deeper. From the story "Henye," here are the brothers Yankev and Yudah.

> When I knew the brothers, their fish-peddling days were behind them. It was during Prohibition and they were making an easier dollar peddling illicit booze. The fish cart, however, was still

in use. For deliveries. The topmost tray, concealing the bootleg booze in the interior of the cart, contained for the sake of camouflage a few scattered pickerel, a bit of pike, a piece of whitefish packed in ice. Yankev, to accommodate expanding trade, had a phone installed in the hall of his house and it rang at all hours, a customer at the other end asking for Jack. Their customers, for the most part Gentile, could not get their tongues around Yankev so they called him Jack. Yudah was called Joe.

The brothers had acquired a bit of English, enough to see them through their business. Their inventory and records were kept in a lined exercise book, in Yiddish. Customers were designated by descriptive terms, nicknames: The Gimpy One on Bathurst, Long Nose on Lippincott. Using their fish carts mocked up with a scattering of moribund fish in the topmost tray, they made their deliveries to Big Belly, Short Ass, The Murderer, Big Tits, The Pale One, The Goneff, The Twister, The Tank.

At the end of the story, Yankev, his first wife dead and he re-married, is talking to Chayle:

" ...You're not happy?"

"Happy," he echoed. "It's like you said—what kind of life is it to be alone?"

All at once he was his old self again. He smiled at my stepmother, a look of mischief coming to his face. "She bought me a pair pyjamas," he said. "Yankev sleeps now in pyjamas, and his missus like a man sleeps also in pyjamas. First thing in the morning she opens up a window and makes exercises. First of all she stretches," he said, demonstrating with his arms aloft. "Then she bends down and puts her ass in the air. And that's some ass to put in the air, believe me. And all day, busy. Busy, busy, busy. With what? To make supper takes five minutes. Soup from a can, compote from a can—it has my *boba's* flavour. A piece of herring? This you never see on the table, she doesn't like the smell. A woman comes in to clean—with what is she busy, you'll ask? With gin rummy. True, gin rummy. They come in three or four times a week, her friends, to play gin rummy. They cackle like geese, they smoke like men. "Dear," my wife says to me, "bring some ginger ale from the frig, the girls are thirsty" —she hasn't got time to leave the cards. Girls, she calls them. Widows! Not one without a husband buried in the ground," he said with sudden indignation. "Dear, she calls me, nu? Before me there was another Dear and she buried *him*. Once in a while without thinking, I call her Henye. She gets so mad, oh, ho, ho. So I make a mistake sometimes, it's natural. How does a man live with a woman all his life and blot out from his memory her name—"

He rose suddenly from his chair, took a handkerchief from his pocket and blowing his nose in it went to the mirror over the sink and peered in it, dabbing at his eyes. "Cholera take it," he said, "there's something in my eye." My stepmother looked away; next minute we heard the sound of a horn. Yankev went to the window. "There she is, my prima donna." He embraced his niece. "Drives a car like a man," he muttered and took his leave.

Yankev's and Yudah's lined exercise book reminds me of a detail from another of Shirley's stories "The Night Watchman." Blum is talking to Pa.

"Did I ever tell you about my old man's bookkeeping system when he ran a grocery store? He bought from wholesalers on credit, and some of his customers bought from him on credit. To keep track of what he owed the wholesalers and what the customers owed him, my old man bought himself a nickel notepad and on one side he wrote 'I owe Pipples,' and on the other side, 'Pipples owes me.'"

Both *The Street* and *A Basket of Apples* delight in and celebrate the magnificent mangling of English by Yiddish speakers. Both were witnesses to their time and place and both got it comically and movingly right.

Cynthia Flood
Short Story Collections: *The Animals in Their Elements* (1987), *My Father Took a Cake to France* (1992), *The English Stories* (2009), *Red Girl Rat Boy* (2013), and *What Can You Do* (2017).
 Novel: *Making a Stone of the Heart* (2002).

Cynthia Flood's stories are surprising in the wide range of their styles. They are stories about parents and children, about wider family relationships, about aging, about dying. They range from elegiac to angry to the oddly focussed comic. There is a trademark quality about Cynthia Flood's writing; it has always a particularity—nouns, nouns, nouns—and rigorous verbs—but at the same time there plays over it an abstracting, directing intellectual quality. The total effect is rather difficult to describe. To say it lumpishly, the writing is a mixture of "hot" and "cool," the heat of detail, the coolness of an interpreting, fierce intellect.

The following paragraph from "The Man, the Woman, and the Witch of New Orleans" will, I hope, illustrate the effect.

> The city of New Orleans, built on clamshells and river sand along a crescent moon of the Mississippi and well below the level of that river, exists in pulsating tension between decay and new growth. A child's wooden wagon left out for a fortnight grows a green skin, while a vine sprouts and begins to twine about the toy. In their elevated graves, in vast glare-white cities of the dead, black and white New Orleanians rot so briskly that one modest tomb may readily hold all that's left of a hundred and seventeen nuns and yet stand ready to take on dozens more. Once, the local foods were highly spiced to delay or mask corruption. Still spiced, they are now refrigerated, frozen, microwaved, convected... but still the spoon sinks into the fragrant, maybe, gumbo, like a foot into the marshes by the Gulf. What lies beneath that surface? What condition is it in? Delicious... . Rot, mould, rust, peel, blister, burst, sag, mildew—against these ferocious verbs the citizenry send forth one noun: paint. Coat upon coat upon

coat of paint, white and cream and pearl and bone and ivory and palest rose. Paint to fill, seal, protect, prevent, maintain. Barely, until next year. Throughout the city, fish and mud smell hairily in the nostrils. Sun and green contend. The full-leaved summer sky is green heat.

Such a paragraph amply repays repeated, slow readings.

Cynthia Flood can move from this complex gumbo to such a comic performance as "Design and Spontaneity," a rendering of a dotty dinner party that reads like a mixture of Beryl Bainbridge and Ivy Compton-Burnett.

Mrs. Mortimer emerged from the kitchen, carrying a cut-glass dish of hot toasted almonds rolled in salt.

"Timothy, what are you thinking of? Introductions. Julian help Webby. Dr. Beardsley, Bessie, a nut. Mrs. T, my dear, it seems more than a month, I do like that dress, wonderful peacock blue. Bessie Beardsley, Mrs. T, my aunt by marriage. A nut? Bessie Beardsley, Webster Willoughby, my uncle by marriage. The living-room, a glass of sherry, a nut, do…"

At the eastern head of his table, Mr. Mortimer aimed his carving knife straight through the animal. "Shall we all hear now from Bessie, on her impressions? The flight? Her recapitulation, so much swifter than our forebears could have dreamed, of their journeys? The sword of the ice-blue river aimed at the heart of the country?"

"You know my stomach, Timothy," said Uncle Webby, confidingly. "I trust there will be no surprises."

"Your digestive tract is surely familiar by now with roast beef and two veg," said Mrs. T, between uncle and niece.

Such sophisticated writing is far more difficult than it appears; it's dancing, yes, but it's Fred Astaire and Ginger Rogers you're watching.

The title stories of the two volumes, *The Animals in Their Elements* and *My Father Took a Cake to France* are both among the most powerful in Canadian writing. In "The Animals in Their Elements," the aging Harry suffers a stroke. He has been living alone save for his cat, Princess. The story is structured around imagery relating to birds—Harry's love of watching them in the maple and walnut trees in his tangled old garden. A mere excerpt violates the texture of the whole but it does allow us to see the delicacy of the writing, the way that style absolutely matches subject matter.

> These unknowns were nurses and doctors, that was all. There was nothing to be said to them. He must just work hard, very hard, to get better. One young doctor, Jewish he must be from the nose, had dark bright eyes, and Harry liked it when he visited. There was a sandbox in which he must feel for letters, to match them with letter-shaped holes in a container. The sand felt silky but it got under his nails. He worked hard, got pretty good at the matching. Now an exercise book. C dash T, put a letter in the middle to make a word. Impossible. No such. Then, as when a bird lands on a rainy branch and the drops frill off the leaves on to those below, there was an infinitely small touch in his head and the letter A presented itself. He smiled. The young doctor smiled too. Then Harry wept, and pointed to the word and wept. Some time later a nurse came saying, "He says to tell you Princess is all right." Belief and incredulity nested together in his mind. No speech. Birds flew distantly over the parking lot behind his plate-glass window.
>
> Some of the food was surprisingly familiar. Shirley had made jelly like this, with bits of fruit suspended in it. Harry wished he knew how, and how to make his left leg work. He thought he was doing his best, but nothing happened. At first young girls helped him to the bathroom but of course he could not go, and finally they brought a man. People got him to move his limbs in a way he saw, but did not yet feel, was rhythmic. In time, in time the leg felt more, though it was ponderous, dragging, with dry skin shaling off like fish scales under an invisible knife. Once,

perhaps a dream? Mrs. Chang was there, grinning at the end of his bed with a paper bag. Later, fat pale buns on his bedtray.

Harry's mental struggles and lapses are suggested by the simplified or broken syntax ("Now an exercise book. C dash T, put a letter in the middle to make a word. Impossible. No such.") His dislocated grasp of his world is suggested in the mysterious "fat pale buns" which appear on his bedtray. ("Once, perhaps a dream?") Birds are used throughout the story because they mean for Harry—beauty? intensity of life? excitement? freedom?—perhaps all these. His sudden apprehension of the letter A is likened to a bird's alighting, a kind of blessing. The possibility that all is well with Princess ("Belief and incredulity nested together in his mind") is capped by the concluding sentence of the paragraph "Birds flew distantly over the parking lot beyond his plate-glass window." He sees birds, the embodiment for him of good emotions, in this case of hope, but they are "distant" still and he remains a prisoner of his body behind plate glass.

Cynthia Flood uses repetition in the writing to great effect. Indicating the slowness of the *meaning* of CAT coming to Harry, she writes, "Then Harry wept, and pointed to the word and wept." Writing of his physiotherapy she says, "In time, in time the leg felt more," the repetition suggesting the repeated exercise movements. Notice, too, that she writes not "his leg," but "the leg," "the" suggesting dead flesh, something that is not him.

It is the accumulation of such small, deft touches which creates a believable world and which delivers delight.

This is writing of a very high order.

Exposing What's There

Cynthia Flood's first two books, highly accomplished and admirable work, were what one might call "traditional modernist." That sounds like an oxymoron until we remember that "modernism" is over one hundred years old. Her first collection, *The Animals in Their Elements*, appeared in 1987, her most recent, *What Can You Do*, in 2017. In those twenty years her work has changed radically.

In the introduction to *Best Canadian Stories 2016*, I wrote "It is received opinion that ageing writers become feeble, and emit fading versions of their earlier flash and filigree. It has been my experience, however, that the older writers in this years' anthology—Pauline Holdstock, Leon Rooke, Cynthia Flood, and Douglas Glover—are growing ever tougher and increasingly exciting to read. As the years pile up, their prose is becoming leaner, faster, cleaner, more demanding of the reader's involvement. In a word, more *urgent*.

In 2001, Flood wrote an article for *CNQ* on Norman Levine. She said that after reading all Levine's work, the writing of other previously admired writers, "seemed to waddle fat-thighed down the page." Although she has explicitly denied being influenced by any other writers in the changes that have overtaken her work, I still suspect that her experience of Levine's writing was not a neutral one.

(Please see the entry on Norman Levine for further reference to her *CNQ* article, wherein she says, "To strip out all that plugs up prose: that is Levine's aim.")

Stripping out all that plugs up prose has been at the centre of modernism from the very beginning, a battle never decisively won. Cyril Connolly caught exactly that oh-so-genteel-mush, that *curled-up-comfy-beside-the-fire-with-a-nice-detective-story-and-a-toasted-crumpet* style in an essay in *The Condemned Playground* (1935).

> ...the rather academic language of the Mandarin class, a style which depends for its force on the combination of adjective and noun or two adjectives and noun:
>
> "With his practical and professional eye, Mr. Cardan thought he could detect in his host's expression certain hardly perceptible symptoms of incipient tipsiness."
>
> That style is the typical instrument of English fiction, and it badly needs tuning.

That disdainful sentence of Connolly's is still precisely the sort of sentence that anglophile readers who deplore life as it now is hold up as a "to the barricades" example of "civilized" writing. The bastion of P.D. James standing impervious against Elmore Leonard's *canaille*.

In the last eighteen years, with increasing economy, Cynthia Flood, countering her own traditional education and her occupation as teacher of college English, has loosened the bonds of grammar, broken formal sentence structures, transmuted description into image, and put her writing on a stark diet. The increasingly austere writing demands more, and increasingly more, of readers.

She wrote to me recently:

> When editing a solid draft of course I try to eliminate everything unnecessary. Not new, but my standards have evidently changed.
>
> Why? I don't know. Age?
>
> When reading novels or short stories now I often get impatient and think *This would be so much better at half the length!* I wouldn't read Knausgaard's shelf of brick-sized novels even if someone paid me well.
>
> (Same for movies. My ideal movie-length remains the classic 90 minutes, and I have to be dragged to anything over two hours).
>
> You know I admire William Trevor, who's generally a concise writer—in stories anyway. (*Felicia's Journey* should have been a short story. Same for *Lucy Gault*.)
>
> I admire Lydia Davis's short fictions—sometimes tiny—very much.

As we follow the trail into Flood's later work, this passing reference should be a very visible blaze to those who know Davis' work. For those unacquainted, *The Collected Stories* appeared in 2009.

She went on to talk about the changes that now increasingly characterize her work:

> With fewer words, I can try to ensure that important ones don't get caught up / swallowed in the predictable machinery of English sentence structure—often cumbersome…
>
> Maybe in writing fiction I have been looking for ways to show not tell? I don't know.
>
> To provide clues—but I don't want reader-detectives.

To lay down a pattern, a design?
Maybe not as strong as lay down.
To suggest.
So a reader will gradually notice. Or *not* notice consciously but still enjoy, keep on reading while certain words (or their cousins) gently reappear, to direct attention. Perhaps that's why I try even harder now to eliminate verbiage?

The change in her writing began with *The English Stories*, a book of linked stories about a small Canadian girl, Amanda, who is taken to England for two years while her father pursues academic interests. Amanda lives first in a residential hotel in Oxford, The Green House, a Dickensian establishment of curdled gentility and a profoundly British silence and secrecy. Later, Amanda is consigned to the savagery of a girls' boarding school.

The stories are essentially concerned with Amanda's acclimatization and acquisition of a new vocabulary. The story "Country Life" affords a good example, Amanda deposited for the night—why, she's not quite sure—in the home of the forbiddingly formal Miss Lucinda Jones. The *oddness* of England, its assumption of superiority, the strangeness of its language are brilliantly suggested throughout, the last five lines of description in the following excerpt rising to image, to what Clark Blaise would call metaphor.

"Can I help you do the dishes?" I asked.

"What shall we do to them?" I shrank—but there was interest in her tone. Miss Jones told me about *washing up*, and we considered why up, not down. Then we went on to dessert and sweet, pie and tart, cookies and biscuits, sweets and candy. Meanwhile her long fingers dipped one plate at a time in the white enamelled pan.

"The coffee cups live in the drawing-room, Amanda." She spread the tea towel across the pan and doused it with scalding water.

I knelt to reunite the cups with their sisters, in a glass-fronted cabinet in a small strange room. In Canada (but that house has been sold and the furniture put in storage) our living room had a ten-foot ceiling and tall windows, tables thick as middens with books newspapers ashtrays photo albums bowls of fruit, battered furniture coated with cat hair, my mother's pastels and my father's watercolours tacked to the walls, disordered bookshelves, a Mexican rug, pots of forced narcissus, their roots concealed by freshwater clamshells from Lake Muskoka. Miss Jones's room was a quarter the size. A bare-legged loveseat and two skirted chairs squarely met a patterned rug. (Was this Persian?) An embroidery frame stood by the leaded window; along the sill, green elephants were sentinels of descending size. On the mantel above the fireplace, a gold-domed clock ticked and tinkled between pencil sketches of a church.

The entire story's final image presents Miss Lucinda Jones—and by implication much earlier pictures in the story too—surrealistically; a perfect presentation of Amanda's vision and understanding; a picture that's sat in my head for years.

Two of the stories stand out from the others as beginning, what we can see in retrospect, as the shift away from the "traditionally modernist." These are "A Civil Plantation" and "Miss Pringle's Hour." The first is a strange story that incorporates swaths of Irish history, particularly of the Elizabethan and Cromwellian periods, and the "plantations," the imposition of what became the Protestant Ascendancy, all this detail as the guarded mental furniture of the history teacher, Mr. Greene, a closet Irishman in this staunchly establishment C of E school. He betrays himself in that teacup world by a slip of the tongue.

I have heard the child Amanda call plimsolls *running shoes* and say *laboratory* with the stress on *bor*, and then witnessed the laughter. One word can kill. Vowels alone can inform just as well as a wrongly-emphasized syllable. Miss Pringle and Miss Hodgson are irreproachably Home Countries, but Miss Lincoln's speech is too carefully not northern, while I suspect that Miss Flower's gentle voice overlies an origin involving coins, counter, and till.

★

At the final tea time this afternoon, I sat as Mr. Greene of Foreign Affairs among the mistresses. My knowledge was held tightly in my head: my origins, my language, the visitations, Amanda's picture, her questions, her mark, her look of hate, my own hate, my recognition of Fitzgerald, my many Notes. All were safe inside.

Mrs. Wilmer said, "How the days draw in!"

"They do, don't they?" responded Miss Flower.

"O rather!" I agreed, rhyming the *a* with *maths*. Thus my sliding tongue gave me away. The chatter of the English ladies ceased. Their eyes observed, their ears decoded. A silence filled Miss Pringle's sitting room.

"Miss Pringle's Hour" is cast in the form of diary jottings and is a triumph of comic characterization. The following gives the flavour.

September 25th, The VIth and the Upper Vth attended the Old Vic's *A Winter's Tale* at the Royal. Meeting Dr Chapple of Clarendon at the interval, I was pleased at our girls' poise. Some of his boys were rambunctious. Dr. C enquired re our university entrances. Of course Clarendon's size and endowments ensure a higher proportion than we can attain, but. The actors performed very well, I thought.

September 30th, News-talk by Mr. Oliver Greene. Amanda Ellis interrupted, to ask a question. No one welcomes more warmly than I the post-war trend of arrivals from other lands in the Commonwealth, as we are now to call it, but the difficulties cannot be denied. The ways of life followed by persons from the Caribbean living in our larger cities, unfortunately in their poorer quarters, are so different from those of native-born Britons as to cause social disruption. Naturally there is nothing of this sort with Amanda, who is physically indistinguishable from her classmates, but.

Mr. Greene is prolix. That man will end his days in some residential hotel, one of those eccentric dodderers crouched by an inadequate fire.

October 4ᵗʰ, Lantern Lecture, The Romans in Britain, Miss Laura Harvie, BA, of the Historial Society. Funds simply must be found to purchase new equipment for such presentations.

Corresp: Old Girl Rosemary Hayton (Clarke) '37 wishes to endow a prize for best Senior essay on a 19ᵗʰ- or 20ᵗʰ-century woman artist. Most generous. I cannot think why she should wish thus to limit the subject-matter.

Mem: Spk Ellis pts re elocution lessons Amanda? RH enq lantern costs.

October 5ᵗʰ, Yesterday was tiring, yet about 2 a.m. I was wakeful (too warm). At the window, my reverie was broken by the sight of Mr. G crossing the Great Lawn and going down the drive. The girls call him Mr. Grey. At that hour, where can the man have been off to? Only distasteful answers occur. Fitz, yes, but Mr. G?

Mem: Spk Fitz, again, re suitable address—Miss Pringle, not simply Miss, which is appropriate should he need to speak to one of the girls. Such distinctions matter. Unlike Mr. Neill, I insist upon outward manifestations of respect. When girls rise on my entrance, I am gratified, for in honouring my position they honour their own.

Oddly enough, it was Mr. G who overheard the Chair of the Council speaking to Dr. C. "Remarkable"—that was the term used—"remarkable, the improvement in tone at St. Mildred's since Pringle became Head." RH was equally delighted. A good reputation among such men is invaluable to a small girls' School. Of course Mr. G told me so as to curry favour. He may think I am unaware of that. The man is a poodle.

Some of the Amanda stories are too long and, I think, should have been more focused. There is a reportorial, "autobiographical" aspect to the stories where the urge *to get in* remembered detail or remembered/embroidered detail, wars with the story as invention or artifice. "Country Life" was worked perfectly; "The Margins Are the Frame," on the other hand, is so crammed it can barely amble forward.

To make clearer what I mean—I remember in the writing of one of my own stories having to do some "research," that word used so pretentiously to mean "looking something up." My "research" for the story was to go out for dinner at a ludicrously pretentious restaurant. I made copious notes throughout: the food, snatches of conversation, the corny band, the processional service, the ostentatious and servile buggering-about with cutlery, my bistro black and white waiter in brown penny loafers, bright pennies in the vamps...

Later, when I settled in to write, I had *pages* of deathless detail that I refused to see clogged forward movement entirely; I had done the "research"—all accurate, wasn't it?—I owed it to events, to the *truth* of the evening, *to get it all in*. I fought this sullen, inert mass for *days* before reluctantly beginning the process, resentfully, of whittling down to telling detail, sniper work rather than barrage. It was the last "research" I ever committed.

With *Red Girl Rat Boy* came a quantum leap. This title and *What Can You Do* and whatever she will write next, are the works that will ensure Cynthia Flood's survival into whatever canon evolves. The stories have an attack that is so fast it is almost invisible, yet almost instantly you know you're in the presence... The authority with which she performs brings to mind Ali's seemingly casual dominance in the ring or the glittering elegance of swordplay. The stories do not flap their emotions about; Flood does not indulge in obvious rhetoric; she would, I imagine, consider such rhetoric as emotional incontinence. It is the very coolness of the stories, that, paradoxically, brands the reader. In *that* particular, not unlike Mavis Gallant.

What did I *mean* by "an attack that is so fast it is invisible?"

I meant the opening four sentences of "His Story, History:"

> Like everyone my age, I contain a young foreigner. Not totally strange, on the beach back there, waves crashing—but now my prostate's doubled, belly tripled. Ears and libido droop, knees refuse, teeth rattle, bionic eyes and bald head glitter. Too often, the mind's engine moves on long-laid rails.

I meant the opening paragraphs of "Eggs and Bones:"

The eggs hit the pan. Too much sizzle. Probably he'd set the heat at 5 again, not 3. For sure he hadn't whisked the eggs long enough, she'd counted the strokes. He'd see the mixture was streaky, then stir too late and disturb the setting process. Kyra lay in their king-sized bed, listening to Norman cook. Likely he's using butter and oil. Stupid. That metal spatula, skr-skrskr. It'll wake Maeve. I can't bear it, truly I can't. Why won't she sleep through the night? Oh lucky me with my mat leave! A whole year to enjoy my baby. Her birthday next week. Use the *plastic* one. Right there, in the utensil jar. That pan's scarred already. The colic's over months ago but still she wakes, wakes, wakes. She has daytime naps, I'm exhausted, I sleep too. No work. I'm thirty. It's time.

He shouldn't scrape yet anyway. Just tip to slide the liquid under, but those eggs'll be nearly cooked now. Frizzled more like.

For Norman, earplugs work, but even if I shove them in till I think they're touching my brain and move her crib right to the end of the hall I hear Maeve. She's not hungry. Won't feed. Cries a while, sleeps again. I don't. I can't. The clock-radio's turned to hide time rushing on, but in May the birds start at four, and if I do sleep it's like an instant till she cries again.

What's he taking out of the fridge? Please not chorizo.

Not just my ears but all of me senses Maeve. Three floors away I'd feel her crying. Mushrooms? I'm starting to work from home. So many women want to do just that, so lucky me. Lucky me? Cheese? The office. I've tried to stay connected, but when I visit there with Maeve it feels unreal. Maybe once I get into my projects? How can I? In all the hours, where's the time? I need sleep. Oh God, he's slicing onion.

I meant, to change the pace, the sombre, slow opening of "Blue Clouds," a story narrated by Jake, the janitor in the hall used by the coms, the Party. The list that ends this excerpt is more than list; it acts as the leitmotif, carries the story's burden. Here, even slow is fast.

Often no one notices the problem, the pattern till a man's in his thirties or even forties. By then he's had several—serious relationships, the comrades say. Serial monogamy, the coms say that too. If his teens were examined there'd be no surprise finding he'd favoured girlfriends with dear little sisters, but here at the hall people mostly arrive in their twenties. Their time before the movement is hidden, except what they pick to tell, and telling is cleaning.

Back up.

Such a man, when he falls for a woman she has a daughter. Maybe two. Could be sons also, but he's not aiming for importance in the life of a small man. It's the small woman he wants. Oh, not to rape, though maybe a hug she'll remember on a birthday, or when she's back from summer camp. No, he wants to implant his image, so if she thinks Man it's him. He puts his arm round her mother, tongue-kisses, turns to smile. *This is how it's done. Your mum likes this.*

An offer to babysit—heard it, seen it. Smiling, the young mum goes off to her CR group. This guy really wants her to be liberated! He plays with the little girl, helps with homework, is fun with her friends, and if she's in her teens lets her know sideways that boys haven't much to offer. He and she chat about how immature they are, she deserves better.

Then, always, he's suddenly charmed by a fresh girl/woman combo.

Break-up, stale mother alone again, seen that too. A child who misses him can be comforted but a teen turns sour, specially to revolutionary mum.

Exceptions, yes. Roy's a carpenter, in his late forties. On him, those years look good. He and Marion and her daughter came to Vancouver from the Calgary branch ten years ago. At the Friday suppers R and M are side by side at the big table. They dance, they picket and poster and go to conventions. Marion's a lifer at the post office, friendly, considerate. Not much for theory. Jennifer just finished high school. Hasn't joined the Youth. Comes to the Oct Rev and May Day banquets, that's all. Sullen.

I asked the old one, "Who's her dad?"

"None of your beeswax," she told me.

The true sign of no nastiness with Roy? He and Marion and Jennifer don't live together. To be under the same roof, that's what the girl-hunters plot, but this mum and her daughter keep their own place.

Enough chit-chat.

The bathrooms at the movement hall are Monday. The Youth can't manage booze, not only them either, so after every week-end, vomit. The divided bucket has cleaning solution one side, water the other, so hot it hurts. Dip mop, use the side-press wringer, repeat. Repeat. Disinfect the wheezing toilets. Rub abrasive cream on porcelain. Shake deodorizing powder on the floor, sweep.

Done, the bathrooms don't look like ads, but they're better than the Cavalier's. Monday's next job that is, down the street. Pub washrooms take twice as long to clean. Shovel, more like. Stinking loops of paper that never reached the bowl, condoms, underpants, butts, coke, bloody pads draped over the pedal-cans, smashed glass, the red crushed wax of lipstick.

I meant the opening of "The Summer Boy:"

Standing in the guest room, Colin looked about. "Why are you making such a fuss?"

"Clean sheets, flowers, a fuss?" Amelia put her arms akimbo.

"Teenage boys don't notice things like that."

"Can't you smell it? Philadelphus. Lovely fragrance."

"He's got this bed for three weeks. Free. Isn't that enough?"

"He's your relative, not mine. And he has a name. Tobias." She began to cough, got water from the guest bathroom as Colin waited.

"I've never met him, nor do I want to. For good reason, I put those people behind me long ago."

"Tobias isn't to blame for his family. He's young, artistic. We're helping him."

"You didn't include me in deciding to do so."

Amelia flicked a grey hair from the shoulder of his jacket. Then she tested the bedside lamp, arranged some art magazines on the night table.

Colin went downstairs and out, to smoke a cigar and weed his herb garden. The low brick wall and box hedge—rosy red, deep green—set off the plantings, defined their place on a dark ground.

In a handful of sentences, Cynthia Flood transports us into her worlds. In "The Summer Boy" these few sentences have set up the plot: Tobias is a teenager from England somehow related to the husband, Colin. Over his grumpy objections, the boy is coming to stay for three weeks. The visit has been agreed to by Colin's wife, Amelia, without consulting him.

But in those few sentences we have learned much more. We've learned things about the marriage. Colin acts the gruff, logical paterfamilias. Amelia is younger than he is but the actual power within the marriage, though she exercises diplomacy. She flicks "a grey hair from the shoulder of his jacket," a "mothering" reflex that both assumes and presumes. He sees her interest in the boy's artistic ambitions as impractical or delusional; she feels the boy deserves warm encouragement. He regards the flowers in the guest room as part of "making a fuss;" she wants him to smell their fragrance. She enjoys their beauty; he has a patch of useful herbs that grow within containing borders, their place "defined" on the "dark ground."

His cigars, too, go some way towards defining him.

Not a single scrap is wasted in this setting-up.

How I wish some of the aspiring writers I work with could grasp the evident lessons these few lines teach, but I have taught literary matters long enough to know that one cannot vitally impart until the student is emotionally and aesthetically ready to receive. Not to be obfuscatory, but I'm talking about, as it turns out in practice, well, oh God! *Satori*.

What follows is also a story from *What Can You Do*, "Dog and Sheep"; it is an engaging experience of Flood's most recent trail-blazing and is given here in full because its particular rhetoric will not allow reference or excerpting.

Late in the afternoon the dog appeared again, around a curve some way ahead on the road.

She had often come trotting back to us, for we were slow, halting often to name and photograph a flower, or to query as our tour guide spoke of local limestone formations. Of French cheese-making. Of the peasant houses (animals downstairs, people up) in the Cathar villages we'd visited. Of the Cathar heresy, whose adherents saw evil and good as equal powers, chose poverty, strove to be kind. Of their betrayers, informants paid in the usual currencies of cash or sex.

"Shocking," we agreed.

French wine-making, too. *Terroir*, very important.

Nearer the dog came, wagging, closer, until those at the front of our walking group cried out. Others halted. In a huddle, we all stared.

Blood covered the dog's muzzle, stained the delicate fur beneath her eyes, dabbled an ear.

"My God, what's she done?"

"Horrible!"

Our cries drove her off a little, puzzled, tail drooping. Through that red mask she peered at us over her shoulder.

Early that morning, this dog had turned up.

As we left the *gîte* where we'd spent the night, we'd spoken of the Inquisition's unsparing work in that particular village. In 1308 every single resident got arrested for heresy.

Our walking tour itself was titled *In The Footsteps of the Cathars*, though most participants had signed up to see the beautiful Pyrenean foothills. Some did feel that faith, if not extreme, might sustain social order? In a good way? One or two, confusing Cathar with Camino, had expected to follow a specific route taken by all the heretics to a singular destination.

"I wonder how many Cathars, total, got burned at the stake."

"Are we going to be so gloomy all day?"

"I'm just glad I didn't live then."

"Tomorrow's the castle of the Really Big Burn."

"Oh no, not rain again!"

At the last house in the village, our guide paused till we all caught up. "Our way starts here."

A single gravestone stood at a field's edge, tilting somewhat and obscured by long, wet grass. *Ici est morte*, we read in our sketchily-remembered high-school French. *Ici est morte / 18 Août 1944 / Castella Pierre / innocente victime / de la barbarie Nazie.*

"Glad I wasn't here for that, either."

Then this dog rose out of a ditch.

A mutt. Thin, scruffy, brown, collar-less, small-eyed. Long, dark nipples swinging. She came close, wouldn't quite allow pats, whimpered, scuttled away, returned to circle and sniff, hung back till she saw where we tended. Then she rushed ahead to wait for us, panting.

"D'you suppose she has puppies somewhere near?"

"Get away!" Our guide thrust his hazel stick at her. She yelped.

"If so, she'll go back to the village," we concluded, going on.

As we were led from one thin grassy path to another, then to a narrow road of beaten earth, light rain continued. The breeze wafted moisture at us, swirled it into loose airy necklaces. On all sides the fields spread out in spring green, shining wet, while in the distance the terrain sloped up, dotted with sheep, to a forested plateau.

"Up there we shall walk," our guide said.

The dog trotted ahead, looking back to check we were still in view.

Behind us sounded a—truck? French. So little! We smiled, moving aside for the vehicle to pass, but it stopped so the three men inside could joke and talk with our guide. They spoke fast. We grasped nothing.

The driver pointed inquiringly at the dog.

"*Problème.*" Our guide shrugged.

More laughter. As the van moved off, the unknown men wiggled their eyebrows at us and waved.

"Foresters," said our guide. "They work near where we walk today. Remove the rotten branch. Inspect for pasts, no, pests."

"How on earth do they manage with that van? *Trop petite!*"

"Earth? Manage?"

The discussion lasted until we neared a larger road. In its middle sat the dog, her head sticking up above the hedge lining the route. She watched us.

"Thinks she's hiding."

"Stupid! She'll get run over. Why the hell doesn't she go back where she came from?"

"Never been trained."

Our guide chased her until she howled and ran off.

"Good!"

We crossed the road and walked alongside a field. Its unknown tall grains swayed close by us, their wet, silky heads making moiré patterns under the breeze. Mesmerizing.

Without notice, our guide turned into a tall green tunnel of shrubs and small trees, a boreen running off at an angle from the field. We'd not noticed the entrance, draped with wet vines.

"Just as well this isn't a self-guided tour!"

"Too right, we'd be lost in no time."

After emerging from the tunnel, we started uphill. Half an hour later we looked back at the valley, a long trough full of silver-green air resembling the great stone troughs in the villages we'd passed through, now empty shapes, once full, sparkling with laundry and the hands of women.

Now we ascended a great staircase, once terraced farmland, the steps blurred by disuse to faint ledges. The rain got serious. We stopped to put on rain pants and jackets, then continued.

After an hour the dog reappeared, wagging madly. Someone reached out to pat. She snapped, cringed, ran.

"Damn that bitch!"

"Maybe her puppies got taken too early, and she's upset."

"Can't we get her back to where we started?"

"You're kidding, right?"

Our dour guide moved on. The temperature dropped steadily, the rain chilled. As hands sought gloves and woolly hats, the dog came near again. She'd stretch out her front paws and drop her head, abasing herself, then look up in hope.

"No! Nothing for you."

We climbed. She came close, sniffed, almost nudged.

"Go home!" Whack of the hazel stick.

She yelped, but stuck around.

When at last we attained the forested plateau, the dog pranced about and shook herself as if happy to be in the dry. So were we. All wrong. Up there, a freshening wind blew rain through the trees and made their foliage shed thousands of cold drops already accumulated.

Our way was stony, muddy, and so narrow that the dog left the track to move among the trees. Some of us tried that too, but low branches and hidden roots made our balance as uncertain as did the stones underfoot. Stepped on, they often slid. We stepped in liquid mud, stepped, stepped among the black pines sheathed in ebony plates. Sweet-smelling fir. The thin grey trunks of *fagus sylvatica*. Holm oaks, festooned with catkins.

"Where's that dog got to?"

"Who cares? Headed back to the village, probably."

"Sensible creature's gone to shelter. Not like us!"

Everyone laughed, except our guide.

"A dog to run about the forest is not good. Higher up on the *montaigne,* wild boar. Deer. Sheep of course. And—wolfs?"

"Wolves."

We went on.

Were those animals watching as we came through their country? Some in our group had seen wild boars on YouTube. Not as large as pigs. Mean tusks, though. One told a story from a TV newscast about a huge sow in Ontario stomping on a drunk, killing him.

A howl sounded from behind, a blundering rush. We turned. Just as the frantic dog reached us, we sensed a blurred motion away, away in the trees—and gone, like a curtain shaken then still.

"Roe deer," said our guide. "Bad animal!" He shook his stick.

The dog's chest heaved. Whining, she skulked off, followed again.

Then the terrain altered. Plateau, *fini*. We started down.

Steepness—odd, to be almost vertical after two hours' walking on the flat! Our feet felt unfamiliar. Trees changed: more conifers, fewer deciduous. *Progress*, we thought. Also we wondered, *Lunch?* Daily, leaving our *gîtes*, we each got ten inches of buttered baguette (we measured) stuffed with meat or fish, plus hard-boiled egg and tomato. Local cheese, a slab. Cold meat, sliced. Fresh salad. Cake. Our guide carried dark chocolate, also a mini camp stove for hot drinks.

We went on.

The rainy twist of trail down through the trees grew steeper. We slowed. The stones now underfoot were larger than those up on the plateau, but they still slipped. Terracotta-coloured mud ran two inches thick, clogging our boots. Our hiking poles became essential for every step, while our guide moved urgently amongst us to point out safe foot placements, repeat *Attention!* Rain fell. Some of us did too, delaying the group to cope with minor injuries.

We murmured of forestry campsites at home, of fire-watchers' cabins. Did our guide plan a lunch-stop at a similar place?

That dog came close again, but at every reaching hand she'd show her teeth. Shouts and rushes drove her off, snarling.

Watch! Attention!

Always the path turned down through the pines to—where? None of us knew. With so many conifers, the forest's ambience dulled. No more wry jokes about *la boue*. Silence, except curses and rain.

Again the dog. On her forelegs, mud reached above the carpal pad.

"Poor thing!"

"Poor thing bit me, remember?"

"She needs people."

"We don't need her."

Another distant noise sounded, *r-rr-rrrrrr*. Not animal. Mechanical, piercing. It'd hurt your ears, close up. *Rrr-r-r-r*.

"Must be the foresters."

"Why haven't we seen them?" What route did they take? Surely that cartoon vehicle couldn't go cross-country like an ATV?

Then our guide loosened his pack. "Time to eat."

Here? Steep slope. Dripping pines. No stumps or rocks to sit on. In a ring of soggy backpacks on the forest floor, we ate standing up.

R-rr-rrrr, further off.

The dog grovelled, whined, begged. Our guide, about to shoo her, aborted his gesture when one of us tossed a slice of ham. Another threw torn bits of baguette. A tomato landed on the mud, a cube of cheese.

Even as the dog swallowed, her pleading glance came again.

"*C'est tout!*" Our guide raised his voice.

"No more, greedy girl."

Some of us ate everything, some repacked a lot. We stretched, or leaned against trees to relax while drinking coffee and tea, well-sugared. The dog sidled amongst us, sniffing at hands, bums, packs.

"Are you deaf? That's *all!*"

Packs on again, poles in hand, *la boue* again.

Down those stony steeps for another nameless time, down, down. More slips, wrenches, bruises. Only the chill rain stayed steady, and the dog slinking off into the trees (who cared what kinds they were?) or weaving amongst us on her muddy paws. Once, near the trail, she squatted.

"Dammit, not here!"

Small dry turds.

How far, how much longer? Some asked, others cringed. Like kids pestering a parent, we knew what our guide would say.

The rain ceased. Unnoticed, briefly. At ten that morning we'd reached the plateau; our watches said five p.m. when we realized that the sound of falling water was MIA.

The steep softened first into a hill, next to a slope. The dog lolloped ahead, out of sight. In bright sunshine, peeling off sodden jackets and hats and gloves, we exited the forest, laughing.

Finally our guide smiled. "Now we see the Kermes oak. Not the holm any more."

Our legs, trembling, sought to adjust as we moved into the valley and across a sunny meadow sprinkled with primula, tricolour pansy, anemone, cowslip, speedwell, all bright-eyed still with rain.

The Pyrenean foothills rose ahead, one crowned with grey ruined teeth, the castle where the greatest immolation occurred. To be bundled alive into fire or to deny their faith: two choices, those Cathars had.

We walked alongside a brook whose current carried a thousand spangles downstream, and reached a gravel road. This, our guide assured us, led to the nearby town where we would spend the night.

Round a curve ahead, the dog appeared again. Came closer, trotting, wagging. Those at the front of our group stopped.

We all stopped.

"Look, horrible!"

"Awful!"

"What's she done?"

Over her shoulder, that puzzled red face, peering.

We hastened forward.

In a depression at the roadside lay a large ewe, fallen.

She nearly resembled an illustration for a children's book, that sheep. Background: blue sky, tall green grass. Foreground: a beautiful creature in her seemingly restful motherly pose, in her roundness, her billowy shining creamy woolliness—but her hindquarters, fully exposed to our view, had been savaged to a bloody mangle. One leg was raw. She could not move.

Patient, full of pain, her large eyes met our gaze.

"Wolf," stated our guide.

"Not—?"

"Her? No no, too stupid, she just sticks in her nose for a taste. Wolf." He pointed up to the steeps we'd just descended.

Some loudly wished for a gun, a knife. Others noted that the sheep was not ours to kill. We walked on along the valley.

The brook, still shallow, grew broader. While fording it, by silent agreement we lured with ham the red-faced dog who'd chosen us. We grabbed her, struggling; we splashed and rubbed her furry yelping face till she no longer looked a murderer. Controlling her thus, we touched her nipples. Hard as horn. No loved puppies, not for years.

At the first farm we reached, our guide went in to leave word of the desperate sheep, so that her owner in this life could be notified and come to end his property's pain.

"They will phone him," he said, returning.

Would this happen before the wolf came back?

We went on. The dog circled near, ran off, came back. No one threw food. No one tried to pat.

Why, we asked ourselves, did this animal, so obviously fearing yet desiring human contact, not have a home?

Did the SPCA operate in France? Even if so, there'd hardly be a branch in the small town.

Why are people so careless?

Why do they not train their dogs?

Why do they not affix identification tags to their dogs' collars, vaccinate the animals, have their teeth checked?

What could we do about the damn dog?

"*La mairie,*" said our guide when we put the matter to him. "We'll take her there."

The town hall was closed, though, by the time we'd walked over the centuries-old bridge (our stream had grown to a river) and threaded our way along the narrow streets, faced with houses washed in white or cream, to the green of the central square. Here stood rubbish bins where we dumped our leftovers, and there a fountain played near a memorial listing locals killed in centuries of wars. A smaller, special stone was dedicated to local *héros de la résistance.* The plane trees' dappled trunks were re-dappled by the late sun among the leaves, and, on one corner of the square, red shutters shielded the windows of our small hotel.

Exhaustion, held back for hours, poured into us. As we entered the lobby, the dog pushed forward too.

"*Mais non*," said Monsieur to the animal that had walked twenty kilometers with us that day. (Thirty, given how she'd run back and forth and circled?) The door, closing, touched her nose.

Later we sat in a pleasant sitting room looking out through small panes to the hotel's courtyard, bright with red pelargoniums. A fire warmed the hearth. Madame, smiling, poured *kir* for us and for guests from other tours. Quite a United Nations we made, really, travellers from every continent.

And here were the foresters again. One exclaimed, "You made so loud noise!" All three laughed. Graceless, we felt. Dumb tourists, trailed unawares by savvy locals.

Another forester chortled, "We found this." A glove, with a clip for attaching to a belt. "Not latched, no good! And this." A candy wrapper.

Barbarians.

The third commented, "That dog with you, we see her often today. No good in the woods. No sense."

"*Ouaf ouaf*, all the time!" agreed Monsieur. "I have let her stay there," and he pointed to the courtyard, "tonight. Then she goes out."

A wicker chair by a puddle offered partial shelter from the rain. Nose on paws, the bitch looked up.

"Out where?"

Monsieur made the face that says *Not my concern*. No, his busy schedule wouldn't feature escorting a stray to the town hall. As for Madame, her mien indicated complete abstention from this topic.

"Couldn't we—?"

Our guide answered, "We leave too early."

After a jagged silence, one forester suggested that he and his fellows return the dog to the village we'd walked from, that day.

"We work there tomorrow. It is her home, yes?"

Who knew?

The glove's owner pocketed it, while Monsieur tossed the crumpled candy wrapper on to the flames. Its silvery coating flared. We all sipped *kir*.

A South African exclaimed, "Dinner smells wonderful, Madame!"

A Scot agreed, then a Californian. We all agreed.

At table, Monsieur discussed the trees on the terrain we'd crossed, admiring specially the strength and longevity of the Kermes oak. In calcareous, pebbly soil it throve, indifferent to that chemistry.

We asked about the semi-deserted villages we'd walked through, the proliferating *À Louer* and *À Vendre* signs, the shut schools, ancient churchyards poorly maintained.

He considered. "Every century has its disasters. These are ours."

Madame nodded. We went on to her hazelnut cake.

All night it rained.

Next day's breakfast featured blackcurrant and apricot jams, made by *la maman et la belle-maman de Madame* from fruit grown in the hotel's garden. Croissants, home-made. We ate fresh Spanish oranges. The foresters were not at table, nor the dog in the courtyard.

Soon the tour's van arrived, to take us to the start of our climb to the site of the great burning. We looked forward to being driven. Our luggage stuffed in, we squeezed giggling on to the narrow seats as our hosts bade us farewell.

In another town at the end of that day we ate a celebratory dinner, laughing, talking, at a table crowded with bottles and cell phones and serving dishes. As we opened the last bottle of wine, some in our group confessed that at dawn they'd heard barks. Opened the red shutters to witness the dog's struggle, the men bundling her into the funny truck.

Where to?

That query segued into *Where next?*

One must reach the airport by dawn for a Munich flight, one for Amsterdam. Sure, share a taxi. Brilliant signage, these

European airports had. A Danube cruise, old pals in Barcelona, a family reunion in Edinburgh—happy plans, though *It'll be good to get home* won several repeats.

Best then to wrap up the evening now, finish packing.

Bustle of bill and tip, purses closing, wallets folded.

That sheep—we spoke of her too. Her great shining eyes, what colour? Some of us thought dark blue, some remembered brown.

*

"Dog and Sheep" is a perfect example of the austerity of Flood's most recent work and of an attack so fast as to be almost invisible. Within a page, we are *in* the small band of cultural tourists being guided *In the Footsteps of the Cathars*. We are seeing what they are seeing and listening to their chatter. Many of the tourists have signed up for the walking tour less for an interest in the Cathars than for the opportunity to experience the beauty of the Pyrenean foothills in the Languedoc.

One or two, confusing Cathars with Camino, had expected to follow a specific route taken by all heretics to a singular destination.

(Camino, literally "path," is an allusion to the famous pilgrim route that ran across Europe to end in Spain in Santiago de Compostela at the shrine of St. James.

The Cathars were an 11th to 14th century Christian sect believing in the idea of two Gods or principles, one being good and the other being evil. The good God was the God of the New Testament, the creator of the spiritual world, the evil God the God of the Old Testament, creator of the physical world. All visible matter, including the human body, was created by this evil God, and was, therefore, tainted with sin. The Cathars offered an escape from the sinful world through a sacrament known as the *Consolamentum* (Consolation). This cleansing and initiatory sacrament having been administered, the postulant was admitted into the ranks of the *Perfecti*.

The Cathars were intensely spiritual and peaceable but their belief flouted the Catholic Church's belief in the one God who created all things visible and invisible. Pope Innocent III, determined to extirpate the dangerously growing heresy, launched the Albigensian Crusade against the Cathars in 1208).

Some did feel that faith, if not extreme, might sustain social order? In a good way?

I *loved* those bleating question marks.
The tourists seem to have a limited interest in medieval history.

We were slow, halting often to name and photograph a flower, or to query as our tour guide spoke of local limestone formations. Of French cheese-making. Of the peasant houses (animals downstairs, people up) in the Cathar villiages we'd visited. Of the Cathar heresy, whose adherents saw evil and good as equal powers, chose poverty, strove to be kind. Of their betrayers, informants paid in the usual currencies of cash or sex.
"Shocking," we agreed.
French wine-making, too. *Terroir*, very important.

The proximity of those last two lines defines the banality of "shocking."
Five subsequent lines of conversation caricature the tourists vividly.

"I wonder how many Cathars, total, got burned at the stake."
"Are we going to be so gloomy all day?"
"I'm just glad I didn't live then."
"Tomorrow's the castle of the Really Big Burn."
"Oh no, not rain again!"

There's something offensive about "total" in the first sentence, slangy, somehow smart-ass, ball cap. And as for the crassness of "Really Big Burn..."
We aren't told *which* castle is being referred to... there were so many: Mont-Aimé, Montsegur, Béziers, Carcassone, Lavour, Cassès,

Minerve, all scenes of mass slaughter and holocausts. No specific castle is named as particularity would run counter to the story's intentions.

This opening is a blitzkrieg of exposition and characterization so skilfully performed that we scarcely notice it *as* performance.

The guide herds up the stragglers.

> Past the last house in the village, our guide paused till we all caught up.
>
> "Our way starts here."
>
> We stood by a single gravestone at a field's edge, a stone tilting somewhat and obscured by long wet grass. *Ici est morte,* we read in our remembered high-school French, *Ici est morte/18 Aout 1944/Castella Pierre/innocente victim/de la barbarie Nazie.*
>
> "Glad I wasn't here for that, either."

The word "either" is interesting because it links *la barbarie Nazie* with the barbarism of the Albigensian Crusade. Interesting, too, that Castella Pierre's grave is untended, obscured, "tilted" and therefore possibly forgotten. Is it interesting that the victim is called "Castella" ("castel" in Italian, "castellan," the governor of a castle), and "Pierre"? Is "Castella" a real French female name?

These tiny details, noticed in my first reading of the story, nicked at me when I read the next sentence: "Then this dog rose out of a ditch."

Rose?

What a *peculiar* word! All sorts of meanings attach to it: religious associations, "come to life again," "rise from the dead," "rise (ascend) into heaven," then "rising" in the sense of "uprising," then the idea of something rising up through water to the surface; I had the strong feeling that I would never have written of a dog that it "rose out of a ditch" unless I had ulterior motive.

It was the word "rose" that alerted me to something going on in this story I hadn't been expecting. As we read further, a sense of unease grows until we realize that we are reading some form of allegory. Yet it isn't the traditional form of allegory; it doesn't have the clunkiness of Bunyan or Spenser's *Faerie Queen*; we are not required to follow the adventures of a protagonist called Pilgrim.

There are no fixed equivalences in this story, no equals = signs. Rather, there are suggestions, notes, chords being sounded, dissonances, all gathering towards a resolution that is a non-resolution. The best way through the story is to follow the progress of events, follow the emotions that events or details arouse.

When she wrote to me about the changes in her writing in the last two books, Cynthia Flood said, as quoted earlier, that she didn't want "reader-detectives," but rather, she wanted the stories to suggest—"So a reader will gradually notice. Or *not* notice but still enjoy, while certain words… direct attention."

Rather than play "reader-detective," I'll point out details in the story that seemed to me suggestive or puzzling, or worth further thought.

The Foresters give me an uneasy feeling. The three foresters in the truck obviously know the tour guide; they talk and joke. They point to the dog.

"*Problème*," says the guide. Shrugs.

The guide says of the Foresters that they work, "To remove the rotten branch. Inspect for pasts, no, pests."

My uneasiness lies with "the unknown men" who "wiggled their eyebrows at us and waved." It is the familiarity that disturbs, the condescension of power.

Towards the end of the story, the Foresters reappear at the hotel and chide the tourists for a dropped glove and a discarded candy wrapper. Are they following the tourists? Are the tourists subject to surveillance? The glove had a clip on it for attaching to a belt. "Not latched, no good," says the Forester. The tourists had also made noise. The dog, too, in their company; not good in the woods.

Those words, *Not latched, no good* resonate, seeming to imply widely, generally, until they represent social orthodoxy.

The *sound* of the Foresters at work: "*r-rr-rrrrr*. Not animal, mechanical. Piercing. It'd hurt your ears close up."

"Mechanical," "piercing," "hurt"—these words carry an underlay of meaning.

Monsieur, the hotel's owner, "…tossed the [offending] candy wrapper onto the flames. Its silvery coating flared. We sipped *kir*."

Flames again. Juxtaposed with the civilized pleasure of sipping *kir*.

And then there's that dog. There are scenes involving the dog that have an oddness about them, a discomfort. The washing of the dog's bloodied face in a brook—uncapturable memories of Sunday School stories and hymns.

As they struggle with the dog, they become aware of her nipples, "Hard as horn. No loved puppies, not for years." This seems somehow full of meaning—but meaning what, precisely?

And then that sheep, beautiful "in her roundness, her billowy shining creamy wooliness," one of the sheep described earlier, the fields "polka-dotted with sheep," a description that might be a description of a naïve painting by Maud Lewis, but this sheep is savaged in its hind quarters, mangled.

> "Wolf," stated our guide.
>
> "Not—?"
>
> "Her? No, no, too stupid, she just sticks her nose in for a taste."
>
> Some loudly wished for a gun, a knife.
>
> Others noted that the sheep was not ours to kill."

A compromise solution is reached; the guide leaves a message at a farmhouse so her owner can come and put her out of her misery.

This scene seems to be telling us something important about the tour group as well as about the dog.

And then there's the very strange scene, heavy with some sort of meaning, of the dog, terrified:

> A howl sounded from behind, a blundering rush. We turned. Just as the female dog reached us, we sensed a blurred motion away, away in the trees and gone, like a curtain shaken then still.
>
> "Roe deer," said our guide. "Bad animal!" He shook his stick.

We need to pause over this. The guide's assertion that the dog had been terrified by a roe deer is *preposterous*, roe deer being quite tiny creatures and in any contact with a dog certain to be the terrified party. And then there is the absurd theatre of his shaking his stick.

At what? Distant, invisible deer? Is that what he wishes his charges to believe?

Something in the forest had terrified the dog. No one actually saw what it was. They registered a blurred motion. "Like a curtain shaken then still." Flood very rarely uses similes so when she does we should pay close attention. A curtain covering what? Revealing what? Surely the right questions to ask?

After this incident, the dog showed her teeth "whenever a hand reached out."

To return to the end of the story. The tourists feel that something must be resolved about the dog.

"Why, we asked ourselves, did this animal, so obviously fearing yet desiring human contact, not have a home?"

The guide proposes that they hand the dog over to the civil authority, take it to the Town Hall, *La Mairie*, but the hall is closed. They walk on towards their hotel. In the town's central square there stood "a large memorial to locals killed in one or another World War." There were also rubbish bins. "A smaller, special stone was dedicated to local *héros de la resistance.*" Flood does not go in for scene painting or decoration; the "smaller stone" sends us straight back to the "tilted" gravestone of Castella Pierre.

In the hotel, sipping *kir*,

> we asked [*Monsieur*] about the semi-deserted villages we'd walked through, the proliferating *À Louer* and *À Vendre* signs, the shut schools, the ancient churchyards poorly maintained.
>
> He considered. "Every century has its disasters. These are ours."
>
> Madame nodded. We went on to her hazelnut cake.

(Another of Flood's savage juxtapositions.)

The warm, comfortable evening continues; "Quite a United Nations we made, really, travellers from every continent."

The next day, the travellers are driven to the site of the great burning;

> The foothills rose ahead, one crowned with the grey ruined teeth of the castle where the greatest immolation had occurred.

To be bundled alive into the flames or to deny their faith: two choices, those Cathars had.

In another town at the end of that day, the travellers

ate a celebratory dinner to conclude the tour, laughing, talking, at a table crowded with bottles and cell-phones and serving dishes. As we finished the wine some of our group confessed that at dawn they'd heard barking. Had opened the red shutters to witness the dog's struggle, see the men bundle her into the funny truck and take her away.

Where to?
That query segued into *Where next?*
Always watch Flood's words.
Confessed
Witness
The struggling dog *bundled* into the van just as the Cathars had been "*bundled* alive into the flames." The repetition is not coinciden-tal. The Cathars, at least, had two choices.

Where next? One was due at the airport by seven a.m. for a Munich flight, one for Amsterdam. Sure, share a taxi. Brilliant signage, these European airports had. A Danube cruise, old pals in Barcelona, a family reunion in Edinburgh…

Another of Flood's signature juxtapositions.
The last two sentences of the story refer us back to that savaged Maud Lewis sheep—"we spoke of her too. Her great shining eyes, what colour? Some of us thought dark blue, some remembered brown."
It is surely difficult by the ending not to see the story as a grim dystopia. Not wishing, though, to be a "reader-detective" I'll close with three general questions reasonable to ask.
How does Cynthia Flood wish us to understand that dog?
Is the Maud Lewis sheep the sheep of the story's title?
Is "sheep" singular or plural?

Keath Fraser

Short Story Collections: *Taking Cover* (1982), *Foreign Affairs* (1985), *Telling My Love Lies* (1996), and 13 *Ways of Listening to a Stranger* (2005).

Novels: *Popular Anatomy* (1995).

Non-Fiction: *Bad Trips* (Ed.) (1991), *As for Me and My Body: A Memoir of Sinclair Ross* (1997), and *The Voice Gallery: Travels with a Glass Throat* (2002).

Keath Fraser is not a writer for lazy readers. *The Oxford Companion to Canadian Literature* says of him: "He is one of the most gifted of the new generation of fiction writers ..." Constance Rooke, in *The Malahat Review*, said: "Keath Fraser is one of the most intelligent writers working in Canada." I wrote, in *An Aesthetic Underground*, about first reading him: "I was later to learn that Keath's work bulges with puns, play, complexities; it is best approached with humility and an array of dictionaries."

In the Kingston Conference issue of *Canadian Fiction Magazine* (No. 65, 1989) Geoffrey Hancock wrote:

> Also unique is his play with language and voices. "Both," said Fraser, "are inextricably linked. Language is at the root of litera-ture, and any work of literature with any sort of integrity has to pay homage to language and it has to keep its attention focussed on the language. Literature that lasts surely has an important foundation in the language on the page."
>
> *Taking Cover*, his first collection, is about the uses and abuses of language, words, communication. One story is appropriately titled "Roget's Thesaurus" ...His fiction has been described as a river of language, sophisticated, colloquial, metaphorical, even surreal at times...

During a panel discussion at the Stratford Festival Conference, Keath said: "The thing that inspires us to write is often, I think, a reaction against the kind of language that we're assaulted with daily, the kind of words—the kind of buzzwords—that drive us up the wall as we watch television and read newspapers. And our desks are the last refuge for us as writers, where we can see how physical and concrete language can be. As writers, we're trying to inspire other people—readers—with examples, with illustrations, of how else language can act, in a way that doesn't have anything to do with the received language or the issues of the day."

There is no one Fraser voice or style—just endless variety and sentences strangely, and sometimes inexplicably, memorable. Here is the old Roget talking in "Roget's Thesaurus":

> My young wife died of tumours the size of apples. That I was a practitioner of healing seemed absurd. It smothered me like fog, her dying, her breath in the end so moist."

How intensely moving! How almost magical.

Or the voice of the Hindu waiter in "Waiting":

> This is a calling like any other, except I was not called. I was not chosen. I was born to it, as some bird to flight. People ask me, what is the secret of waiting? People ask me, do you like waiting? Okay, no one asks me, but I have a mind to tell them ...

The voice of Maurice Ringspear, psychotic monster, in the opening of "Healing":

> That summer my countrymen were in the news abroad. A violinist was found nude, gagged, dead at the bottom of an airshaft at the Metropolitan Opera House in New York City. In August, the Playmate of the Year died in a West Los Angeles house when a shotgun blew away her face; she was from the West Coast too. We all were. Even the one-legged cancer victim, the most famous of us, hopping across Canada on an aluminum hinge. Only I survived.

The narrating voice in "Le Mal de l'Air":

> Miles, on the other hand, started smoking Dutch cigars, drinking Domestica wine, and at night dropping his front

tooth and plate in a glass of water made rabid by an extra Polydent tablet.

In the story "Foreign Affairs," Silas, suffering from MS, long confined indoors, taken out in a wheelchair, hungry to see the world:

> That evening she takes him strolling along English Bay to the bathhouse, where they park to watch the sea festival. His aroused vision of the world dilates. Like Krish [his dog] he drools. His gaze is determined to cover everything. The filmy blouses of thin-strapped, heavy-breasted girls in white jeans and black heels. Helium balloons shaped like silver salmon tied to the wrists of Oriental infants. Bowling pins in the air around a juggler's head.

These snippets—every one—mesh with the world's particularities and catches them in "physical and concrete language."

"Le Mal de l'Air"

The following paragraphs share with the reader my first experience of encountering Fraser. You are with me as I open the envelope.

In the foreword to *82: Best Canadian Stories,* Leon Rooke wrote, "This is winsome stuff, gladdening to the heart, necessary to life and limb. The 'best' writer—our position of faith—is always the stranger, the writer not heard from yet."

I wrote the following essay about Keath Fraser for *The New Quarterly* describing the central joy of editing, the joy of finding, in Leon's words, "the writer not heard from yet."

> I first encountered Keath's writing in 1981 when I was editing Oberon's *Best Canadian Stories* with Leon Rooke. I remember I was sitting in the kitchen with a moody cup of coffee eyeing the morning's pile of manila envelopes. I ripped one open and glanced over the opening sentence. The story was entitled "Le Mal de l'Air." This is what I read:

"Suppose he had a three-day-old festering on the elbow, ate pork at his mother's on Sunday and got sick: his wife would rather blame his illness on bee-stings than on worms in a good woman's meat."

Huh?

The second sentence:

"Bees she believed just as likely to cause nausea and the shakes as they were a slowly puffed-up arm."

By now I was intrigued.

By the time I'd finished the first paragraph I realized I'd found a writer of strange power and accomplishment. I read the entire story sitting there in the kitchen in a state of mounting excitement.

Here's the paragraph in full:

Suppose he had a three-day-old festering on the elbow, ate pork at his mother's on Sunday and got sick: his wife would rather blame his illness on bee-stings than on worms in a good woman's meat. Bees she believed just as likely to cause nausea and the shakes as they were a slowly puffed-up arm. Her responses were intemperate and increasingly persistent. She had been to the doctor who could find nothing wrong inside her long, splendid body. Once she took her cello to the Gulf Islands and played on the beach for a pair of misplaced whimbrels. She wasn't happy. You had to conclude that something had infected their marriage. "Or am I just getting bitter," wondered the discomfited Miles, "as the two of us grow alike?"

What a *mysterious* paragraph this was. What could I make of it? It was alive with differing cadences, tones, and levels of diction. It was full of movement. It was busy. The first sentence changed pace at the colon, changed from a colloquial tone to something more formal. Then followed the playful *buzz* of "bees she believed." Then in the third sentence the diction changed again, becoming Latinate, echoing perhaps the words of a doctor or psychiatrist.

But why did he use the words "a good woman's meat"? Why was she good? The word seemed to come from the unnamed wife rather than from Miles. Was it perhaps in defense of the mother whom Miles has accused of bad housewifery? In the word "good" were we hearing an incredibly compressed version of their quarrel?

The simple inversion of "Bees she believed" stressed the irrationality of her belief. The strong stresses falling one after the other prepared us for the "intemperate" responses in the next sentence. And I wonder if Keath intended us to be thinking of the phrase "bees in her bonnet."

But what on earth were "misplaced whimbrels"? According to the *Shorter Oxford*, whimbrels were "various small species of curlew." According to *Webster's New World Dictionary*, "any of a group of European shore birds resembling the curlew, but smaller, with a pale stripe along the crown: they breed on the islands north of England."

So did that mean the whimbrels were "misplaced"—put in the wrong place—because they're supposed to be in Europe and not on the Gulf Islands? That made no sense whatever, so I consulted W. Earl Godfrey's *Birds of Canada* and discovered that *Webster's New World Dictionary* had let me down. Whimbrels were not confined to Europe. There is a North American whimbrel also known as the Hudsonian curlew. One population of whimbrels winters in California and nests in northwest Alaska and Canada. It is a spring and autumn transient in British Columbia and common on the coast.

So a reasonable reading of "misplaced" would be that this particular pair of whimbrels hadn't migrated at the right time. But "misplace" also means "to bestow (one's love, trust, affection, etc.) on an unsuitable or undeserving object." So the whimbrels, by playful extension, are also "misplaced" because they are receiving the misplaced attention of Miles' wife.

The whimbrel sentence captured the wife's "intemperate" quality perfectly. The slightly sad vision of a woman on a beach playing the cello to an audience of two birds suggested about the wife hysteria, drama, theatricality of emotion. Yet at the same time the sentence was comic, of course, and the brief sentence "She wasn't happy" reinforced the comic tone.

But the comic tone also had the effect of making me wonder about Miles. What sort of husband would react in that way to his wife's distress?

And worrying at the paragraph again—*why* "whimbrels"? Did he just like the sound of it? Did he choose it for comic effect? Did he swell the sentence up with ornithological exactitude so that he could deflate it the more comically with: "She wasn't happy"?

(In 1986, at the Kingston Conference, Keath was to say: "For me pleasure is the ability to bury a reader in the story even if we don't understand it at all. Have respect for the mystery. A fiction is more than understanding; it's perception and delight." So his advice to me would probably be to relax and reread.)

Miles is "discomfited." I suspect that some readers might have read that as "discomforted," meaning essentially "made uncomfortable," but "discomfited" means something much stronger: "1. Originally, to defeat; overthrow; put to flight; hence 2. To overthrow the plans or expectations of; thwart; frustrate."

And this harsher word fits perfectly with the picture the paragraph paints of marital discord.

(In Keath's choices of words, secondary meanings often seem to obliquely thicken the story's stew. The verbal noun "festering," for example, has a secondary meaning of "rankling," meaning "embittering," which accords with the word "discomfited.")

Another aspect of this busy paragraph is the sounding of the story's emotional notes: "festering," "sick," "illness," "nausea," "infected."

I read recently a book of art criticism by Robert Hughes called *Nothing If Not Critical* and was struck by the following passage on Manet. Hughes is referring to a painting from 1866 called *The Fifer*.

> Manet's sense of touch was extraordinary but its bravura passages are in the details: how the generalized bagginess of a trouser leg, for instance, rendered in flat, thin paint and firmed up with swift daubs of darker tone in the folds, contrasts with

the thick creamy white directional brush strokes that model the curve of a spat. The ceaseless intelligent play of flat and round, thick and thin, "slow" and "fast" passages of paint is what gives Manet's surface its probing liveliness. There is nothing "miraculous" about it, but it was not the result of a mechanically acquired technique either. It is there because, in his best work, Manet's inquisitiveness never failed him; every inch of surface records an active desire to see and then find the proper translation of sight into mark.

Although it is always dangerous to compare painting and writing, I thought the paragraph a useful way to think about how writing works. "The ceaseless intelligent play of flat and round, thick and thin, 'slow' and 'fast' passages of paint"; those words are surely pregnant with suggestion for a way of approaching Keath Fraser's writing.

I was so impressed by Keath's work that I offered to help him get a collection published. What could I do but love the man who wrote this sentence: "His dinner lay in him like hooves."

Hooves!

There's a simile to savour.

Louis K. MacKendrick of the University of Windsor, a critic noted for his generous and unusual engagement with the work of younger writers, has written well on Keath Fraser in an essay in *Canadian Fiction Magazine* (No. 65) and in *Writers in Aspic* (Ed. J. Metcalf, Montreal: Véhicule, 1988).

Mavis Gallant

Short Story Collections: *The Other Paris* (1956), *My Heart Is Broken* (1964), *The Pegnitz Junction* (1973), *The End of the World and Other Stories* (1974), *From the Fifteenth District* (1979), *Home Truths* (1981), *Overhead in a Balloon* (1985), *In Transit* (1988), *Across the Bridge and Other Stories* (1993), *The Moslem Wife* (1994), *The Selected Stories of Mavis Gallant* (1996), *Paris Stories* (2002), *Montreal Stories* (2004), and *Going Ashore: Early and Uncollected Stories* (2009).

Novels: *Green Water Green Sky* (1959) and *A Fairly Good Time* (1970).

Plays: *What Is to Be Done?* (1983).

Non-fiction: *Paris Notebooks* (1986).

It is not really possible to treat the work of Mavis Gallant and Alice Munro in the same way I have treated the work of most of the writers on the Century List. Mavis Gallant has written so many stories and comes at them in such a variety of ways that brief quotation cannot suggest typical voice or style. Alice Munro's stories have been getting longer and longer—verging almost on the novella—and are complex with time shifts and subtle digression so that limited quotation, again, cannot suggest overall flavour. There is little doubt that they are the commanding writers in Canadian short fiction—and therefore in Canadian literature; the debate amongst writers concerns which is better than the other. Alice Munro's career has been more visible, but many readers and writers think that Mavis Gallant's rather cold eye and stringent intellect will age better.

In 2006 Mavis Gallant was honoured in New York City at the reading series Selected Shorts. To an audience of more than seven hundred, Russell Banks delivered this tribute:

> From her early twenties, when she left Montreal for Paris, she became a writer whose life and work resisted the narrow confines of national identity. In some ways this has been a small liability—not to her work, certainly, quite the opposite—but perhaps to the shape of her public career. Her fame, if you will. She has not been a writer who represents and is thus claimed for the exclusive appreciation of a single national literary readership. She's not the exclusive property of Canadian cultural consciousness, its witness and celebrant. She's not a French writer, certainly, not even a French writer who writes in English. She's not North American or European. She's a world writer who happens to tell her stories in the English language. She would probably hate me for saying this, but in an important way, like my

colleagues here tonight, Michael Ondaatje and Jhumpa Lahiri, she's a post-postmodern writer, a post-postcolonial writer, a post-multicultural writer, one of those artists who refuse the hyphen and reject the claims of national fealty. She belongs to no one but herself and therefore her work belongs to all of us.

Apart from living abroad and writing about "damn foreigners," another possible reason for her tardy acceptance is that her stories make big demands on the reader. They are complex, highly intelligent, wry, and ironic. In remarks quoted in the introduction to my anthology *Making It New: Contemporary Canadian Stories*, Clark Blaise said of her work "... what, pray tell, is the difference between a Mavis Gallant story when she's working at her richest and fullest and most polyphonic and someone else's novel? It's just that the novel becomes smaller and thinner than her story."

By "thinner" Blaise means thinner in texture, less rich in detail, less particular, less rooted in the real world. Her rootedness in the real—often a reality that seems "foreign" to the Canadian consciousness—is another possible reason for the slowness of her acceptance in Canada. She is a writer passionately interested in politics and we have to be able to recognize a wide range of reference and allusion to European history and culture if we are to respond adequately to the experience of her stories. In an interview by Debra Martens, Mavis Gallant says of "The Pegnitz Junction": "I wrote it in high spirits, and it was such fun to write because a great deal of it has some references to German writing—parodies and take-offs and skits and all sorts of things that people didn't get ..."

In the *Canadian Fiction Magazine* interview by Geoff Hancock, she gives some background for her deep interest in politics. She talks of "being twenty-two, being the intensely left-wing political romantic I was, passionately anti-fascist," and seeing the first pictures out of the concentration camps. She was bewildered that Germany could have allowed this to happen. And she thought: "If we wanted to find out how and why this happened it was the Germans we had to question. There was hardly a culture or a civilization I would have placed as high as the German."

Thinking back, she comments: "I never lost interest in what had happened, the *why* of it, I mean. Nothing I ever read satisfied me... I had the feeling that in every day living I would find the origin of the worm—the worm that had destroyed the structure. The stories in *Pegnitz Junction* are, to me, intensely political for that reason. It is not a book about Fascism, but a book about where Fascism comes from. That is why I like it better than anything else. Because I finally answered my own question. Not the historical causes of Fascism— just its small possibilities in people."

Her interest in politics is not in party politics, in advancing a theory or a cause. She is concerned with the emotional lives of individuals and families within social and political structures. In the Debra Martens interview (*So To Speak: Interviews with Contemporary Canadian Writers* edited by Peter O'Brien, Montreal: Véhicule Press, 1987) Mavis Gallant says: "I would think that everything is political, in a certain sense, in people's lives. They don't always realize it; they're either the victims of it or not aware of it... I don't think I could consider people, even in a small domestic entanglement— even if I didn't mention it or write about it—without saying what the structure was that they lived in, and what created it, and what at that particular moment was acting on it ..."

But her concern is always the individual within the structure rather than the structure itself, the particular rather than the abstract.

If all this sounds off-puttingly rigorous, start *The Selected Stories* backwards and read first the four richly comic stories about Henri Grippe. And if I have somehow made her sound rarified, think of the simple and earthy power of what she wrote for me in *Making It New*.

> Like every other form of art, literature is not more and nothing less than a matter of life and death. The only question worth asking about a story—or a poem, or a piece of sculpture, or a new concert hall—is, "Is it dead or alive?"

Essential reading is *Canadian Fiction Magazine* No. 28 (1978). Pages xvi and xvii in the preface to *The Selected Stories of Mavis Gallant* offer a fascinating description of the typical genesis of her stories. Constance Rooke gives a sensitive reading of the story "Irina" in *Writers in Aspic* (Ed. J. Metcalf Montreal: Véhicule Press, 1988).

An important profile of Mavis Gallant by Janice Kulyk Keefer appeared in *The Macmillan Anthology (1)* edited by me and Leon Rooke (1988).

In order to stress Mavis Gallant's signal achievements in the story form I have included a tribute I wrote recently. Similarly, I have included a reading of an Alice Munro story. Some quotation from interviews is repeated but deliberately retained.

> *A talk given on the occasion of the unveiling of a plaque by the Writers' Chapel Trust at St. James the Apostle Anglican Church in Montreal on October 9, 2015, to celebrate and honour the work of Mavis Gallant.*

In the academic year 1983–84, Mavis Gallant was writer-in-residence at the University of Toronto and was awarded during her tenure the Canada-Australia Literary Prize, an alternating award designed to deepen the two countries' knowledge of each other's literature. The Australian High Commission in Ottawa arranged a luncheon in her honour in a private room in the National Arts Centre. Mavis had apparently requested my presence.

We had been in touch by correspondence prior to this. In 1978 she'd had kind words for my novella *Girl in Gingham,* and in 1982 she'd written an essay to accompany two of her stories I'd anthologized in *Making it New*, an essay called "What is Style?," which she later plundered to use in the introduction to her *Selected Stories*.

I strolled up to the NAC and found the room. I was alone except for a man fighting starched napery on a makeshift bar. Then Mavis sailed in ahead of her escort, a visibly cowed suit from External Affairs. Mavis inspected the table and went around reading all the name-cards.

Picking up a card that was beside her own, she said, "I have no intention of sitting next to *that* odious little man!" She switched the name card of this eminent Canada Council functionary, seating me beside her. He, with further juggling, was put at the greatest possible remove.

"He accepts a salary from the Canadian government," she said, "and comes to Paris making speeches espousing separatism."

Lunch proceeded with a litany of complaints from Mavis about the interminable line-ups at the Ontario Health Insurance office, the architectural brutality of the Robarts Library, the sullen ugliness of this windowless—eyeless, she said, in Gaza—National Arts Centre, the tardiness of professor Sam Solecki in providing her with a typewriter, the appalling manners of that very bearded man, you know—flapping a hand—in Alberta...

She spread about her a certain tension and constraint.

I thought of the various occasions on which my wife Myrna and I had walked past her apartment building in Paris, No. 14 rue Jean-Farrandi, in the sixth arondissement, not even daring to *think* about intruding to pay our respects.

After dessert, waiters refilled the glasses and the high commissioner rose and made a deft and graceful little speech ending with the words:

"And now let us drink a toast to Mavis Gallant and to the day she sets foot on our shores."

In a very loud voice, a Lady Bracknell, "a HANDBAG!" voice, Mavis said, "GO to Australia! I have no intention of GOING to Australia! Why would anyone think ... I'm in the middle of a book. Who *in their right MIND...*"

★

We can only imagine the misery of Mavis Gallant's childhood.

In "What is Style?" she obliquely refers to "the grief and terror that after childhood we cease to express." Her British father died young, yet the child Mavis was taught to believe, until she was thirteen, that he had returned to England. Heartbreakingly, when you think about it, she wrote about those years, "I kept waiting for him to send for me."

Mavis' mother is best described by that splendid American phrase, "a piece of work"; she was spectacularly unstable, being arrested for cross-dressing and other violations of the then-prevailing codes of sexual conduct, public this and that, big-amy, that sort of thing. Mavis was essentially abandoned, aban-doned to boarding school and the tender mercies of rigidly uned-ucated nuns. After the age of ten she was in the care of guardians. She ended up in New York at the Julia Richman High School for Girls at East 67th and Second Avenue.

Terry Rigelhof, who has been sharing his biographical research with the co-editors of Mavis' *Journals,* which is being prepared in New York, wrote to me the other day, "Did you know that she was right at ground zero at the birth of the Bund in New York in 1936?" He went on to say, "I have it on the authority of one of the editors at the *New Yorker* that many of the leading Bundists not only sent their daughters to Julia Richman but congregated in the neighbourhood. Mavis's adolescent essay "Why I am a Socialist" seems to have been written in response to the political ferment at the school, though it's hard to tell because within a year or eighteen months of her enrollment, she was expelled for truancy. She thought the New York Public Library offered a better education."

(The General Jewish Labour Bund was a secular socialist move-ment founded in 1897 in the Russian Empire. It split during the Revolution into communist and socialist factions, was revisited as a secular democratic socialist movement mainly in Poland, was dec-imated there by the Nazis, and reborn in the US, spreading from there to many other countries, including Canada.)

Mavis's prying mother found "Why I am a Socialist" and responded, "You had better be clever because you will never be pretty."

(I take this detail from "The Linnett Muir Stories," in *Home Truths,* from a piece called "In Youth is Pleasure." I treat this detail as factual rather than fictional because the Linnet Muir "stories" are manifestly *not stories at all* but lightly veiled memoir or autobiog-raphy. One only has to look at the *shapes.* When one considers the date of the book (1981) it is perhaps not fanciful to see the "Linnett" stories as in the tradition of the New Journalism—that fruitful blur-ring of fact and fiction. Joan Didion's books, for example, *Slouching Towards Bethlehem* (1968), *The White Album* (1979), Truman Capote's *In Cold Blood* (1965), Norman Mailer's various excursions in the field.

Mavis arrived back in Montreal at the age of eighteen. She was living entirely independently. She spread the impression that she was older. Her "library" consisted of "a few beige pamphlets from the Little Lenin Library purchased second hand in New York. I had a picture of Mayakovsky torn out of *Cloud in Trousers* and one of Paddy Finucane, the Irish RAF fighter pilot, who was killed the following summer."

(Mayakovsky was a communist, later Soviet, poet, artist, Futurist. *Cloud in Trousers* was his most famous book of poetry.)

The little detail of the photograph of Mayakovsky brings to my hopelessly meandering mind an autobiographical fragment by Beryl Bainbridge about venturing to London's lure.

> I left the North of England when I was sixteen and ran away to London, taking with me in a brown carrier bag from Lewis's, my best skirt and jumper, a box of paints, my ration books and a framed photograph of Rasputin.

How precious and adorable, these young rebels!

Unless, of course, they happen to be *your* daughter.

She got herself an office job where she soon became known as "Bolshie," a cartoon character of the period who went around "carrying one of those black bombs with a sputtering fuse," also common British slang in that British immigrant-staffed office for one who was awkward by nature, constitutionally in opposition, deriving, of course, from Bolshevik.

When she was twenty-one she was taken on at the Montreal *Standard* by its art director, the painter Philip Surrey, himself a Trotskyite. She moved on to become a staff writer on the *Standard*, writing gritty, contrarian articles on such topics as the failure in integrating immigrants and their exploitation in what amounted to "truck" systems. The more radical of Mavis' friends were painters and some of the actors at the Montreal Repertory Theatre.

The RCMP routinely harassed Party members under Section 98 of the Criminal Code. This section was declared illegal by Parliament in 1937, but in that same year, Quebec, under the Union Nationale, passed the anti-communist Padlock Act. This act was not declared *ultra vires* (that is, beyond Quebec's legal power as being under federal rather than provincial jurisdiction) until 1957.

Terry Rigelhof's research shows that Philip Surrey was visited by the RCMP in 1949 or 1950, their intention to investigate Mavis' political affiliations and activities. It must be remembered that 1950 was the opening year of disgustingly hysterical McCarthyism in the US, and remembered, also, that the activities of the RCMP and the FBI were not unconnected. The RCMP were additionally Standing on Guard following the revelations of Igor Gouzenko in 1945. Surrey fended the RCMP off but the situation was considered grave. John McConnell, proprietor of the *Standard* and patron of the arts (he was instrumental in the career of Maureen Forrester) gave Mavis a year's salary and an open return ticket to Montreal, much, according to Terry Rigelhof, to the vast relief of McConnell's wife, and Mavis left for Europe.

I have gone at such great length into Mavis's childhood and political convictions because both inform all her mature work, work that was grudgingly received in Canada—standard, dreary nationalism suggesting that stories set in Europe rather than in Canada were of no concern to *us*. Her first five books were not even published in Canada and her reputation among the literati was not really rehabilitated until Geoff Hancock brought out a Mavis Gallant Special Issue of *Canadian Fiction Magazine*, in 1978, and I'm happy to tip a grateful hat to him for this.

The second book of the unpublished five was *Green Water, Green Sky*, a still-unappreciated novel. It appeared from Houghton Mifflin in 1959. Below is the opening paragraph, sounding in images all the notes of the book's burden:

"the morning muck"
"the soft, dull slapping"
"the outrage" of his cousin's hair across his face.

How wonderfully un-Canadian such writing is; in 1959, in Canada, Mavis Gallant was writing in a league of her own, a league of one.

They went off for the day and left him, in the slyest, sneakiest way you could imagine. Nothing of the betrayal to come showed on their faces that morning as they sat having breakfast with him, a few inches away from the Grand Canal. If he had been given something the right length, a broom, say, he could have stirred the hardly-moving layer of morning muck—the orange halves, the pulpy melons, the rotting bits of lettuce, black under water, green above. Water lapped against the gondolas moored below the terrace. He remembered the sound, the soft, dull, slapping, all his life. He heard them say at the table they would never come here in August again.

They urged him to eat, and drew his attention to the gondoliers. He refused everything they offered. It was all as usual, except that a few minutes after he was in an open boat, churning across to the Lido with Aunt Bonnie and Florence. Flor and Aunt Bonnie pushed along to the prow and sat down side by side on a bench, and Aunt Bonnie pulled George towards her, so he was half on her lap. You couldn't sit properly: her lap held a beach-bag full of towels. The wind picked up Flor's long pony-tail of hair and sent it across George's face. His cousin's hair smelled coppery and warm like its colour. He wouldn't have called it unpleasant. All the same, it was an outrage, and he started to whine: "Where are *they?*"

The last of those five books not published in Canada was *The Pegnitz Junction,* which was published first in New York, in 1973, by Random House and, in 1974, in the UK by André Deutsch. I can't resist here a bibliographic meander. The first edition of *Pegnitz* is now quite scarce. I remember being one afternoon in William Hoffer's Vancouver warehouse and gazing at case after case of pristine copies of the book; Bill, in piratical mode, had bought from Random House the entire remaindering. On the other hand, he had almost nothing of Alice Munro's early work. "I didn't buy it when they were coming out," he said. "I just didn't rate her."

Silly man.

The Pegnitz Junction is, I think, Mavis' best book. That, or *From the Fifteenth District.* It is certainly the most radical book in technical terms. It clouds our ability to read it if we think of it in Canadian terms, if we are comparing it to such contemporaneous titles as Margaret Laurence's *The Diviners* (1974), Marian Engel's *Bear* (1976), Hugh MacLennan's *Return of the Sphinx* (1967), W.O. Mitchell's *The Vanishing Point* (1978), Carol Shields' *Small Ceremonies* (1976).

Mavis Gallant lived in Paris and read routinely in English, French, and German. Her influences and genius were not provincial. If we are to enter through her rhetoric and techniques into the emotional worlds of her stories we should more fruitfully be considering her in the light of such writers as Samuel Beckett and, say, Harold Pinter. *Waiting for Godot* was first performed in Paris, in 1953, twenty years before the appearance of "The Pegnitz Junction," and Beckett had been writing in French and English for twenty years before *that*. Pinter's extraordinary plays, *The Birthday Party*, in 1958, ranging through *The Caretaker* (1960) to *Old Times* (1971) and *No Man's Land* (1975).

When I was rereading "The Pegnitz Junction," a novella that on one level recounts a train journey, the comparison that came immediately to mind was the journey by car in V.S. Naipaul's *In a Free State*, a journey into ratcheting fear. Neither book is essentially concerned with a literal journey.

The central facts, intellectual and emotional, in Mavis's Europe, are Franco, Mussolini, and Hitler, the faces of fascism, and the stories in "The Pegnitz Junction" probe what it is in us, the man in the street, as it were, that makes us culpable in the horrors of the twentieth century.

Her subject matter is "loss and bewilderment"—people displaced, uprooted, bereaved, impoverished, living in countries foreign to them, the century's walking wounded. Mavis's own history of "loss and bewilderment"

> I kept waiting for him to send for me

fuses with the greater losses. The helpless children in her work (*never* sentimentally observed) are the victims of injustice, autocratic authority, and power—who wields it and how, a question often buzzing in the events of the stories. These innocents set up reverberations into ideas of social structure, politics, the leaders and the led.

In the story "An Autobiography," from *Pegnitz Junction*, the narrator says "... what I have wanted to say from the beginning is, do not confide your children to strangers. Watch the way the stranger holds a child by the wrist instead of by the hand, even when a hand has been offered."

Another meander is forced upon me. A friend, Nancy Baele, sometime-visual arts critic for the Ottawa *Citizen* and friend of Mavis Gallant, whom she visited annually and corresponded with, told me recently that Mavis had said that her two favourite writers of the twentieth century were Elizabeth Bowen and Penelope Fitzgerald. Further, that of Elizabeth Bowen's work, her favourite book was *The House in Paris* (1935). Of this book Mavis said, "The conversation of the two children in front of the fireplace is one of the most shining things I've ever read."

The portrait of Véronique in "An Autobiography," an unaccompanied child of four dispatched by her parents by plane, consigned towards the care of strangers, is fierce with anger and compassion. It is a moving portrait, both of child *and* narrator, and sounds plangent notes, which shimmer inside the story both backwards and forwards. The more deeply we respond to the veracity and vitality of the portrait of Véronique, the more profoundly do we understand and sympathize with the narrator because the brilliant structure of the story, a juxtaposition of two seemingly separate blocks, employs Véronique to illuminate the narrator's life.

"An Autobiography" brings clamorously to mind Clark Blaise's remark: "...what, pray tell, is the difference between a Mavis Gallant story when she's working at her richest and fullest and most polyphonic and someone else's novel? It's just that the novel becomes smaller and thinner than her story."

> I fastened her seatbelt, and she looked up at me to see what was going to happen next. She had been dressed for the trip in a blue-and-white cotton frock, white socks, and black shoes with a

buttoned strap. Her hair was parted in the middle and contained countless shades of light brown, like a handful of autumn grass. There was a slight cast in one eye, but the gaze was steady. The buckle of the seat belt slid down and rested on one knee. She held on to a large bucket bag—held it tightly by its red handle. In the back of the seat before her, along with a map of the region over which we were to fly, were her return ticket and her luggage tags, and a letter that turned out to be a letter of instructions. She was to be met by a Mme. Bataille, who would accompany her to a *colonie de vacances* at Gsteig. I read the letter toward the end of the trip, when I realized the air hostess had forgotten all about Véronique. I am against prying into children's affairs—even "How do you like your school?" is more inquisitive than one has the right to be. However, the important facts about Mme. Bataille and Gsteig were the only ones Véronique was unable to supply. She talked about herself and her family, in fits and starts, as if unaware of the limits of time—less than an hour, after all—and totally indifferent to the fact that she was unlikely ever to see me again. The place she had come from was "Orly," her destination was called "the mountains," and the person meeting her would be either "Béatrice" or "Catherine" or both. That came later, the first information she sweetly and generously offered was that she had twice been given injections in her right arm. I told her my name, my profession, and the name of the village where I taught school. She said she was four but "not yet four and a half." She had been visiting, in Versailles, her mother and baby brother, whose name she affected not to know—an admirable piece of dignified lying. After a sojourn in the mountains she would be met at Orly Airport by her father and taken to the sea. When would that be? "Tomorrow." On the promise of tomorrow, either he or the mother of the nameless brother had got her aboard the plane. The Ile-de-France receded and spread. She sucked her mint sweet, and accepted mine, and was overjoyed when I said she might put it in her bag, as if a puzzle about the bag had now been solved. The stewardess snapped our trays into place and gave us identical meals of cold sausage, Russian salad in glue, savoury pastry, canned pears, and tinned mineral water. Véronique gazed onto a plateau of food nearly at shoulder level, and picked up a knife and fork the size of gardening tools. "I can cut my meat," she said, meaning to say she could not.

Wanting to show readers *how* Mavis Gallant embodies "loss and bewilderment," impoverishment, diminishment, life in the wreckage of Europe, I can do no better than to point to the masterly opening paragraphs of "His Mother," a story in *From the Fifteenth District* set in Budapest. Mavis Gallant does not illustrate such abstractions as "loss and bewilderment" but rather *embodies* them in detail, in the ratty realness of unbrushed hair and an old fur coat worn as a dressing gown. These paragraphs are seemingly effortless, unmarked by verbal fireworks, the voice meditative, elegiac, the whole intensely moving:

His mother had come of age in a war and then seemed to live a long grayness like a spun-out November. "Are you all right?" she used to ask him at breakfast. What she really meant was: Ask me how I am, but she was his mother and so he would not. He leaned two fists against his temples and read a book about photography, waiting for her to cut bread and put it on a plate for him. He seldom looked up, never truly saw her—a stately, careless widow with unbrushed red hair, wearing an old fur coat over her nightgown; her last dressing gown had been worn to ribbons and she said she had no money for another. It seemed that nothing could stop her from pestering him with questions. She muttered and smoked and drank such a lot of strong coffee that it made her bilious, and then she would moan, "God, God, my liver! My poor head!" In those days in Budapest you had to know the black market to find the sort of coffee she drank, and of course she would not have any but the finest smuggled Virginia cigarettes. "Quality," she said to him—or to his profile, rather. "Remember after I have died that quality was important to me. I held out for the best."

She had known what it was to take excellence for granted. That was the difference between them. Out of her youth she could not recall a door slammed or a voice raised except in laughter. People had floated like golden dust; whole streets of people buoyed up by optimism, a feeling for life.

He sat reading, waiting for her to serve him. He was a stone out of a stony generation. Talking to him was like lifting a stone out of water. He never resisted, but if you let go for even a second he sank and came to rest on a dark sea floor. More than one of her soft-tempered lovers had tried to make a friend of him, but they had always given up, as they did with everything. How could she give up? She loved him. She felt shamed because it had not been in her to control armies, history, his stony watery world. From the moment he appeared in the kitchen doorway, passive, vacant, starting to live again only because this was morning, she began all over: "Don't you feel well?" "Are you all right?" "Why can't you smile?"—though the loudest sentence was in silence: Ask me how I am.

After he left Budapest (got his first passport, flew to Glasgow with a soccer team, never came back) she became another sort of person, an émigré's mother...

Her interest in politics is not in party politics, in advancing a theory or a cause. She is concerned with the emotional lives of individuals and families within social and political structures. In the Debra Martens' interview (in *So to Speak: Interviews with Contemporary Canadian Writers*. Montreal: Véhicule Press, 1988) she says:

> I would think that everything is political, in a certain sense, in people's lives. They don't always realize it; they're either the victim of it or not aware of it ... I don't think I could consider people, even in a small domestic entanglement—even if I didn't mention it or write about it—without saying what the structure was that they lived in, and what created it, and what at that particular moment was acting on it ...

But always her concern is the individual *within* the structure.

Bearing these ideas in mind, and bearing in mind, also, that Mavis Gallant breathed an international air that had been charged by such as Beckett, Pinter, and Gunter Grass (these three names simply shorthand for the idea of internationalism), the following quotation from near the beginning of *The Pegnitz Junction* begins to blossom slowly into something much more complex than a bizarre altercation in a cheap hotel; with rereadings we come to see this scene as being, in musical terms, a prelude.

The *dramatis personae*: Herbert, a thirty-one-year-old divorced man with a young son, little Bert, and Christine, Herbert's girlfriend, who is just twenty-one. They are German, on holiday for a week in a Paris hotel, which is slated for demolition.

> Christine woke up alone at five. The others were awake too—she could hear little Bert's high-pitched chattering—but the bathroom was still empty. She waited a polite minute or so then began to run her bath. Presently above the sound of rushing water, she became aware someone was pounding on the passage door and shouting. She called out "What?" but before she could make a move, or even think of one, the night porter of the hotel had burst in. He was an old man without a tooth in his head, habitually dressed in trousers too large for him and a pajama top. He opened his mouth and screamed, "Stop the noise! Take all your belongings out of here! I am locking the bathroom—every door!"
>
> At first, of course, she thought that the man was drunk; then the knowledge came to her—she did not know how but never questioned it either—that he suffered from a form of epilepsy.
>
> "It is too late," he kept repeating. "Too late for noise. Take everything that belongs to you and clear out."
>
> He meant too *early*—Herbert, drawn by the banging and shouting, kept telling him so. Five o'clock was too *early* to be drawing a bath. The hotel was old and creaky anyway, and when you turned on the taps it sounded as though fifty plumbers were pounding on the pipes. That was all Herbert had to say. He really seemed extraordinarily calm, picking up toothbrushes and jars and tubes without standing his ground for a second. It was as if he were under arrest, or as though the porter's old pajama top masked his badge of office, his secret credentials. The look on

Herbert's face was abstract and soft, as if he already lived this, or always had thought that he might.

The scented tub no one would ever use steamed gently; the porter pulled the stopper, finally, to make sure. She said, "You are going to be in trouble over this."

"Never mind," said Herbert. He did not want any unpleasantness in France.

She held her white towelling robe closed at the throat and with the other hand swept back her long hair. Without asking her opinion, Herbert put everything back in her dressing case and snapped it shut. She said to the porter in a low voice, "You filthy little swine of a dog of a bully."

Herbert's child looked up at their dazed, wild faces. It was happening in French; he would never know what had been said that morning. He hugged a large bath sponge to his chest.

"The sponge isn't ours," said Herbert, as though it mattered.

"Yes, it's mine."

"I've never seen it before."

"It's name is Bruno," said Little Bert.

We should slowly pick up that there are undercurrents in the story. In the passage I have referred to as "prelude," the drunk or epileptic porter denouncing them for running a bath "too late" and Herbert's rational response that the porter means "too early," and Herbert's acceptance of the outrageous situation, his refusal to "stand his ground for a second"—something strange is happening here and we should be alerted.

It was as if he were under arrest, or as though the porter's old pajama top masked his badge of office, his secret credentials. The look on Herbert's face was abstract and soft, as if he had already lived this, or always thought that he might.

The porter's last words are: "Dirty Boches, you spoiled my holiday in Bulgaria. Everywhere I looked I saw Germans. The year before in Majorca. The same thing. Germans, Germans."

At the railway station there is a bronze plaque on the wall.

> The plaque commemorated a time of ancient misery, so ancient
> that two of the three travellers had not been born then, and
> Herbert, the eldest, had been about the age of little Bert.

We must assume from context that this railway plaque commemorates the deportation of French Jews to the camps.

As they settle into their carriage Christine refuses Herbert's offer of newspapers and starts reading her paperback of Deitrich Bonhoeffer's essays.

(Bonhoeffer was a German Lutheran theologian and pastor. In a letter to Reinhold Niebuhr, he wrote: "I have come to the conclusion that I have made a mistake in coming to America. I must live through this difficult period of our national history with the Christian people of Germany. I shall have no right to participate in the reconstruction of Christian life in Germany after the war if I do not share the trials of this time with my people."

He was arrested, in 1943, for his resistance to anti-semitism and sent to Buchenwald. He was hanged at Flossenbürg in 1945.)

Herbert talks to little Bert about having lunch early on the French train because the German train at Strasbourg would not have a restaurant car. His actual words are "Because there will be no facilities on the second transport."

Transport.

With that dreadful word, Mavis Gallant is signalling to us not only that Herbert is stultifyingly pompous, but that the journey we are about to share has correspondences with, ineradicable connections to, that "time of ancient misery," the locked cattle-car transports of the *nuit et brouillard*.

She is first going to immerse us in Herbert, Christine, and little Bert and then, through them, in the experience of Germany past, in Germany present; she will show us pictures and let us listen to voices as she quests for understanding of that "time of ancient misery." These details of the seeming surface, as they accumulate, take on the story's emotional burden.

And a quotation from the story "Old Friends."

A commissioner of police joins a popular young actress for lunch. He has known her since she was a struggling unknown. Back then, he had once tried to pick her up on a train at night, thinking her to be a prostitute. Since those days he has had her past investigated and now considers her to have been unjustly arrested and sent to transit camps as a child; she was, after all, only *partly* Jewish, and she should not have been "forced to mingle with Poles and Slovaks, and so on." She has now become, for him, in a reversal of roles, a reversal of power, a kind of necessary pet, his last connection to youth and vitality.

> She is laughing, so she must be pleased. She is giving the commissioner her attention. On crumbs like these, her laughter, her attention, he thinks he can live forever. Even when she was no one, when she was a little actress who would travel miles by train, sitting up all night, for some minor, poorly paid job, he could live on what she gave him. She can be so amusing when she wants to be. She is from—he thinks—Silesia, but she can speak in any dialect, from any region. She recites for him now, for him alone, as if he mattered, Schiller's "The Glove"—first in Bavarian, then in Low Berlin, then like an East German at a radio audition, then in a Hessian accent like his own. He hears himself in her voice ... he is laughing so hard he has a pain; he weeps with it. He has to cross his arms over his chest to contain the pain of his laughter. And all the while he knows she is entertaining *him*—as if he were paying her! He wipes his eyes, picks up his fork, and just as he is trying to describe the quality of the laughter ("like pleurisy, like a heart attack, like indigestion"), she says, "I can do a Yiddish accent from Silesia. I try to imagine my grandmother's voice. I must have heard it before she was killed."

And in that last, seemingly casual sentence, "before she was killed," the axe falls.

Martha Gellhorn, journalist and short-story writer, is quoted in Caroline Moorhead's biography:

It was in Dachau, she said, that she really understood for the first time the true evil of man. "A darkness entered my spirit" and "there in that place in the sunny early days of May 1945" she stopped being young. Later she said, "It is as if I walked into Dachau and there fell over a cliff and suffered a lifelong concussion, without recognizing it."

In that seemingly casual remark of the young actress, Mavis Gallant swings the axe. "Each work of literature," said Kafka, "must be an axe to break the frozen sea within us."

For one so "passionately anti-fascist," as Gallant describes herself, "Ernst in Civilian Clothes," the jewel in the crown of *The Pegnitz Junction*, is a wonder of imaginative compassion. It fuses Gallant's attempts to understand the roots of fascism with her emotional need to explore the trauma of wounded childhood and to employ those wounds as a bedrock truth in the later, wider world. "Ernst in Civilian Clothes" essentially revolves around two scenes, two words: the French word *maman* and the German child-word meaning "mummy": *mutti*.

The story concerns Ernst and Willi, two men now in their thirties who, as boys, were captured in Germany by the Americans and shipped as prisoners to France. Ernst had been in the Werewolves, Himmler's ineffectual attempt to create a partisan force operating behind Allied lines. In the French prison camp, Ernst, seeing that the food is plentiful in the section for French Foreign Legion recruits, decides to sign up. As the story starts, he has just been demobilized from the Legion, his time served. Mention is made of his having fought in Indo-China, in the siege of Dien Bien Phu, where the French were defeated by the Viet-Minh led by General Giap (1946–54). He would also inevitably have served in the Algerian War against the Front de la Libération Nationale.

(I cannot resist urging on the interested reader a book that marked me deeply—*A Savage War of Peace: Algeria 1954–62*, by Alistair Horne.)

Before his capture, Ernst buried his identification papers and his arms outside a village of which he remembers only that, "It begins with L." On the run, "he vomited bark and grass and the yellow froth of fear."

Before being taken,

> He walked all one night to the town where his mother and stepfather were. The door was locked, because the forced-labour camps were open now and ghosts in rags were abroad and people were frightened of them. His mother opened the door a crack when she recognized the Werewolf's voice (but not his face or his disguise) and she said, "You can't stay here." There was a smell of burning. They were burning his stepfather's S.S. uniform in the cellar. Ernst's mother kissed him but he had already turned away. The missed embrace was a salute to the frightening night, and she shut the door on her son and went back to her husband.

In the "locked freight car" to France—a wry allusion to the deportation of the Jews *from* France—Ernst glimpses the rubble of Mainz and subsequently attests to its being his birthplace. His birthdate, too, shifts lower when he learns in the camp that those under eighteen are given double rations. So his release papers from the Legion stated his date of birth and his place of birth incorrectly but they are official papers validated by officialdom: "his identification is given substance by a round purple stamp on which one can read *Préfecture de Police*."

Again: "He pledged his loyalty to official papers years ago—to officers, to the Legion, to stamped and formally attested facts."

Life to Ernst seems shifting, dreamlike, phantasmagorical.

Willi, meanwhile, continues to believe that the Americans sold their prisoners at fifteen hundred francs a head. *To whom* is not clear. I take this as being some sort of confusion in Willi's head, perhaps deriving from Eichmann's cash-dickerings for Hungarian Jews, in 1944. (See *Kastner's Train*, by Anna Porter.)

> Ernst, the eternally defeated, could know the difference between victory and failure, if he would apply his mind to it; but he has

met young girls in Paris who think Dien Bien Phu was a French victory and he has let them go on thinking it, because it is of no importance. Ernst was in Indo-China and knows it was a defeat. There is no fear in the memory. Sometimes another, younger Ernest is in a place where he must save someone who calls *"Mutti!"* He advances; he wades in a flooded cellar. There is more fear in dreams than in life. What about the dream where someone known—sometimes a man, sometimes a woman—wears a mask and wig? The horror of the wig! He wakes dry-throated. Willi has always been ready to die. If the judge he is waiting for says "This is true, and you were not innocent," he says he will be ready to die. He could die tomorrow. But Ernst, who has been in uniform since he was seven, and defeated in every war, has never been prepared.

History, real or mythological, has little meaning for Ernst. As he trudges through the Jardin des Tuilleries he sees the black sculptures of Mercury, of the Rape of Deidamia, of the Roman emperors, as mere shapes amidst the ranks of the winter trees black against the bleak sky.

(The text prints *Deidamia* for *Deianeira*. She was the wife of Hercules who was "raped" (i.e., "carried off") by the centaur Nessus.)

Willi, meanwhile, has remained in France, eking out an existence as a guide and interpreter for German tourists, a translator, and actor playing bit roles as S.S. officers in films about the war.

Ernst, waiting in Willi's apartment on the rue de Lille to leave the next day for Stuttgart and a promised labouring job, is wearing civilian clothes "as normal dress for the first time since he was seven years old."

His Austrian mother was desperately poor even after she married his stepfather, and when Ernst put on his Hitler Youth uniform at seven it meant, mostly, a great savings in clothes. He has been in uniform ever since. His uniforms have not been lucky. He has always been part of a defeated army. He has fought for

Germany and for France and, according to what he has been told each time, for civilization.

Willi keeps a scrapbook of newspaper clippings about World War II.

> Willi is waiting for... the rational person who will come out of the past and say with authority, "This was true" and "This was not." The photographs, the films, the documents, the witnesses, and the survivors could have been invented or dreamed. Willi searches the plain blue sky of his childhood and looks for a stain of the evil he has been told was there. He cannot see it. The sky is without spot.
>
> "What was wrong with the Hitler Youth?" says Willi. What was wrong with being told about Goethe Rilke Wagner Schiller Beethoven.

(Wearing my writer hat, I'm fascinated by how Mavis Gallant uses non-punctuation to dig more deeply into Willi.)

On this day of waiting for Willi's return from escorting German tourists to Napoleon's Tomb and a strip joint in Pigalle, Ernst overhears the uproar in a neighbouring apartment.

> Early in the morning, the mother's voice is fresh and quick. The father leaves for work at six o'clock. She takes the child to school at a quarter to eight. The child calls her often: "*Maman*, come here." "*Maman*, look." She rushes about, clattering with brooms. At nine she goes to market, and she returns at ten, calling up to her crony that she has found nothing, nothing fit to eat, but the basket is full of something; she is bent sideways with the weight of it. By noon, after she has gone out once more to fetch the child for lunch, her voice begins to rise. Either the boy refuses what she has cooked for him or does not eat quickly enough, but his meal is dogged with the repeated question "Are you going to obey?" He is dragged back to school weeping. Both are worn out with this, and their late-afternoon walk is exhausted and calm. In the evening the voice climbs still higher. "You will see, when

your father comes home!" It is a bird shrieking. Whatever the child has done or said is so monstrously disobedient that she cannot wait for the father to arrive. She has to chase the child and catch him before she can beat him. There is the noise of running, a chair knocked down, something like marbles, perhaps the chestnuts, rolling on the floor. "You *will* obey me!" It is a promise of the future now. The caught child screams. If the house were burning, if there were lions on the stairs, he could not scream more. All round the court the neighbours stay well away from their windows. It is no one's concern. When his mother beats him, the child calls for help, and calls *"Maman."* His true mother will surely arrive and take him away from his mother transformed. Who else can he appeal to? It makes sense. Ernst has heard grown men call for their mothers. He knows about submission and punishment and justice and power. He knows what the child does not know—that the screaming will stop, that everything ends. He did not learn a trade in the Foreign Legion, but he did learn to obey.

In Willi's scrapbook he [Ernst] turns over unpasted clippings about the terrorist trials in Paris in 1962. Two ex-Legionnaires, deserters, were tried—he will read to the end, if he can keep awake. Two ex-Legionnaires were shot by a firing squad because they had shot someone else. It is a confusing story, because some of the clippings say "bandits" and some say "patriots." He does not quite understand what went on, and the two terrorists could not have understood much, either, because when the death sentence was spoken they took off their French decorations and flung them into the courtroom and cried, "Long Live France!" and "Long Live French Algeria!" They were not French, but they had been in the Legion, and probably did not know there were other things to say. That was 1962—light years ago in political time.

Ernst is going home. He has decided, about a field of daffodils, My Country. He will not be shot with "Long Live" anything on his lips. No. He will not put on a new uniform, or continue to claim his pension, or live with a prostitute, or become a night watchman in Paris. What will he do?

When Ernst does not know what to do, he goes to sleep. He sits on the floor near the gas heater with his knees drawn up and his head on his arms. He can sleep in any position, and he goes deeply asleep within seconds. The room is as sealed as a box and his duffelbag an invisible threat in a corner. He wades in the water of a flooded cellar. His pocket light is soaked; the damp batteries fail. There is another victim in the cellar, calling *"Mutti,"* and it is his duty to find him and rescue him and drag him up to the light of day. He wades forward in the dark, and knows, in sleep, where it is no help to him, that the voice is his own.

Ernst on his feet, stiff with the cold of a forgotten dream, makes a new decision. Everyone is lying: he will invent his own truth. Is it important if one-tenth of a lie is true? Is there a horror in a memory if it was only a dream? In Willi's shaving mirror now he wears the face that no superior officer, no prisoner, and no infatuated girl has ever seen. He will believe only what *he* knows. It is a great decision in an important day. Life begins with facts: he is Ernst Zimmerman, ex-Legionnaire. He has a ticket to Stuttgart. On the twenty-eighth of January, in the coldest winter since 1880, on the rue de Lille, in Paris, the child beaten by his mother cries for help and calls *"Maman, Maman."*

What historical, psychological, sociological insights does the story offer?

None.

Mavis Gallant does not descend into pallid intellectualism; she does not traffic in such ersatz wares.

In the *Canadian Fiction Magazine* Geoff Hancock interview with Mavis Gallant (*CFM* No. 28) she says:

> Try to put yourself in the place of an adolescent who had sworn personal allegiance to Hitler. The German drama, the drama of that generation, was of inner displacement. You can't tear up your personality and begin again, any more than you can tear up the history of your country. The lucky people are the thoughtless ones. They just slip through ...

She wishes us to *experience* something of Ernst's life. She offers us not an analysis of "a mercenary's" feelings but an entry into *Ernst's* feelings, one man on January 28 in an apartment in Paris on rue de Lille, a man shabbily discharged from the Foreign Legion, a real, singular man, in an exactly caught Paris where the early morning café windows are "fogged with the steam of rinsed floors," where "the Metro quais will smell of disinfectant and cigarette butts," and where the smell of chestnuts burning in the vendors' braziers is "more pungent than their taste."

And finally, Mavis Gallant gave me, among so many gifts, a simple question to emblazon on my banner as I hoist my old carcass up on to Rosinante and urge her forwards yet again towards the windmills, a question that so cleanly cuts through all the clutter and baroque obfuscations of recent criticism.

She wrote: "Is it dead or alive?'"

Zsuzsi Gartner

Short Story Collections: *All the Anxious Girls on Earth* (1999) and *Better Living Through Plastic Explosives* (2011).

Zsuzsi Gartner's debut story collection in 1999, *All the Anxious Girls on Earth* was, to be fanciful, like an explosion in a dictionary warehouse. Words, phrases, references, allusions, movie titles, pop songs, trademarks, sifted down through veils of wavering smoke onto discombobulated readers.

The stories had no plots in the traditional sense of "plot"; they were improvisations, performances, wild dances with language. "Wild" but laser-accurate in their observations and recordings of city life, in their nailing of trademarks, fads, horrible urban habits.

...Costco-size Prego jars, and empty four-litre plastic milk jugs.... These sociological mappings and verbal exactitudes remind me of a remark made by another brilliant performer, Stanley Elkin.

> What I enjoy about fiction—the great gift of fiction—is that it gives language an opportunity to happen. What I am really interested in after personality are not philosophical ideas or

abstractions or patterns, but this superb opportunity for language to take place.

This will immediately open eyes for some readers and baffle others.

(I was an instant convert to Stanley Elkin years ago after reading, in his second novel, *A Bad Man* (1967), the character Feldman's observation of a girl lifeguard in a white bathing suit, "the dark vertical of her behind like the jumbo vein in shrimp.")

Zsuzsi Gartner, too, is habitually funny and funny because manically *accurate*:

> The child has everything it could possibly want and now it comes to you, this evening after the first day of junior kindergarten, and says, "I'd like some pyjamas."
>
> This child who already has a goldfish and rabbits (yet unnamed), a music box with one of those tiny ballerinas that pop up and twirl slowly to *Swan Lake*, a porcelain tea set bearing the likeness of that little Parisienne Madeline, a skipping rope (yet unused), a horse (named Conan, after her favourite late-night talk-show host), her own homepage and internet account, and an Air Miles card boasting 29,342 points...
>
> What kind of place is this school where children of all races and abilities learn together in harmony and yet claim to *all* have pyjamas? (Note: Find out who this Italian pedagogue Montessori really is and what kind of social experiment he or she is up to.) You might as well be sending the child to that public school down the block where syringes litter the schoolyard like space debris and twelve-year-old girls hanging around the sagging metal fence claim to be able to do outrageous things with their sturdy, black-licorice-stained lips.

Surely, even to those not yet addicted to language, the use of the word "sturdy" in its context is worthy of multiple brownie points?

What, then, are Zsuzsi Gartner's stories *about*?

A question best approached obliquely.

Until very recently, CanLit was rural, inward, and backward-looking. Smith's novels, *How Insensitive, Noise, Muriella*

Pent, and *Girl Crazy* reveal our cities. Hugh MacLennan and Robertson Davies, for example, were unable to *see* cities. Our younger writers, amply aided by American predecessors, shone spots and floods. Robertson Davies, blurbing Marian Engel's silly novel, *Bear,* pontificated that the book, which recounts the "affair" of a lady librarian in Northern Ontario with a tired bear, shows "the necessity... to ally ourselves with the spirit of one of the most ancient lands in the world. In our search for this spirit, we are indeed in search of ourselves."

Phooey!

Russell Smith and Zsuzsi Gartner's characters share, rather, the view of the eighteenth-century Anglican divine, Sydney Smith, who wrote: "I have no relish for the country; it is a kind of healthy grave."

Zsuzsi Gartner says of one of her characters:

> ... the you that walks in the city with a bounce in your step, cocky, stepping out among moving vehicles, not bothering to cross at intersections; dodging cars in some mad, happy dance or yelling at drivers who cut you off on your bike. Places to go, people to see. Out of my way, hombre! The insistent hum in the air addictive music to move by. Adrenaline snaking through your body like electric light, the voltage so high in your eyes that the lashes burn to the touch, vibrating until you practically lift off. In the city you are hardly earthbound.

So what are Zsuzsi Gartner's stories *about?*

"The opportunity for language to take place," etched observation and invention, the precision and timing of comedy, all in the service of what is encompassed in the word "City."

Here a story begins:

> The former teen terrorist, sitting on the back porch—which isn't really a back *porch* as such but a fire-escape overlooking an alley lined with three-foot fennel gone to seed, the deranged beauty of panic weed bursting through a seam in the pavement, graffiti-splattered garbage cans, some so dented by angry

ex-boyfriends behind the wheels of circa 1981 Camaros that they looked doubled over from a sucker punch (as well as blue boxes heaped with wine bottles, Costco-size Prego jars, and empty four-litre plastic milk jugs because these buildings backing onto the alley house many growing, fatherless children, two of whom wobble by below on second-hand in-line skates pushing at each other and yelling, "Don't be such a fag!"...

Why resist?

Paul Glennon
Short Story Collections: *How Did You Sleep?* (2000) and *The Dodecahedron or A Frame for Frames* (2005).

One of the more acerbic of my female writers at the Porcupine's Quill said that Paul Glennon's work stands in the same relationship to Literature as M.C. Escher's does to Art. She clarified this by saying that the sort of people who liked Escher wore plastic shields and multiple ballpoints in their shirt pocket. This tart comment probably reflects an instinctive defence of the norms of social realism. Paul Glennon's is a territory into which Ray Smith, Leon Rooke, Diane Schoemperlen, Patricia Robertson, and Douglas Glover also stray. It is a territory which encompasses farce, whimsy, metaphysics, surrealism, pastiche, and play. The spirit and practice of Jorge Luis Borges stand close.

Glennon has written of his interest in Oulipian principles, "that is on the principles of the Ouvroir de la Littérature Potentielle (OuLiPo). OuLiPo is a group of mostly French authors who create literature based on highly arbitrary constraints of their own making. Amongst the most famous of these are Georges Perec's *La Disparition*, a novel written entirely without the letter E and Raymond Queneau's *Exercices de Style* in which the same object is described over and over in different rhetorical styles."

On the home front, Diane Schoemperlen's novel *In the Language of Love* was "structurally based on the 100 words of the Standard Word Association Test, originally devised by Carl Jung. It's an intriguing list, the first five words being: Table, Dark, Music, Sickness, Man. The last five words are: Street, King, Cheese, Blossom, Afraid. I conceived of this structure early in 1988 but did not begin writing it until August 1990. The form was compelling and clear but it took me that long to figure out what the book was going to be *about*."

My acerbic author at the Porcupine's Quill would probably consider Paul's and Diane's writing as "like farting Annie Laurie through a keyhole. It may be clever but is it worth the trouble"— Gulley Jimson's immortal words, in Joyce Cary's *The Horse's Mouth*, to Sir William and Lady Beeder concerning her watercolours. As should be obvious through my insistence throughout this book on the centrality of artifice, hers is not a position I share.

We might do well to remember that Gulley Jimson was attacking in Lady Beeder's work the trite, the worn-out conventions.

> Sir William got out an easel and a big portfolio, in red morocco with a monogram in gold. And he took out a big double mount, of the best Bristol board, cut by a real expert, with a dear little picture in the middle. Sky with clouds, grass with trees, water with reflection, cows with horns, cottage with smoke and passing labourer with fork, blue shirt, old hat.

Paul Glennon's stories are very much not "old hat." In "Chrome," for example, a man awakes to see the world as if everything had been coated in chrome:

> I lifted the pillow off my head and put my hand in front of my face, slowly examining the gleaming metallic curves of my palm and fingers. My hand was featureless except for little splinters of wire that used to be body hairs... Nothing looked dirty. Balls of dust and lint in floor corners looked like brooches of finely wound silver wire. The breakfast cereal on my spoon seemed more like highly specialized parts for a European car or appliance ...

The danger of such writing, it seems to me, is that it is easy to descend into mere cleverness and to lose touch with emotion;

the challenge is to domesticate the fantastical and invest it with feeling.

"The Museum of the Decay of Our Love," the first story in *How Did You Sleep?*, seems to me to do just that, triumphantly. The husband visits the Museum and tours the various exhibition halls—The Colonial Period, The Revolution, The Republic, The Civil Wars, The Reconquista, The Junta.

In the Civil Wars Hall:

> All the small space would accommodate were paintings, a few small icons with peculiar compressed perspective and a dozen wide, mostly brown and gloomily realistic battle paintings.
>
> The director gestured quickly to the icons as we passed. "Aloofness, Intellectual Pride, Disdain, Domestic Drudgery, Ennui, Justified Resentment, Estrangement, Sorrow Inconsolable" …
>
> His voice was a drum roll of vibrato as he read off the battle names: "the Stand-off in the Kitchen, the Long March, the Night of the Rebuff, the Marsh Wars, the Campaign of the Chaco, the Mountain Stronghold, the Final Meeting."

A bravura performance. And *strangely* moving.

Douglas Glover

Short Story Collections: *The Mad River* (1981), *Dog Attempts to Drown Man in Saskatoon* (1985), *A Guide to Animal Behaviour* (1991), *16 Categories of Desire* (2000), *Bad News of the Heart* (2003), and Savage Love (2013).

Novels: *Precious* (1983), *The South Will Rise at Noon* (1988), *The Life and Times of Captain N.* (1993), and *Elle* (2003).

Non-Fiction: *Notes Home from a Prodigal Son* (1999), *The Enamoured Knight* (2004), and *Attack of the Copula Spiders* (2012).

Douglas Glover is the author of six story collections and three novels. The last, *Elle*, won the Governor General's Award for

Fiction in English in 2005. Normally I would represent him by the selected stories, but *Bad News of the Heart* is published by Dalkey Archive in Normal, Illinois and may prove awkward for Canadian readers to obtain. *16 Categories of Desire* would be a good substitute.

Glover's stories are comedies of unhinged sadness. Professor Lawrence Mathews at Memorial University has written of them, "His art aims to reveal not 'the meaning of life' but 'only the mystery of it, its insolubility, its resistance to meaningful explication.'"

The narrating "I" in "State of the Nation" might be speaking for many of Glover's protagonists when he says:

> I am out of there, a crushing weight on my chest—heartburn or love, I can't tell which.

Glover's protagonists, some in mental hospitals, others wandering lost, are trying to escape "emotional confusion and darkness."

> … In session with Dr. Gutfreund, I had once let slip (possibly under the influence of sodium pentathol injections administered surreptitiously) details of my youthful fascination with "lifelike" mechanical toys. What did I mean by lifelike? Gutfreund had demanded. He was always trying to get me to explain myself to myself, which I understand is standard therapeutic technique.
>
> What did I mean by lifelike? I meant moving about, performing complex and repetitive actions up to and including making simple speeches. I loved my little tin drummer boy, a barking dog that turned somersaults when wound up and a frog that hopped. I also loved automated bank tellers, self-serve gas stations and vending machines (there was one in the hospital cafeteria which I took to calling Mother.)
>
> Somehow, I told Gutfreund, these machines managed to essentialize all that was good in life while subtracting the emotional confusion and darkness. You never saw a vending machine

beat an old woman to death for her handbag, I said. With a machine you know where you stand.

Over these wildly funny stories of despair broods the fathering spirit of Samuel Beckett; it is possible to hear something of the familial cadences in "My Romance":

> I call it love, for want of a better word—I don't know what it is really. Beyond us there is a void, and inside us there is a void. At the centre, the self is inscrutable. We ride the dark, lunar surfaces of unknown objects our whole lives long; we are receivers of messages the provenance of which is as obscure as death itself. It seems to test us, to drown us, grow us, betray us, destroy us. Before it, we are alone. And yet between this void and the shallow dogmas of psychotherapeutics there remains some residue, some faint sediment of—what? The thing you can't see for looking at it, the thing disappearing at the corner of your eye, the thing not conceived in any of your philosophies, the thing that is not the void and not the half-crazy, shambling beast of desire that dogs our lives (what the Buddhists call "the little self"). This is the place where loves resides, if love resides.

Glover is profoundly interested in rhetoric and reveals his many tricks-of-the-trade in an interview with Melissa Hardy entitled "Essential Furniture of the World" in *Paragraph* Volume 13, No. 1 (1991) and in the transcription of a panel discussion "The Theatre of the Page" in *The New Quarterly: Wild Writers We Have Known* Volume XXI, Nos. 2 and 3.

The dedication of *16 Categories of Desire* reads, perhaps unsurprisingly, *This book is for my dog Nellie.*

Terry Griggs

Short Story Collections: *Quickening* (1990), *Quickening* [re-issue] (2009), and *The Discovery of Honey* (2017).

Novels: *The Lusty Man* (1995), *Rogue's Wedding* (2002, reprinted as *The Iconoclast's Journal* in 2018), *Thought You Were Dead* (2009), she has also written the Cat's Eye Corner trilogy for younger readers, and the YA title, *Nieve* (2010).

The stories are usually set in Manitoulin Island, Ontario, where Terry Griggs grew up and where her parents owned a fishing camp. "This land included miles of shoreline, forests, fields, a river, a bay in front of our house, etc., and it was the work of my childhood to get to know every inch of it." She was not, she says, much of a reader when a child.

> Which is not to say that there weren't other sources of story. You need look no further than the Catholic Church for a packed and bizarre fund of that. As well, anecdote came with the summer breezes, for our camp was always full of people, many of them American (never tight-lipped), and many of whom returned year after year—so you got the ongoing saga. In town there was a whole community of interwoven narratives of which I was aware (to a degree) and a part. Hence my immediate attraction to *Under Milk Wood* when I later encountered it—I had lived the form.

Her tomboyish spiritual attachment to the natural world, her later imaginative recreation of that world—"The ice was still in the bay. The ones who live below, the green-haired women with blue bodies and flowing black dresses ..."—her participation in anecdote and gossip and the stories she was told of saints, martyrs, and miracles and her sharing in what in one story she called "the communal daydream," all this is mixed together, pure recollected detail and imagined magic, no dividing line between them, to form her own myth of Manitoulin and its characters, a Canadian counterpart to Dylan Thomas' lovely village of the very Welsh-sounding Llareggub, Bugger All spelled backwards.
    Here is the *feel* of that mythic landscape, the opening two paragraphs of the story "A Laughing Woman."

> A laughing woman with flame-coloured hair and a dress green as leaves wanders down the road and it's summer, luminous summer, the sun dropping haloes and scarves of light. Clothes are cast off, shades are raised. Putty-soft babies, born and coddled

in the long winter, are put out on lush new grass and later, in photos, are seen to be playing with sunspots and flashing bolts. Summer spreads over the island like a thousand voices carried over water, like a thousand tongues of fire, engulfing, inciting.

Even the ghosts, packed like larvae in the earth, grow restless and refuse to stay put. Mari knows this. Within sight of her place, down the hill on the other side of the road, lies a graveyard. Evenings sitting on the front step with Whip beside her, chasing birds in his sleep, she watches them rise like brume. Some drift toward town, others stay close, anchored to the last of their possessions—mossy bones, names carved on stone, a spelling of themselves they no longer understand. It fascinates her, how they weave like swifts through the falling dark caught in patterns of unrest that never vary... .

In her interview in *Writers Talking* she said:

But stories, yes... Possibly it's the form I'm best suited to, as I love language—charged, heightened—and style and narrative. (You know, I do find it annoying when critics say I pay no attention to the story in stories, simply because it is not done the usual way, or they can't be bothered to read with a degree of attention.) As Elizabeth Bowen has said, "The short story avoids routine, it is the most fluid and experimental of forms." At a time when even literary novels are becoming more formulaic, the story may be the best and most artistically open place to play.

Play is present in every Griggs story, play couched in an eruption of baroque language—perhaps she'll forgive me if I go so far as to say *rococo*. Lovely, endless verbal invention. Lava thrown into the night sky and then running in glowing rivers of gold. The creation of myth demands excess.

In my *Freedom from Culture: Selected Essays 1982–1992* I quoted Griggs as writing:

If anything, a story is a complexity, a puzzle, an involved telling, and it is form that makes available to us a story's intricacies and depths as well as its surface. Form carries out intention, that of plot and character naturally, and that of the writer who may be after a certain texture or density in the prose, or who may have something else up her sleeve. Something private but there nonetheless for discovery. Like the generative impulse behind "Suddenly," which was simply to define in narrative terms the word "suddenly." The result being a head-on collision of the dictionary and the short story that gives "Suddenly" its episodic and immediate character, as if it is saying, "I am this, and this, and *this!*"

Form in my stories often takes its cue from the dominant metaphor. In proper metaphor fashion the story becomes in structure, in its very bones, what it is about. (Everything, imagery, symbolism, just piles into the metaphor like kids into a station wagon and the story takes off.)

I was, for some reason, much moved years ago when Griggs told me that before she settles to the day's prose she reads poetry to spiritually prepare herself for what faces her.

Two brief quotations from "Man with the Axe."

First, the almost symphonic:

All that week her ear itches with a telltale trickle of melt like a tap dripping somewhere, and soon water speaking in a hundred, then a thousand voices through rocks and trees and shifting earth ...

Second, the domestic:

Erie had been listening all that week to thaw, a trickle of melt tickling her inner ear, the sound of water dripping off the eaves, *drip* into that handful of bare stones by the corner of the barn, *drop* off the branches of the forsythia out front. Like tears, she thought, cold tears.

Like poetry, I thought.

Terry Griggs is interviewed in *Writers Talking* Edited by J. Metcalf and Claire Wilkshire (Erin: Porcupine's Quill, 2003). There is another important interview conducted by Michael Carbert in *Carousel Magazine*, No. 11, 1996.

Steven Heighton
Short Story Collections: *Flight Paths of the Emperor* (1992), *On Earth As it Is* (1995), and *The Dead Are More Visible* (2012).
 Novels: *The Shadow Boxer* (2000), *Afterlands* (2005), *Every Lost Country* (2010), and *The Nightingale Won't Let You Sleep* (2017).
 Poetry Collections: *Foreign Ghosts* (1989), *Stalin's Carnival* (1989), *The Ecstasy of Skeptics* (1994), *The Address Book* (2004), *Patient Frame* (2010), and *The Waking Comes Late* (2016).
 Non-Fiction: *The Admen Move on Lhasa: Writing & Culture in a Virtual World* (1997), and *Workbook* (2011).

A travel writer said that for thousands of young men and women from the States, Canada, and England, teaching English in Japan or Korea has become almost a rite of passage, the twentieth century equivalent of the Grand Tour.
 In the *Writers Talking* interview Heighton says:

> We easily found jobs teaching English—like thousands of other *gaijin*, foreigners—and an eight-tatami flat in Osaka. During our ten busy, happy months there I strove to learn the language, mainly from a second-hand book published a few years before by two elderly, venerable Tokyo philologists. Page by page, chapter by chapter, the sentences the student was asked to render into English grew more disturbing and macabre. *Shitai*—corpse or cadaver—was one of the first words I was required to learn.

Heighton is unashamedly romantic in his attitude to literature. He offers interesting comments on romanticism in an interview in *The Notebooks* and in *Writers Talking* he said: "At the turn of the millennium being a true rebel means being, by postmodern standards, unabashedly uncool—an aesthete, devoted to the old pursuit of truth and beauty in artistic form."

The most powerful of his stories in *Flight Paths of the Emperor*—"The Beautiful Tennessee Waltz" and "Five Paintings of the New Japan"—deal with his narrator's romantic veneration of the "old Japan" only to find that for the Japanese the situation is more equivocal. Of his young Japanese friends at The American Dream café in "The Beautiful Tennessee Waltz" he writes: "At first we had seen each other as spiritual guides to remote Promised Lands, then discovered our maps were obsolete, our purposes at odds. We were falling out of love, but at first we would not give up. I pestered them with queries about Mishima and the Emperor. I patronized them and they patronized me.... They stopped mentioning my 'quaint obsession' with the old culture, and when I ordered saké (only old people and foreigners drink saké) they smiled beatifically and said nothing."

Not all, however, is sensitive exploration of West meeting East. Heighton is too much a poet not to revel in the rich comedy of Japanese English. Here from "Those Who Would Be More Visible," the narrator is riding home after the day's teaching.

> My favourite moment on the ride "home" to my tatami closet: as the train crossed under the river and climbed out of the tunnel and shot into the open night, a long line of huge neon billboards reared across the river like false-front structures in a midway, luminous and festooned—a commercial phantasmagoria of imagery and Japanese script and twisted English, all mirrored in the sluggish Ara. On a towering billboard, a wry *gaijin*—seemingly James Coburn—sipped whiskey above a slogan rendered in gothic script, as if it were a plug for a prog rock band: OF YOU DREAM, BE HANDSOME CAD, FOR YOU PARTY LIFE AND NIGHTIES OF BACHELOR FUN.

In the splendid comic story "A Man with No Master," the narrator is kidnapped from the Amanogawa American English School

English Language
Made Not Exactly Easy But
Helpful For Your Better Life.

by Katana-san and a man the narrator calls Ray-Ban, because of his glasses. They are *yakuza* hired by a rival school. They take him to a bar where the TV is playing Kurasawa's *The Seven Samurai*. Ray-Ban gets progressively drunker talking at the film.

"In the belly!" urged Ray-Ban. *"Like a dog!"*

Heighton talks about what kind of writer he is in the *Writers Talking* interview.

> Writing of what she knows, the chronicler of home renews or reorients our view of the familiar, showing us how strange and foreign the domestic really is. ("She" because I think first of Alice Munro.) Writing of what he doesn't know, so as to discover it in the telling, the explorer of "away" makes the foreign and exotic feel as familiar as home. ("He" because I think first of Malcolm Lowry and Paul Bowles.) Clearly I was that second kind.

And here is Heighton making the foreign and exotic restaurant *Yume No Ato* as familiar as home in that truly masterful story "Five Paintings of the New Japan."

> I was the first foreigner to wait tables in the *Yume No Ato*. Summer enrollment was down at the English school where I taught so I needed to earn extra money, and since I'd been eating at the restaurant on and off for months it was the first place I thought of applying. It was a small establishment built just after the war in a bombed-out section of the city, but when I saw it the area was studded with bank towers, slick boutiques, coffee shops and flourishing bars and the *Yume No Ato* was one of the oldest and most venerable places around. I was there most of the summer and I wish I could go back. I heard the other day from Nori, the dishwasher, who works part-time

now in a camera store, that our ex-boss Mr. Onishi has just fought and lost a battle with cancer.

"We have problems here every summer," Mr. Onishi sighed during my interview, "with a foreign tourist people." He peered up at me from behind his desk, two shadowy half-moons drooping under his eyes. "Especially the Americans. If I hire you, you can deal to them."

"With them," I said automatically.

"You have experienced waitering?"

"A little," I lied.

"You understand Japanese?"

"I took a course."

"Say something to me in Japanese."

I froze for a moment, then was ambushed by a phrase from my primer.

"*Niwa ni wa furu-ike ga arimasu.*"

"In the garden," translated Mr. Onishi, "there is an old pond."

I stared abjectly at his bald patch.

When Heighton's first novel, *The Shadow Boxer*, appeared, the *Independent on Sunday* (UK) wrote of it:

> Steven Heighton's first novel comes out of its corner with both fists swinging... Essentially the story of one man's troubled love affair with literature, *The Shadow Boxer* fizzes with life and energy, its prose a heated mix of lyricism and muscularity. A bravura performance... a post-beat bildungsroman of the sort that isn't written anymore... its adhesion to the old vanities of authenticity and the primacy of experience [make it] nothing less than a full-blooded argument with postmodern trickery. Intense and poetic... has a swaggering, larger-than-life quality.

Exactly the same could be said of *Flight Paths of the Emperor* and *On Earth as it Is*.

See Heighton's interview in *The Notebooks* edited by Michelle Berry and Natalee Caple Toronto: Random House, 2002.

Jack Hodgins
Short Story Collections: *Spit Delaney's Island* (1976), *The Barclay Family Theatre* (1981), and *Damage Done by the Storm* (2004).

Novels: *The Invention of the World* (1977), *The Resurrection of Joseph Bourne* (1979), *The Honorary Patron* (1987), *Innocent Cities* (1990), *The Macken Charm* (1995), *Broken Ground* (1998), *Distance* (2003), *The Master of Happy Endings* (2010), and *Cadillac Cathedral* (2014).

Non-Fiction: *Over Forty in Broken Hill* (1992) and *A Passion for Narrative: A Guide for Writing Fiction* (1994).

When I was rereading Jack Hodgins' books and thinking about the shape and composition of the Century List, I was in two minds about the work. I had never been a great fan of *Spit Delaney's Island*; its "parable" quality had never persuaded me. *The Barclay Family Theatre* had to be the decider. But that, too, posed a problem because I liked three of the eight stories but found that the remaining five made me, for a variety of reasons, cringe. Compounding this mixed response was the knowledge that it involved one of my prejudices and that therefore my judgement might well be skewed or unfair. And the considerable weight of Hodgins' reputation in Encyclopedias, Guides, and Companions militated against my instincts. I decided to attempt to explain my judgement and let readers make up their own minds.

The stories in *The Barclay Family Theatre* I liked were "More than Conquerors," "The Lepers' Squint," and, with reservations, "The Plague Children." The other stories I thought cute, overwritten, and "folksy." If you liked these other stories you'd call their humour "broad"; if you didn't, you'd call the humour "crude" or "plonking." If you liked them, you'd say they were "expansive" or "full of zest for life"; if you didn't you might say they were "formless" or "sprawling." But for me "folksy" remains the central reason for my baulking.

I have an uncontrollable distaste for populist work. There is the prejudice naked and unapologetic. I find this folksy quality in the work not only of Jack Hodgins but in W.O. Mitchell, Bill Gaston, Alden Nowlan, Hugh Garner, W.D. Valgardson, W.P. Kinsella, and

Ken Mitchell among others. It is a minor but persistent strain in Canadian writing.

Is this simply class prejudice on my part? Or is it more complicated? Folksy, it seems to me, wants to turn back the clock. Folksy wants to praise the "simple," wants to renounce "literature" and revert to "good old-fashioned story-telling." Folksy wants to undo modernism; folksy wants to banish "story" and restore "tale." And in the process it makes language cruder, simpler, less demanding, and in its pandering to "approachability" betrays a hundred years of very sophisticated thought, feeling, and effort. So, yes, I do think that rather more than class is involved.

In Hodgins' story "Invasions '79," Bella Robson's academic son James becomes enamoured of a Russian girl in distant Ottawa. Bella, at the insistence of her daughter, Iris, flies from Vancouver to investigate. James' "... speciality (when anyone asked) was some old poem she'd never had the pleasure of reading. Its title went something like *Toil Less and Crusade*, though she couldn't guarantee that she'd remembered it right."

Troilus and Criseyde.

Groan.

Dear Sweet Old Mum.

The flavour of this laboured comedy can be tasted in what follows.

> There was little ambiguity, however, when Iris called one evening in late October. "You'd better come see this for yourself," she said. "Your brilliant son has got himself involved with the Russians!"
>
> Bella Robson nearly dropped the receiver. Was it possible? This might be the end of a decade that had seen the whole world trying to act like friends, but to her a word like "Russians" still conjured up images of barbed-wire fences and spies and firing squads. Iris assured her it was even worse that that. "A woman."

Iris meets her mother at the airport.

> "Well, he's not in the salt mines *yet*," she said, stepping forward to take her mother's tote bag from her hand. Her tone of voice

made it clear that she didn't expect this state of affairs to last long. "But I can tell that his phone's been tapped."

Bella Robson felt her heart skip a beat but she kissed her daughter's cheek and told herself to stay calm. "If you can tell," she said, "it must be amateurs who are doing it."

Iris lifted her eyes to the ceiling. "If it's amateurs who throw him in jail, will that be all right with you too?"

Despite the Encyclopedias, Guides, and Companions, this reads to me like Amateur Hour.

Bill Gaston's stories, too, are rambling, episodic, anecdotal, some not much more than expanded jokes. He is capable of much more powerful work. Indeed, I selected a story of his, "Honouring Honey," for *Best Canadian Stories 07*. But his conversational, collo-quial style contains the built-in weaknesses of verbal simplicity and restricted vocabulary.

Consider this paragraph about the landlady Mrs. Barastall in "The Walk," one of the better stories in *North of Jesus' Beans* (1993).

Maybe the worst part about the boarding house was having to sit beside old Mrs. Barastall, in front of the TV, with nothing to say. He thought he could smell her: under the waft of flo-ral cheapness an ominous undertone of something a little sour. Andy joked to himself that Mrs. Barastall was the only reason he did well in school, forced as he was away from *Cheers* and *Twin Peaks* to be alone in his room with his books.

In truth, because of the old woman he watched more TV than he ordinarily would have. For one, she seemed to like the same programs he did. But it was more that he found it hard to walk by—harder than her own family did, in any case—with-out sitting down and watching a show with her. She was, in his opinion, too often left alone, especially after her cancer was diagnosed.

And now he was starting his fourth year here!

Friends would still ask how he could stand living "with, you know, other people around." They seemed to love being away from their families, and would speak with dread, only half joking, about a coming Christmas. Andy knew now that boarding houses were weird. He didn't know himself why he stayed. He didn't really like it, but he didn't really hate it.

The only interesting sentence in the four paragraphs is the untypical one: "... under the waft of floral cheapness an ominous undertone of something a little sour." And I'm not totally at ease with "undertone" when we're talking about a smell. The last three sentences, on the other hand, are about as plonkingly flat as it is possible to get. (For the concept of "plonking" see Stephen Potter's *The Theory and Practice of Gamesmanship* (1947) and *One-Upmanship* (1952)).

At one time, I was in correspondence with W.D. Valgardson, who told me that he deliberately wrote in a simple manner because he was writing for "the people." I was astonished at such naïveté in one who had studied at the Iowa Writers' Workshop.

Valgardson wrote four story collections: *Bloodflowers* (1973), *God Is Not a Fish Inspector* (1975), *Red Dust* (1978), and *What Can't Be Changed Shouldn't Be Mourned* (1990). In the late seventies and early eighties he was widely considered one of Canada's most important story writers. Even the usually level-headed George Woodcock rated him a leading practitioner. It was never an estimate I shared. I would imagine that today Valgardson is scarcely read at all, his career a warning shot across the bows of those who would structure anthologies and make Lists.

In *Kicking Against the Pricks* (1982) I wrote: "I recently re-read all [Valgardson's] work when I was compiling an anthology for school children; I was appalled to discover that there was not a single story that was not suitable."

Hugh Hood

Short Story Collections: *Flying a Red Kite* (1962), *Around the Mountain: Scenes from Montreal Life* (1967), *The Fruit Man The Meat Man & The Manager* (1971), *Dark Glasses* (1976), *Selected Stories* (1978), *None Genuine Without This Signature* (1980), *August Nights* (1985), *A Short Walk in the Rain* (1989), *The Isolation Booth* (1991), *You'll Catch Your Death* (1992), and *After All!* (2003).

Novels: *White Figure White Ground* (1964), *The Camera Always Lies* (1967), *A Game of Touch* (1970), *You Can't Get There From Here* (1972), *Five New Facts about Giorgione* (1987), and *The Camera Always Lies* [reissue] (2015). *The New Age Series: The Swing in the Garden* (1975), *A New Athens* (1977), *Reservoir Ravine* (1979), *Black and White Keys* (1982), *The Scenic Art* (1984), *The Motor Boys in Ottawa* (1986), *Tony's Book* (1988), *Property & Value* (1990), *Be Sure to Close Your Eyes* (1993), *Dead Men's Watches* (1995), *Great Realizations* (1997), and *Near Water* (2000).

Non-Fiction: *Strength Down the Centre: The Jean Beliveau Story* (1970), *The Governor's Bridge is Closed* (1973), *Scoring: The Art of Hockey* [Illus. Seymour Segal] (1979), *Trusting the Tale* (1983), and *Unsupported Assertions* (1991).

Hugh Hood was the author of ten story collections, the last, *After All!* appearing posthumously, in 2003. Hood's work is so stylistically various that no one volume of the ten conveys his range so I have chosen to represent his work by *Light Shining Out of Darkness and Other Stories*, the volume I selected for the New Canadian Library, in 2001, and named after a story in *Around the Mountain*, a title presumably referring to the opening verses of the Gospel According to Saint John.

If we come to Hood's work expecting it to be like the mainstream we are likely to be disappointed and baffled. A Hugh Hood story is an experience unto itself and it is a demanding one. In the introduction to *The Isolation Booth*, Hood wrote: "Almost all my work is designed to be read silently by very intelligent and attentive readers, a large majority of them women, three or four times."

It is not only, however, the range and vigour of Hood's mind and its occasional eccentricities which challenge the reader but also the depth of his religious beliefs. Religious belief permeated his every thought. As it was with Wordsworth that "the meanest flower that blows can give / Thoughts that do often lie too deep for tears" so it was with Hood and Canadian Tire and Mac's Milk stores, with advertising flyers, with the packaging of Air Canada meals; the presence of God was everywhere apparent to him. When he published a story entitled "The Fruit Man, the Meat Man, and the Manager," a story about three employees of a grocery store, I can still remember his *astonishment* that I had not immediately grasped that they had correspondences with the three persons of the Holy Trinity.

If we do not share his beliefs, must these stories then be alien to us? Do they exclude us?

Hugh was aware of the problem but remained serene. In the introduction to *Around the Mountain* he wrote:

> My religion makes its predictable appearance in the composition of the book. I have always been a religious believer, a Catholic by birth, upbringing, and mature conviction. While I always draw a distinction between religious conviction and ideology I realize that most secular discourse does not. Catholic belief is far from incidental to the production of *Around the Mountain*. Whether faith and dogma have here degenerated into disingenuous propaganda is a question for readers of other ideological persuasions to propose to themselves.

Hood is far too sophisticated a writer, far too subtle and refined, to topple into didactic mode. His religion is the emotional ground of his being, not a series of debating points he wishes to score. His tendency is always to celebrate and question rather than instruct. One does not have to be Catholic to see-saw with the narrator at the end of "Going Out as a Ghost"; one does not have to be a Catholic to understand and share in the joy and celebration that is "Getting to Williamstown."

Hood's religious convictions had an almost inevitable influence on the forms of his stories. In the introduction to *Flying a Red Kite* (The Collected Stories: Volume 1. Porcupine's Quill) he recalls the writing of one of the stories: "'Fallings from Us, Vanishings' has always seemed to me to be the first story in which I am writing wholly as myself, not as a version of Faulkner or Styron or Thurber or Joyce. It has the strongly allegorical cast, the echoes of medieval romance, the Wordsworthian aesthetics and psychology, and the perhaps somewhat abstract quality of my later work."

Hood had limited interest in plot or character and a decreasing interest, as time went by, in evocative writing. He often mentioned as conscious influences on his work Dante, Wordsworth, and Spenser; his mind dwelled on the *Purgatorio, The Prelude, Tintern Abbey, The Faerie Queene, The Shepheardes Calender.* Because he was working deliberately outside the conventions of his time, because he was reinvigorating allegory, he was more or less forced to invent new shapes for his stories.

Or does the slight bafflement some of his stories occasion stem from the possibility that we are bringing to his work conventions that do not apply? Is it possible that Hood should not be considered as in the modernist traditions and conventions at all? Perhaps he was writing inside a Catholic tradition much in the way that Morley Callaghan was, the tradition of homilies and *exempla,* a form W.J. Keith calls "moral fables," a form that would have been familiar to him from childhood?

However we approach his large body of work, I remain utterly convinced that *Around the Mountain,* an evocation of Montreal life, should be central in a Canadian canon. Endearingly innocent, Hugh Hood wrote *Around the Mountain: Scenes from Montreal Life* in 1967, believing that it would sell to tourists wanting a souvenir of Expo '67.

> In those days I was spending a lot of time out at the Montrose Record Centre on Bélanger, west of Montée Saint-Michel. As you come over from the centre of town, east on Jean-Talon or Bélanger, you'll be struck by the flatness and lack of charm of this neighbourhood. I've forgotten the boundary streets, if in fact I ever knew them. It's *calme plat, terne,* though you might be interested by the Italian neighbourhood between Papineau and D'Iberville, lots of *gelata* parlours and *sartorie.*

With this book he perfected a trademark style, a mastery of the seemingly casual, what I described once as "an informal formality, a heightened vernacular," a creation more complicated than it seems.

W.J. Keith has written an invaluable, jargon-free book on Hood's stories called *God's Plenty: A Study of Hugh Hood's Short Fiction.* Enthusiastically recommended.

Getting to Williamstown

In a letter dating from the mid-eighties and addressed to "The poet Metcalf," Hugh Hood wrote:

> I had a blinding insight the other day in conversation with Noreen, one that I think is both beautiful and true, and it is this. The regionalism of Canadians at the present time is the secular and as it were post-Christian version of English Canadian Protestantism, with the identical mental characteristics, the parochialism, the hole-and-cornerism. It has been described to a T by Matthew Arnold in *Culture and Anarchy* and he would spot it at once. A Catholic by definition is a Universalist, *"quod ubique, quod semper,"* as Newman never tires of repeating. You can't be a Catholic regionalist—it's an untenable mental contradiction, but you can certainly be a Protestant regionalist, it's the nature of the beast. A Québecer who has abandoned Catholicism gives his allegiance to the idea of the nation and the national unity and coherence of a people, whom he imagines as an orthodoxy. The PQ was the natural successor of the worst aspects of Québec Catholicism.
>
> (Voice intervenes, what brilliant stuff this is!!)
>
> But an English Canadian Protestant, instead of making hay with the notion of private witness, essential to both Calvinism and Lutheranism, and the insistence on individual definitions of doctrine and assent in religion, when once he turns to total materialistic secularism finds his private doctrine and witness in his locality and in the opinions of himself and his nearest neighbours, and finally, of course, like all enthusiasts in his own personal view of things. So he insists on the superiority of all things Saskatoonian over the formal modalities of any other burg. He then cries up the superiority of his Saskatoonian suburb, his street, his block on the street, his little home, himself, and the cycle is complete. The sociology of the arts enforced by a Protestant view of artistic value. I note that English Canada, as e.g., the Toronto *Globe and Mail,* has invariably been hostile to

Catholic experience and thought, and that Catholic universalism has been alien to EngCan.

I note further that Catholic Christianity has been more receptive and welcoming to the arts than any other ideology or system of doctrines. Dante, Haydn, Titian, Raphael, Hood. DON'T STEAL THIS IDEA. I WANT TO WRITE IT UP.

I am quoting from this letter because it suggests something of the pleasures and difficulties of reading Hugh Hood's work. He addresses me as "The poet Metcalf" because at that time we were pretending to disdain poets but also because it was a favoured locution of P.G. Wodehouse and Hugh knew that its use would amuse me. This casual (for him) letter reveals him both as intellectual and as a passionate Catholic. And as a touch quirky. The letter is both earnest and funny at the same time. The range of reference and allusion is completely typical: P.G. Wodehouse, Dante, Matthew Arnold, Cardinal Newman, Calvin, Luther, Haydn, Titian, Raphael... Hood.

(Modesty was not one of Hugh's many sterling qualities.)

And finally, the verbal play, the comic shifting levels of diction: "all things Saskatoonian," "the formal modalities of any other burg."

Should we read Hood as a Catholic apologist? Can we read him in any other way? Is he a writer of realism in the modernist manner or a writer of allegory?

In such a story as "Getting to Williamstown," is Williamstown, Ontario, to be read as heaven?

Well, yes and ... no.

W.J. Keith, in his *God's Plenty*, navigates with his usual sensitivity.

Hood announced in an interview as early as 1972, "Everything I write is an allegory, there's no question about that," but most commentators at that time were obsessed with his realism to the exclusion of any other literary mode. He may well have regretted that statement when he encountered the equally narrow focus of later allegorizing critics. Indeed, in another interview a year later he insisted that he was "not just an allegorist," while his claim to being "*both* a realist ... and a *transcendentalist allegorist*" followed five years after that. It is surely a mistake to assume that every Hood fiction must invite the same kind of analytical approach. Because his work often responds to allegorical interpretation, there is no reason why all his narratives should aspire to a higher dimension of meaning. I can see no point, for instance, in scrutinizing "The Dog Explosion" in search of erudite profundity.

At the same time, Hood was always deeply conscious of the reflection of the divine or spiritual world on the secular or material world, and vice-versa. In the Struthers interview, he asserted: "I think bringing together the spiritual intelligence and the world of the senses and the world of the incarnate is the fundamental task of every thinker whether he's a poet or a theologian." Or, he might have added, a writer of fiction. And because Hood is an artist, the most impressive statement of the principle occurs within a fiction when, in *A New Athens*, one of May-Beth Codrington's paintings is seen as presenting "the vision of the heavenly and eternal rising from the things of this world." Such an approach can, I suppose, at least loosely be termed "allegorical," but more important, in my view, is the way Hood expects us to be aware of the one while experiencing or imagining the other. When the narrator in the central story of *Around the Mountain* arrives at the top of Mount Royal, it is not to transcend "the things of this world" but to look back down on them from above. The weakness of so much allegorizing of Hood's work is that it tends to leave the realistic level behind in its earnest search for abstract truth. In Hood's work, however, the realistic is illuminated and recognized as sacred by its relation to the divine.

In my account of individual stories within this book, I have often preferred to employ the term "moral fable," employed by F. R. Leavis a generation ago (and now, of course, unfashionable) when discussing such works as Dickens's *Hard Times* and James's *The Europeans*. "I have called *The Europeans* a 'moral fable,'" Leavis wrote, "because a serious intention expresses itself in so firm and clear an economy of organization, and the representative significance of every detail in the book is so insistent." Such a description fits Hood's work well, and allows for the almost "fabulous" departure from strict realism in certain of his writings that therefore draw attention to a larger meaning. At the same time it avoids the more rigid associations of "allegory."

"Getting to Williamstown" is a story of total metaphor. Williamstown is at once a real town and at the same time a destination towards which Mr. Fessenden has been striving for years. Of the old house there he dreamed of buying he says, "It is a heavenly place."

"Now we are coming to Williamstown; the trees are growing plentiful."

And, "The fields were expansive and rich, peaceful, ah, God!"

But the demands of dailyness always carry the family away to Maitland or to the Town of Mount Royal.

"It's three o'clock and we'll have to make up time if we're going to be in Maitland for dinner. The highway straightens and we get up to fifty, going straight west away from heaven."

Or back to the Town of Mount Royal where, Mr. Fessenden says, "There are no trees…" and where "Without noticing it, the citizens live in an arid plain where the grass yellows in May."

The trees, the fields, sunlight, Williamstown's gleaming white building, all are "an island of green under the sun," a haven, a heaven that Mr. Fessenden has been "getting to" for years, a haven and a heaven he is conscious of as "these six bear me kindly up the aisle."

And throughout the story and observed with love, the daily detail, the magical gas pump, the glittering and lethal meat slicer, the arc of white letters on the window of the general store spelling out SALADA TEA.

Hugh saw God everywhere manifested.

Ubique.

Semper.

"Getting to Williamstown" is a quiet gem of a story. It has lived and grown in my atheistic mind for years and has achieved importance in short-story history not only for its originality but by virtue of having been published, in 1966, in Martha Foley's *Best American Short Stories* along with stories by William Faulkner, William Maxwell, and Flannery O'Connor.

Isabel Huggan

Short Story Collections: *The Elizabeth Stories* (1984) and *You Never Know* (1993).

Memoir: *Belonging: Home Away from Home* (2003).

I'll concentrate my attention on *The Elizabeth Stories* because I have a personal attachment to the book. In the seventies and early eighties, when I was editing *Best Canadian Stories* for Oberon Press, I read an issue of the Saskatchewan magazine *Grain*. The issue contained a story—I'm almost certain a *first* story—by Isabel Huggan called "Celia Behind Me," which was so precisely written, so rich in detail, so moving, that I felt compelled to find the author and, like Oliver, ask for more. After coaxing and cajoling on my part and prevarication and bewailing on hers, *The Elizabeth Stories* evolved and were launched into the world to delight thousands in the book's various editions.

The eight stories chronicle the childhood and adolescence of Elizabeth Kessler, who grows up in Garten, an imaginary small town with a Mennonite hinterland, based, presumably, on Elmira, Ontario. *The Elizabeth Stories* is the same kind of book as Alice Munro's *Lives of Girls and Women* and Mary Borsky's *Influence of the Moon*, an evocation, that is, of an enchanted time and place. Though Elizabeth did not find Garten enchanting.

The older Elizabeth, looking back, writes: "By all odds, I should have been dragged down by the life I led as a child in Garten. I should still be there, or somewhere like it, forced under by my upbringing and all the expectations around me. But luck was with me, and small pockets of defiance multiplied beneath my surface, keeping me afloat, preparing me for that final escape."

Of her ballet classes described in "Jack of Hearts" Elizabeth writes, "Along with most of my friends, I had been enrolled in Saturday morning classes at the age of seven. We were beginning that long process of instillation, the steady drip, drip, drip of Values onto our skulls and into our brains. If our parents could only control our lives long enough, we would eventually achieve grace, tidiness and frugality."

Elizabeth's home life is economically sketched in, as are her parents Frank and Mavis. Here is Elizabeth with a schoolfriend, Rudy, in his father's butcher shop, eating salami. "... he divided the pile so we each had a handful of the spicy meat. It was foreign and exciting, the kind of food I never had at home. For although my father's background was German, as it was for many of the people in the town, my mother's was English, and she deplored garlic and anything the least bit European as being not quite clean."

Elizabeth's early transgressions (usually sexual) cause her mother to cry "I'll never be able to lift my head on this street again!" and "How will I be able to hold my head up in this town again?"

Frank, stuffy, stodgy, rigid, is sketched with sprightly strokes by his comments on Mavis' friend, honorary "Aunt" Eadie.

> As much as my mother admired her friend, my father disparaged her. He was critical not only of the way she dressed ("flashy") and looked ("hair is never that colour in nature.") but even of the way she laughed ("she has a loose laugh, Mavis, loose!"). She was in a word flamboyant—the epitome of all that Frank Kessler loathed and feared.

(That second "loose," with its exclamation mark, strikes me as exquisitely funny.)

Elizabeth, meanwhile, nurtures "small pockets of defiance" and continues preparing for "that final escape." Even church camp offers an escape from Garten:

> ... I learned more about God's glory at Camp Zion than I had ever known, and during Bible study I memorized the Beatitudes and several long scripture passages by heart. I learned to make a fruit basket of popsicle sticks, and a wooden plaque on which I glued alphabet macaroni to read GOD IS LOVE... By the third summer, even though Sharon and Amy chose a co-ed camp closer to home, I would have let nothing come between me and Camp Zion. I didn't need friends from home; I was just as happy to leave them behind, to concentrate on these brief, intense friendships with

girls from Brantford, Hamilton, London, St. Catherines. These were girls who could teach me about life outside Garten, who knew about things I had never encountered— Chinese egg rolls, pizza, perverts in movie theatres, how to steal stuff from stores, how to wad your brassière with Kleenex (I didn't need to and for that had some status), how to slick your hair back into a ducktail and wear your blouse collar turned up at the neck. Endless, the things there were to discover at Camp Zion.

"They Desire a Better Country"—the motto of the Order of Canada. *Desiderantes meliorem patriam*. I, personally, desire a MUCH better country. Sometimes in moments of mental and emotional weakness, I daydream of a national curriculum. I daydream of teacher-training institutions razed, of pedants ejected, of Mrs. Gundy silenced, of pedagogues from OISE harried to exhaustion along Bloor Street. I daydream of a national curriculum in history. Of a national curriculum in literature for secondary-school students. I daydream of teaching the beautiful deployment of language, the sheer *pleasure* of *Lives of Girls and Women, A Basket of Apples, Influence of the Moon, The Elizabeth Stories* ...

Dayv James-French
Short Story Collections: *Victims of Gravity* (1990), *What Else Is a Heart For?* (1998), and *The Afternoon of Day Five: Revised Stories 1987-1994* (2006).

In my 1992 book, *The New Story Writers*, I wrote about Dayv as follows:

> Innovative shapes must be forged in a language which is precise and quick to the touch. This is not to say that the writing must be "poetic" or fancy in any way, rather, it must be precise, concentrated, and above all, appropriate.
>
> As an illustration of those qualities, I'd offer the first paragraph of Dayv James-French's "Contacts":

Looking directly forward from the top of the stairs, Wayne can see Angela in the bathroom. She's sitting in the middle of the tub, her back rounded and pink, with an expression of intense concentration focused above the taps on the far wall. Her hair is twisted up, to keep it dry, but a strand has loosened and curls down the side of her neck An epaulet of bubblebath dots one shoulder. She doesn't look anything like a child: her plump eleven-year old body appears through the steam like a voluptuous woman's. Wayne, helplessly, feels nudged by an emotion inappropriate for a father. He's been taken by surprise.

James-French was one of the least radical of these younger writers, but his touch in a story is easily recognizable. When I first read his work I was reminded of listening to Thelonius Monk—the same sort of dissonances. I don't mean "dissonances" in terms of sound; I mean, rather, a denial or distortion of shape or significance convention would have led us to expect. He achieves these disquieting effects in a variety of ways; one is by using an odd kind of focus, an extreme close-up, say, or a scene pictured from an odd angle which we have to puzzle over to decipher. By observing things in extreme close-up, he often renders the everyday as mysterious as it actually is.

The first six paragraphs or so of "Contacts" are packed with implication and image which reverberate on into the story and which the story amplifies and elaborates. The brilliance of the writing in these paragraphs only reveals itself on subsequent readings, only reveals itself within the context of the whole story. And that is exactly as it should be.

Many years ago I started messing about with what I privately called "Degas angles." A "Degas angle" was something seen from an odd vantage point or was something *incomplete*. I'd started consciously thinking about this when I realized that Degas' paintings had been structured, in part, by the *accidental* qualities of photography, that he'd painted bits of people,

people partly out of the frame to capture an *unposed* quality, a "realness" which painting had never done before. An example of a "Degas angle" in my own work would be the sight of "Father's" head with its two wings of white hair seen through the bannisters mounting the stairs in the story "Single Gents Only." And the sight of Father attempting to light the geyser in the bathroom, the view partially blocked by the back of the boy in the brown dressing gown. I've never talked to Dayv about this so far as I can recall, so it's most unlikely he derived his angles from me.

And we do, of course, have cinema in common.

Do writers *really* get together and discuss "Degas angles?"

Well, no.

Like all other creative people, writers only discuss money.

But even the most secretive and intuitive among them are wrestling with formal concerns whether they'll talk about them or not. Some writers give a great deal of conscious thought to technique while others, for whom writing is magical, prefer not to pry into the mysteries, believing that ratiocination might destroy their ability to perform. Doug Glover, who luxuriates in theory, stands at one pole, Steven Heighton at the other; the others range between.

Dayv James-French, in *his* comments on form, deplores the "excessive genteel *tidiness*" of such writers as Katherine Mansfield. I was particularly struck by his words because in an interview published in the University of Guelph's *Carousel* magazine I'd said:

> One of the problems with the epiphany story is that it reached a kind of perfection fairly early on and then it became, in the hands of lesser writers, far too *neat* a way of parcelling up a bit of experience. There's a sense in which the epiphany story presents a piece of life and then makes a comment on it. In other words, when the form is less than greatly handled it becomes merely another version of the moralizing sort of story it was invented to supplant.

In the best work of the writers of my generation in Canada, what we've arrived at are forms that allow us not to be neat. We have struggled through to forms that are our own voices. Our stories are probably less defined, more ambiguous, shifting. We've given ourselves up, in a more abandoned way, to imagery. And by that I absolutely *don't* mean that we stud our puddings with raisins of simile and metaphor. I mean we create images—scenes, rather, which in their richness, detail, complexity, and sometimes mystery have the power of images in dreams, and these images draw the reader into them and from that *experiencing*, varieties of meaning will evolve for the reader.

We draw readers into our verbal performances. They are inside. They can't *observe* the story from the outside. This is why rhetoric's so important and why a knowledge of the tools of the trade adds to the reader's pleasure.

As I'm saying this I have in mind some of the almost dream-like stories Alice Munro writes—stories like "Meneseteung." Such stories as Norman Levine's "Something Happened Here." The almost hypnotic monologues of such Rooke narrations as "Mama Tuddi."

Here is Dayv James-French, then, on what he calls "A-ha!" stories:

> Without especially planning to be innovative, I see I have rejected the (post-)Freudian model of writers who thrilled me in my teens, especially Lawrence and Mansfield. I'm not interested in duplicating that kind of genteel *tidiness.*
>
> Were I a different sort of writer, I might say that my stories take their shapes from *present-ing the past*, that is, constructing the parallel lines of memory and moment, sensibility and sensation. While I eschew the deliberate reflexiveness (and self-congratulation) of post-modernism, I work to create a kind of corporate voice in a short story, a mediation between the writer and the narrator, so that the story is clearly a *written* performance.
>
> I don't use a beginning-middle-end structure in my stories, preferring to start as close to the end as possible, then backing up to the central image. I don't place the "ideas" on the surface,

or in the spotlight. This may be a reaction to the neatness of the fiction I grew up with—all those bloody pompous men drawing battlefields so they could behave heroically under fire. With all respect to those who were personally involved, the two wars of my lifetime (Vietnam and the Gulf) were sloppy, inconclusive affairs. They were "about" something, and in time they were over, but they did not end with closure.

Life is just too complex to be presented in traditional, or even modern forms. A story needs to be taut, but if it's linear and suggests a complete resolution (What I call A-ha! Stories), then I think it's dishonest, television in type. What I do, instead, is give shape to domestic realities in a past-and-present construction that makes sense out of chaos without imposing order.

Mostly, I don't deliberate over technique, preferring to let the story dictate its own shape. I'm (slowly) learning to trust the stories' own voices, to listen rather than tell.

The "untidiness" of Dayv's stories, their skewed shapes, the way they deny the shape we expect them to have, that they *ought* to have, their refusal to "impose order"—their very shapes are another aspect of "dissonance," of those marvellously jarring Thelonius Monk chords.

The experience of reading a Dayv James-French story is often like buttoning up a many-buttoned overcoat only to find when one has reached the top that one is holding a button for which there is no buttonhole. Or the other way round.

And the coat feels funny.

What follows is a (necessarily) long quotation from his story "Cervine." Even from this excerpt, the reader ought to be able to sense what I was trying to convey by "odd kind of focus" and "skewed shapes" and "dissonance." The massive moose, quite real in the largely drained pool, at the same time grows massive as an image in the story and leaves one with a coat feeling very funny indeed. Funny peculiar, not ha-ha, that is.

"Cervine" is a glittering performance.

(*The cast of characters*: Dan is the husband, Laurie his (relatively) new wife. Joshua is Laurie's son from a previous marriage and is visiting for the holidays. As the excerpt opens, Joshua has just returned from the mall, where he has sneaked an unauthorized haircut, to a household of rising tensions.)

Not quite human-looking, is what Dan thinks.

Joshua is wearing an athletic top like an undershirt, but banana yellow and deeply scooped at the neck and under the arms. Where his skin shows, it isn't much more than a beige film over his bones. He's standing at the kitchen door, not quite leaning against the wall behind him, although his upper body slants back as though he's been arrested in the act of entering the room. Neon-green Spandex bicycle shorts girdle his body from waist to knees. Dan winces at the flatness of the crotch, looks down at the unlaced high-top sneakers, as incongruously huge as the paws of a puppy of mixed pedigree.

"What's upset your mother," he starts, trying to formulate a line of logic, some way to suggest that Laurie might have a point about Joshua looking weird, and then he realizes that Joshua's clothes are not the issue. Laurie must have picked them out, possibly after she made Joshua try them on. Dan tries to take in the hair without actually staring; it's a modified brushcut, with a short pigtail on one side at the back, a tuft rising over the forehead. The rest of his scalp is bushy as a hamster. Two snips with a scissors would bring everything into line. But, Dan thinks, why bother? If Joshua is going to dress like an android, there's no point in looking like a person from the neck up.

Joshua is looking at something slightly above and beyond Dan's right shoulder, through the aluminum screen door, into the yard. He's probably embarrassed, having a stranger witness his being an object of maternal disapproval. He might even be thinking of Dan as another *guy*, and be suffering some reduction in status. It's an oddly endearing thought, flattering, and Dan claps his palms together as though something has been settled, to indicate he's not going to finish whatever speech he'd started.

In front of him, Joshua snaps his arms up, like he's reaching for a long pass, or shielding his eyes from bright headlights on a dark road. His skin loses its colour, fading from beige to pale grey to white. The tips of his ears turn pink, then red. He makes a noise in his throat, a noise that sounds like *moof, moof.*

He's having a *heart* attack? Dan thinks, his own heart suspending itself between beats. Sweet Christ, a *stroke*?

There's an odd rustling all of a sudden, an artificial sound, as though someone in special effects were crunching potato chips against a microphone to suggest the crackling of a forest fire. The sound seems to be coming from all four corners of the room. Nausea rises in Dan's throat. He is scared in a way he's never been frightened of anything in his life. There's nothing in his senses but fear. A low, low note, operatic in its physicality, thrubs through the air, through Dan's head, entering each ear and being cancelled out in the middle of his brain. From temple to temple, he's an empty space; the eye of a hurricane, a gaping fissure in the earth's crust. Whatever is dangerous is external. With no room for thought, purely by instinct, he steps back, one hand swinging wildly behind him for the crash bar on the screen door. At the moment he feels it give, he reaches out and pulls Joshua towards him and rolls the two of them out into the pale yellow evening. A second later—less than a second—he shouts "Out! *Laurie*, get out of the *house!*"

Joshua twists away from Dan and yells, "Mom!" He's short of breath—Dan may have been squeezing him in his arms—but he recovers a nearly normal tone to say, "Don't yank me *around*," and he smacks the back of his hand against Dan's upper arm before taking the five or six steps to the edge of the deck. Again, he yells, "Mom!"

"Sweet—" Dan's urgency evaporates the moment he hears Joshua's voice. It's quiet again. There wasn't an earthquake (he realizes that had been his concern). The house will not fall in on itself. Laurie is safe. Where he was fearful, now he feels glassy and hollow, fragile still. He's confused. "What was that all about?"

"I tried to tell you." Joshua calls out another impatient, "Mom!" He turns and points at the pool. "It's a moose."

Mossy antlers large as whale bones; dark brown fur, seemingly acres of it, short as a cow's; a great dewlap under its neck like a woolly mailpouch. Dan can't take it all in. The animal dominates the pool the way a car takes up most of the space in a garage. The moose's hind hooves are flat on the bottom of the deep end. Through the water, rippling with shallow crests and troughs, the globes of the knee-joints seem to shrink and swell. Its shorter forelegs are braced on the slope of the pool. In the huge head with its fleshy overlip, white-less eyes the size of grapefruit look comparatively tiny and stupidly expressionless.

Mark Anthony Jarman
Short Story Collections: *Dancing Nightly in the Tavern* (1984), *New Orleans is Sinking* (1998), *19 Knives* (2000), *My White Planet* (2008), and *Knife Party at the Hotel Europa* (2015).
Novels: *Salvage King Ya!* (1997).
Non-Fiction: *Ireland's Eye: Travels* (2002).
Poetry Collections: *Killing the Swan* (1986).

Mark Anthony Jarman published *Dancing Nightly in the Tavern* in 1984. Thirty-four years ago, now. He published it at a time when such short story writers as W.P. Kinsella and W.D. Valgardson were much in vogue. It is not surprising, then, that not much attention was paid. Jarman wasn't particularly interested in nationalism or regionalism or racial minorities. It would be rather difficult to extract from his stories any moral certainties or comforts. He was not interested in what nationalist political claptrap habitually describes as "telling our own stories."

Jarman's not your man for pablum.

His characters want something but don't know what.

Ray hasn't eaten, has a vision of himself being rolled somewhere, caught with others in the Depression, a post office mural, a Hopper painting, in the U.S.A. Think positively, Ray counsels himself. As what we came for eludes us, so we will replace it. At the food bank there is cheese. Hot coffee and three-bean salad in those cheery church basements ...

This is not the fucking Depression, I will not line up for their handouts, gnaw the bureaucrats' cheddar. There is a bone stuck in my throat. I want, I don't know, something.

Right from the start, Jarman went for the jugular of language. A contemporaneous review of *Dancing Nightly* suggested that he might have been influenced by Jack Kerouac, but this observation is more true of the characters' wallowing in alcohol and drugs than it is of stylistic influence. Kerouac's a rather flabby writer; Jarman is madly fierce. He reminds me less of Kerouac than of the Cormac McCarthy of *Blood Meridian*.

His landscapes are mythic landscapes of the mind, a mind drunk or drugged with hopelessness. His cities are visions of violence and madness and remind me of Nathanael West's *Day of the Locust*. His prose is not the delicate register of sociological markers or the accumulation of realist detail for its own sake. His is a prose of apocalyptic incantation.

Here in "Cowboys Inc." are Jankovitch and Ironchild on the road.

... swinging hard across the blue plains and raggedy-ass cottonwood, the endless flight through pale aspens and truckstop botulism, K-mart snakeskin cowboy boots, cheating songs, box elders. This is just after the grain elevator blew over to Missouri: burnt for days and they couldn't get at the bodies. In the blind pigs and roadhouses lizards cringe under the crashing rain of Wurlitzers and chicken bones.

That is the Jarman voice.

For which we should give thanks.

And while Mark Jarman was blowing and honking and screaming these fervent solos, academe ignored him and placidly munched on Marion Engel.

Some reviewers have described Jarman's characters as "blue-collar," but the colour of their collar is wildly beside the point. Jarman's men and women live outside society, on the edge of imminent horror. Most, as in "Men Ought Always to Pray and Not to Faint" are dying for the day's first fix or drink.

> Outside it hurts to open my eyes. The pink flamingoes still have price tags on them. Heat steams in the road, the moss-backed elms dry, ready to crumble or burst into flame. I am running with sweat and toxins.
>
> My father moved to the north side to labour in the huge diesel shop, trains humping all night inside the grass berms, flowering my childhood dreams, metal, swearing and coupling. I am parched. My mouth forms phrases. I have the beer.

Not all the stories are equally successful, but Jarman had the talent and the literary wisdom to understand, from the beginnings of his career, that *words* and their deployment were his answer and salvation. He had the insight and courage to sacrifice grammar and punctuation and tradition to grab immediacy.

Douglas Glover offers a fascinating tribute in his essay "How to Read a Mark Jarman Story," published in his collection, *The Attack of the Copula Spiders*.

Mark Anthony Jarman's career unfolded—exploded—into *New Orleans Is Sinking*, *19 Knives*, and *Knife Party at the Hotel Europa*. *Dancing Nightly in the Tavern* is a glittering book, the first expression of a literary samurai.

Susan Kerslake

Short Story Collections: *The Book of Fears* (1984) and *Blind Date* (1989).
Novels: *Middlewatch* (1976) and *Seasoning Fever* (2002).

Susan Kerslake's stories are unconventional. She dispenses largely with plot and character and centres on a voice and a consciousness that's often in extreme situations. A woman trapped in a car crash slowly regaining consciousness and becoming aware of her injuries.

A woman gripped by fear in a heart specialist's examining room awaiting the results of tests.

> The room is dusty. Peculiarly furnished with a large conference table—probably one left over—a sink, several rolls of cheap paper towels, no holder... There is nothing to read except the plug in the sink: Crane.

The observations of a woman abducted at gunpoint from a shopping mall and taken to a rooming house.

> Sitting at the bottom of the bed, on the heap of sheets and blankets that seemed to be trying to get away, he would hunch forward, restraining his shaking hands under his armpits and peer at her, the curve of her breast through the pale orange gauze of her blouse, the dip between her thighs where the print cotton skirt hung like a hammock. He wasn't interested, just curious; her kids looked at centipedes the same way. Under his breath he would mumble, "I have such difficulty ..."

The thoughts and fears of old Emily in a single room in a slummy neighbourhood.

> Cupping her palm over her mouth and nose, she sniffed the familiar circus of peanut butter, soap, stale cleaning cloths, bleach. Through it all she could identify the unique musk of her old body. Her skin had always been soft and smooth. Now wrinkles slid down in it. Now she could pluck folds and they would peak like beaten egg whites.

The writing is intense, electric, the reader thrown in at the deep end of *medias res*. The writing is usually held in an extremely tight focus. Kerslake's interest is not in resolutions to what she starts but in the movement of minds. The experience of reading her is rather like listening to Pablo Casals playing the Bach suites for unaccompanied cello; the music burrows and winds ever deeper into itself. It is tinged with obsession.

The writing is so unusual that only quotation can suggest its qualities. Here is a series of brief excerpts from "Push-Me Pull-You," about a woman who admits herself to hospital because of unbearable pains in her head. She is given drugs:

> A drug rushes into action; I can feel it taking over, spreading like water over the sand castles of brain.

In a lucid interval:

> The world is small; it has gathered right around me; a little light, warm air, the slight touch of cotton, the scent of ironing and antiseptic, silence.

Attempts between the administering of drugs to get out of bed:

> There is a lady on the other side of the hall. She is holding onto the railing with both hands, humps of fat show through the back of her robe. On the floor is a puddle. She rolls her face from side to side. I never help anyone here. One nurse will coax her on down the hall. An aide will mop the floor and wipe the smear of drool off the wall. I watch from my side of the wall. No one watches me; from time to time I actually believe no one is watching me.

Awake at night:

> Looking in the mirror above the sink, I thought I saw my soul fluttering on the surface of my eye. I was afraid it would escape, and death, a small maggoty thing, would invade the black hole to lick up the shine.
>
> ...
>
> It is dark in the rooms. Light from the nursing station whispers to the walls in the corridor. Sneaking in the rooms, it lights like metallic dream birds on the shiny surfaces of steel and glass. In the bed next to me there is the ghostly shape of a woman. She moans, the sheets are too heavy, too rough for her. I have never

seen her face. I don't know if she even has a face, perhaps there is nothing but the moan; grey pulsing lips as large as her head. They always keep the curtain drawn. For a long time I didn't know if anyone was there. I didn't want to see her—it. There was a smell. Antiseptics could not camouflage the green edges. I imagined her seeping into the sheets, dripping off the rubber mattress cover. In the night I would step on her. She wasn't real. It would take more than shadow and smell. This was some sort of test: reality. Or reality—your reality. Do you think this woman is real? Slippery question. If only my head were clear. Be careful.

The building is breathing through its vents. I get up. The floor is cold. It feels so good ...

Susan Kerslake offers a strange music, original and deeply imagined, one that, once heard, is difficult to forget. It is heartening that *The Book of Fears* went through three printings.

Shaena Lambert

Short Story Collections: *The Falling Woman* (2002) and *Oh, My Darling!* (2013).
Novel: *Radiance* (2007).

Shaena Lambert is, in my view, an extraordinary talent. She has a honed ability to move into stories in a way that seems, superficially, to be comfortably traditional but the deft Who-When-Where stuff is given substance, weight, and surprise by seemingly casual detail which becomes entirely persuasive and rich in significance and by word-choices that pierce. Reading her, I am continually excited by each new subtlety.

The opening of the story "The War Between the Men and the Women" can serve as an illustration of the above in action:

It is 1968 and there is a war between the men and the women. Jane hears it on the radio, where for the first time women's voices read the news; and she sees it at school, where the art teacher, Miss Hannah Shapiro, has started going bra-less, great wandering breasts shifting this way and that under soft denim; and there it is, on the bus: women travelling into Vancouver from the islands displaying gloms of hair under their arms.

At home things are still as a knife blade...

The word "gloms," with this meaning, and as a noun, would seem to be a Lambertian invention from the American slang "to glom" (onto) and is inexplicably and splendidly ugly. The "wandering" breasts under "soft denim" is lightning caricature.

The glory, verbally, of this opening page is the tenseness of the dinner table, the silent slicing of the ham, the tenseness between the father and the mother and daughter caught so brilliantly in the sentence:

"At home things are still as a knife blade."

This is what I think of as writing at high voltage.

Shaena Lambert is also very funny and in this mixture of focused observation, devastating verbal accuracy, and comic spirit reminds me of the work of her friend, Caroline Adderson, in her recent work *Ellen in Pieces*.

She makes her freighted scenes seem effortless. Here from "Oh, My Darling":

> The night before as he lay on the bed, Callum put aside his magazine to tell you he wanted to trace his family roots. You assumed he meant to Sweden or possibly, on his mother's side, to Scotland. You were tidying and turning off lights. When you glanced up, Callum had a blown-back look, as though he had stuck his head from a car window.
>
> "Nessie," he said, I think I have aboriginal blood in me."
>
> Poor Vanessa. You stared at your blue-eyed husband. Even his underwear looked Scandinavian; soft flannel boxers in off-white. You raised an eyebrow, but your heart lurched. There you stood, solid as a tree trunk, with your hennaed hair and puckered arms, and you felt as though the floor had plummeted a dozen

feet, like the deck of a boat. Callum is a partner in a law firm specializing in aboriginal treaty cases. His new articling student, Connie, is Haida, of the Eagle Clan. She looks it too, with her aristocratic nose and black eyebrows, hair falling to a slash at her chin line.

Even the *smells* of her writing astound:

A young man with dreadlocked hair danced toward her ...Up close the man smelled of the brine in feta cheese ...

(From "Crow Ride")

She cuddled against him, then they both flipped, and he snuggled against her back, cupping her breast. His underarms smelled, not unpleasantly, of baked beans. Slowly, as though working a complex and ancient fountain, he began to press her breast. He squeezed, pressed and then improvised with a light jiggle. Anna felt a flicker of irritation.

"Don't." She lifted his hand away.

Shaena sent me the following notes on her short-story writing beginnings and present practice; much food for thought here *and definitely not baked beans.*

Grit, Scrapbooks, Jelly Jars—A few Thoughts on Writing Stories
1. Grit and motion.

My stories usually begin with a thought or an idea that has grit to it. It sticks in my mind. I write it down in my notebook. Often the grit has to do with seeing a situation from two or more angles. There's some irony at the centre. But more often the story starts to grow from an image or an image cluster.

In my story "Crow Ride," for instance, I had two initial ideas. The first was a fact: all the crows in Vancouver head east at sunset to roost in an abandoned building in Burnaby. The second was my ongoing fears and worries about teenage drug use—Ecstasy, Ketamine, Crystal Meth. These two things sat side by side in my mind and in my notebook, but I couldn't figure out a story. Then one day, my 24-year old son mentioned a mass bike expedition—a crow ride!—where dozens of young people follow the crows to where they roost. With the idea of *movement* I had my title, and was suddenly excited to enter the story, though I still had only two disparate pieces of grit to go on. Still, I'd found a spring out of which the action could flow. Not too long before I had read Eudora Welty's brilliant story, "No Place for You, My Love," where two lovers take a trip from New Orleans down into the steamy gulf coast. I had also read that Welty was stymied by how to write her story until she hit on the idea of putting her characters "on the road." I decided in a flash that my main characters would take a trip too—from that "safe" west side of Vancouver, through the downtown eastside, to the place where the crows roost. From that day to night. I didn't realize, as I sat down to write the first draft, that this would be a trip to the underworld, a chase, in a sense, after a dead child. That came later.

2. Capturing energy

Years ago, I took a writing workshop with Margaret Atwood. I was fairly new to writing stories and over the moon to have been selected for her class. On about day three, I put up my hand and said, sheepishly but rather proudly too, that I sometimes didn't want to get my fingers in and change what I'd written in a first draft, because it seemed to have come with a particular kind of force, in a particular set of words. Those words had energy, I said, and subsequent rewrites wrecked that force. "Any advice?" She looked at me for a long time, coolly, and then she said, "*That* is an idea you should get rid of."

It was, she said, an essentially Romantic (capital R) idea, one that pictured creativity as a single, great spasm. "In general," she finished by saying: "an idea should become more interesting—not less interesting—the more you work on it."

This stuck with me. The appraising look. The good but somewhat scathing advice. And of course I do agree; a story needs to "thicken," to develop layers, to pose new mysteries as you go deeper. It needs to morph and shake off skins. Still: I stubbornly continue to believe that early drafts, if they are good, can have an energetic force to them—a force that can be caught, and then passed from draft to draft, becoming, no matter how the words change, an energy container for the piece. Every word may change, but the aliveness at the story's core will stay.

Nevertheless, most of what's been written in a first draft— *the actual words*—may need to be chucked.

3. The scrapbook technique

After I have a draft I leave it for weeks or even months in order to "let it dry," as one would with watercolours. You can't work when they're wet. Then, when I'm ready to go to work, I print out the pages and lay them in a large scrapbook, single-sided, leaving room to write in longhand all around the piece. By having the original in front of me, tactile and available, I never have to fear "losing it," or "wrecking it" —emotions that can make me stall out. At the same time I can drift, consider, and work around the edges, asking myself questions, making no distinction between writing the piece and writing about the piece. This allows me to explore every aspect of it, without trying to "sound good," which can be the death of stories. Interestingly, by freeing myself from "sounding good," I often find that what I've jotted in the margin, a note to myself, is exactly the wording I want.

4. An occasional chrysalis

There is another thing that sometimes happens; I discover that this elaborately built story draft had actually been a chrysalis. It surrounds a small, live thing, which is the only *really interesting thing* to pursue. This means throwing everything else away and going after this bit of life at the centre. When this used to happen to me, I would groan and moan and thrash around, not believing it, wasting weeks in disbelief. Now I try to move faster.

5. Doors and windows

Years ago, when I hadn't yet written a full, satisfying story and was struggling and confused, I read Flannery O'Connor's famous essay on symbols and surface, in her book *Mystery and Manners*. This essay had a huge impact on me. Her theory that symbols (and I think we could add in theme here as well) can only be created when the writer pays close attention to the surface details of life; how things smell, taste, look, feel. This is fascinating and true. If you want to talk about death, life, youth, eternity, redemption, you can only do it through dirty socks, rancid butter, mustard stains, a flock of geese. But if you find the right images, and poke at them, and play with them, they can become doors and windows, revealing hidden layers. To me these doors and windows are like "the gate cards" in Tarot— seemingly minor cards, usually in the practical pentacles suit, which, because of their very earthliness, their mundanity, magically reveal deeper meanings with close study.

To render the physical world in such a way that it gives off meaning—a kind of world under the world of the story—is close, I think, to what E.M. Forster talks about when he mentions "prophesy" as one aspect of fiction. Some work has it, and some doesn't. Some writers always remain secular. They don't cross over. But others do.

My favourite story writers are able to do this. With Henry James, for instance, you can feel the huge weight of a secondary meaning beneath the surface of his stories. And the Aliveness! Talk about closure. In his brilliant story, "The Beast in the Jungle," you can actually feel the jaws (of the story and of the beast) snapping shut at the end, like fate. William Trevor, Lorrie Moore, Alice Munro (think of what she does with faces!), John Cheever, Barry Lopez, Kafka, Flannery O'Connor—they all have this quality. As for Nabokov, he actually makes this idea—the remarkable way that

everyday objects are freighted with an inner (and sometimes terrifying) symbolism—the subject of his brilliant story, "Signs and
Symbols," about a boy who is incurably mentally ill and his struggling Russian immigrant parents. The boy's illness is, in essence,
that he attributes wild spirit and meaning, voice and personality
to the inanimate world. Nabokov shows how the story's opening
image, "a basket of fruit jellies in ten little jars," which the parents
choose to take to their son in the institution, can be a symbol of
paralyzing futility, of a cruel and wasteful universe. Yet these jars,
"yellow, green, red," while continuing to hold waste and suffering
(and many other things), manage to morph luminously by story's
end to hold, as well, the parent's unstoppable love.

Margaret Laurence
Short Story Collections: *The Tomorrow-Tamer* (1963) and *A Bird in the
House* (1970).

Novels: *This Side Jordan* (1960), *The Stone Angel* (1964), *A Jest of
God* (1966), *The Fire-Dwellers* (1969), and *The Diviners* (1974).

Non-Fiction: *A Tree for Poverty* (1954), *The Prophet's Camel Bell*
(1963), and *Long Drums and Cannons: Nigerian Dramatists and Novelists
1952-1966* (1968).

Memoirs: *Heart of a Stranger* (1976) and *Dance on the Earth: A
Memoir* (1989).

The stories collected in *The Tomorrow-Tamer* were published, largely in
Canadian literary magazines, between 1956 and 1963. *The Tomorrow-
Tamer* is better written than *A Bird in the House*, the language a touch
brighter, the stories, though with an ideological edge, slightly less
sentimental. I find in general that Margaret Laurence's early work is
better than her later efforts; I can reread *A Jest of God* but cannot again
plough through *The Stone Angel* or, *much* worse, *The Diviners*.

The Writers' Trust of Canada invited me to deliver the 2017 Margaret
Laurence Lecture and what follows is a part of what I had to say.

After living in England for a decade Margaret Laurence returned
to Canada in 1970 as the author of *The Tomorrow-Tamer*, and

other titles about Africa, and *The Stone Angel*, *A Jest of God*, *The Fire-Dwellers*, and *A Bird in the House*, books set in Canada. Her presence and her work created wild enthusiasm and she became almost instantaneously the poster-woman of CanLit. Compared with what preceded her in Canada and with what was contemporary with her in Canada, her writing was undeniably important. Her books struck readers as vibrantly new and as at the leading edge of Canadian writing. She died in 1987.

Time's Kaleidoscope has tapped her work into a different shape. My old friend, the Vancouver antiquarian book dealer, William Hoffer, also dealt in painful truths and was given to quoting among other brilliances and scurrilities the following thought:

With the passing of time we stand the more clearly revealed.

Listen to these sentences from the story "The Drummer of All the World," published in 1956, wherein Mathew, the son of a missionary, is returning to Ghana on the eve of its independence from England. The red umbrella this extract mentions was part of the paraphernalia of Ashanti tribal rank and nobility. Mathew concludes:

We were conquerors in Africa, we Europeans. Some despised her, that bedraggled queen we had unthroned, and some loved her for her still-raging magnificence, her old wisdom. But all of us sought to force our will upon her.

My father thought he was bringing Salvation to Africa. I do not any longer know what salvation is. I only know that one man cannot find it for another man, and one land cannot bring it to another.

Africa, old withered bones, mouldy splendour under a red umbrella, you will dance again, this time to a new song.

Setting aside the question of whether these explanatory sentences of summation ought to be in the story at all, the essential point to be made is that the writing is recognizable now as *historical* writing. It recognizably belongs to a particular period and its literary traditions, traditions which ran counter to the traditions of modernism which informed the most powerful work of the twentieth century. The passage's self-conscious rhetoric and studied cadences will find a place in a literary museum rather than being read with a flashlight under the blankets.

I will not raise the question of whether or not bones can wither.

(As to the "ideological edge," a socialist rosiness of vision was almost a given in the early sixties and after the translation into English of Frantz Fanon's *The Wretched of the Earth* in 1963 became *de rigueur*. That "Africa… you will dance to a new song" in the passage from "The Drummer of All the World," quoted above, resulted not in The New Jerusalem but in Idi Amin and a slew of other such rotting monsters.

I was reminded of that naiveté when recently I tried to reread a John Steinbeck title to see how it made me feel; I was embarrassed.)

It has become very much clearer in the 30 years since her death that Margaret Laurence's writing was less the beginning or expression of something new and much more the culmination and probably best expression of a tradition of writing that was poised to disappear. Her work makes certain advances on the work of such writers as Morley Callaghan, Sinclair Ross, Ernest Buckler, W.O. Mitchell, and Hugh MacLennan. But she never fully embraced modernism; she teetered on the brink of doing so, most notably in *A Jest of God*, but nearly always fell back into the tradition from which she emerged. Consider another passage from "The Drummer of All the World." Mathew bumps into his boyhood best friend, Kwabena:

"Oh, I am a medical orderly." His voice was bitter. "An elevated post."

"Surely you could do better than that?"

"I have not your opportunities. It is the closest I can get now to real medical work. I'm trying to get a scholarship to England. We will see."

"You want to be a doctor?"

"yes"—He laughed in an oddly self-conscious way. "Not a ju-ju man, you understand."

Suddenly I thought I did understand. With me, he could never outgrow his past, the time when he had wanted to be another kind of doctor—a doctor who dealt in charms and amulets, in dried roots and yellow bones and bits of python skin. He knew I would remember. How he must have regretted betraying himself to me when we were both young.

I wanted to tell him that I knew how far he had travelled from the palm hut. But I did not dare. He would have thought it condescension.

The construction of this passage—dialogue or picture followed by commentary and summation—is entirely typical of Laurence's work. It accounts for her great popularity at the time she was writing. She did the work for the reader; she showed a little and explained a lot. She was spoon-feeding the reader. She was, in a word, easy. And it is that loose easiness that will explain why in the future her reputation will decline.

The seed of self-destruction is sowed even in the first line of the quoted passage.

"Oh, I am a medical orderly." His voice was bitter. "An elevated post."

The spoken words "An elevated post" are, in context, obviously bitter. We do not need a PhD to understand that, do we? We are bright enough to know that an orderly is not "elevated." But Margaret Laurence added in the explanatory spoon-feeding sentence, "His voice was bitter." This merely clogs up the works. It also reveals a very un-modernist mistrust of the readers' ability to read. Good readers will drift away from such repetitive irritation, seeking work that will involve them more by letting them work, by letting them become participants in the creation of the work.

When I wrote that "the seeds of self-destruction" lay in that sentence, what I actually had in mind was not seeds but rebars—the reinforcing rods in concrete.

Some years ago Myrna and I were on an archeological tour of bronze age sites in Greece. I was chatting with one of the venerable accompanying Oxford archeologists as we drove from Piraeus into Athens. Ghastly expanses of raw concrete lined the highway, most of them fresh-poured to house visitors to that year's Olympic games. He was explaining to me that ancient stone buildings survived because of the antique methods of construction.

"Compressive stresses," he said, forcing his palms together, "strategic tying with strips of lead."

Rebars, he said, are destroying modern buildings from inside because damp penetrates to the rebars and they begin to rust spreading corrosion out into the concrete.

Dismissing the relentless concrete ugliness around us with a cheery wave, he said, "No point in bemoaning. Take the long view. Always take the *long* view. In a hundred years they'll all have fallen down. Though knowing Greece, possibly considerably sooner."

Am I proposing, then, seriously proposing, that a short story, or even a novel, can be criticized for, even invalidated by, a few less-than-perfect sentences? Is a single sentence important? Isn't the point to get one's point across? Isn't a sentence a pretty simple thing?

How to answer... You see, getting one's point across isn't the point. The point isn't the point. And yes, the single sentence, in a sense, does, carry the weight of the entire structure. And no, a sentence isn't a simple thing. Oh, dear! I can see I'll have to get at this, if I can, in a roundaboutish way.

A few years ago, I was walking across the park in Russell Square near the British Museum. Myrna and I were staying at the Russell Hotel, a rather Gormenghast-ish edifice that boasts a room called The Virginia Woolf Bar and Grill. It was, to my sorrow, closed for refurbishment. I would definitely have had a

Virginia Club or a Woolf Burger. Just imagine, ghastly snob that she was, how appalled she would have been!

Coming towards me on the path were two men deep in conversation. I was talking to Myrna and paid no attention to them other than to register that one was tall and the other of average height. As they passed us, the smaller man was saying earnestly: "I do like something of a creamy consistency on my porridge."

I know these were his exact words as I had stopped in my tracks and written them in my notebook knowing them to be beyond price.

Later, I started playing with this unconsciously comic utterance and soon arrived at a different arrangement.

What I wrote was this:

"Not necessarily milk or cream," he said, "but I do like something of a creamy consistency on my porridge."

So I invented "Not necessarily milk or cream" and I inserted a "he said"; I'd felt the sentence needed a build-up towards "porridge." The slightly odd placement of "Not necessarily milk or cream" suggests the speaker is finicky. The "he said" acts largely as punctuation of delay, and delay in reaching "porridge" makes arrival funnier.

Later still, I played with a second version. What would happen if I moved "porridge" from its end position to an earlier position in the sentence, giving the *weight* of the sentence to "something of a creamy consistency"?

Like this:

"Not necessarily milk or cream," he said, "but I do like on my porridge something of a creamy consistency."

Finally, I arrived at what I thought was the funniest version of all, a sentence exquisitely performed:

"Not necessarily milk or cream," he said, "but I do like on my porridge

and here the words go into italic
something of a creamy consistency."

The average reader would probably say that all the versions say the same thing, the only element of invention being the words "Not necessarily milk or cream." But the average reader would be wildly wrong. The three versions that follow the first verbatim recording of the sentence are moving words into different positions for a rhetorical purpose. The three versions are moving step by step towards the suggestion of character. Through a single line of speech, if played with carefully enough, a character begins to emerge; if I listened to more of him I'd soon see what he *looked* like; a story might emerge.

Moving "porridge" to an earlier position in the sentence begins the creation. The speaker emerges more vividly as old-fashioned, precise, pedantic, an old fusspot.

When I make the next change by italicizing (i.e. giving weight in delivery) to "something of a creamy consistency," there seems to be floating in the words a hint perhaps that the speaker is gay.

I'd thought I was finished with it but then a fourth version, a tweak, suggested itself. In this final version, I chose not to include in the italicized words the word "something" because in this particular sentence "something" is what I think of as a "weakener"; it muffles the sentence. By not italicizing it, a space in the speaking of the sentence is created; the reader is forced to pause for a beat before pronouncing the forceful "of a creamy consistency" and that pause makes the italicized words even more portentous.

Imagine yourself on a stage.

Here's what it sounds like:

"Not necessarily milk or cream," he said, "but I do like on my porridge something (PAUSE—then intensely) of a creamy consistency." By the time I'd finished messing about, the speaker struck me as a possible refugee from a Harold Pinter play.

We have come a long way from Margaret Laurence's sentence, "His voice was bitter," and I apologize for all that round-the-mulberry-bush, but no, a sentence isn't a simple thing. Each sentence is a brick in the construction of a house.

Each sentence exerts compressive stress.

All of the foregoing "porridge" is an illustration of what I have been trying to nudge readers towards for years: that *how* something is written is *what* is being written.

I'm much in agreement with Nick Mount's comments on Margaret Laurence's work in his recent history *Arrival: The Story of CanLit*. Of *A Bird in the House*, he writes:

> The stories are a step up from magazine melodrama, popular fiction lit up by a dose of symbolism and reflection on serious subjects. As Honor Tracy said in her review for the *New York Times*, "Were this collection to be judged by women's magazine standards, she would doubtless receive an A-plus." Like most of Laurence's fiction, it strikes me as an enjoyable and even important read in its day, but not good enough to survive its time. The respect other Canadian writers had for her has kept too much of Laurence's work around past its best-before date.

Elise Levine
Short Story Collections: *Driving Men Mad* (1995).
 Novels: *Requests and Dedications* (2003) and *Blue Field* (2017).

You can take a paragraph almost at random from any of the stories in *Driving Men Mad* and you will realize immediately that Elise Levine plays her prose as a musical instrument. In this she shares interests with Mark Jarman, Norman Levine, Terry Griggs, and Michael Winter. She cuts and compresses, stretches, squeezes to produce writing that ranges from aria to incantation.

Here's a paragraph from "Boy":

> In Perry I play burnball every day after supper, making do with Mike Hires, a retard from Special Ed. class. Slap-slap down the road, smoking ball against glove faster-fast through the long twilight, everything flattened to two boys one creature purely boy, and a sound like spitting.
>
> There are days and days of this.

The paragraph immediately raises questions of grammar and meaning and we have to accept two narrating voices. But the difficulties are easy to overcome; they tend to melt away if you read the passage aloud and surrender to the sounds of incantation.

Levine is something of a magician; she makes language perform. Silk scarves appear, doves flutter, the Ace of Spades rises through the deck at her command. Here from the story "Angel" is the voice in monologue of the young lesbian abandoned by Angel; she is rehearsing the history of their love. The wild cityscapes of the story are not backdrops but rather embodiments of the narrator's passion; they fulfill the same function as the cityscapes in the short stories of Mark Jarman.

> It was midnight, Angel, and I'll never forget. We did it in doorways up and down Church Street, my back against rotting wood or my hamstrings hurting, crouched down on grey concrete, the club where I'd cruised you receding as we twisted down alleyways and across half-empty parking lots. You wooed me that night and I could hear my breath whistling in and out of me and when you pulled my shirt up and over my head and tossed it—just like that, in the middle of the street—it was like a ghost floated up inside me and fluttered out of my mouth, my white shirt sailing up over Parliament Street, and the next morning I saw it lying on the streetcar tracks at Queen and Sherbourne.

Or this, rather astonishing, recreation of desire rising:

> You racked up those balls like a pro and beat those old dykes in their black leather vests who lovingly took their hand-crafted, mother-of-pearl-inlaid cues from monogrammed cases and everyone stood around, and I counted each sudden click as you knocked the balls down, always where you said you wanted them and it was like each click that night brought me closer to something, each click a notch cut closer through the tension thick as the blue smoky bar or the heavenly sweet smell of amyl in the bathroom, and looking up I could see the smooth moves shaking it out there on the dance floor but all I could hear was you, calling, Six ball in the corner pocket, and click, Nine ball

in the side pocket, and all night long I felt I was moving, Angel, really moving.

Incantation again, the play of alliteration.

In the interview in *Writers Talking*, Elise Levine says of the way she works:

> ... writing is a process of excavating what is embedded, an extended drive to fill in the centres of the truth of a character. I think of a mouth spotlit, opening and closing in a blacked-out theatre. I flirt with notions of some strange, operatic experience, part Monteverdi, Messiaen, Ligeti, PJ Harvey—equal parts aria and recitative, with performers well-versed in the uses of extended techniques. Ahistorical, forever playing away on a lost stage, in a pocket out of time. My job is to press my forehead against the stage door and peek through a peephole, and try to describe, as faithfully as I can, what I see and hear.

What is particularly interesting about this is that the peephole view doesn't even let her see *all* of the stage; she is looking at a scene with everything inessential and surrounding cut off from view. Because of the peephole she is looking at the distillation of a distillation. She is looking at something viewed in a way which makes the scene or action seem strange. Things are presented to us in such a light or with such a magnification or in bewildering close-up that the everyday becomes exotic. When I read Elise's account, I thought of Shklovsky's *ostranenie*—"making strange." (Shklovsky, Viktor Borisovich. Russian Formalist. *The Technique of the Writer's Craft*, 1928.)

In the same interview, she wrote:

> As the piece begins to emerge as a whole, I try to shape (the material feels plastic, three-dimensional). I try to listen as hard as I can for the way the piece should sound (the material is musical, involving timbre and pitch, pulse and rhythm and hypermetre, it unfolds over time, is, like music, abstract). I try to look as hard as I can (fast flat lines or textured and painterly), to imagine.

Content dictates form, form equals content: I keep going, and if I'm lucky, I at times find myself awed in the presence of this beautiful, mysterious tautology.

And for a digestif—emotionscape again—here is the night security guard at the Boulevard Club in "Testing, Testing":

> Once on a moonless night when I'd been up two days straight, maybe more, my scalp tingly and tart with Black Beauties, I took the dog outside the club to do her business. As I waited for her to finish, I could dimly make out the marina sailboats rocking, the trees in the nearby park swaying. I could hear the occasional baying of what seemed to be every solitudinous beast of night, from the lost cygnet I saw jerking disconsolately into and out of the water to the stray Canada goose bruising the night sky over Lakeshore Drive. The lights of the city shone to the north, blurring with those from passing cars. Everything, in every place I looked, was speeding ahead, so fast I could barely catch the drift.

Such originality has cost Elise Levine dearly. Again in the *Writers Talking* interview:

This "finding an expressive language" means, she says, "risking being labelled 'unconventional,' 'poetic,' 'experimental'—these underhandedly pejorative terms that smack of a conservative, underimagining, reactive view of literary fiction very much in contrast to commonly held views of other contemporary arts."

Keath Fraser has written on the stories of Elise Levine, "How As Writers Do We End?," in *The New Quarterly volume xxi. Nos. 2 and 3*.

Norman Levine

Short Story Collections: *One Way Ticket* (1961), *I Don't Want to Know Anyone Too Well* (1971), *Thin Ice* (1979), *Why Do You Live So Far Away* (1984), *Champagne Barn* (1984), *Something Happened Here* (1991), *The Ability to Forget* (2003), and *I Don't Want to Know Anyone Too Well: Collected Stories* (2017).

Novels: *The Angled Road* (1952) and *From a Seaside Town* (1970).

Poetry Collections: *Myssium* (1948), *The Tight-rope Walker* (1950), and *I Walk by the Harbour* (1976).

Non-Fiction: *Canada Made Me* (1958).

Norman Levine stands at the very centre of achievement in Canadian short-story writing. His masterful stories are already a familiar part of our mental and emotional furniture. Everyone has their own favourites, but I could not imagine Canadian literature without such stories as "By the Richelieu," "A Small Piece of Blue," "We all Begin in a Little Magazine," and "Champagne Barn."

The stories may be familiar—but they are decidedly not comfortable. In them, Levine conveys various forms of displacement, of discontent, of alienation, of loss. Like Alexander Marsden, the roundabout-maker in "A Canadian Upbringing," Levine left Canada "because he [felt] the need to accept a wider view of life." Levine stands aside, observing life's to and fro; he has elected to be a permanent outsider as immigrant, as resident alien, as writer, as Jew.

The Cambridge Guide to Literature in English says of Levine's work: "Written in a tight, economic prose style, his stories evoke places vividly and frequently focus on social outsiders, the problems of the writer's life and his Jewish-Canadian upbringing." *The Oxford Companion to Twentieth-Century Literature in English* says: "Levine's spare, understated prose style is seen at its best in his short stories. Predominantly first-person narratives, they exhibit a keen eye for external details, but their prime concern is with the subjective experience of the outsider."

While Levine's writing always *seems* clear and simple, the stories themselves are far more complicated than the simplicity of language suggests. One might say that his work is as simple or as subtle as the people reading it. The stories usually function as an accretion of images—all of which contribute to the story's emotional current, adding tiny detail to what will be the finished shape. Levine refuses to explain or interpret his scenes for us, requiring us, in a sense, to *compose* the story for ourselves. It is that act of composition that turns these stories into such powerful emotional experiences.

Consider "Champagne Barn," for instance. We are treated to a range of scenes and images: the Senior Citizens' Home where one of the residents, Mr. Tessier, has watched sixty-eight corpses carried out over the years; the mindless chatter of the narrator's mother; a restaurant meal with the narrator's spinster cousin, who is in her forties and still a virgin; a meeting with a childhood friend who has become a butcher; a tour of the decaying neighbourhood of the narrator's childhood. The story ends with the hack, hack, hack of the butchers' choppers in Reinhardt Foods. The last line: "I would carry that sound with me long after I left."

As we will carry this story with us. Levine has created a world in this marvellous story—a world deftly suggested and then nailed with telling detail. He forces us to compose meaning from the seemingly random encounters and events in five days of the narrator's life. Through the vividness of his detail (steely master that he is) he moves us to brood on the narrator's life, a brooding which overflows the story's bounds and compels us to confront our own direction and mortality.

This way of writing is essentially poetic and it is no surprise that Norman Levine's first two books were collections of poetry: *Myssium* (1948) and *The Tight-Rope Walker* (1950).

> The beat and the still
> And the beat, caught, lift,
> Of the rook and the gull
> Over sea, roof, hill
> Disturb this place from sleep.

Of these lines he wrote: "It was the first line—describing the way the bird flew—that made me realize that the leaner the language the more ambiguous it becomes, and the more suggestive... The more you tell—the more you are keeping the reader out from bringing his or her experience in. So if you can reduce a thing to a minimum like 'The beat and the still'—then the reader brings his or her associations to that. So contrary to what people think: the more cryptic you are the more resonance there is." (Metcalf, J., and J.R. Tim Struthers, eds. *How Stories Mean*. Erin: The Porcupine's Quill, 1993.)

Levine's work has resonated with readers in England and Europe for many years. Canada has been slower to respond. *The Times* (UK) said that Norman Levine's work was marked by "timeless elegance." *Encounter* said: "Norman Levine is one of the most outstanding short-story writers working in English today." *Le Monde,* a paper not given to rhapsody, compared him with Chekhov.

★

Levine and I were in fairly close contact. I have long admired the integrity and courage of his artistic life. We both left our countries of origin and I once said to him that I thought he had made the right decision and that I had probably made the wrong one. He replied that we had both made decisions that suited our personalities.

After a brief stint in London, Levine moved to St. Ives—"silence, exile, cunning"—and began forging his style, the main preoccupation of most modernist writers. Levine's mature work is marked by its fragmentation, unorthodox grammar, and denial of cadence. We can imagine the effect upon his youthful work of daily contact with such blossoming abstract painters as Peter Lanyon, Terry Frost, Patrick Heron, Roger Hilton, and Bryan Wynter, all of them preoccupied with their own technical innovations.

Levine wrote: "If it hadn't been for St. Ives, and especially the painters I grew up with, I wouldn't be the writer I am."

> Another thing I got from the painters was the need for immediacy. When they finished a painting they wanted me to see it in their studio. And there it was. At a glance. Through the eyes. Onto the nervous system. I remember thinking: how could I get this immediacy in writing? And I remember Peter Lanyon telling me, in his studio, that all that mattered was the work. "You take something from life. Make something from it. Then you give it back to life."

In an interview with Cary Fagan in *Descant 40* (Spring 1983), Levine said:

> ... the visual is very strong for me. I believe a writer, or anyone, should have a good pair of eyes. If I can see something and describe it in very plain language that's about as much as

anybody can do. The straitjacket of language deadens any kind of emotion, any kind of excitement. You're always working within a deadening effect which language has on the feelings which you've experienced through your eyes. So you've got to somehow get this excitement from the feeling that helps you select the kind of words in the order that will give you some of that excitement when you read them. That sounds complicated but it isn't. It's very simple.

In a special Levine issue of *Canadian Notes and Queries*, Cynthia Flood wrote brilliantly on the evolution of Levine's style.

Like a painter himself, Levine lays down colour, line, mass, dimension, angle.

All vegetation was killed by the sulphur that the wind carried from the Sinter Plant. You could see the direction of the wind. It was like a scar in the landscape. In the distance, on either side, I could see more hills with the blue-black outline of growing trees on them. But here everything was dead. The rocks the colour of ashes and the burned-out remnants of trees sticking up like a field of gibbets.

That was 1958. An older Levine would peel out "You could see, It was like, I could see, on them" and "sticking up like a field of gibbets" (he is not a simile fan), but the simple diction and spatial clarity continue.

She had kept everything neat and clean. Now a thin layer of dust was on the furniture and on the wooden floor. and on the leaves of the plants in the front room. The earth was dry. I watered the plants. Looked in the fridge. A few potatoes were sprouting. The pears were bruised...

That's 1991...
We must see the images singly, if we're to read Levine.

Past Bytown Museum that always seemed shut. Past the jail with its high, small greystone walls. Up Laurier Bridge. The horse straining.

So precise. To reach this plainness, Levine abandons plain sentences.

The glare from the snow. Washing hanging out. The long winter underwear. Then by an open crossing with the red arm flashing in and out like a heartbeat, the cars waiting on either side. Why can't I settle for this?

To strip out all that plugs up prose: that is Levine's aim. Articles, linking verbs, clause-breeding relative pronouns, wordy modifiers—dangerous. They draw attention to themselves. Worse, they smother energy. Readers, rolling along the shiny habitual rails of subject and predicate, enter the familiar sentence-tunnel knowing when the verb will arrive and the terminal light appear. We read to reach an expected end. That habit Levine wants to break. We are to *look*. Outside the train.

The following passage, from the late story "Soap Opera," describes the narrator's mother's apartment. The narrator is staying in the apartment while visiting his mother, who is in hospital and thought to be nearing her end.

I opened the door of her apartment. In the half-light I could see the three small rooms. Brought the suitcase in, quickly drew the curtains, and opened the windows. All the clocks had stopped.

The place looked as if it had been left in a hurry. In the kitchen, dishes on the draining-board were upside down. In the bedroom the large bed was not made. A dress was on the back of the rocking-chair. Two-tone, beige and brown shoes were under the bed. The calendar had not been changed in two months.

She had kept everything neat and clean. Now a thin layer of dust was on the furniture and on the wooden floor. And on the leaves of the plants in the front room. The earth was dry. I watered the plants. Looked in the fridge. A few potatoes were sprouting. The pears were bruised and had started to go rotten. I couldn't understand why Sarah hadn't tidied up. There was some half-used cottage cheese, a bottle of apple juice, a tin of *Ensure*. The cupboard, by the sink, was packed with tins as if for a siege. I made a cup of coffee, brought it into the front room, sat by the table and started to relax.

I had not been here on my own before. How small and still. And full of light. The chesterfield set, from the house, was too large. She brightened the settee with crocheted covers—banks of red, yellow, green—that kept slipping down. And cushions with embroidered leaves of all kinds. The same was on the chair, by the side of the window, overlooking the street and the small park. (The Lombardy poplars are gone. But the gazebo is there. And the kids throwing a ball around.) On the other side of the window, against the wall, a large black and white television was on the floor. No longer working. Its use, to support the plants on its top. Beside it: the glass-enclosed wooden cabinet with her best dishes, best cups, saucers, the Chinese plate that goes back to my childhood, the Bernard Leach mugs and bowl that I brought back on visits from St. Ives. On top of the cabinet a family tree. Small, round, black and white photographs in metal frames hung from metal branches. Father and mother, in the park by the river, some fifty years ago. Sara and I... when we were around ten and eight.. the people we married... our children... with their husbands... their children..."

The first things to remark on about this passage is its simplicity, its fidelity to detail, its seemingly documentary quality. What *he* sees is what *you* get, narrator as camera. But is this, in fact, what Levine is up to? For though I would insist absolutely that each detail is itself absolutely—the stopped clocks are stopped clocks, the dust is dust, the bruised pears are bruised pears—the slow (plodding, say the insensitive) accumulation of physical detail, because of the context, (the old woman lying in the hospital, death possibly approaching), the accumulation of physical detail begins to turn into an emotional "atmosphere," each detail, while always itself, becomes something larger than itself. *Not* a symbol, God save us! But a tremor in the near-invisible web Levine is spinning.

Given the context of the possibility of the mother's death, can we persist in reading these paragraphs as flat documentary?

"In the half-light."
"All the clocks had stopped."
"left in a hurry"
"the calendar… had not been changed in two months."
"now a thin layer of dust was on the furniture"
"and on the leaves of the plants."
"The earth was dry."
"The pears were bruised and had started to go rotten."
"packed with tins as if for a siege."
"crocheted covers that kept slipping down."
"with embroidered leaves"
"The Lombardy poplars are gone."
Television 'No longer working."
"On top of the cabinet a family tree. Small, round, black and white photographs in metal frames hung from metal branches. Father and mother, in the park by the river, some fifty years ago. Sara and I… when we were around ten and eight… the people we married… our children… with their husbands… their children…"

Things broken, slipping, abandoned, bruised, stopped…
Flat documentary?
Or something much closer, perhaps, to… poetry?
It is not irrelevant to add that Levine's postgraduate work was on Ezra Pound and so the precepts of Imagism would have been entirely familiar to him.

Some Secondary Material

Norman Levine is at present best represented by *I Don't Want to Know Anyone Too Well: Collected Stories.*

CNQ (Canadian Notes and Queries) No, 60 (2001) was a special issue on Levine's work and contains the brilliant essay by Cynthia Flood from which I have quoted.

CNQ 70 contains Alison Oldham's essay on early Levine, "The Gentleman in the Attic."

Interesting comment by Levine on his own work appears in *Making It New: Contemporary Canadian Stories* (Ed. John Metcalf) Toronto: Methuen, 1982 and in *Canadian Classics* (Ed. John Metcalf and J.R. Struthers) Toronto: McGraw-Hill Ryerson, 1993. See also a truly strange discussion of the story "A Small Piece of Blue," which can be found in *Writers in Aspic* (Ed. John Metcalf) Montreal: Véhicule Press, 1988.

*

Norman Levine died in 2005. I wrote the following obituary for *The Independent* at the request of his daughter, Carrie.

It was written in great sorrow and as an act of homage.

Norman Albert Levine, writer: born Rakow, Poland, 22 October 1923; married 1951 Margaret Payne (died 1978; three daughters), 1983 Anne Sarginson (marriage dissolved); died Darlington, Durham, 14 June 2005.

In the late forties, after having served as a pilot and bomb-aimer with the RCAF, flying Lancasters out of Leeming, North Yorkshire, Norman Levine decided to leave Canada's cultural desert and return to an England he had come to admire. What had attracted him, he wrote was "seeing paintings, hearing concerts, reading new books and *New Writing*. And, especially, seeing how the English lived and behaved in wartime."

In those early days he was introduced in a Thames-side pub to poet George Barker who said to him: "Sorry, chum, nothing personal. But coming from Canada, you haven't got a chance."

Levine, who died at the age of eighty-one on June 14, 2005, spent many years of his life in St. Ives, Cornwall, proving George Barker profoundly wrong. Like all modernists, he spent his life forging and honing a signature style. His was fragmentary and imagistic, prose stripped to the bone, conventional expectations of rhythm denied forcing the reader into a new, intimate, and uneasy relationship with the word on the page. His most important story collections were *Champagne Barn, Something Happened Here, By a Frozen River,* and *The Ability to Forget.*

Canada has never recognized Levine's amazing talent and achievement. Canada's cultural nationalists have never forgiven Levine for his 1958 autobiographical travel book *Canada Made Me.* The book closed with the words, "I wondered why I felt so bitter about Canada. It was foolish to believe that you can take the throw-outs, the rejects, the human kickabouts from Europe and tell them: Here is your second chance. Here you can start a new life. But no one ever mentioned the price you had to pay, and how much of yourself you have to betray."

Written at the beginning of a boosterish period, this rather sour look at Canada's underbelly closed for Levine the possibility of Canadian publication. It was to be seventeen years before another Levine title appeared in Canada.

Levine was always by temperament and choice an outsider. As a Jew, as a resident alien, as an immigrant, he was always on the margins observing with an unsentimental eye. His stories usually have an elegiac quality and typically explore loss, impermanence, and the fragility of human hopes. He wrote in the story "Soap Opera": "... whenever I go to a new place and walk around to get to know it, I inevitably end up in a cemetery."

The son of an impoverished fruit-peddler who plied his trade with a horse and cart, Levine at eighteen volunteered for officer training and was sent on a course to take what he used to call "gentleman lessons." These he duly learned but he belonged to no class or cause. If he believed in anything it might have been Chekhov.

If Levine was ignored in Canada, his reputation in England and Europe was high. The *Times Literary Supplement* described his work as "masterly." *The Times* talked of his "Timeless elegance..." and *Encounter* wrote: "Norman Levine is one of the most outstanding short story writers working in English today."

In Europe his German translator was Nobel laureate Heinrich Böll, and in recent years his work has been translated in Holland, Switzerland, and France.

Younger writers in Canada now are slowly discovering his work and some have been directly influenced by his stylistic experiments. Michael Winter, a young writer directly influenced, said of him: "His style is not one that appeals to a lot of people, but a lot of writers marvel at his talent... His economy of so little saying so much—when you try to write like that, you realize how hard it is to capture things accurately and truthfully with very few words. He was a writer's writer."

Annabel Lyon

Short Story Collections: *Oxygen* (2000) and *The Best Thing for You* (2004).

Novels: *The Golden Mean* (2009) and *The Sweet Girl* (2012).

At the Stratford conference, Diane Schoemperlen illuminated Annabel Lyon's stories by quoting from Raymond Carver's 1981 essay "On Writing."

> I like it when there is some feeling of threat or sense of menace in short stories. I think a little menace is fine to have in a story. For one thing, it's good for the circulation. There has to be tension, a sense that something is imminent, that certain things are in relentless motion, or else, most often, there simply won't be a story. What creates tension in a piece of fiction is partly the way the concrete words are linked together to make up the visible action of the story. But it's also the things that are left out, that are implied, the landscape just under the smooth (but sometimes broken and unsettled) surface of things.

"... the things that are left out... ." Hemingway said almost exactly the same thing. Omission, we might say, is one of the main keys to reading Annabel Lyon. She came early and honestly to the idea. In an interview with me in *Writers Talking* she wrote: "My dad taught me to write when I was small. He had been a journalist and newspaper editor for many years and taught me some particularly ruthless lessons about style that I've had trouble giving up. The main one, which I've accepted as dogma, was to cut out all extraneous words. If you've said something in six words and you can say it in four, you're obliged—by logic, by aesthetics, by Occam's razor, by principles of elegance and an acquired radar for pretentious bullshit—to say it in four."

"… the landscape just under the smooth (but sometimes broken and unsettled) surface of things."

Her story "Tea Drinks" opens with this menacing sentence:

"Finally she takes me aside to tell me you just can't treat people that way. This is in the garage, behind the house. I try to look preoccupied. I finger the blade of my jigsaw, frowning."

The omission in the opening of the story "Black" reels us helplessly in:

> The old woman upstairs is taking a long time to die. Downstairs, Jones is making some phone calls. Jones calls Barry and Edith, and Tom and Anna, and Jack and Ruby and Glen. He calls Larry and Kate and Bridget and Amy. He calls Foster. He calls Susy and Morris.
>
> "God, Jones,' Morris says. "I'm so sorry."
>
> "But will you come?" Jones asks.
>
> Morris pulls on the phone cord, stretching Jones' voice out and letting it seize back to coils, a kid with bubble gum, finger to tongue. "Do you really think," Morris says. "At this point, I mean."
>
> "Yes," Jones says.
>
> "I mean, considering."
>
> "Yes."
>
> "Will Lorelei be there?"
>
> "Lorelei, Lorelei," Jones says. "Are you coming or not?"

And so on.

The rest of Susy's life—in this opening excerpt she is five—is conveyed in a series of brief imagistic takes until she dies at the age of eighty-five.

The story "Things" is reduced to lists:

> In the grocery store I buy tortillas, juice, milk, condoms, soap. I worry the cashier will write to my mother and tell her I buy tortillas, juice, milk, condoms, soap.

In the narrator's building is a tenant called Calla. The story moves forward in stripped, intense image blocks. Omission intensifies the focus.

> Calla has a social worker named Pippa. Pippa has a braid. She gives Calla sample budgets and meal plans, and encourages her to go on outings with the Group.
>
> Calla brings her sample sheets to my door. She says, Macaroni and carrot sticks? Whole-grain banana bread?
>
> Also, Calla dislikes the people of the Group. She says they make too much noise at bus stops.

The effect of omission is to involve us more actively in the story; we have to create it for ourselves, to write it for ourselves using Annabel Lyon's suggestive notation. We might recall Norman Levine's remark "the more cryptic you are the more resonance there is."

At the end of our interview in *Writers Talking* Annabel wrote:

> Amazingly (for a [1] first book of [2] short stories from a [3] small press) it was widely reviewed, and well-reviewed, and the criticisms—lack of structure, brevity, opaque character motivations, cuteness in the prose—were criticisms I had already levelled at myself, and was trying to address in my new stories. So I was happy.

This proclamation of a veering more towards the mainstream is already being fulfilled, though the writing remains what Caroline Adderson describes as "sparky." In Annabel's novella, "Palaces," in *The New Quarterly* No. 102 (Spring 2007)—Bonny, Mary, and Jack in mildly inebriated conversation:

"You guys are always talking about computers," Bonny said. "Computers or motorcycles. Amscray, ackjay. We're having girl talk."

"Speaking of motorcycles," Mary said.

"Yeah, speaking of motorcycles," Jack called from the next room.

"Oh, he's fine," Bonny said. "I was exaggerating before."

Bonny's boyfriend rode a motorcycle. She had shown up an hour earlier saying it was all over.

"He has all these little habits that just get on my nerves," Bonny said. "Food habits, toilet habits, you know what I'm talking about."

The change is clear. The earlier Annabel would not have accommodated us with: "Bonny's boyfriend rode a motorcycle. She had shown up an hour earlier saying it was all over." And although I understand why she made the change, part of me hankers still for the glittering obscurities of such stories as "Stars," "Tea Drinks," and "Awake."

Alistair MacLeod

Short Story Collections: *The Lost Salt Gift of Blood* (1976), *As Birds Spring Forth the Sun and Other Stories* (1986), and *Island: The Collected Stories of Alistair MacLeod* (2001).

Novels: *No Great Mischief* (1999).

I emigrated to Canada in 1962, sailing on the *Carinthia* from Liverpool. Just before this I went on a farewell holiday with two university friends to the Outer Hebrides. We crossed from the Kyle of Localsh to the Isle of Lewis, landing at Stornaway. Fishing boats were coming in, the sea silver and utterly still and in the silver, black rounded shapes like floats or buoys which soon turned out be the heads of harbour seals following the boats. They heaved themselves up the stone steps onto the dock and whuffed and honked for fish. Their breath was memorable.

We were put in the postman's van who took us on his route until he found a cottage willing to accept us. The landscape was harshly beautiful and haunted by a great weight of history. The people we met were friendly but formal. The crofter had a few acres of land, a cow, a fishing boat, and a shed where he wove tweed. He had been a steward on a P. and O. liner and had travelled the world; his three sons all had degrees from Edinburgh University. We went out along the cliffs together and shot rabbits for a stew.

The family invited us to attend a party they were having on Saturday night, friends and neighbours dropping by to record messages in Gaelic and to sing "mouth music" for relatives in Cape Breton, a place, so they said, in Canada. The singing went on all evening, fuelled by liquor that had bypassed officers of Customs and Excise. At minutes to midnight everyone got up to leave. The Sabbath was upon us.

I have visual and emotional memories of Lewis and of the island's way of life, so I can easily empathize with Alistair MacLeod's love of Cape Breton and with the grip it must have had on his heart. But my task is to talk not about love of place and past but about writing. The stories in *Island* are presented chronologically; the first, "The Boat," was published in 1968, the last, "Clearances," in 1999. The first six stories are indeed stories; that is, they have elements of plot, character, and dialogue. The last ten stories are not really stories in any conventional sense at all, and to approach them with conventional expectation is to be disappointed. There is little dialogue and any forward movement tends to get arrested by descriptive detail; scenery is extensively "painted," a way of life is depicted by a cataloguing of *things*. The effect is rather folkloric, rather like looking at a primitive painting.

> The kitchen is small. It has an iron cookstove, a table against one wall and three or four handmade chairs of wood. There is also a wooden rocking-chair covered by a cushion. The rockers are so thin from years of use that it is hard to believe they still function. Close by the table there is a washstand with two pails of water upon it. A washbasin hangs from a driven nail in its side and above it is an old-fashioned mirrored medicine cabinet. There is also a large cupboard, a low-lying couch and a window facing upon the sea. On the walls a barometer hangs as well as two pictures, one of a rather jaunty young couple taken many years ago. It is yellowed

and rather indistinct; the woman in a long dress with her hair done up in ringlets, the man in a serge suit that is slightly too large for him and with a tweed cap pulled rakishly over his right eye. He has an accordion strapped over his shoulders and his hands are fanned out on the buttons and keys. The other picture is of the Christ-child. Beneath it is written "Sweet Heart of Jesus Pray for Us."

The woman at the stove is tall and fine featured. Her grey hair is combed briskly back from her forehead and neatly coiled with a large pin at the base of her neck. Her eyes are as grey as the storm scud of the sea. Her age, like her husband's, is difficult to guess. She wears a blue print dress, a plain blue apron and low-heeled brown shoes. She is turning fish within a frying pan when we enter.

This passage is entirely typical.

MacLeod cut dialogue to a minimum. The stories avoid drama, avoid action. They are static. The foregoing quotation from "The Lost Salt Gift of Blood," where detail smothers, is typical of the later work. A story like "The Road to Rankin's Point" collapses completely under what comes to feel like verbiage.

The sun is rising above the mountains and touching the freshly washed earth. The raindrops glisten and sparkle, and the fog and mists that hang above the dirt roads of high places rise and vanish toward the sky. The bobolinks and red-winged black-birds bounce and sing from the tips of their springing willows. Orange butterflies glide and float on the drafts of air and the chattering squirrels and chipmunks sprint along the fallen logs like busy proprietors doing morning inspection. The earth is alive, refreshed and new.

When MacLeod wants to stress the beauty and virtuous simplicity of Cape Breton and enhance the nobility of his elemental characters, he does so in rather crude contrasts. The son leaving Cape Breton in search of a larger life in the story "The Vastness of the Dark" gets a lift from a travelling salesman from Toronto—a rather obvious representative of the world beyond the Island—whose main expressed interest is in casual sexual intercourse with the small-town women left widowed by mine disasters.

Or this from "The Last Salt Gift of Blood":

> And perhaps now I should go and say, oh son of my *summa cum laude* loins, come away from the lonely gulls and the silver trout and I will take you to the land of the Tastee Freeze where you may sleep till ten of nine. And I will show you the elevator to the apartment on the sixteenth floor and introduce you to the buzzer system and the yards of the wrought-iron fences where the Doberman pinscher runs silently at night.

This is not exactly subtle.

And again, there is the question of sentimentality. I can imagine Alistair countering such a charge by claiming *unabashed* sentimentality.

It may be that the most fruitful way of looking at Alistair MacLeod's work is to think of the stories not as stories in the modernist tradition, but as hybrid mixtures of memoir, folk tale, and sketch. "To Everything There Is a Season" is certainly a memoir, and "The Closing Down of Summer" is much nearer meditation than story. These are pieces of writing that are hymns to the past, celebrations, meditations. As one of the stories puts it, "songs of loss." We should listen for the skirl of lament. We should, perhaps, read these pieces with the ballads in mind, such ballads as "The Bonny Earl of Murray," "Sir Patrick Spens," "The Twa Corbies." Joyce Carol Oates, in her afterword to *The Lost Salt Gift of Blood*, says: "If I were to name a single underlying motive for MacLeod's fiction, I would say that it is the urge to memorialize, the urge to sanctify." Which is the perfect explanation for the loving, but fictionally inappropriate, description of the kitchen quoted earlier. These stories do not take the same aim as, say, Katherine Mansfield or James Joyce or Ernest Hemingway. Their aim, I would say, is bardic.

> After a while they begin to sing in Gaelic, singing almost unconsciously the old words that are so worn and so familiar. They

seem to handle them almost as they would familiar tools. I know that in the other cars they are doing the same even as I begin silently to mouth the words myself. There is no word in Gaelic for good-bye, only for farewell.

This narrator remembers then a lyric from the fifteenth century.

> I wend to death, knight stith in stour;
> Through fight in field I won the flower;
> No fights me taught the death to quell –
> I wend to death, sooth I you tell.

> I wend to death, a king iwis;
> What helpes honour or worlde's bliss?
> Death is to man the final way –
> I wende to be clad in clay.

Alexander MacLeod
Short Story Collections: *Light Lifting* (2010).

Alexander Macleod is the author of the story collection *Light Lifting* (2010). It is an extraordinary book by any standards, but as a first book it is astonishing. The stories are more than ambitious in their reach and brilliant in execution; they are grounded in acute observation of the physical world, yet in their final impacts are reaching out towards more spiritual concerns; the glimpsed or implied visions most of the stories offer are bleak, the dominating mood is elegiac.

Nearly all the stories share a peculiar property; they seem (if I'm allowed this illogicality) to be profoundly about surfaces; they *seem*, at first, to be almost conventional in their structure and implied destinations yet somewhere in the story our solid expectations shift beneath our feet and what we had taken for simple "realism" leaves us suddenly staring down into a fault, a chasm, an abyss.

Some of the stories suggest themselves as almost total metaphors.

"Miracle Mile," for example, is a story about two boys, runners, who are competing at the national level. The story takes place "the day after Mike Tyson bit off Evander Holyfield's ear"—a truly Blaisian opening where the story "many times *is* its beginning, amplified."

The opening event of "Miracle Mile" is the two boys ritually racing a freight train under the tunnel between Detroit and Windsor, a sequence which, like the Mike Tyson reference, opens a vista on competition, contest, and death.

The story's title is the name journalists bestowed on the Roger Bannister/John Landy race in Vancouver, in 1954, a race where the story's narrator claims that Landy, who had previously established faster times than Bannister, only *seemed* to stand a chance of winning.

> [Landy] knew exactly where Bannister was coming from—he just couldn't do anything to stop it. For the whole last lap Bannister is right behind, tall and gangly and awkward and just waiting, deciding when to go.

The narrator claims that on the video Landy is obviously

> dead before he even starts the last lap. It's one of those things you recognize if you've been through it yourself....
>
> When a guy is done, he's just done and no amount of fighting can save him... We called it "rigging," short for rigor mortis. When your body started to constrict—when parts of you gave out like that, dying underneath you at exactly the moment you need something more—we called that rigging.

The image of Bannister for the whole of the last lap "right behind" Landy, "tall and gangly and awkward and just waiting," suggests to my mind a praying mantis, agent of destruction, a vision, along with the subsequent reference to "rigging," which identifies racing with merciless violence.

In the pre-race minutes of mental preparation, the narrator thinks about his decision to give up competition and we are given a different vision.

> If I ever have a kid, I think I'll let them participate in the grade school track meets when they're little, but that's it. Before it gets too

serious, I'll move them over to something else like soccer, or basket-ball, or table tennis. Something with a team or something where you can put the blame on your equipment if it all goes wrong. But when my child is still little, I'm definitely going to push for the grade school track meet because it never gets better than that. In the grade school track meet, you give the kids one of those lumpy poly-ester uniforms and they turn all excited. They get the day off school and they get to cheer for their friends and maybe they get picked to be one of the four that runs the shiny baton all the way around the circle without dropping it. At the grade school track meet, they give out ribbons that go all the way down to the "participant" level and if you do well, they read your name over the announcements at school so everybody will know about it. You get to pull on a borrowed pair of spikes and go pounding down that long runway before you jump into the sand. It's always hot and sunny and maybe your parents let you buy a drumstick or one of those over-priced red-white-and-blue popsicles from the acne-scarred high-school kid who has to ride around on a solid steel bicycle with a big yellow cooler stuck on the front. Maybe the girl with the red hair is there, the girl from the other school, the girl who wins all the longer races like you do. Maybe the newspaper takes a picture, you and the red-haired girl, standing on the top step of a plywood podium, holding all your first-place ribbons in the middle of a weedy field while all the dandelions are blowing their fuzzy heads off.

That's how it should always be. The stands should always be full of parents who don't know anything—people who can't tell the difference between what is really good and what is really bad—but they're there anyway, clapping and shouting their chil-dren's names, telling to "go" and "go" and "go." You see why it's so nice. The lanes are crowded with kids clunking their way home to the finish line and trying so hard. They go sailing way over the high jump bar—it looks so easy—and they come down on the other side, rolling softly into those big, blue fluffy mats. It's sunny and everybody's laughing and everything is still new.

All that disappears when you get serious. At the very top end—and, when you come down to it, Burner and I were still far from the *real* top end—it's completely different. Everything starts to matter too much and there are too many things that can go wrong and everybody knows the difference between what is really good and what is really bad. It comes back to the numbers. At the top end, we count it all up and measure it out and then we print the results so everybody can see. The guys I raced against were the mathematical totals of what they had done so far. That was it. Nobody cared about your goal or about what you planned to do in the future. It might take two full years of training to drop a single second or just a couple tenths off your personal best but you couldn't complain. We were all in the same boat. For us, every little bit less was a little bit more.

Really, it's the opposite of healthy. People will do anything to make those numbers go down. Some of them gobble big spoonfuls of straight baking soda before a race even though they know it gives you this brutal, bloody diarrhea an hour later. That's nothing. It's even legal. They can't ban you for baking soda, but I know guys who cross over, guys juiced up on EPO and guys who just disappear for a year and then come back like superstars. They say they've been training at altitude on some mountain in Utah, but everybody knows they've been through the lab, getting their transfusions, and playing around with their red blood cell count.

The story ends in a particularly successful manner. All story writers know that endings are possibly the most difficult part, artistically speaking, of the entire construction.

(See Clark Blaise's essay "On Ending Stories" in his *Selected Essays*. "The opening anticipates the conflict. The ending immortalizes the resolution.")

At the end of "Miracle Mile," the narrator and his running mate, Jamie Burns, are jogging through the streets surrounding the stadium, calming down after the race, cooling off. Jamie, known as and addressed as "Burner" (a nickname full of suggestions and resonances) has just won glory on the track; the narrator has informed him before that race that he has decided to stop competitive running and retire from the obsessive training, dieting, illicit cortisone injections, isolating concentration, bleeding feet.

As they jog along, a gang of kids on bikes passes them and are cheeky and taunting. Burner, uncontrollable in his aggression and testosterone, starts to run after them. The story ends like this:

> One of the boys, a kid wearing a tough-looking camouflage T-shirt, zipped around us and swerved in tight to cut me off. As he pulled away, he shot us the finger and said "Nice tights, loser."
>
> I glanced over at Burner and said "Let it go," but it was too late. His face was tightening up and that angry stare was coming back into his eyes. He wasn't looking at me.
>
> "Hey," he yelled and you could feel the edges hardening around that one little syllable. He pulled ahead of me and started tracking them down. I was caught unprepared and a step behind and I couldn't figure out how we had managed to arrive at this point. Burner was charging again and the kids were running. They didn't know. There was no way on earth they could have known. The little girl was pedalling as fast as she could and there was this strange, high-pitched, wheezing sound coming out of her, but there nothing she could do. Burner had already closed the gap and his hand was already there, reaching out for the thin strands of her hair. It all disintegrated after that. He must have been a foot taller than the oldest one.

The ending engages us precisely because it is ambiguous. "…the kids were running. They didn't know. There was no way on earth they could have known."

And… "It all disintegrated after that."

What did the kids not know?

After what?

We assume violence.

What "disintegrated?"

The story turns us back into itself.

However brilliant and compelling in its evocation of the world of running, is this a story about running? Or is it possibly a story "about," *the intellect's eagerness to foreclose,* the life of the artist and the price such a life exacts? Or other things?

> ... but I never met a balanced guy who ever got anything done. There's nothing new about this stuff. You have to sign the same deal if you want to be good—I mean truly good—at anything. Burner and I, and all those other guys, we understood this. We knew all about it. Every pure specialist is the same way so either you know what I am talking about or you do not.

Exactly.

Whatever the reader wishes to read into it, the story is pleasurably rich and chewy in all its dimensions and suggestions and sounds shimmering on into the silence the story leaves behind.

MacLeod's non-Blaisian, *non*-resolution of the story leaves us entangled in it. The emotional and technical success of this gambit intrigued me, so I asked the question all writers ask of each other: Who do you read?

> You're right to assume that I am influenced by American writers—that's definitely true—but I've been teaching courses on the Canadian short story for more than ten years and I think that has shaped my work in more direct ways. Norman Levine is important to me, as he is to so many people, but I've spent more time studying my dad and Clark Blaise and Alice Munro and Mavis Gallant and Guy Vanderhaege. In Atlantic Canada, I like the Newfoundlanders very much and I think Lisa Moore and Lynn Coady and Jessica Grant are all great. In the rest of the country, the younger writers I admire include Annabel Lyon, Michael Christie, Deborah Willis, Eden Robinson, and Sarah Selecky. Outside Canada, the Irish writers have been very kind to me, both personally and professionally, and I know that I have learned so much from John McGahern, Anne Enright, Colm Toibin and Claire Keegan, as well as the super Scots: John Burnside, Ali Smith and Andrew O'Hagan. The Americans who matter to me in significant ways obviously include Flannery O'Connor, Richard Ford, Raymond Carver and Denis

Johnson, but also Jhumpa Lahiri, Benjamin Percy, Wells Tower, Lorrie Moore, George Saunders, Valerie Sayers and Bonnie Joe Campbell. The poet Elizabeth Bishop is also very important to me. Any writer who is doing something interesting in an interesting way will hold and reward my close attention and I am continuously impressed by my young, as yet unknown students....

(*Letter.* June 19, 2014)

There isn't a dud story in *Light Lifting* and, as an editor and anthologist it's rare for me to be able to say that. I do have favourite stories, however, and they are "The Loop," "The Number Three," and "Wonder about Parents."

"The Loop" is narrated by a young boy, Allan, who delivers prescriptions and pharmacy goods on his bicycle for Mr. Musgrave, proprietor of the Musgrave Pharmacy. In his delivery bag he carries blood-pressure medications, antacids, laxatives, the plastic bottles of pills in their little white bags, eye drops, candy, denture cream, cans of Chef Boyardee, and calcium supplements, which he delivers to the aged in assisted-living homes, the shut-ins, the men on disability from injuries sustained while working on the assembly line.

Most feared by the local kids is the horrible Barney, reputed to be a boy-fancier. Allan always leaves his delivery safely outside the front door.

> He was famous mostly for his hernia. It was this red pulsating growth about the size of a misshapen grapefruit and it bulged way out of the lower left hand side of his stomach. It seemed like something impossible, like one of those gross, special effects from an alien movie that was supposed to make you think there was a smaller creature in there. Just the shape of it, and the way it stuck out of him, and how it seemed to come right at you, could make a person squirm if they weren't used to it. But he refused to get it fixed and he was always making a big deal about how tough he was and how it didn't bother him at all. He thought it was funny to pull back his shirt and scare the little kids as they walked by.

> "It ain't hurting me," he used to say. And then he'd poke at
> this own stomach just to prove it was true. The finger would
> go deepdown into the grapefruit and when he pulled it out, the
> creature inside would kind of tremble.

(A lovely example of how the movement of the prose suggests the
child-voice.)

Allan is exposed, in his rounds, to a variety of sufferings and
eccentricity. After he helps in shifting a sideboard, one of her refin-
ishing hobby-jobs, Mrs. Hume gestures round the furniture-stacked
apartment and says, "Which one of these do you want? ... Just
choose and I'll leave it to you in my will."

Allan reflects, "I could tell she wasn't joking, but at that stage in
my life I don't think she knew there was nothing I needed less than
a china cabinet."

Sometimes what he did and saw was less comical.

> It seemed, sometimes like I knew too much about things I wasn't
> really supposed to know at all. Like the first time your eyes touch
> on a bad case of bedsores—the kind that can eat big, fist-sized
> holes right through your flesh just from laying down in one spot
> for too long. The first time you see that, you can't look at any-
> thing the same way anymore. The Musgrave job was full of stuff
> like that. There was an old man who asked to help rub in the
> eczema cream for his legs and when I kneeled down to touch
> him, even as softly as I could, large flakes of his skin came off
> in my hands like red fish scales. And there was another lady on
> McEwan who needed me to read her the fine-print directions on
> a package of glycerine suppositories.
>
> "I don't know why in the hell they write everything so small,"
> she complained to me while I waited outside the bathroom door.
> "Just tell me what it says. Are you supposed to run them under
> the water before they go in?"

The final scene of "The Loop" involves Allan administering CPR to
Barney.

His body was just a thing, like a pile of laundry in the middle of the room, as still as the furniture.

After the resuscitated Barney, whose mouth had tasted of "ravioli and the beer and the white paste," is stacked into the ambulance, Allan, in the story's last paragraph, reflects that:

> More than anything I wanted to go home and be exactly my own age for as long as I could. That was my new plan. I would go home and lie on my bed and stare at the Guy Lafleur poster on my wall and love the way he didn't need a helmet. Then I'd eat nothing but junk—just twizzlers and blow pops and lik-m-aid fun dip—and I'd listen to my music as loud as I wanted. Maybe I'd watch *The Dukes of Hazard*. I thought about Bo and Luke Duke and how they never killed anyone and never used guns. Instead, they used to tape a stick of dynamite to one of their arrows and fire it straight into the bad guy's hideout and blast the whole thing into a pile of splinters and falling straw. That would be just about right, I thought. It would be great to just sit with them in the backseat of the *General Lee* and scream as loud as you could as they punched the gas and their orange car started up its long flight across the river, over to the other side, where no one could follow and you always got away.

Those last, almost casual words "and you always got away," strike us with the force of the defibrillator paddles. They drive us back into the story and reposition both Allan and us; with those words, the story is shocked into a different shape. We understand, overwhelmingly, that Allan has been taught on his daily rounds that nobody "got away," that he will share the fate of Barney and the suppository lady, and the lady with "a big yellowish cyst."

Mr. Musgrave, looking through a glossy flyer from Shoppers Drug Mart, once remarked gloomily of his pharmacy: "We're a dying breed."

This is knowledge that Allan has been unconsciously approaching throughout the story.

I was very interested in "Wonder About Parents," a story about infestations of lice and a baby daughter with a high and dangerous fever. I was much moved by the intensity of this love story, but my initial interest was sparked by its punctuation (or lack of it) and its sentence fragmentation. I wondered if I was seeing the influence of Norman Levine and wrote to MacLeod to enquire.

This was his reply:

I don't have any major stylistic influences that would guide the way I use punctuation, sentence structure or grammar in my stories. Most of the time, I am just trying to match the content of the story to the feel of the prose and I spend most of my time and energy reading it aloud over and over again, trying to get the rhythm and sound and the pace of the individual lines and paragraphs to come together in the right way. In the story "Wonder about Parents," I was trying to capture that sense of a committed but exhausted intimacy that all young couples with kids share and I wanted the story to sound and feel like that disjointed rush of life that dominates this phase of adulthood. In my experience anyway, when there are lots of young kids around and life is running full tilt, there's far more need than there is capacity to meet that need, and the individuals involved in this mix—the parents / former lovers—hardly ever speak to each other in full sentences anymore. Though they are sharing all these very powerful experiences nearly every day, most of those moments just slide by in a great hurried blur that never ever really settles down long enough to take the form of a full quiet reflection or a properly formatted, grammatically correct, thought. I didn't really do it on purpose, but I think that's why the punctuation faded in importance and everything else ended up running together into one long, mixed up memory of intense times. I wrote "Wonder about Parents" to hit on that one particular feeling and since that feeling really isn't present in the same way in the other stories, that's why it stands out a bit. The same applies to the runner story or the car story or the swimming story. They all have different concerns and different physical dimensions so I wrote them all with different tones and different rhythms and different kinds of pacing and acceleration. Other people may think they all sound the same, but to me, they feel like completely different projects.

(*Letter*, June 19, 2014)

Nothing could persuade me faster than the following scene from "Wonder About Parents" to pursue this book immediately.

Rows of moulded seats with metal arm rails that make it impossible to lie down. A Saturday night crowd during the holidays. Woman with plastic bag socks. She has a shopping cart full of empty pop cans parked outside the sliding door. A guy sleeping across from us, legs splayed wide like an upside down "Y." Small separate bruises on the right side of his face. Ambulances rolling in and out. Stretchers. Overdoses. Bar fights. A man with a knife stuck right through his hand. Nurse tells him to leave it in and wait for further instructions. Triage.

We fill out our forms and huddle. Health Cards from a different province. Suspicion. You may have to pay for this up front and get reimbursed when you return home. Her temperature keeps rising. Wheezing when she breathes. Brown pus around her eyes. They take blood and urine samples right away. Then we wait.

Five hours. Six.

They have her hooked up to a machine. Tubes and wires. A long strip of paper, like a sales slip, scrolling out. Something inside draws a continuous erratic line over the narrow graph paper. It goes up and down. Sometimes rests for a long plateau. The nurses consult it every time they come in the room. We have no idea what it means. When we ask, they say: more data for the chart. There are numbers, too. Three of them. Two for blood pressure, we think, and then something else. A single flashing light, but no sound. The bulb is purple. Blinks on and off. Fluctuates. A silent rhythm, picking up and coming back down. Her heart, most likely, but it seems too slow sometimes.

I come to relieve her. 10:30 at night. Freezing outside. Other things will happen, but we will never live clearer than this. I take off my boots. She puts hers on. Car outside waiting in temporary parking. Meter running. The heater will stay warm if we switch fast enough.

She just went down, she says. Probably be up for something to eat in two or three hours. New bottle of formula in the fridge at the nurse's station.

Okay, good. There's spaghetti waiting for you.

I hold her. All her weight collapses in to me and we both cry. Quiet empty corridors in the hospital. Nothing happening. All the overhead lights turned down.

When are they going to let us go?

I don't know. Have to wait till they say something.

She puts on her winter coat. Turns to leave.

I move to the chair. The upholstery is hard blue vinyl. Cleaning staff wipe it down every morning with a spray bottle of disinfectant. I push it back so the recliner part kicks up. It is about two-feet wide, hard metal support bars running below the surface. You can go down, maybe, but you cannot sleep here. The place where you wait for the next day to come.

I get one of the thin pillows from the shelf in the bathroom. Look up and see her at the end of the hall. Waiting by the elevator. Her head shaking. The numbers descending. I call her name as I move, almost run, down the corridor in my sock feet. Meet her on the way. Kiss.

Stay, I say.

Please stay.

She smiles.

We go back. Squeeze onto the vinyl chair. Her legs between my legs. Arms hanging over the side. Heads touching. Everything forced together. Darkness in the room. Our baby makes no sound. Only the bulb from the machine now. Inscrutable purple light flashing on the ceiling. Like a discotheque, maybe, or the reflection of ancient fire in a cave.

K.D. Miller

Short Story Collections: *A Litany in Time of Plague* (1994), *Give Me Your Answers* (1999), *The Other Voice* (2011), *All Saints* (2014), and *Late Breaking* (2018).

Novels: *Brown Dwarf* (2010).

Non-Fiction: *Holy Writ* (2001).

K.D. Miller's first book, *A Litany in Time of Plague*, owes its title to the Elizabethan poem "In Time of Pestilence," by Thomas Nashe, whose refrain at the end of each verse is:

> I am sick, I must die.
>> Lord, have mercy on us!

When I was a schoolboy I used to copy out poems that spoke to me into a large ledger that had *Accounts Receivable* in gold on its black cover. I copied out Nashe's poem because I was so taken by its third stanza:

> Beauty is but a flower
> Which wrinkles will devour;
> Brightness falls from the air,
> Queens have died young and fair,
> Dust hath closed Helen's eye.
> I am sick, I must die.
>> Lord, have mercy on us!

It was the third line—*Brightness falls from the air*—that captured me, captivated me; it seemed then to say all the world. What it actually meant was not clear to me and still isn't, but I remain captive to its magic.

The stories in *Litany* are a carefully constructed interweaving whole concerning Arley, family friend "uncle" Raymond Mayhugh, author, and lover of Robbie. The stories move from Arley as a child to Arley growing up to become the actress "Lee," to Raymond, voluble, flirtatious, monstrous, to his death in a home.

The stories in the voice of Raymond Mayhugh are not stories about the plague of AIDS; they are—vital difference—stories about

455

Raymond and Robbie. Miller has cast them in the form of monologues or soliloquies spoken and thought by Raymond. All the stories in *Litany* are *performances* and it is with the word performances
that I must start presenting the brilliant achievement of K.D. Miller.

But before considering the stories in that intended sense, I'd like
to mourn—deplore?—that her fiction wasn't performed nationally
on CBC. I can remember listening when I was a boy to the radio
broadcasts of Beckett's *All That Fall* and *Embers*, both plays not only
first performed on but commissioned by the BBC. How could the
CBC have missed the massive power of the three Mayhugh stories—"Author of," "A Litany in Time of Plague," and "Lifesaver"?
How could they have missed the profoundly moving pair of stories
in the recent *All Saints*, "Still Dark" and "Ecce Cor Meum?"

And how could they have missed Miller herself as performer?
I have vivid memory of her performing "Lifesaver"; the dramatic
"punctuational" *clicks* she made as Raymond sucked his diminishing
Lifesaver; it was searing.

Brightness has certainly fallen from the airwaves; we seem now
condemned to listening to effete and comfy young afternoon men
on the CBC discussing macramé and their new mountain bicycles.

Because performance is the essence of Miller's writing and
because, if we are to receive her well, we must position ourselves
as audience in a theatre, I feel it important that she sketch in her
growth as an actress.

(All the quotations by K.D. Miller are taken from *Writers Talking*
(2003), edited by John Metcalf and Claire Wilkshire. I must also
admit to having had a presence, though minimal, in the editing of
four of her story collections.)

> The exercises I did in acting classes to train my powers of concen-
> tration, observation, and emotive memory still serve me well as a
> writer…What I learned as a director comes in handy too. I was taught
> to "parse" a script, then go over and over a single line or bit of busi-
> ness until it worked. The recommended formula was one hour of
> rehearsal per minute of performance. As a writer, I still think in terms
> of segments of action—acts, scenes, and "beats," like heartbeats.

Sometimes when a story appears to be dying, I turn back into a director and try to revive it as I would a play. "Why isn't anything *happening?*" I bark at the hapless page. "What are you supposed to be *doing?*"

From what ground did the young actress at the university in Guelph spring?

Hamilton, you say?

In the fifties?

I was very taken with Susan Coolidge's "Katy" books, especially *What Katy Did at School*. I had a *thing* about boarding schools, and was convinced that if I could attend one, I would be a completely different person. Someone like Rose Red, the girl in the Katy books who is loved in spite of, or perhaps because of, the "scrapes" she keeps getting into. Rose Red was likely the first of a character type I've always admired in fiction and in life—someone who not only sticks out like a sore thumb but takes pride in doing so.

I had the first part down pat. In school I used to look at other little girls—docile, feminine, interested only in their dolls, their hair and the contents of their plastic purses—and envy what I took to be their easy, uncomplicated lives. For all I might admire Rose Red, I still yearned to fit in with the crowd. My high marks and my artistic talent tended to put me in the spotlight, as did my "compositions," which teachers liked to read aloud to the class. Though I was not friendless, I lacked a social role model. When it came to dealing with my peers, I more or less had to make it up as I went along.

So I became a watcher and a listener. I would observe ordinary exchanges between people, then run them over and over in my mind like films. Anything spontaneous or natural was strange to me. Maybe that's what made me an artist. I've always felt a strong impulse to depict my own life. To enact it somehow. Record it.

What else had tilled the ground?

My first published story, "Now, Voyager," is narrated by an unnamed "I" who idolizes an eccentric, slightly glamourous elocution teacher living up the street. Well, an eccentric, slightly glamorous elocution teacher *did* live up the street. Marie Jean, or Miss Jean, as I called her in fiction and in life, was like a little dot of colour in the greyness that was Hamilton in the fifties. Her French name and her being Catholic were enough to make her exotic in my eyes. But there was also the way she spoke—as if words were more than conveyors of information. As if they had colour and shape. As if speech could be music, or painting, or even dance.

Besides the influence of Miss Jean, there was my mother's girlhood infatuation with movie stars, which she managed to pass on to me. I still have the book of charcoal sketches she did from photographs in movie magazines of the thirties and forties—Bette Davis, Clark Gable, Joan Crawford, etc. She and I would check the *TV Guide* each week to see what was going to be playing on *Saturday Night at the Movies*. All that week, she would act out bits for me of *Now Voyager, Dark Victory* or whatever melodramatic weepy we were going to see. By the time Saturday night rolled around, I was so pumped that the real thing could not possibly live up to my expectations. But for days afterwards, I would be Greer Garson in *Random Harvest* or Barbara Stanwyck in *Stella Dallas*. "You like *old* people!" a classmate accused me one day when we were listing our favourite movie stars. It was true. I was living in the wrong decade.

At Guelph she came under the influence of the drama teacher Robert Shafto. She relates how his coaching and directing, seemingly dictatorial, were actually "one of the greatest kindnesses I have ever received."

But back to high school. For all the experience and confidence I was gaining I was also picking up every bad stage habit going. I had a good voice and a strong presence. Unfortunately, I also had an eye and ear for theatrical cliché. My acting was essentially mimicry—all slick, hollow surface.

I was riding for a fall, and I took it, in first year university. At Guelph, I began to learn the hard way what Rosalind Russell meant when she said, "Good acting is standing up naked and turning around very slowly."

On opening night, it was obvious that I was making a brilliant debut. The compliments I was getting from both students and faculty all but drowned out Robert Shafto's pointed silence.

After a couple of weeks of Acting 100, I began to relax with him. He was a gentle, courteous teacher who managed to find something positive to say about what each of us was doing. An early assignment was a dramatic reading of the poem "Richard Corey." He used my delivery of the phrase, "he glittered when he walked" as an example of taking a line and making it one's own. So one day I asked him what he had thought of my performance last semester.

Decades later, I still remember every word of his reply. "You were acting from the chin up," he said. "Nothing was felt. There was no heart. No gut. Furthermore, you were monitoring your every word and gesture in such a self-complimentary manner that I was nauseated. As late as three days before opening, I was begging your director to replace you. Any other actress in the department, script in hand, would have been an improvement."

Those words look so cruel in black and white. In fact, they constitute one of the greatest kindnesses I have ever received. Shafto was saying what I had been suspecting for some time. My first reaction was relief, followed by a growing exhilaration. The false apprenticeship was over. At last I was going to start to learn to act.

It was like returning to the womb. Being remade, cell by cell. "You took a step forward," Shafto would say after calling *Cut*. "I did not understand that forward step. And *my* not understanding it was a direct result of *your* not understanding it. Please take that step back. And if you do step forward again, do it for a *reason*. Do it because you *want* something, and taking that step is the *means* of getting it." And so it would go, with every step, every gesture, every word, every tear. Nothing superfluous was allowed—nothing affected or easy or just thrown in for show. ("It should *cost* you something to act!") Cliché, he impressed upon me, was the hallmark of dishonesty. Worse, of cowardice.

And the way to reach an audience was not to play directly to them but to make them cease to exist through total immersion in the character and the world of the play.

Needless to say, what I was learning during those thirteen weeks in Robert Shafto's class was not just how to act but how to live. And how to write. To this day, whenever I get bogged down in pedestrian prose, I hear Shafto's crisp diction in my ear: "It's too *easy*. It's not *costing* you anything. Take that step back and start again."

Space precludes my talking about all the stories in *Litany* and how they are interconnected so I'll concentrate on the stories about the very theatrical author Raymond Mayhugh. What Raymond has to say is usually both funny and desperate. In the following, we share Raymond's morning-after thoughts:

So more out of boredom than anything else, I had my latest aco-lyte spend the night. And the night was fine. Oh my, yes. But the trouble with nights is they have mornings stapled to them.

And all the mornings are the same. The coffee. The eyes above the rim of the coffee mug, following me around the kitchen. Me wanting so much to say, "Look, you're a sweet treat in the dark but a bloody bore by daylight, so just *go*."

But instead, I say, "How about something kind of eggy, with vegetables and herbs?" I learned, centuries ago, that if I say, "How about a frittata?" I'll be met with a blank stare. It takes at least two years of university to get the smell of their mother's cooking out of most of them.

I know that. But even so, when we get down to clinking and chewing, I'm still on tenterhooks, wailing for, "Hey, this is a really good omelette." Someday, someday, I am going to heave my plate at somebody's vestigial pimples and shriek, "It's a frit-tata, you fucking little ignoramus! It's a frittata!"

And oh, dear, what do we talk about? What *can* we talk about?

But such is my beloved. Shit. Remember that schoolyard song, "Nobody likes me, everybody hates me, I'm going to the garden to eat worms"? Well, here it is, folks. Raymond Mayhugh's *mood* for the day. Day? Hell, I've been working up to this for half the week. So let's really do it, huh? Let's give it a real go.

Raymond having lunch with Robbie, his sometime lover, and the man he would attend on and attend to in the hospice where Robbie will lie dying of AIDS, the Robbie that will flood Raymond with memories as he, too, in old age, sits dying in a home.

Anyway. I bitched on cheerfully to Robbie about that, and about editors and advances, blah-blahing away. Oh, I love myself when I'm with book. I'm a blur. I never slow down. Everything but the book just melts into distance behind me.

Everything, that is, except too, too solid Robbie. He stayed right in front of me, and the minute I paused for breath stopped me dead by talking about his soul. His *soul*. He actually used the word.

"You know, Raymond," he began in that self-deprecating way that used to get to me, "I've been looking at my life a bit too, lately. I've begun thinking again about the state of my soul."

Now, Robbie does this kind of thing. I was at a barbecue with him once, where everybody was riding along happily on a bubble of beer. All of a sudden Robbie looked up and said, "When the Indians were here, the sky was black with birds." Pop.

Well, I refused to be popped. The calamari had arrived, thank God, so I speared one and held it up. "Does anyone else know about this?" I asked conspiratorially. It's what I used to say to him in bed.

"About what? My soul?"

"No. Calamari in lemon-garlic butter. Does anyone else—Oh, never mind." God, I hate it when someone won't carry the ball.

"I'm sorry, Raymond," he said, and I had to smile. When Robbie says he's sorry, he not only looks and sounds sorry, he really is. He has one of those faces that don't change. Even at forty-two, he still looks like an English choirboy. Longish hair, collar up, ears straight out. Eyes.

"I'm sorry," he repeated. "It's just something that's been on my mind lately. More and more I find myself thinking back to the way I was when we first met. You remember, don't you, how I couldn't look at three telephone poles without seeing Calvary? Well, I'm starting to think that maybe I really was on a pilgrimage that—" he shrugged and gave that deprecating smile again "—that underwent a little detour."

Oh, God. I was bored with this kind of talk when I was an undergraduate. I got bored with it again when Robbie and I had our little affairette twenty-two years ago, and he dumped one religious crisis on me after another. I mean, my phone would ring at some ghastly hour of the morning (on top of everything else, Robbie's an early riser), and I would hear, "Raymond? Are you awake?"

"I am now."

"I had to tell you. I had to tell *someone*."

"What?"

"I kept a vigil last night. I dozed off once or twice, but I meditated most of the time. And Raymond, it *came* to me."

"What did? The ghost of Christmas yet to come? I hope you helped him."

"Oh, Raymond. I mean I realized something. About myself."

"Well, what, Robbie? I'm on tenterhooks."

"I realized that I'm an accidental Christian!"

The trouble with a statement like that is you can't tell someone to fuck off for making it. "Robbie, what the hell are you talking about?"

"I'm talking about me, Raymond. I just realized that I am a product of western Christendom. My ethos, my world view, my frame of reference, everything is essentially Christian. So there's no more need to struggle with my faith. It's a given, like my hands, or my eyes, or—"

"Robbie, take two altar boys and call me in the morning."

Well, over lunch, I felt the old familiar boredom setting in again. So I decided to head it off. "Robbie," I said, "about your alleged soul. Two things. First, nobody's come back to tell us what's on the other side of the big D. We're not even sure there's anything to worry about, one way or the other. Second, supposing somebody does come back and says, here's the scoop. If you're good, you spend eternity sitting on a stream of Jacuzzi bubbles, sipping Chablis. But if you're bad, you stand forever in a cashier's lineup listening to 'Attention, K-Mart shoppers' over and over again. So what? What do you do? Change the past? Change what you are? Start taking the homeless out for dim sum?" I speared another tiny perfect squid and gestured at him with it. "There's no piece of paper inside the box this board game came in, telling you the rules in seven languages." I twiddled the squid in the lemon-garlic butter and put it in my mouth. "Where's all this soul crap coming from just now, anyway?" I asked when I had swallowed. "You're not dying, are you?"

"Well," he said, "yes. I suppose I am." Then he reached out, put his hand on my wrist and said, "I'm sorry, Raymond."

Few Canadian writers are capable of writing as sophisticated as this. This quoted passage is studded with little pleasures—"too, too solid Robbie" flicks, in passing, Hamlet's "O! that this too too solid flesh would melt..." Hamlet's cry about death and suicide in the soliloquy are not essential to what K.D. is doing here—just a grace note.

Not many writers are capable of such precise caricature as:

> Even at forty-two, he still looks like an English choirboy. Longish hair, collar up, ears straight out. Eyes.

Raymond's aggressive query about how Robbie might atone for his sins:

> So what? What do you do? Change the past? Change what you are? Start taking the homeless out for dim sum?

Of these stories starring Raymond Mayhugh, K.D. wrote:

> A motive. A sense of the character's rhythm. A growing feeling of empathy with that character. These are the things an actor

takes along on what is essentially a journey of discovery. To write Raymond was to play with him, which in turn was to learn to love him.

Raymond's death in the Home is played with an intensity and power unequalled in anything in my experience of Canadian prose. "Lifesaver" builds slowly, following his meanders into memories, his erotic dreams, his still acerbic commentary on his surroundings when he starts from sleep, his fierce mental resistance to capitulating to his keepers.

We should be moving again soon. A couple of the kids have hauled the old dear back into her chair and are trussing her up. Smiling, cheerful, the way they always are. Must be on drugs. Or maybe the money's good.

The little letters have worn off my Lifesaver, Robbie. It's as smooth as an inner tube at the beach now.

My God. Inner tubes. I haven't thought about inner tubes in years. Getting all shiny and tight and fat in the sun. Almost burning our shoulders and the backs of our knees, while our bums sag through the holes into the cold lake.

The sun's so bright I can see it shining pink through the backs of your ears. And it's turned the hair on your arms into white down. There you go, paddling away in your inner tube, scooping at the water with cupped hands.

Robbie? Aren't you going out a little deep? Robbie, you're going out too far. Robbie! Why don't you turn around? You're getting smaller. Farther away. Robbie, come back! Come back right—

What? I'm sorry? What was that, nurse? No. No, I wasn't saying anything. Yes, I'm quite all right, thank you. Pardon? Oh, yes. I do still want to go. Of course I do. Why wouldn't I want to go? I said I would, and I will.

Robbie, where the hell are we going? I'm not about to ask this kid pushing me. It doesn't do to let them know what planet you're really on.

Let's see. We were stopped. Now we're moving again. Great big long caravan of us. It's mid-afternoon, to judge from the light through the windows we're passing. Too late for lunch. Too early for supper.

Wait a minute. Here it comes. Activity Time! In the Activity Room! How *could* I have forgotten? Come on, Raymond. Work up a little enthusiasm. It's *nice* of them to try to stimulate us into a semblance of life now and then. Balances the death-counselling they give us free of charge.

The grim cavalcade proceeds:

Jesus, I can feel my heart beating. Careful, Raymond. Somebody might take your pulse and discover you have one. Probably against regulations.

Maybe it's the Lifesaver. Sharp little wafer on my tongue now. Turned my spit into raspberry wine. Amazing what artificial flavouring can do. The other day the Lifesaver nurse gave me grape and it brought back all my lovers. Starting with you, my sweet and twenty. Didn't we have an afternoon.

Remember? You were nothing but eyes, Robbie. Watching me. All over. Your mouth is watching me. Your nipples. Your cock, not even hard yet, but I swear it can see me. The pink ends of your toes are little eyes, watching.

And I don't know what to do. No. That's not it. I don't know where to start. I want everything, all at once. I can't move. I can't ask you for anything, I want you so much.

So you put out your hand. There. I can take your hand. I take it and I kiss it. And then my lips draw back and my teeth just take over.

Gently, gently, I *gnaw* you, Robbie. I feel your skin sliding over your tendons, over your bones, as I roll your knuckles tenderly between my teeth.

And then I'm gnawing your cheekbones, then your lips, feeling the hint of your own teeth under them. And then your collarbones, your ribs, the points of your pelvis.

You smell all over of my spit, Robbie. And we've both come by the time I'm teething on your toes.

And I must have fallen asleep afterwards, because now you're trying to wake me. Whispering my name in my ear. That's nice. I like that. Your breath in my ear. Mister Mayhugh. Mister Mayhugh. What, are you playing a game or something? I'm *Raymond*, for God's sake. What's this business about Mister—

Oh. Oh. I'm sorry, dear. I just dozed off there for a second. Thank you for waking me. Thank you very much, dear.

And here we are at last. In the Activity Room. All ready for Activity Time.

Raymond drifts off and remembers Robby in Terry House.

The phone rang the minute I got home from seeing you. You looked so young while I was feeding you your supper. With your neck so thin, and your ears sticking out against the pillows. But the minute I got home the phone rang and a nurse said, you'd better come right back. He's going.

You were going all the time I was nudging and honking through rush-hour traffic, Robbie. And you were still going when I was in the elevator on my way up to your room. But when the elevator doors opened, there was the nurse standing there. He's gone, she said. Just now.

And all I could say was, where?

I open my eyes again. Still in the Activity Room. Some of them around the table smile a welcome back. The male nurse turns the pumpkin so I can see the face he's carved. Now he's putting a candle inside. Lighting it. Dimming the room lights.

And it's all dark now. Except for the face.

Oh. Well.

This *is* a surprise.

All the times I tried to imagine how it would be, I never thought it would be like this.

So familiar.

So close.

Your breath, a tickle near my nose. Then your mouth, a soft, slow pressing. A silver thread of saliva stretching between your lips and mine.

Robbie, I can still

What a daring ending!

The voice, at last, stilled.

Raymond's sudden *recognition* of death:

Oh.

Well.

This *is* a surprise.

I was very forcefully reminded of Henry James' words on experiencing the stroke leading to his death:

So here it is at last, the distinguished thing!

But K.D. informed me that she drew on Margaret Laurence's final line of *The Stone Angel*:

And then

K.D.'s work is less visual, less lyrical, than say, Alice Munro's or Norman Levine's because she favours voices talking, but that said, one of her descriptive lines in "Lifesaver" that shimmers for me concerns Raymond and Robbie at the lake playing in their inner tubes.

Inner tubes, "Getting all shiny and tight and fat in the sun."

So immediate, so real I can even smell them, yet at the same time so oddly erotic.

Is it the word "getting"? Are these tubes tumescent?

Miller published *Litany* in 1994; twenty years later, in 2014, she published *All Saints,* a volume that was reviewed in *Macleans* magazine under the headline: "Hallelujah! A Canadian classic is born." In between, she'd published, in 1999, a volume of stories, *Give Me Your*

Answer. It is unfortunate that I don't have space to talk about that book because I suspect that it may well contain some of her very best work. The stories grapple with hard and gritty material; they make us uncomfortable; they offer no answers; they are full of pain.

In *Writers Talking* she spoke about my own involvement in *Answer* and mentioned a letter I'd written to her that I only vaguely remember:

> John's editorial notes to me, though few, have always had a theatrical ring. "The effect of that final page should be one of a slowly closing fist," he wrote in regard to "Author of." And when I almost abandoned my second collection, *Give Me Your Answer*, because it was getting too autobiographical for comfort, he issued a call to arms: "You are a writer. That's what you do. That's what you are... What's really important is for your work to sparkle and to last. You won't connect with other people unless you connect with the primal material of your life and wrestle it to the ground with elegant and powerful language... the unpalatable truth is that if you wish to be important as a writer your allegiance must not be to people but to the perfected arrangement of words on paper."

All Saints is a distinguished collection and certainly *ought* to become "a Canadian classic" but, of course, won't unless we read it and *recognize it*, a remark that applies to so many of the titles discussed in this book.

I want to draw particular attention to two of the stories in *All Saints*; what I have to say about them and about ways of approaching them I intend as applying to all the stories in the book and to Miller's work in general.

The two stories are "Still Dark" and "Ecce Cor Meum"; they are discrete as stories but are connected by having in common the same characters, Simon, the vicar, and Kelly, a parishioner, who desires him. There is nothing much in either story requiring elucidation, but pleasure can be deepened if the reader surrenders to the performance as we do when a Paul Schofield, a Kenneth Branagh, a Gielgud, or an Olivier commands the stage.

Miller's work is typically theatrical. We often use the word "theatrical" to mean "affected," "excessively emotional," "histrionic." I'm using it here in the flatly literal sense of "of the theatre." What I'm suggesting is that readers, for this particular writer, *position themselves* as audience in the stalls watching and listening to the action on the stage.

The opening of "Still Dark" is pure theatre.

> Simon closes the door of his office behind him. Locks it. Checks that it is locked. Turns and wades through the dark until he nudges the edge of his desk. Works his way around to his chair and sits.
>
> He pulls open the bottom left drawer, bunches the hanging files together and reaches into the cavity at the back. Touches a softness that always surprises him, like the fur of a sleeping animal.
>
> While his eyes adjust to the dark, he lifts the sweater out, holds it up and shakes it gently. Telling himself again that he should be keeping it in a plastic bag. Telling himself again that he shouldn't be keeping it at all.

You can see Simon in the gloom and you can see the lights coming up just sufficiently to let you see him taking out the sweater. The brilliant use of "wades" and "nudges" builds what the actor is doing; the words might be stage directions. It has always been my experience that theatre is much more tense, intense, than film; theatre is a far less passive experience.

This slow, intense introduction, which suggests, in retrospect, so many things—guilt, furtiveness, sensuality, obsession—opens out into italicized speech, memory, phone conversation replayed with Kelly, the sweater's owner, concerning its whereabouts, the interview she'd conducted earlier with him for the parish magazine remembered, re-created, the interview after which she'd left the sweater behind, *then*, in an amazing stroke, Miller has Simon conduct with the sweater he's draped over the chairback facing his desk *The Reconciliation of a Penitent*, the act of confession from the

Book of Common Prayer. Who among all our writers but Miller could have invented antiphonal responses between a penitential vicar and a sweater. But she makes it seem so natural in context, so emotionally real.

Then another mode of speech takes over, another scene begins. Simon gets up and braces his hands against the wall below the crucifix that his bipolar wife had made from oddments (pure theatre, this) and confesses again to what he feels to have been his negligence which contributed to her suicide. His racked confession rehearses the pain of his marriage, the mess her illness had made of his career, the confusion of his present desire.

The pulse of the story never flags, the voices never stop. Miller has no need to bark at this story, *"Why isn't anything happening?"*

By the last couple of pages—brilliant detail this—the lights have lifted enough for him to be able to see—keeping us *in* that office, *at* that desk—"the holes in the top button of Kelly's sweater and the criss-cross of thread."

The ending of the story continues to involve us precisely because it *isn't* a resolution, *isn't* an ending. We are left wondering what will happen; we are left exactly where we ought to be, still stuck in the emotions of these lives.

This is the story's non-ending:

> He gets up, goes around to the front of his desk and lifts the sweater off the back of the chair. Shakes it gently and folds it. Stands looking down at it in the growing light. It's as soft as ever in his hands. He raises it to his face. And still that hint of Ivory soap.

I'm probably importing far too much of myself into the story but the detail here makes me think of a priest celebrating one of the seven sacraments, then taking off his stole, folding it and kissing it.

There are hints in the language of these sentences, "soft," "gently," "in his hands," "to his face," and the sensuality of the lingering scent of Ivory (surely not *merely* proprietary?) that hint at the direction but in the end the story remains undirected, ambiguous, turning us back into itself to continue involving us with the lives we've been living in.

"Ecce Cor Meum" is a companion piece to "Still Dark," the same situation seen from Kelly's position rather than Simon's. The story opens thus:

> Polyp.
>   Funny little word. Sounds botanical. A bed of flowering polyps. Gather ye polyps while ye may.

Kelly is sitting in a Starbucks drinking coffee while waiting to have a bone density scan in the medical building she's just left after blood tests with her own doctor and the speculum insertion that has confirmed a polyp on one side of her cervix.

During the bone density scan, Kelly dozes off to the repetitive *Wheenga! Wheenga!* as the machine slowly travels up her body; she drifts into an erotic reverie, she and Simon in a car, they are heading for his cottage, she is fondling him as he drives, the wood-smoke smell of his red flannel shirt.

When the machine stops and she is released, she makes her way over to All Saints, where Simon is to conduct the service for Ash Wednesday.

When Kelley's mind wanders to "Gather ye polyps while ye may," Miller is using an allusion to a poem again just as she did in the title of her first book, *A Litany in Time of Plague*. The reference here is to the poem by Robert Herrick "To the Virgins, to Make Much of Time" which was published in the collection *Hesperides* in 1648. I quote the first and last verses because, with this allusion, Miller is sounding one of the story's main emotional themes.

> Gather ye rose-buds while ye may,
>   Old Time is still a-flying;
> And this same flower that smiles today
>   Tomorrow will be dying.
>   [...]

> Then be not coy, but use your time,
> And while ye may, go marry;
> For having lost but once your prime,
> You may forever tarry.

Though Herrick was an ordained priest, he was something of a rois-
terer, a friend of Ben Jonson and his circle, an ardent royalist in the
Civil War losing his benefice during the Commonwealth, and living
for some time with a mistress, Tomasin Parsons, who was nearly
thirty years younger than he was and with whom he was thought to
have had an illegitimate daughter; by "marry" in "To the Virigins," I
rather doubt he *meant* "marry"; *autre temps, autre moeurs.*

The story ends with Simon's Ash Wednesday sermon and with
Kelly awaiting his return to the choir loft, where the service has
been held, to talk to her after he has finished bidding farewell to the
other parishioners.

It is important in understanding the story to know that Ash
Wednesday is the first day of Lent and always falls forty-six days
before Easter, the commemoration of Christ's crucifixion and resurrection. (The forty weekdays of Lent are devoted to fasting and
penitence in commemoration of Christ's fasting in the wilderness.)
In Roman Catholic churches of the Latin Rite (and High Anglican
churches) this service prepares congregations through prayer, repen-
tance, and self-denial to better appreciate Christ's death and resurrection. Ashes from burned palm crosses of the preceding year's
Palm Sunday are blessed and the officiating priest makes a cross in
ash on the foreheads of worshippers. Ash Wednesday additionally
reminds worshippers of the need to prepare for a holy death.

Simon conducts the service.

"The Lord be with you," he begins.
Together they respond, "And also with you."
"Let us pray."
They lower the kneelers and slump into position.
"Almighty and everlasting God," he reads from the prayer
book, "you despise nothing you have made ... "

Polyp.

" ... Create and make in us new and contrite hearts, that we, worthily lamenting our sins and acknowledging our brokenness ... "

It's there. Inside her. Growing. Right now.

In Simon's sermon, he makes reference to the oratorio written by Paul McCartney, *Ecce Cor Meum*, the title taken from an inscription McCartney found in a church beneath a depiction of the crucifixion. The words in Latin mean Behold My Heart. Simon refers particularly to an interlude in the oratorio that is an elegy for McCartney's wife, Linda, who died of cancer.

Kelly resists Simon's ease and fluency

You're so good at this, Simon. You charm your way through a service. Just the right balance of light and serious. The way you charm your way through a phone call. A lunch.

This entire sequence of Ash Wednesday service is a new take on antiphonal response. Simon preaches; Kelly resists him in her thoughts. This makes, of course, for drama. We are witnessing a silent battle.

As "Still Dark" used Simon's dark study as a stage, most of "Ecce Cor Meum" uses Kelly's mind as a stage. What she is thinking is not presented to us by an omniscient author as "she thought," "she felt," "she was afraid of"—that distancing stance—but rather we are plugged directly into Kelly's mind as she argues, fears, remembers, dreams—the pages are alive with action; that action is her voice. "To the Virgins, to Make Much of Time" and the elegy for Linda McCartney, dead of cancer, are the bookends, as it were, of the story.

Simon concludes his sermon:

"So we can certainly begin Lent by receiving ashes as a reminder that our lifespan is limited. But we shouldn't stop there. We need to go on to acknowledge the thing in our life that most frightens us, most pains us. The thing we are most reluctant to face. It doesn't have to be death, though it can be. It can be the need to confront someone and say, 'You have hurt me.' Which is the first step on the road to forgiveness. Or it can be the need to tell someone that we love them. Whatever it is, I suggest you enter this season of Lent with the intention of saying, in effect, *Ecce cor meum*. Behold my heart."

He goes to the altar rail and picks up the brass bowl. He turns back to them and recites, "We begin our journey to Easter with the sign of ashes, an ancient sign, speaking of the frailty and uncertainty of human life." Then he gestures them forward.

At the close of the service, Kelly sits waiting for Simon's return.

That's the tradition. If you need to talk to the priest, you stay in your pew after the service.

Simon will not be long in saying goodbye to the seven people who have attended the service.

Her eyes fill again. Spill over. It's not dying that she's most afraid of. What she's most afraid of is picking out a valentine with a safe nothing of a message inside. Then deciding not even to send that.

She wipes the wet off her cheeks, then pushes her bangs back off her forehead. Too late, she remembers the ash. Now her fingertips are black. She stares at them.

Then she draws her fingertips down one cheek, then the other.
A sign for Simon.
She hears his footsteps approaching.

Her heart is thumping against her breastbone. She takes in a deep breath. *Ecce cor meum*. Lets it out. *Behold my heart*. Breathes in. *Ecce cor meum*. Out. *Behold my heart*.

And there the story ends. Or doesn't end. Like the ending of "Still Dark," this ending leaves us hanging, Kelly with pounding heart,

Simon's footsteps approaching. And, like the ending of "Still Dark," we are turned back into the story, not released from it.

Had she ended it by revealing "what happened next," the story would have changed its shape entirely, becoming deformed and a much lesser thing, dismissible, a Harlequin "romance."

Throughout this book I have said that the *what* of a story is always less interesting than the *how*, that the how *is* the what. A grimly reductive mind could say that "Ecce Cor Meum" is a story about a neurotic woman who is sexually attracted to her priest. A further aspect of her neurotic anxiety is the fear that she is dying of cancer.

The real life of the story, however, is not in this *what* but in what Kelly sees and hears, in her thoughts and feelings, memories and reflections. The opening scene of the story in Starbucks is full of delights in the way Miller *builds* Kelly. Kelly wants a refill of coffee and wonders if that's the word.

> These places have their own language, and she doesn't come into one often enough to pick it up.
>
> *I don't belong in the world.* She made Simon laugh with that. She'd just handed his Blackberry back to him after examining it. It's true. At some point, it all just started to elude her. Starbucks and Blackberries and iPods and iPads and YouTube. And young female celebrities who all look the same and all seem to be leading the same disastrous life. It all just makes her feel old. At fifty-seven. Meera, the young Hindu woman she works with, asked her the other day if her church forbids cell phones. She couldn't get over the fact that Kelly still doesn't have one. "Anglicans don't really forbid anything," Kelly said. "We just decide we're above it."

So much in Miller's creation of Kelly, so much *going on*.

While Kelly is quelling romantic thoughts of Simon by repeating her mantra: *Create in me a clean heart. And renew a right spirit within me*, she hears a toddler at a table behind her asking the same question over and over.

"Loo lah-bee?" Each time, the mother answers, "When Grandma comes."

Breathe in. *Create in me—*

"Loo lah-bee?"

"When Grandma comes."

Why is this little scene there in the context of words from the *Common Prayer*? Was Miller putting this there as a parody of or commentary on liturgical antiphonal response, a meaningless question and an evasive answer? I felt this quite strongly but didn't want to be assertive without asking Miller's intention. She said that she'd written it simply as part of the "ground" of the story, as accurate and establishing detail, but that what I was feeling was quite possibly a meaning that had been lurking in what she'd written, one of those gifts from the dark, from "the current," that made a fuller kind of sense retroactively.

It's also entirely possible, of course, that she was treating my enquiry with kind diplomacy.

The richness of this story can be better grasped if the reader reads aloud, slows down, or tries various passages as if on a stage or in a recording studio. This might sound absurd, but "Still Dark" and "Ecce Cor Meum" are essentially scripts, acting copies of plays, musical scores; to hear the music is essential to understanding. Best to overcome the embarrassment and accept this; rehearse.

"...the three stories narrated by Raymond Mayhugh in *Litany in Time of Plague*," she wrote in *Writers Talking*, "all gave me a chance to act with my pen—great fun."

More seriously, she wrote:

> I'm told that muscians are encouraged to hum or sing a difficult passage of music they are trying to master. The act of taking the notes in, of becoming their instrument, can break down technical and psychological barriers between player and score.

Sound advice for readers too—"becoming their instrument"; that says so succinctly what I've been trying to suggest.

She went on to say:

> For four years when I was in Vancouver, I was employed by the BC Library Services Branch to tape-record books for the blind. I narrated works by Alice Munro, Margaret Laurence, Margaret Atwood, Marian Engle, Audrey Thomas, Mavis Gallant, and many other authors who were coming into their own in the mid-seventies. Though I didn't realize it then, that job was in large part my training as a writer. Not only was I being exposed to significant new works, but I was acting as their "instrument." I'm still convinced that the best way to appreciate a piece of writing is to read it aloud.

She concluded with:

> Whatever it's all about, it's not about prizes or best-seller lists. (Though I wouldn't turn my nose up at either.) As I confess in my third book, *Holy Writ*, I have a relationship with writing— one that is akin to my relationship with God, and is at the very centre of my life. That makes writing both dangerous and dear. To do it badly—to play safe, take it easy and not let it cost me anything—is to betray what is best in me. But to do it well? That is to stand up naked and turn around very slowly.

A Wholly Unawarranted, Though Pleasurable, Digression.

When I've extolled the pleasures to be found in K.D. Miller's work—most recently in *All Saints*—the reaction has sometimes surprised me.

Anglican like Barbara Pym, do you mean?

Though perhaps I shouldn't have been surprised. As Australian writer Shirley Hazzard put it: "We may now say 'Barbara Pym' and be understood instantly."

My answer has always been that one couldn't make such a comparison, as Pym is a writer of high comedy. Her novels glitter. Miller, though often very funny, is not a comic writer at all. *The Oxford Companion to English Literature*, in an entry so brief as to seem disapproving (possibly on ideological grounds), describes Pym's work as "satirical tragi-comedies of middle class life" containing "distinctive portraits of chuch-going spinsters and charismatic priests; many of the relationships described consist of a kind of celibate flirting."

K.D. Miller's stories confront sadness less obliquely.

The other essential difference between Miller and Pym (setting aside the impossible to set aside—style) is that Pym is writing of and within the baroque intricacies of the British class system, her first books appearing in the fifties before massive social change had weakened the earlier patterns.

The Pym story is simply told. Between 1950 and 1961, she published six novels to a generally delighted critical reception. Her seventh book, *An Unsuitable Attachment*, was rejected by her publishers, Jonathan Cape. They cited low sales figures (three thousand copies or so of each of her previous titles), figures they claimed scarcely allowed them to break even. The villain in the piece seems to have been the newly appointed go-getter editor, Tom Maschler, who favoured, according to Pym, "Ian Fleming and Len Deighton and all the Americans they publish…"

For the next fourteen years she was everywhere rejected.

She was resurrected when, in 1977, *The Times Literary Supplement* (TLS) published a list, chosen by eminent literary figures, of the most over- and underrated writers of the century. Two of the arbiters, quite independently, cited Barbara Pym as the most underrated, the only living writer to be so distinguished. The two eminences were Lord David Cecil and Philip Larkin.

I hope some of the following quotations from reviews may lure a few readers into the Pym world.

When the posthumous *A Very Private Eye: An Autobiography in Diaries and Letters* (Ed. Hazel Holt) appeared in the US, the publisher's advance publicity notice read: "Barbara Pym's novels are so quintessentially English that even English publishers hesitated to put them out."

With her resurgence, parallels were drawn, by some, with Jane Austen.

The poet Anthony Thwaite wrote: "Her characters are all ... meticulously impaled on the delicate pins of a wit that is as scrupulous as it is deadly."

Philip Larkin wrote: "Barbara Pym has a unique eye and ear for the small poignancies and comedies of everyday life."

No Fond Return of Love was reviewed enthusiastically by Siriol Hugh-Jones in the *Tatler*:

> A delicious book, refreshing as mint tea, funny and sad, bitchy and tender-hearted, about what it is like to be a fading lady in her early thirties living in North London and trying to soothe the niggling pangs of disappointed love with hot milky drinks and sensible thinking... I love and admire Miss Pym's pussycat wit and profoundly unsoppy kindliness, and we may leave the deeply peculiar, face-saving, gently tormented English middle classes safely in her hands.

An Unsuitable Attachment, rejected in 1963, remained unpublished until after her death in 1980. Philip Larkin wrote of it in a foreword:

> *An Unsuitable Attachment* now that it is finally before us, clearly belongs to Barbara Pym's first and principal group of novels by reason of its undiminished high spirits. For although the technique and properties of the last books were much the same, there was a somberness about them indicative of the changes that had come to her and her world in fifteen years' enforced silence. Here the old confidence is restored: "Rock salmon—that had a noble sound about it," reflects the vicar, Mark, at the fish and chip shop, buying supper for his wife Sophia and their cat Faustina, and the reader is back among their self-service lunches and parish bazaars and the innumerable tiny absurdities to be found there. It is perhaps the most solidly "churchy" of her books: Mark and Sophia in their North London vicarage are at its centre, and the Christian year—Harvest Thanksgiving, Lent and Easter—provide both its frame and background. "One never knew who might turn up in Church on Sunday," Sophia thinks,

and it is this kind of adventitious encounter that once again sets her narrative moving.

(The possibly abstruse humour in the unworldly Vicar's reflection, "Rock Salmon—that had a noble sound about it," lies in the fact that "rock salmon" was the name invented to foist upon fish-and-chip shop patrons the flesh of a small species of shark known as Dogfish.)

Quintessential Pym for me, lines I find exquisitely funny, are these from *A Few Green Leaves*.

> "Do you see many foxes here?" Isobel asked.
>
> "Oh yes—and you can find their traces in the woods," said Daphne eagerly. "Did you know that a fox's dung is grey and pointed at both ends?"
>
> Nobody did know and there was a brief silence. It seemed difficult to follow such a stunning piece of information.
>
> "How fascinating!" said Adam at last. "That's something I did *not* know, I must look out for it when I next take a walk in the woods."

Some of her diary entries I also find quite unforgettable:

> Mr. C in the Library—he is having his lunch, eating a sandwich with a knife and fork, a glass of milk at hand. Oh *why* can't I write about things like that any more—why is this kind of thing no longer acceptable?

> To Dr. S. He told me about a pacemaker... which must be removed at death as it is likely to explode in the crematorium. (He said I could use it in a book.)

> Lunched at the Golden Egg. Oh, the horror—the cold stuffiness, claustrophobic placing of tables, garish lights and mass produced food in steel dishes. And the egg-shaped menu! But perhaps one could get something out of it. The setting for a breaking-off, or some terrible news or an unwanted declaration of love.

It is horrible to imagine how she bore the fifteen unjust years of imposed silence, crushingly sad that she did not live long enough to see her career, her life, vindicated in the glowing reviews *An Unsuitable Attachment* received on its publication in the United States.

> The publisher must have been mad to reject this jewel. The cut-glass elegance of her precise, understated wit sparkles, her understanding of the human heart gleams more softly but just as bright.
>
> *Washington Post*

> *An Unsuitable Attachment* is a paragon of a novel, certainly one of her best; witty, elegant, suggesting beyond the miniature exactness the vast panorama of a vanished civilization.
>
> *New York Times*

...beyond the miniature exactness the vast panorama of a vanished civilization—how *profoundly* the reviewer engaged with Barbara Pym's book.

To end this meander on a lighter note, of the two eminences who salvaged Barbara Pym's career, Philip Larkin is surely known to all. Or should be. The other *arbiter elegantiae* is less widely known. Lord Edward Christian David Gascoyne Cecil was Goldsmiths' Professor of English literature at Oxford from 1948-69. He is noted for books on the poet Cowper, on Lord Melbourne, Thomas Hardy, Jane Austin, and Charles Lamb. His lectures drew considerable attention. His lisping, class-throttled accent and eccentricities of delivery left an indelible impression.

Kingsley Amis butted heads rather with Lord David during the oral defence of his B. Litt thesis and Cecil's made-to-measure feathers were ruffled; the degree was not granted. Amis was advised by friendlier academics that rewriting the thesis would be futile because if Lord David were hissy he would ensure that he again chaired the thesis defence committee with the conclusion foregone.

The desired degree would doubtless have been described by Philip Larkin and Amis himself (along with *Beowulf, Trolius and*

Criseyde, and *The Faerie Queene*) as "ape's bumfodder," but it would have been useful in job applications and, down the years, Lord David's rebuff rankled.

Many years later, Amis took revenge in his *Memoirs*, performing in print one of the deadly impersonations for which he was famous, Lord David Cecil at the lectern.

> For much of male Oxford, especially undergraduate Oxford, Lord David was a bit of a joke, one with a touch of lower-middle-class resentment often lurking in it. It was not so much the dramatic, Leslie-Howard good looks, nor even the clothes, which were not particularly extravagant, but mannerisms, the mobile head and floating hands, and above all the *voice*. John Wain got a lot of both matter and manner with his imitation (appropriated by me without acknowledgement until now) of the opening of a standard Cecil lecture: "Laze... laze and gentlemen, when we say a man looks like a poet... dough mean... looks like Chauthah ... dough mean ... looks like Dyyden.... Dough mean ... looks like *Theck-thpyum* (or something else barely recognizable as "Shakespeare")... Mean looks like Shelley (pronounced "Thellem" or thereabouts). Matthew Arnold (then prestissimo) called Shelley beautiful ineffectual angel Matthew Arnold had face (rallentando) like a *horth*. But my subject this morning is not the poet Shelley. Jane... Austen...

Lisa Moore

Short Story Collections: *Degrees of Nakedness* (1995) and *Open* (2002).

Novels: *Alligator* (2005), *February* (2010), *Caught* (2013), and *Flannery* (2016).

In *Writers Talking* Moore wrote:

> A fully-formed story is a rare occurrence for me. I keep a daily journal, switching from the computer to a hard-cover black notebook throughout the day. The journal is full of dialogue, dreams, images, gestures and scenes. It's a journal of impressions rather

than facts. My fiction almost always develops from these notes. I write the journal without looking for any cohesion or theme, though over a two-month period I usually find the material has an internal order that can become a short story. I have a kind of illogical belief that certain images are magic, super-saturated with meaning. I write fast in my journal because I want to sneak up on those moments and snag them before I know what I'm doing. Too much scrutiny at this stage can make things fusty.

In further discussion of images—absolutely central to her work— she goes on to say:

Recently I have been learning to edit video on my computer at home. A shot of my daughter and me in a vaulted alleyway in France. We're holding hands and spinning in a circle, our hair flying out behind us. I try cutting the speed halfway through the spin so when our feet hit the pavement the sound is distorted, drawn out, a reverberating *thwack*. It takes more than an hour to edit less than half a minute. Around one o'clock in the morning when vibrant, frenetic pixels have implanted themselves onto my retina for good, it occurs to me that the written word is dead. That a hundred years from now the image will have taken over. The language of images will proliferate and evolve at a tremendous speed. The video blur on the screen in front of me—a splash of orange shirt, the blue shutters—all a swarming mass of tiny pixels seems to be far more *living*, more full of possibility than anything I could write. One frame of video contains so much detail. It would require several pages of writing to capture what the eye devours in a second. At one in the morning, writing seems destined to lose its privileged position as a form of communication.

But she then reverses her position:

Norman Levine, in an interview with Michael Winter, once said the less a writer gives the reader the better. Levine is referring to what McLuhan calls a cool medium: a medium in which the audience does most of the work. The reader is a fully engaged participant in the act of creation. It's that ambiguity, or coolness, that draws me primarily to writing rather than to the visual arts in the end.

Lisa Moore creates stories by the accretion and juxtaposition of images; the difference between us is that she is far more radical. Sometimes it is not immediately clear what the images add up to; my experience of her work suggests that meanings will emerge if the reader stops trying to intellectualize the work, if the reader absorbs the full impact of each building block rather than trying immediately to articulate a meaning for the whole structure. Lisa Moore does not travel in straight lines.

Here's the sort of thing she means. From "Haloes":

There's a photograph of the house my parents built together when it was just a skeleton. Blond two-by-fours like a rib-cage around a lungful of sky. They worked back to back shifts in the restaurant they sold before I was born. The house was built on the weekends. I never once heard my parents make love, or saw them naked together. But the photograph of the two-by-fours is like walking in on them, unexpected. The house without its skin. Their life together raw, still to come.

Or this from "Ingrid Catching Snowflakes on Her Tongue":

I like sitting on the staircase listening to our house. The gravelly voice of the coffee maker in the kitchen, something metal turning over in the dryer, the ebbing of canned laughter from behind a bedroom door on the third floor. Mike's daughter Mary rubbing against the tub, flaccid splashes. The house is a skeleton and our moods surge along the wiring, spilling through the pipes, circulating like currents of heat. Living under the same roof with someone else shapes you both, the way liquid takes the shape of its container.

Sometimes her images are almost surreal:

When Mike and I make love, a blush comes into his cheeks and the tips of his ears. That's my private colour for him, almost plum. The first time we were together we were behind the row housing under criss-crossing clotheslines, white shirts laughing with their bellies. We were drunk and his tongue in my ear sounded like a pot of mussels boiling, the shells opening, the salty shells clicking off one another, a riot of tiny noises. I got the flu. He made a pot of tea: cinnamon, cloves, apple and orange chunks. The next day we made love in his new house, empty of furniture except for a couch, covered with satiny parakeets, belonging to the former owners. Streetlight poured in. A plastic bag of chicken breasts glowed on the floor where I'd dropped it.

It's of considerable interest to me that Lisa Moore has been reading Norman Levine and has been influenced by his experimentation in the story form. She is already, in her first book, beginning to abandon conventional punctuation in the search for intensity, immediacy. The influence of Norman Levine must date to 1993, when the Porcupine's Quill re-published *From a Seaside Town* and *Canada Made Me* and sent Norman on a reading tour of the Maritimes. While in St. John's, Norman was interviewed by Michael Winter, editor of the literary magazine *Tickle Ace*, a meeting which seems, over the years, to have had significant ramifications.

The interview with Lisa Moore in *Writers Talking* was conducted by Claire Wilkshire, writer and fellow-member of the fiction collective *The Burning Rock*.

Addendum (written some seven years after the foregoing.)
In "Rings within Rings", an interview with Leesa Dean which appeared in *The New Quarterly* No. 133 (Winter 2015), Lisa Moore and Leesa Dean talk about Lisa's time at the Nova Scotia College of Art and Design.

In *Alligator*, for example, she wanted to create something that would, like Jackson Pollock painting, resemble a portrait without a singular focal point. "Pollock would lay a huge canvas on the floor and just throw paint on it," she explained. "Usually in the composition of a painting you have highlights and colour, things that draw the eye around the canvas so that your eye is moving all the time between these points of interest. But Pollock was creating a kind of flatness where there was no particular point of interest. All of the squiggles of paint were the same. Because the image was the same all over, it almost gave the sense of going on to infinity." Her desire was to mimic Pollock's technique by creating what she called "a democratic portrait of St John's, displayed from several vantage points."

The connection between Pollock and portrait seems to me at best muddy and while formal experimentation interests me, I think the desire to mimic in language Pollock's adventures in paint is foredoomed; one cannot spatter words over a huge canvas because words, stubbornly, convey reference while paint is innocent.

I would offer mildly the criticism that Lisa Moore is sometimes trapped by her delight in pictures and surfaces, a painter's delight, and insufficiently marshals these pictures to serve a driving narrative and emotional purpose. This probably explains why the endings of some stories seem unresolved or not to have emerged inevitably from the body of the story. The reader comes to feel too often that she seems to be walking aimlessly, no real destination in mind; this was exactly the criticism John Updike levelled at the stories of Sylvia Townsend Warner.

The novels that have followed the two story collections have deepened my unease.

Alex Good seems to share my unease. In *Revolutions: Essays on Contemporary Canadian Fiction*: "... Moore sometimes has three of four wonderful sentences on a single page. That she can have three or four awful sentences *on the same page* is something I have no good explanation for."

Alice Munro

Short Story Collections: *Dance of the Happy Shades* (1968), *Something I've Been Meaning to Tell You* (1974), *Who Do You Think You Are?* (1978), *The Moons of Jupiter* (1982), *The Progress of Love* (1986), *Friend of My*

Youth (1990), *Open Secrets* (1994), *The Love of a Good Woman* (1998), *Hateship Friendship Courtship Loveship Marriage* (2001), *Runaway* (2004), *The View from Castle Rock* (2006), *Alice Munro's Best Selected Stories* (2006), *Too Much Happiness* (2009), *Dear Life* (2012), and *Family Furnishings: Selected Stories 1995-2014* (2014).

Novels: *Lives of Girls and Women* (1971).

I would urge on readers all these individual titles.

"The finest writer of short stories working in the English language today." *The Times* (UK).

"That Munro is a great writer of short stories should go without saying. She is also one of the two or three best writers of fiction (of any length) now alive." *Sunday Times* (UK).

"… quite possibly the greatest short story writer at work today." *Daily Telegraph*.

"She is one of those few living writers who, in the way of the greats, must simply be read." *The Globe and Mail*.

I've chosen to reprint the following essay on Munro's "Walker Brothers Cowboy" because many readers have mentioned how helpful they had found it. I wrote it for my critical anthology *Writers in Aspic* (1988).

I could just as easily have honoured Monro by writing about other great favourites of mine such as "Royal Beatings," "White Dump," "The Moons of Jupiter," or "Meneseteung" but the latter story has had over a dozen essays written on it and three by J.R. "Tim" Struthers in the American journal *Short Story*, a special issue he guest-edited in Spring 2013.

I also wanted to direct attention to "Walker Brothers Cowboy" because I feel that much lip service is paid to Munro and often without much real understanding. The "companion piece" to "Walker Brothers Cowboy" is the story in *Dance* called "Images."

In her book, *Mothers and Other Clowns: The Stories of Alice Munro* (1992), a book apparently much respected in academic circles, Magdalene Redekop, associate professor in the English Department at Victoria College, University of Toronto, wrote of the story "Images":

The first time I read this story I assumed that the mother was dying and many of my students made the same assumption. There is an ambiguity in the story: the mother could as easily be dying as giving birth.

There is no ambiguity whatsoever.

If an associate professor at the University of Toronto and the flower of Canada's youth can so misread a story from Alice Munro's first book, an engagement with her earliest work does not seem to me redundant.

The Signs of Invasion
Alice Munro's "Images"

In my 1972 anthology, *The Narrative Voice*, Munro recorded that a Toronto critic had said that the roofed-over cellar in "Images," home to the eccentric and delusional Joe Phippen, "symbolized death, of course, and burial, and that it was a heavy, gloomy sort or story because there was nothing to symbolize resurrection." Munro went on to vehemently deny all this, saying, "So I get to say, don't I, whether a house in the ground is death and burial or whether it is, of all unlikely things, *a house in the ground?*"

Professor Magdalene Redekop, Professor (now, thank God, Emerita) wrote of the house in *Mothers and Other Clowns: The Stories of Alice Munro* (1992), "The journey leads to Joe Phippen's underground house, to a place of shadows that suggests primordial depths, Plato's cave, and 'fairy stories.'"

WHAT!

"Primordial" means "existing at or from the beginning of time" and the depths of Joe's cellar were probably twelve to fifteen feet.

How Plato got in there defeats speculation.

Set against this claptrap, the stub-your-toe realness of Del Jordan's wondering eye "pretending not to look at anything"; "several thick, very dirty blankets of the type used in sleighs and to cover horses"; "the terrible smell of coal oil, urine, earth and stale, heavy air," and the Christmas candies Joe gives her, "which seemed to have melted then hardened again, so the coloured stripes had run. They had a taste of nails."

Professor Redekop is a professional obscurator, a tiresome word-chopper, who seems unable to tell the difference between Hades and a hole in the ground.

In very brief summary, "Images" is set up into four sections, sections I think of as movements in the musical sense of the word. The first opens in the present with conversation between the child, Del Jordan, and Mary McQuade. The child pretends not to recognize her because "It seemed the wisest thing to do." Mary McQuade responds by saying, "If you don't remember me you don't remember much," adding, "I bet you never went to your Grandma's house last summer. I bet you don't remember that either."

Those opening lines leave us with the question of why it seemed to the child "the wisest thing to do" to not recognize Mary.

The story then moves back to the previous year and Del's grandfather dying under the care and supervision of Mary McQuade. The connection in the child's mind between Mary and death is established. The story then moves back into the present of the first six lines with the reappearance of Mary, who is now tending Del's very pregnant mother. The child is suspicious and fearful "trying to understand the danger, to read the signs of invasion." Part of the danger in the child's mind is not just the association of Mary with death but the closeness of her father with Mary.

In the second section of the story, Del accompanies her father as he checks his trapline. Joe Phippen appears carrying an axe and, unseen by Ben, stalks closer and closer. Del "never thought, or even hoped for, anything but the worst." Ben talks to Joe in a kindly, calming way until Joe gradually recognizes him. He leads them back to his roofed-over cellar, his house in the ground, where Del listens to the talk and watches wide-eyed as Joe's sullen tomcat laps whiskey from a saucer. Joe rants about "them Silases" who, he claims, persecute him and aim to "burn me and my bed." Eventually, the child falls asleep on the filthy couch.

The third section of the story recounts the journey home, Ben carrying Del part of the way. He sets her down at a point where she can see their home half a mile away below them. She does not at first recognize it. Ben instructs her about what she must not mention when they get there.

The final brief section shows them, with Mary, at the supper table. Del's father "looked steadily down the table at [her]" and "dazed and powerful with secrets, I never said a word."

The story is wonderfully rich in its physical detail, a Christmas pudding of a story, *stuffed* with sixpences, yet in its narrative line, presented in images, it is as delicately precise and graceful as a wine glass held to the light.

Professor Redekop wrote of "Images":

> There is an ambiguity in the story: the mother could as easily be dying as giving birth.

There is, of course, no ambiguity whatsoever.

It is not stated that the girl-narrator's mother is pregnant but we are presented early enough in the story with the facts that the mother is in bed and that the family has shipped in a cousin, Mary McQuade, who is a Practical Nurse, to care for her. Were she dying, the adults presumably would not have carried on family life with such coarse joviality and horseplay, and Del would not have been allowed onto the bed to pester her for attention.

We are offered a scene early on that spells out the situation.

> My mother's hair was done in two little thin dark braids, her cheeks were sallow, her neck warm and smelling of raisins as it always did, but the rest of her under the covers had changed into some large, fragile and mysterious object, difficult to move. She spoke of herself gloomily in the third person, saying, "Be careful, don't hurt Mother, don't sit on Mother's legs."
>
> Given over to Mary's care, she whimpered childishly, "Mary, I'm dying for you to rub my back." "Mary, could you make me a

cup of tea? I feel if I drink any more tea I'm going to bob up to the ceiling, just like a big balloon, but you know it's all I want." Mary laughed shortly. "You," she said, "You're not going to bob up any-where. Take a derrick to move *you*. Come on now, raise up, you'll be worse before you're better!" She shooed me off the bed and began to pull the sheets about with not very gentle jerks.

Mary McQuade's bracing comments and laughter leave no room for "ambiguity" in our understanding. To be plonking, if we can't grasp "large, fragile and mysterious object," "like a big balloon," "derrick," and "worse before you're better!" we'd be better to spare students our guidance.

At the same time, it is equally obvious that the girl *is* thinking about death and danger, and about the possible connection of child-birth with death, and the connection of Mary McQuade with death and the threatening nearness of Mary McQuade with her father. It's a mix-up. It is not that she doesn't *know* her mother is pregnant and what that means. Obviously she knows. What the story deals with is what the child *feels* about the whole situation and what she feels need not make adult sense.

We are presented with *how* this guarded child is feeling through—no surprise—images. Though it *was* a surprise in 1967–8 in Canada. It was so surprising as to be revolutionary, Canada having been largely oblivious of modernism and still dwelling in Jalna.

After the opening exchanges with Mary in time-present, the story goes back to time-past, the previous summer at Grandma's house. The images suggest what the child can't articulate; the job of composition is left up to us.

Her grandfather has withdrawn to the largest front bedroom, where he lies in bed in the shuttered gloom, "with his white hair, now washed and tended and soft as a baby's," cared for by Mary McQuade. The child is put to sleep in a crib "not at home but this was what was kept for me at my grandma's house." Most of what the child feels, rather than can articulate, is conveyed by the repeti-tions and play of *white* and *dark*, *black* and *white*, *hot* and *cold*, *bright* and *dull* and allusions to *babies*.

To hammer this out: the grandfather's *white* hair "soft as a baby's," *crib* (twice) *"white* night shirt and pillows" making a white island in the "near-darkness. Sitting in the "near darkness" (with the meaning of "nearly," "almost" *and* "soon to happen") Mary McQuade in her *white* uniform who "waited and breathed." So the two islands of whiteness in the near-darkness are Mary McQuade and the dying grandfather.

(How *clever* is "waited and breathed"; Mary, still alive, breathing, waiting for cessation of the old man's breath but *also*, in one word, suggesting the total, awful silence in the room, so quiet one can her breathing.)

No wonder that the child "pretended not to remember" Mary, that not remembering "seemed the wisest thing to do."

The world outside the grandfather's room is a world of life and light. In her room, "the dazzle of outdoors—all the flat fields round the house turned, in the sun, to the brilliance of water-made light-ning cracks in the drawn-down blinds."

The tension-building play of white and black culminates in this:

> … the ceilings of the rooms were very high and under them was a great deal of dim wasted space, and when I lay in my crib too hot to sleep I could look up and see that emptiness, the stained corners, and feel, without knowing what it was, just what every-body else in the house must have felt—under the sweating heat the fact of death-contained, that little lump of magic ice. And Mary McQuade waiting in her starched white dress, big and gloomy as an iceberg herself, implacable, waiting and breathing. I held her responsible.

Writers working in the lyric mode tend to produce writing that operates on two levels simultaneously. There is the surface level of conventional writing—informative, denotative, narrative—and then there is a level beneath the surface level that tells the story again, simultaneously, but in connotative emotional terms by a series of repeated words (and variations on them) and by details that rein-force that dominant feeling. The second, lower level is the emotional "blood," as it were, of the obvious flesh; it is, as it were, the story in shorthand.

If you now went back over the quotations and underlined *dim*, *crib*, *hot*, *emptiness*, *stained*, *heat*, *dark*, *baby*, *ice*, *white*, and *iceberg*, you would be following the emotional narrative, quite possibly unconsciously, but your feelings would be manipulated.

This idea, this aspect of craft, is so important to understanding how this story in particular works and how many stories in general work, that I'll illustrate it again by a passage in Alice Petersen's story "Nothing to Lose" in *Worldly Goods*, a passage fresh in my mind as I was working with her recently.

Constance, in her story, is employed in a wool shop that has three half-mannequins of female figures in the window that are dressed, seasonally, in the differing garments Constance has knitted. Her employer, the shop's owner, Rory Leggelt, proposes to her—after she has worked there seven years and just before she is off to Venice for a holiday—that she take a percentage, become a partner in the shop, and that she knit *him* an argyle sweater as a token of her commitment. She feels dubious about what "commitment" might entail.

In Venice, she enjoys her holiday and has a friendly little affair with a large Australian she meets. On the morning after her return to Montreal, she approaches the shop to report for work.

> There had been no perceptible change in the weather in the week since Constance had been away from Montreal. Even though it was September, the dry city sidewalks waited to burn in the fresh shadows of morning. Constance caught a whiff of rot from the alleyway behind the charcuterie. A row of lanterns in punched-out metal had been strung up along the front of Amelle's shop but the same birdcages still hung in a cluster around the door.
>
> There was one new thing. The graffiti artist had finished painting the wall across the road from the wool shop. The yellow bricks had become home to a sea-green girl with wistful eyes the size of dinner plates and hair that streamed down the wall towards the alleyway like the tentacles of a great, yearning octopus.

The lights changed again and still Constance hesitated to cross the road to the wool shop. She sighed, knowing that Rory Leggelt was standing behind the shop door, peering out between the silhouettes of the half-women, waiting for an answer about percentages and the argyle sweater.

She knew that after she passed through the shop door it would shut fast behind her with a sound that went *thlock*. And the cold air would blow and she would feel quite drained, as if she were wearing only her slip.

And if at that moment, instead of watching her through the glass, Rory had opened the door; if he had only spoken her name through the morning air, she might have gone across to him and willingly entered the shop, closing the door behind her. She would have made a loop and wound the yarn around her finger, casting on over a hundred stitches before beginning the voyage, to and fro, up the length of his back to his shoulders.

Instead, and Rory Leggelt was forever puzzled as to why, for she never sent as much as a postcard to explain herself, Constance moved off down the alleyway, passing along under the wave of the green girl's hair and into the shade of a small-leaved acacia...

Again, if you went back over the passage and underlined *dry, burn, shadows, whiff, rot punched-out, strung-up, cages, hung, tentacles, half-women, thlock, shut fast, cold air, blow, drained, closing the door behind her, wound the yarn, voyage, to and fro*, you are revealing the story's emotional pattern.

The final sentence, of course, reverses the pattern so that Constance passes below the graffiti girl whose hair is no longer seen as capturing and imprisoning "tentacles," but as a "wave," and onto pavement not "dry" or "burning" but in "shade."

And I am only skimming the surface of Petersen's story. Earlier, and not at that point lodging in our conscious mind, it is revealed that Constance has a ridge on her finger, a callous raised by knitting.

I think of these links of significant words as the *shadow-narrative* or *the underlay*; the "prose" story proceeds on one level, an "informational" level, while simultaneously the *shadow-narrative* carries the richness of meaning, the "poetic" level. The pulp of the fruit, and its essence, the juice.

The really interesting question is whether writers do this consciously or unconsciously; I tend to think that in the first burst of rough work the process is largely unconscious but in the rewriting the patterns are recognized and deliberately worked, though I can speak only of my own practice.

"Images" starts, then, from the child's memory of her grandfather's dying and what she saw as the agency in this of the white-clad Mary McQuade, "waiting in her starched white dress, big and gloomy as an iceberg herself, implacable, waiting and breathing. I held her responsible."

The word "implacable"—meaning "that cannot be appeased," "inexorable"—is so authoritatively placed; it stops the flowing of the sentence with its commas and with the strong stresses of its pronunciation.

As the story moves into the present, the small Del Jordan decides that pretending not to recognize Mary McQuade "seemed the wisest thing to do," even if Mary was not wearing her starched white uniform; that it didn't make her less dangerous and might merely mean that "the time of her power had not yet come."

It's difficult to be precise about Del's age in the story but I would imagine somewhere around five and a half, or six, still young enough to be thinking magically.

Del fears and dislikes Mary McQuade on all levels; she dislikes her smell, which she associates with sickness, with "a preparation rubbed on my chest when I had a cold." There is a nasty taste, too, in all the food Mary McQuade cooks and even perhaps "in all food eaten in her presence."

Del "doubted that she was asked to come. She came, and cooked what she liked and rearranged things to suit herself, complaining about draughts, and let her power loose in the house. If she had never come my mother would never have taken to her bed."

And then there's something new in the air that Del's aware of but is unable to define. She keeps it under observation.

"My father, too, had altered since her coming."

"His teasing of Mary was always about husbands."

"...all these preposterous imagined matings..."

The horseplay between them: he throws at her, but misses, a fork she has deliberately given him, a fork with a broken tine; in retaliation, she chucks the dishrag at him. Of which horseplay, the ludicrous Redekop writes:

> The narrator's father is the victim of Mary McQuade's practical jokes and their pattern of interaction is consistent with what anthropologists know of the relation between permission to joke and kinship structures.

Well, glad we got *that* cleared up.

Del doesn't know what all this horseplay might mean but sees it as a threat. It is almost as if she and Mary are in a contest for Ben's affections. I don't think it perverse to suggest an unconscious sexual rivalry on Del's part.

> At supper-time it was dark in the house, in spite of the lengthening days. We did not yet have electricity. It came in soon afterwards, maybe the next summer. But at present there was a lamp on the table. In its light my father and Mary McQuade threw gigantic shadows, whose heads wagged clumsily with their talk and laughing. I watched the shadows instead of the people. They said "What are you dreaming about?" but I was not dreaming, I was trying to understand the danger, to read the signs of invasion.

In this last paragraph of the story's first section, the first sentence—"At supper-time it was dark in the house, in spite of the lengthening days"—is not padding or intended as meteorological information; it points up that, despite natural expectation of increasing light, the house is still dark; it strengthens the feeling of affairs being unusual, unnatural. It is preparing us for "gigantic shadows," monster heads, ogres, as are "dark" and "shadows," which hark back to the dying grandfather in the darkened room. It is, if you like, the film's musical soundtrack, the "underlay."

Before looking at the story's second section, I'd like to comment on some of the beauties of Alice Munro's writing, the magic of her detail. Ben Jordan's family background: "uncles broke wind in public and said, 'Whoa, hold on there!' proud of themselves as if they'd whistled a complicated tune."

Those farting uncles remind me—very Munro, this—of Rose in "Royal Beatings" (*Who Do You Think You Are?*) provoking and luring her unwise younger brother, Brian, into singing in Flo's presence,

Two Vancouvers fried in snot!

Two pickled arseholes tied in a knot!

Under Mary's influence, Ben reverts to family ways "eating heaps of fried potatoes and side meat and thick floury pies."

("Side meat," a word probably only used now in rural Canada and America, meaning fried salt pork. Munro's work treasures and celebrates these words from a fading or lost rural past; she is custodian, curator.)

Ben's boots are a vivid caricature of their owner.

His boots were to me as unique and familiar, as much an index to himself as his face was. When he had taken them off they stood in a corner of the kitchen, giving off a complicated smell of manure, machine oil, caked black mud, and the ripe and disintegrating material that lined their soles. They were a part of himself, temporarily discarded, waiting. They had an expression that was dogged and uncompromising, even brutal, and I thought of that as part of my father's look, the counterpart of his face, with its readiness for jokes and courtesies. Nor did that brutality surprise me; my father came back to us always, to my mother and me, from places where our judgment could not follow.

What an extraordinary piece of writing! It demands many re-readings; it is prose reaching towards poetry.

When I was writing about Mary Borsky's *Influence of the Moon* I called attention to "luminous and holy detail," in her work, the child's-eye reception and apprehension of the physical world. Alice Munro's work is filled with "holy detail," though some of it is invented rather than remembered; in the essay "The Colonel's Hash Resettled," quoted in the "Precious Particle" chapter, she mentions specifically that she never accompanied her father on his trapline, that Mary McQuade was pure invention. But memory and invention are more or less the same thing; invention rises out of the deep pool of memory and emotion and is simply an emotional extension of what is actually remembered. Munro herself has said that these inventions were not exactly inventions so much as things she "found," that is to say, found in her head, gifts from the dark. And whether actual memory or found, "it is all deeply perfectly true to me, as a dream might be true."

And with those words, we reach the area many writers do not wish to probe or discuss, the magic place; this is what I was talking about in the "Precious Particle" chapter when I wrote of "the power, the mystery, the joy of the birth of images from the dark." Alice Munro does not like talking about inspiration or technique and usually smilingly deflects queries, professing ignorance, often saying "I don't really think about that kind of thing." She does, of course, and around the time of the publication of *Dance of the Happy Shades* we often talked technique. She also pretends to be much less widely read than she is, another of her Keep Out! tactics.

In the "Colonel's Hash" essay she did go some way towards explaining herself:

> There is a sort of treachery to innocent objects—to houses, chairs, dressers, dishes, and to roads, fields, landscapes—which a writer removes from their natural, dignified obscurity, and sets down in print. There they lie, exposed, often shabbily treated, inadequately, badly, clumsily transformed. Once I've done that to things, I lose them from my private memory.

She fears abstraction and "the intellect's eagerness to foreclose." That "magic place" and its gifts is one of the crucial sticking points in discussing literature; one either grasps what she means by "treachery" to chairs and dishes, to the "holiness" of *things*, or one does not. I'm reminded of the probably apocryphal response of Louis Armstrong to a lady who asked him what jazz *was*: "Lady," he is alleged to have replied, "if you've got to ask, you're never gonna know."

The second section, or movement, of the story recounts the day on the trapline and the advent of Joe Phippen with his axe. Father and daughter set out and their walking is captured in the wonderful sentence, "My father's boots went ahead."

This conjures up the little girl plodding behind. In the struggle over the uneven and frozen ploughed earth, bent forward with effort, head down, no time to look around, the world narrowed to the relentless boots ahead, boots she must not let down by showing weakness.

(Often in Alice Munro's work, one is halted by a sentence that expresses something in such a compressed manner, so precisely, that regardless of context, it gives a jolt of pleasure in her technical mastery and an expanding aesthetic delight as one realizes how perfectly, how absolutely, the sentence exists.

"My father's boots went ahead."

Another such sentence a little later in the story; Joe Phippen with his axe: "'Ben Jordan,' the man said with a great splurt, a costly effort, like somebody leaping over a stutter."

"Splurt" is likely Munro's invention but is obviously forged from "sputter" and "spurt" and possibly "splurge." "Costly effort" and "like somebody leaping over a stutter" use these *physical* difficulties in speaking to express Joe's *mental* slowness in recognition and mental difficulty in formulating his slowly dawning comprehension. In other words, Joe doesn't stutter; his brain does.

I can't remember quite this kind of thing in a lifetime of reading. What joy to luxuriate in such a sentence.)

Father and daughter at the riverside. When Ben shows her the drowned rat in his trap and explains that its death had been merciful, "I did not understand or care. I only wanted, but did not dare, to touch the stiff, soaked body, a fact of death."

The advent of Joe Phippen with his murderous axe is foreshadowed by the narrative's "underlay"; forgive my, by now, obvious italics.

Ben's "skinning knife, its *slim light blade.*" The Wawanash River, "*silver* in the middle where the *sun hit it* and where it *arrowed* in to its swiftest motion. That is the current, I thought, and I pictured the current as something separate from the water, just as the wind was separate from the air and had its own *invading shape.*"

(Notice that "invading" is a deliberate echoing of the earlier, "I was trying to understand the danger, to read the signs of invasion.")

Joe's axe "*gleaming* where the *sun caught it.*"

I wouldn't be wildly surprised if the idea of "current" carried over to "as if *struck* by *lightning*" and "like a child in an old *negative electrified* against the *dark noon sky* with *blazing* hair and *burned-out* Orphan Annie eyes" in the paragraph quoted below—actually I feel certain that this is the case but won't insist as I have a horror of setting even a foot in Redekop territory.

Del's reaction to Joe's silent closing-in on her father:

> People say they have been paralyzed by fear, but I was transfixed, as if struck by lightning, and what hit me did not feel like fear so much as recognition. I was not surprised. This is the sight that does not surprise you, the thing you have always known was there that comes so naturally, moving delicately and contentedly and in no hurry, as if it was made, in the first place, from a wish of yours, a hope of something final, terrifying. All my life I had known there was a man like this and he was behind doors, around the corner at the dark end of a hall. So now I saw him and just waited, like a child in an old negative, electrified against the dark noon sky, with blazing hair and burned-out Orphan Annie eyes. The man slipped down through the bushes to my father. And I never thought, or even hoped for, anything but the worst.

(This passage gains a strange rhetorical power from the switch from the past tense in the first sentence to the present tense in the fourth.)

"All my life I had known there was a man like this..." It's been a very short little life, so how was Del so "knowledgeable" about death? Natural nightlight-fears explain some of it, but we must also cast back to the stories her mother used to tell her before becoming Mother, stories about the murder of the "Princes in the Tower and a queen getting her head chopped off while a little dog was hiding under her dress and another queen sucking poison out of her husband's wound; and also about her own childhood, a time as legendary to me as any other."

These ancient murders were events not differentiated in the child's mind from the equally distant tales of her mother's childhood and so became for the child unsurprising expectations in her own life. This foreshadowing early in the story can't, of course, be grasped as such at first reading.

Ben talks to Joe in a matter-of-fact way while really caressing him, gentling him like a spooked horse, until Joe recognizes him. With writerly skill, Munro uses the conversation between the men not only to navigate a tense, dramatic moment in the narrative but also to sketch in Ben's essential kindness and courtesy. Joe, disarmed, as it were, leads them back to his roofed-over cellar.

Del sits on the dirty couch "pretending not to look at anything" but wide-eyed. Joe pulls out from behind the stove where it's been hiding the huge tomcat with "sullen eyes" and, to entertain his guests, pours something from a Mason jar into its saucer.

"Joe," says Ben "that cat don't drink whiskey, does he?"

(The Mason jar, as container, immediately tells Ben that the liquid is bootleg whiskey and probably, in proof, near-lethal. Mason jars were, and are, the standard-size containers for moonshine, another fading rural custom.)

The cat laps up the saucerful and then walks away "sideways" as Del sits listening as Joe rants about his phantasmagorical enemies, the Silases, and demonstrates, with a blow from his axe that splits the rotten oilcloth on his table, what he will do to these persecutors. Ben "said nothing but tested the axe blade with his finger." We are intended to imagine, I feel, that the edge is blunt.

Eventually, "Overcome with tiredness, with warmth after cold, with bewilderment quite past bearing, I was falling asleep with my eyes open." So ends the second movement of the story.

The Canadian Short Story

The third section demands especially careful reading, and for that reason it's necessary to quote it in its entirety.

> My father set me down. "You're woken up now. Stand up. See. I can't carry you and this sack of rats both."
>
> We had come to the top of a long hill and that is where I woke. It was getting dark. The whole basin of country drained by the Wawanash River lay in front of us—greenish brown smudge of bush with the leaves not out yet and evergreens, dark, shabby after winter, showing through, straw-brown fields and the others, darker from last year's plowing, with scales of snow faintly striping them (like the field we had walked across hours, hours earlier in the day) and tiny fences and colonies of grey barns, and houses set apart, looking squat and small.
>
> "Whose house is that?" my father said, pointing.
>
> It was ours, I knew it after a minute. We had come around in a half-circle and there was the side of the house that nobody saw in winter, the front door that went unopened from November to April and was still stuffed with rags around its edges, to keep out the east wind.
>
> "That's no more'n half a mile away and downhill. You can easily walk home. Soon we'll see the light in the dining room where your Momma is."
>
> On the way I said, "Why did he have an axe?"
>
> "Now listen," my father said. "Are you listening to me? He don't mean any harm with that axe. It's just his habit, carrying it around. But don't say anything about it at home. Don't mention it to your Momma or Mary, either one. Because they might be scared about it. You and me aren't but they might be. And there is no use of that."
>
> After a while he said, "What are you not going to mention about?" And I said, "The axe."
>
> "You weren't scared, were you?"
>
> "No," I said hopefully. "Who is going to burn him and his bed?"

502

"Nobody. Less he manages it himself like he did last time."

"Who is the Silases?"

"Nobody," my father said. "Just nobody."

There has always seemed to me more going on in this section than a brisk read delivers. Of course, from our general experience of reading, we expect some kind of denouement, climax, resolution at the end of a story. But towards what end has this story been tending? I am not being dogmatic in what follows; I am suggesting a reading of this movement of the story, a matter of tentativeness, nuances, but prompted by the very strong feeling that under the sway of the surface waves, beneath the seaweed growth and silt, lies a definite shape, a deck perhaps, a hull.

"'When *I* use a word,' Humpty said in a rather scornful tone, 'it means just what I choose it to mean—neither more nor less.'" I need to talk about this penultimate movement scrupulously; I have a horror of straying into the *Through the Looking-Glass* world of Redekop.

The first difference in this section from the rest of the story is the rather obvious one that this is the first place where the description is, as it were, wide-angle; we share the child's looking out over a vista. The camera pans over the "whole basin of country," taking in bush, fields with scales of snow in the furrows, tiny fences—then moving closer to bring up grey barns satellite to farm houses, and finally narrowing in on *one* house, hers. At first, she does not recognize it.

It is the opening five sentences, however, that alert me, that give me the feeling that more is being said here than what seems to be being said.

It's important to hold in mind the last words in the preceding section, "I was falling asleep with my eyes open." Such an *odd* detail. It turns out that the third section is much concerned with seeing.

"My father set me down. 'You're woken up now. Stand up. See. I can't carry you and this sack of rats both.'"

These are not unusual words for a father to say. "Stand up" implies that the sleepy child is not doing so completely, is still perhaps leaning against his arm or thigh. "See," is followed by the panoramic description and her slow recognition of the familiar seen from a different angle. The implication, *in context*, is that her angle, her view of things, is changing too.

Munro doesn't often use single words as complete statements; they should jolt us.

"You're woken up now," instead of the more usual "You're awake now," seems to suggest that something *has wakened* her. Something other than being set down. "Stand up. See," sound to me as if they might be read as "You're now aware of... Stand on your own two feet. See the world anew. See what is really there. See with eyes that have been opened."

There is considerable difference between "Look" and "See." See usually means the *ability* to see or understand. *Can you see that? I see what you mean*, while Look usually means look *at* something. *If you look over there, you'll see...* In the context of this passage, it would have been more natural for Ben to have said something like "Look at the view," or "Look towards the bottom of the hill." When you think about it, "See" the landscape is a rather peculiar usage. Had Munro added, "he said, pointing," it would sound more colloquial but, significantly, she leaves it as stark command.

Here I might well be fanciful but these injunctions of the father—Stand up. See—have an almost Biblical ring to them, Jesus to the young man cured of palsy, that sort of tone, *Arise...take up thy bed... and walk...* (Matthew 9:6).

These possible meanings I take to be Munro's intentions. I am not asserting that we're meant to read them as the conscious thoughts or conscious feelings of Ben or Del. Munro is letting us see and understand more than her characters can articulate.

Del, *not needing to be carried anymore*, can manage the "easy walk home"; soon she'll "see the light" where her mother is. She wakes when her father sets her down. He is finding it difficult to carry both her and the sack of rats. Proximity to these dead creatures that, earlier in the story, she "did not dare touch," these, "facts of death" no longer seem to concern her.

When Ben asks her, "You weren't scared, were you?"

"No," I said hopefully.

A charming "No"—she hoping that was the required answer and also a way of saying, "Just a little bit but I hope I won't be any more."

We should recall her first sight of Joe in his "drab camouflaging clothes": "All my life I had known there was a man like this and he was behind doors, around the corner at the dark end of the hall." Now, Del has seen that man in plain view and sat on his dirty couch and shared his melted candies with their runny stripes. And now she sees her old fears in the beginning of a new light.

Her last wavering doubts, voiced in her questions about the axe and the Silases who want to burn Joe and his bed, are dismissed by her father; it is simply Joe's habit to carry about the axe, nothing more; and the Silases, Ben explains, are just Joe's make-believe enemies.

Del has seen the bogeyman and he is "Just nobody."

The description of the landscape, a landscape rather like a David Milne dry point—and Del's dawning recognition of her own house seen from a new vantage point, raise the whole section into what Clark Blaise would firmly think of as metaphor. We might compare this section with the final section of "A North American Education."

The brief final section of the story works as a natural and elegant conclusion; it is not obtrusive in the way that the ending of "Walker Brothers Cowboy" was; there is nothing of that worked, tacked-on feeling. It gives, I feel, some justification for my reading of the language leading up to it.

"'Eat your supper,' Mary said, bending over me. I did not for some time realize that I was no longer afraid of her. 'Look at her,' she said. 'Her eyes dropping out of her head, all she's been and seen.'"

We understand "all she's been and seen" as ordinary colloquial rural speech, words on the same pattern as "Look at what you've gone and done," words that mean "all the places she's been to and the things she's seen." But it's possible Munro also wishes us to see that "all she's been" can also mean "the person she has been" and, it is implied, "now isn't."

In the interrogation about the cat and the whiskey, her father "looked steadily down the table" at her, and she, "prepared to live happily ever after... dazed and powerful with secrets... never said a word."

I first heard this story read by an actor on Robert Weaver's *Anthology* program on the CBC before it was published in *Dance of the*

Happy Shades. I had the electric experience of *recognizing* it. Exactly what I was trying to do, Alice Munro had marvellously accomplished. Hearing that story was the portal to the rest of my life.

CASTING SAD SPELLS
Alice Munro's "Walker Brothers Cowboy"

Most of the fifteen stories collected in *Dance of the Happy Shades* had been previously published in magazines. Two or three, however, were specially written to enlarge and complete the volume and among these later stories were "Images" and "Walker Brothers Cowboy."

Both are interestingly different from most of the other stories in the book and represent a stylistic change. They are more highly wrought than previous stories, the rhetoric at a higher pitch, the images more intense, the painting of detail more vibrant.

While some of the stories in *Dance of the Happy Shades* were first published in such literary magazines as *The Fiddlehead* and *The Canadian Forum,* others were first published in *The Montrealer* and *Chatelaine.* None was "commercial," but all were traditional in form and one or two might be criticized for being overly explicit. The two stories written especially for the book, on the other hand, seem more consciously "literary"; they are more complex than the others not only in language but in form and they make no concessions to popular expectation.

That one of these stories is *called* "Images" directs us to the nature of the change in Alice Munro's work at this time; she is beginning to relinquish conventional plot and is beginning to work in what is essentially a poetic manner, letting images and the accumulation of detail carry the story's line and emotional weight. She withdraws in these stories far more than she had previously as commentator or explicator and allows the reader to come into more unmediated contact with the imagery.

Not surprisingly, "Images" and "Walker Brothers Cowboy" also exhibit a concomitant change in form. The structures of the stories are unlike anything she had attempted before and they emphasize and enhance the primacy of the image. "Walker Brothers Cowboy" is divided into three sections; the first is introductory, the second is amplification and extension of the essential melody in the first, and the third concludes and returns us to the opening section by way of allusion and repetition. The important thing to realize about the first section is that it is, in itself, an image. It cannot be read conventionally as an aspect of plot, for read in that way it makes little sense. If we approach it looking for the "story," looking for the "what happens," we will prevent ourselves from seeing what *is* there; we must give ourselves up to language and to image. The first section is the whole story in miniature; it contains, in essence, all that is to come in sections two and three. It might not be entirely fanciful to suggest that there is about the story something almost sonata-like, but however one wishes to think about the structure of "Walker Brothers Cowboy" some sort of analogy with music seems inevitable.

Before considering this opening section, however, it is important to pay attention to the narrating voice, because the pleasure we should take in Alice Munro's skilled handling of the narrative conventions is a rich part of the story's larger pleasures. Both "Images" and "Walker Brothers Cowboy" are initiation stories, stories about the gaining of knowledge, and so the effectiveness of them depends to a certain extent on our sharing the child's innocence and on our growing with the child towards understanding. Although the narrator of "Walker Brothers Cowboy" is actually the Jordan girl, grown up and looking back at her childhood, the writing is intended to suggest a young girl's voice and sensibility. The use of the present tense in narration—a device which in the hands of a lesser writer could have induced numbing monotony—is varied here with subtle craft and goes a long way in itself towards suggesting youth and simplicity.

Consider again the following passage:

> He has a song about it, with these two lines:
> And have all liniments and oils,
> For everything from corns to boils ...

> Not a very funny song, in my mother's opinion. A pedlar's song, and that is what he is, a pedlar knocking at backwoods kitchens.

Up until last winter we had our own business, a fox farm. My father raised silver foxes and sold their pelts to the people who make them into capes and coats and muffs. Prices fell, my father hung on hoping they would get better next year, and they fell again, and he hung on one more year and one more and finally it was not possible to hang on any more, we owed everything to the feed company. I have heard my mother explain this, several times, to Mrs. Oliphant who is the only neighbour she talks to. (Mrs. Oliphant also has come down in the world, being a school-teacher who married the janitor.) We poured all we had into it, my mother says, and we came out with nothing. Many people could say the same thing, these days, but my mother has no time for the national calamity, only ours. Fate has flung us onto a street of poor people (it does not matter that we were poor before, that was a different sort of poverty), and the only way to take this, as she sees it, is with dignity, with bitterness, with no reconciliation. No bathroom with a claw-footed tub and a flush toilet is going to comfort her, no water on tap and sidewalks past the house and milk in bottles, not even the two movie theatres and the Venus Restaurant and Woolworths so marvellous it has live birds singing in its fancooled corners and fish as tiny as fin-gernails, as bright as moons, swimming in its green tanks. My mother does not care.

In the lines, "Not a very funny song, in my mother's opinion. A ped-lar's song, and that is what he is, a pedlar knocking at backwoods kitchens," I think we are hearing in the repetition of "pedlar" and the implied "that's what you are" the child echoing something of the mother—though sharing none of her bitterness.

The next two sentences present the girl's voice. Notice how the voice is suggested by "the people who make them into capes and coats and muffs" instead of, say, "furriers." The sentence follow-ing these, however, with its succession of "ands" and its final com-ma-spliced conclusion represents not so much the girl's voice as the girl reproducing the oft-heard monotony of her mother's litany of complaint.

Next, the mother is quoted directly, though without quotation marks—an omission perhaps meant to suggest that this remark is made often and always in the same words, that the remark has become ritual. The words in the next sentence, "but my mother has no time for the national calamity, only ours," sounds rather sophisticated for the girl but we are meant to take them, I think, as her perception because of the words "these days." Perhaps such a phrase as "national calamity" was current on the radio or in newspapers. Had Alice Munro intended us to read this sentence as if spoken by the adult looking back, she would have used different tenses and "those" days as opposed to "these."

Note, in the following sentence, that in "Fate has flung us …" we are again intended to hear, at a remove, the mother's vocabulary and histrionics. The long concluding sentence, which also suggests the mothers' voice with its *No, nor, not*, then modulates back into the simulation of the voice of the child, a voice suggested not merely by subject matter but by the rhythm of the "ands" and by the syntax of "Woolworths so marvellous …" and by the sentence's rhythmically awkward conclusion.

It's important to remember that in a writer like Alice Munro we are reading prose that is more subtle than much of what now passes for poetry; it's necessary to be alert to the play of voice because it is only by paying close attention that we can savour the story's fullness.

The first paragraph of the first section is a beautifully compressed piece of writing that all at once suggests the girl's voice, gives us information about the family's straitened circumstances, and sketches the relationships within the family. The particular love the girl has for her father is also established.

The description of the walk down to the lake presents a physical and emotional landscape. Alice Munro has rightly always resisted symbol-seekers and reductive reading insisting that a spade is indeed and always a spade, but the accumulation of physical detail in this opening section obviously functions as more than topographical survey.

The evening games of the children they pass are "ragged, dissolving." The children "draw apart, separate into islands of two or one… occupying themselves in… solitary ways."

The sidewalks are "cracked and heaved"; father and daughter walk past a factory with "boarded-up windows." And then the town "falls away in a defeated jumble of sheds and small junkyards... we enter a vacant lot... and there is one bench with a slat missing on the back ..."

Father and daughter sit and look at the lake—"Which is generally grey in the evening, under a lightly overcast sky, no sunsets, the horizon dim." Further along is a lifeguard's "rickety throne" and further off still are the docks where the grain boats load, boats that are "ancient, rusty, wallowing."

This landscape, then, is a suitable background to the Jordans' descent into urban poverty and it suggests something of the defeat and bleakness of Ben Jordan's emotional life.

The third paragraph of this opening section is rather curious. Why is it there? What does it contribute? Tramps wander up from the "dwindling" beach and climb the "shifting, precarious path." Such meetings are, we learn, not infrequent but they always frighten the girl. The paragraph tells us directly that the father is "hard up" and his actions suggest that he has sympathy for the tramps, perhaps even some fellow-feeling for he, too, has come down in the world.

The incident described is obviously important. The paragraph contains only the third sentence of the section actually spoken. It concludes with a line whose rhythms and word placements are deliberate: "My father also rolls and lights and smokes one cigarette of his own."

The use of the word "one" suggests that the father does not smoke a great deal, perhaps cannot afford much tobacco. The deliberateness of the sentence echoes the deliberateness of the act; the rhythm tells us that it is a *rationed* ritual and pleasure. We are meant to assume that the manufacture and smoking of a cigarette are something of a performance, something done deliberately and at significant junctures.

The story will return us to this incident.

The final paragraph contains the fourth line of actual speech in this first section: "Well, the old ice cap had a lot more power behind it than this hand has." There is in this, perhaps, a faint suggestion

of the ineffectual, of the father's powerlessness against the indignities of poverty. The section concludes with the child trying to think
about Time and Change and wishing that everything would always
remain safe and the same. This passage obviously looks forward to
the concluding two paragraphs of the entire story and thus links
beginning and end.

The body of the story, the second section, now amplifies what we've
already been given, in concentrated form, in the first. We learn the
history of the family's decline into poverty and we learn, in greater
detail, how the girl feels about her parents.

The girl is humiliated by the mother's pretensions to gentility
and resists recruitment to her views: "I pretend to remember far less
than I do, wary of being trapped into sympathy or any unwanted
emotion."

The mother uses her various ailments as a weapon against the
father and as a means of holding onto him.

"He goes back once again, probably to say goodbye to my
mother, to ask her if she is sure she doesn't want to come, and hear
her say, 'No. No thanks, I'm better just to lie here with my eyes
closed.'"

The girl doesn't actually hear these words spoken on this occasion. She doesn't have to; she's heard them many times before. The
girl's sympathies and feelings are entirely for the father.

It's probably important at this point to say something about those
sympathies and feelings and about Alice Munro's young female narrators in general. At the end of "Walker Brothers Cowboy," the girl
has begun to grasp something of the complexities of her father's
life, about its sadness, about paths not taken; she has sensed the
meaning of mysteries and has begun to learn things about herself as
a female. Exactly *what* she has learned is neither described nor articulated, but "Walker Brothers Cowboy" is charged with a sexuality
we should not ignore.

The same is true of "Images." Too many readers, I think, have
assumed too firmly that "Images" is concerned with the child's
learning simply about death; they seem to have given insufficient

weight to the story's sexual concerns. They seem to have overlooked the fact that Mary McQuade, Death's harbinger, has come to the house to deliver the girl's mother of another baby, that the girl is making a connection between death and birth and sex and being female, that Mary McQuade is always being teased about possible husbands. The child watches the shadows cast by her father and the flirtatious Mary McQuade and tries "to understand the danger, to read the signs of invasion."

The narrator in "Images" is slightly younger than the narrator in "Walker Brothers Cowboy," but in both cases the stories are richer for us if we realize that they are narrated by a girl very sensitive to the sexual currents around her, who is hungry for sexual knowledge, and who is eager to learn how this sexuality will affect *her* life. Both stories are, in a way, as much about sexuality and the female role as the far more explicit "Boys and Girls."

(Adolescent sexuality is, of course, the main subject and focus of *Lives of Girls and Women*, the next book Alice Munro was to write.)

The girl, then, rejects her mother's embittered gentility and cleaves to her father. The father deals with their poverty and with their having come down in the world by maintaining a façade of jollity. He amuses the children with his improvised songs, with his patter, jokes, and comic self-mockery. There is even a suggestion of the father as artist turning his trials into "the song." Father knows the shortcut out of town; he represents, for his children, the "hope of adventure."

He bears the weight of the family on his shoulders.

He attempts to coax his wife into laughter by performing for her amusingly "rude" sales routines. The daughter says: "… and she would laugh finally, unwillingly."

The father's territory is a desolate landscape, "flat, scorched, empty," with dust hanging over the dirt roads and with "falling-down sheds and unturning windmills" on the decaying farms; all this forms the background for, and is the counterpart of, the father's emotional life.

The event which is the turning point of the story is the emptying of the chamber pot out of the window. He is not actually hit: "The window is not directly above my father's head, so only a stray splash would catch him."

But splashed or not, the event is the final degradation, the final straw. He picks up the suitcases "with no particular hurry" and walks back to the car "no longer whistling." He sits in the car, which is raucous with the laughter of his son and daughter exulting in the naughtiness of *pee* and in the exquisite pleasure of pee having been poured out of a window. He sits there and does not start the car until he has rolled and lighted a cigarette. And it is this at the pivotal point of the story which should return us, if only for a moment in memory, to the scene in section one with the tramp.

Sitting there, smoking that deliberate cigarette, Ben Jordan reaches a decision. He starts to drive. He tells his son not to tell his mother about the pee because she wouldn't see the joke. In other words, her sympathies would not be for Ben's humiliation; her anger would be directed against him for working at such an "ungentle-manly" job. The boy wants to know if the incident is in the "song." Ben says that he'll try to work it in. But he isn't singing.

The conversation with the daughter is both naturalistic and yet full of significance: "'Are we still in your territory?' He shakes his head."

He is heading *out* of his territory, both physical and emotional, and he is neither singing nor being amusing. He is heading towards the house of a woman he *might* have married, a woman who would not have suffered headaches. He is driving so fast over the pot-holed roads that all the bottles clink and gurgle and are in danger of being broken, the bottles that are the source of his livelihood. He is driving in full flight both away from the scene of his humiliation and towards someone who can offer comfort.

Nora, not recognizing him at first, says: "Have you lost your way?"

It's a poignant question for us as readers, for by now we've realized that he'd lost it years before. This sudden appearance of Ben Jordan is an immense shock to Nora: "'Oh, my Lord God,' she says harshly, 'it's you.'"

The heavy stresses fall on every word.

When asked if she's got a husband hiding in the woodshed, her laugh is "abrupt and somewhat angry." (Though we get the impression that Ben knows full well that she's unmarried.) When she is reintroducing Ben to her mother and explaining that he is now married, she speaks "cheerfully and aggressively" as though challenging her mother to comment. The blind old mother has not spoken to Ben for many years, yet recognizes his voice instantly. We are to assume, then, that at one time Ben and Nora were extremely close.

We are told little about their past relationship. Like the daughter, we must try to piece things together. It would not be unseemly to guess that one strong reason for the failure of their relationship was that Ben Jordan was Protestant and Nora Catholic. The bigotry in Ontario in the twenties and thirties was virulent. Nora *digs with the wrong foot*—a Protestant Irish expression meaning, "She's Catholic—she's not one of us," "She's not our sort."

Whatever the reasons for the collapse of the relationship, Nora is the sister who has remained unmarried at home to care for her blind mother. One sister is married with children, the other is a teacher in western Canada, financially independent, who hasn't been back to the farm in five years. The "faint sour smell" that the girl smells in the kitchen is metaphorically the smell of frustration and disappointment.

When Nora reappears, washed, scented, changed into a flowered dress and more "sociable and youthful," Ben says of the flowers on the material that he'd never known there were green poppies. Nora's reply is both flirtatious and blunt: "You'd be surprised all the things you never knew."

Nora and Ben drink whiskey together. Nora's having a bottle other than for "medicinal purposes" marks her as a woman out of the ordinary, a woman morally suspect. The girl is fascinated by the fact that her father is drinking because her mother has gone out of her way to tell the girl that he never does. We are to assume from this, I think, that Ben once drank more than the occasional nip but has been weaned from it—and from other enjoyable bad habits. His drinking days were those he spent with Nora. The implied background here is the puritanical connection between nonconformist protestantism and the temperance movement. Ben's wife in her "good dress, navy blue with little flowers, sheer, worn over a navy-blue slip. Also a summer hat of white straw, pushed down on the side of the head, and white shoes I have just whitened on a newspaper on the back steps" is the embodiment of arid respectability and Protestant religiosity.

It is at this point that Alice Munro starts to tinge Nora's speech with Irish syntax and rhythms.

(Implied social, religious, and historical backgrounds are precisely what give Alice Munro's stories their dense, textured feel. A single line of dialogue such as Ben's "Keep it in case of sickness?" vibrates with meanings that soon will have to be explained to a young and urban readership.

How should we read Ben's enquiry? Is it serious? Is it seeking an answer to questions not being directly asked? Is it jocular?)

Ben next performs for Nora a version of the chamber-pot incident. His daughter remarks on the discrepancy between what she'd seen happen and his account of it. As usual, Ben is turning his disappointments and humiliations into entertainment for others. There is a sense, too, that it is only by refashioning reality that he is able to bear it; in his created version of the incident he emerges a "hero in the ranks of Walker Brothers," even if his heroism is Chaplinesque.

Nora laughs "almost as loud as my brother did at the time"— the brother who's been told not to mention the incident at home because his mother wouldn't be "liable to see the joke." Ben then entertains Nora with his sales spiel and his song.

We are reading a scene which is parallel to the scenes alluded to earlier, where Ben tries to coax his disapproving wife into laughter, where her laughter, finally, is "unwilling;" in this scene, then, she and Nora are being compared and contrasted. Ben's clowning is, in both cases, a kind of offering, a kind of courtship.

The scene immediately following, the scene where Nora dances with Ben's daughter, is curious; this, we feel, is no ordinary dancing lesson; it is uncomfortable, faintly disquieting. The girl is aware of sexual currents even if she doesn't understand them; we the readers, however, understand the girl as a surrogate.

What is faintly disturbing about this scene—and the child's presence in it—is Nora's unladylike heat and arousal, an excitement which is conveyed through the child's registering of "her strange gaiety, her smell of whiskey, cologne, and sweat. Under the arms her dress is damp, and little drops form along her upper lip, hang in the soft black hairs at the corners of her mouth."

Nora waltzes the girl to a stop in front of Ben and says: "Dance with me, Ben."

"I'm the world's worst dancer, Nora, and you know it."

She stands there in front of him "her breasts... rising and falling under her loose flowered dress, her face shining with the exercise, and delight."

She asks him again.

"Ben."

My father drops his head and says quietly, "Not me, Nora."

The whole of this dancing passage is a masterly piece of writing. The second time that Nora asks Ben, she is not asking him to dance. She does not say "Ben?" She says, "Ben." She is both offering and claiming.

(And is Ben's "Not me, Nora" simply negative, or does "Not me" imply someone else, perhaps? Another, or others, who helped Nora drink half the whiskey because she doesn't care for drinking alone? Or are we to accept her statement, "I can drink alone but I can't dance alone"?)

Ben's declining the invitation is a sad acceptance, on his part, of duty, of the choices he has made in life. The scene peters out in painful conversational small-change and ends in silence. Nora stands close to the car in her "soft, brilliant dress," a dress which is flamboyant, possibly even slightly vulgar—and so very different from the dress described earlier, Ben's wife's dress, which is "navy blue with little flowers."

The third and last section of the story restates and returns us to the story's first section; the story's last sentence—a reference to the Lake—returns us to the story's opening sentence.

The father does not behave on this afternoon as he usually does. He does not buy the usual pop or ice cream. He buys licorice. We realize that this is to mask the smell of the whiskey when he gets home but the girl does not. She does, however, feel and share her father's sadness, although she is unable to articulate its nature. She has caught some of the heated sexuality and sadness in Nora's front room and, without understanding why, knows instinctively that these are matters not to be mentioned to her mother. Alice Munro—not, of course, for the first time in the story—uses the girl's innocence and naivety to twist the emotional screws. The daughter, utterly devoted to her father, resolves that the mother will learn nothing of the afternoon from *her*. She guesses that the most serious material to be kept from the mother must be the dancing lesson and the whiskey. This loyal innocence on her part somehow intensifies the sadness of what it really is that her father wants kept secret—the desolation that his life has become.

The girl feels confident that her little brother won't betray anything because "he does not notice enough." The most he might remember would be "the blind lady, the picture of Mary." With these two references, Alice Munro turns us back into the story before opening the throttle, as it were, for the story's conclusion.

The two flat references suggest again the sadness of Nora's life and its mystery for the narrator. The picture of Mary would only be found in the homes of Roman Catholics, those who *dig with the wrong foot*, words which now seem "sad to me as never before, dark, perverse." The "blind lady," Nora's mother, is recalled for us sitting in the faintly sour-smelling kitchen with a drop of silver liquid welling from the sunken eye, "a medicine, or a miraculous tear."

This is an example of the command of odd detail which makes Alice Munro's prose so rich and persuasive. It is so *peculiar* yet so real that we are persuaded it could never have been invented. At the same time, it renders the scene almost iconic, as though the old lady's silver tear is a tear for all human sadness and suffering.

The penultimate paragraph of "Walker Brothers Cowboy" has always troubled me. It feels as if Alice Munro is straining for rhetorical effect and impact. While it is true that the girl's feeling about her father's life is expressed in terms of fairy tale and enchantment, the syntax seems far less the girl's than the author's. I have never been quite sure what Alice Munro *meant* by this paragraph; usually she writes with precision and economy, but the writing here is vague and ambiguous. I am tempted to say that it is slightly pretentious.

Clark Blaise, in a brief essay entitled "On Ending Stories," describes two basic kinds of endings in modern stories:

> There are only two kinds of endings: those that lead you back into the story, and those that lead you— gently or violently— away. I associate the first kind of ending with de Maupassant and Chekhov, and with modernists who adapted those stories for their own purposes—Hemingway, Joyce, James. Of authors who lead away from the story, who wish to emphasize the artifice of the story, or wish to address the reader directly, I associate dozens of our contemporaries. Impatience with art is as old as faith in art; the choice of ending is the battlefield for those particular feelings.
>
> You are aware of stories that end with a let-down. "That's it? It's over?" you ask yourself. There's a Hemingway story (there are many Hemingway stories like it) that ends, "Bill selected a sandwich from the lunch basket and walked over to have a look at the rods." That's an ending? Norman Levine can fade out in the same way. It's subversive of course, a subversion of the expected neatness of closure, the gathering up of narrative and thematic threads, the welling-up of music, the frozen gesture that summarizes *the whole meaning of the story...* We realize that the short story initially paid its debts to theatre, or to fable; audiences expected a big pay-off at the end. When it didn't happen, it was revolution, it was art.
>
> I think of these endings as the most disturbing. They hit a glancing blow at the reader but generally ignore him. By approximating the most casual of voices, they manage (in the hands of masters) to sound most urgent. By ignoring us, they speak to us directly ...
>
> Endings that lead us away from the story can do so gently or abruptly. The most traditional kind of ending is the one that serves

as a prose equivalent to the theatrical last scene, the rising of music and receding of the camera as lights go out, one by one, and characters fade off together in a figurative sunset. Such endings announce a faith in continuity, order, harmony—no matter what particular horrors may have been investigated in the story. They are sophisticated and traditional ways of updating the old "happily ever after" ending so familiar from fables. Even if the endings are thematically "sad," they are formally (or cosmically) "happy"; they lead away from the specific exemplum (the story) to a generalized harmony. They are religious in form, if not in content.

How can you detect such an ending? Well, they *sound* like endings. From Eudora Welty (a prime influence on Alice Munro) we get,

> Outside the redbirds were flying and criss-crossing, the sun was in all the bottles on the prisoned trees, and the young peach was shining in the middle of them with the bursting light of spring...

From Margaret Laurence's first collection,

> The sea spray was bitter and salt, but to them it was warm, too. They watched on the sand their exaggerated shadows, one squat and bulbous, the other bone-slight and clumsily elongated, pigeon and crane. The shadows walked with hands entwined like children who walk through the dark."

Let's look more closely now at the penultimate paragraph of "Walker Brothers Cowboy." It is too "literary," too wrought. It strives for the second kind of ending that Blaise talks about, the symphonic ending. What Blaise didn't mention in his essay, but which is typical of "symphonic" endings, is that the writers consciously or unconsciously heighten their language. Elevated rhythms and archaic syntax tend to creep in. We may well hear biblical echoes in grammatical constructions or in repetitions. Sense sometimes capitulates to incantation.

What is meant *exactly* by "my father's life"? What does the word "life" mean? Why would that life be "flowing back from our car"? Back to where? To Nora? Or is it "flowing" in the sense of, say, blood from a wound? Or are we to understand "flowing" as meaning something like "diminishing, emptying" in the manner of a deflating balloon?

Is it "life" that is "darkening and turning strange," or is it "the last of the afternoon?" In what way can we really compare a "landscape" and a "life"?

Is this language believable in the girl's mouth? Are these apprehensions totally credible in this child?

These confusions are compounded because in the final paragraph Alice Munro produces a *second* ending—an ending of the *first* type described by Blaise, the "let-down" ending. Thus the story ends symphonically and then ends in deflation. The result is somewhat of a mess.

Alice Munro made interesting comment on the endings of her stories in an interview with J.R. (Tim) Struthers. The interview was published in Louis MacKendrick's *Probable Fictions: Alice Munro's Narrative Acts*.

> **TS:** ... Something that interests me is your sense of the fashions of fiction-writing at certain periods.
>
> **AM:** Well, when you've been writing for a while, you can't help but be aware of this. You may flatter yourself that you're not influenced by fashions, but I certainly am. That is, I don't adopt a fashion in order to get published somewhere or in order to win critical acclaim. It's just that there is a current way of saying things which seems effective, and so one begins to experiment with that way and to use it. And then later on, it seems possible to say things in another way. And these are actually fashions.
>
> **TS:** Could you identify a number of the fashions—magazine fashions, perhaps—that ...
>
> **AM:** Oh, I wouldn't get that definite. I don't mean this thing... you know the way you used to be advised to read about the

market [laughter] and then write stories for the market. I don't mean at all that kind of thing because I was never interested in it. But, for instance, when I read over my stories of the '50s... and I've never been an innovator or an experimental writer. I'm not very clever that way. I'm never ahead of what's being done at the time. So in those stories in *Dance of the Happy Shades* there's an awful lot of meaningful final sentences. There's an awful lot of very, very important words in each last little paragraph. And that's something that I felt was necessary at the time for the stories to work. It must have been a prevalent fashion. That's the idea I got that it was necessary. But it wasn't something any market was demanding or any critic was demanding. It was the way I felt that you made a story most effective. And now, I would go back, if I could rewrite most of those stories, and I would chop out a lot of those words and final sentences. And I would just let each story stand without bothering to do the summing up, because that's really what it amounts to.

TS: I remember when you read "Postcard" at Western in the mid-'70s.
AM: I know I often chopped ...

TS: You dropped the last paragraph when you read the story.
AM: And if I ever do a final edition of all those things, I'll drop the last paragraphs. God knows if I'm right or not. That is just the way I feel now. Isn't it true that Henry James went through and made a lot of his early stuff more difficult and obscure later on? And I believe that Frank O'Connor continued writing stories over and over even after they'd been published. I haven't seen the different versions, but the point I'm making is just that it's not even that you are necessarily improving the story. You are telling it the way you see it now. And you have no idea what improvement means. You're just telling it the way it seems to work now. And I could go on and on doing my stuff over and over that way. I wouldn't do any of the stories in *Dance* quite the same. And that's why the rewriting after a while gets to be such

a strange thing. I rewrite stories now, and my editors don't like them as well as earlier versions. And sometimes they may be right. There's a point after which you're not sure what you're doing with the rewrites.

It is gross impertinence to rewrite a writer, but I've often thought "Walker Brothers Cowboy" could be improved by cutting most of the last section so that with the necessary adjustments the story could have ended with the father saying: "I don't know. I seem to be fresh out of songs. You watch the road and let me know if you see any rabbits."

Or—even better—it could well have ended with Nora in her brilliant dress making an unintelligible mark in the dust of the car.

I suspect that's precisely where the story *did* end and that the final four paragraphs were added later. On the other hand, it must be remembered that this story appeared in Alice Munro's first book. Her writing since then has grown ever more dazzling. Few short-story writers in Canada, even now, would be capable of matching the opening paragraph of "Walker Brothers Cowboy" for precision, economy, and grace.

> After supper my father says, "Want to go down and see if the Lake's still there?" We leave my mother sewing under the dining room light, making clothes for me against the opening of school. She has ripped up for this purpose an old suit and an old plaid wool dress of hers, and she has to cut and match very cleverly and also make me stand and turn for endless fittings, sweaty, itching from the hot wool, ungrateful. We leave my brother in bed in the little screened porch at the end of the front veranda, and sometimes he kneels on his bed and presses his face against the screen and calls mournfully, 'Bring me an ice-cream cone!' but I call back, 'You will be asleep,' and do not even turn my head.

Kathy Page

Short Story Collections: *As In Music* (1990), *Paradise and Elsewhere* (2014), *The Two of Us* (2016), and *Dear Evelyn* (2018).

Novels: *Back in the First Person* (1986), *The Unborn Dreams of Clara Riley* (1987), *Island Paradise* (1988), *Frankie Styne & the*

Silver Man (1992), *The Story of My Face* (2002), *Alphabet* (2005), and *The Find* (2010).

Endless Invention, Amazing Variety

On the Kathy Page shelf in my library there's a June, 1982 issue of the British magazine *Writing Women* (Vol. 1 No. 3). It contains Kathy Page's first publication, two stories entitled "The Politics of the Superficial Become the Poetry of Surfaces" and "A Leaf in the Works." The magazine came from the library of Angela Carter and bears her ownership signature on the first page.

I'd admit to bibliomania, but I mention the magazine not from musty pedantry but because it introduced the young Kathy Page as feminist/socialist, and the fortuitous link to Angela Carter could be seen as indicating a direction in Page's future work.

The first five books she wrote were published in England but not in North America. Of the next six, following her move to Canada in 2001, three were published in Canada and in England, the last three in Canada alone.

Back in the First Person and *The Unborn Dreams of Clara Riley* are explicitly feminist. *First Person* details the aftermath endured by Cath Sheldon after she accuses her ex-boyfriend, Steven Blake, of raping her. Cath recounts months of police incredulity and bullying, medical callousness, and legal delays. After all the courtroom theatrics have played out, Steven Blake is acquitted for lack of corroborating evidence that the act had been non-consensual

The narrative is very readable, its detail carefully built and convincing, yet ultimately it reads more like a work of journalism than a work of the imagination, probably because it follows, in plot terms, an exterior sequence of events leading to and culminating in a trial; which is to say that plot dictated the book and held her captive. It's probable that, at the time of writing the book, she'd have considered my opinion, at best, ridiculous.

Unborn Dreams is set in the Edwardian years. It is about the life of Clara Riley and her husband, Michael. Clara ekes out a livelihood toiling as a laundress while Michael works as a carpenter's labourer. Clara has suffocated her first baby and aborts a second, an abortion arranged and financed by Mrs. Audley Jones, the suffragette wife of an Admiral. Clara washes and irons Mrs. Audley Jones' clothes and linens and is treated by her as something of a Cause. Clara's sins are a torment for Michael, who is a devout Catholic. Again, the situation results in a trial and Clara is convicted and imprisoned, abortion and its procurement then on the statute books as a crime.

The writing is lively and the period research is so well-handled as to be scarcely noticible, yet the temptation is to shrug so-what and say, yes, but that was *then*... A differing way of looking at the book is that she is looking back to direct our attention towards those same forces that still oppress women: poverty, a class system that is reflected in the law and its administration, lack of educational opportunity, lack of representation in social and political structures.

The book undeniably has an agenda, designs upon us, and perhaps because of this suffers literary weakness. Michael, for example, seems not to strongly exist outside his fervent Catholicism; Mrs. Audley Jones is little more than a lay figure; we do not see and hear her as anything more than a spokesperson for suffragette concerns. When the Admiral learns of her possible indictment, he consigns her to Peacehaven, a Private Residence for the Insane.

Here is Michael, brooding in the courtroom as he waits for the trial of Mrs. Audley Jones to start, a trial that will not take place, as her counsel enters an application to the court that will exempt her from trial on the grounds of insanity.

> Michael hates the Admiral's wife. She encouraged Clara to want more than she was meant to have, she gave her that coat, fed her with dainty sandwiches and cake so as she'd always want it: it was her fault for tempting. And that Admiral's wife was after votes for women and it was one of those that threw the brick that sent glass into that girl's face. He hates Mrs. Audley Jones, he's come to see her in the dock... and Clara, he might glimpse her from behind, in the dock as well, his wife that grew so tender but never sung a lullaby, that nursed him but never nursed a

child. A devil beneath, he mutters to himself, the Devil has many guises. And a blind eye often weeps.

Such a passage brings to mind the Villain in silent films mugging over the Heroine, who is clad in gauzy garments and tied down across the railroad tracks.

In a passage immediately following, Mr. William Elverton, Counsel for the Prosecution, stands before judge and jury, outwardly calm but gripped by his need to dominate.

> ... beneath the gracefully gathered folds of his gown, each one of his muscles pulls to its utmost and is counterbalanced by the pull of its opposite, so that he stands locked and each movement feels like an abrupt and temporary escape from paralysis. His penis erect, even his toes are stiff, but the voice that issues from his bolted body is smooth splendid...

We are to understand that Counsel has a hard-on for Mrs. Audley Jones and Clara Riley.

(In *Cassell's Dictionary of Slang,* edited by Jonathan Green, *hard-on* is partially defined as:

> Noun. (late 19C+) an erection; thus *have a hard-on for*, to want something very much, to like or dislike a person particularly.)

But having an *actual* erection rather than a metaphorical one seems to be edging into unintentional farce.

Kathy Page co-edited with Lynne Van Luven a book of essays about body parts entitled *In the Flesh*; she contributed an essay, "Hand over Hand."

> Long ago, during the Second World War, my father penned hundreds of letters to my mother, which she kept; recently, with both parents' permission, I read them. Dad's writing was smaller than mine, more restrained; the letter shapes, and the ways of linking them, quite different from those I was taught. But I see

> a similarity in the way we put words on the page: a certain lack
> of care for the taught form, a hurtling, hurried look that comes
> from badly wanting to say what's in our hearts and minds.

This description of handwriting suggests to me what it is that's at
the centre of my dissatisfaction with Kathy Page's first two books.
She is "hurtling and hurried," while I've come to believe that what's
in our hearts and minds is best served by a cold mastering of technique. In her early work, Kathy is expressive, while I see manipulation as writing's goal.

By manipulation, I mean that though there is much in my own
heart and mind, my goal is not to express that but, by artifice and
rhetoric, to cause *readers* to think and feel. Many readers are repelled
by such deliberation, such "coldness."

With his usual weary brilliance, Oscar Wilde pronounced upon this
notion well over a hundred years ago in his essay "The Critic as Artist."

> A little sincerity is a dangerous thing, and a great deal of it is
> absolutely fatal.

To be scrupulous, I must record that these first two novels were published by the prestigious new press for women writers, Virago, and
that both received appreciative reviews from the literary community.

Though I felt that *Unborn Dreams* was too much touched by a
"documentary" impulse, by an almost journalistic concern, there
were passages in it, significantly, nothing to do directly with the plot,
that pushed me towards excitement and expectation for future work.

Clara remembering her Sheffield childhood:

> Sheffield was darker even than London, dirtier too, but it was
> smaller and you could see the edges of it: you could imagine
> getting away, follow with your eyes the railway tracks snaking
> off into the distance. She used to run up hills to see what was on
> the other side. There was always a shifting layer of smoke, but
> if she got high enough she could just see the blues and greens
> and purple beyond. She remembers the reddish earth in winter,

and the cabbage fields that were a metallic green, quite different from the green of pastures.

This is writing of a different order from much of the book, writing about Clara's unarticulated desire for more, for "away," for "beyond." The "metallic green" of cabbage fields has stayed with me for years.

That desire for a larger world is again sculpted in this lovely oil-and-water image:

> "This work I'm doing for Mr. Holden," Michael says as they turn into Hyde Park, "is very good class. He's using walnut and mahogany, even where it won't be seen. Blunts a plane in half the time of deal. And twice the weight. You'll have seen it in Penley Square, walnut: it's got the grain all swirled together, a pattern like oil and water mixed." Clara sees it perfectly, the oil and the water, then the wood on Mrs. Audley Jones's dressing table reflected in the three mirrors you can tilt to see your back and sides. She can also see their own small mirror, propped on the mantelpiece, moved each morning to the sink for Michael's shaving. Their mirror reflects a much smaller piece of the world. Body and soul, she hungers for walnut and mahogany, for huge, glittering reflections, the smells of polish and out-of-season flowers.

(The word "deal" is a British usage, a noun meaning pine wood.)

The following passage, Clara accompanying Michael to Sunday mass, is a bravura performance; when I first read her work this was the Kathy Page I was waiting for:

> The church is so dark that she can see only the windows, huge expanses of multi-coloured light delicately veined with black. The place is full of quiet endless echoes. She holds on to Michael until the last possible moment, he, not having gazed at the windows can still see in the dark, and guides her to an empty pew, then crosses the aisle to sit among the men. Smells like autumn

in here, she thinks, damp and bitter and sad. Michael is kneeling, head bowed, eyes dropped shut final as blinds. He won't look at her now she's here. She wants, impossibly, to hold his arm as slowly in the shuffling silence she returns from not-here to find she is pressed hard, kneeling on wood, while the church groans with miserable, endless chanting and organ chords, each note as long as it possibly could be, like they're trying to make you weep. Each sound takes hold of her and pulls and wrings inside. She feels herself setting solid inside her Sunday best dress and new coat from Mrs. Audley Jones: Clara Riley with her feet growing cold holding the little black book shut when everyone else's is open, following the standing and kneeling like a bad dancer in the chorus line. Church is like cleaning floors, she thinks, and her knuckles crack loudly as she pulls herself up again using the book ledge. All around her they are praying for forgiveness, in almost-unison, begging to be cleansed, steady rhythms of chant thudding and falling at the end of each breath. Yes, it's like rinsing in the sink, the sound of it, oh Lord, they're all washing their dirty souls in the huge stone walled sink of the church. She keeps her eyes open throughout the prayer, watching the swaying row of bowed heads in front of her and comparing the set of individual pairs of shoulders. She watches Michael's profile. His face seems sealed up like a stranger's, without the glimpse of his half-blue eyes. His hands rest useless on his knees like sleeping kittens: he's not there, she realises. Just as she was somewhere else walking along in the sunshine this morning, so now he's somewhere else even farther away, not himself. That's the real reason, she thinks, glad to understand.

The pattern in the nearest window is Mary dressed in a thousand fragments of blue, and an angel in gold and red. Pie-faced Mary she thinks, with amusement and a touch of jealousy: better than sneaking the bundle up a stranger's drive at dusk, to call your bastard the Son of God and turn it all to the good... And now they're queuing up for communion, Michael glancing at her from the corner of his eye. She looks away. There's something in her insides that writhes at the thought. It's Sunday, the day of ease, the church windows may filter their meagre allowance of light into a coloured gloom, but outside she knows is bright and clear. The bone-dry biscuit, the blood-bitter wine. No.

Page's third novel, *Island Paradise*, a dystopia set in a not-distant future, is a strange mishmash of a book that received unwarranted praise, quoted on the dust jacket, from Maggie Gee and Malcolm Bradbury. Gee's endorsement didn't surprise me as she has written an apocalyptic vision of nuclear holocaust (*The Burning Book*) and another book set against a background of ecological disaster (*Where Are the Snows?*) But I did find Bradbury's praise surprising.

Page attended the University of East Anglia in Bradbury's MA course in creative writing. She had signed up initially as she wanted to work with Angela Carter, but Carter had been diagnosed with lung cancer, forcing her resignation.

Bradbury taught American literature at UEA and also ran the creative writing school. His novels and stories seem to be not much regarded these days, but I was captured when I was at university by his novel *Eating People Is Wrong* (1957) and have read him steadfastly and with joy ever since: *Stepping Westward, The History of Man, Rates of Exchange...* Some of his neglect may be reaction to his finding so much modern criticism comical; difficult, of course, if you're a writer, not to.

Page organizes her society in capital letters. Everything is owned and managed by the State. Universal Peace was achieved by The Unfought War. The forces of Law and Order are The Surveillance. The populace is housed in blocks called Residentials. Random or organized violence has been eliminated and occurred only in the past, known as the Time Before. People killed are described as the Untimely Dead. Raw materials and power are derived from Planet Three. An unknown Entity is attacking Planet Three. The details of this conflict and other news are broadcast daily on the huge and ubiquitous public Telescreens. In return for this peaceful and productive society all citizens are subject to Timely Death, that is, euthanasia at the age of fifty or so.

Sounding somehow familiar? It should. *Island Paradise* is a stew of influences. The main meat ingredients must be Orwell and

Bradbury—*Animal Farm* and *Nineteen Eighty-Four* and Ray Bradbury's *Faherenheit 451*. A pinch, perhaps, of H.G. Wells' *A Modern Utopia*? A dash of Kurt Vonnegut's *The Sirens of Titan* or *Cat's Cradle* or even *Player Piano*? A faint taste one can't quite identify... possibly William Golding? And easily identified, Aldous Huxley's *Ape and Essence* and *Brave New World*. I'm merely guessing.

I've spent time on these three early books because they are not available in Canada and are likely out of print in England.

It is with her fourth book, *As in Music and Other Stories*, that Kathy Page begins to move towards the centre of this book.

Here though, I must briefly divert to mention the three splendid novels that followed that first book of stories: *Frankie Styne and the Silver Man*, *The Story of My Face*, and *Alphabet*. With the last two titles Page moved up through the echelons of British publishers into the ranking press Weidenfeld and Nicolson. I have no need to comment on the books, as they are easily obtainable in Canada, two of them republished by Biblioasis, with the third soon to follow. I can suggest how engrossing they were in this household, how lost we were in them, by mentioning that *Alphabet* occasioned two days of cheese sandwiches and *The Story of My Face* was phone-off-the-hook and a regime of cold ham slices.

As in Music, not published in Canada, contains fourteen stories. When she was assembling *Paradise and Elsewhere*, her first short-story collection in Canada, she moved six of the stories from *Music* into *Paradise* and added eight more previously uncollected.

Caroline Adderson interviewed Kathy for *The New Quarterly* when *Paradise* appeared and excerpts from the interview are indicated as CA/KP.

> **CA/KP:** What happened was that when I decided to stop procrastinating and put together a new collection of stories, I sorted through what I had and realised that there was not one but nearly two books' worth and that it would work far better to separate the realistic and the fabulous stories, as opposed to mixing them together. I sent both collections to Biblioasis. John Metcalf immediately accepted the realistic collection, but was

reluctant even to read *Paradise and Elsewhere,* such was his prejudice against the genre. I more or less had to beg him even to look at it and after several months—well into the editing of the other book—he did so, with a heavy heart: dreading, he told me later, both the read and the letter he would have to write to me afterwards. But once he began, he was smitten and Biblioasis decided to publish it before the other collection.

Mildly ashamed (but only mildly) at this public parading of my prejudices—*I must put my pyjamas in the drawer marked pyjamas, I must eat my charcoal biscuit which is good for me*—contrition, contrition—I bought and read, in expiation, Angela Carter's *The Bloody Chamber* (1979) and *Black Venus* (1985).

(See also the Century List entries on Paul Glennon and Patricia Robertson for further evidence of reluctance.)

Many years before reading Kathy Page, I had read Margaret Atwood's *Murder in the Dark, Good Bones,* and *The Tent.*

Angela Carter (she was one year behind me in the English Department of Bristol University) and Margaret Atwood are obviously very clever indeed but neither avoids didacticism and neither makes me suspend disbelief and neither *moves* me.

Kathy Page does.

Caroline Adderson gets right to the heart of my prejudice in the following exchange about the story "Low Tide."

> **CA:** "Surrender to the unconscious" explains a lot about these stories. You pull off some astounding feats and the only way I can see that you've made it work is by following the inner logic of the narrative. I mean, you'd hardly sit down and say, "Oh, I know! I'll write a story where a seal emerges from the ocean as a woman and later turns into a bird!" One couldn't consciously pull that off without the story seeming utterly contrived and plot driven. But when I finished "Low Tide" it struck me that you'd achieved the perfect conclusion, one that is both surprising and inevitable. Do you think, then, that the reason so much genre writing is bad (hence the literary

prejudice against it), is because the writers are going at it from the outside rather than the inside?

KP: That's just it. And perhaps if you come at it from the outside trying to conform, the structural mechanics become more visible, whereas really it is better (more immersive) for the reader to be unaware of them? Just as in sports or juggling, it's best not to over-think... "Low Tide" is one of the newest stories in the book and was wonderful to write. I had the selkie myth in mind, of course, but wasn't interested in merely repeating it with different props and costumes.

I'm mainly a realistic writer and sometimes, especially when writing a novel, do a vast amount of research. I'm often meticulous about the accuracy of setting or mileu. But there's another part of me which yearns to go elsewhere, beyond the life-like animations of things that might plausibly happen in everyday reality or in historical time, and that yearning is where *Paradise and Elsewhere* comes from.

Who were Page's influences in this non-realistic tradition? In this excerpt from a letter she refers to some of them.

KP: I feel the early eighties were a rich time for non-realistic writing. Magical realism in the form of García Márquez's *One Hundred Years of Solitude* had been available for a decade or so, and Isabel Allende's *House of Spirits* came out in 1982. Both of these writers integrate the magical, ghostly and surreal with the recognisable world, and again, they do so Kafka-fashion by making it emotionally necessary and as physically real. Marquez's short story "A Very Old Man with Enormous Wings" can almost be read as a manifesto for his way of writing.

Angela Carter, for example, followed her stunning and utterly uncategorizeable dystopian/mythical novel *The Passion of New Eve* with an equally wonderful set of rewritten fairy stories, *The Bloody Chamber*. Reading Carter was as exciting as reading Kafka. It was thrilling to see how, by means of intricate and playful prose, quite the opposite of the simple styles the tales were originally cast in, Carter could break rules, expose assumptions, turn stereotypes inside out, all at the same time as being utterly charming and avoiding any temptation to set up an alternative orthodoxy. She was debunking the hidden messages and admonitions of our culture and offering possibilities for a new era, one in which Grandma's wisdom became questionable and the wolf and the girl might get to go to bed together, and Bluebeard, a serial killer, could be stopped by maternal intervention. Carter was a mistress of setting and cast her stories in a hinterland between dream and reality: again, this is something I've learned a great deal from. A.S. Byatt is another wonderful British writer, steeped in literary history, folk-tale and myth, who knows how to slip between the everyday and the otherworldly, how to blend the two. Sara Maitland likewise; she has a spiritual side to her work which I find off-putting but her early-eighties collection *Telling Tales* was also influential.

When editing story collections, I've often said to the writer, "OK. Here we are with (say) ten short stories. This is going to be the book you launch upon the world and that we hope is going to launch you. Now...
Which two stories in the typescript are the weakest?"
As soon as this question is asked, the answer is usually suddenly obvious. This is a strange and valuable truth. The weakness had not been so obvious before the question was put and the question could not have been put at an earlier stage without demoralizing the writer. It is as if the question suddenly brings the "odds against" into close focus for the first time. The question invites self-triage, as it were; the writers are pitted against their personal bests. They are suddenly forced to consider their pages not merely against the competition in the marketplace, but against nebulous but weighty tradition. The realized weakness of two stories, the *comparative* weakness, is not usually depressing and often leads to renewed determination "to purify the dialect of the tribe."
(Such an approach to a body of work was honed by my friendship with the painter Tony Calzetta, to whom this book is dedicated. Tony advocates a rapid tour of any new show to locate the

best painting, a painting that immediately consigns all the remaining paintings to second rank, freeing him to then locate the source of cheese and wine.)

When Kathy and I were editing *Paradise* there were two stories in the mix I thought were thinner than the rest, thinner in texture, and therefore thinner in feeling, too obviously vehicles for ideas. (They were entitled "Big Man" and "Yesterday's Astounding Events.")

Oh, how I distrust ideas!

I suggested to Kathy she jettison them and replace them with two new ones. The selkie story, "Low Tide," that Caroline and Kathy were talking about in the interview excerpt was one result, "We the Trees" was the other. Both stories are clear survivors in any triage operation.

> **KP:** "Low Tide" was written quite quickly (for me) to fill a gap in the book. *Paradise and Elsewhere* has several stories with desert settings and I felt it needed a watery story. The selkie stories came to mind: the notion of the seal woman as an exile, a captive, yet at the same time one who might love her captor, has always haunted me. In the traditional stories, she is often tricked or caught, with the man hiding her seal skin so that she cannot return to the water. I found myself wanting a different beginning—more motivation on the selkie's part—and I ended up with a seal woman who actively sought out new experience and a true mate. I also knew the story began at low tide, when the seabed is at its most exposed and the sea is on the verge of its return, and that the man my seal-woman met would be a lighthouse keeper. The rest—the story of an intense sexual relationship that begins with great promise yet becomes abusive—unfurled as I wrote. About halfway through I knew that the story would end with escape and flight: that if she could shapeshift once, then she would and must do so again at the end, and instead of returning, she would go further on.

I'll concentrate on "Low Tide" to suggest the magical quality of the entire collection.

(The only thing I found to grump about in the entire book was the names of the primitive characters in the primitive backwater described in "Lambing." They were called Ax, Crow, Hammer, Sling, Gull, and Lark.

In William Golding's *The Inheritors*, his Neanderthal characters are called Lok and Fa. I sometimes entertain the thought of writing a story set in some post-holocaust future in which the regressed, mutated characters are called Aubrey, Cecil, Noel, and Evelyn.)

Here is the opening paragraph of "Low Tide," the selkie, pelt shed, emerging from the sea as a human.

> It was hot, the sky a bowl of blue; waves slapped against the rock. I remember still the astounding sensation of the air on my face, stomach, shoulders, back and limbs—all over, like invisible hands. How it was to stand upright on new legs and feet: utterly strange, yet easy, and then, a moment later, such a feeling of weight! The land's pull made each step an intentional thing and turned mere standing into an act of resistance. Intensely aware of my new flesh, I waded ashore and walked along the beach, leaving my prints in damp, newly exposed sand: my heels, the balls of my feet, my ten toes.

At the far side of the bay is a small island with a lighthouse the only habitation. A man is watching her approach. He says he is her husband; he calls her Marina.

> He said he was my *husband*. He kept the lighthouse, and as well as that, he was a kind of artist, one who used science in the service of beauty, he said. Surely I remembered that? And the bed he had built for us on the third floor of the tower? Our wedding day, the drunken priest? The night of the storm?
>
> "I remember none of it," I told him. I was sitting on a pile of sacks in the stern of the boat. The ocean was flat and glossy, as the tide flowed in and bit by bit filled up the bay. It rippled gently as if there were muscles beneath its skin. Reflected light flickered on our faces. The man who claimed to have married me looked away a moment, then back.

"That may be for the best," he said. "Everything will be better this time, Marina, I promise you. I'm very sorry. I think I had every right to be angry, but I never meant to hurt you."

Naturally, I marked the word, *hurt*. And yet I knew that it was not me that he spoke of, and he seemed sincere. I liked his smoothness, the lean, muscular look of him, his strong-fingered hands, the intensity of his gaze. And that first time, constrained as we were by oars shelved to each side of us and by the struts and seats but most of all by being in a small vessel floating on the roof of my former world, can only be called exquisite: sex so gentle in its beginnings, so constrained and restrained—yet only seeming so, for within those limits our bodies' sensations were amplified like voices trapped in a cave, and at the end, shuddering, we broke free of all bounds, left the world and returned to it as if new. I saw, afterwards, that his hand bled from where he had slipped it between me and the floor of the boat.

The bloodied hand foreshadows.

Clarence Morgan's odd statements and questions lead us, ominously, into past events in the lighthouse.

He pulled me close and reached under the jacket to feel the slippery heat between my legs. His hands shook as he unfastened the horn buttons, and soon we made good use of the table.

How willing I was! He liked that. Likewise, I told him, and he liked that too. Both of us were greedy for pleasure. But more than that, I craved the deep forgetting at the heart of the act of love, that shedding of the trivial particulars that separate one being, one species, from another. Our desires were attuned, our bodies spoke. He fitted me. I liked him well, from the length and firmness of what he called his member to the gleam of his body hair in the firelight and the long muscles of his arms and legs. He seemed a good mate, even though after the act he must ask, whispering, his lips to my ear, his hands restless on my skin,

"Did you open yourself like this to him? Even if you did so, I do forgive you, because you have returned. But tell me, please."

"I don't understand," I said and pulled away.

We would not be persuaded by the story if it wasn't rooted in the everyday of lighthouse-keeping, or Mr. Morgan's photography, of Marina's study of Mr. Howard's tome on meteorology—*cirrostratus, cumulonimbus*—wouldn't be persuaded if we could not feel the everpresent wind bending the grasses and stunted trees towards the mainland, if we could not see the clouds the wind pushes across the sky, could not smell "ozone and kelp and emptiness."

Despite the ceiling ventilation it was unbearably hot near the light. Below, in the watch room it was cooler, and there, at five in the morning and five in the afternoon, without fail, we re-filled the kerosene, and wound the clockwork tight. It was a circular room, with strong oak floors to support all our supplies and equipment, and generous windows all around to let in light. There was a desk, where the lighthouse records were written, and shelves where they were kept; a narrow door led out to the observation platform. The platform was also used to support the ladder when the light room windows were cleaned after heavy storms, and in any case, according to regulation, no less than four times a year. Also in the watch room was a bed built out from the wall: Why, he said, add in a journey up and down the spiral stairs when night observations needed to be taken? And why be separated? Why stay down in the gloom of the cottage, when there was so much light to be had and we could see each other so very well?

"I shouldn't believe in you," he said, looking up into my face while I knelt astride him on that bed, rocking, squeezing just enough to keep us both on the brink of our double descent, "but I must."

I always believed in him. But at night my underwater dreams seemed just as true: the dives and twists, the impossible grace and freedom of a lost world. More than once I woke in tears and the feeling lasted for days: a terrible grief and longing to be where I could no longer survive. All I could do then was gaze out to sea, or walk the shore cursing myself for being careless; I yearned for that dense, oily fur, the fat-sheathed musculature beneath. There was no remedy. But if he was gentle, he could ease me back to the pleasures of our life on the island off East Point, where gulls and terns and albatrosses soared and wheeled and plummeted into the water, and the wind blew clean and constant, bending the low grasses and the wildflowers and the few small trees back towards the mainland, and bringing with it the smells of ozone and kelp and emptiness, while all the time the clouds it pushed across the sky stretched and grew and shrank and grew again.

Still surrounded by the sea, I lived on land, a wife of sorts. I practised my letters. I learned how to keep the record. In a single sentence, that ran across the width of the book, I must include the weather, any passing vessels, any incidents, and the state of the equipment and supplies. I learned about the winds and Mr. Howard's names for the clouds: the veils of cirrostratus, the ominous mounds of cumulonimbus, heavy with rain. I learned how to trim the lamps and clean the parts of a lens, how to use the telescope, how to calculate distance, read a chart and judge the course of a ship.

Marina's gradually *becoming* Marina is suggested, reinforced by brief but powerful scenes such as her assuming the clothes that had belonged to the real Marina.

He reached into the chest and pulled out two small shapeless pieces of fabric.

"For your legs," he explained. "Would you please just try them?"

The material I later learned was made from moth cocoons and the finest water-repellent wool of a special breed of sheep; all clothes then were made from beasts and plants.

At the end of the story, Marina, tired of crazed abuse and increasing cruelty, escapes by transforming herself again and becoming a bird. We are to assume that the bird she becomes is a mollymawk, an albatross—"I watched them slip and soar," she says of them earlier, "and it lifted my heart."

> Out there on the platform, buffeted by the winds, I breathed in the cold salt air and watched the seabirds, marvelling at the way they stayed together, and at the steady beating of their wings, mile on mile. The largest birds, the mollymawks, pass without apparent movement or effort through the air; their wings fixed, just barely tilting from side to side to ride the currents like waves, they simply turn their heads the way they wish to go... Such huge birds, the mollies, yet it was as if they had no weight. I watched them slip and soar and it lifted my heart. I longed for the bird-feeling and imagined it: the ocean and the land spread out beneath in intricate detail, but also in depth and with extraordinary focus. In my mind's eye I saw as if from very far above the rocks the island and the tower where I myself stood looking out. The wind blew steadily to the east and the air seemed to offer itself to me. And I would not go back inside, would not endure another night with Clarence Morgan, the clockwork beneath us unwinding itself cog by cog until the next time it must be set, and the next, and the next. Ignoring his call, I climbed onto the rails, balanced for one terror-stricken moment then gave myself to the wind. Immediately I felt the new strength in my chest and back, the structural dominance of two great limbs.
>
> The water below was almost pink. Just two wing-beats, and I was rising fast. I could no longer hear his call, and did not look back, for the air is a kind of ecstasy, a far freer thing than even a swimmer could believe.
>
> Yet I'll admit that come spring, on my way to the grounds, I did return, and landed on a low cliff to watch my former keeper, on the beach below, set up a new version of his camera. The apparatus was directed at the seals sunning themselves on the rocks. He was thinner and older than I recalled. He had broken his

promise not to hurt me, and there was a gun slung over his shoulder which I knew he might use. Yet even so, watching him, I felt for the first time the need to open my wings wide and stretch my neck to its utmost, then tuck my head deep down this way, then that, to stretch and bow and tread out the steps of our dance. A sound came out of me, part shriek, part moan: oh, look at me! For looking is the beginning of the dance. He must see me exactly as I am and what I do, the exact way of it, and I, likewise. And by scrupulous imitation, turn on turn, we come to see better and prove to each other that we see, and what we see. We must show that each can and will exactly follow the other, or, failing, try again...

Hearing me, the keeper turns and reaches for his binoculars. He faces me, but gives no sign of recognition or sympathy. My call dies in my throat; I put myself into the wind, run, and scull hard until the updraft bears me and I ride suddenly without effort and free of the earth's jealous pull; I soar above vast ocean into the even vaster air. I must fly on to the place where I will meet my kind, and find the one with whom I can perfect the dance.

Albatrosses mate for life and their courtship rituals are a kind of patterned dance where each must follow the other's movements exactly, the two becoming, as it were, one.

The dance is so central to the story's meaning yet Kathy, because of the story's structure, cannot describe it fully because a partner is missing, so I'll digress somewhat to describe the dance itself and what it means, not in albatrosses, but in cranes. Different species but similar performance, the significance the same.

In 1987 I was in Ljubljana, the capital of Slovenia, then still a republic within Yugoslavia. I was on a lecture tour arranged by External Affairs talking in all the Yugoslavian capitals about Canadian Literature. Driving from the airport to Ljubljana, I saw standing by the side of a stream in a misty meadow two huge white birds. The taxi-driver told me they were cranes, that they wintered in North Africa and returned to Europe every year to the same nest, a great platform of rushes they'd made in the stream near an old stone bridge. Cranes, he told me, mated for life.

Later, I returned to that place and watched their courtship ritual. I was so moved by it that I used it as the finale of my novella *Forde Abroad*.

After much fanning of tail feathers, pacing, parading, jumping into the air together, simultaneous bowing to the nest:

> One of them stretched its long, heron-like neck straight up into the air and gave forth a great trumpet blast of noise, harsh and unbelievably loud.
>
> *Krraaa-krro.*
>
> The other bird straightened the S of its neck and replied.
>
> *Krraaa-krro.*
>
> And then the two birds paced towards each other until their breasts were touching and began to rub each other's neck with their heads, long swooping-and-rising caresses, their beaks nuzzling at the height of the embrace.

Kathy Page describes this ritual I've described as "the dance," and she is exactly right.

So this astonishing story of seal-woman-bird, and demented lighthouse-keeper, unlike much of its genre, somehow becomes believable and moving, rising in its finale almost to song, to a paean of love-as-relationhip.

The stories in Kathy Page's second book, *The Two of Us*, are in naturalistic mode and I'll look at two of the sixteen to suggest the range of pleasures they offer. The two stories are "The Last Cut" and "Northern Lights." There are other stories in the collection that are particular favourites, "The House on Manor Close," "Red Dog," "The Two of Us," "It is July Now," all memorable performances but space prevents my visiting them. What amazes is her versatility.

"The Last Cut" is about a hairdresser, Eric, who is pressured into staying long beyond closing hour to attend an old customer, Mrs. Swenson, whose cut, she insists, must be done that day.

> Mrs. Swenson was one of Renée's regulars, but Eric had once or twice cut her hair, which he remembered she wore in a

knot at the back. She was maintenance, rather than style, middle-aged, very low-key.

He waits in the empty salon, waits past the time of the appointment, waits in increasing irritation until "a small woman in a much-too-large coat pushed in through the big glass door."

"I'm afraid we're closed," he said.
"Sorry!" she said in Mrs. Swenson's voice.

The gaunt figure wearing a beret has been undergoing chemo.

Eric cuts what remains of her hair and helps her choose a becoming hat from the variety she has brought with her.

The story confounds our expectations. What looks as if it's going to be a heart-rending story about a cancer victim turns subtly into a story about Eric; it could even be read as a story about art and its function. By the time we reach the end of the story, we realize that Mrs. Swenson has been almost a prop, a stage device to illuminate the play's real star and subjects.

Eric is built very carefully. That he is gay is made fairly obvious early on, but as we settle down to read a "gay-hairdresser story" Page builds this deliberate cliché into an experience that is both surprising and as exhaustingly moving for us as it is for Eric.

After his work has been interrupted by dealing with Mrs. Swenson on the phone, he returns to his work on his client.

Back at the mirror, he apologized profusely, misted Cara's hair, unclipped the top section, combed, then paused with the scissors poised.

"You're sure?" A brief nod: she was absolutely certain.

He liked that, and he liked the way she watched his hands go about their work—interested, expecting the best. No anxiety. He knew already that she could carry off the bold asymmetrical cut she'd chosen, and this, for him, was what it was all about: creating a splendid surface that gave pleasure, enhanced the face, drew others in. Something that emphasized the best points of a personality, and served as status symbol—armour, even, if required. The dramatic statement. The perfect product. The finishing touches. *This* he was good at. Not social work. Not—

"Let me guess," he said to Cara. "Media?" Her eyebrows leaped up, a fresh smile formed.

"PR."

"Close."

During the cutting of Clara's hair, he struggles with his feelings of guilt and anger, revisiting old wounds, old slights.

He might be useless with sickness, crying, or babies, but he could do chat. Also gifts, surprises, places to go. He always knew exactly what to buy for his sisters' kids at birthdays and Christmas: jackpot every time.

"You spend too much," Emma said to him once, taking him aside in the kitchen. "What are you trying to make up for?" She'd put the flat of her hand on his chest. "It's okay. You don't need to."

"I don't know what you mean," he said.

In this next quotation we can see Page beginning to build Eric into something more complex than a tradesman; there's nothing missing but there's something there unexpected.

Sprigs of hair gathered around their feet and the junior swept them away. Cara talked about an art gallery event she was organizing, and Eric nodded, his comb gliding through the damp, well-conditioned hair. Periodically, his eyes flicked up to meet hers in the glass. Eight or more hours a day he talked in the mirror like this. After work, if he went straight into some kind of social situation, he missed the mirror, felt at the same time not quite there and overexposed.

Was there something missing in him?

He finishes his work on Clara. His changed scissors make a new sound, "faint but very sharp and pure." Slowly, Kathy Page is beginning the build of Eric as an artist, not obviously so and much open to interpretation, but the ritual aspects of the haircut are rehearsed, "compliments and thanks," and, a flourish, "the final removal of the cloak." That final line of the quotation: "At the end of a cut, he liked to shake hands." This is both an assertion of himself and a tribute—going both ways—to artistry. One would be unlikely to shake hands with, say, a plumber.

> He pumped up the chair, combed again, changed scissors and leaned in close, aware of the different sounds the new pair made—faint but very sharp and pure. Soon would come the blow-dry and the shoulder brushing, the showing of the back of the head, the nods, smiles, compliments and thanks, the final removal of the cloak. It was silly to let the thought of Mrs. Swenson get in the way of these things, all of which he enjoyed, but it did. He was already thinking that he must check the room at the back, make sure it was properly set up, clean and warm enough. Anger washed over him, then guilt, which he struggled to repudiate: So that's how it is. We're not all the same. What I do is worth *something*.
>
> He reached for the finishing spray. Cara closed her eyes and the air filled with a delicate, rosemary-scented mist.
>
> "There," he told her, and she tossed her head to see the way it moved.
>
> "Perfect!"
>
> At the end of a cut, he liked to shake hands.

The theatricality of haircutting is played up in the following quotation wherein Eric prepares to cut what is left of Mrs. Swanson's wisps.

> "Thanks for fitting me in. Next week," she said, "after the chemo, I'll be feeling very bad, so it had to be now."
>
> It was every bit as difficult as he'd thought. Every bit. He swallowed back the sour taste in his mouth. If he could have run, he would have.

"Actually, Mrs. Swenson—Susanna," Eric told her, as brightly as he could, "you're looking very well." He aimed to go on from there to say that she might be surprised, when the hair was gone, by how interesting the face can look. Then he could have suggested removing the beret. But something—something that came from Mrs. Swenson rather than from him—prevented all of this. He remained perched on the stool, and for a long moment she studied herself in the mirror, examining her own image carefully, as if to remember it. Fronds of grey hair peeked out from under the edge of the beret.

"I lost weight," she said with a shrug. "Do you have kids yet?" Eric explained how he wasn't the settling type.

[...]

Eric groped for words, found none, stared back at her.

"I'm sorry," he began.

"Ach—it's only *hair*," she interrupted, suddenly looking away. "Please start."

So there it was: the once-long dark-honey hair, now in a short, greyish bob, thinning in patches. He stood behind her; their eyes met in the glass. Out of habit, Eric ran his fingers through the hair and smiled at the mirror-woman looking steadily back at him.

"I have some hats in my bag," she said. "I don't normally wear one and I didn't know what to get. I trust you'll help me choose the best one afterwards?"

He managed a nod, picked up the comb, explained how he would approach it in stages, and then made a pretense of sectioning the head. It was as if he were on stage, in a play.

What happens next is a piece of writing so extraordinary, so beautiful that I must quote all of it. The massage of Susanna's skull is an act of love and creation wherein Eric loses himself, loses all sense of time, an act that makes the long day past seem insubstantial as a dream. When the massage is over, Eric retreats to the washroom, where he weeps.

He emerges to help Susanna choose a hat. She tries on one after another, passing to him "an Elizabeth Taylor turban affair" while she tries on a pilot's hat with ear flaps.

Eric lowers the turban, settling it on his own head.

This odd action seems to me the very heart of the story. It is susceptible to various readings but all centre on what we are to think and feel about Eric. In this particular instance, I'm more than content to resist "the intellect's eagerness to foreclose" and simply gaze upon the beturbaned Eric; the longer and more concentratedly we gaze upon him, the more the story will, to use Seamus Heaney's lovely word, *discover* itself.

"Please, get rid of it!" Her papery lids sank protectively over her eyes. He turned on the electric razor. Lightly, he pressed the crown of her head until she had lowered it enough, then he worked up from the nape, exposing the entry of the spinal cord into the skull, the curves to either side, the broad plates of bone.

Some styles involved shaving the sides only, or thin bands and patterns across the entire head, but a whole head, plain as an egg—he'd never before had a client who wanted it, though, of course, in this situation, *wanted* was not the correct word. The cleared area was a bluish white, cold looking, like some kind of stone; but at the same time, as he worked, he could feel the warmth rising from her scalp.

The shaver hummed busily as he pushed the last of the soft fuzz aside, first one side and then the other. He noticed how her skull was deep from front to back, squarish at the sides, and gently domed on top; shaved, it looked oddly larger than before. He switched off the razor, slipped it in its pouch and ran his fingertips lightly over her head, checking for anything missed. Her skin, stretched over the dome of bone, was warm and slightly oily. Where the hair had been growing more strongly or had been protected from the razor by dips in the skull were rough patches, like velvet rubbed against the grain.

Her eyes closed, her forehead pulled down, her eyebrows bunched tight. The whole face was tight. It was not what he planned, but Eric's fingers found the right place, just above the pivot of her jaw; slowly, he rotated the skin there and the tissues beneath until he felt them, and then her entire jaw, loosen.

He progressed little by little, downwards along the lower ridge of the skull. He supported her forehead with his left hand and continued with the right, pressing firmly into the muscles and tendons at the top of the neck where her spinal cord entered the skull—a smooth column suddenly lost, like a train swallowed by a tunnel. He raised her head again, let her balance it, then worked slowly all over the side and top of the scalp, moving the skin infinitesimally this way, then that. She let out a sigh. He placed his hands, the fingertips just separated, on her hairline and then moved them very slowly back over the entire head. When he reached the neck, he brought them closer and then kneaded the muscles there. At the end, he cupped her head in both hands before resting them gently on her shoulders.

Looking up, he saw in the mirror his neat and familiar self, standing behind an older woman who seemed half space-alien, half baby.

"There," he said. "There, it's done now, Susanna."

Her eyes were still closed. He waited.

When Susanna saw herself, she put her hand to her mouth to catch the shriek that leaped from it. She turned to face him, breaking the mirror's spell. He wiped the moisture from under his eyes with his forefinger.

"I don't see why *you're* crying," she told him. "It *is* a shock, but I feel...not too bad. I feel better."

"Excuse me. I'm sorry!" he said, "Very sorry." There was nothing to apologize for, she said. *Please*, she said again, she did want him to help her with the hats. It would only take a minute.

Eric adjourned to the washroom. He closed his eyes and surrendered, allowed the sobs to work their way through him, amplify themselves in a room made of slate and glass. When he emerged, red-eyed, exhausted, Susanna waited calmly in front of the mirror wearing a purple knitted hat that rose to a point above her head, with plaited strings that dangled down the sides. It was like something an elf might wear.

"So?" she asked, tilting her chin, pouting a little. Exposing her bald head again, she removed the hat, offered it to him, reached into her bag and brought out an Elizabeth Taylor turban affair, purchased at a charity store, she said. She sat up straighter, raised her eyebrows.

"What do you think? Is it me?" she asked. "Or this?" She handed him the turban, pulled on a pilot's hat with earflaps, then a checkered cap.

"Susanna," he told her solemnly, but half-smiling, as he lowered the turban onto his head, "the thing is, Susanna, with good bones like yours, you can probably carry off any of these."

He sat in the back room of the salon, wearing the turban, and watched her try on the other hats. What he'd said was true. The oversized cap, the skullcap, the striped bobble hat, the felted wool helmet with a peacock feather on the side, the fine-knit toque, the white fluffy synthetic fur, the astrakhan: every one of them suited her. The first cut of the day seemed like something that had happened in a film, or a dream. He had no idea what time it was.

"Northern Lights" appeals to me both as a reader and writer. The story it tells is straightforward and uncomplicated, the marriage of a driven woman and an unambitious husband. Joe started as an aspiring artist; with the passing of time "he still sketched but the painting got lost." Christina wrote her books "about sugar, slavery, tobacco, rubber, chocolate—and that meant travelling."

He became a "home-husband" and looked after their two children, Ben and Andrea. She, meanwhile, forged through the academic ranks. The marriage grew rocky. The following brief paragraph encapsulates the years and delivers us back to the present.

He met lots of other women as he carted Ben and Andy around. He had an afternoon-sex phase. A whisky-drinking phase. Depression, which eventually led to the job on the nightline. For a while, in the middle of all this, he understood that Christina was ashamed of him. At one point, she moved another man into the house, a small, bearded semiotician from Hamburg, but Joe stayed drunkenly put, and Gustav eventually departed. And then, suddenly, somehow, their friends were divorcing and amazed at them for being still together. "Home-husbands" became briefly fashionable and they were pioneers. Ben left home, then Andrea. They had done the whole thing.

Christina is offered a plum job in a Canadian university and she makes active plans to take it. Joe slowly realizes that he is, if not happy, then content with where he is.

"Supposing I've changed my mind, suppose I want to stay here," he begins, "would you still want to go, for yourself?" His head clears, as if from years of fog. His body settles firm around his bones. He fixes her face, studies it, looking for clues.

"I have resigned, Joe," she says. Not what he asked.

"They'd have you back."

"Not this year! What is this? Talk about appalling timing," she says, and she's absolutely right. "This is what you always wanted," she says and, again, she's absolutely right, but his heart pounds and his voice rings out.

"Answer me, please—would you still want to go? Is this for you or me? Sorry," he adds more quietly.

"It is an incredible chance, Joe," she says, "Not just my job. For a new life."

But, Joe is thinking, I want the one I have! I want to know what Paula looks like with her new haircut. Whether Dave ever writes his screenplay, or Mary Coates got to Birmingham… The place where he lives surrounds him. It's a raft—solid, well made—and if he clings to it, it will protect him from Christina's plans, from his own acquiescence, from anything.

"I'm sick of being jerked about," he says.

"We've been here nearly ten years!"

"If you're doing it for me, I don't want to go, okay? I don't want to go. I hope that's clear. Are you doing it for me, or for you with me on the side? That's my question—so answer it, will you, please!"

She turns on the light by the bed. They face each other, just a few secrets each between them. Her eyes are bright, the skin around them ever so slightly creped. "I want to stay here. Us to stay here," he says, sitting there on the bed with his thinning hair and soft belly, his unpainted pictures, the empty house all around. He's desperate for a drink he mustn't allow himself.

"Just when I've made it work out, in the end!" she says. Her voice tears at its edges—at him too—but the fact is, she still has not told him: Is she doing it for him, or for her, with him on the side? He has never been so angry, not in his entire life. It's a massive charge, running through him, like a kind of electrocution. He could burn up, strike out—but then it hits him that after all this time, she and he are still the same as they ever were, only more so.

Everything dissipates. Her face is just a blur. Her clothes sigh as she moves towards him. Outside, it's very dark.

"Joe?" she asks, "Joe, why cry now?"

That's how the story ends. This has so far been the story's skeleton or armature. What did I mean by saying I admired and envied the story's architecture?

Joe realizes involvement and a measure of contentment in his neighbourhood and street as he is on his way home from working as a volunteer manning phones helping the homeless find shelter. What follows is the heart of the story, a loving streetscape and, if such a word exists, hearscape; it stands in contrast and in opposition to the new life in Canada.

A new life. A fairy tale. And indeed, among the photographs she had brought to show him, the couple who had preceded them, wearing puffy jackets trimmed with fur, skied across a frozen lake towards a wooden house backed by snow-laden trees. He did not ask: When did you apply for this?

[...]

It's fully dark now, the streetlights pooling on the pavement. He walks the few hundred yards home, passing a blowsy girl waiting for a different bus and the hunched, grey-haired man who always seems to be at the corner of their street, smoking and watching his terrier defecate in the gutter. Joe passes him with a nod, walks on, taking in the gardens—one wildly fertile, a miniature jungle, the dark shapes of bushes and plants bursting out of the small space. Its owner, often seen wearing a blue checked housecoat to water and trim, is sitting inside with the curtains open and the TV on. Another patch is paved in stone, with just one large pot containing a eucalyptus tree to one side of the door, a galvanized watering can at the other. He has never seen the person it belongs to but they have a piano and play like a god, though it's unpredictable—sometimes he catches it for several days on end, then not at all for months... How many thousand times has he seen, smelled and heard all this, this typical semi-suburban London street with trees and Victorian houses, this place where people come to bring up kids and not be totally broke? Why is it still so interesting?

At the gate to their house, he stops, listens to the distant purr of the traffic on the main road. A telephone rings, a light is turned off, a breath of wind runs through the plane trees. The next-door neighbour (and there's another story) puts a bottle on the step, a particular, hollow, chinking sound which makes Joe know he will miss doing so himself, and that he will also miss the milkman, Dave, an extraordinary fellow with a passion for Dostoyevsky who says he was once was a priest and, after his shifts, goes home to work on a movie script that will knock the world flat. And he will miss Carol, two streets away in the estate, who stops by or calls once a week or so to share what further sense she's made of her mess of a life. She's in her seventies. He met her during his drinking phase; she's still in hers.

"Are you there?" she'll say. "It's this: there is no Continuity." Or, "I'm pretty sure that there is no Essential Self. Most people can fool themselves, but because of the life I've lived, I can't." Or, "There's only Memory, dear. I'm hanging on to mine by the skin of my teeth." She hasn't called so often lately, and he realizes, as he thinks of her, that this could well be because he's going. In two weeks' time. They have a leaving party planned.

The neighbour setting down an empty milk bottle for the milkman to collect in the morning, "a particular, hollow, chinking sound"— such observed and heard detail is precisely what propels Kathy Page into the front rank of story writers,

But what did I mean by saying I admired the *architecture* of this story? To answer that question, what follows is the opening of the story.

"London," his caller is saying. "I'm in London, by the road. In a phone box." She has a worn but once-rich voice, a faint accent he can't at first place.

"So what's the situation?" Joe adjusts his headset, ticks some boxes on the form. Opposite him, Paula is making one of her Blu Tack animals as she listens to her own call. She makes them every night: elephants, whales, a giraffe with a matchstick neck, even the occasional human being, naked and less than chaste— none of them bigger than the top digit of a thumb.

"I need somewhere to sleep," Joe's caller says.

"Can you tell me how come?"

"I'm forty years old and I've never had anywhere to damn well go," she says, "so how do I know how bloody-well come!"

"I'm sorry," he says, as they were taught, "but I need to ask these questions in order to help." There is no reply, just breathing.

"Date of birth: you must have been born in... '59?" he says.

"No," she says. "Fifth of May, 1935. It says so."

"You would be sixty-two, then," he says. There's a long pause. He expects her to argue, braces for it. But when she does eventually reply, her voice is small and disappointed, like something shrunk in the wash.

"I might be," she says. "I must be, then, mustn't I? I have to get back to Birmingham," she tells him, her voice still small, but firm.

"This is a London service. All I can try to do is get you a hostel place here," he says. "I can do that." *Vacancies: female 3, male 4,* the screen in front of him reads. He presses *next.* "Westminster," he says, "Southwark or—"

"Birmingham," she interrupts. "Birmingham, not somewhere else. It has Birmingham on my birth certificate. That's where I should be. Best all round. It's people not being in the right places that makes everything so hard, so very hard as they are, very hard and falling apart all the time, just violence and misery! If it's two thousand miles away or two miles away, same difference—it's no good, no damn good! Do you understand? The right place stops you breaking up in bits. People should go to there, wherever it is. You must know that. If you don't, you're in the wrong, fucking, damn place yourself." She's breathing hard.

"When were you last in Birmingham?"

"I remember—" she says brightly, "it had a green door."

"Can you remember the road name?"

"No," she says. Then: "Yes! *Gallstone Drive*. I think it was thirty-six or sixty-six. Call them. They know me there. Tell them Laura."

"I'll put you on hold, Laura," he says. "Gallstone Drive," he hisses at Paula, who is taking a call at the desk opposite, and enjoys seeing her try to keep a straight face. He calls emergency social services in Birmingham. *Gallstone Drive!* But there is a place she might mean, the woman there says: a number thirteen Galveston Road is her best suggestion. It's what used to be called a "home."

"Might be the place," Laura says, anxious. "Ask about the green door."

As we read this beginning, we must see Laura as a batty old woman so confused or drunk as to make little sense; by the time we reach the end of the story—or when we reread—we see that Laura is talking exactly to the centre of Joe's emotional quandary:

> It's people not being in the right places that makes everything so hard, so very hard as they are, very hard and falling apart all the time, just violence and misery!

What a brilliant construction! I can't think of another Canadian writer who has so boldly constructed a story whose lyrical ending is foreshadowed and underpinned by what, at first reading, seems opening irrelevance.

Kathy Page's most recent book, *Dear Evelyn*, is composed of the best stories she has yet written. The linked stories mainly concern Harry Miles and the woman he marries, Evelyn Hill, though in later stories their three daughters play increasingly important roles. Through linkage, the book has some of the qualities of a novel but its emotional power resides in the imagery of the stories as discrete creations.

The stories follow Harry from boyhood until he meets Evelyn and marries her. Their life is interrupted by Harry's service in the Second World War. On his return, his career in municipal construction begins:

> Timber, Labour, and Economies of Scale with Multiples of Units, while behind him the radio plays and the girls squeal delightfully in their bedroom across the hall. It is just like the army but without the noise and excitement.

As the marriage plays out, Evelyn becomes more and more the dominant partner. Harry, who adores her, suppresses his artistic yearnings and labours to provide for them and to build a new house far away from "the narrow soot-stained terraces where they both began."

Evelyn becomes less dear as the stories move on in time; she behaves autocratically, is swept by her emotions, brooks no interference in or modifications of her plans, withholds her sexual favours, and grows intolerant and touchy to the point of seeing Harry largely as a messy intruder in her home's routine, neatness, and décor.

Harry is, by nature, a committed person. In many ways much stronger than Evelyn, he can bend to Evelyn's wind without feeling compromised or diminished. His nature is suggested in his reaction, as a schoolboy, to Shakespeare's sonnet 116:

> He noticed the image of the ship, the many iterations of what love was not, puzzled over *the remover to remove*. He

was excited by the poem's extremity. It seemed to him that choosing to make a commitment even to the edge of doom would in some way that he could not begin to explain enlarge a person.

By the final, wrenching stories in the sequence, Evelyn has consigned the incontinent Harry to an "assisted living facility."

The story "Desperate Glory" suggests some of the richness and depth of all the stories in *Dear Evelyn*. The title is taken from these lines in Wilfred Owen's poem "Dulce et Decorum Est":

> My friend, you would not tell with such high zest
> > To children ardent for some desperate glory
> > The old Lie: Dulce et Decorum est
> > Pro patria mori

Would not tell the "old Lie" if you had seen what Owen had seen.

The story concerns the young Harry's involvement with a new teacher of English, Mr. Whitehorse, who is a veteran of the horrors of the Great War and who attempts to engage the boys in poetry. Harry is probably his one success. Mr. Whitehorse, soon nicknamed by the boys "Dark," "Whitearse," and "Workhorse," has a glass eye and facial scars from shrapnel; he brings to the reading of poetry an unusual gravity.

One of the pleasures of this story is, for want of a more accurate word, its handling of "sociological" background or, more bluntly, "class," a matter addressed directly, and indirectly, by loving depiction of place and history.

> He'd been awarded a scholarship to cover most of the fees. They had bought the uniform second hand: cap, boater and blazer with *Pour Bien Desirer* and the portcullis sewn in gold on the breast pocket. Each evening his mother sponged and pressed the uniform while he slept, and each morning she rose early to pack lunches for him and his father and brother. Then it was a half an hour's walk between two worlds.

His father had accompanied him the first day. It was straight all the way once they reached Earlsfield Road; as the hill picked up, the shops thinned out and the terraces grew progressively bigger, until they detached themselves from each other at the top, where they sported stained glass, carved gables and attic rooms for the maids. The road ran close to the railway, past Spencer Park, where the roof of the Royal Patriotic Building became visible above the trees, and on to the Roundhouse and Battersea Rise. The school gates, right next to the railway line, were unassuming. But through them you could see a gatehouse and a tree-lined path. The school had an ancient charter and had moved out from the city fifty years ago into a steep, red-brick building with a tower, arched windows and a courtyard, a warren of a place surrounded by gardens and huge, perfect playing fields.

A sixty-pounder from the Great War, given in recognition of the school's sacrifice, was parked in the grounds in front of the main entrance. The day began with prayers in the dark wooden chapel, and the Officers' Training Corps was all but obligatory. Boys had the use of a library and a swimming pool and ate their lunches at long tables in a room flooded with light; they learned Latin, calculus and physics, modern languages, mathematics, rugby and rowing.

"You'll not get this chance again. Pay attention and speak up, but be polite," Harry's father said at the gate. His hand glanced heavily from his son's shoulder, as if to push him on and in, then he strode away, already late for his job at the United Metal Works.

Harry's scholarship opened for him a world that was impossible to glimpse from State schools; his drilling in the Officers' Training Corps, more or less compulsory in all public schools, ("public" in the UK meaning private and fee-paying) resulted in the Second World War in his immediate commissioning as a second lieutenant. As an officer, his social world and class "ranking" were once again expanded, enlarged.

Albert Miles had started out on lathe, moved up to setting the machines. He knew his numbers, enjoyed reckoning and brought it to every aspect of his life—even laid out his allotment garden with exact measurements and calculated yields in advance. From their early years he'd drilled both sons in mental arithmetic. At Harry's age, his older brother, George, was a natural whose lightning calculations became a party-piece. But George was also drawn to roaming the commons, shooting neighbours' cats with his pellet gun, and begging rides on motorbikes. He didn't *apply* himself.

Harry did not have the same gift, but found a kind of satisfaction in numbers. They were a means to an end. He excelled in the London County Council Scholarship Exam because he badly wanted to and it was clear to him that what they were looking for was obedience to the task, to the given facts and the rules. You must take the time to understand exactly what was required, write the calculation in neat, well-aligned columns without errors, then state the correct answer in a well-constructed sentence free of spelling or punctuation mistakes: They travelled seven thousand miles in six months. They consumed fifteen apples per family per week. The journey lasted four days, three hours and ten minutes. Answers must be underlined, using a ruler. No smudging.

Parsing sentences started out in a similar vein, but the bare sense that arose from the relationship of one part to another was only the beginning of what the words might say to you, of where the thread of meaning might lead. Harry half hated and half loved words, held them in a kind of squeamish fascination because of their very slipperiness, because they could take you anywhere at all, including somewhere you did not wish to go, and because his father trusted only facts, and, despite the lack of application, preferred George: George this, George that, George the other, who had now talked his way into a half-decent job in the Gramophone Works and was in everyone's good books again.

Mr. Whitehorse's idealistic teaching of poetry carried a concomitant belief in the importance of the natural world and of a person having their being most fully within a history. "A pastoral vision was something they carried inside them, in what Yeats had called their deep heart's core, and it was part of the poet's task to keep that vision alive."

The boys almost immediately reduced "deep heart's core" to "old fart's bore," but in Harry these feelings and ideas seeded and took root.

> Withering and keen, John Clare had called winter. The cast iron radiator beneath the window was barely warm, but Harry sat close enough to press his left leg against it, absorbing all its heat. He had come to enjoy the poetry class more than anything except for games. He liked chemistry too, and there was a similarity: explosions, transformations. You never knew where the lesson would go, what would happen, how you might feel, what you might discover or be forced, suddenly, to think about.
>
> Another train passed, its whistle hooting mournfully, like some huge mechanical owl. The railway, Whitehorse told them, had changed everything. It ran along what had once been a field's edge and the boundary of a mediaeval estate, and set the boundaries of the school's current property. Just forty years ago the streets they walked to come to school had been open fields. The old landscape and the people who had tended it persisted in the names of places and streets: Lavender Hill. Southfields. Earlsfield. Osiers Road. And the rural life of Northamptonshire which John Clare had depicted so lovingly over a century ago was changing even as he wrote, and that, surely was why the poem seemed to ache with nostalgia, a word derived from Greek words for pain or longing, and for home... Harry, looking out at the snow, thought suddenly of his father, in summertime, bringing home along with the usual vegetables, a bunch of red and purple dahlias that he'd grown on their allotment by the cemetery. The way his mother's face opened up as she set them in the jar.
>
> They considered "The Lake Isle of Innisfree," page 405, and "Upon Westminster Bridge," page 399.
>
> Human kind, Whitehorse said, should not be separated from the natural world. A pastoral vision was something they carried

inside them, in what Yeats had called their *deep heart's core*, and it was part of the poet's task to keep that vision alive.

Old fart's bore, someone wrote on a scrap of paper. The back of the class shook with laughter, but Harry screwed the note up and shoved it into his inkwell then had to surreptitiously dry his fingers on his trouser leg when Whitehorse invited him to read.

Page performs brilliantly this handing-on of the torch or baton from Mr. Whitehorse to Harry when Whitehorse asks Harry to read an unnamed poem by an unnamed poet. Here is how she handles this scene, paying readers the compliment of their knowing the poem or guessing correctly which poem it must be.

> It was the last poem in the book, page 539, on the left side: four verses, twelve lines in all. Harry ran his eyes over it, drew breath.
>
> It was hot, and a train stopped unexpectedly. That was all: the name of the place, a man coughing. Heat, haystacks, plants and birds: it was a poem in which nothing happened. And yet as he read, the words remade the room. There was a silence, when he finished, in which he at least felt the heat and heard the birds.
>
> "What did you think of it?" Whitehorse asked.
>
> He'd noticed that the sentences either stopped before the lines' ends, or ran over them, so that you did not so much notice the rhymes, which in any case came only alternately, and in the final stanza, loosened their grip yet further. He'd noticed that, and more, too much to say.
>
> "Different, sir," he said.
>
> Whitehorse gave an almost imperceptible nod, then switched his attention to the class in general, swivelling his head this way and that in the slightly exaggerated way of his to which they were all now oblivious. "This writer, I believe, will turn out to be one of the twentieth century's most important poets," he said.

The poem that Harry reads is called "Adlestrop" by Edward Thomas, who was killed in the Great War in 1917. It is a poem that captures

and expresses all that Mr. Whitehorse wished to give Harry. By with-
holding the actual lines, Page is creating *Harry's* experience of the
poem.

(For those curious—

Alderstrop

> Yes. I remember Alderstrop
> The name, because one afternoon
> Of heat the express-train drew up there
> Unwontedly. It was late June.
>
> The steam hissed. Someone cleared his throat.
> No one left and no one came
> On the bare platform. What I saw
> Was Alderstrop—only the name
>
> And willows, willow-herb, and grass,
> And meadowsweet, and haycocks dry,
> No whit less still and lonely fair
> Than the high cloudlets in the sky.
>
> And for that minute a blackbird sang
> Close by, and round him, mistier,
> Farther and farther, all the birds
> Of Oxfordshire and Gloucestershire.

The poem holds an important place in the history of poetry. It should,
perhaps, be considered as a part of the imagist movement though
Thomas tended to be a fence-sitter rather than a combatant in the war
between the opposing poetic camps. "Adlestrop" itself perfectly illustrates this; the first two stanzas are imagist in their unadorned intensity
while the last two stanzas, in their awkwardness and stilted diction—
haycocks dry, No whit, lonely fair, cloudlets etc.—belong equally firmly
in the Georgian camp. But however flawed, the poem is unignorable
because of the laconic magic of the first eight lines.)

The story ends sadly—as it had to. The majority opinion of the class was that all the poets were likely "nances." Mr. Whitehorse himself...?

"Boys, I have to let you know that I am not prepared to modify my curriculum in response to ill-considered parental opinions, and so must leave you unexpectedly." His one-eyed gaze lingered momentarily on Davis and Smart. "A pity. The First Master will take this class until the end of term. And I thank you for your kind attention. I believe we have learned something together this year, and now I must wish you all good-bye, godspeed, and good luck."

The class chorused their goodbyes and clattered out of the room, but Harry sat on by his window in a pool of spring sunshine, unable to leave, to move at all.

"Miles," Whitehorse said, "come here." So he rose, took a few steps and stood, acutely aware of gravity, next to the oak desk.

"You have an ear for verse. I would have put you forward for the Reader's Prize, but under the circumstances I've not been asked to nominate. So—" Whitehorse reached down for his briefcase, extracted a book, "I hope you will enjoy Thomas's collected poems." A slim volume, bound in cream with red lettering: Harry gulped for air, unable to staunch the tears.

"Sorry, sir!"

Whitehorse put a hand on his shoulder, and left it there.

"Why should you be sorry?" he said. "It's good to feel things. Though the day must go on. Here—" He offered a tobacco-smelling handkerchief, and steered Harry towards the door that led to the outer stairs.

"Will you find another teaching post?" Harry asked, as they began the descent.

"Don't trouble yourself. Something will turn up," Whitehorse said. "Do you know Shelgate Road?" he asked conversationally. "About half a mile, Clapham way? Thomas grew up there, at number sixty-one. Walked the same streets as you when he was a boy."

What did he mean by connecting them in that way? Harry wondered, then, and periodically afterwards —concluding only in middle age that his teacher had very likely meant no more than to be friendly and matter of fact.

A brief hand-shake at the bottom of the staircase, and then they parted. Harry never saw the man again. But he kept the book: To Harold Miles, for outstanding work. With all good wishes, David Stanley Whitehorse, his teacher had written on the flyleaf, in the careful copperplate he had learned long before the war, when he was himself a boy.

Alice Petersen
Short Story Collections: *All the Voices Cry* (2012) and *Worldly Goods* (2016).

I did not start writing until I came to Canada as a graduate student [from New Zealand]. Being an immigrant renders me a tourist in two countries—it's a good kind of distance to have for the observing part of being a writer. I can also worry less about what people will think. As a student I wrote ghastly poetry. Fortunately unpublished. I could not write fiction while I was studying—I felt too crushed by the weight of the literary canon. After I finished up I felt easier about imagining great writers to be kindly mentors rather than unreachable stars. My studies did help, though. Working on Borges made me think a lot about plot and about the individual voice. Working on Gertrude Stein taught me to write on and not care and not to assume that anything has to be a certain way, just because it's always been done that way.

I feel fortunate to have had certain years of my life when two writers with very strong voices, Jorge Luis Borges and Gertrude Stein were the focus of my interests. One drop of either writer in your own work and you're sunk.

More about influences. One would love to have it all spring straight from the head, but that's not the truth of it. If you write, you should be reading, always. Influence is a difficult side effect of reading but it must be dealt with. I do reread stories and paragraphs and ask myself "how did that writer approach this problem?" I think that's a valid way of learning, but when it comes to the actual writing, I think that every writer knows when imitation is getting the better of originality.

I brought away three ideas from my academic years that were useful to writing. One was from T.S. Eliot's "Tradition and the individual Talent"—the idea that there is a tradition, a Platonic Bookshelf that gets reordered and reshuffled when a new talent comes along, so it's worth giving writing a shot, just in case you end up on The Shelf. From Borges, I gathered that there are no new stories, but that every writer has the right to retell those stories with a unique voice. Again, advice that is liberating for the novice. And lastly, from the example of Gertrude Stein's life, I learned not to be daunted, but to write on.

(Alice is disapproving of my frivolous (and ignorant) attitude to Gertrude Stein. Though much of her writing does put me in mind of the now nearly forgotten English versifier Villiers David's couplet:

> *Has any man who's ever read a line*
> *Discovered meaning yet in Gertrude Stein?*

perhaps Alice in her charity will teach me how to read her.)

In terms of influence, we might as well start with Katherine Mansfield. For New Zealand writers, Katherine Mansfield's work is second nature—to be lived with but also to be treated warily in terms of worrying about over-influence. My mother kept a copy of Katherine Mansfield's works in the glove box of the car. I spent a lot of time waiting in the car while my older sisters had their music lessons. After I'd finished the most interesting pages of the car manual (cigarette lighter, window function, etc.) I'd read a Mansfield story. A phrase like "I seen the little lamp" from "The Doll's House" sums it up really—it's not just the significant object, it's the wondering voice that goes with it that makes the story live.

All New Zealand writers have to make their peace with Mansfield, to accept her genius and then to make an effort to move the genre onwards. Mansfield was the master of the significant detail, the chilly moment, the gesture that changes everything. All hers are the tiny incremental moments that make up our ways of being. Mansfield taught me to look properly at the spaces between people, to listen to the ways they communicate and to notice what they find important. Mansfield was also utterly dedicated to her work. She worked like the blazes. And then she died. There's something to be remembered and learned there.

I did not come across the stories of Alice Munro until my first Christmas in Canada—a dear friend gave me a copy of *Open Secrets*. I was hooked from the start. Alice Munro's stories are so strong, her writing so subtle, with that dark ungoverned streak at the heart of things. Fabulous. I felt the same way reading Alice Munro's stories of Ontario and BC, as I did at the age of sixteen, reading a sonnet by James K. Baxter set in an Otago landscape. Literature could indeed be made with the material to hand. It was very liberating.

Alice Munro. I could go on about her a lot. I came to her work at the time when I was just inching my way out of academia. There she was, alive and writing about her life, her invented communities, her history and landscape. Suddenly it seemed possible to write and be alive (i.e., not two hundred years in the grave) at the same time. And of course, she had such an effect upon the very form of the short story, with her innovations in the relation between time and narrative. She spins out this long narrative line and then suddenly sends down a spiral of time, to way back when, then it comes bobbing back up again to the present moment, but infused with new information that gives the narrative another pulse forwards. In lazy hands this becomes a shaggy-dog approach to the short story, but in Munro everything still counts, still tends towards the simultaneous arrival of key character and reader at the given, inevitable moment. It's a different take on the "slice of life" short story that has a compact time frame—Munro makes us see that the "life" in "slice of life" has a long history. There's a great pleasure for the reader in that. Sometimes, short stories can seem short on ingredients, but Munro's stories are always satisfying because of the way she treats time.

And the darkness, the wildness of Munro. You don't have to be good all the time in a Munro story. Good grief, the things her people do—that hem of that nice woman's coat, trailing through, what was it, brains? Where she stepped over a dead body in her hurry to get to the next one. Utterly unforgettable.

I think of the short story as bubble or a drop of water, compact and teeming with life to its very edges. The short-story mode magnifies the moment in time, the raised eyebrow, the sign between couples, the shift in thinking, that can turn the course of a greater story that goes on beyond the bounds of the story that is told (since a water drop has the potential to be part of a larger body). I like this intensity. In my own stories I try (and of course it is just trying—the theory can be much more successful than the practice!) to focus on moving towards that salient moment, and I do it using all the old techniques of image or significant detail or slowed movement. I like to arrive with the reader at that moment, so that they understand with me. This element of shared understanding is central to how good stories have their effect.

Look, I do the thing, I pile up the pages by telling the story and asking myself what it's about until it's all been covered, then much later I pull the story out of the pile of pages, reducing forty pages of long hand to twelve typed pages. Much later, after I've looked at what I've done by instinct and examined what find of form and mode I automatically adopted to tell that particular story, I shape it with every tool in the work box of tradition, to round it out and make it sing. I guess the academic training in modernism gives me easy access to that tradition, since the modernist era was the era of the short story.

What are those tools? Images and details that encapsulate or suggest the story as a whole. Colours and moods that bind a story together. Previous experiences that make characters' reactions inevitable. Surprises that break the frame. What frame? Any frame. Not stinting on language either, but trying not to slobber all over the page.

I am glad to have had years of classical music training, since music gives me different ways of thinking about structure and the lines that flow through a story from beginning to end. I read my stories aloud to catch the cadence of the sentences. I get a lot of pleasure from the aural quality of sentences. I am interested in the way a sentence arcs and lands. When I was small I used to listen to records of Vivien Leigh reading children`s stories. There was a sentence from a story by Alison Uttley that finished up like this: "… but she kept the poker by her side while she drank her milk"—I never forgot that. The dread and the rhythm and the need for the kind of security provided by pokers and milk.

I think of writing as being like papier mâché. We start with life, of course we do. But we rip it into tiny pieces and recon-stitute it into the art object, the story, which is something else entirely. But, like papier mâché, sometimes the occasional word is still legible on a specific fragment, but the rest of the context has been torn away. But I know. I know where it comes from.

A mosaic teacher told me that to make good mosaic, you have to be willing to smash the tile, to really smash it. If the frag-ment of tile is too large, it speaks of itself too loudly and not in relation to the other fragments. I find this advice useful when it comes to drawing on life for writing stories.

(*Letters* May 17, 2014 and May 21, 2014)

Alice Petersen's style is rather difficult to write about, to pin down. It has a brilliant accuracy though an accuracy which is peculiarly hers.

A deer has just come out of the woods. Dainty best describes the pattern of spots on her sides, like icing sugar on a coffee cake, and the tender white flame of a tail.

How *odd* is the word "tender," how marvellously accurate the deer's colour and the shapeless shapes like powder dusted on the flanks;

yet accurate as the description is, there's at the same time something quirky about it, funny almost in the accuracy of its incongruity. Coffee cake!

Or this:

> … she was the first to see the weasel slipping along under the rock fall, its dark body undulating like an animated moustache.

Or this:

> Hattie. Her real name was Heliotrope. Her mother had been an artist's model back when there were only two models in the whole city of Dunedin and all decent New Zealanders considered modelling to be tantamount to prostitution. Heliotrope. What a name for a child. It was preposterous, redolent of ragged satin undergarments strewn over an ancient carpet.

That last sentence is crammed with vivid suggestiveness, very rich, full of sensual suggestion, of seedy grandeur, while being at the same time oddly comic when connected to the name "Heliotrope."

Or this:

> He stopped before a pool of snow water. An object lay at the bottom of it. It was a metal disk, dull and serrated: a winch, a gear, cog-like. It could have been Champlain's Astrolabe, only that had already been found.
>
> Astrolabe sounded like one of the drugs that Cynthia had been prescribed for depression….

Or this prescription for avoiding sexual entanglements in middle age:

> Still, Colin shied away from the physical logistics of entanglements. He worried about his weight and the moment of displacement; if a woman should invite him to share a bath with her, for example. And of course love does not last and does not improve, but only atrophies. Do not all the novels demonstrate

it? The fever that does not bring about death or lifelong separation from one's parents abates and clears up. One only has to survive the dangerous years (15–35) as mentioned above; to build a life raft of useful things strapped together with webbing—a good pepper grinder, a modest wine collection, the complete recordings of the Beethoven string quartets, a gaseous golden retriever called Calliope—and then one is ready to ride out the tempests.

The fever of passion which "clears up," like acne, the *fragments shored against my ruins* as T. S. Eliot has it, which include "a good pepper grinder" and "a gaseous golden retriever." Colin's character here so brilliantly and concentratedly evoked and nailed utterly in that characteristic "gaseous."

(*Why* "gaseous" is so perfect in the context rather than "incontinent" or "farty" and *why* "gaseous" is so wonderful when linked to the name Calliope would take me half a page I do not have.)

What I'm attempting to say about Alice Petersen's writing is that, sensual as it often is, there plays over it all a tremendous intelligence, a cool, *assessing* quality and perhaps deriving from that, a dry *fino* sense of humour, a Tio Pepe take on life.

It may seem odd, then, that I want to draw attention to an uncharacteristic story in *All the Voices Cry*, the story "Scottish Annie," the story of a day's outing for an old woman remembering her mother and her childhood.

I am attracted to stories that have a ballad-like feel about them, polished by repetition and time. From my own published work, the stories I like best are those that have a sense of musical wholeness about them—the voice, the form, the individual details and the story within feel meshed and complete by the time the story is done. "Scottish Annie" is one of these.

"Scottish Annie" came about as the conjunction of two things. The first was a drive through Seacliff, the cliffside settlement where the famous asylum that once housed Janet Frame used to stand. I said to my sister, "It's always sad in Seacliff."

So we discussed that feeling. And then I thought, but it can't be always sad here—what kind of a story about Seacliff would not be sad? Earlier on the same trip we had walked under trees where banana passion fruit flowers were flowering on vines. These are purple flowers with blue stamens, very exotic, tropical and surprising in the chilly south of New Zealand. I wanted to put one in a story, and it showed up in this hard-bitten life of Annie's, like the love she finds with young Dr. Whooping Cough, which is also tropical and surprising.

In "Scottish Annie" the lyrics of the song "Robins and Roses" encapsulate the dream of love in a cottage, but it's also a song that's been in my head since childhood. We used to play it on a 78, on a gramophone that had been in my mother's family. Oh the pleasure of winding up the mechanism, of putting in the needle, of listening to this cracked voice crooning on about an idyll that included afternoon tea. I'll never forget that. So, the song is my personal fragment. And of course I also wanted the story to be like a song; like a rehearsed family story, so that was also part of it. Gertrude Stein used to talk about listening to the "bottom nature" of people, which I think is probably the most awkward phrase in the universe, but I guess my version of "bottom nature" is the songs that characters sing about themselves, and I say song deliberately, because a song is a rehearsed, shaped structure, like a family myth.

(*Letter.* May17, 2014)

Ruby, the narrator of "Scottish Annie," a volunteer, takes residents of a retirement home out for drives, and on the day this story happens she is driving Mrs. Webster through Seacliff, where Mrs. Webster wants to see the ruins of the old house where she was born and raised. The house used to look out onto the Seacliff Asylum.

Ruby thinks of the asylum: "It was a grand old place, the asylum at Seacliff, majestic and crenellated. They had proper lunatics in those days."

Then Mrs. Webster launches into the story of her mother, "Scottish Annie," and her affair with the lodger, a medical resident at the asylum, Mr. Reginald Hooper, called by the children Dr. Whooping Cough.

> Mr. Currie was on his way up the hill to look at Dolores who had hoof rot. He smelt the smoke and ran to the house. I saw the fire too, because I was that baby, you know. It's one of my earliest memories, poking a stick at a piece of wood where the paint has swelled up into lovely soft bubbles. Mr. Currie ran into the burning house and he found our Mum and the lodger passed out on the bed. Entwined they were. At noon. And her not even wearing a wrapper. Mr. Currie had to get it off the hook on the back of the door. First he brought our Mum out, and then Mr. Currie, such a brave man, went back in for Mr. Hooper. After that there was nothing that could be done to save the house. Dry as tinder it was under the rafters. You must have been able to see the flames far out at sea…
>
> Mr. Currie laid Mum and Mr. Hooper side-by-side on the cold grass and covered them with a blanket. And the hill beside the house there is so steep that the bodies were almost standing up. Carbon monoxide had come creeping up on them. Well. They came round eventually. No harm done, and everyone said that it was a miracle. Even Mr. Currie said that, because if they had both died, who would have looked after all us kids?
>
> Well, Mr. Hooper did the decent thing, and he married our Mum, took her on with the five kids and even had another one. That's my younger brother Neil. He's up in the Ross Home now. And Mr. Hooper's parents, they also did the decent thing and disowned him.

The story is more complicated than "ballad" or "family myth," for it is as much about Ruby as it is about Mrs. Walker but I leave it to the reader to discover its pleasures.

There is a quality about Alice Peterson's stories that I've avoided saying anything about because I feel inadequate to do so. There plays around them a particular light. There's a lucidity both intellectually, and, inexplicably, like a physical quality of enveloping brightness.

It is a special intensity of light, a luminosity, which confers both calm and heightened sensitivity. If I had to say what that light is like I would think about the light in St. Ives; I would think about the steps leading up to the Chapter House in Wells Cathedral; I would think about the light in Sir Norman Foster's Queen's Room at the British Museum and the glory of the light in the Lady Chapel at Ely Cathedral. And still feel myself groping to explain. If talking *connoisseur*, paintings, say, or pots, the word "presence" would be in the air.

Gayla Reid
Short Story Collections: *To Be There With You* (1994) and *Closer Apart* (2002).
    Novels: *All the Seas of the World* (2001) and *Come from Afar* (2011).

If there is one fault to be found with Gayla Reid's stories it is that some them have unsatisfactory endings. This could be said of more than one of the writers among these fifty. It is the endings of stories which present the biggest challenge for story writers. Think of a gymnastic performance. The athlete can demonstrate fluid mastery on the bars or rings, each series of movements rhythmically flowing into the next, but the clinching moment for the performer is the dismount, the moment that stops and caps the sequence. If the performer buckles, takes a half-step back on landing, is forced into an unnatural stance to maintain balance, then the performance is marred and the audience feels an inevitable disappointment. If, on the other hand, the dismount is perfect—bang!—the entire performance seems logical and inevitable and our pleasure in it is an aesthetic one. Commentators say of a perfect conclusion that the performer has "nailed" the landing.

I loved the lyric detail and texture in such stories from *To Be There with You* as "Sister Doyle's Men" and "Uncle Reg and the Wide Brown Land" but thought that neither was "nailed." However, "To Be There with You" is a perfect performance and its ending resonates. And resonates.

    It is narrated by a young woman working as a reporter in the Vietnam War. Here is one of the story's movements. Its quiet horror burns backwards into itself when we reach the domesticity of the image of Ron "coaxing his kids to eat up their peas."

We'd start off drinking at the Grand, then go on to those make-shift places that had sprung up along the beach front—little round huts, they were. I'd try to get Ron and the others to talk about the war. What about Dak To? (Dak To was where the main U.S. fighting was going on.)

What about it? They spoke of the cricket scores back home.

Sometimes in one of these bars you saw a soldier crying his eyes out. "Ratshit," his mates would say. Then look away. We are in a bar. It's not long since Ron's best mate, Johno.

A chap called Ian comes up. He's young and he's really hand-some. Ian starts slapping Ron on the back, in a familiar way that is part friendly, part hostile. "Zip 'em right down the middle, mate," Ian says. "Whaddya say, mate? Zip 'em right down the middle."

He's very drunk.

"Beauty, mate," Ian goes on. "One for you and one for me."

Ron, who's quite a bit older, says, "Take it easy, mate. Just take it easy, eh."

But Ian keeps on keeping on.

"One for you and one for me. What do you say? Ripper, mate."

Ron gets up and punches him in the stomach, hard.

That shuts him up.

I didn't see it as any big deal—Ron's punching him. They were all pretty physical men.

What interested me was what Ian had said.

I'd heard it before.

After the drinking and fucking had been pushed to the limit, and Ron was almost asleep, out of it, he'd mumble, under his breath but loud enough for me to hear: "One for you and one for me."

He could have been back home coaxing his kids to eat up their peas.

But I didn't think so.

I should explain why I include Gayla Reid in the Century List if I have reservations about some of her work. She is there because she is powerful and, for me, *unignorable*. She has, to echo a book title, the right stuff. I commend her in the hope that she'll return to the arena to nail her landings *bang* with aplomb.

Patricia Robertson
Short Story Collections: *City of Orphans* (1994) and *The Goldfish Dancer* (2007).

I usually lie in bed for an hour after waking and turn over what a night's sleep has cast up. On the morning after re-reading *City of Orphans* I found that in my mind was a book by John Livingston Lowes called *The Road to Xanadu* read when I was sixteen or seventeen, a book about Coleridge's reading. I was also thinking about that murky tome, Coleridge's *Biographica Literaria*. Specifically, I was thinking about Coleridge's distinction between Imagination and Fancy. Fancy, Coleridge, claimed was governed by Imagination. Fancy, he said, is a mode of memory; its associative power collects from the artist's past, words, images, rhythms etc. which it delivers to Imagination, which then fashions these raw materials into Art.

Why was this fusty stuff in my mind? I hadn't the faintest interest in Coleridge's obscure musings and considered wide swathes of the *Biographia Literaria* incomprehensible.

The other thing in my mind was the first two lines of the song sung in *The Merchant of Venice* while Bassanio is contemplating the caskets:

> *Tell me, where is fancy bred,*
> *Or in the heart, or in the head?*

For Shakespeare, the word "fancy" usually meant "love" or "infatuation," though he sometimes used the word to mean "creativity" or "imagination." What Coleridge meant by "Fancy" is still open to much Germanic debate.

I slowly realized that Shakespeare and Coleridge were nothing to do with Patricia Robertson. I was simply thinking about the word itself, not those specific contexts. I was thinking about *City of Orphans* and the word "fancy"; the word "fancy" meaning something like "fanciful," "whimsical," "something based on imagination rather than fact." And I realized that in this entirely convoluted manner I was preparing to confront another of my prejudices.

Patricia Robertson writes two kinds of stories; most are rooted in the real world while others are what I think of as "fanciful." In *City of Orphans* there are two "fanciful" stories, "Finn Slough" and "Arabian Snow." I've usually felt that fanciful stories have lesser power and authority than stories rooted in the real world. The "real world" I consider a more imagined world. Even things straightforwardly *remembered*, are, in a way, imagined. Though I don't feel that way about Paul Glennon's fanciful stories. The difference, perhaps, is that Glennon's stories are charged with feeling.

For example, in "Arabian Snow" Gabriela gives birth to Minna and starts dreaming of a past life when she was a princess in Norway and betrothed to an Arabian prince.

> They'd begun in the hospital. On the second night, the baby asleep in the crib beside her, Gabriela woke with the sheets in her fists, the pillow damp with sweat. She'd been somewhere among sand dunes, palm trees, minarets, her face covered in a white veil... In the afternoon, drifting in and out of sleep, she walked through a courtyard of turquoise tiles where a fountain sparkled in sunlight and a nightingale sang in a cage ...

The "dream-story" is told in italicized paragraphs woven into the non-dream story of Gabriela and Minna.

> *My father promised three pairs of gyrfalcons to the traders when they came to Bergen in their djellabas, asking for the master falconer to the king ...*

Much more typical of Patricia Robertson's work—and much more imaginative—are these paragraphs from "Counting":

> On Saturdays we visit Auntie Edna. My mother puts Billy in his push-chair and we walk up the avenue and under the railway

bridge to the high street. Past Bentley & Son Greengrocers, past Boots' Chemists and the sweetshop, rows of jars with silver lids, to Old Lyme road where we turn right. Past Hall's Toffee Works with its warm sweet smell, cauldrons pouring a thick gleaming brown stream into moulds. Under the chestnut trees at the edge of the park with the black metal hobby horses and the Peter Pan statue. After the last houses there are fields with daisies in them. We go through a stile and follow a cowpath which comes out in Wheaton Crescent, where my aunt lives.

Today my aunt is standing in the kitchen with flour streaks in her hair, making buns and custard. My mother takes a pile of newspapers off a chair and sits down to talk. She holds Billy on her lap but he struggles down and my aunt gives him a saucepan and wooden spoon to play with.

I find the language of "Arabian Snow" meretricious. I cannot escape the feeling that such stories are manufactured.

On the other hand, *hurrah!* for that saucepan and wooden spoon. Patricia Robertson has command of a range of styles and rhetorics and with them she embodies one fairly constant theme—her characters seek to make sense of their lives and grope towards larger and more expansive visions through acts of imagination. The expatriate narrator in "City of Orphans" loves hopelessly a beautiful boy prostitute; in counterpart he tells, lying on the grave, a continuing and comforting story of hope to the spirit of a child who died in 1893; Simon in "Pretty Bangs" turns away from the delusions of the conventions and vows to create in the world—astonishment; Stefan Czerwinski, detainee in a Canadian labour camp in the First World War in the story "Ice Palace," sustains himself against the brutalities with a vision of female beauty.

When theme and feeling and language fuse, Patricia Robertson creates paragraphs that are positively burnished; here is the narrator in "City of Orphans," a story set in a North African city:

That night I lay in the airless heat of my room listening to the cries of the old quarter, comforting and abrasive as a cat's tongue.

What would entice that sulky boy to stand behind shutters at my balcony window while I ran my fingers down his spine? I wanted to see that pink mouth open, the neck arch, hear him cry out as I bit into downy skin. I pressed my face into the pillow but still he stood there, smiling at me from beneath those long lashes. My little life of carefully counted coins, chalky fingers, bottles of wine—the same life I had, in mid-life, left behind me—lay about me like a husk. Peter stood at a doorway visible only in outline, poised to enter, his face turned away from me.

Leon Rooke

Short Story Collections: *Last One Home Sleeps in the Yellow Bed* (1968), *Vault* (1973), *The Love Parlour* (1977), *The Broad Back of the Angel* (1977), *Cry Evil* (1980), *Fat Woman* (1980), *Death Suite* (1981), *The Magician in Love* (1981), *The Birth Control King of the Upper Volta* (1982), *A Bolt of White Cloth* (1984), *Sing Me No Love Songs I'll Say You No Prayers* (1984), *How I Saved the Province* (1989), *The Happiness of Others* (1991), *Who Do You Love* (1992), *Muffins* (1995), *Narcissus in the Mirror* (1995), *Oh No I Have Not Seen Molly* (1996), *Art. Three Fictions in Prose* (1997), *Oh! Twenty-Seven Stories* (1997), *Who Goes There* (1998), *Painting the Dog: Selected Stories* (2001), *Balduchi's Who's Who* (2005), *Hitting the Charts: Selected Stories* (2006), *The Last Shot: Eleven Stories and a Novella* (2009), *Pope and her Lady* (2010), *Wild World in Celebration and Sorrow* (2012), *Fantastic Fiction and Peculiar Practices* (2016), and *Swinging Through Dixie* (2016).

Novels: *Fat Woman* (1980), *Shakespeare's Dog* (1983), *A Good Baby* (1989), *The Fall of Gravity* (2000), and *The Beautiful Wife* (2005).

Plays: *Krokodile* (1973) and *Sword/Play* (1974).

Poetry Collections: *Hot Poppies* (2005) and *The April Poems* (2013).

Leon Rooke has published more than three hundred short stories, most of them written before the year 2000. Representing him by one collection is impractical so I have chosen two selections which attempt to do justice to his range. They are *Painting the Dog* and *Hitting the Charts*. These volumes together present thirty-six stories, which give a fair sampling of his achievement.

Rooke has been one of the driving and shaping forces in Canadian literature over the last forty years or so. His influence on the short story is incalculable. He is an exuberant performer of his own work and performance is the fundamental key to understanding him. His stories are nearly all voices talking, monologues, soliloquies, the reader button-holed. In addition to his novels and stories, he has written numerous plays and has had a lifetime involvement in the theatre. To grasp Leon, one simply has to listen. This seems, today, blindingly obvious and simple, yet for years many readers were unable to hear him. The dutiful search for "meaning" rendered it the more elusive. All we have to do is listen to the voices and take pleasure in the spate of language washing over us, the torrent of lovely words. Meaning arrives through our acquiescence, through our delight in the performance.

The other key to reading Leon Rooke is to realise that his stories are improvisations. Think of him as a tenor sax player and the story as a jazz improvisation. Relax into what he's playing.

Rooke's body of work, his teaching, and his many performances over the years have helped to give the short story in Canada a new and different emphasis. Here are a few snippets of the multiplicity of voices that call to us, invite us to come in.

> Here's a story.
>
> Although it has been going on for years, the crucial facts are fresh in my mind so I will have no trouble confining myself strictly to what's essential. Nothing made up, have no worry about that. I live in this world too: when my wife, lovely woman, tells me that people are tired of hearing *stories,* they want facts, gossip, trivia, how-to about real life, I'm first to take the hint. So this is plain fact: yesterday my foot was hurting. The pain was unbearable. I was in mortal anguish and convinced I'd been maimed for life.
>
> (The opening of "The Deacon's Tale.")

> We got fifty-two (52) kids in the nursery, the Henny Penny Nursery, only one teacher, and she's retarded. They come to me, the parents of these kids do, and they say, "Sir, Mr. Beacon, excuse us, sir, for butting in like this, but some of us parents, mostly those of us

you see right here, what we've noticed is that Mrs. Shorts, running
your place, well, sir, to make no bones about it, she's retarded."
(The opening of "Some People Will Tell you the
Situation at Henny Penny Nursery Is Getting Intolerable.")

Voice, characterization, the psychology of the scene and its comedy—all are delivered by commas.

Oh, crafty Rooke!

You have heard about Mama Tuddi. If you got eyes and ears or
a brain in your head then you know that Mama Tuddi is a big
celebrity, that she have her own show The Mama Tuddi Show
on TV and radio where she sell soft drinks by the bottle and the
crate, especially on TV where everyone know what she look like
and how much she enjoy her work.
(The opening of "Mama Tuddi Done Over.")

There are almost as many voices as there are stories.

William Faulkner wrote: "Beginning with *Sartoris* I discovered that
my own little postage stamp of native soil was worth writing about and
that I would never live long enough to exhaust it, and that by sublimat-
ing the actual into the apocryphal I would have complete liberty to use
whatever talent I might have to its absolute top. It opened up a mine of
other people, so I created a cosmos of my own. I can move these people
around like God, not only in space but in time." Leon's multiplicity of
characters and voices are his cosmos and he is the God who creates and
disposes. And rarely deigns, if not in the mood, to fully explain.

Although I advocate the best approach to Rooke's work as relaxing
into it and absorbing the spate of language washing over us, I'm well
aware that many readers object to what they consider his rampant
and meaningless floods of verbiage. So let me revisit this contention.

In 1981, I was haggling with Jack David, publisher of ECW, about bringing out a collection of Rooke's stories entitled *Death Suite*. Jack phoned me
during these negotiations and asked if I really did stand behind this work,
if I really thought it of great importance. I assured him that I did.

Soon after, he called me again and said, "I heard him read last night. *Now* I get it. I just wasn't hearing him off the page."

Rooke does not set out to write carefully planned masterpieces. Rather, he picks up his sax and noodles about on that melody in his head to see what will happen. I wrote about his noodling in *Canadian Classics*, an anthology I edited with J.R. 'Tim' Struthers, in 1993.

> He rarely leaves his stories alone. He's always revising and rewriting. Between Canadian publication and subsequent American publication, stories and novels grow longer. There's a sense in which a Rooke story is never *finished*. We could consider a printed Rooke story in much the same way we might consider a transcribed solo by Charlie Parker; perhaps both are best served by a recording of a live performance.
>
> There are dangers, of course, with this approach to fiction. Improvisation is not always inspired; it is not always coherent either. Some might say that Rooke is a captive of language and rhetoric, that too many of the stories are, in Horatio's rebuke to Hamlet, "wild and whirling words." It does sometimes seem that Rooke has sacrificed meaning to energy, that he shares Stanley Elkin's belief, not that "less is more" but that "more is more." How well will his work stand up over time as *writing*? Might we be forced to say ruefully years from now, "Well, I guess you had to be there"? Or can we train ourselves well enough to hear the music that is on Rooke's pages?

The contention that Rooke sacrifices meaning to unbridled rhetorical exuberance, to oratorical hijinks, deserves examination.

What follows is an excerpt from an unpublished novel, *The House on Major Street*, the typescript's first two pages. They are what, in a conventional novel, would be described as exposition.

```
Help, help! Ours is a house occupied by the blind,
the deaf, the mute, the totally helpless! We
are lame, we are crippled, we are maimed and
tormented, socially inept, bunglers of the
first rank, mental midgets, bereft of hope! We
crawl about on hands and knees, we cry out,
(Help, help!) We crouch in dark corners, en-
```

treating our captors: *(What have we done? Why are you doing this to us? Mercy! Mercy!*

Help, help!

Hurry, friends, with news of our desperate plight. Inform the police, the military, the press, the very topmost, exalted despots of our great country. Barons of the left, moguls of the right, pillars of the very centremost centre. Our dye is cast, our pigment set. The shit has hit the fan.

Oh, help us.

Forget latitude, longitude, write down this address: two-six-eight (268) Major, a stone's throw from Bloor Street's best. Heart of the heart's heart. Artsyfartsy land. A scholar's digs. Turn where you see the Bloor SuperSave. Red brick house (renovated Not, and no plans to). Lacy windows, how many bodies buried in the basement, beaten shrubs by the front walk, rubbish aswirl, snow a mile high.

You can't miss it. Extreme measures are called for, don't even *think* negotiation. Too late, too late. Beseech our liberators to arrive with tanks, flame throwers, scud missiles, pots and pots of chicken soup; have phantom jets strafe our house and thousands of enraged crusaders lay siege to our door. Be warned, many will die ...

Be cool.

Hang easy.

Save us.

We perish by the hour.

+++

The sober mind might wonder why tanks, flame-throwers, scud missiles, and phantom jets are necessary to subdue and liberate a detached residence in the Annex. Who are these captives and these "thousands of enraged crusaders"? Crusaders? Why would it take "thousands" to besiege a house in the Annex?

Where would they park?

But more to the point, why is the text printed in different type sizes? Whose voice is the larger type? Whose is the smaller? Could the larger text be the public voice of the captives, the smaller the voices of the individual captives? Is the larger type possibly a clandestine communiqué? Who *are* the captors?

I have read the entire novel and haven't a clue.

As a writer reading, the main thing I notice (detail, always detail) apart from the swooping and soaring registers of diction, is that Rooke has written "Our dye is cast" when presumably he intended to write "Our die is cast"; "dye" meaning "a colouring agent" while "die" is singular of "dice." The interesting thing to me is that "dye," in its incorrect sense, carries him in the heat and turmoil of creation to the word "pigment," presumably some such thought as oil paint drying or fresco hardening, and the word "cast" leads him to "set," the word "cast" being thought of not as "thrown" but as molten metal poured into a mould. His mind at play.

Or, maybe "dye" is meant to suggest the illiteracy of the captives? Though that doesn't explain "pigment" popping up.

Who knows?

After the asterisk, the story hares off in a new direction.

+++

```
The one window of Tallis Haley's second-floor
room looks out over an exquisite garden. In
this garden stands a fine sculpted fountain,
erected overnight by unseen hands. So it
seems. Because when Tallis Haley — the comet,
man! Weird light! Watch that little shit go! —
was removed from Children's Hospital and re-
stored to his own bedroom, the next-door site
was a rubble-strewn field. He remembers this
```

clearly. Yes, and rolling hills, trees, swollen streams. Muskrat and chipmunk, *buffalo*!

From a high limb you could see all the way to
Winnipeg. Turn a snitch and there was Buffalo.

Another century.

Each night now, in the dead of night, no less
than a dozen women perambulate, with elaborate cries of ecstasy and considerable expertise in the charm area. Graduates of the
Arthur Murray School, he supposes. Lawrence
Welk as well, but zippier. Bit more flash, you
know. A dream. Oh, it's a dream, by any one's
account. Bewitching, yes, a joyful ceremo-
ny. And every night, you understand, which is
hard on a boy in his comate status.

Fantastic events unfolding, here at 268 Major.

Ask Daisy, ask Emmitt, inquire of anyone.
These women frolic, they dance, they weave
the spell of divine and harmonious rites.
Even in the cold, even in softly-falling
snow, they come. They loosen their smocks,
they relieve themselves of all encumbrances:
naked, they cavort about the cascading fountain, as if exorcising themselves of daredev-
il demons, of weights carried for centuries.
Unyoked. Women in overdrive.

Phantoms, Tallis sometimes thinks, from the
innocent beyond. No males allowed. No means
no. Keep your distance, Jack.

Later in the night, they form a chain of
hands and snake away, fade like white sheets
aflit in wind. Going, going, gone…

Woo me, fine maidens, into the nimble, heathery
hereafter. Bind me with the invisible strands of

```
your invisible net flung from the great beyond.
Take me to that place of the grazing buffalo.
```

I will refrain from comment. Except to say that the first passage has a certain energy because it is *voice*; this second section, largely descriptive, but seen vaguely, sags.

And I might add that the sentence "They loosen their smocks, they relieve themselves" has done its dire and unintended work before the words "of all encumbrances" arrive.

Rooke's stories, on the other hand, are nearly all taut and vibrating; the restrictions of the form create intensity. The novel, a more expansive creature, allows for writing more relaxed. The only two of Rooke's novels that attain the intensity of the stories are *Fat Woman* and *A Good Baby* (1989) and they are novels mainly of voice.

But what does *Rooke* think he is doing?

He defends his practice in his foreword to *The Happiness of Others* (1991), a volume that brings together his best stories from the first two books he published in Canada, *The Love Parlour* (1977) and *Cry Evil* (1980) and from *The Broad Back of the Angel* (1977) published by the Fiction Collective in New York.

> My stories began appearing in US magazines in the late fifties and early sixties, at a time when many young writers were insisting that the old short-story imperatives of beginning, middle, and end—as with other rigid conventions—needed revitalization. That the form, generally, without abandoning tradition altogether, required a refurbishing. Eisenhower's conservative hue had largely coloured the social and political life in the US through the fifties, and this same conservative pall was to be seen in many of the literary arts, especially the short story. We were seeking more open forms, fresh angles of approach to material—a new poetics for fiction—while most editors were still expecting the "well-built", formally repetitious, and realistically endowed works that had prevailed through the thirties and forties...
>
> The writers of the generation beginning and/or emerging during that period, myself among them, were on the prowl for

new strategies, new methods of presentation, a fusion of fresh and disparate techniques in the deployment of *story*, stylistic innovation, new skins that one might inhabit, rearrangements in the depiction of place and time and character, a certain discourtesy in the unfolding of plot, displacement of description, new configurations in story structure, a reshaping of beginning, middle and end that more accurately mirrored human thought—were on the prowl, that is to say, for an international insignia, for a revamped, uninhibited muse. "Models,' as the thing these writers were in pursuit of, is too grandiose a word and was, except for Chekhov's stories, an alien, suspect, concept, as they innocently, or deliberately, set out to rejuvenate the form. Raymond Carver, Robert Coover, Grace Paley, William Gass, Leonard Michaels, Cynthia Ozick, Joy Williams, Joyce Carol Oates, Richard Brautigan, Russell Banks, John Gardner, and Donald Barthelme are a few on the American side who spring quickly to mind.

In 2004, I wrote a piece on Leon's work for an anthology celebrating his achievements. The book was called *White Gloves of the Doorman* and was edited by Branko Gorjup. What follows is an excerpt from:

This Here Jasper Is Gittin Ready to Talk

In a book called *Singularities* edited by Geoff Hancock in 1990, Leon contributed a piece which reads in part as follows:

I don't have many rules for the writing of short fiction. One of them is, if a thing is going wrong, then start over. If it is going nowhere, then give it up, or start over. If it goes a while, and stops, then you stop too because maybe you have gone as far as the story wants you to go. Which often means, of course, starting over. The piece lays down its own laws; that's another thing I mean. That's why many very intelligent, very gifted literary people who want to write, can't. They operate under the fallacious notion that the writer is Creator—God, whereas the intervention of another sort is more frequently the case. The thing, at a certain point, and usually at the start, creates itself. It is of value, or it isn't. Does it matter so much anyway, since the story that awaits the telling awaits as well the teller, and as many aren't found as are.

Another glimpse into the nature of Rooke's inspirations and inventions appears in my 1982 anthology, *Making It New*, an essay of his called "Voices."

In the Geoff Hancock interview in *Canadian Fiction Magazine* (Leon Rooke Issue, 1981) Leon said:

> I've also written ten or fifteen stories that came out of no-where. I sat at the typewriter, typed out one sentence, and that sentence invited another sentence and that demanded a third. Several hours later I had the first draft—even sometimes the final draft— of a story. These stories happen very fast and where they come from or where they're going I don't know until I get there.

In case I have been too fanciful or insufficiently precise in my talking about Leon's work I would like to illustrate his approach by talking about a particular story and examining it. The story I wish to consider is "Saks Fifth Avenue" from the 1984 collection, *A Bolt of White Cloth*.

If the reader stops the eyes from flitting over the page numbers I give and actually *reads* "Saks Fifth Avenue" consulting those numbers, much is revealed about how a Leon Rooke story works—or doesn't. The reader will see, as through an inspection panel, the heart of the furnace.

> Jazz groups play what are called "head arrangements," rehearsed, memorized introductions, statements of the tune. The various instruments in the band then improvise. Some sessions sparkle; the head arrangements are crisp, the solos inventive, galvanized.

On other nights all that musicians seem able to deliver is competence; solos noodle around, everyone seems to be going through the motions, there is no spark. And sometimes it happens that one of the musicians breaks out of the noodle pudding into something suddenly emotionally charged.

Something like this happens in "Saks Fifth Avenue."

The story starts: "A woman called me up on the telephone. She was going to give me twenty thousand dollars, she said. I said come right over, I'm not doing anything this evening."

No explanation is offered about the money. At the end of the story the woman appears, gives him the money, and the story ends with his counting it. This is the frame of the story, those parts analogous to the head arrangements in a tune.

After launching the story in this way, Rooke next introduces Coolie, Cecil's wife. They bicker interminably. Coolie abuses Cecil relentlessly while polishing her nails and watching television. Cecil meanwhile, at her suggestion, polishes his shoes and muses about this and that.

The shoe polish is kept in an old box from Saks. Cecil wonders where the box came from. It seems that the box is going to form a riff in the story but that direction peters out.

Coolie almost mechanically abuses him.

The writing is tepid, repetitive, banal. This is not because Rooke is not capable of better writing. It is because Coolie and Cecil no longer hear each other.

"Habit: me with my dishes, Coolie with her words."

At the same time, it is also true that Leon is noodling, unsure of where he's going and why. The story, thirteen pages in, is beginning to founder. And then that magical thing happens and Leon leans into the story and starts to blow.

Cecil wonders what it would have been like if he and Coolie had had a child. And in a lyrical outburst Cecil conjures up his imaginary son as together in the kitchen they cook Spezzatino di Vitello. This solo is tight, builds beautifully, and for the first time this story achieves genuine emotion. Then the story slumps again for five pages until Cecil then imagines a daughter. Again

Leon plays a fiery solo. Then again the story slumps. The lady with the money arrives and Leon plays one last solo about a little Peruvian girl Cecil's going to give money to and the story then expires.

These three solos occur in "Saks Fifth Avenue" in *A Bolt of White Cloth* on pages 133–134, 139–140, and page 143. Any reader ought to be able to feel the intensity of these passages, the way they differ from the material that surrounds them.

It is obvious that I don't consider "Saks Fifth Avenue" a success but it serves perfectly to illustrate the improvisational way in which Leon works. He always runs the risk of falling off the high wire, but *taking* the risk is a part of writing's attraction for Leon.

"Saks Fifth Avenue" suffers also from being a hybrid, an attempt to mix a rendition of an unhappy marriage with elements of fantasy or fable. We remain unconvinced by Cecil and Coolie as people, baffled by the lady bringing the unexplained money. Leon's work, paradoxically, gets "realer," more deeply emotional, the more stylized it is, the further he gets away from anything approaching realism.

Of course, there are plenty of times when he gets it right with the very first note and blows fiercely through to triumph. *Then* he gives us such gorgeous performances as "The Deacon's Tale," "Hitting the Charts," "Winter Is Lovely, Isn't Summer Hell," "Mama Tuddi Done Over," and "Some People Will Tell You the Situation at Henny Penny Nursery is Getting Intolerable,"

"For Love of Madaline," "For Love of Elenor," "For Love of Gómez," "Leave Running," "The Deacon's Tale," "Wintering in Victoria," "If You Love Me Meet Me There," "Memoirs of a Cross-Country Man," "Biographical Notes," "Mama Tuddi Done Over," "Winter Is Lovely, Isn't Summer Hell," "Hitting the Charts," "The Birth Control King of the Upper Volta," "The End of the Revolution and Other Stories"... My list could go on.

To some readers, it may seem that Rooke's very subject is *words*, that his subject is *the saying itself*, that he abandons himself

to shallow post-modern hijinks. I see him as a much more traditional figure. It is true that he had an explosive impact on the
stodge of Canadian writing, that he shattered tired formula fiction,
that he created new, uncomfortable shapes, but the new shapes,
far from being nihilistic, were expressing, exploring fiction's traditional concerns afresh.

Bernard Malamud described the short story as "the multifarious
adventures of the human heart," a phrase that sums up the essence
of Rooke's creations.

Rooke's collection *The Love Parlour* (1977), his first book in
Canada, was reviewed by Clark Blaise:

> Oberon's little volume is a feast. "If You Love Me Meet Me
> There" and "Memoirs of a Cross-Country Man" are so intense,
> so perfectly implanted as *voice* (post-modernism's victory over
> modernism) as to be unparaphrasable.
>
> One doesn't "enter" such stories in the conventional sense.
> Instead they enter you.

He continued:

> I judge the Oberon collection of Rooke's short fiction to be the
> most technically accomplished, most perfectly realized, and
> easily the most psychologically sophisticated ever published in
> Canada.

an accolade bestowed now nearly half a century ago, a succeeding
half a century of endless invention and accomplishment.

Rebecca Rosenblum

Short Story Collections: *Once* (2008) and *The Big Dream* (2011).
Novels: *So Much Love* (2017).

I've always been surprised—and rather depressed—by CanLit's
meat-and-two-veg-ness, by its middle-class avoidance of chronicling
or exploring large segments of the population and wide swathes

of common Canadian experience. Change has been slow and very recent indeed.

Milestones in that slow change are Norman Levine's stories and his dyspeptic travelogue *Canada Made Me*, Brian Moore's sad Irishman in *The Luck of Ginger Coffey*, Frank Paci's tradition-bound Italians and their rebellious offspring, Wayson Choy's portraits of Chinese-Canadian life. I was excited, too, by Sharon English's first story collection, *Uncomfortably Numb,* because among much else, it offered an intense picture of the life of high-school students. An equally unexplored territory was traditional Canadian society as viewed by immigrants. In 1997, I published *Buying on Time* by Antanas Sileika. I have always treasured the following scene between the narrator's splendidly solid Lithuanian father and his neighbour "English." The family is living like troglodytes in the excavated basement of what will eventually be a house in a new subdivision.

> "Your cat," said Mr. Taylor to my father, "has been running across my lawn"... My father pondered the words. The relationship between our cat and Mr. Taylor's lawn was impossibly remote to him. What could the one have to do with the other?... Clearly there was a problem, or this English would not be there, standing in his shirt and tie in the ruts by our subterranean home. My father strained to imagine the problem.
>
> "It shits on lawn?"
>
> "No, no," Mr. Taylor said. "That is not what I meant."
>
> "It pisses on flowers?"
>
> "It merely walks. I do not want your cat to walk on my lawn."
>
> ...
>
> "I fix," my father said.
>
> Mr. Taylor would have been happy to leave it at that, to take his victory against the foreigner and return to his evening paper, but my father gestured for him to stay where he was...
>
> He came out with the cat in his hand... He carried the cat by a handful of skin behind its head, and he held it out to Mr. Taylor.

> "I told cat not walk on lawn, but it doesn't listen. Bad cat. You tell it."

Rebecca Rosenblum is another writer exploring the lives of unchronicled Canadians. Her stories are peopled by waitresses, young singles with part-time jobs, students, office techies, street hustlers, warehouse labourers, Vietnamese immigrants, all the players of the big city's underclass with limited or bleak futures. These are people the *literati* have, in the past, avoided, drawn their skirts away from on the bus.

How skilfully and economically Rebecca Rosenblum creates a character and a world. Taste the first two paragraphs of her story "ContEd."

> Eva's place is busiest in the evenings—lots of fried cheese and ass-grabbing near midnight. We're supposed to close at one, but drunk people are hard to scatter. It's good tips, and I got used to sloppy pub scenes when I hung around with Riley, my ex. I just don't like getting home so late there's not enough time for sleeping, cooking, errands, let alone reading. *Tax Answers* is boring, but I understand if I concentrate. When I'm tired, I wind up staring at the same page until I fall asleep. The book cost $60.
>
> By the time I get to the campus I have ten minutes to find the classroom. I meant to stop and eat. I meant to look calm and smart, not confused and late. The Continuing Education people sent me a map that I can't follow, a little notebook, a ruler, a pen, all printed with *ContEd*. As I walk, I keep thinking ContEd isn't a real word. My feet hurt and the interconnected buildings make no sense; when I look out a window I'm across the street from where I started.

How skillfully these two paragraphs begin to sound the emotional notes of the story; seemingly casual, seemingly merely scene-setting, seemingly almost conversational, they are anything but.

Or taste the first two paragraphs of "Fruit Factory."

> I wake up and it's dark. When I pull the alarm clock towards me to stop it screaming, my fingers turn green in the glow from the 4:30.

I kick off the sheets and stand up before I can think. The sidewalk is right outside our basement window and there aren't any curtains. I look out, but there aren't any feet so I hike my gray T-shirt up and off. My hair statics and crackles. I pick up the black bra from the floor under the window and hook it on. Then I put on a different gray T-shirt. I step into the crumpled figure eight of yesterday's jeans and pull them up over the underwear I've already got on. I look back at the clock as I smooth down my hair with the palm of my hand. It's 4:34. I have enough time to wash my face and drink a glass of juice today before I get the 4:49 bus to work. This is Monday.

"Joséefruitsbonjour."

"Hi, is Mike there, please"

"NoI'msorryhe'snot. MayItakeamessage?"

"Travaille-t-il aujourd'hui?"

"Uh...   iln'estpasici...   je   pensequ'non. Voulezvouslaisserunmessage?"

"Oh, no, that's ok. Je peux rappeller."

"Okbon. Mercimadame."

"Bye."

After the snack truck leaves, we have a few minutes before the 9 a.m. orders, so Jean and Sami stay out in the gravel lot, chucking yams at the cat...

What density of information conveyed with such disguised skill and craft! Fact and feeling conveyed seemingly effortlessly.

Days are like days are like days. When you wake up at 4:30 in the morning, it's a lot like not waking up at all. Tuesday is like Monday, except it is raining.

How much I admire the way she manages such things as that! And the brilliant evocation of place:

Hop Stop was a grayed plank building barely larger than a school bus, the sort of place you never entered unless you lived around the corner or were lost...

Magazines of glossy skin girls, wild blond hair the same colour as their faces. Spongy Twinkies also the same pale bronze. Lightbulbs Triscuits tampons carpet-deodorizer cough-drops hand warmers ice tea of various brewings. Plastic slushie urns with their spinning churns.

The impact of the lack of punctuation!

The detail that *pins* the place definitively—*carpet-deodorizer!*

To chronicle and explore new literary subject matter, to capture it, demands a new vocabulary, a new use of language; one can't write about office techies as Rebecca does in *The Big Dream* in the orotundities of Robertson Davies. The worlds of the people she is writing about are defined in many ways by money and consumerism and their worlds are therefore full of brands and product names. English, often fragmentary or oddly inflected, is not the only language of this world. Food is important in these stories because the characters are chronically hungry. Language must bend and torque to capture the new.

(This stretching and straining of language for exactly the same purpose can be heard in other writers on the Century List—Mark Anthony Jarman, Zsuzsi Gartner, Leon Rooke, Terry Griggs…)

Here are the opening paragraphs of "After the Meeting," from *The Big Dream*.

After the meeting was over, we got in Wayne's car, since he was the only one who had a car, and started driving back into town. We figured we'd go to Martin's, but on the way we picked up a 2-4, a pizza, and a box of Jos. Louis. Since we were all unemployed now, the beer was domestic and the pizza was from this Iranian place by the highway, but I wouldn't compromise on the Jos. Louis.

"Metro brand is shit," I told Danvir. He shrugged but I could tell he agreed.

As we walked down the alley to the basement, Martin said, "They shoulda let us take our stuff, like the stuff from our desks. They shouldn't have made us go straight-aways, 'cause it'll suck to take all that on the bus if Wayne's not there."

"And I *won't* be there, man—all I got in that desk is the manual and some Craisins."

"Mmm, Craisins," is what I said, because I had skipped breakfast thinking I'd get a muffin from the caf to eat at my desk while I worked, only there was no work that morning because we were busy getting laid off.

Rebecca Rosenblum's work reminds me, in an oblique way, of something that Miles Davis wrote in his autobiography about hearing Dizzy Gillespie and Charlie Parker playing together at the Riviera Club in Billy Eckstine's band in St. Louis, in 1944.

I've come close to matching the feeling of that night in 1944 in music, when I first heard Diz and Bird, but I've never quite got there. I've gotten close, but not all the way there. I'm always looking for it, listening and feeling for it, though, trying to always feel it in and through the music I play every day.

Rebecca Rosenblum is also "always looking for it, listening and feeling for it..." and that is what I love and honour in her work.

Robyn Sarah

Short Story Collections: *A Nice Gazebo* (1992) and *Promise of Shelter* (1997).

Poetry Collections: *The Space Between Sleep and Waking* (1981), *Anyone Skating on That Middle Ground* (1984), *Becoming Light* (1987), *The Touchstone: Poems New and Selected* (1992), *Questions About the Stars* (1998), *A Day's Grace* (2003), *Pause for Breath* (2009), *My Shoes Are Killing Me* (2015), and *Wherever We Mean to Be: Selected Poems 1975–2015* (2017).

Non-Fiction: *Little Eurekas: A Decade's Thoughts on Poetry* (2007).

To have one's nose bloodied from time to time can be salutary. I remember, when we were readying *Promise of Shelter* for the Porcupine's Quill being charmed by the detail within the stories, by the acuity of observation, but somewhat troubled by the *shapes* of the stories. They seemed to me, like Gayla Reid's, not quite "nailed."

I wrote to Robyn suggesting that the story closings needed more—well, I didn't know what, but, well, *oomph*.

Robyn replied at great length, a letter of kindly intent but undeniably stern. She explained that I simply didn't know how to read her, that I was bringing to her work a set of modernist conventions and expectations that did not really fit with her intentions or practice. She showed me how to read her and I have remained appreciative and grateful.

When Kim Jernigan and I were planning the *Wild Writers We Have Known* conference at Stratford, we decided to invite two story writers who were also poets to talk about the ways that being a poet influenced being a story writer. Steven Heighton and Robyn Sarah delivered lectures on the topic under the title "Ringing Changes: The Poet's Hand in the Short Story."

Steven Heighton said:

> Robyn Sarah and I have been asked to speak not just in general but in specific, personal terms. Discussing the seminar in advance, we discovered that we'd coined remarkably similar phrases to suggest what we, as poets who often write fiction, attempt to do. In Robyn's case "serial resonance" is a good description of what she does in fiction almost all the time; in my own case "serial illumination" describes a form I sometimes use (while at other times I write more traditional fiction). What both terms suggest is a poetics of echo and increment, calling to mind the rhetorical force through artful echoing of key words or phrases, or even images. Both Robyn's and my terms seek to describe texts that accrue meaning and momentum via a slow accumulation of juxtaposed words and images, rather than by following the old "line of rising action" to a conventional climax and dénouement.

Robyn Sarah then traversed the same ground.

> Insofar as short stories have become more compressed—and the new techniques of storytelling do demand great

compression—the ear is more important in the writing. As stories become discontinuous, told in imagistic segments with white space around them like separate "beads" of prose loosely strung together, each bead in its compression becomes a sort of poem, and wants a poem's or a joke's perfection of timing—the ear attentive at the level of the syllable. Hence, the "poet's ear" in the short story ...

Both of us have hit on a structural principle based not on a line of dramatic action or sustained single narrative, but on serial variations spun around an idea, an image, or a phrase... I tell one story that is digressive and free-associative—like a person who begins to tell a story, then says "that reminds me ..." and continues in this vein, weaving in and out of the primary story. I use this structural principle to set up a series of thematic echoes that cumulatively build a mood or explore an idea. In "Looking for My Keys" [in *Promise of Shelter*], the story begins as being, literally, about a set of lost house keys. As the narrator explains how she happened to lose them—in the process, confiding details of her daily life and routines—the story subtly shifts into being about her personal sense of security, first as an individual and then, as one who is loved. Subsequently, as Hasidic neighbours appear in her narrative, it shifts again, introducing the idea of security based on faith and cultural connectedness. These levels enter the text successively, like lines in a musical fugue, until they are all intertwined—by which point the word "keys," and the idea of losing them, should be resonating in more than one frequency wherever it occurs.

And what does this method of accrual and echo look like? In "Looking for My Keys," the narrator leaves her keys on the hood of a parked car while changing hands with awkward shopping bags.

It seemed too much to expect that the car would still be there, but I walked back over to where I remembered stopping. The car was gone, but even from half a block away I could see something lying on the curb, gleaming in the sun, right where the car had been. I came closer and there were my keys, waiting for me, winking. It's funny how vividly I remember this moment, the immense satisfaction of picking up my keys from the pavement. The squareness and rightness of my keys being *right there*, exactly where I'd figured I must have parted with them. A little feat of memory, a successful exercise of self-knowledge, proof that I could always recover what was important, even if I temporarily lost sight of it.

The children were happy with the newly painted table, and even happier when—having painted it—I was inspired to go out and buy four old Windsor-style chairs in a used-furniture store, and to paint them the same colour. Our old chairs, a scruffy and mismatched assortment of leftovers, went out on the back porch. "It's so nice in here now, Mummy," said my son, "like a *real* person's kitchen, like my friends' houses." And I was a little shocked at this glimpse of how I'd been living, not noticing the shabbiness, unaware that my children noticed, calculated, compared.

Much has changed since then. My keys are not even the same keys, since I and my children now live in my friend's house, a few blocks away. My peach-coloured coffee mug broke, long before I moved. Since my friend had a perfectly good kitchen table set, a solid oak one that had belonged to his grandparents, there was no need for me to keep my pink table when we decided to live together; but I didn't want to part with it altogether, so it is now at my friend's chalet in the country. Sometimes when we go there I look at it and think about how painting it was the beginning of my being good to myself, after a long time of living numbly from day to day, in the wreckage of my failed marriage. The colour of it warms me, it is the colour I remember waking myself up with.

That "resonating in more than one frequency" isn't difficult to grasp. Once it's been pointed out to you. Robyn Sarah reprints "Ringing Changes: The Poet's Hand in the Short Story," along with Steven Heighton's essay, in her sparkling collection *Little Eurekas: A Decade's*

Thoughts on Poetry (Biblioasis, 2007). Both essays also appear in *The New Quarterly* Volume XXI, Nos. 2 and 3. *Wild Writers We Have Known.*

Diane Schoemperlen

Short Story Collections: *Double Exposures* (1984), *Frogs & Other Stories* (1986), *Hockey Night in Canada* (1987), *The Man of My Dreams* (1990), *Hockey Night in Canada & Other Stories* (1991), *In the Language of Love: A Novel in 100 Chapters* (1994), *Forms of Devotion* (1998), *Red Plaid Shirt* (2002), *By the Book: Stories and Pictures* (2013), and *First Things First: Selected Stories* (2016).

Novels: *Our Lady of the Lost and Found* (2001) and *At a Loss for Words* (2008).

Non-Fiction: *Names of the Dead: An Elegy for the Victims of September 11* (2004) and *This Is Not My Life* (2016)

What follows, "Forging New Shapes," is the introduction I wrote, in 1991, for Diane's *Hockey Night in Canada and Other Stories*. Since then, her technically inventive stories deploying digression and discontinuous narrative, brave new shapes, have won the Governor General's Award for Fiction.

Forging New Shapes

When I was editing *Best Canadian Stories* in the 1970s I can remember receiving stories submitted by Diane Schoemperlen who was then living in Canmore, Alberta. I didn't accept any of these stories but the name lodged in my mind; it joined my list of the names on which to keep a more than casual eye.

Years later—in 1987—I accepted from Diane two stories for the first *Macmillan Anthology*, stories entitled "A Simple Story" and "The Man of My Dreams," the latter being the title story of the collection she went on to publish with Macmillan in 1990. Diane reminded me when I was talking to her recently that when I accepted these two stories, I had written her a letter saying that she had finally won through to a recognizable "Diane Schoemperlen story." (I also seem to remember going on to say that she now had to avoid the danger of repeating herself, of becoming the captive of the strategies she had developed.)

When I started writing in the early 1960s, I faced exactly the same problems she faced, exactly the same problems that each new generation or grouping faces. The writers I was particularly associated with—Hugh Hood, Ray Smith, Clark Blaise, Alice Munro—were all struggling to create new shapes and forms for their stories. The shapes we had inherited from Hemingway and the other great American writers had hardened into an orthodoxy, a classicism, had become what Kent Thompson called "academy stuff." Those shapes were *their* shapes. What young poet today would dedicate himself to writing, say, the villanelle? We could not write *our* stories in *their* voices.

Each of us tackled the same problem in different ways but we were all well aware of what we were attempting. I would say, looking back now, that we succeeded so well that we created considerable difficulties for the younger writers who would follow us. It would have been difficult to avoid the challenge of stories like "Silver Bugles, Cymbals, Golden Silks," "Walker Brothers Cowboy," "Gentle As Flowers Make the Stones," "A North American Education," "A Small Piece of Blue," and dozens of other immensely powerful and original works.

(I rush to point out, however, that I am not trying to assert the beginnings of a Canadian tradition in the short story. The idea that an hermetic Canadian literary tradition exists or can evolve is one of the nuttier nationalist fantasies. On the other hand, I know from conversations that some of the younger story writers were influenced by Canadian writers of my generation. Just as they were influenced, though, by American and British writers and, in translation, by writers from Italy and Chile. So rather than positing the birth of a Canadian native tradition I'd be more comfortable suggesting that some Canadian writing has moved out into the mainstream of writing in English).

For the first time since the mid-1970s, I can see now a new formal upheaval taking placed in Canada. Younger writers are everywhere forging new shapes which are *their* shapes. This formal upheaval is not, of course, merely some matter of "technique," some sort of nuts-and-bolts messing about which might well provide fascinating shop-talk for writers but which is of no interest to readers. What readers must understand is that the shape of a story *is* the story. There is no such thing as "form" and "content." They are indivisible; they *are* each other. New shapes are new sensibilities.

Diane is one among a growing number of serious young fiction writers who are allowing us to see and feel in a new way. Other names that spring to mind are Keath Fraser, Linda Svendsen, Dayv James-French, Terry Griggs, Douglas Glover, and Steven Heighton. All are concerned in very different ways with the same task.

The stories in *Hockey Night in Canada and Other Stories* can be read as a record of Diane's struggle towards the kinds of stories in her most recent collection, *The Man of My Dreams*. This is not to be patronizing. The remarkable thing about *Hockey Night in Canada and Other Stories* is that all the stories hold up well. All contain surprises, felicities, pleasures.

In 1976, Diane attended a six-week summer writing workshop in Banff. For one of those weeks she was taught by Alice Munro. Some of the stories in this collection—I'm thinking of "The Long Way Home," "Hockey Night in Canada," "Clues," and "Crimes of Passion"—suggest to me the influence of the Alice Munro of such stories as "Walker Brothers Cowboy" and Images."

Then there are the transitional stories, which are attempting to break away from the influences, such stories as "First Things First," "Frogs," and "Notes for a Travelogue."

And then there are achieved new forms in such stories as "Life Sentences," "This Town," and "True or False."

But even in her earlier and more conventional stories, Diane's work could not be confused with Alice Munro's. And as she develops could not be confused with that of any other young writer in Canada.

Diane's territory is not rural or small town but is rather the gritty urban world of the Safeway, the laundromat, the café whose orange vinyl seats are patched with black electrical tape, a world where men dream of women who are "queens" but settle instead for women they think of as "utility grade," a world where women yearn for true love but end up trading gross recipes for Lazy Day Lasagna and Inside-Out Ravioli.

Life in this world bruises Diane Schoemperlen's heroines in their affairs and relationships and failing marriages and they learn and record small wisdoms with a tough, rueful humour:

> Last August I met this guy Dean at a party. I remember thinking he looked a little tired but I didn't see that as a serious problem at the time. He fell asleep at the party but then we'd all had quite a bit to drink and he wasn't the only one. He looked like a child when he was asleep. It wasn't until later that I discovered this is true of many people and is not an accurate measure of one's character.

Indeed, it is Diane's humour which is, for me, the central pleasure of her work. Nearly all the stories are marked with a sly humour which is wry and dry and sometimes as painful as ingested ground glass:

> She thought of her cousin Denise back in Hastings whom she had always been told had married late in life. For years, the whole family had treated Denise with a hopeful sympathy, as though there were little else she could be expected to do at such an advanced age beside marry a widower or keep working forever at the Bank of Montreal. Ruth had recently figured out that Denise actually got married at twenty-eight. Her husband, Howard Machuk, was a gynecologist who'd never been married and he gave her everything she could possibly want, including a dishwasher for her thirty-first birthday.

Diane creates this work with loving detail and detail itself—trade names, brand names, the banal language of advertising, the plenitude of deliberately flat fact—forms one of her comic devices.

I'm beginning to suspect that she is building, story by story, the Schoemperlen world. I mean by this that as she continues to write we'll begin to pay her the ultimate compliment of recognizing certain things we see as essentially details from a

Schoemperlen story. I will never again see an orange vinyl seat patched with black electrical tape without being immediately reminded of her observing eye. And can there *really* be a dish called Inside-Out Ravioli? But one *knows* it's true.

If someone were to ask for an example of the sadly funny world of Diane Schoemperlen, I'd give them to read the following paragraph from "Notes for a Travelogue." Sharon and Grant are two years into a failing marriage and take a week's holiday camping in an effort to hold matters together. On the first night they pitch their tent in the dark in a campground. The paragraph describes the next morning.

> Morning reveals a white Winnibago squatting just down the way, fat with sleeping strangers. There seems to be ten or twelve of them, with interchangeable heads, emerging one by one in various states of half-dress. The children race down to the lake in a pack while the adults put the coffee on. They holler blindly back and forth at each other through the tree cover—warnings, discoveries, the breakfast menu. While I'm waiting my turn in the fibreglass outhouse, a white poodle licks amiably at my ankles. Grant pumps up the Coleman stove and breaks eggs seriously into a metal bowl.

This paragraph is crammed with pleasures: the Winnebago "fat with sleeping strangers," the choice of the words "amiably" and "seriously." But the real joy of the paragraph in its context in the story is the way it seems to suggest and stand for and comment on the state of Sharon's marriage.

Welcome to the world of Diane Schoemperlen.

Adventures in the Absurd

For readers previously unacquainted with Diane Schoemperlen's work, the following look at "Red Plaid Shirt" will illustrate how a typical Schoemperlen story is put together, how it works, and why it is constructed in the way it is. Despite winning the Governor General's Award for Fiction in 1998, for *Forms of Devotion*, Schoemperlen's reputation is oddly muffled; it is as if Alice Munro and Margaret Atwood have sucked all the oxygen out of the room; our culture, such as it is, seems unable to accommodate the rich range of our writers. More than one hopeless reader has said to me that they'd been shy about asking for her books in stores or at the library because they were unsure of how to pronounce her name.

(It's "Shump.")

"Red Plaid Shirt" was first published in 1989, and in the years succeeding has become an almost iconic creation for younger writers; its influence can still be seen in endless variations on its technique in stories and "life-writing" (vile term!) in the literary magazines from coast to coast, though no one I'm aware of has equalled the depth and delicacy of Schoemperlen's creation.

"Red Plaid Shirt" is structured as follows: it is made up of discrete sections, each of which is introduced by naming a particular garment in the narrator's closet of memory: Red Plaid Shirt, Blue Cotton Sweatshirt, Pale Grey Turtleneck, White Embroidered Blouse, Yellow Evening Gown, Black Leather Jacket, Brown Cashmere Sweater, Green Satin Quilted Jacket. Each garment evokes a past love affair, inevitably disastrous.

At the conclusion of each memory evoked by a specific garment, the narrator lists all the disparate things the colour of the garment brings to her seemingly scatty mind. For example, the Red Plaid Shirt segment ends with an unpunctuated list of associations *Red* holds for her, unpunctuated to simulate the flow of haphazardness.

> Red: crimson carmine cochineal cinnabar sanguine scarlet red ruby rouge my birth stone red and blood-red brick beet-red bleeding hearts Queen of fire god of war Mars the colour of magic my magic the colour of iron flowers and fruit the colour of meat dripping lobster cracking claws lips nipples blisters blood my blood and all power.

This seemingly random list has a strange power as one reads it in its place in the story—it shines a sudden little light towards paths of intertwined thought and feelings—Mars, iron, war, bleeding, blood, meat drippings, cracking claws, my blood, all power.

Another path: hearts, Queen, magic, lips, nipples.

When we have read and digested the entire story in all its segments, we can see, looking back, that this "random" list is foretelling Daniel's bloody attack on "you" in the segment entitled Brown Cashmere Sweater that results in the Emergency Department and a hostel for battered women.

These lists at the end of each garment-section were intended, she once told me, as a "chorus" commenting on the central action. She also said she wanted them read as integral parts of each segment, that she'd laboured on them, sounding them aloud, until she got the rhythm and repetitions they demanded.

It struck me that these lists were akin to, intimately akin to, what I describe in the entry on Alice Munro as "underlay" or "shadow-narrative," soundings of the emotional depths; the list words are the recorded echoes coming back.

(Here's a meander absolutely *forced* upon me. This whole idea of "underlay" and Schoemperlen's "chorus" may have a relative in Laurence Olivier. I was struck by Kenneth Tynan's brilliant first book, *He That Plays the King*. It was published in 1950, when Tynan was twenty-three! In a chapter called "Heroic Acting Since 1944," Tynan wrote of Olivier's *Richard III* at the New Theatre in 1944:

> From a somber and uninventive production this brooding, withdrawn player leapt into life, using the circumambient gloom as his springboard. Olivier's Richard eats into the memory like acid into metal, but the total impression is one of lightness and deftness. The whole thing is taken at a speed baffling when one recalls how perfectly, even finically, it is articulated; it is Olivier's trick to treat each speech as a kind of plastic vocal mass, and not as a series of sentences whose import must be precisely communicated to the audience: the method is impressionist. He will seize on one or two phrases in each paragraph which, properly inserted, will unlock its whole meaning: the rest he discards, with exquisite idleness. To do this successfully he needs other people on the stage with him: to be

ignored, stared past, or pushed aside during the lower reaches, and gripped and buttonholed when the wave rises to its crested climax. For this reason Olivier tends to fail in soliloquy—except when, as in the opening speech of *Richard*, it is directed straight at the audience, who then become his temporary foils. I thought, for example, that the night-piece before the battle sagged badly, in much the same way as the soliloquies in the *Hamlet* film sagged. Olivier the actor needs reactors: just as electricity, *in vacuo*, is unseen, unfelt, and powerless.

When I first read this, when I first read *a kind of plastic vocal mass* and *one or two phrases… properly inserted, will unlock its whole meaning…* I felt like Cortez's men looking at each other

> *… with a wild surmise—*
> *Silent, upon a peak in Darien.*

"Red Plaid Shirt" is written entirely in the rarely used second person. The narrator is addressing "you," her younger self. Or, at least, that's how *I* read it. But other readings are possible so I'd better let Diane comment.

J.R. "Tim" Struthers conducted an interview with Diane in 1999, published in *Wascana Review* in 2005 and entitled "Illustrated Fiction: An Interview with Diane Schoemperlen."

TS: I'd like to ask you a question concerning "Red Plaid Shirt." Had you ever read anything else in the second person?

DS: I had, actually. I read *Bright Lights, Big City* by Jay McInerney and, unlike many people, I really liked it. I liked the voice. I liked whatever it does to tell something in the "you" point of view. I really enjoyed it. I wouldn't write a whole novel in it like he did. But I think it worked for a short story. Not everybody likes it. I have had one person say to me after I read the story that she felt "assaulted" by my story, which I thought was a bit much.

TS: I think that would be a more appropriate description of the disturbing voyeuristic effect of the second-person narration of the story "Eyes" in Clark Blaise's collection *A North American Education*.

DS: It's a very forceful person, maybe simply because it doesn't get used a lot, so I think when you're reading or hearing something in the second person you're *really* listening because it's so different and you don't quite know how to take that "you." I mean, is it "me," is it "you," who is it?

The red plaid shirt was bought for the narrator by her visiting mother one summer in Banff. She felt it was "flattering against your pale skin, your black hair." The shirt was made of "100% pure virgin wool." The Western Outfitters store in which the mother bought the shirt had "a saddle and stuffed deer head in the window." Think about that "innocent" detail.
The plaid shirt

> reminded you of your mother's gardening shirt… You picture her kneeling in the side garden where she grew only flowers— bleeding hearts, roses, peonies, poppies—and a small patch of strawberries. You picture her hair in a bright babushka, her hands in the black earth with her shirt sleeves rolled up past the elbow. The honeysuckle hedge bloomed fragrantly behind her and the sweet peas curled interminably up the white trellis. You are sorry now for the way you always sulked and whined when she asked you to help, for the way you hated the dirt under your nails and the sweat running into your eyes, and the sweat dripping down her shirt front between her small breasts.

The story's final garment-section, Green Satin Quilted Jacket, will link us back to these seemingly unimportant details, pulling them into a different shape, investing them with unexpected weight.
(Follow, in retrospect, the "underlay.")
The shirt segment then moves forward in time.

> You were wearing the red plaid shirt the night you met Daniel in the tavern where he was drinking beer with his buddies from the

highway construction crew. You ended up living with him for the next five years. He was always calling it your "magic shirt," teasing you, saying how it was the shirt that made him fall in love with you in the first place. You would tease him back, saying how you'd better hang onto it then, in case you had to use it on somebody else. You've even worn it in that spirit a few times since, but the magic seems to have seeped out of it and you are hardly surprised.

The "magic" seeps out continually and we are treated with each succeeding garment to a highly selective series of "autobiographical" vignettes of the narrator's love life ("autobiographical" because of the "you," read by me, again, as addressed to the narrator's younger self), vignettes which feature much drink, drama, violence, heartache, and a parade of wildly unsuitable men given to what, in our mealy-mouthed times, is called "inappropriate behaviour."

Following are excerpts from Black Leather Jacket, an account of the narrator's life with the biker, Ivan.

Ivan used to take you on weekend runs with his buddies and their old ladies to little bars in other towns where they were afraid of you: especially of Ivan's best friend, Spy, who had been hurt in a bike accident two years before and now his hands hung off his wrists at odd angles and he could not speak, only make guttural growls, write obscene notes to the waitress on a serviette, and laugh at her like a madman, his eyes rolling back in his head, and you could see what was left of his tongue

You would come riding up in a noisy pack with bugs in your teeth, dropping your black helmets like bowling balls on the floor, eating greasy burgers and pickled eggs, drinking draft beer by the jug, the foam running down your chin. Your legs, after the long ride, felt like a wish bone waiting to be sprung.

Then in the next paragraph the narrative changes gear.

You never did get around to telling your mother you were dating a biker (she thought you said "baker"), which was just as well, since Ivan eventually got tired, sold his bike, and moved back to Manitoba to live with his mother, who was dying. He got a job in a hardware store and soon married his high school sweetheart, Betty, who was a dental hygienist. Spy was killed on the highway: drove his bike into the back of a tanker truck in broad daylight; there was nothing left of him.

What an ignominious end to Ivan (the Terrible)!

The bizarre and comical lace through nearly all Diane's work in complicated ways. I quote again from the Tim Struthers interview in the *Wascana Review*; for reasons of space, I'll have to plunder rather than quote in full.

> **DS:** ...people have said of some of my things I've written that I'm cynical and what not. I'm really not.
>
> ... I have a rather sharp sense of humour... but that doesn't mean I'm cynical... some review said I had a vision as grim and bleak as Samuel Beckett... I was aghast!
>
> ... I took exception to it... Just because I'm aware of the absurdity of life—or whatever you want to call it—doesn't mean that I'm cynical... I have some pretty grim and bleak moments and I know those moments are in the writing. But overall I really think of myself as an optimist.

Later in the interview, she says: "I think that irony, which I use a lot in my work because that is how I see the world, is a slippery thing."

I have a suspicion that the unnamed reviewer who compared her work to that of Beckett was not only silly but possibly unaware that Beckett is simultaneously grim *and* funny; some of his excursions in language, the comic exactitude of the "sucking stones" performance to take an obvious example, are verbal equivalents of W.C. Fields' vaudeville routines with a warped billiard cue. Or Lucky, in *Waiting for Godot*, thinking: a "think" that starts as a parody of academic discourse:

> *Given the existence as uttered forth in the public works of Puncher and Waltman of a personal God qua qua qua qua white beard qua qua qua qua...*

"Qua" meaning "as being," the ablative singular of "Qui" meaning "who." It *also* means absolutely *nothing*—the sound an animal makes. Recently I was in the Boboli Gardens in Florence and my head was turned sharply by a woman saying to her toddler in Italian baby-talk, while pointing to a duck on the ornamental lake, "Look at the qua-qua!"

With the section, Brown Cashmere Sweater, we return to Daniel, whom we met first in Red Plaid Shirt.

> Brown Cashmere Sweater that you were wearing the night you told Daniel you were leaving him. It was the week between Christmas and New Year's which is always a wasteland. Everyone was digging up recipes called Turkey-Grape Salad, Turkey Soufflé, and Turkey-almond-Noodle Bake. You kept vacuuming up tinsel and pine needles, putting away presents one at a time from under the tree. You and Daniel sat at the kitchen table all afternoon, drinking hot rum toddies, munching on crackers and garlic sausage, playing Trivial Pursuit, asking each other questions like:
>
> What's the most mountainous country in Europe?
> Which is more tender, the left or right leg of a chicken?
> What race of warriors burned off their right breasts in Greek legend?
> Daniel was a poor loser and he thought that Europe was a country maybe somewhere near Spain.

The description of that period between Christmas and New Year's is also a picture of the emotional "wasteland" ("you"'s word) that the relationship has become for "you." She is acknowledging, perhaps the long-suppressed view, that Daniel is a bit dim and "a poor loser" in more than a card-game sense. The description is both funny (the desperate recipes, the triviality of Trivial Pursuit), and at the same time very unfunny. Follow the "underlay": wasteland, digging up, vacuuming up, tinsel, pine needles (dry, fallen), putting away, Trivial Pursuit, tender. And "burned off" Amazonian breasts; the police photographer later in this sequence photographs you's "left breast, which has purple bruises all over it where he grabbed it and twisted and twisted."

The next paragraph, still through specific detail, burrows into the real nature of you's disenchantment, disaffection.

> This night you have just come from a party at his friend Harold's house. You are sitting on the new couch, a loveseat, blue with white flowers, which was Daniel's Christmas present to you, and you can't help thinking of the year your father got your mother a coffee percolator when all she wanted was something personal: earrings, a necklace, a scarf for God's sake. She spent most of the day locked in their bedroom, crying noisily, coming out every hour or so to baste the turkey, white-lipped, tucking more Kleenex up her sleeve. You were on her side this time and wondered how your father, whom you always secretly loved the most, could be so insensitive. It was the changing of the guard, your allegiances shifting like sand from one to the other.

In other words, in abstracting words, the violent, rather pathetic Daniel is seen not simply for what he is but as embodying the general insensitivity of traditional maleness; Schoemperlen is writing about the emotional gulf between women and men. Imagine what a dogmatic dog's dinner Margaret Atwood would have made of this! But Schoemperlen blends her disillusionment with buoyant and defiant comedy.

(Recall the Howard she refers to in the first section of this entry on her: "Her husband, Howard Machuk, was a gynecologist who'd never been married and he gave her everything she could possibly want, including a dishwasher for her thirty-first birthday.")

And "you"'s poor mother "crying noisily" ("noisily," purposefully) but emerging every hour or so, "white-lipped," to baste the turkey; wounded emotions still subservient to a sense of marital and culinary duty. This sentence so complicatedly funny.

When "you" tells Daniel she is leaving him,

> Daniel grips you by the shoulders and bangs your head against the wall until the picture hung there falls off. It is a photograph of the mountains on a pink spring morning, the ridges like ribs,

the runoff like incisions or veins. There is glass flying everywhere in slices into your face, into your hands pressed over your eyes, and the front of your sweater is spotted and matted with blood."

("Glass in slices" always stops me because of its unusualness. I expect to read "splinters" or "shards" but "slices" does strange double duty as, somehow, simultaneous noun and verb. Discomfortingly vivid.)

On the way to the hospital, he says he will kill you if you tell them what he did to you. You promise him anything, you promise him that you will love him forever and that you will never leave.

All the writing about the visit to the hospital and what follows in the shelter for battered women is recorded flatly. A lesser writer would have expressed and elaborated on "you"'s emotions but statements *about* emotion do not make us feel.
"She felt sad."
Well, yes, ok.
Noted.
Instead, Schoemperlen makes a move that is so simple yet so clever that it causes in me "a sharp intake," as P.G. Wodehouse would have written, of writerly breath. She shifts the focus away from "you" and onto Daniel and lets a simple statement about him evoke emotions in the reader about him *and* about the observing "you." This simple statement moves us to emotional judgement and towards vivid empathy for her physical and emotional wounds.

The nurse takes you into the examining room. Daniel waits in the waiting room, reads magazines, buys a chocolate bar from the vending machine, then a Coke and a bag of ripple chips. You tell the nurse what happened and the police take him away in handcuffs with their guns drawn.

I can imagine an uninspired teacher of creative writing reprimanding a beginner for "repetition" in "wait/waiting" and for "needless detail" and "padding" in the vending-machine purchases.

I would go so far as to say—pure impertinence—that the line about Daniel's purchases could have been improved had Diane *named* the magazines he is flipping through, *People* magazine, say, or *Canadian Living*; had she *named* the chocolate bar, *Mars Bar*, say, *Snickers*, *Hershey's*; had she *named* the chips, *Lay's Ripple Cut* or some-such. Naming, branding, would somehow intensify our understanding of his callousness, his seeming obliviousness to the awfulness of what he has done.

The vivid familiarity of a brand name would intensify the simultaneous existence of ordinariness and the violent and bizarre. I often think that such simultaneity is one of Diane's preoccupations. That simultaneity occurs again in the paragraph about the women's shelter where "The woman with the broken cheekbone has two canaries in a gold cage that she carries with her everywhere like a lamp." The reader either rises to the intended irony of canaries in combination with lamp—or doesn't.

And while on the subject of brand names and ordinariness, all of Schoemperlen's lists, recipes, song titles, descriptions of meals and drinks, of what people wear, their cats, their house plants, colour schemes, appliances, the snatches of overheard conversation—it is all part of a purposeful creation of a world, a kind of brash painting, a kind of pop-poetry. I'm reminded, on the wing, as it were, of Rauschenberg's "combines," Joseph Cornell's boxes, the paintings of Richard Hamilton and R. B. Kitaj. Diane's own forays into the visual arts can be most lushly seen in her recent *By the Book*.

When I wrote earlier of "The Red Plaid Shirt" becoming an iconic creation in its influence on younger writers, it was the form of the story that influenced them rather than anything verbal or visionary. Diane's work evolved into this method of plotting—improvising on letters of the alphabet, or quotations from handbooks on grammar or psychiatry—as ways of reinvigorating the traditional linear movements of plot. It was a way of finding a new way of looking and seeing. It was a new way of capturing a life, a way she saw as closer to reality—no, make that "a way she *felt* as closer to reality"—than a Beginning/Middle/End story with its imposition of coherence upon life's evident chaos and tumbling randomness. It was a way of jolting the reader about, of insisting every page or so on a refocussing, of forcing uncomfortableness.

(Norman Levine was doing much the same much earlier, forcing us, uncomfortably, to *look*. As Cynthia Flood, quoted earlier in the entry on Levine, put it:

> Readers, rolling along the shiny habitual rails of subject and predicate, enter the familiar sentence-tunnel knowing when the verb will arrive and the terminal light appear. We read to reach an expected end. That habit Levine wants to break. We are to *look*. Outside the train.

Schoemperlen, however, was not a *conscious* theoretician. Norman Levine *was*, though it took him quite a long time to achieve fully on the fictional page what he had been feeling and thinking about for years. Diane said to me recently that she made these "experimental" shapes "to see if I could make them work," that it was playing around with these shapes that, more than anything else, "filled me with creative joy."

In her most recent book, *First Things First: Early and Uncollected Stories*, she writes in the preface:

> ... while some of these early stories were written in a more traditional manner, my fascination with innovative forms and structures was there from the beginning. There are several stories written in short sections, many containing lists of one sort or another, one modeled after a true-or-false questionnaire and another set up as a multiple-choice test. The story "Life Sentences," written in 1983, is a kind of fill-in-the-blanks interactive piece, where sometimes the missing word is obvious and sometimes not. I can't honestly say what gave me the confidence to think I could do all these different things. What made me think I could just break the "rules" of conventional story writing and do it however I wanted?

> In the introduction to my 1991 collection, *Hockey Night in Canada and Other Stories*, John Metcalf wrote: "What readers

must understand is that the shape of a story *is* the story. There is no such thing as 'form' and 'content.' They are indivisible; they *are* each other. New shapes are new sensibilities."

This makes perfect sense to me now but how did I know that then? I don't think I did, at least not consciously. Reviews of my work over the years have often referred to me as a writer who is "challenging the short-story form." I can assure you that never once in my life have I sat down at my desk and thought, "Now what can I do to challenge the short story form this time?"

But challenge the form is exactly what she did.

To return to the final garment-section of "Red Plaid Shirt," the section entitled Green Satin Quilted Jacket. This section links back to the first section, Red Plaid Shirt, and closes the story in what I'd have to call a quintessential Schoemperlen ploy (and play); Green Satin Quilted Jacket does not close the story at all but opens onto the beginning of a new relationship, a relationship "you" wishes to be "transparent." In plot terms, we are left dangling; in emotional terms it is clear where "you" is headed.

The final sentence of the segment and of the whole story reads:

More than anything, you want to hold his hands across the table and then you will tell him you love him and it will all come true.

Can this *Harlequin* pap be the grim-as-Beckett Schoemperlen? Fear not, and read on.

The section is so important in the overall structure of the story that I must quote it in full.

GREEN SATIN QUILTED JACKET

in the Oriental style with mandarin collar and four red frogs down the front. This jacket is older than you are. It belonged to your mother, who bought it when she was the same age you are now. In the black and white photos from that time, the jacket is grey but shiny and your mother is pale but smooth-skinned, smiling with her hand on her hip or your father's thigh.

You were always pestering her to let you wear it to play dress-up, with her red high heels and that white hat with the feathers and the little veil that covered your whole face. You wanted to wear it to a Hallowe'en party at school where all the other girls would be witches, ghosts, or princesses and you would be the only mandarin, with your eyes, you imagined, painted up slanty and two sticks through a bun in your hair. But she would never let you. She would just keep on cooking supper, bringing carrots, potatoes, cabbages up from the root cellar, taking peas, beans, broccoli out of the freezer in labelled dated parcels, humming, looking out through the slats of the Venetian blind at the black garden and the leafless rose bushes. Each year, at least one of them would be winter-killed no matter how hard she had tried to protect them. And she would dig it up in the spring by the dead roots and the thorns would get tangled in her hair, leave long bloody scratches all down her arms. And the green jacket stayed where it was, in the cedar chest with the handmade lace doilies, her grey linen wedding suit, and the picture of your father as a small boy with blond ringlets.

After the funeral, you go through her clothes while your father is outside shovelling snow. You lay them out in piles on the bed: one for the Salvation Army, one for the second-hand store, one for yourself because your father wants you to take something home with you. You will take the green satin jacket, also a white mohair cardigan with multicoloured squares on the front, a black and white striped shirt you sent her for her birthday last year that she never wore, an imitation pearl necklace for Alice, and a dozen unopened packages of pantyhose. There is a fourth pile for your father's friend Jack's new wife, Frances, whom your mother never liked, but your father says Jack and Frances have fallen on hard times on the farm since Jack got the emphysema, and Frances will be glad of some new clothes.

Jack and Frances drop by the next day with your Aunt Jeanne. You serve tea and the shortbread cookies Aunt Jeanne has brought. She makes them just the way your mother did, whipped, with a sliver of maraschino cherry on top. Jack, looking weather-beaten or embarrassed, sits on the edge of the couch with his baseball cap in his lap and marvels at how grown up you've got to be. Frances is genuinely grateful for the two green garbage bags of clothes, which you carry out to the truck for her.

After they leave, you reminisce fondly with your father and Aunt Jeanne about taking the toboggan out to Jack's farm when you were small, tying it to the back of the car, your father driving slowly down the country lane, towing you on your stomach, clutching the front of the toboggan which curled like a wooden wave. You tell him for the first time how frightened you were of the black tires spinning the snow into your face, and he says he had no idea, he thought you were having fun. This was when Jack's first wife, Winnifred, was still alive. Your Aunt Jeanne, who knows everything, tells you that when Winnifred was killed in that car accident, it was Jack, driving drunk, who caused it. And now when he gets drunk, he beats Frances up, locks her out of the house in her bare feet, and she has to sleep in the barn, in the hay with the horses.

You are leaving in the morning. Aunt Jeanne helps you pack. You are anxious to get home but worried about leaving your father alone. Aunt Jeanne says she'll watch out for him.

The green satin jacket hangs in your front hall closet now, between your black leather jacket and your raincoat. You can still smell the cedar from the chest and the satin is always cool on your cheek like clean sheets or glass.

One day you think you will wear it downtown, where you are meeting a new man for lunch. You study yourself in the full-length mirror on the back of the bathroom door and you decide it makes you look like a different person: someone unconventional, unusual, and unconcerned. This new man, whom you met recently at an outdoor jazz festival, is a free spirit who eats health food, plays the dulcimer, paints well, writes well, sings well, and has just completed an independent study of Eastern religions. He doesn't smoke, drink, or do drugs. He is pure and peaceful, perfect. He is teaching you how to garden, how to turn the black soil, how to plant the seeds, how to water them, weed them, watch them turn into lettuce, carrots, peas, beans, radishes, and pumpkins, how to get the kinks out of your back by stretching your brown arms right up to the sun. You haven't even told Alice about him yet because he is too good to be true. He is bound to love this green jacket, and you in it too.

You get in your car, drive around the block, go back inside because you forgot your cigarettes, and you leave the green jacket on the back of a kitchen chair because who are you trying to kid. More than anything, you want to be transparent. More than anything, you want to hold his hands across the table and then you will tell him you love him and it will all come true.

GREEN: viridian verdigris chlorophyll grass leafy jade mossy verdant apple-green pea-green lime-green sage-green sea-green bottle-green emeralds avocadoes olives all leaves the colour of Venus hope and jealousy the colour of mould mildew envy poison and pain and snakes the colour of everything that grows in my garden fertile nourishing sturdy sane and strong.

The garment-segment Green Satin Quilted Jacket is itself divided into five basic blocks of writing. The first centres around "you"'s childhood and her desire to wear the green jacket to play dress-up, and, later, to attend a Hallowe'en party at school wearing the jacket as part of her costume as a Mandarin. She pictures her mother cooking and looking out over the kitchen sink at the black winter garden hoping that her rose bushes will survive.

The first block is Schoemperlen in intense lyric mode. We must never assume that detail in a Schoemperlen story is gratuitous. The green jacket belonged to "you"'s mother, who bought it when she was somewhat younger than "you" now is, the "you" sorting through her dead mother's possessions. In family photos, her mother is wearing the jacket, "smiling with her hand on her hip or your father's thigh."

A happy pose, confident, possessive of her young husband, a little provocative.

This youthful confidence and assertiveness is further suggested in the mother's clothes the child-"you" wants to play dress-up in, "her red high heels and that white hat with the feathers and the little veil that covered your whole face." Later, "you" wanted to wear the green jacket to a Hallowe'en party where she would be the only mandarin among the "witches, ghosts, or princesses, with your eyes, you imagined, painted up slanty and two sticks through a bun in your hair."

The intention of the passage is not only to flesh out and realize "you"; it is also to reintroduce, more insistently than in earlier garment-sections, the idea of "dressing-up," of disguise, of pretending to be someone one is not.

The veil "that covered your whole face."

If we think back at this point about the story's earlier sections, "you" has appeared in various guises, usually subservient to men she both desires and thinks she needs, yet feels mildly contemptuous towards.

She lived for five years with Daniel, who thought Europe was a country maybe somewhere near Spain. With Ivan, she became a biker's "old lady" until Ivan married his high-school sweetheart, Betty, a dental hygienist. She clung to the hope that Dwight would stop being an unreliable slob; she dresses for New Year's Eve in a Yellow Evening Gown only to encounter her date, Fernando, with a woman on his arm, his previously unannounced wife. When she first encounters Fernando, she realizes that Peter, the aspiring jazz musician, "has an inferior bone structure."

All these affairs and relationships have in common the fact of "dress-up"; for each succeeding man she adopts a new disguise, she dresses the part. This aspect of the story is stated most obviously after the decline into respectability of Ivan the Biker.

You wear your leather jacket now when you need to feel tough. You wear it with your tight blue jeans and your cowboy boots. You strut slowly with your hands in your pockets. Your boots click on the concrete and you are a different person. You can handle anything and no one had better get in your way. You will take on the world if you have to. You will die young and in flames if you have to.

(Schoemperlen is full of delicate effects to which we need to be sensitive. The pathetic braggadocio of the repeated "if you have to.")

The opening section of Green Jacket prefigures its final section.

The other emotional concern that runs through the first section is the role of the mother. She refuses to let "you" dress up in the satin jacket; she refuses pleas.

> She would just keep on cooking supper, bringing carrots, potatoes, cabbages up from the root cellar, taking peas, beans, broccoli out of the freezer in labelled dated parcels, humming, looking out through the slats of the Venetian blind at the black garden and the leafless rose bushes.

I want to return to that garden in a moment, but let us look a little more closely at that sketch of "you"'s mother. The tallying of the labelled and dated packages conveys the tedium of the routine of cooking; Schoemperlen details the contents of the packages as a "short hand" portrait of the mother, equating the one with the other. *Dated* packages, while being a realistic detail, also conveys the idea of time and time passing. Eliot's *I have measured out my life in coffee spoons*, that sort of feeling is intended here. This feeling invests "the slats of the venetian blind" with the suggestion, perhaps, of prison bars. Yet at the same time, as she looks out on the black garden, she is humming. We remember also her noisy weeping over the gift of the coffee percolator yet her hourly emergence to baste the turkey. The implication is that this is an incarceration she accepts.

The "leafless rose bushes" in the black garden.

> Each year, at least one of them would be winter-killed no matter how hard she had tried to protect them. And she would dig it up

in the spring by the dead roots and the thorns would get tangled in her hair, leave long bloody scratches all down her arms.

Once tuned into the writing, it's difficult not to read this as emblematic of her emotional life and its costs. Follow the "underlay." It has an almost D.H. Lawrence feel to it, though lacking his stridency.

What is *really* interesting is to see that this passage sends us back to the Red Plaid Shirt section, where the mother gardening is, again, a central image—"in the side garden" (not the *main* one, we imagine, where serious vegetables grew) "where she grew only flowers."

With first in the list of blossoms, "bleeding hearts." We are being steered to see the mother's flower gardening as a continuing struggle against a bleeding heart (think percolators) and as an assertion of the need for beauty and… Surely I don't have to go on thumping the tub?

But "you" are sorry now that you "hated the dirt under your nails and the sweat running into your eyes," sorry that you turned away from your mother's life only to drift into failed entanglements, your mother, "the sweat dripping down her shirt front between her small breasts." Impossible in this story not to think of Amazons burning off their right breasts and "you's" left breast "which has purple bruises all over it where he grabbed it and twisted and twisted."

The green jacket "you" desired to dress up in is denied her, and remains, until her death, in the cedar chest with other of her mother's treasures, "handmade lace doilies, her grey linen wedding suit, and the picture of your father as a small boy with blond ringlets." Treasured and romantic fragments shored against her ruins.

The next movement of the story—the whole thing is so rich, so poetic that I'm thinking in terms of music—is "you" sorting though her dead mother's possessions, one pile for the Salvation Army, one for the second-hand store, "one for yourself because your father wants you to take something home with you."

There's a fourth pile for her father's friend Jack's new wife Frances, because they've had hard times since Jack "got the emphysema." (The delicately dabbed in "the" of country speech nailing class and education.)

Here the segment changes direction, sounding the sombre notes of male irresponsibility and violence. Jack and Frances and Aunt Jeanne drop by the next day to pick up the bags of clothes and after they've left Aunt Jeanne reveals that Jack's first wife, Winnifred, died in a car crash, Jack driving drunk.

> And now when he gets drunk, he beats Frances up, locks her out of the house in her bare feet, and she has to sleep in the barn, in the hay with the horses.

Aunt Jeanne and "you" and her father reminisce about how, out at Jack's farm, her father used to tie their toboggan to the back bumper of the car towing small "you" on her stomach "clutching the front of the toboggan which curled like a wooden wave."

"You" admits for the first time how frightened she had been by "the black tires spinning snow into her face." Her father is astonished; "he thought you were having fun."

In the final section of the story, "you" is meeting the new man downtown for lunch. She studies herself in the mirror wearing the green jacket and decides "it makes you look like a different person: someone unconventional, unusual, unconcerned... You get in your car, drive around the block, go back inside because you forgot your cigarettes, and you leave the green jacket on the back of a kitchen chair because who are you trying to kid. More than anything, you want to be transparent. More than anything, you want to hold his hands across the table and then you will tell him you love him and it will all come true."

"...around the block" has an idiomatic ring to it. "...who are you trying to kid" is her renunciation of wearing literal and figurative disguises, of pretending to be who she is not.

Here the language of the writing changes again, and Schoemperlen's buoyant humour surfaces. For what is the "new man" like? This *paragon* she has found?

The new man is "a free spirit," he eats "health food," "paints well, sings well," has just completed an "independent study" of eastern religions.

(How sneaky, snarky, that word "independent.") Doesn't smoke, drink, or do drugs. He is "pure" and peaceful." He is teaching "you" how to garden, (this refers us back to her mother whose gardening was existential) how to turn the black soil. He teaches her "how to get the kinks out of your back by stretching your brown arms right up to the sun."

To crown all, this "free spirit" plays the dulcimer.

Dulcimer!

I said to Diane that I thought "Dulcimer" was wildly over the top, a dulcimer being an ancient instrument, a zither-like thing played by being struck with hammers. The only thing possibly worse would have been playing that early ancestor of the spinet, the virginals.

This ghastly man is so obviously boringly wonderful, a walking compendium of fads, so obviously in sheep's clothing, that given "you"'s track record, he is bound to turn out to be, at the very least an Axe-Murderer or Serial Dismemberer.

Who is she trying to kid?

The "chorus" provides an interesting commentary.

*

Further critical material can be found in "The New Story Writers" in my *Freedom from Culture: Selected Essays 1982–92*.

Carol Shields

Short Story Collections: *Various Miracles* (1985), *The Orange Fish* (1989), *Dressing Up for the Carnival* (2000) and *Collected Stories* (2004). Novels: *Small Ceremonies* (1976), *The Box Garden* (1977), *Happenstance* (1980), *A Fairly Conventional Woman* (1982), *Swann: A Mystery* (1987), *The Republic of Love* (1992), *The Stone Diaries* (1993), *Larry's Party* (1997), and *Unless* (2002).

Poetry Collections: *Others* (1972), *Intersect* (1974), and *Coming to Canada* (1992).

Plays: *Departures and Arrivals* (1990), *Thirteen Hands* (1993), *Fashion Power Guilt and the Charity of* Families [with Catherine Shields] (1995), *Anniversary: A Comedy* [with Dave Williamson] (1998), *Women*

Waiting (1983), *Unless* (2005), *Larry's Party—the Musical* (2000), and *Thirteen Hands and Other Plays* (2002).

Non-Fiction: *Susanna Moodie: Voice and Vision* (1976) and *Jane Austen* (2001).

I have never been interested in Carol Shields' novels, considering them rather lukewarm, muted, women's-magaziny. There is no technical innovation, no challenge in them. Dialogue tends to be ill-managed. I thought I had Carol Shields pegged. Domestic, a bit sentimental, twee. Imagine my astonishment, then, when I read *Various Miracles* and later *The Orange Fish*. Observation was acute, language was tight and vibrating, form was dense and packed.

I asked Shields what had happened and she didn't really seem to know, describing the stories in *Various Miracles* as more or less a visitation, a sudden liberation. Stoddart had little clue as to the value of the collection and released it as a paperback original. It did not create much critical stir, though writers were acutely aware of it. A copy in fine condition is hard to find. Four years later Stoddart released *The Orange Fish* in hardcover. The two collections remain much more important than *The Stone Diaries* and *Larry's Party*, for which she was awarded medals and prizes.

Carol was a little more articulate in an interview with Eleanor Wachtel:

Wachtel: Your fiction took a more experimental turn in 1985 with *Various Miracles*. What happened?

Shields: I discovered the old storyteller's voice, the omniscient narrator. I'd never tried it before and I wanted to. I thought I would write a book of short stories, because you're not bound to one particular voice. I could tell stories from close up or from far back. I wanted to tell stories from children's point of view. I wanted to do all the narrations. The other thing I realized as I wrote those stories was that I could get a little bit off the ground and let the story find its own way. I decided to let that happen, let it go where it seemed to go, even if it didn't make any naturalistic sense.

Here is the "social arbiter" Georgia Willows from the story "Good Manners."

> Promptly at three-thirty each Tuesday and Thursday, neatly dressed in a well-pressed navy Evan-Picone slub silk suit, cream blouse and muted scarf, Georgia Willows meets her small class in the reception area of the MacDonald Hotel and ushers them into the long airy tearoom—called, for some reason, Gophers—where a ceremonial spread has been ordered.
>
> Food and drink almost always accompany Mrs. Willows' lectures. It is purely a matter of simulation since, wherever half a dozen people gather, there is sure to be a plate of sandwiches to trip them up. According to Mrs. Willows, food and food implements are responsible for fifty per cent of social unease. The classic olive pit question. The persisting problem of forks, cocktail picks and coffee spoons. The more recent cherry-tomato dilemma. Potato skins, eat them or leave them? Saucers, the lack of. The challenge of the lobster. The table napkin quandary. Removing parsley from between the teeth. On and on.

How this deft, light, sparkling opening leads on to Mr. Manfred's "tube of pink, snouty, dampish flesh" and matters even darker, cannot even be guessed at. This is a dazzling story.

Ray Smith
Short Story Collections: *Cape Breton Is the Thought Control Centre of Canada* (1969), *Lord Nelson Tavern* (1974), and *Century* (1986).

Novels: *A Night at the Opera* (1992), *The Man Who Loved Jane Austen* (1999), *The Man Who Hated Emily Bronte* (2004), and *The Flush of Victory: Jack Bottomly Among the Virgins* (2007).

Ray Smith's originality and importance lie in the fact that from the very beginning of his career he turned away from the conventions of realism and started to write stories totally unlike those of early twentieth-century masters of the form. His achievement has been undervalued by those who want Canadian literature to "tell our own stories to ourselves," an aim he would consider crude and vulgar. He might shudder just a trifle to consider this, but there is about his writing a Firbankian quality, a glittering artifice, a dandyism.

In an invaluable introductory essay in *Cape Breton...* entitled "The Age of Innocence" (1989), Smith describes his work as belonging to the Alternate Tradition, the tradition that stems from Laurence Sterne's *Tristram Shandy*.

> [The stories are] part of a body of work called 'speculative fiction.' Generally ironic in tone. Aesthetic in approach; which means, I suppose, an indirect approach to many social and political problems of the world around us. This is in clear contrast to the other rising [in 1971] body of writing which includes things like revolutionary writings, the new journalism, documentary novels and the like, all of which try to grapple directly with the aforesaid social and political problems. I should emphasize, or repeat, that speculative fiction doesn't ignore the world, but approaches it somewhat indirectly. The telling point is that all these types have pretty much rejected the whole creaking apparatus of the... psychological-realism (or whatever it's called) form of writing.
>
> Some big dogs in speculative fiction: Jorge Luis Borges, Vladimir Nabokov. Coming big dog: Kurt Vonnegut, Jr. Prominent younger dogs: Thomas Pynchon, John Barth, Donald Barthelme, Richard Brautigan.

Ray once said to me, "Being a Canadian, of course I have no language." We might well look at all his work as a love affair with other languages, other dialects, other tribes in their heartlands. *A Night at the Opera* immerses us in the German city of Waltherrott and in its opera *Der Hosenkavalier*, written by the city's favourite son, Carl Maria von Stumpf. The stories in *Century* luxuriate in Paris of the *belle époque*, contemporary Venice, the pampered world of

Austrian ski slopes, and in the ordered elegance of Edinburgh's New Town. His novel, *The Flush of Victory: Jack Bottomly Among the Virgins*, embraces and celebrates the horribly colourful Strine, the Australian vernacular.

What sort of linguistic razzle-dazzle was Ray Smith up to in the late sixties when he was forging a style? A close reading of "The Age of Innocence" and of Ray's commentary on "Colours," in my anthology *Sixteen by Twelve*, will help. One of his central concerns was getting rid of what he thought of as the lumber of scene and setting. I'll take just two examples to suggest the kinds of devices he was inventing.

In the story "Colours" the protagonist Gerard wishes to ask questions of an exotic dancer called Patchouli. Ray is mainly concerned with getting Gerard from A to B and doesn't wish to waste narrative time on conventional description of the night club setting. This was his solution:

> So, after Patchouli had read Gerard's note and agreed to the interview, Gerard pushed past the chorus (laughter, sweat, smoke, gaping mouths) into the wings and, led by the man with six fingers, came and sat in her dressing room.

The five words in parentheses are, in effect, a montage. A montage that makes *us* make an instantaneous montage in our minds of all the musicals and showbiz/gangster nightclub scenes we've watched in countless movies. Once he's done it, it's not difficult for us to grasp, but his having *invented* it suggests we're in masterful hands.

Here's another example of Ray at play from the opening of the second section of "Peril":

> Period watched the carousel from a distance. Between him and the carousel stretched a green lawn with tree shadows like continents on a map. The lawn was so flat that Period had the impression (as had also many before him) that the lawn could be rolled up on a pole and carried away. (The carpet movers stout, slow, their cloth caps ...)

When he's finished deflating the lawn-as-carpet cliché what does he want me to do with the carpet movers?

stout, slow, their cloth caps ...

I'm not completely sure, but I think he wants from me something like: British. Black-and-white. Late fifties. Ealing Studios. Possibly involving Alec Guinness ...

These, and dozens more, are the sorts of games these stories play.

Useful discussion can be found in *The Montreal Story Tellers: Memoirs, Photographs, Critical Essays (Ed. J.R. Struthers). Montreal: Véhicule Press, 1985.* And in an essay of Ray Smith's called "A Refusal to Mourn the Death, by Bullshit, of Literature in the Eighties" in *Carry on Bumping. (Ed. J. Metcalf) Toronto: ECW Press, 1988.*

Russell Smith

Short Story Collections: *Young Men* (1999) and *Confidence* (2015).

Novels: *How Insensitive* (1994), *Noise* (1998), *The Princess and the Whiskheads* (2002), *Diana: A Diary in the Second Person* (2003), *Muriella Pent* (2004), and *Girl Crazy* (2010).

Non-Fiction: *Men's Style: The Thinking Man's Guide to Dress* (2005).

Russell Smith is the author of three novels, a novella, two collections of short stories, *Young Men* and *Confidence*, and a work, written under the pen name Diane Savage, which old-fashioned booksellers would have catalogued under the heading "Curiosa."

Only in Russell Smith's work would one read dialogue like this:

> "What a herman. What a fucking howie. You are a dorb, you know that? You are a total dorboid. You rot my bag."

Only in Russell would we read:

> "Come on, you know what I've heard. That you're more than friends with that incredible babe with the weird name."
> "Leyalla. Leyalla Brown. Yes, we've been kind of—"
> "Doing it. Sinkin' the pink."
> "Danny, really, sometimes you talk like a—"

"Bonk city. Bonk-o-rama. Good for you. I mean seriously, congratulations. She is incredible."

Only Smith could write such *good* parody of wine-speak:

> "It's not special, I know," he said, pouring, "but it's the most expensive bottle the shitty little liquor store near here had, and I was lucky to get the last eighty-nine, the rest were ninety-threes or some such. I actually don't mind it. A little thin, but with some earth, country earth, a hint of duck footprint, you know, an echo of a sort of honking, braying –"

Smith's fictional worlds are restaurants, raves, the offices of magazines, catwalks, fashion shoots. His restaurants are run by celebrity chefs "chain-snorting cocaine." They are staffed by anorexic, coked-out "Alpha Babe" waitresses. They post Dress Codes that read:

> No running shoes
> No rugby shirts
> No fucking nice sweaters
> (Make an *effort*, for fuck's sake)

They are patronized by neurotic girl fashion photographers like Nicola, "Nicola the Ebola babe," whose hair is dyed the colour of "toxic waste."

But always, here and there, a lyric touch:

> Behind him, in the open kitchen, Manuel was doing a special of quail and orange glaze; there was the odd *phuff* of a tablespoon of Grand Marnier catching fire, then the warm smell of burned sugar in the air.

A lovely invention, that *phuff*. Persuasive *spelling*.
The homelife of Smith's young men is usually straitened, cash-strapped, grubby.

"GONNA STROKE YOU UP," boomed the car stereo.

James felt his chair vibrating. Above the bass, the boys outside were shouting at each other.

"She's a cow, man. She's a fucking *pig.*"

"You fucking know shit, Armando. Fuck you, man. Stop pulling the hair out of my ass."

"Suck my hairy –"

To his momentary relief, someone cranked up the booming even louder, and the voices were lost. He watched his water glass slowly edge across his desk. He wondered what a seismograph would read in his neighbourhood on any midafternoon ...

Next door, the teenage girls responded to the boys with their romantic tune, the little stereo stretched to breaking, fizzing with white noise. "*And I. Will always. Love you.*" Cigarette smoke in his room. The girls were home all day these days; school out, parents at work. If he put his head out the window he would be able to see them on the sundeck below, in their shorts and T-shirts, smoking, fighting, frequently sobbing. He thought of their long hair, the lipstick and braces, newly Neeted legs glistening in the sun, and tried not to.

It should be obvious by now that I have an extravagant regard for Russell Smith's writing. As I've said before, comparison with early Kingsley Amis is not inappropriate, the exuberant Amis of *Lucky Jim, That Uncertain Feeling, I Like It Here,* and *Take a Girl Like You.* Interesting, too, to note that Smith is adept, as was Amis, at mimicry. His dialogue is impeccable, his eye merciless. Another influence on his work is Evelyn Waugh; I've not confirmed this, but I sense in *How Insensitive* the ghostly presence of *Vile Bodies.*

With such masters of language as his mentors, how could Russell Smith not be gilded?

Linda Svendsen

Short Story Collections: *Marine Life* (1992).

Novels: *Sussex Drive* (2012).

Marine Life is a collection of linked stories related by Adele Nordstrom, often called by her mother, "Coconut" or "Mince Pie," about her father, Humphrey, her stepfather Robert, her sisters Joyce and Irene, her mother June, and her dangerous alcoholic brother, Ray. The matter of the stories, loves and terrors, heartbreaks, marriages and divorces is common enough but what is so astonishing is the economy and elegance of the telling.

Alice Munro wrote of the work: "Linda Svendsen's stories are stunning—so easily embodying such terrific power."

Marine Life is among the crown jewels of Canadian short stories. Here is Adele at the age of fourteen in the story "Flight":

> ... After beating Penny at ping-pong, I biked home. At the bottom of the crescent I could make out my mother and second oldest sister on our front porch. I pedalled hard and pretended I was going to crash into them. "No brakes," I shouted. "Save the children and run for your lives."
>
> At the last second I swerved, crushing a clump of daffodils. They hadn't budged. Joyce still wore sunglasses, although there was nothing to shield her eyes against. "Hi, gang," I said. "Why're you sitting out here in the dark?" The lamp on my bike beamed across their laps and they seemed hypnotized by a family of moths going tizzy in the light. It was then I realized something wasn't right. I said, "What happened?"
>
> "Joyce is leaving Eric," Mum said carefully, and I was struck by that word *leaving*. Joyce had not actually *left* yet, although her body was beside ours and not his. "She's going to stay with us until she's on her feet."
>
> "Oh," I said.
>
> "I'll let her tell you. I'm going to bring the mower in before somebody steals it." Mum stepped over the zigzag of half-cropped lawn and tugged the machine out from under the dogwood. She called over the rattle, 'Doesn't the grass smell good?' and disappeared into the garage. She was crying.

How poignant and how *very* elegantly put together.

The stories, cumulatively, become very dense; we become deeply involved in the complexities of the Nordstrom family's emotional life. This impression of density and detail is, in a sense, strange because Linda's influences are American minimalist; she studied at Columbia in New York with Gordon Lish.

All of the stories are lit with a deadpan humour.

> I turned on the air conditioning and we listened to it. Here I was on my wedding night with my father, sitting on a bed, possibly a vibrating one, in a Queens motel.
>
> "Marriage," Dad said, "as I'm sure you've learned during your extensive and, need I add, expensive schooling, is life's most difficult proposition."
>
> "There are no happy marriages," I said. "Only unexamined ones."
>
> "Who says that?"
>
> "Me," I said.

And a vignette of June, Adele's scatterbrained mother:

> About 2 a.m. she fetches a small china box and places it before me. She opens it and spreads tiny molars and bicuspids and incisors on the table, beside our saucers, and tells me it's my first set of teeth.
>
> "You're kidding," I say.
>
> "No," she whispers. "I'll always keep your teeth."

Adele at the age of ten, ice-skating with her father, Humphrey, on one of his Saturday visitation days:

> I hugged the side every few feet. The only way I knew to brake was to slam into the wood. The ice was strewn with teenagers, the normal sort and a mentally retarded bunch. One of them took over the penalty box, pounded his mitts together, and screamed "Santa" each time Dad whizzed by, until he was given a needle.

Linda wrote the following commentary for me when I was assembling the anthology *Second Impressions* (Ottawa: Oberon, 1981).

Frederick Busch, an American novelist and short story writer, says good fiction is "the song inherent in the fighting through of people who share a room or house or bed or child or journey: they fear to perish of one another, or without each other, and yet, calling each other dead, they won't lie down." I tend to go along with this stance—looking for the "song" of a story in its style and language, looking for why it had to be told in just this exact way, a particular voice. Leonard Michaels says, "Every story has the language of its own occasion." Storytellers tell the same tales over and over, and what makes these births, deaths and separations new and vivid is the voice (language, tone, the timing). What is told, when and how it's told.

Equally important is Busch's idea of "fighting through." And not simply "fighting." One can see that on television. "Fighting through" implies that things are not black and white, that events have tender repercussions. A story that does not try for its character, or *try* its characters, cannot hold, or move. And that's what I hope my writing will do. As Busch swears, "Serious writing... is dangerous writing. It makes us, with our secrets and lies, hurt. It doesn't keep the darkness out. Nothing so safe; it lets the darkness in." And Elizabeth Hardwick once said in a seminar, "It's like that slap when you finally feel the caress in it."

... When I write a story, I'm writing it to a particular person, a mind that I want to parry things with, somebody I'd like to confide in. Happily, so far, this imaginary audience has not been too removed from the rest of humanity, so I could be addressing practically anybody. And then I like to believe I tell an emotional kind of truth. I take scraps from my experience (perhaps envy, an infatuation) or something that excited me in somebody else's, and then make up. Maybe tell it how it should have happened. Sometimes I simply have an ending—a final image or a strong feeling or a phrase—and write what would have had to happen to get there. Robert Bly might say it's "a growing into a sense of what's inside" or as Stanley Elkin demands, "What does this story know unconsciously?"

I write slowly. After I figure out what's happening, the basic events, I re-write them so that they interest me. I guess this is the "song" part. I want to be lured by my own words: I like them to bite. Sometimes I say to myself, "If you could read only this story in the world, how would you want it to be?" And then I have to make it match a high expectation, as best I can ...

Audrey Thomas
Short Story Collections: *Ten Green Bottles* (1967), *Ladies and Escorts* (1977), *Real Mothers* (1981), *Two in the Bush and Other Stories* (1981), *Goodbye Harold, Good Luck* (1986), *The Wild Blue Yonder* (1990), and *The Path of Totality* (2001).
· Novels: *Mrs. Blood* (1970), *Munchmeyer and Prospero on the Island* (1971), *Songs My Mother Taught Me* (1973), *Blown Figures* (1974), *Latakia* (1979), *Intertidal Life* (1984), *Graven Images* (1993), *Coming Down from Wa* (1995), *Isobel Gunn* (1999), *Tattycoram* (2005), and *Local Customs* (2014).

According to the rules I've set myself, I must represent Audrey Thomas' achievement by what she herself has selected in *The Path of Totality*; if I were free to do otherwise I'd probably have chosen *Ladies and Escorts*.

The first five books were published by small or literary publishers, the three subsequent collections by Viking Penguin. (*Two in the Bush* is actually not new work; it draws a mixture of stories from *Ten Green Bottles* and *Ladies and Escorts*.) I am recording these dry details because they turn out to be important.

The most striking stories in *The Path of Totality* are "If One Green Bottle... ," "The Albatross," "Salon des Refusés," "Two in the Bush," "Joseph and His Brother," and "The More Little Mummy in the World." The stories are tightly written, demanding, experimental, four of them using techniques of collage. All are incisive. And all of them are drawn from collections published by small literary publishers.

When we turn to the stories published by Viking Penguin in *Goodbye Harold, Good Luck* and *The Wild Blue Yonder*, the writing has undergone a sea change. The stories have become loose and baggy, sometimes not far removed from anecdote and gossip. What once was taut is now flabby; what once was direct and urgent is now garrulous. The stories seem to drive to no emotional end. The experience of reading them—I am talking of such stories as "The Dance," "In the Groove," "Ascension," and "Survival of the Fittest"—puts me in mind of watching episodes of *Neighbours* or *Coronation Street*, bright and chatty while they're going on, but when they've stopped going on, unnourishing and oddly unmemorable.

These later stories seem unbalanced in their length and detail. Even an interesting one such as "Local Customs" almost collapses under its embroidery of detail, as does "The Dance." Excessive detail furs and clogs the writing, slows and muffles. What follows is an excerpt from "The Survival of the Fittest," which in no way advances plot, delineates character, or adds depth to theme. It is uncontrolled wordiness and is, unfortunately, not untypical.

> Her mother tried to imagine Heather standing in her flat—her "apartment"—in Boston, talking into a telephone, maybe a fancy one like one of those she saw advertised the week before when she went to pay her telephone bill. There were pictures of all sorts of telephones, for executives and people in a hurry, telephones with memories, telephones without cords, Princess phones in pretty colours, even telephones for the kiddies— shaped like Snoopy or Mickey Mouse. One advertisement had amused her in a grim way, an ad for a "grannie phone." There was a picture of a sweet-looking, white-haired lady, face down on the carpet, and underneath the words—"Thirty seconds after she fell, help was on the way." It seemed you just yelled "help help" and the telephone picked up the sound of your voice. It was the same as dialling 999. When her turn came at the counter she said to the girl, "Grandpas fall down as well" and pointed to the ad. The girl was busy; she didn't even smile.
>
> "I don't know, I'm sure," she said, handing back the change and dismissing her. "Next," she called, as Mrs. Hutchison moved away.

Dialogue, which in the earlier stories had been crisp, here wilts into archness and art-denying shapes.

Here is the divorced Martha to her daughter Anne in "Breaking the Ice."

> ... Martha said, "A friend of mine is coming Friday morning."
> "A friend of yours?"
> "A new friend. His name is Richard. I think you'll like him.'
> (Please like him, said the mother's heart to the child's. I like him.
> I like him a lot.) 'He has a daughter, just about a year older than
> you."
> "What's her name?"
> "Anne, the same as yours. We'll have to call you Anne One
> and Anne Two."
> Her daughter's voice was cold. "Nobody's going to want to
> be Anne Two."
> (*Please*, said the mother's heart to the child's. What do you
> know about loneliness? Oh please.) "Well," she said, "we can call
> you Anne T. and her Anne L. No discrimination there."

The younger Audrey Thomas would not have perpetrated this.

In the introduction to *The Path of Totality* she writes of the stories "a lot of them have to do with language, with my love of words ..." In this case, such a love is not a virtue. She self-indulgently permits her narrators to meander into etymology and word play.

The story "Mothering Sunday" begins with this daunting paragraph.

> Hail Mary, Wounded art Thou among Women. That's what it
> means, doesn't it? Still, there in the French: *blesser:* to harm, to
> hurt, to injure, to wound. "*C'était une blessure grave.*" *Se blesser,*
> to wound oneself. In English we can trace the word back to
> *blod.* Hail Mary, Blessed art Thou among Women. All the Marys
> bleed.

My comment would be: *C'est un blather grave.*

Audrey Thomas' contribution to the short story in Canada was her early and surefooted use of collage techniques, work on which younger writers can still draw. In their time, in the context of Canadian writing, these early stories were trailblazing.

Guy Vanderhaeghe

Short Story Collections: *Man Descending* (1982), *The Trouble with Heroes* (1983), *Things As They Are* (1992), and *Daddy Lenin and Other Stories* (2015).

Novels: *My Present Age* (1984), *Homesick* (1989), *The Englishman's Boy* (1996), *The Last Crossing* (2002), and *A Good Man* (2012).

Plays: *I Had a Job I Liked. Once* (1992) and *Dancock's Dance* (1996).

I know absolutely nothing about Guy Vanderhaeghe's upbringing and education. I read his work as it appeared in the literary magazines in the late seventies and eighties. I remember publishing "What I Learned from Caesar" in *Best Canadian Stories 1980*. His work was obviously stronger than most that surrounded it in the magazines. But rereading him now prompts me to *imagine* his literary self-education. I say "self-education" as his degree work at the University of Saskatchewan was in history rather than literature.

Consider these quotations from "The Watcher," a story published in 1980.

> And in the midst, in the very eye of this familial cyclone of mishap and discontent, stood Grandma Bradley, as firm as a rock. Troubles of all kinds were laid on her doorstep. When my cousin Criselda suddenly turned big-tummied at sixteen and it proved difficult to ascertain with any exactitude the father, or even point a finger of general blame in the direction of a putative sire, she was shipped off to Grandma Bradley until she delivered. Uncle Ernie dried out on Grandma's farm and Uncle Ed hid there from several people he had sold prefab, assemble-yourself crop-duster airplanes to.

And this:

> The yard was little more than a tangle of thigh-high ragweed and sowthistle to which the chickens repaired for shade.

And this:

> In 1958 Grandma Bradley would have been sixty-nine, which
> made her a child of the gay nineties—although the supposed
> gaiety of that age didn't seem to have made much impress upon
> the development of her character.

The prose is well-mannered, formal, slightly old-fashioned. The
diction is elevated, the verbal comic effects very slightly ponderous, contrived, *worked*. From where does all this derive? Whose
work and influence helped forge this style? The *Oxford Companion
to Canadian Literature*, in another entry by Professor Staines, says
that Vanderhaeghe writes "in the prairie tradition to which its
author is indebted"; as practitioners of that "tradition" Staines cites
Margaret Laurence, Sinclair Ross, and Robert Kroetsch. As though
they were snowed in north of Pukatawagan with nothing to read
but each other—Margaret Laurence with all her years in Africa
and England, Sinclair Ross with his interest in Proust and Claude
Mauriac, Robert Kroetsch with his PhD in creative writing from
the Writers' Workshop at the University of Iowa and his years of
teaching "post-colonial" literature at Binghampton, New York. That
"prairie tradition" is—again—nationalist invention, mentally lukewarm Loony Tunes.
   ... putative sire ...
   ... repaired for shade ...
   ... much impress ...
   The *sort* of writer I seem to hear behind these quotations—possibly an eccentric view—is someone more like Stephen Leacock than
Robert Kroetsch. Almost certainly British rather than American.
What I *imagine* is simply something like this: in Vanderhaeghe's childhood and adolescence Saskatchewan was doubtless far more British
than it is now. The books available to him in schools and libraries
would, I imagine, have been fairly British in flavour. Canadian writing was not much of a force. The *kind* of writing exhibited in the
quotations need not date back to Leacock; it need not have come
from one particular writer or group of writers. It was a kind of

educated British *generic* writing. It was, simply, what "writing" was. Vanderhaeghe's distinction was that he turned away from it realising the power and delights of the demotic.

Consider this quotation from the same story:

> My parents didn't own a television and so my curiosity and attention were focussed on my surroundings during my illnesses. I tried to squeeze every bit of juice out of them. Sooner than most children I learned that if you kept quiet and still and didn't insist on drawing attention to yourself as many kids did, adults were inclined to regard you as being one with the furniture, as significant and sentient as a hassock. By keeping mum I was treated to illuminating glances into an adult world of conventional miseries and scandals.
>
> I wasn't sure at the age of six what a miscarriage was, but I knew that Ida Thompson had had one and that now her plumbing was buggered ...

This splendid descent into the overheard vernacular can stand for what Vanderhaeghe set out to do in his short fiction: wean himself from the style and diction he'd been early influenced by, funny as it often is, and connect into the vernacular and demotic. As his work progresses, he abandons good-mannered formalities and produces, instead, beautifully heard paragraphs like these farmers at a family gathering in the story "Reunion":

> The conversation ran on, random and disconnected. There was talk of the hard spring, calf scours, politics, Catholics, and curling. Totting up the score after four drinks, Jack concluded hard springs, calf scours, politics, and Catholics weren't worth a cup of cold piss. That seemed to be the consensus. Curling, however, was all right. Provided a fellow didn't run all over the province going to bonspiels and neglect his chores.

That paragraph leaves me envious.

In the splendid story "King Walsh," he writes of some poor and frugal farmers who "squeeze a nickel until the beaver shits."

As he relaxes into the demotic he even writes in the voice of an adolescent. "… nobody ever accused Pop of being a religious fanatic by no means. He goes to confession regular like an oil change, every five thousand miles, or Easter, whichever comes first."

When Vanderhaeghe is not aiming at the comic, his increasingly austere style—a style he has won through to—is compelling. Here, from "A Taste for Perfection," is Ogle in a hospital ward unknowingly suffering from a brain tumour.

> The sudden glare of the light in the bathroom glancing off rubbed enamel and spanking bright tiles hurt his eyes. The place smelled of antiseptic and somebody else's turds.
>
> Ogle examined his face in the mirror over the sink. It seemed to him that the left side of his face had altered, although he couldn't be sure. There was a sensual droop to the eyelid, and the corner of his mouth felt a little slack and lacking in decision. He flexed the fingers of his left hand and made a weak fist; he felt faint.
>
> He sat down on the toilet seat, lit his cigarette, entwined his long legs about one another and meditatively scratched his shin. All he wanted now was four ounces of Scotch, neat. That would make this an occasion. The cigarette smoke hovered around his head, a blue nimbus.
>
> "A drink, a drink," he declaimed to the opposite wall, hoisting an imaginary glass, "my sterile, christly kingdom for a drink." Ogle attempted a suitably ironic smile but the stiff, resisting muscles of his face informed him he had failed and produced only a grimace. *There is something radically wrong here,* he thought.
>
> On the other side of the door, Morissey spoke indistinctly to a character in his dreams.
>
> "Die in your sleep, you old prick," Ogle answered him.

Guy Vanderhaeghe by Nicholas von Maltzahn in *Profiles in Canadian Literature*, Series 8 is well worth a visit.

Kathleen Winter

Short Story Collections: *boYs* (2007) and *The Freedom in American Songs* (2014).

Novels: *Where Is Mario?* (1987), *Annabel* (2010), and *Lost in September* (2017).

Non-Fiction: *The Road Along the Shore: An Island Shore Journal* (1991) and *Boundless: Tracing Land and Dream in a New Northwest Passage* (2014).

The two emotional poles in Kathleen's childhood were being uprooted from a warm family life in the north of England and emigrating to Newfoundland; this move rendered her "foreigner" in both places. She has written movingly and comically about this uprooting in "You Can Keep One Thing." (It is not unreasonable to assume that "Maggie" in this story and "Marianne" in later ones are remembered and imagined earlier selves.)

Of her doting grandmother, she writes:

> After dinner Grandma read her own tea leaves. "Two pieces of money are coming from far away." She rattled through her chronic bronchitis. She wore scarlet lipstick and a black wig, and ate lemon bon bons, for her diabetes, out of a paper bag, and she let me have as many as I wanted. "Someone is going to get a ring." She took out the cards and read those. "Beware a dark man. That must be the rent man. If he comes we won't open the door."

In Newfoundland, new lessons had to be learned.

> It's Mom here, not Mam. Desks are destes. Ghosts are ghostes. Chimneys are chimleys. I put my hand up and said, "Can I go to the toilet, please," and they gave me a talking lesson at recess.
> "You have to call it the bathroom."
> I told Dad and he said, "That's silly, there's no bath in it."
> "Those aren't fish fingers either," I told him. "You have to call those fish sticks."

She enshrines the texture of her childhood memories—and I mean "enshrines" literally—in such paragraphs as…

> I ate blackberries behind the allotment fence while Dad checked his cold frames and measured his leeks with a ruler he designed that measures the bulb underground… We went to Les's allotment and measured the length of his giant white Californian rabbits, then we went to find out how the pigeon races were going, and there was a lot of intrigue around that, with baskets and flags and rushing on trains to Morpeth and Gateshead…

Readers may be reminded by "with baskets and flags and rushing on trains to Morpeth and Gateshead" of the magical worlds of Dylan Thomas in *Portrait of the Artist as a Young Dog* and *Under Milk Wood* and Mary Borsky in *Influence of the Moon,* of Linda Svendsen's *Marine Life,* of Mordecai Richler's *The Street,* and of the book by Kathleen's brother, Michael Winter's *One Last Good Look.*

(See the notes on Mary Borsky in the Century List.)

Kathleen wrote to me recently about the beginnings of her literary career, a romantic quest to San Francisco and Paris:

> I managed to get to Paris because Jacob Siskind, Ottawa music and arts journalist, wrote me a letter of reference that convinced the Canada Council to give me my first writing grant. Jacob came to Carleton University where I was studying toward a journalism degree and taking a lot of wretched courses, and he filled in for an absent professor for a couple of months, and introduced the class to Shostakovich. I was writing poetry and stories all the time and had done so as long as I could remember, and there was something so sympathetic about Jacob Siskind that instead of handing in a journalistic assignment I plucked up enough courage to give him one of the stories. When he handed it back to me he asked me two things: was I psychologically all right, and did I have any more stories. I told him I thought I was mentally safe, though I could understand, from the story I gave him, why he might have considered me imperilled—for one

thing, I remember it ended with the narrator dissolving into the wall of an empty room. I gave him more stories and he told me they had something, they were real stories and I was a real writer and should continue. This was the first time anyone had told me this, though I knew I was a writer and not a journalist and it gave me confidence—and also money, as his letter meant the CC gave me six thousand dollars to write stories.

I hitchhiked to Gander Airport and got a plane to England. For a couple of weeks I looked after my granddad, who was blind and had other health issues and lived alone in South Shields, sending my mother copious letters about his home health care worker and his situation. Then I got a bus to the Channel and got on a boat and went to Paris, where my real writing could resume.

I checked into a cheap hotel called Hotel St. Christophe. The toilet was a communal hole in the floor on the staircase but there was a Juliet balcony with geraniums and the room had a bidet. I ate chocolate croissants every morning and bought a thick packet of green onionskin paper and began writing my novella, *Where Is Mario?* I walked a great deal, and wandered into Shakespeare & Co., whose proprietor was George Whitman—I believe his shop was a reincarnation of Sylvia Beach's shop—I mean I think he opened it as a sort of new installment of her shop, or in honour of her shop, which I think closed during the Second World War. When I got there George was working on cutting and pasting the shop's periodical newsmagazine—the pages were all over the counters and shelves—and when I told him I was a writer he asked me if I could proofread it. In exchange, he gave me a nook at the top of some stairs, that had a desk in it, and a manual typewriter. The nook looked down over the whole bookshop, shelves and shelves of books, with interesting people coming in, and, I seem to remember, a lovely resident cat. I proofread a couple of issues of the magazine during my time in Paris, and daily I went upstairs to the nook and worked on *Where Is Mario?*, which is set in Paris and is a sort of fragmented document of some of the real things that happened to me there, along with scenes from my imagination and fairy-tale elements and ephemeral musings. I was 23 or 24. Customers would come in and browse and once in a while they'd notice me clacking away upstairs—it wasn't really a room up there, more like a hidden landing, half church pulpit and half secret cupboard—and some of them would get very excited at the thought there was an actual writer working on a manuscript just over their heads, as Hemingway and all the rest had done, etc... all that romantic literary stuff. I got a real kick out of that. When I wasn't proofreading or writing there, I walked around Montmartre and along the river and under the bridges and up and down winding streets, totally alone except for Italian jazz pianists and a Japanese singer with a convertible and a few other non-Parisians who followed me around hoping I'd sleep with them.

I didn't start writing the Marianne stories until after I returned penniless from Paris (and Naples, where I'd had to hide in a hotel basement living on stolen sausage and spinach sandwiches and hiding out from an Egyptian with a gold tooth who tried to steal my passport and gave me a white gift-wrapped box which I did not open and whose contents I never found out.... I escaped by fleeing on the midnight express back to Paris, where I met a vaga-bond couple who let me sleep in their beautiful apartment owned by someone rich and absent, an apartment from whose windows I drew some of the illustrated scenes for Mario while I kept writing it)... I returned to Newfoundland and had no money but went to use a pay phone on Water Street and all the coins in the phone tumbled onto my feet, which kept me going for a while. A painter whose work I'd written about in the paper saw me on the street and told me to come with her to a tiny fishing outport 45 miles away, and I got in her old car and went there, and this was the place where all the Marianne stories, or most of them are set. As soon as I set foot in that little place I knew it was a kind of magic I'd never seen before. The willows at the roadside were shiny and red, and the old-fashioned garden roses were fragrant and not modern, and the old women who lived along the road were crazy and they loved me and I hung out in their kitchens and drew roosters on burlap sacks for them so they could make hooked mats. I found a falling-down house to rent from an old fisherman for hardly any money, and stayed there three years and wrote the Marianne stories there. This was right after Paris. "A Plume of White Smoke" was the first Marianne story I wrote, and as soon as I sent it to a magazine I got an acceptance letter and the same happened with the others and I realized that was what people wanted. They didn't want fragments of dreams about lost Mario in Paris. They didn't want stories whose protagonists dissolved into the walls at the end. They wanted real things about old women who worked in fish plants and for whom the scent of a banana was exotic. I still haven't completely gotten over this.

In a recent letter Kathleen said to me, about *Where Is Mario?*... "Don't be too unkind. I still love otherworldly things."

Where Is Mario? is as romantic as the pilgrimage to Paris and the labours in the Shakespeare and Co. book shop.

...Mario lays his hands between my shoulders and my shoulders change into birds...

I give thanks that she returned to *this* world, the world of "A Plume of White Smoke" and "The Worship Centre."

... The street was dark. It was raining. The streetlamps had silver lines streaming down to the dead flowerbeds at their bases. A sleek, wet German Shepherd walked with Marianne, his fur soaking through her skirt to her leg, then he turned up Colonial Street, his claws clicking the pavement.

In 1991 Kathleen published *The Road Along the Shore,* a selection from her diary, sketches, snatches of conversation, oddities, occurrences. In the Introduction she wrote:

St. Michael's is the second of three communities located on a little road off the main southern shore highway, about a half-hour's drive from St. John's. The road runs first through Burnet Cove, and ends at the wharf in Bauline.

The first time I went to St. Michael's, snow was quietly falling into the silver spaces among bare alder branches beside the road. It was a humble and quiet scene, filled with power and grace.

I had never lived in nature, in a land not wounded. The beauty of this place called me. I moved there when I was offered the chance to rent Lewis Melvin's old house whose kitchen window looked out over Gull Island, Green Island and Great Island. I lived alone.

I was searching for the source of life, for God. Over the next two years I would search the tidal pools, trout ponds and deep speckled midnight skies, and take refuge from loneliness in the kitchens of the people who fished and cut wood and cared for their families along the shore. I was a lost soul, and for me St. Michael's was a place of spiritual growth, because the place is charged with the energy of God's creation.

And that seems to me a useful entry point into Kathleen Winter's work.

Michael Winter

Short Story Collections: *Creaking in Their Skins* (1994) and *One Last Good Look* (1999).

Novels: *This All Happened* (2000), *The Big Why* (2004), *The Architects Are Here* (2007), *The Death of Donna Whalen* (2010), and *Minister Without Portfolio* (2013).

Non-Fiction: *Into the Blizzard: Walking the Fields of the Newfoundland Dead* (2014).

Aiming for immediacy, he has stripped his writing down to a simplicity that makes the world strange in its intensity. In an interview in Natalee Caple's *The Notebooks* he said "I want to describe sex (and everything else) in a new way, and when you write in a new way, it can seem hard to read or difficult."

This statement should remind us of Hemingway's statement, quoted earlier, from *A Moveable Feast*: "Since I had started to break down all my writing and get rid of all facility and try to make instead of describe, writing had been wonderful to do. But it was very difficult, and I did not know how I would ever write anything as long as a novel. It often took me a full morning of work to write a paragraph."

In dialogue, Winter banishes much conventional punctuation. He dismisses entirely "he said" and "she said." Often he introduces a speaker simply with a colon. It produces something like a playscript. Here is an example of the effect from the story "Second Heart."

> In the morning, Junior:
> Gabe. Come on.
> What's up.
> We're getting Dad a load of wood.
> He's got lots of wood.
> Come on, Gabe. He's got bad feet. I got the saw in the truck.
> I got gas and oil. I even made you a little sandwich. Just half a
> load. We'll be done by one.
> Is Dad going?
> Dad can't be at that any more.
> I'm too stiff.
> Just you and me against some trees.
> They take the truck and go in Lady Slipper Road again.
> That deadfall stuff is rotten, June.
> Are you catching on?
> Junior parks where they were parked before. And get out. It's
> cold and low light. Grey rolling nimbus. Junior takes an axe from
> behind the seat.
> Okay.
> Junior: You can't guess?
> A sweat creeps into Gabe's armpits.
> There's a moose in there.

Along with this stripping down of the prose, Winter compresses too, using something like a prose "shorthand." Here's an example from the story "Lustral."

> At the end of summer I invited Femke to my parents' cabin.
> Get out of the city, see some woods. We hitchhiked and it's

easy. People assumed we were a couple, which, secretly, excited both of us. We played cribbage and read Edgar Allan Poe. The flax and monkshood. A fire on the beach for hotdogs and a tin of beans.

The blue-flowering flax and monkshood are slipped in as shorthand for "idyll," "beauty," "romance."

Another Winter ploy is omission. Reviewers have described him as a minimalist and have linked him with Hemingway and Carver, but his work looks and sounds like neither. It does, however, have things in common with Norman Levine and Winter has acknowledged Levine as an influence.

His style is not one that appeals to a lot of people, but a lot of writers marvel at his talent... His economy of so little saying so much—when you try to write like that, you realise how hard it is to capture things accurately and truthfully with very few words. He was a writer's writer.

Another of the complexities of what Michael Winter does as a writer is his unconventional handling of time. Natalee Caple asked him about this in her interview in *The Notebooks*.

NC: Your timeline loops as if to suggest that memory and time are continuous and connected. How do you think about time when you are writing? What do the flashbacks and braided memories tell the reader about the narrator and the story?

MW: Okay, an example. In October, a brief snowfall. The hoods of all the cars covered in the snow. And suddenly we are thrown back into the previous winter. Or the previous winter hurtles forward to us. And then you see one bare hood, which must be due to a hot motor. And that hood connects to summer. In these moments, as in reflection, time seems to coil like a rope and touch at points and connect. So to be linear with events seems false to the practice of being conscious, and to be.

Winter also shares that impulse to enshrine that I was writing about in the section on Mary Borsky—Alice Munro's "every last thing, every layer of speech and thought, stroke of light on bark or walls, every smell, pothole, pain, crack, delusion, held still and held together—radiant, everlasting." Though he'd probably be embarrassed to put it that way. But in a more muted way he's saying the same sort of thing to Natalee Caple in *The Notebooks* interview:

> I asked Norman Levine this question. About why his protagonists are always writers. And he said he's not interested in making things up. And I feel the same.

Scrupulous attention to the world and something of Hemingway's "making" instead of "describing" obviate the need for invention and lead to such glorious writing as the following paragraph from the story "Wormholes." I have read it dozens of times and am still slightly stunned by its strange power.

> The beer kept me from coming. You know how I come quickly. And she was pleased when she saw how hard an orgasm I had with her. She went to the toilet, which you can see from the bed. She came back to bed and we lay there for a few minutes. We listened to the people upstairs argue. She smoked. She said she had to go. I said you can stay. I can make you an egg. But she got up and all that nakedness.

Essential interviews with Michael Winter are to be found in *The Notebooks* and *Writers Talking*. Russell Smith rather brilliantly wrestles him to the ground in *Wild Writers*.

Shortly after publication of *One Last Good Look*, Michael Winter announced in an interview that he was abandoning short fiction because he could not afford to write it anymore. *One Last Good Look* had earned him a great deal of artistic capital; it seems to me that, sadly, book after book since then, though earning him coin of the realm, has squandered his real wealth, his reputation as an artist.

The sense I have of squandered talent was reinforced by a perceptive sentence in Alex Good's fine polemic *Revolutions: Essays on Contemporary Canadain Fiction*: "A lot of young Canadian writers seemed to be following identical paths: proceeding from a promising volume of short stories to a series of increasingly clumsy and overwritten novels."

*

And here a concluding digression is called for. Caroline Adderson, Steven Heighton, and Michael Winter are the only three Canadian writers I know who acknowledge the influence of another Canadian writer on their work. Caroline Adderson gives a nod to Michael Winter and Lisa Moore; Michael Winter to Norman Levine. Steven Heighton acknowledges the general influence of my 1982 anthology *Making It New* and mentions specifically that his lovely "Five Paintings of the New Japan" was modelled after my story "Gentle as Flowers Make the Stones"—both stories involving the ongoing translation of a poem.

It has been borne in on me during the last forty years that it is unusual to find Canadian writers who even *read* other Canadian writers. The only exception to this generality that I know of is T.F. Rigelhof. It is not at all unusual to find aspiring writers who have never read Leon Rooke, Clark Blaise, Norman Levine, Keath Fraser, Mavis Gallant... Similarly, older writers remain resolutely ignorant of Caroline Adderson, Michael Winter, K.D. Miller, Sharon English... while all of them seem to be cognizant of, say, Lorrie Moore or Lydia Davis.

If the country's *writers* do not read each other—an aesthetic and competitive necessity, one would have thought—why should we expect an audience to read us? If *writers* do not care, why should anyone else? And the anecdotal evidence of that collegial indifference is overwhelming. Is it that Canadian writers hold Canadian achievement in contempt?

I often find myself thinking of Michael Harris' words: "I cannot believe after many years of writing, editing, and collecting experience that there will ever be a Canadian literature."

It is difficult to suppress the thought that Canadian writers are the engineers of their own defeat.

One might wish that some Canadian critics and readers might stray for a while through such books as Matthew Arnold's *Essays Literary and Critical*, Eliot's *The Use of Poetry and the Use of Criticism*, *The Sacred Wood*, *Notes towards the Definition of Culture*, and *What Is a Classic?* Through George Saintsbury's *A History of English Criticism*. Through T.E. Hulme's *Speculations*. Because we must at some point—beyond the inanities of *Survival* and the maunderings of postmodernists—give thought to Canadian literature's hierarchy.

The Century List will, I hope, provide a starting point for a consideration of our achievement in the short story in Canada in the twentieth century and the opening years of the twenty-first. Trampling already on the heels of that achievement are young writers readying their first collections: their accomplishments will inevitably pull history and taste into a different shape and, to use Evelyn Waugh's words, the "order of precedence" will shuffle ranks to accommodate them.

Would You Mind Repeating That? I'm Not Quite Sure...

"In a bloated culture distracted by shoddy goods, stories are an invaluable commodity. Stories are handcrafted gems; they reflect the expertise and experience of their maker. Stories finally survive because of the passion of the story-writer."

From: *Selected Essays*. Clark Blaise.

"A book, a story... 'must be the axe for the frozen sea within us'."

From: A letter to Max Brod. Franz Kafka.

"What I advocate is the notion of paintings as beings, not representations."

From: Catalogue notes. Claude Tousignant.

"I think of myself as a maker of images. The image matters more than the beauty of the paint... I suppose I'm lucky in that images just drop in as if they were handed down to me... I always think of myself not so much as a painter but as a medium for accident and chance... I don't think I'm gifted; I just think I'm receptive."

From: A filmed interview. Francis Bacon.

"Learning to paint is literally learning to use paint."

From: Recorded conversation. Lucian Freud.

"You take something from life. Make something of it. Then give it back into life."

From: An interview with Norman Levine.
The quoted words of Peter Lanyon.

"And more and more my own language appears to me like a veil that must be torn apart in order to get at the things (or the Nothingness) behind it. Grammar and Style. To me they seem to have become as irrelevant as a Victorian bathing suit or the imperturbability of a true gentleman. A mask."

From: A letter to Axel Kaun, 1937. Samuel Beckett.

"No writer worth a damn is a national writer or writer of the frontier or a writer of the Renaissance or a Brazilian writer. Any writer worth a damn is just a writer. That is the hard league to play in. The ball is standard, the ball parks vary somewhat, but they are all good. There are no bad bounces. Alibis don't count. Go out and do your stuff. You can't do it? Then don't take refuge in the fact that you are a local boy or a rummy, or pant to crawl back into somebody's womb, or have the con or the old râle. You can do it or you can't do it in that league I am speaking of."

From: Ernest Hemingway.

"The region is something the writer has to use in order to suggest what transcends it. His gaze has to extend beyond the surface, beyond more problems, until it touches that realm of mystery which is the concern of prophets."

From: An address to the Georgia Council of Teachers of English.
Flannery O'Connor.

"When filmmakers 'adapt' a novel for the screen, they're really turning a novel into a short story."

From: *Selected Essays.* Clark Blaise.

"If I go to the National Gallery and I look at one of the great paintings that excite me there, Rembrandt, Velazquez, it's not so much the painting that excites me as that the painting unlocks all kinds of valves of sensation in me which return me to life more violently."

From: A filmed interview. Francis Bacon.

"If you can *talk* about it why paint it?"

From: Conversation. Francis Bacon.

"It is Olivier's trick to treat each speech as a kind of plastic mass, and not as a series of sentences whose import must be precisely communicated to the audience: the method is impressionistic. He will seize on one or two phrases in each paragraph which, properly inserted, will unlock its whole meaning; the rest he discards with exquisite idleness. To do this successfully, he needs other people on the stage with him: to be ignored, stared past, or pushed aside during the lower reaches, and gripped and buttonholed when the wave rises to its crested climax…"

From: A review of Olivier's *Richard III* (1944). In *He That Plays the King: A View of the Theatre*. Kenneth Tynan.

On his studio:

"I feel at home there in its chaos because chaos suggests images to me."

From: Conversation: Francis Bacon.

"Klee wanted each of his works to be autonomous, an object in its own right. He wanted to demonstrate that the most considerable kinds of picture-making have less to do with mimesis, with making from the outside in, than with self-generation, making from the inside out. The point of art was, in the words of Klee's best-known aphorism 'not to reproduce the visible, but to make visible'. Most of the images in Klee's pictures therefore emerged during the process of creation. The picture was finished, Klee said, when 'he stopped looking at it and it started looking back."

From: Catalogue of the Tate Exhibition. Paul Klee.

"Prose is not to be read aloud but to oneself at night, and it is not as quick as poetry, but rather a gathering of insinuations..."

From: *The Oxford Companion to Twentieth Century Literature in English*. Quoted by Jenny Stringer (Ed.) from Henry Green.

"Since I had started to break down all my writing and get rid of all facility and try to make instead of describe, writing had been wonderful to do. But it was very difficult, and I did not know how I would ever write anything as long as a novel. It often took me a full morning of work to write a paragraph."

From: *A Moveable Feast*. Ernest Hemingway.

"I can quite easily sit down and make what is called a literal portrait of you. So what I am disrupting all the time is this literalness, because I find it uninteresting."

From: A filmed interview. Francis Bacon.

"It is no use telling me there are bad aunts and good aunts. At the core, they are all alike. Sooner or later, out pops the cloven hoof."

From: *The Code of the Woosters*. P.G. Wodehouse.

Only a writer with a tin ear could write:
'the cloven hoof pops out'.

The comic core is 'pops'; 'out pops', in its reversal of the expected form of words, is given added comic power, and the sentence ends with the power *image*. Any reader puzzled as to the meaning of 'the cloven hoof' would be better employed knitting.

From: A communing with his *Diary*. John Metcalf.

A notebook entry of Malamud's when writing *Dubin's Lives:* "The sentence as object—treat it like a piece of sculpture."

From: A review of Malamud's *Idiot's First*. S.K. Oberreck.

"We are born to die, but in between we give this purposeless existence a meaning by our drives... The greatest art always returns you to the vulnerability of the human situation."

From: A filmed interview. Francis Bacon.

"I read [Evelyn Waugh's] *Decline and Fall* and *Vile Bodies* over and over, as if they were poems."
From: *Reliable Essays: The Best of Clive James.* Clive James.

"Style always obsessed him. 'Properly understood, style is not a seductive decoration added to a functional structure; it is of the essence of a work of art', he wrote. 'The necessary elements of style are lucidity, elegance and individuality; these three qualities combine to form a preservative which ensures the nearest approximation to permanence in the fugitive art of letters'."
From: *Evelyn Waugh and His World.* (Ed. David Pryce-James).
Waugh's words are quoted by David Lodge.

"My editor at Random House Joe Fox, used to tell me, 'Stanley, less is more.' He wanted to strike—oh, he had a marvellous eye for the 'good' stuff—and that's what he wanted to strike. I had to fight him tooth and nail in the better restaurants to maintain excess because I don't believe that less is more. I believe that *more* is more. I believe that less is less, fat, fat, thin thin and enough is enough."
From: The *Paris Review* Elkin interview.

"What I adore about fiction—the great gift of fiction—is that it gives language an opportunity to happen. What I am really interested in after personality are not philosophical ideas or abstractions or patterns, but this superb opportunity for language to take place."
From: The *Paris Review* Elkin interview.

The character Feldman in Stanley Elkin's *A Bad Man*, talking about a girl lifeguard in a white bathing suit, says that he sees, 'the dark vertical of her behind like the jumbo vein in shrimp'.

"English writers, at forty, either set about prophesying or acquiring a style. Thank God I think I am beginning to acquire a style."
From: *The Diaries of Evelyn Waugh.* (Ed. Michael Davie).

"He mentioned last year, when he read at Washington University, that one can't discuss a story by moving off into the ideas the story generates. The meaning is in the fiction and the fiction is the meaning, he dogmatically told me."

From: A review of Bernard Malamud's
Idiot's First by S.K. Oberreck.

"Like every other form of art, literature is no more and nothing less than a matter of life and death. The only question worth asking about a story—or a poem, or a piece of sculpture, or a new concert hall—is, 'Is it dead or alive?' If a work of the imagination needs to be coaxed into life, it is better scrapped and forgotten."

From: "What Is Style?" Mavis Gallant
in *Making It New* (Ed. John Metcalf).

Henry IV, Parts I and II

"The most treasurable scenes in these two production were those in Shallow's orchard: if I had only half an hour more to spend in theatres and could choose at large, no hesitation but I would have these. Richardson's performance, coupled with that of Miles Malleson as Silence, beak-nosed, pop-eyed, many-chinned and mumbling, and Olivier as Shallow, threw across the stage a golden autumnal veil, and made the idle sporadic chatter of the lines glow with the same kind of delight as Gray's *Elegy*. There was a sharp scent of plucked crab-apples, and of pork in the larder: one got a sense of life-going-on-in-the-background, of rustling twigs underfoot and the large accusing eyes of cows, staring through the twilight. Shakespeare never surpassed these scenes in the vein of pure naturalism: the subtly criss-crossed counterpoint of the opening dialogue between the two didderers, which skips between the price of livestock at market and the philosophic fact of death ('Death, saith the Psalmist, is certain; all must die') is worked out with fugal delicacy: the talk ends with Shallow's unanswered rhetorical question: 'And is old Double dead?' No reply is necessary: the stage is well and truly set, and any syllable more would be superfluous. The flavour of sharp masculine kindness Olivier is adept in: for me the best moment in his *Hamlet* film was the pat on the head for the players' performing dog which accompanied the line: 'I am glad to see thee well'."

From: *He That Plays the King*. Kenneth Tynan.

Clive James visiting Tynan in his canyon home near Los Angeles where Tynan is dying of emphysema:

"… he was the stylist of his time: the true star critic. One of the things that made him so, apart from his turn of phrase, was what he called his limitless capacity of admiration. When I said that Hemingway's style had fallen apart in the end, Tynan read aloud from that marvellous passage where Hemingway, towards the close of his life, talked about the Gulf Stream's ability to take in any amount of junk and still run clean again after a few miles. I could tell that Tynan was talking about his lungs; and Hemingway was wrong, of course; but the prose sounded like holy writ in Tynan's strained voice as the hot sunlight inexorably ate its way into the absurdly green lawn. Tynan was giving me a final lesson in what lasts: the style impelled by the rhythm of the soul, breadth of feeling with a narrow focus. Any youngster who wants to get into this business should find a copy of Tynan's first book, [written when he was 23] *He That Plays the King* and do what I did—sit down and read it aloud, paragraph by paragraph."

From: *Unreliable Memoirs* (Vol. IV) Clive James.

"Style in writing, as in painting, is the author's thumbprint, his mark… I am thinking now of prose style as a writer's armorial bearings, his name and address."

From: "What Is Style?" Mavis Gallant
in *Making It New.* (Ed. John Metcalf).

"Complaining about the style in Dan Brown novels is like complaining about the food in a brothel."

From: A newspaper review. Andrew Pyper.

"Even today, and to an alarming degree [social] background remains a factor in any Englishman's perception of the arts, because it is such a factor in his perception of society—to the extent that even the most aesthetically sensitive critic finds it hard to purge himself of the supposition that the arts serve social ends.

Cleverness is no safeguard against this peculiar obtuseness, of which F.R Leavis, still volcanically active during my time at Cambridge, was merely the most flagrant example."

From: *Reliable Essays: The Best of Clive James.*

"If he'd wash his neck, I'd wring it."

From: A remark concerning F.R. Leavis attributed to Sir John Sparrow, Warden of All Souls.

Richard Gilman concerning Regina O'Connor, Flannery's mother.

"One evening at dinner she [Regina] said to me, while Flannery stared at her food in embarrassment, 'Now I want you to tell me what's wrong with those publishers up there in New York. Do you know how many copies of Mary Flannery's have been sold? Three thousand two hundred and seventy-eight, that's how many copies of Mary Flannery's novel have been sold, and there is something very wrong with that, they are not doing right by her.' I said that Farrar Straus was a fine publisher and that *The Violent Bear It Away* wasn't the kind of novel likely to have a big sale. And then I added that Flannery's reputation was more and more secure and that was the important thing. 'Important thing!' she snorted, 'reputations don't buy groceries'."

From: *Flannery O'Connor: A Life.* Jean W. Cash.

"Philip Roth loved Malamudian sentences such as this near the end of 'The Bill': 'He tried to say some sweet thing but his tongue hung in his mouth like dead fruit on a tree, and his heart was a black-painted window.' Or there was the opening of 'Idiots First' which Daniel Stern so admired: 'The thick ticking of the tin clock stopped. Mendel, dozing in the dark, awoke in fright. The pain returned as he listened. He drew on his cold embittered clothing'—the 'thick' ticking, the play-off between 'in the dark' and 'in fright', the 'return' of something before the 'stopping' of the beginning, the daring of 'embittered' clothing."

From: *Bernard Malamud: A Writer's Life.* Philip Davis.

Evelyn Waugh

"... the necessary elements of style are lucidity, elegance, individuality... Lucidity does not imply universal intelligibility. Henry James is the most lucid of writers, but not the simplest. A great deal of what is most worth saying must always remain unintelligible to most readers. The test of lucidity is whether the statement can be read as meaning anything other than what it intends...

Elegance is the quality in a work of art which imparts direct pleasure; again not universal pleasure. There is a huge, envious world to whom elegance is positively offensive. English is incomparably the richest of languages, dead or living. One can devote one's life to learning it and die without achieving mastery. No two words are identical in meaning, sound and connotation. The majority of English speakers muddle through with a minute vocabulary. To them any words not in vulgar use, are 'fancy' and it is, perhaps, ignoble deference to their susceptibilities that there has been a notable flight from magnificence in English writing...

...Individuality needs little explanation. It is the hand-writing, the tone of voice, that makes a work recognizable as being by a particular artist (or in rare decades of highly homogeneous culture, by one of a particular set.)"

From: "Literary Style in England and America" from *A Little Order*. (Ed. Donat Gallagher.) Evelyn Waugh.

Muriel Spark

"The artist, she said, was 'a changer of actuality into something else' and because literature 'infiltrates and should fertilise our minds' 'ineffective literature must go.' By 'ineffective' she meant the 'marvellous tradition of socially conscious art,' 'the representation of the victim against the oppressor'. The problem with social realism was that it offered surrogate absolution. We rise from it chastened but all the more determined to be an oppressor rather than a victim. It encourages 'the cult of the victim' and, wherever this exists, 'there will be an obliging cult of twenty equivalent victimizers.' No, the 'art of sentiment and emotion' had to go. 'In its place I advocate the arts of satire and ridicule'. It was a moment in history, she insisted, 'when we are surrounded on all sides and oppressed by the absurd.' Sharp, unsentimental intelligence was required to unnerve and paralyse it. The function of art was to give pleasure—'that element of pleasure which restores the proportions of the human spirit' and 'is the opposite and enemy of boredom and of pain'—but the 'cult of the victim is the cult of pathos, not tragedy.' It was exhausted. We had to recognize 'the ridiculous nature of the reality before us' and mock it. 'We should know ourselves better by now than to be under the illusion that we are essentially aspiring, affectionate and loving creatures'."

From: The Blashfield Foundation Address, May 1970, quoted in *Muriel Spark: The Biography*. Martin Stannard.

Raymond Carver

"He is not a particularly quotable writer. That's one of his virtues, that he never tried to achieve a beautiful line. It's the steadiness and quietness of his prose that creates his sense of reality. You never get the feeling, 'Oh, yeah, the writer got off a good one there'. That's never in his work. I can read things that are more brilliant on the surface, but they don't go to the heart of things the way Ray's work does. He gets there in a very quiet, unassuming way, but he's only apparently simple. It takes art to do what he does."

From: *...when we talk about Raymond Carver.*
(Ed. Sam Halpert.) Tobias Wolff.

"...The more people attacked Ray, the more I realized he was an important writer... A number of established sensibilities didn't want him in the city. There's a Russian saying: 'When you enter the city, the geese begin to cackle.' But then some big names weighed in on his side."

Ibid. Leonard Michaels.

"The stories seemed very fresh to me, and extremely gripping and dramatic. I thought they attempted to give language to things—to moments in life—which, until you read his story, you never realized existed importantly. You knew they existed, but Ray made them

hold a great deal—those moments. As with all great work, his stories made you pay close attention to life."

Ibid. Richard Ford.

Concerning Terry Southern: "... the essence of the man was never
on the screen anyway: not even in *Easy Rider* or the best bits of *Doctor
Strangelove*. The essence was in *Candy* and *The Magic Christian*, and
in some of the factual stories in *Red Dirt Marijuana and Other Tastes*.
I never stole anything from him but I admired his colloquial tone.
(Listen to Aunt Livia in *Candy* and ask yourself if Ring Lardner, J.D.
Salinger or Philip Roth ever eavesdropped on everyday conversation
with quite so acute an ear."

From: *Unreliable Memoirs*. (Volume IV). Clive James.

Sherwood Anderson

"The prose Anderson employs in telling these stories may
seem at first glance to be simple: short sentences, a sparse vocabulary, uncomplicated syntax. In actuality, Anderson developed an
artful style in which, following Mark Twain and preceding Ernest
Hemingway, he tried to use American speech as the base of a tensed
rhythmic prose that has an economy and a shapeliness seldom found
in ordinary speech or even oral narration. What Anderson employs
here is a stylized version of the American language, sometimes rising to quite formal rhetorical patterns and sometimes sinking to a
self-conscious mannerism. But at its best, Anderson's prose style in
Winesburg, Ohio is a supple instrument, yielding that 'low fine music'
which he admired so much in the stories of Turgenev."

From: *Introduction* by Irving Howe to a reprint
of *Winesburg, Ohio* from Wildside Press.

"Cinema's 100 years seem to have the shape of a life cycle: an
inevitable birth, the steady accumulation of glories and the onset
in the last decade of an ignominious, irreversible decline." Thus
begins Susan Sontag's essay 'The Decay of Cinema', published
in the *New York Times* in 1966. Hers is a story of an art form
corrupted by commercial imperatives, of the darkened theatre's

rituals disappearing in the age of video and television: "Images now appear in any size and on a variety of surfaces... The sheer ubiquity of moving images has steadily undermined the standards people once had both for cinema as art and for cinema as popular entertainment."

From: *TLS* review of "The Decay of Cinema".
New York Times. 1996. Susan Sontag.

"... a debate between William Styron and the actor Ossie Davis. It was Mr. Davis' contention that in writing *The Confessions of Nat Turner* Mr. Styron had encouraged racism... and it was Mr. Styron's that he had not. David Volper, who had bought the motion picture rights to *Nat Turner*, had already made his position clear: 'How can anyone protest a book' he had asked in the trade press, 'that has withstood the critical test of time since last October?'"

From: *The White Album*. Joan Didion.

Clark Blaise
"... the local volcano is smoking and getting ready to blow. Gather the children, don't look back, head for the shore, man the life rafts. The writers, and readers [of short stories] are looking at fleeing footprints. They've [the former inhabitants] seen something, they've smelt the sulphurous flames...

The point I'm getting at is the essential short story gesture, as opposed to the novel's. We [short story writers] are not in the business of establishing any of the *whys*. The preconditions are fine where they are; they were built by another civilization, carved out by different glaciers and hurricanes. Novelists like those things, journalists can deal with them, memorists need to get to the bottom of them. The story traces what lingers after the whirlwind, after the fracture. Or before it. We're not in the business of establishing the reasons, social historic, economic, psychological, why things happen. They've already happened. As a character in Malamud's "Take Pity" says "How did he die?" and the answer comes back, "Broke in him something. That's how." "Broke what?" "Broke what breaks.""

... By turning away from the need to explain too much, to create, construct, and establish, the story opens a space that is not available to the novel.

... Stories are the membrane we sling around discontinuity and chaos, the whole insolence of a universe that does not respond to cause and effect, or consequence, and antecedent. They are the voice we give to chaos, anonymity, quotidian derangement.

Story is the permanent avant-garde, it can draw its immediate inspiration from art, technology, philosophy, myth, newspapers, sports, a letter and overheard scrap. Some blessed soul can write novels on little more, but novels are about resolution and completion. Story is about destruction, the slipping away."

From: "The Craft of the Short Story"
from *Selected Essays*. Clark Blaise.

"Hints and fragments, the great modernists have taught us, can leave a much stronger impression than a story where both detail and themes are explicitly laid out. ... Derek Walcott keenly described the aesthetics of fragmentation in these words: 'Break a vase, and the love that reassembles the fragments is stronger than that love which took its symmetry for granted when it was whole.' Much of modern art takes its passion from the idea that the world is a shattered vase which is impossible to repair except through an act of the imagination."

From: "Make-Believe Books and Imaginary
Libraries: From Rabelais to Seth". Jeet Heer.

"If you want to write serious books you must be ready to break the forms, break the forms."

From: V.S. Naipaul in conversation recorded by
James Wood in his essay collections *The Fun Stuff*.

Robert Hughes in 2004 writing about Lucien Freud's lonely crusading belief in figurative painting and portraits:
"Every inch of the surface has been won, must be argued through, bears the traces of curiosity and inquisition—above all,

takes nothing for granted and demands active engagement from the viewer as its right. Nothing of this kind happens with Warhol or Gilbert and George or any of the other image-scavengers and recyclers who infest the wretchedly stylish woods of an already decayed, pulped-out postmodernism."

Oscar Wilde:
  "Everything matters in art except the subject."

Index of Names and Book Titles

Acknowledgements

My thanks to Emily Donaldson for the genial rigour of her copy-editing; to Chris Andrechek for his design and patient typesetting; to Katherine Barber's *The Canadian Oxford Dictionary*, a grateful tug of the forelock; to Dan Wells, publisher of Biblioasis, for his incisive and commanding editing, a publisher whose taste and vision are transforming CanLit into literature in Canada.

I have made extensive use of quotation throughout *The Canadian Short Story*, from quoting Katherine Mansfield's "Miss Brill" in full to shorter quotations from the works of writers under discussion as well as those who I thought shed light on what I was trying to impart. I have referenced all of these in the index at the back of the book. I made use of these quotations entirely for pedagogical purposes, and as such consider their usage fair and reasonable.